THE FIFTH QUARTER
HARD COURT

MIKE DAWSON

:01

First Second
New York

:01

First Second

Published by First Second
First Second is an imprint of Roaring Brook Press, a division of Holtzbrinck
Publishing Holdings Limited Partnership
120 Broadway, New York, NY 10271
firstsecondbooks.com
mackids.com

Library of Congress Cataloging-in-Publication Data is available.

Our books may be purchased in bulk for promotional, educational, or
business use. Please contact your local bookseller or the Macmillan Corporate
and Premium Sales Department at (800) 221-7945 ext. 5442 or by email at
MacmillanSpecialMarkets@macmillan.com.

First edition, 2022
Edited by Mark Siegel and Samia Fakih
Cover design by Kirk Benshoff
Interior book design by Mike Dawson and Sunny Lee
Printed in China by 1010 Printing International Limited, Kwun Tong, Hong Kong

Drawn digitally using a Wacom Cintiq tablet, colored digitally in Photoshop.

ISBN 978-1-250-24435-2 (paperback)
10 9 8 7 6 5 4 3 2 1

ISBN 978-1-250-24434-5 (hardcover)
10 9 8 7 6 5 4 3 2 1

Don't miss your next favorite book from First Second!
For the latest updates go to firstsecondnewsletter.com and sign up for our enewsletter.

BY ART
WE LIVE

For Aliza

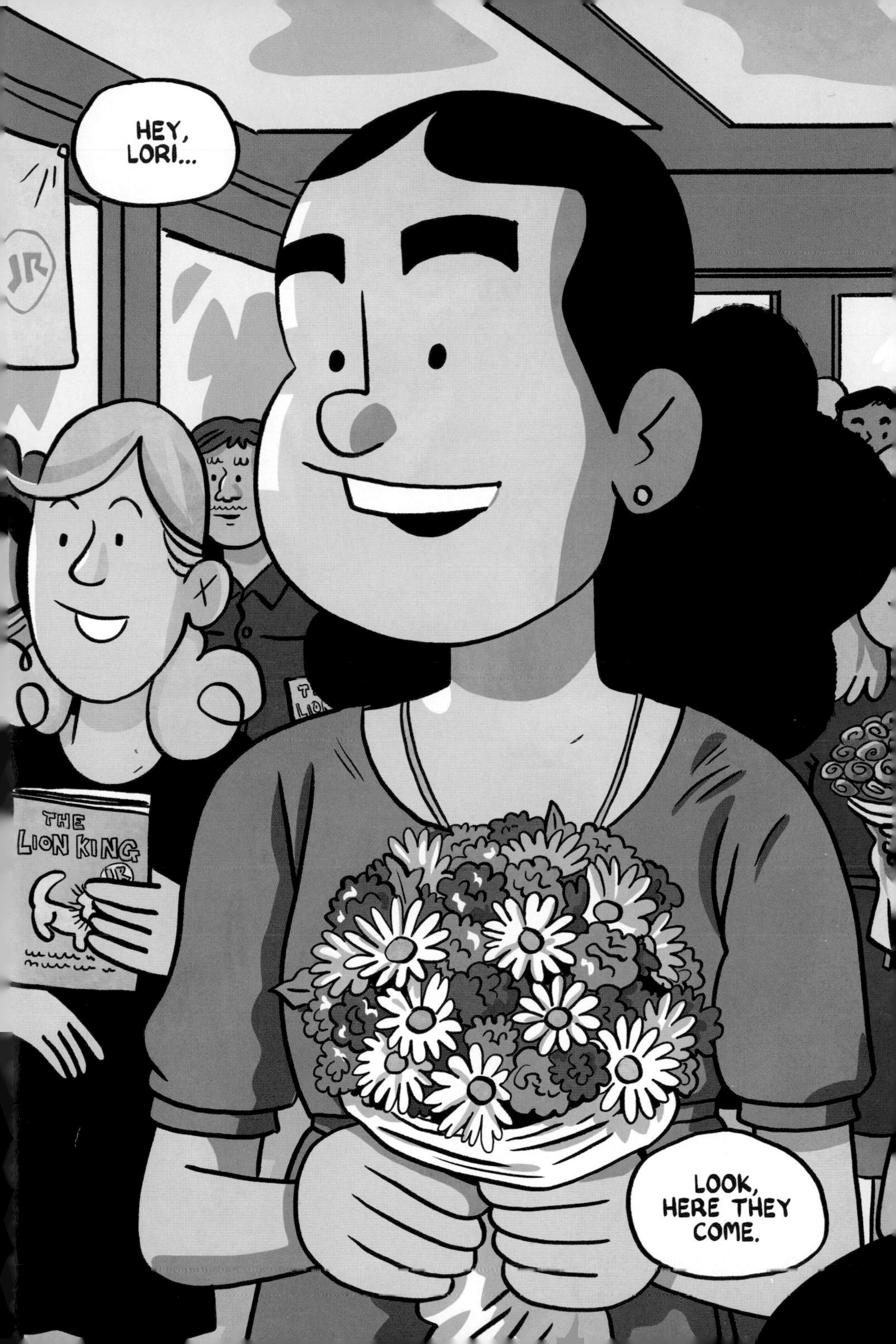
HEY, LORI...
THE LION KING
LOOK, HERE THEY COME.

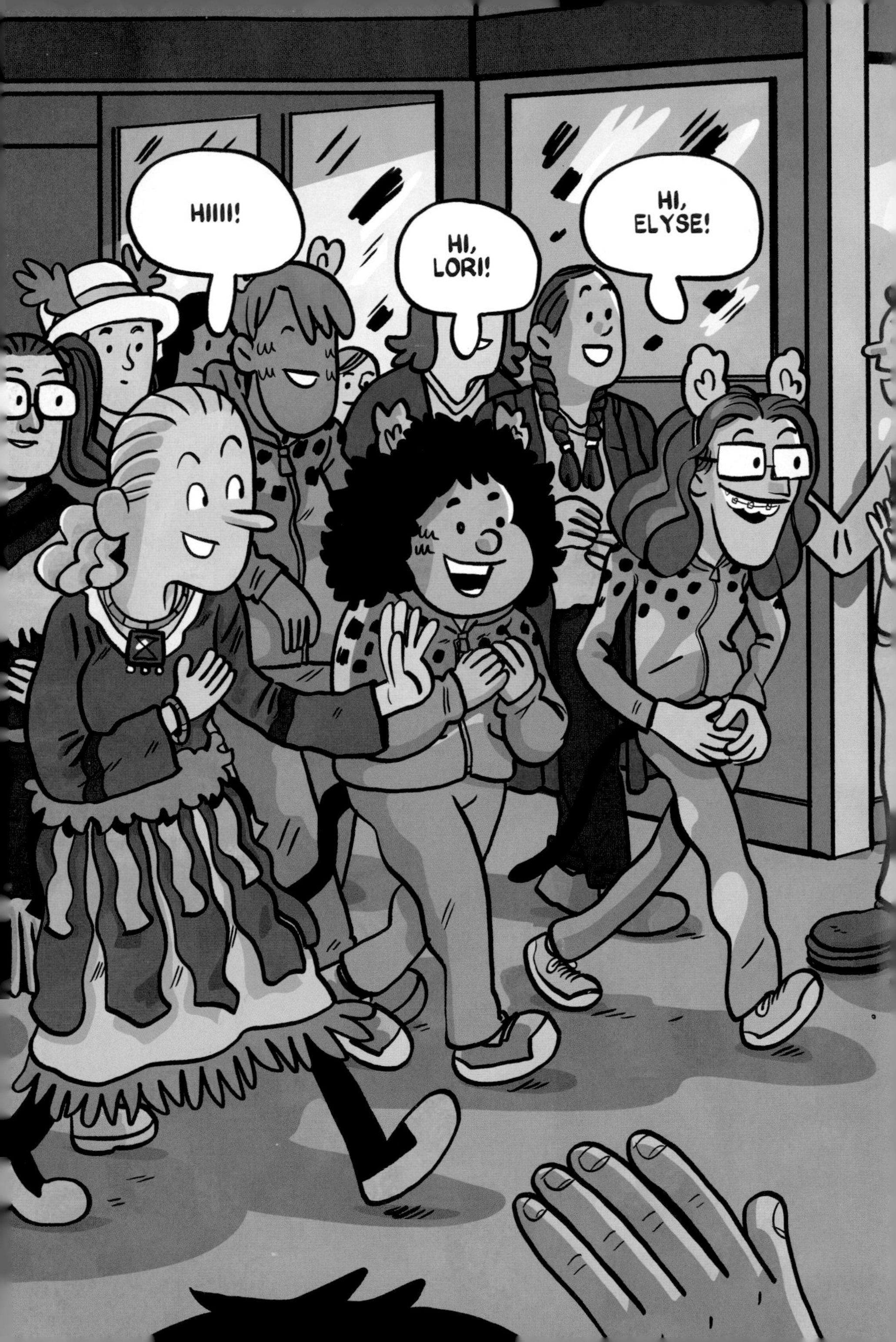
HIIII!
HI, LORI!
HI, ELYSE!

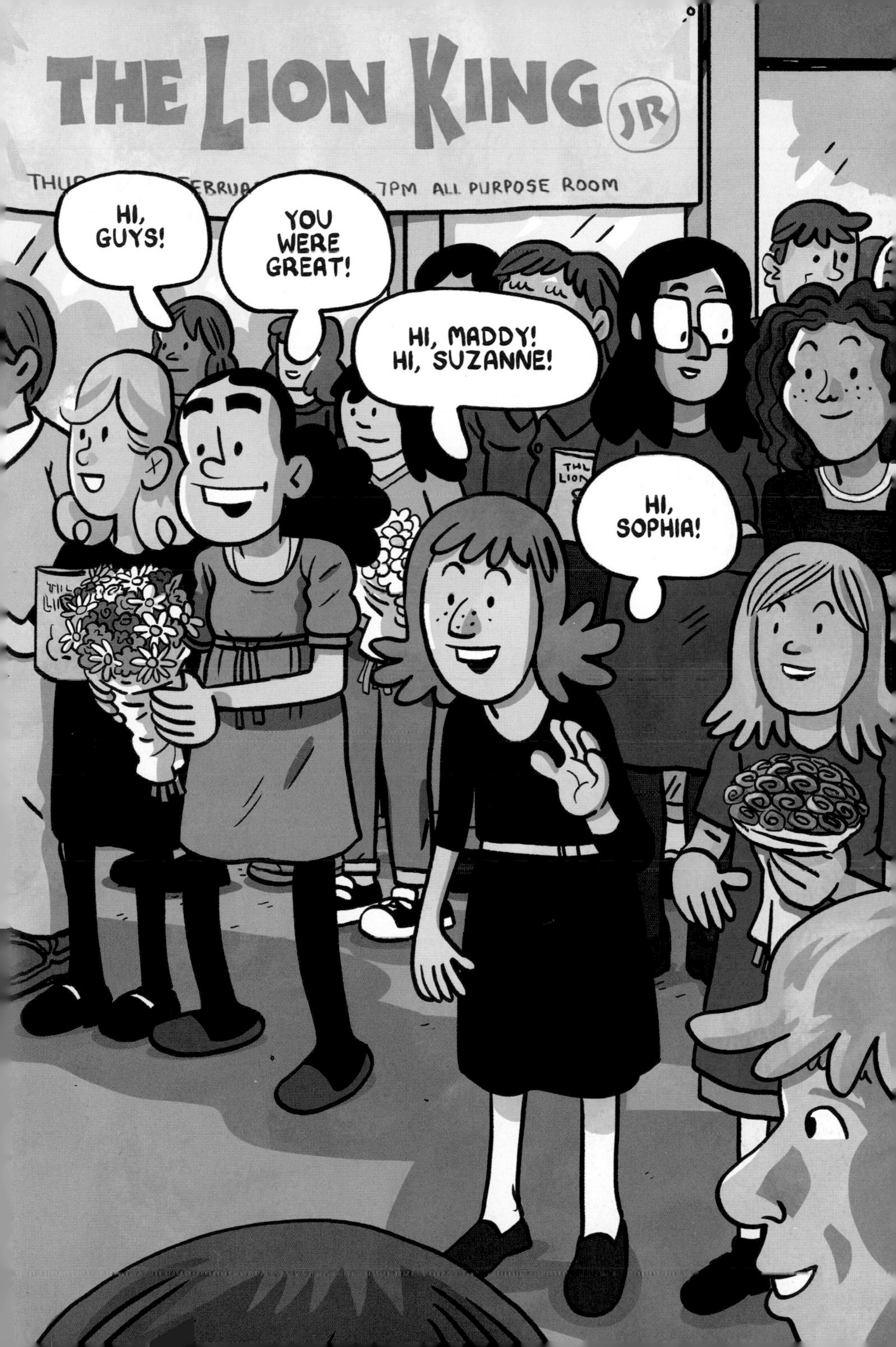
THE LION KING JR
THUR... FEBRUA... 7PM ALL PURPOSE ROOM
HI, GUYS!
YOU WERE GREAT!
HI, MADDY! HI, SUZANNE!
HI, SOPHIA!

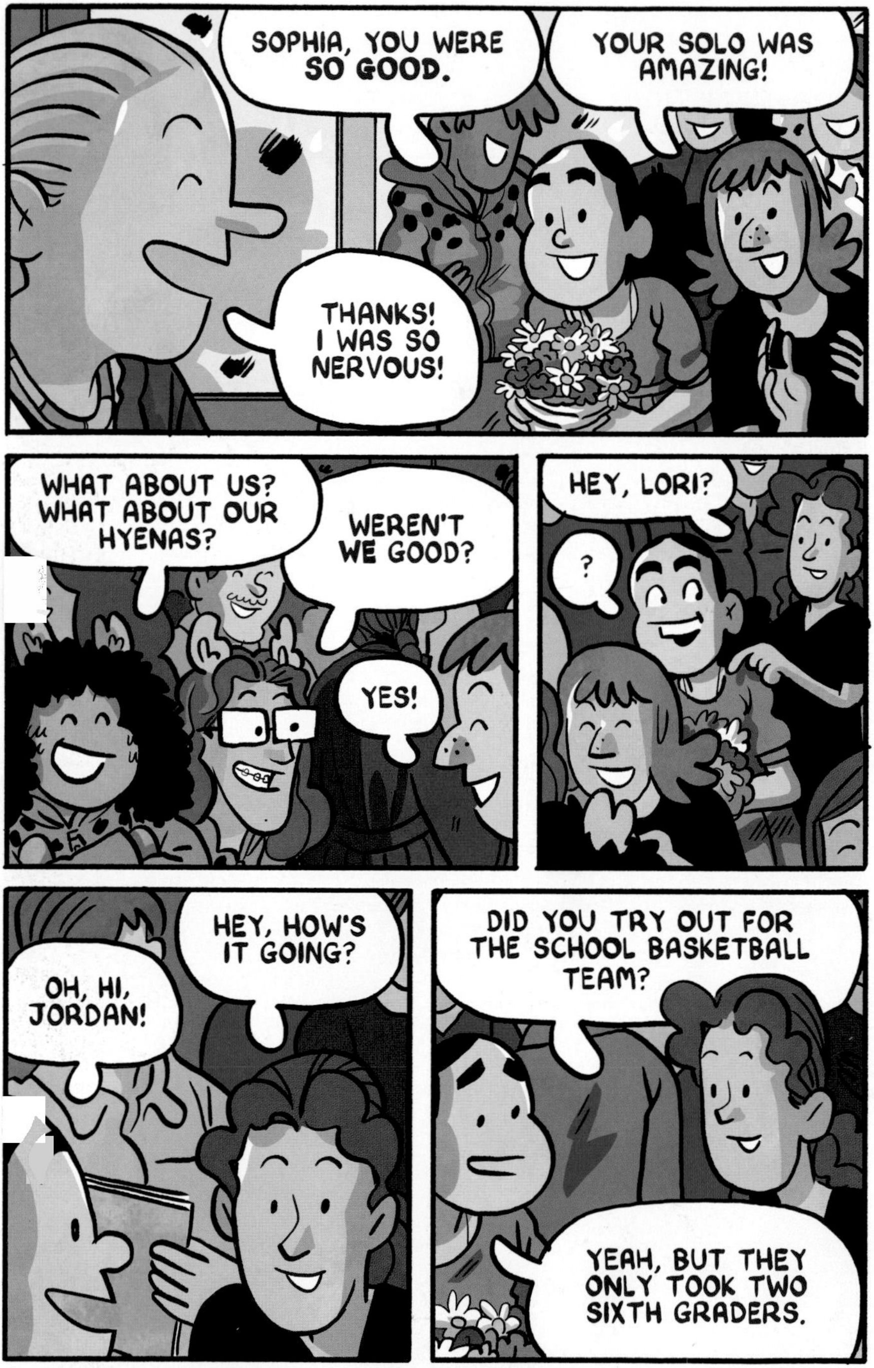
SOPHIA, YOU WERE SO GOOD.
YOUR SOLO WAS AMAZING!
THANKS! I WAS SO NERVOUS!
WHAT ABOUT US? WHAT ABOUT OUR HYENAS?
WEREN'T WE GOOD?
YES!
HEY, LORI?
?
HEY, HOW'S IT GOING?
OH, HI, JORDAN!
DID YOU TRY OUT FOR THE SCHOOL BASKETBALL TEAM?
YEAH, BUT THEY ONLY TOOK TWO SIXTH GRADERS.

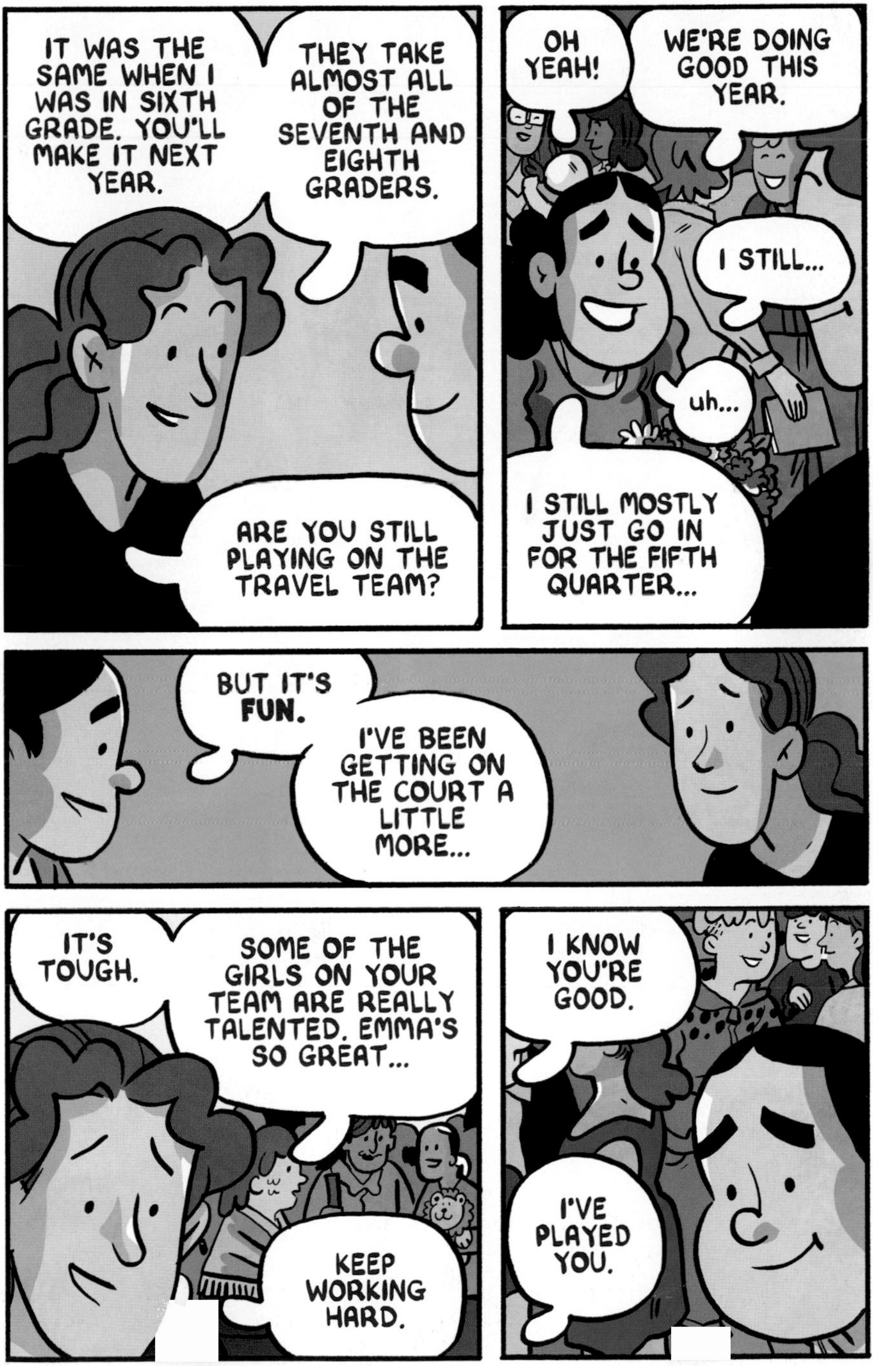
IT WAS THE SAME WHEN I WAS IN SIXTH GRADE. YOU'LL MAKE IT NEXT YEAR.
THEY TAKE ALMOST ALL OF THE SEVENTH AND EIGHTH GRADERS.
ARE YOU STILL PLAYING ON THE TRAVEL TEAM?
OH YEAH!
WE'RE DOING GOOD THIS YEAR.
I STILL...
uh...
I STILL MOSTLY JUST GO IN FOR THE FIFTH QUARTER...
BUT IT'S **FUN.**
I'VE BEEN GETTING ON THE COURT A LITTLE MORE...
IT'S TOUGH.
SOME OF THE GIRLS ON YOUR TEAM ARE REALLY TALENTED. EMMA'S SO GREAT...
KEEP WORKING HARD.
I KNOW YOU'RE GOOD.
I'VE PLAYED YOU.

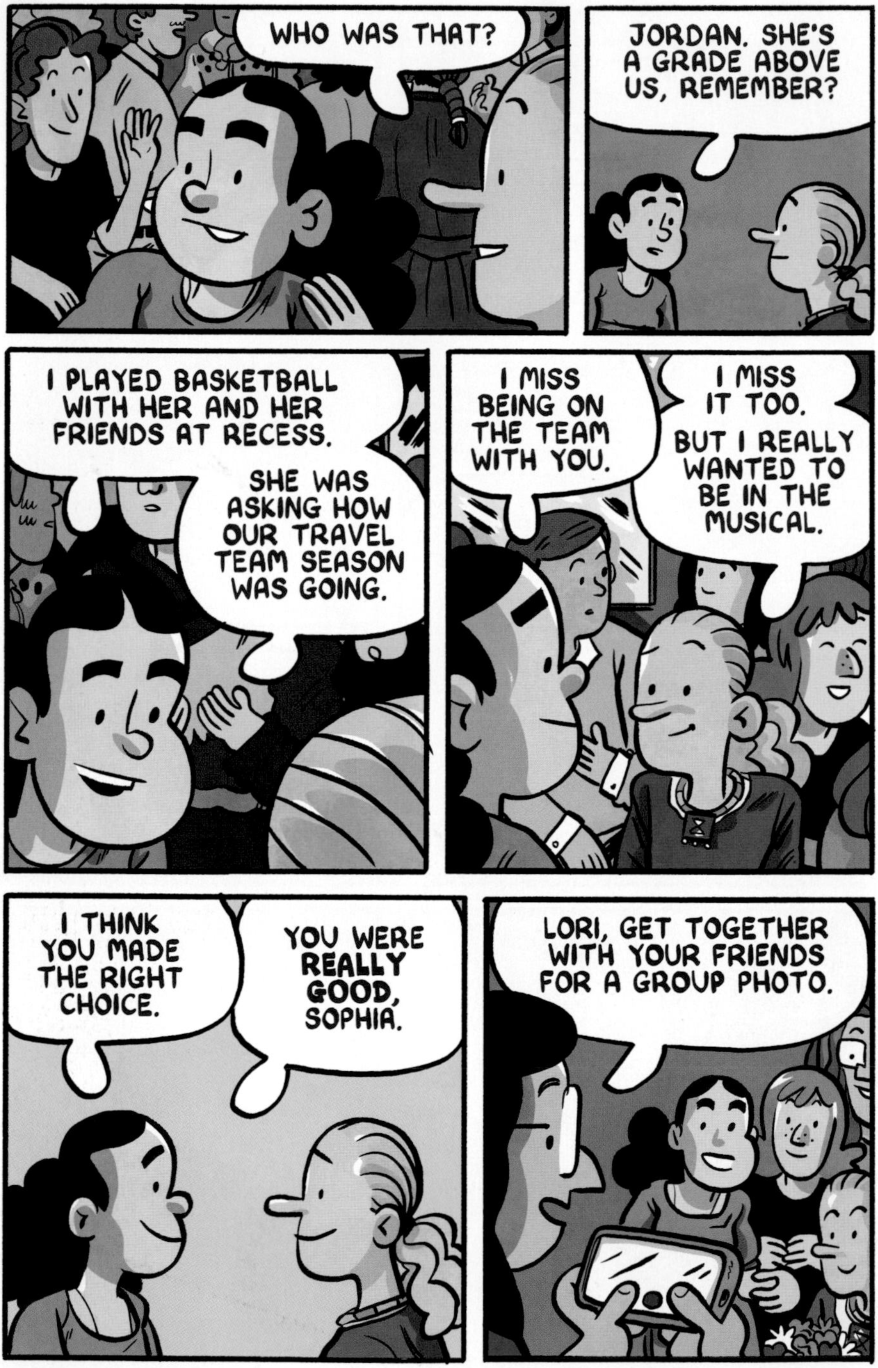
WHO WAS THAT?
JORDAN. SHE'S A GRADE ABOVE US, REMEMBER?
I PLAYED BASKETBALL WITH HER AND HER FRIENDS AT RECESS.
SHE WAS ASKING HOW OUR TRAVEL TEAM SEASON WAS GOING.
I MISS BEING ON THE TEAM WITH YOU.
I MISS IT TOO.
BUT I REALLY WANTED TO BE IN THE MUSICAL.
I THINK YOU MADE THE RIGHT CHOICE.
YOU WERE **REALLY GOOD**, SOPHIA.
LORI, GET TOGETHER WITH YOUR FRIENDS FOR A GROUP PHOTO.

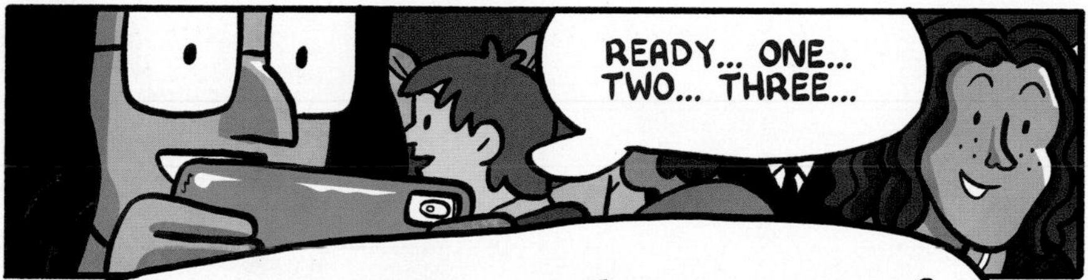
READY... ONE... TWO... THREE...

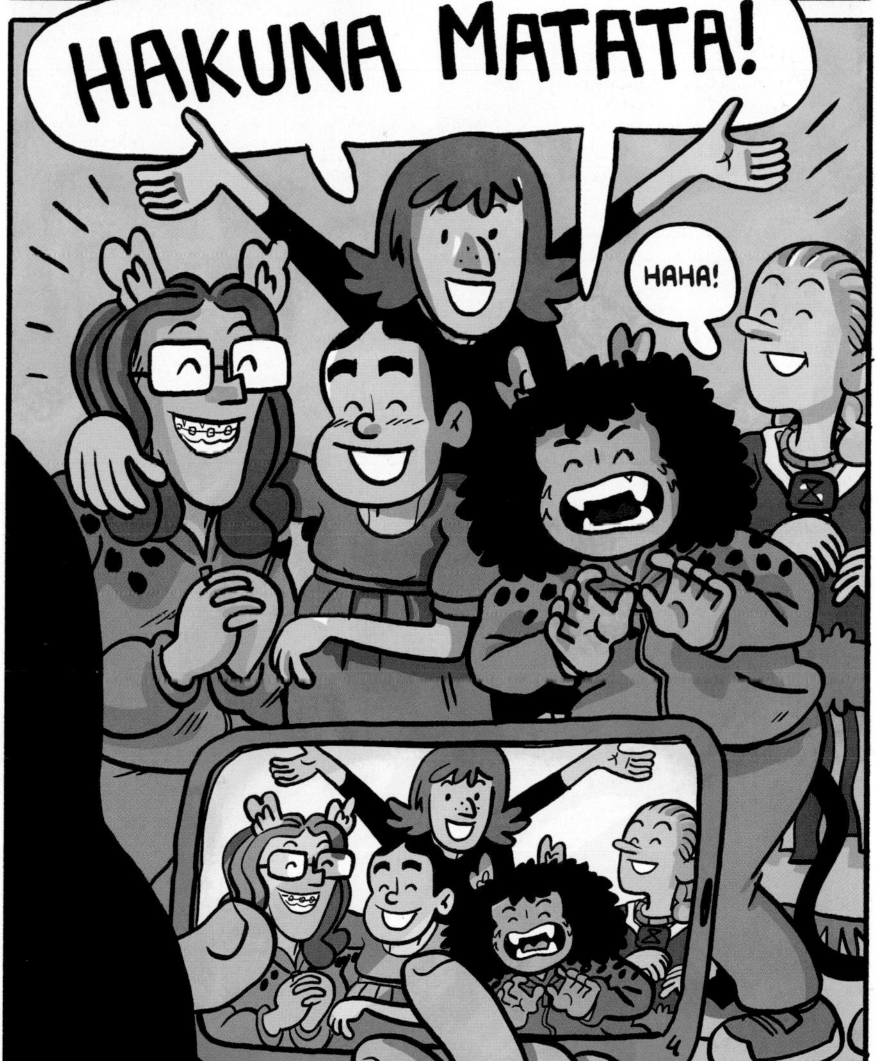
HAKUNA MATATA!
HAHA!

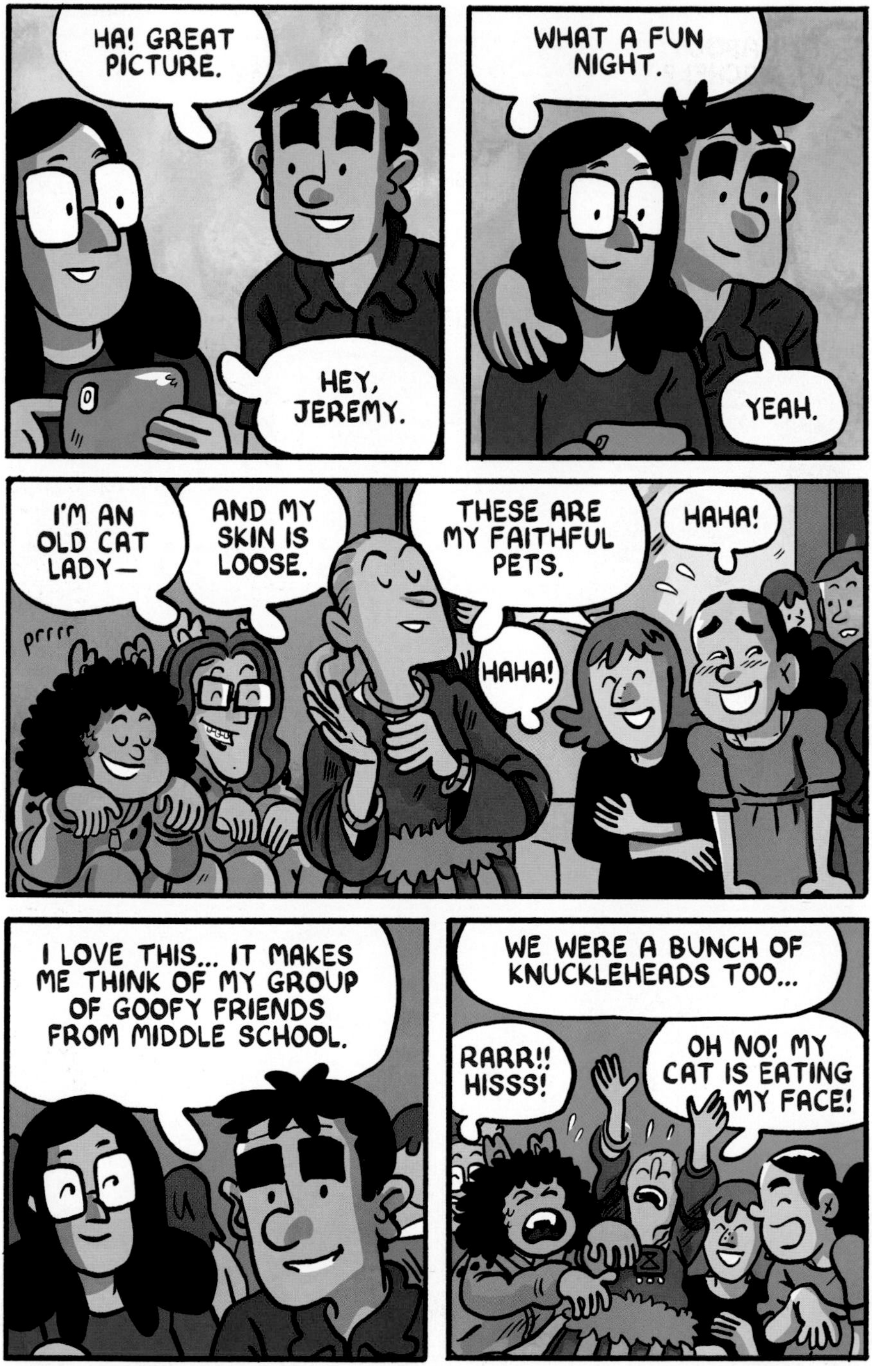
HA! GREAT PICTURE.
HEY, JEREMY.
WHAT A FUN NIGHT.
YEAH.
I'M AN OLD CAT LADY—
AND MY SKIN IS LOOSE.
prrrr
THESE ARE MY FAITHFUL PETS.
HAHA!
HAHA!
I LOVE THIS... IT MAKES ME THINK OF MY GROUP OF GOOFY FRIENDS FROM MIDDLE SCHOOL.
WE WERE A BUNCH OF KNUCKLEHEADS TOO...
RARR!! HISSS!
OH NO! MY CAT IS EATING MY FACE!

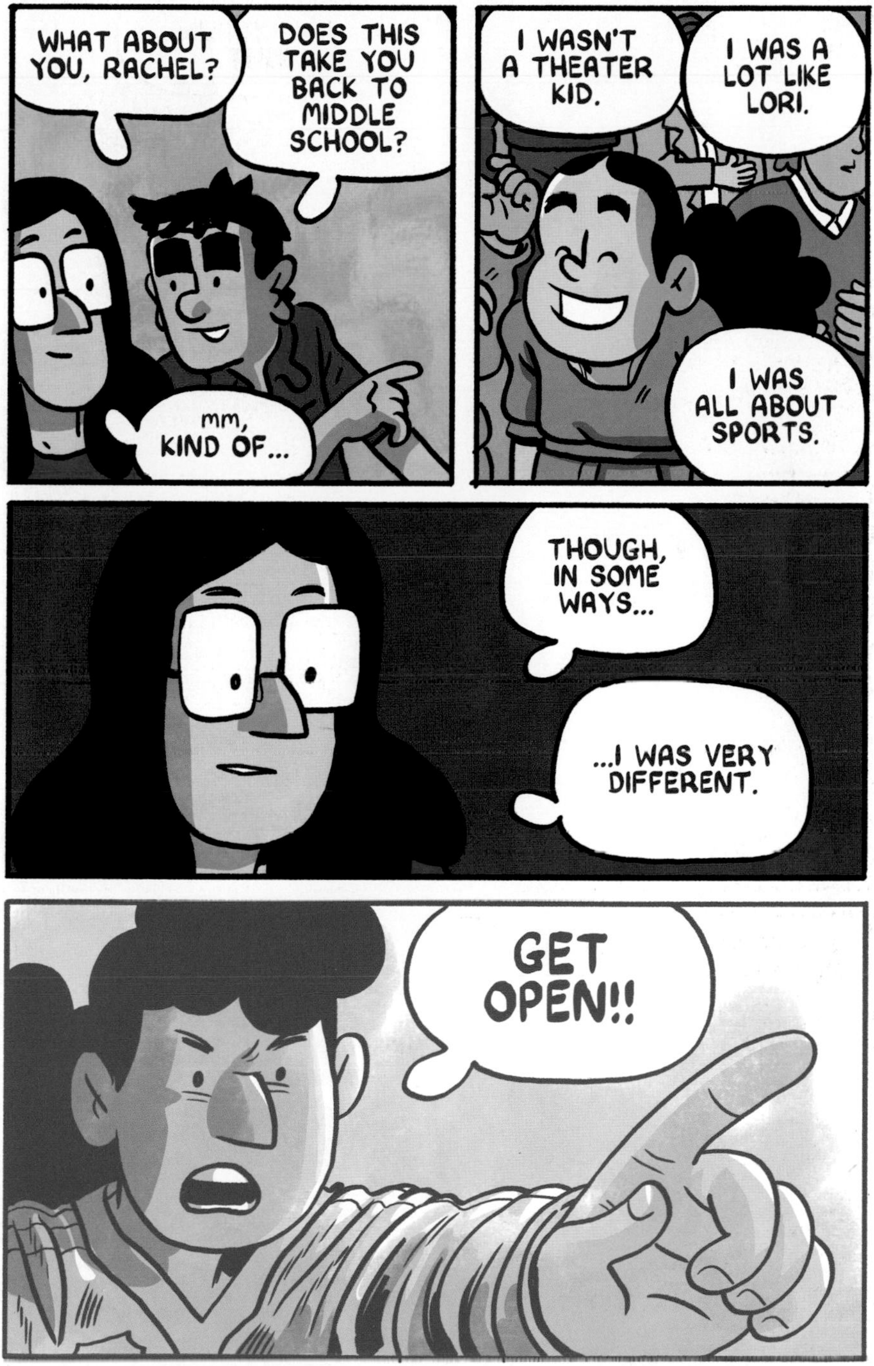
WHAT ABOUT YOU, RACHEL?
DOES THIS TAKE YOU BACK TO MIDDLE SCHOOL?
mm, KIND OF...
I WASN'T A THEATER KID.
I WAS A LOT LIKE LORI.
I WAS ALL ABOUT SPORTS.
THOUGH, IN SOME WAYS...
...I WAS VERY DIFFERENT.
GET OPEN!!

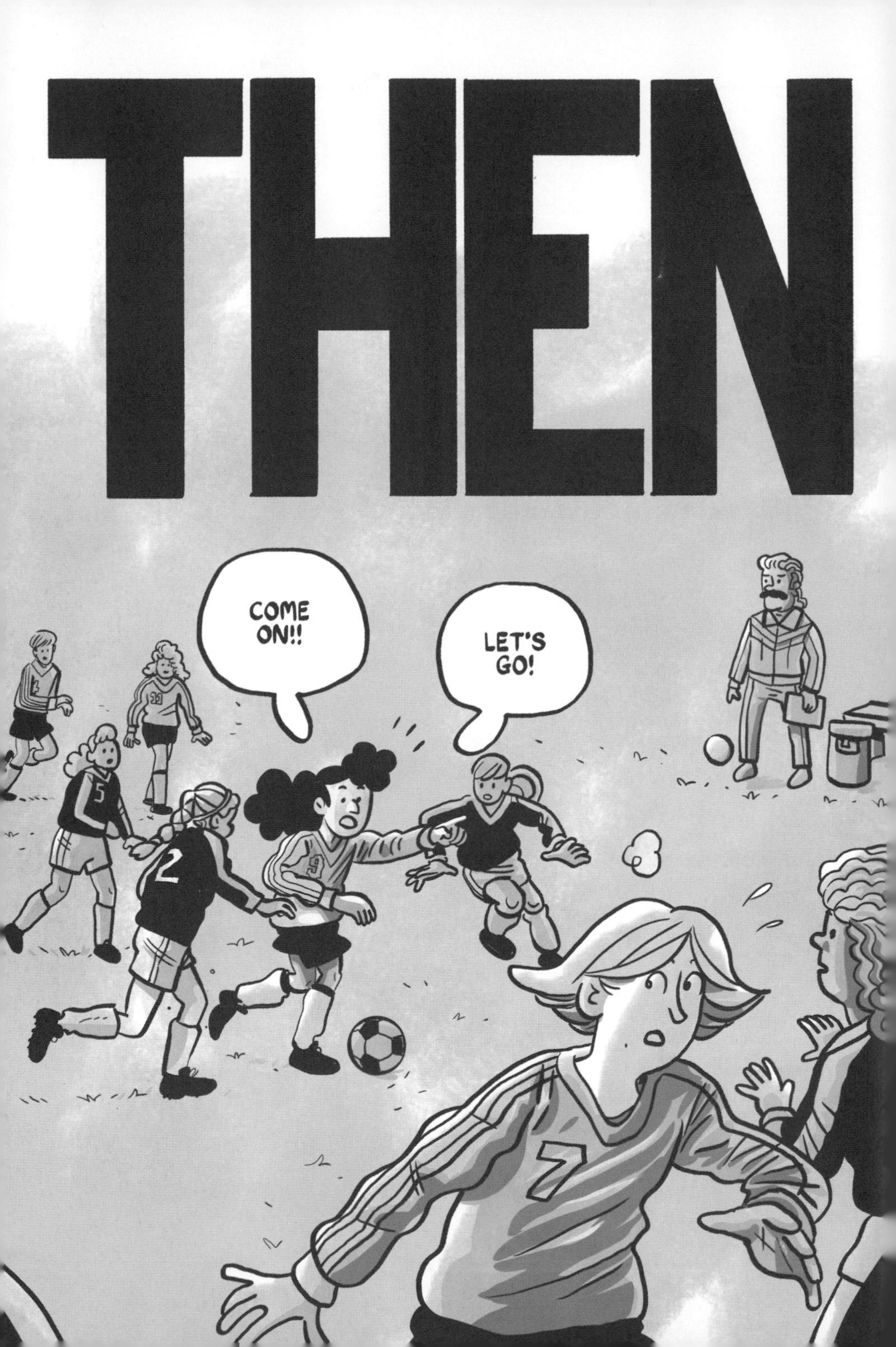
THEN
COME ON!!
LET'S GO!

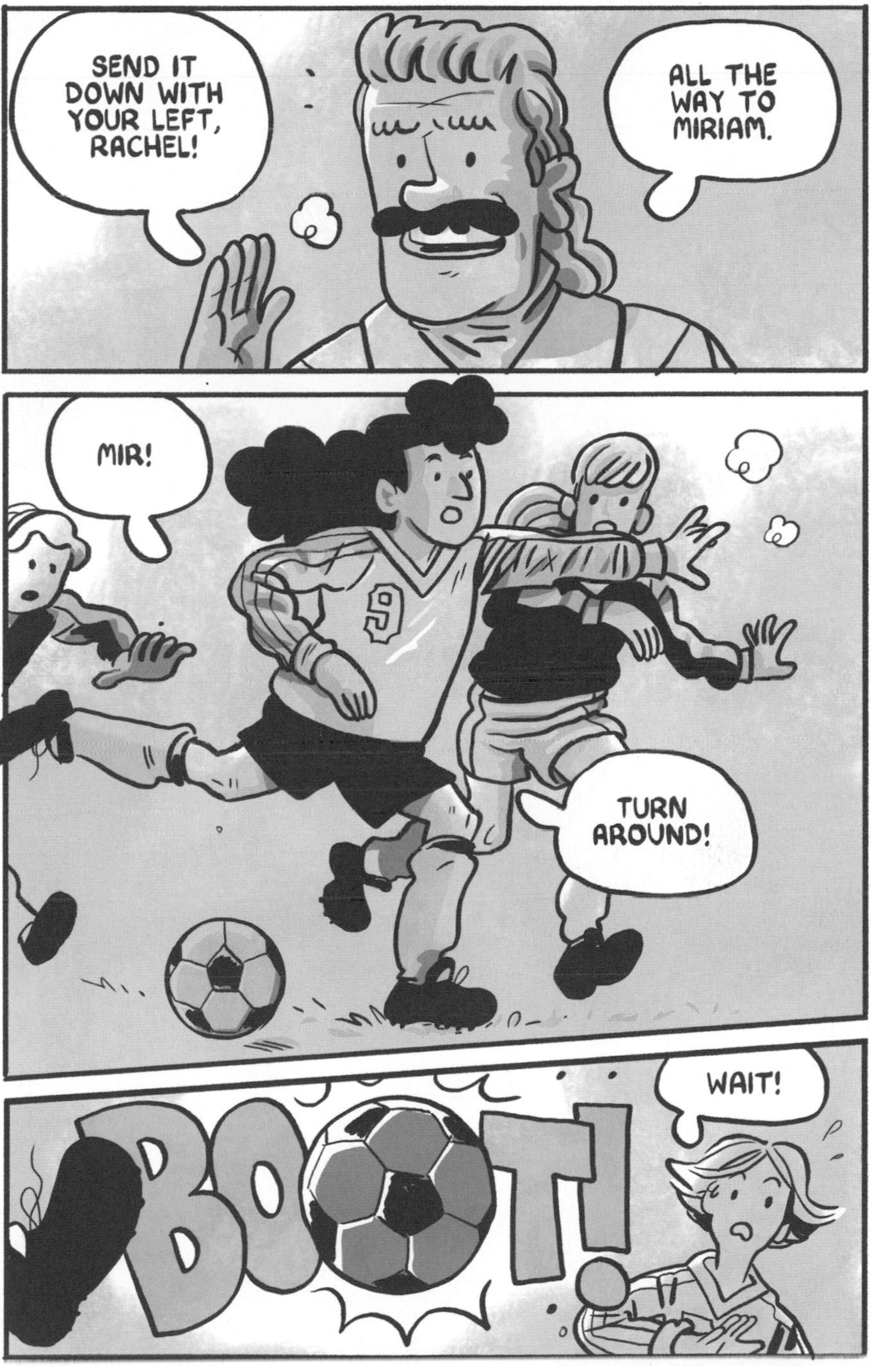
SEND IT DOWN WITH YOUR LEFT, RACHEL!
ALL THE WAY TO MIRIAM.
MIR!
TURN AROUND!
WAIT!
BOOT!

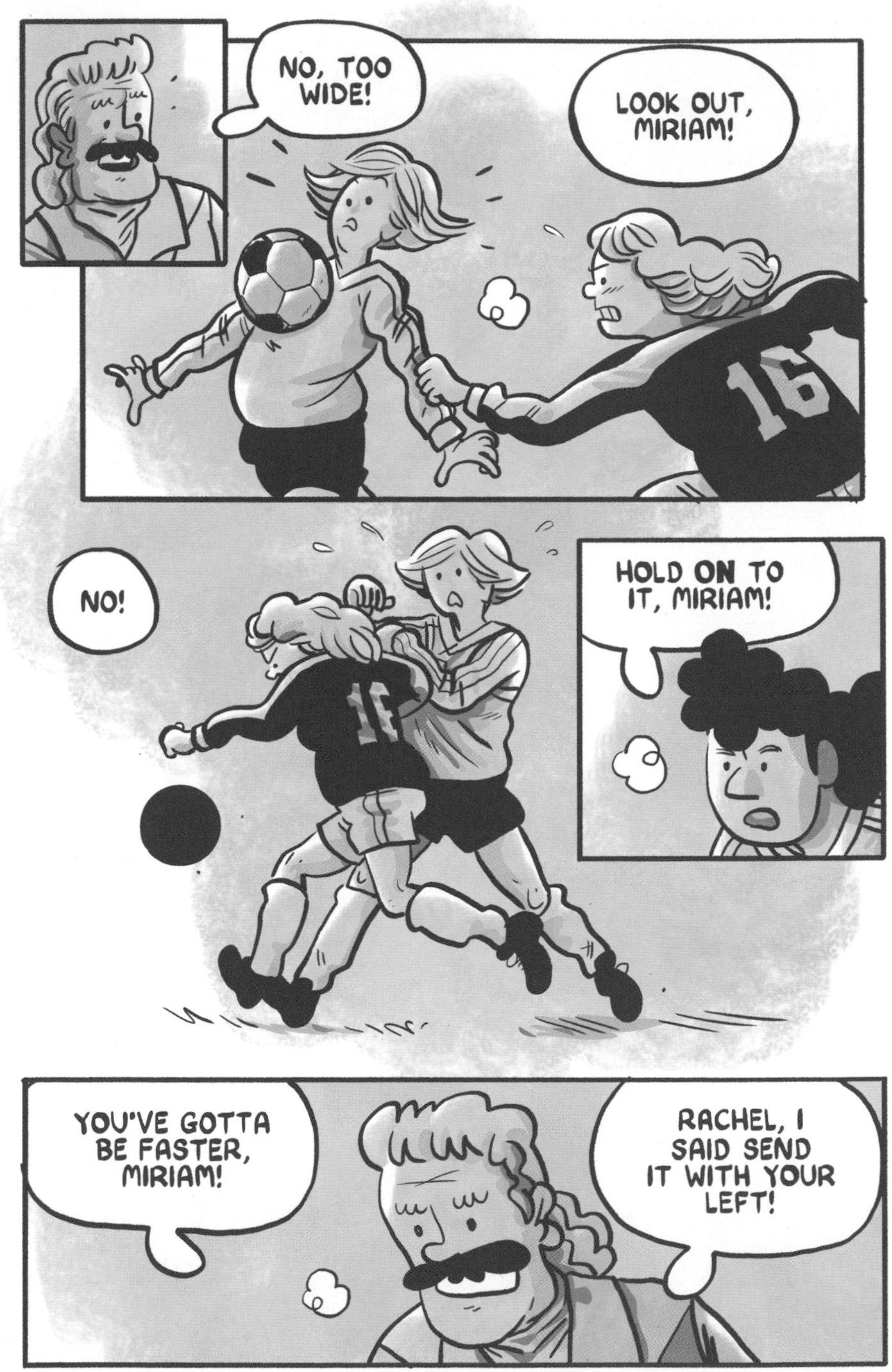
NO, TOO WIDE!
LOOK OUT, MIRIAM!
16
NO!
16
HOLD ON TO IT, MIRIAM!
YOU'VE GOTTA BE FASTER, MIRIAM!
RACHEL, I SAID SEND IT WITH YOUR LEFT!

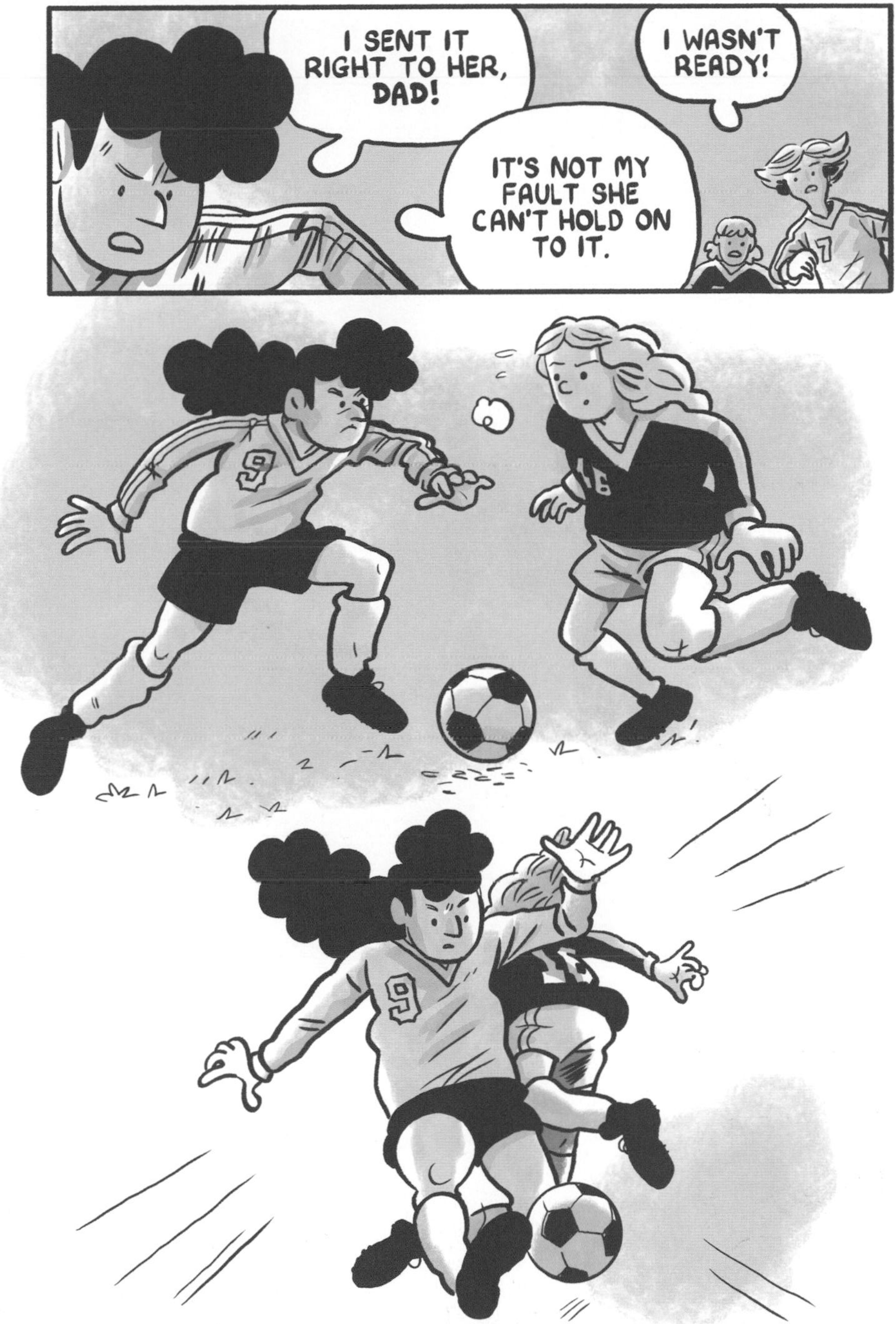
I SENT IT RIGHT TO HER, DAD!
I WASN'T READY!
IT'S NOT MY FAULT SHE CAN'T HOLD ON TO IT.

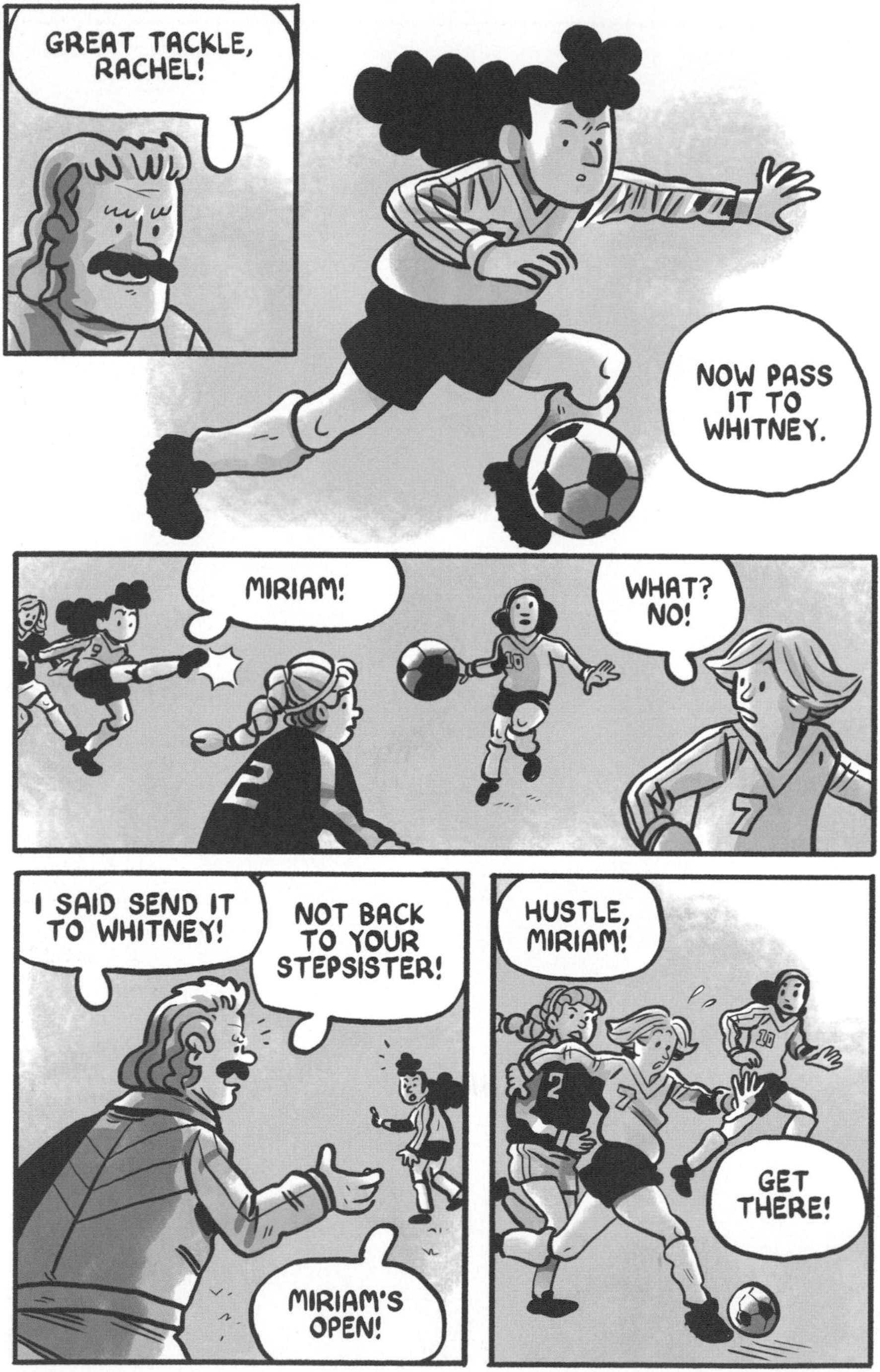
GREAT TACKLE, RACHEL!
NOW PASS IT TO WHITNEY.
MIRIAM!
WHAT? NO!
I SAID SEND IT TO WHITNEY!
NOT BACK TO YOUR STEPSISTER!
MIRIAM'S OPEN!
HUSTLE, MIRIAM!
GET THERE!

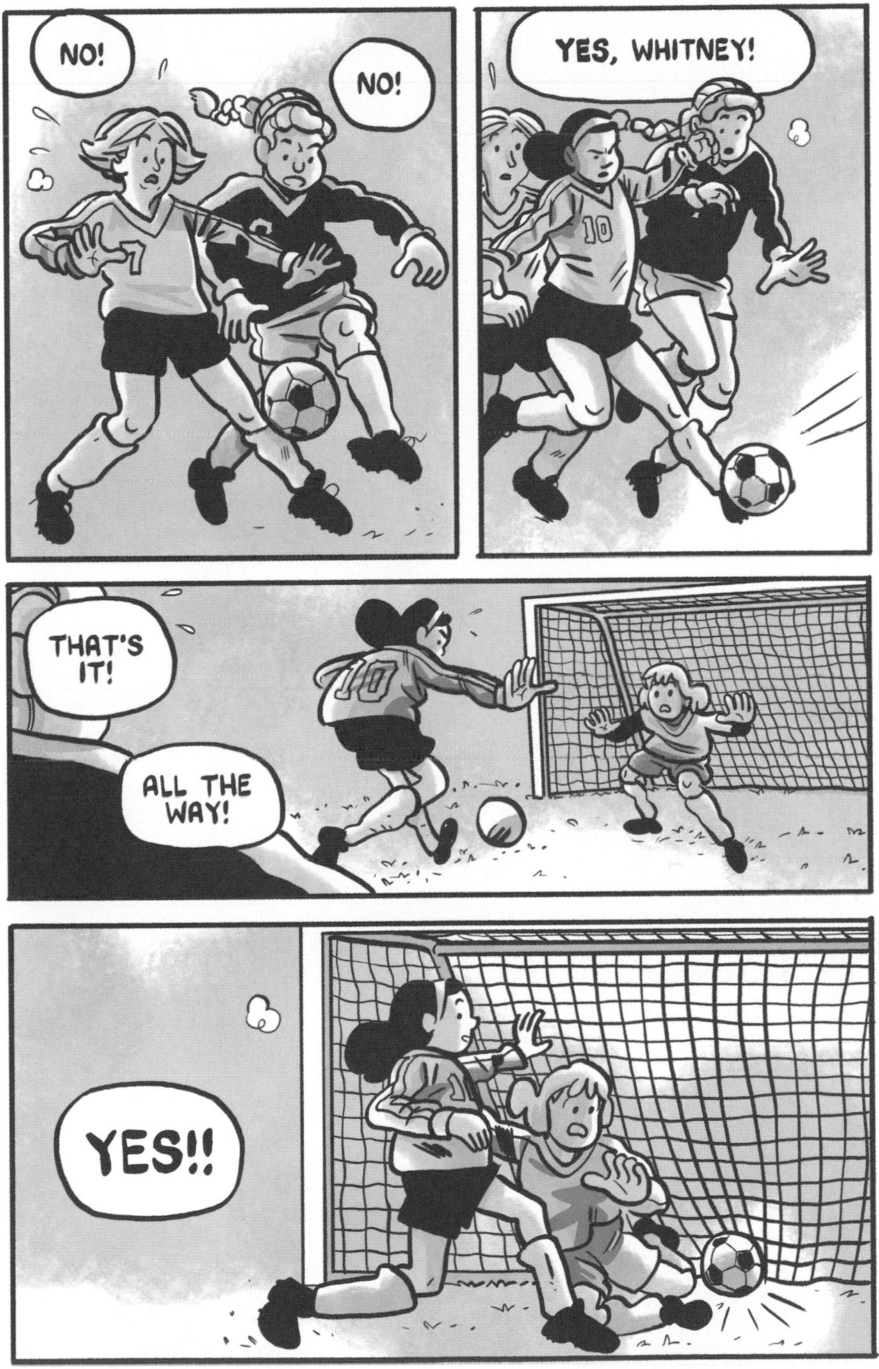
NO!
NO!
YES, WHITNEY!
THAT'S IT!
ALL THE WAY!
YES!!

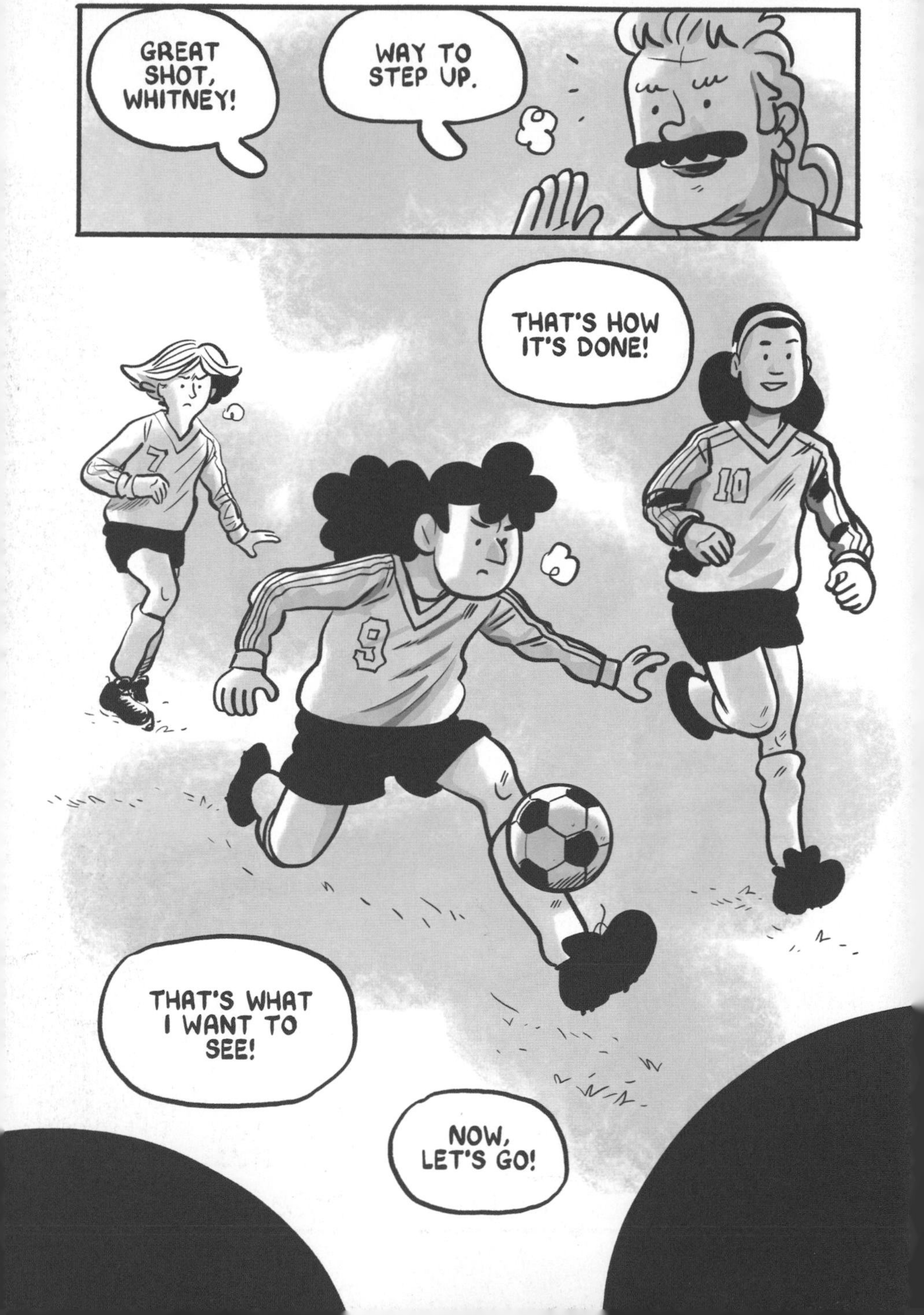
GREAT SHOT, WHITNEY!
WAY TO STEP UP.
THAT'S HOW IT'S DONE!
THAT'S WHAT I WANT TO SEE!
NOW, LET'S GO!

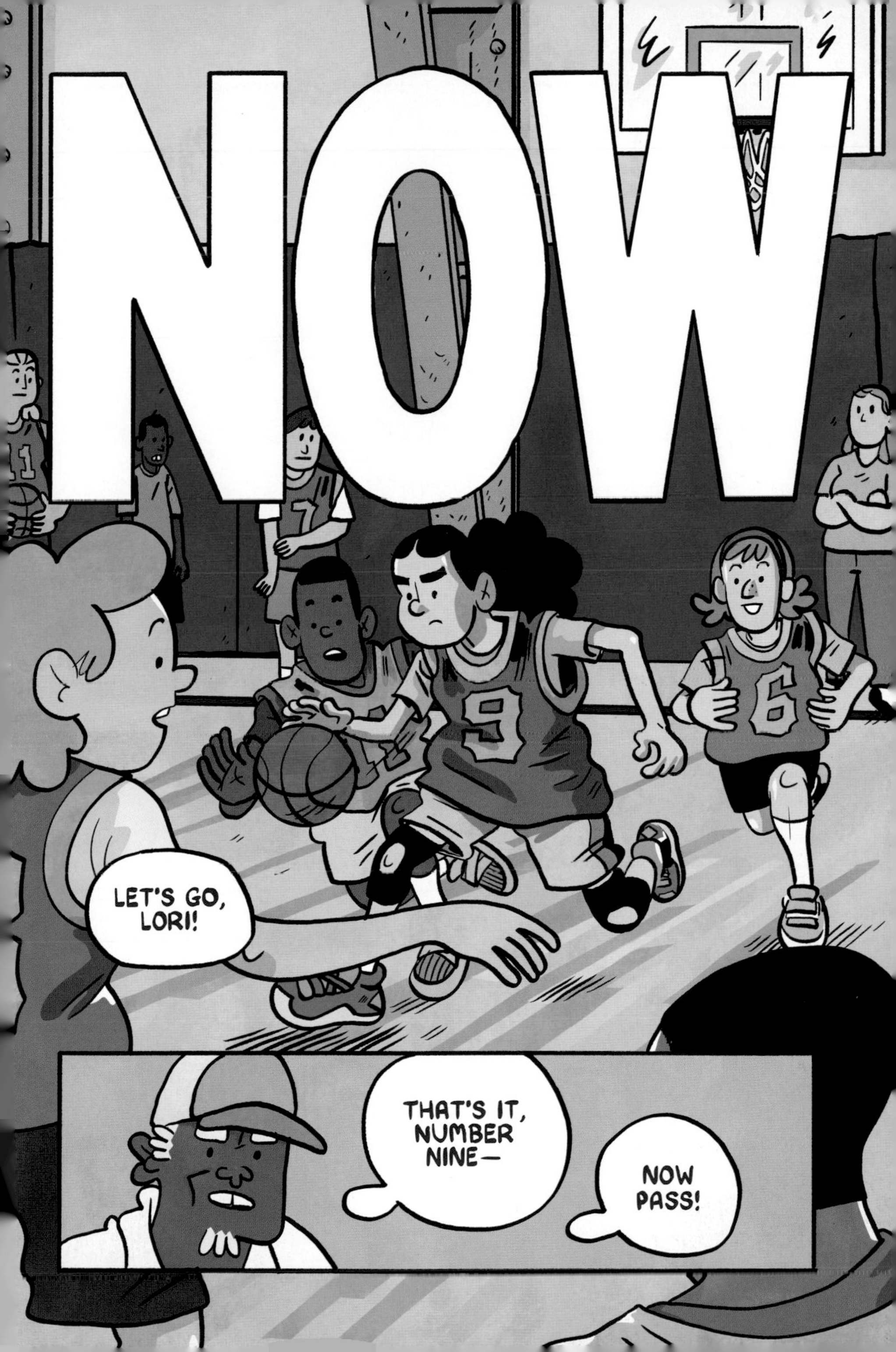
NOW
LET'S GO, LORI!
THAT'S IT, NUMBER NINE—
NOW PASS!

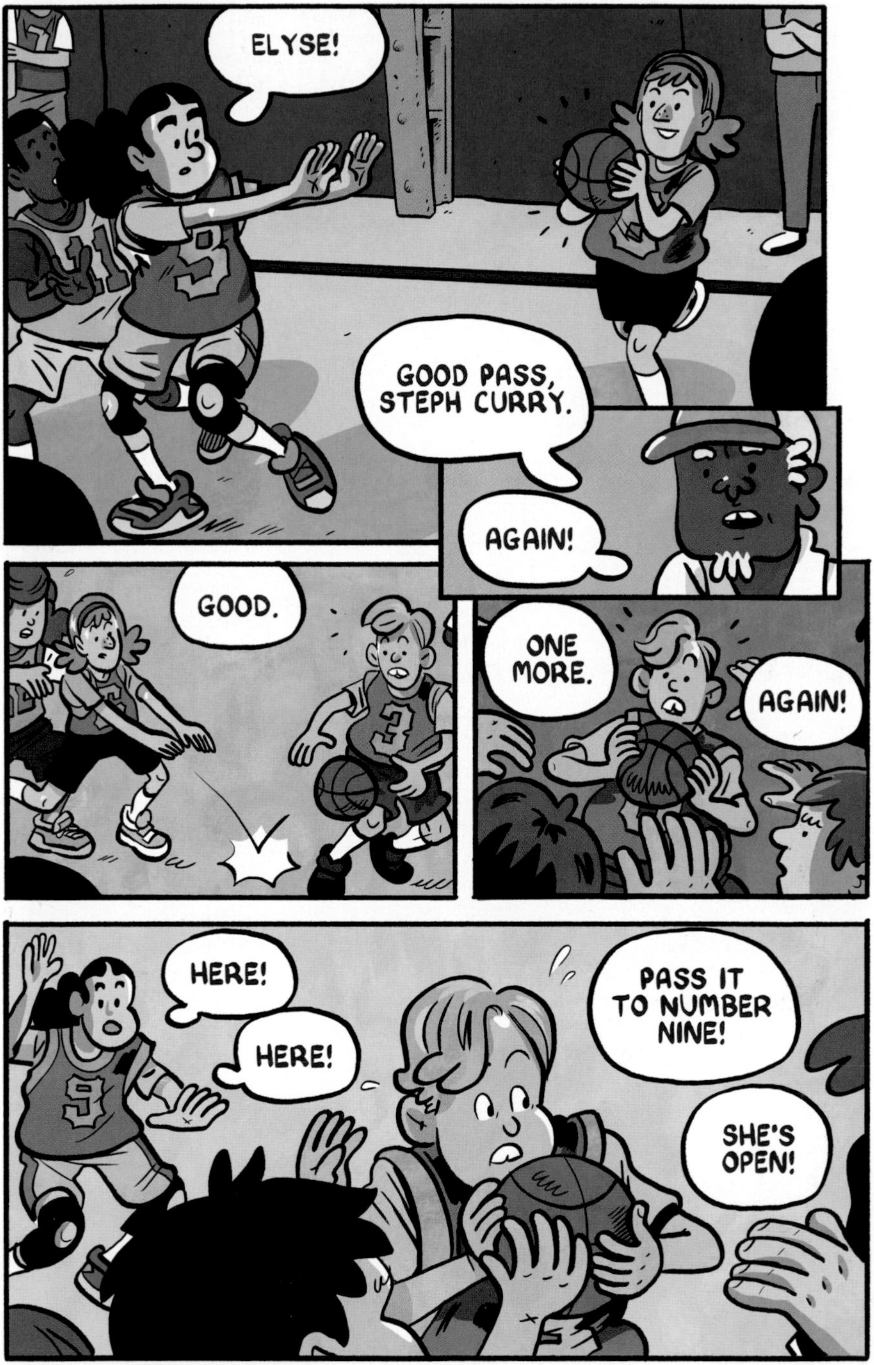
ELYSE!
GOOD PASS, STEPH CURRY.
AGAIN!
GOOD.
ONE MORE.
AGAIN!
HERE!
HERE!
PASS IT TO NUMBER NINE!
SHE'S OPEN!

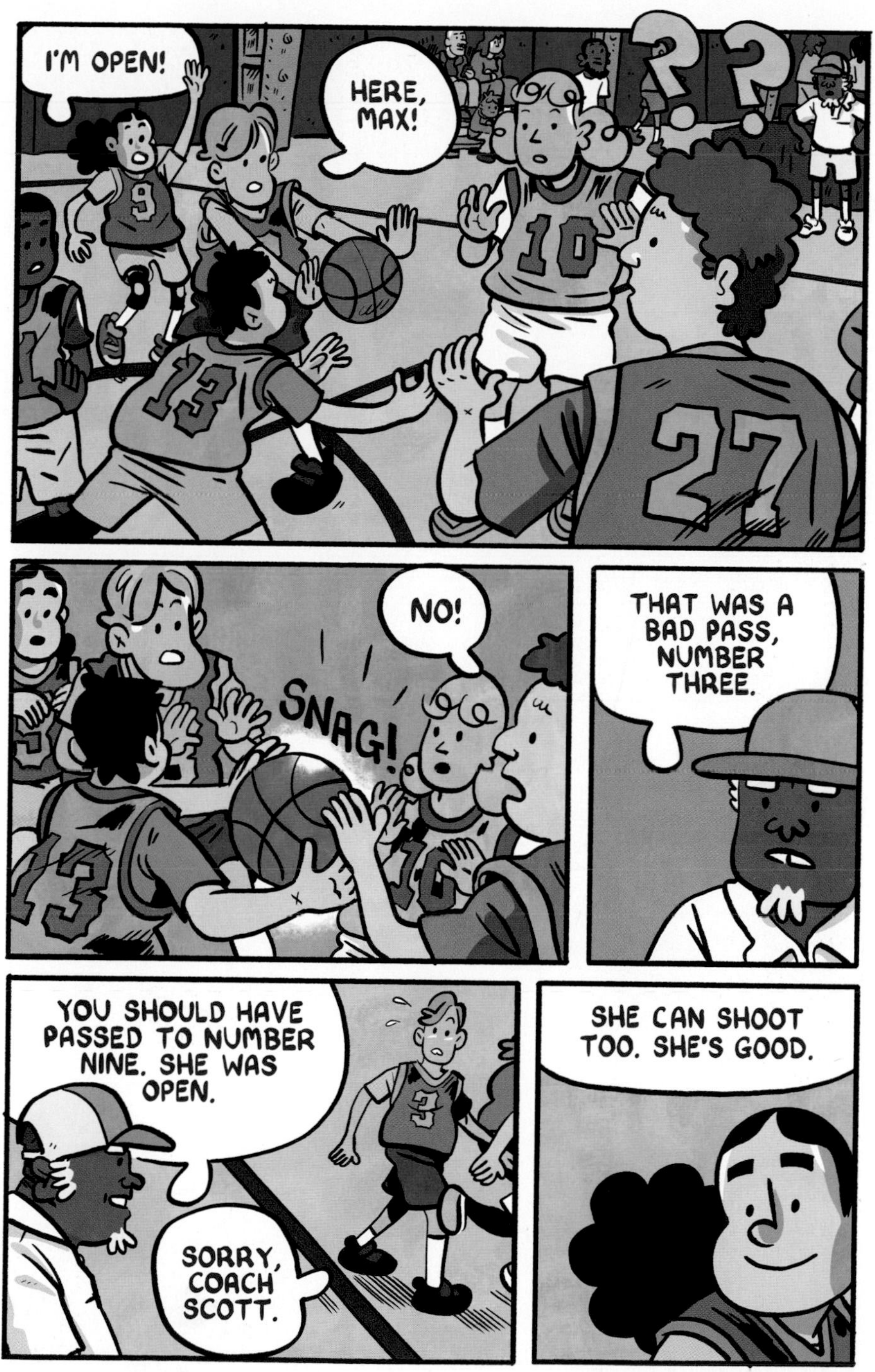
I'M OPEN!
HERE, MAX!
??
NO!
SNAG!
THAT WAS A BAD PASS, NUMBER THREE.
YOU SHOULD HAVE PASSED TO NUMBER NINE. SHE WAS OPEN.
SORRY, COACH SCOTT.
SHE CAN SHOOT TOO. SHE'S GOOD.

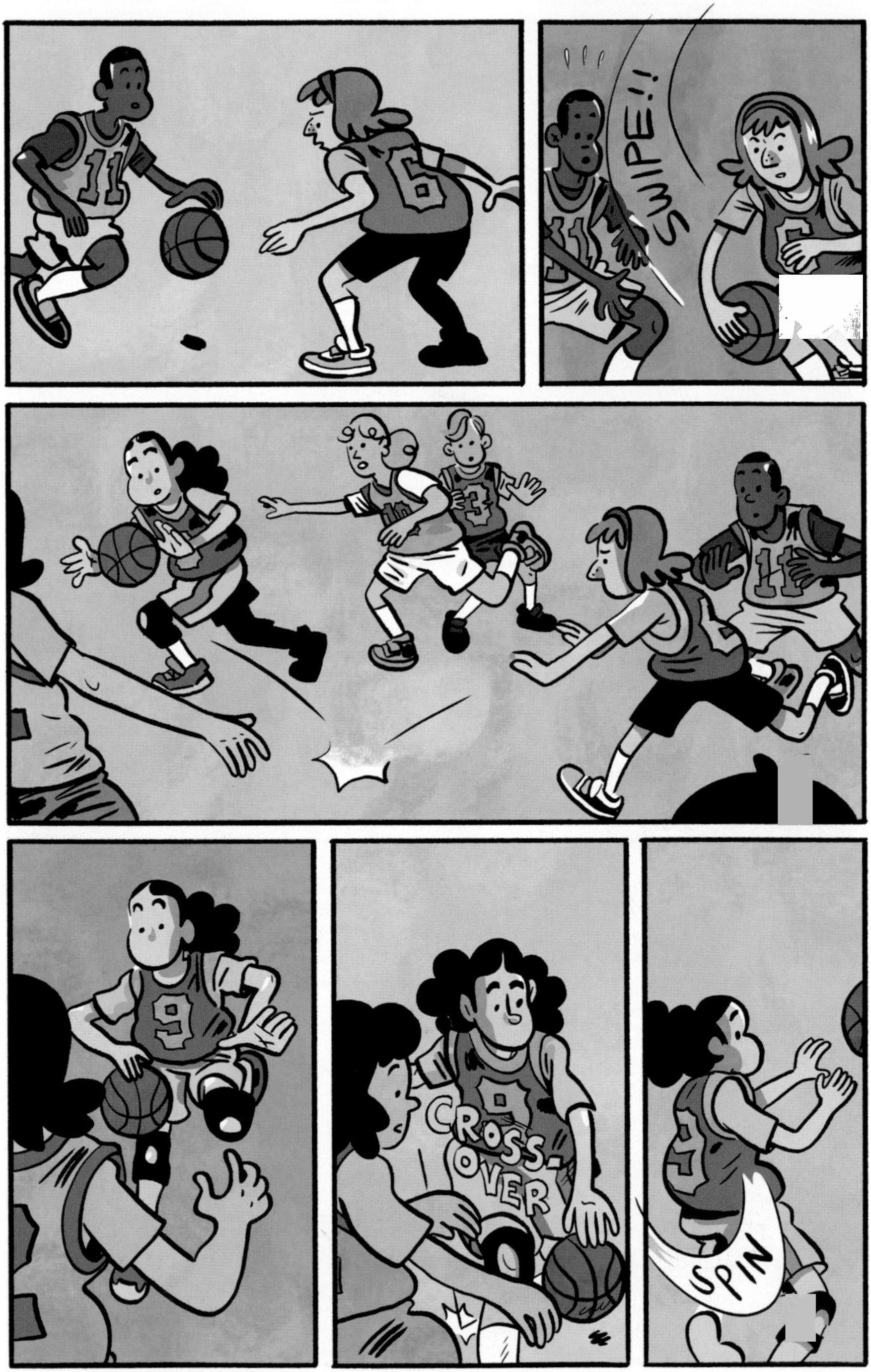
SWIPE!!
CROSS-OVER
SPIN

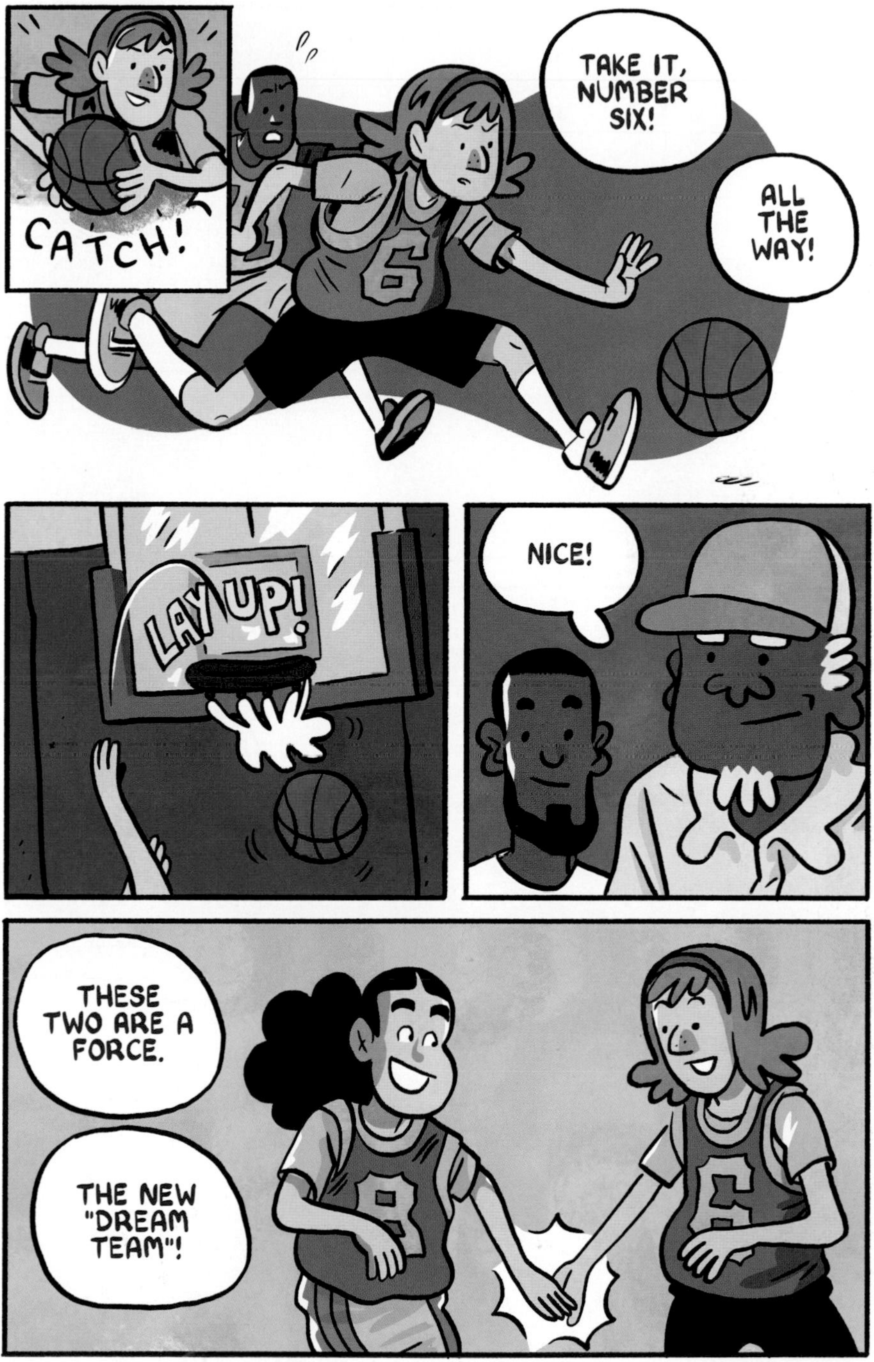
CATCH!
TAKE IT, NUMBER SIX!
ALL THE WAY!
LAY UP!
NICE!
THESE TWO ARE A FORCE.
THE NEW "DREAM TEAM"!

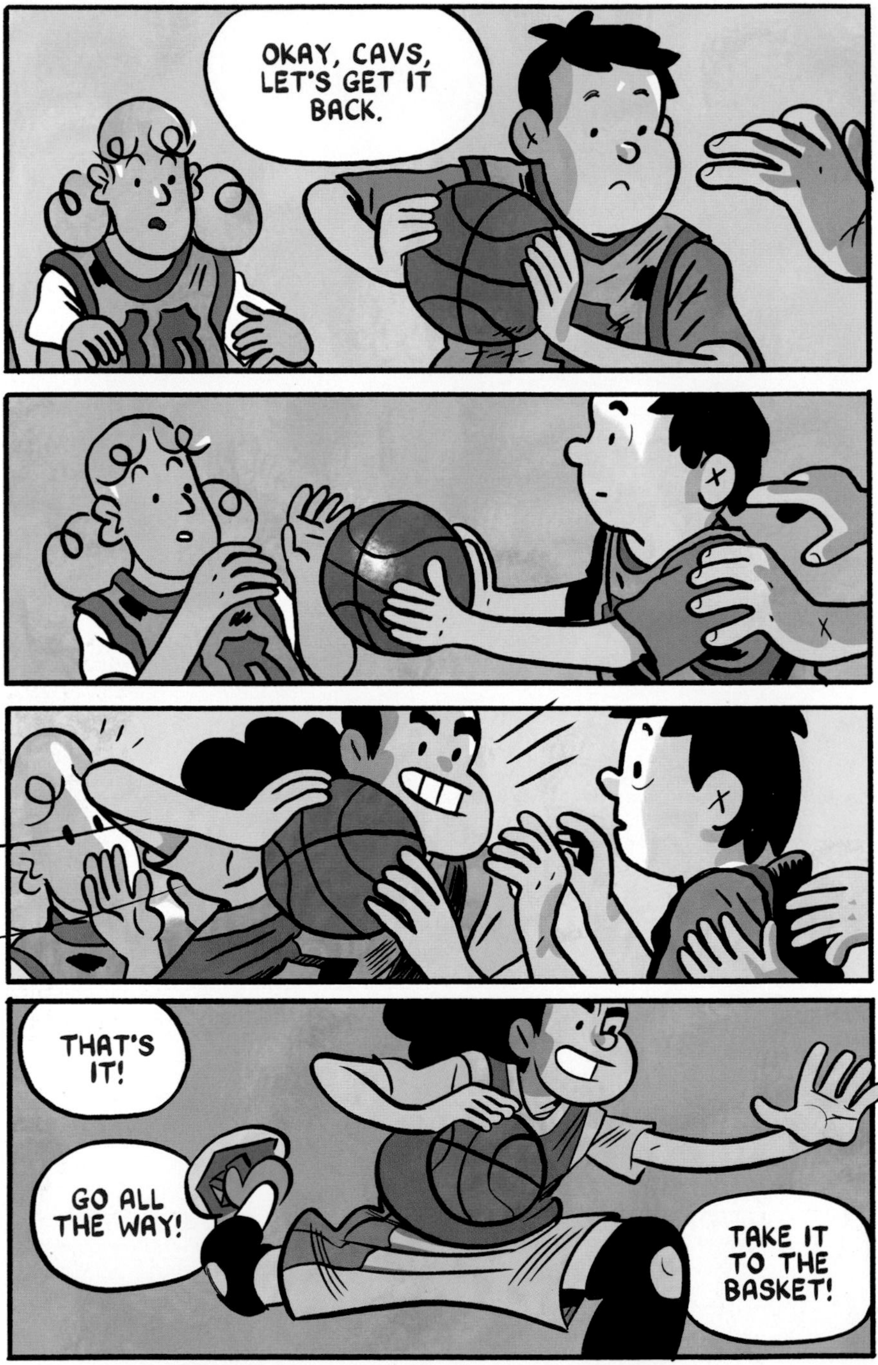
OKAY, CAVS, LET'S GET IT BACK.
THAT'S IT!
GO ALL THE WAY!
TAKE IT TO THE BASKET!

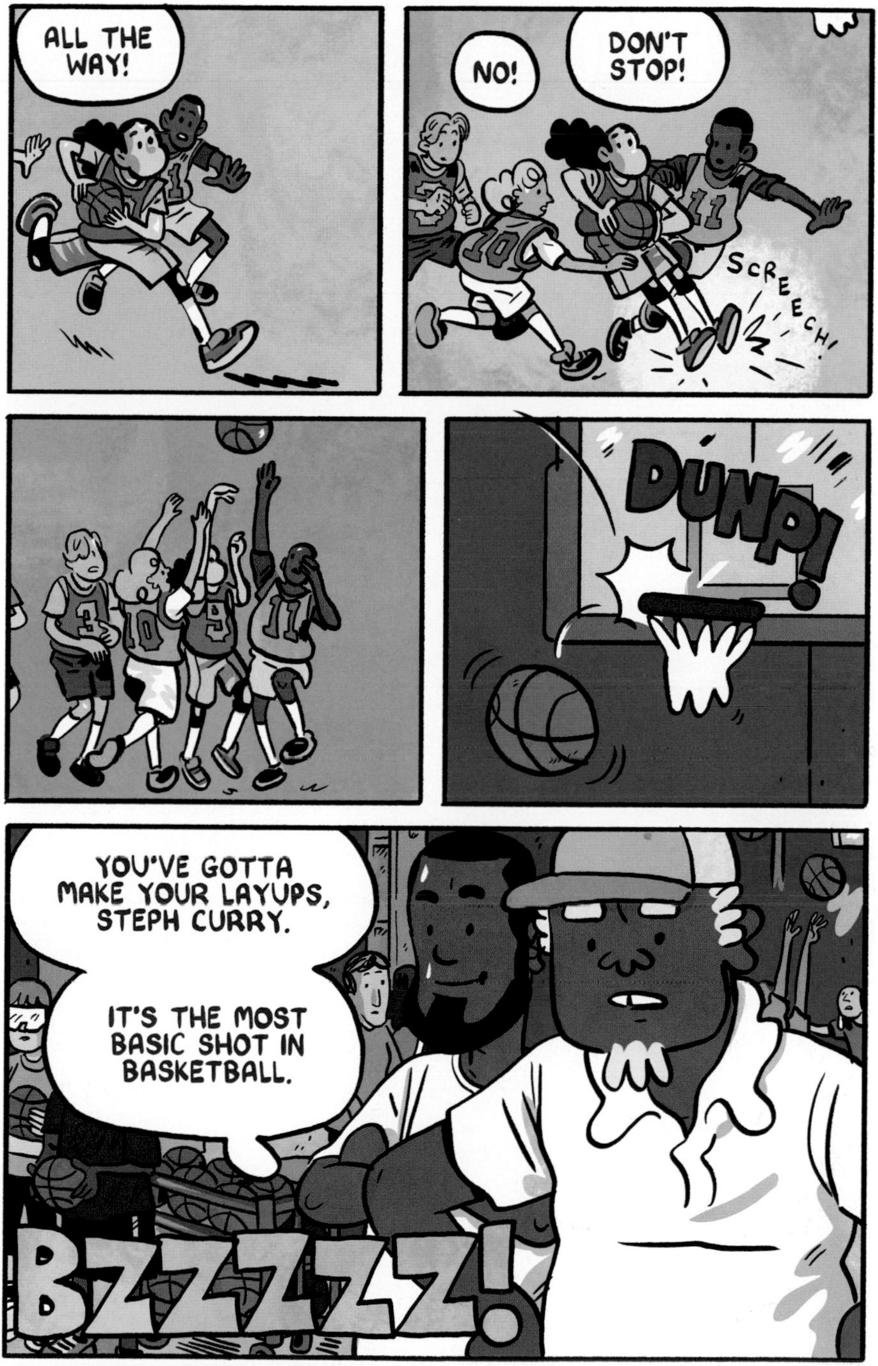
ALL THE WAY!
NO!
DON'T STOP!
SCREEECH!
DUNP!
YOU'VE GOTTA MAKE YOUR LAYUPS, STEPH CURRY.
IT'S THE MOST BASIC SHOT IN BASKETBALL.
BZZZZZZ!

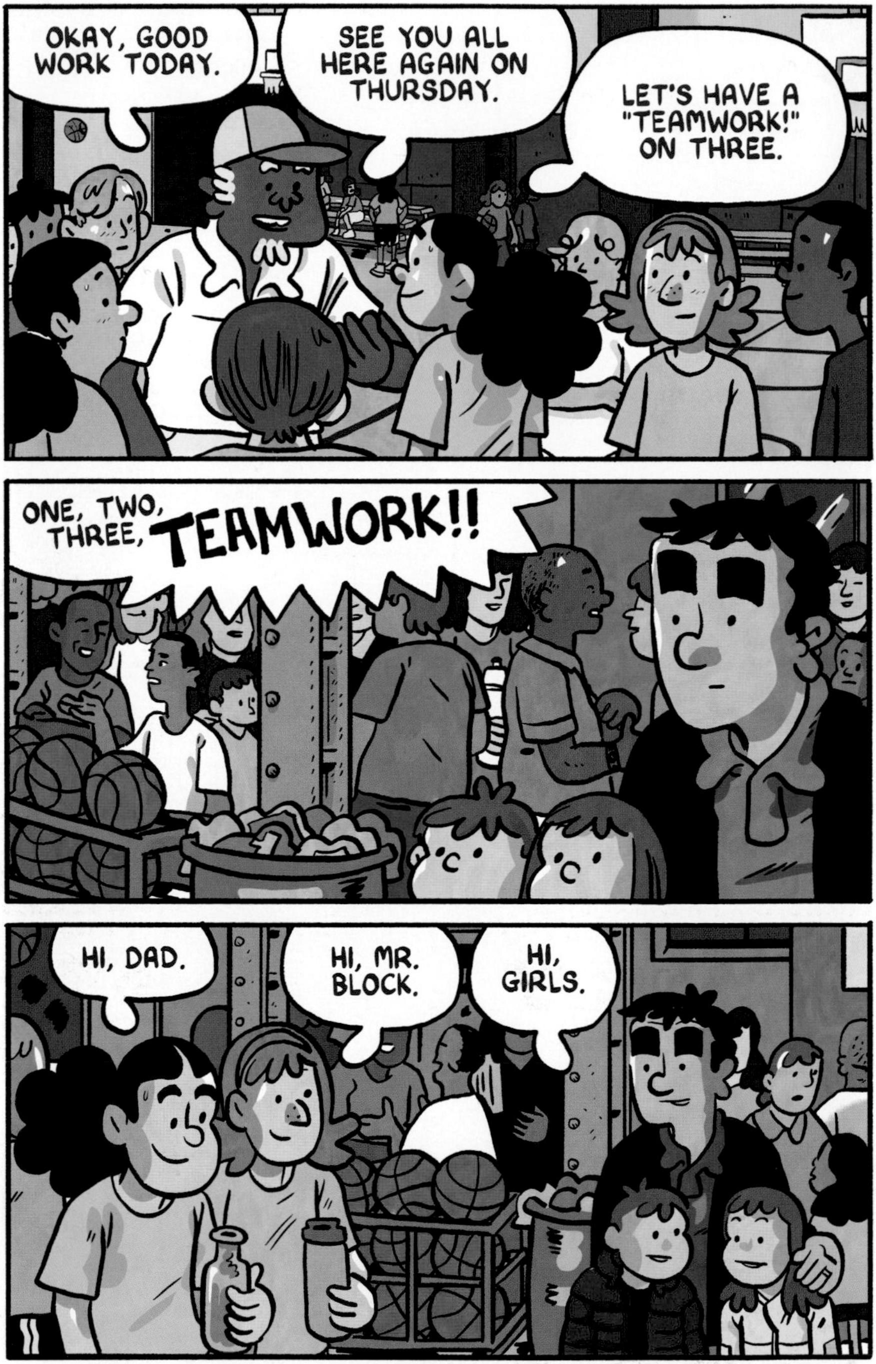
OKAY, GOOD WORK TODAY.
SEE YOU ALL HERE AGAIN ON THURSDAY.
LET'S HAVE A "TEAMWORK!" ON THREE.
ONE, TWO, THREE, TEAMWORK!!
HI, DAD.
HI, MR. BLOCK.
HI, GIRLS.

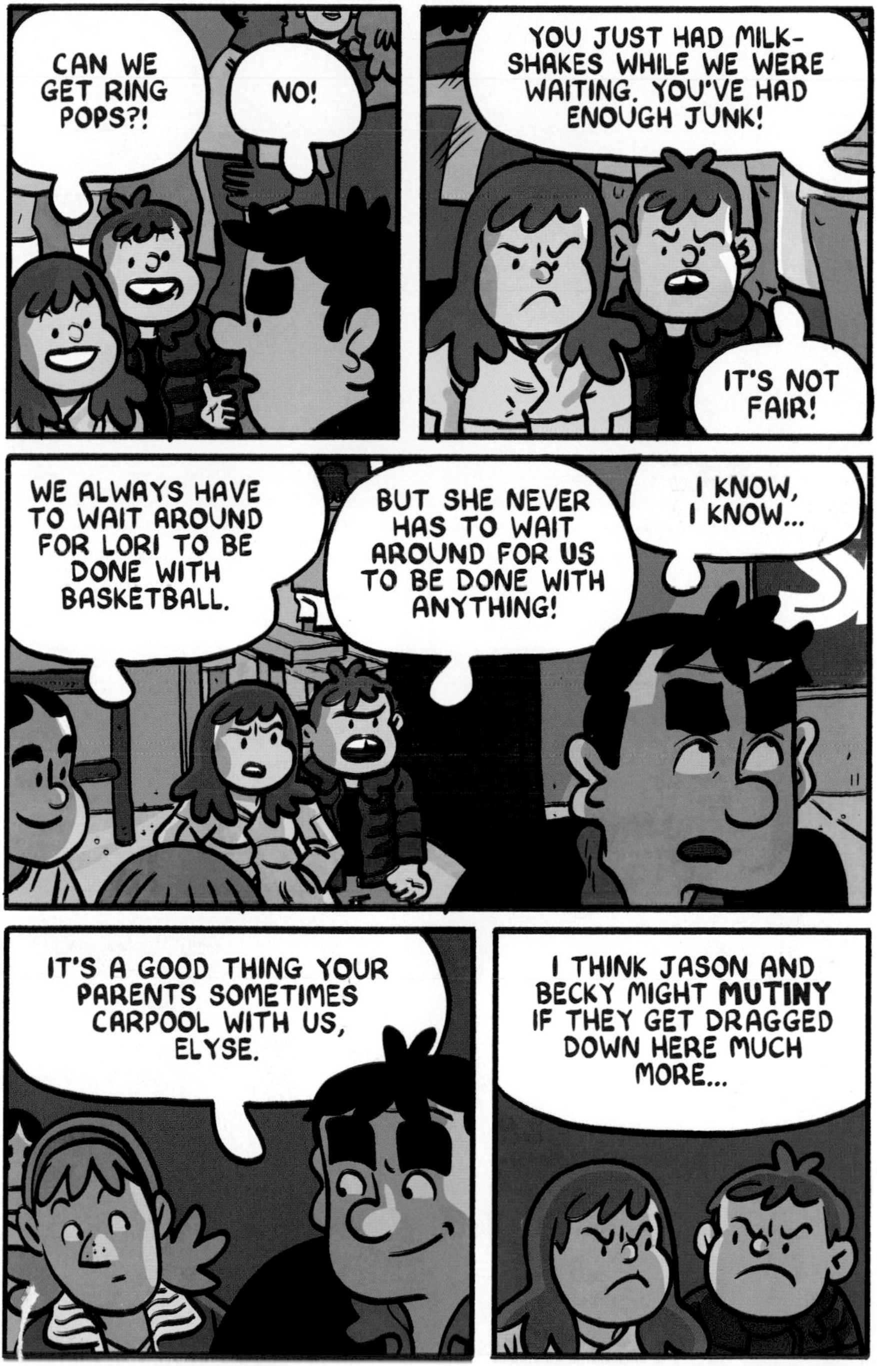
CAN WE GET RING POPS?!
NO!
YOU JUST HAD MILK-SHAKES WHILE WE WERE WAITING. YOU'VE HAD ENOUGH JUNK!
IT'S NOT FAIR!
WE ALWAYS HAVE TO WAIT AROUND FOR LORI TO BE DONE WITH BASKETBALL.
BUT SHE NEVER HAS TO WAIT AROUND FOR US TO BE DONE WITH ANYTHING!
I KNOW, I KNOW...
IT'S A GOOD THING YOUR PARENTS SOMETIMES CARPOOL WITH US, ELYSE.
I THINK JASON AND BECKY MIGHT MUTINY IF THEY GET DRAGGED DOWN HERE MUCH MORE...

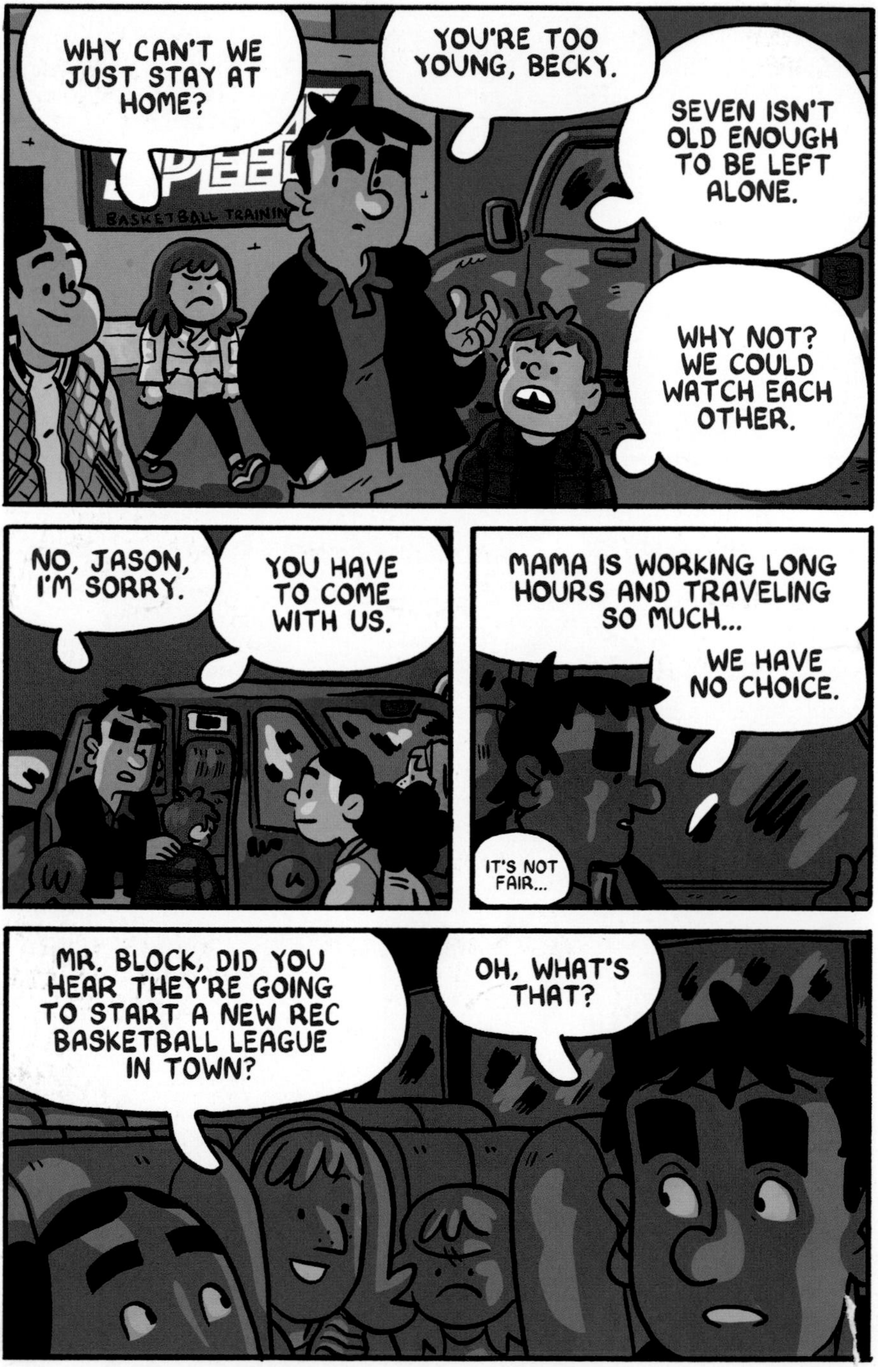
SPEED
BASKETBALL TRAINING
WHY CAN'T WE JUST STAY AT HOME?
YOU'RE TOO YOUNG, BECKY.
SEVEN ISN'T OLD ENOUGH TO BE LEFT ALONE.
WHY NOT? WE COULD WATCH EACH OTHER.
NO, JASON, I'M SORRY.
YOU HAVE TO COME WITH US.
MAMA IS WORKING LONG HOURS AND TRAVELING SO MUCH...
WE HAVE NO CHOICE.
IT'S NOT FAIR...
MR. BLOCK, DID YOU HEAR THEY'RE GOING TO START A NEW REC BASKETBALL LEAGUE IN TOWN?
OH, WHAT'S THAT?

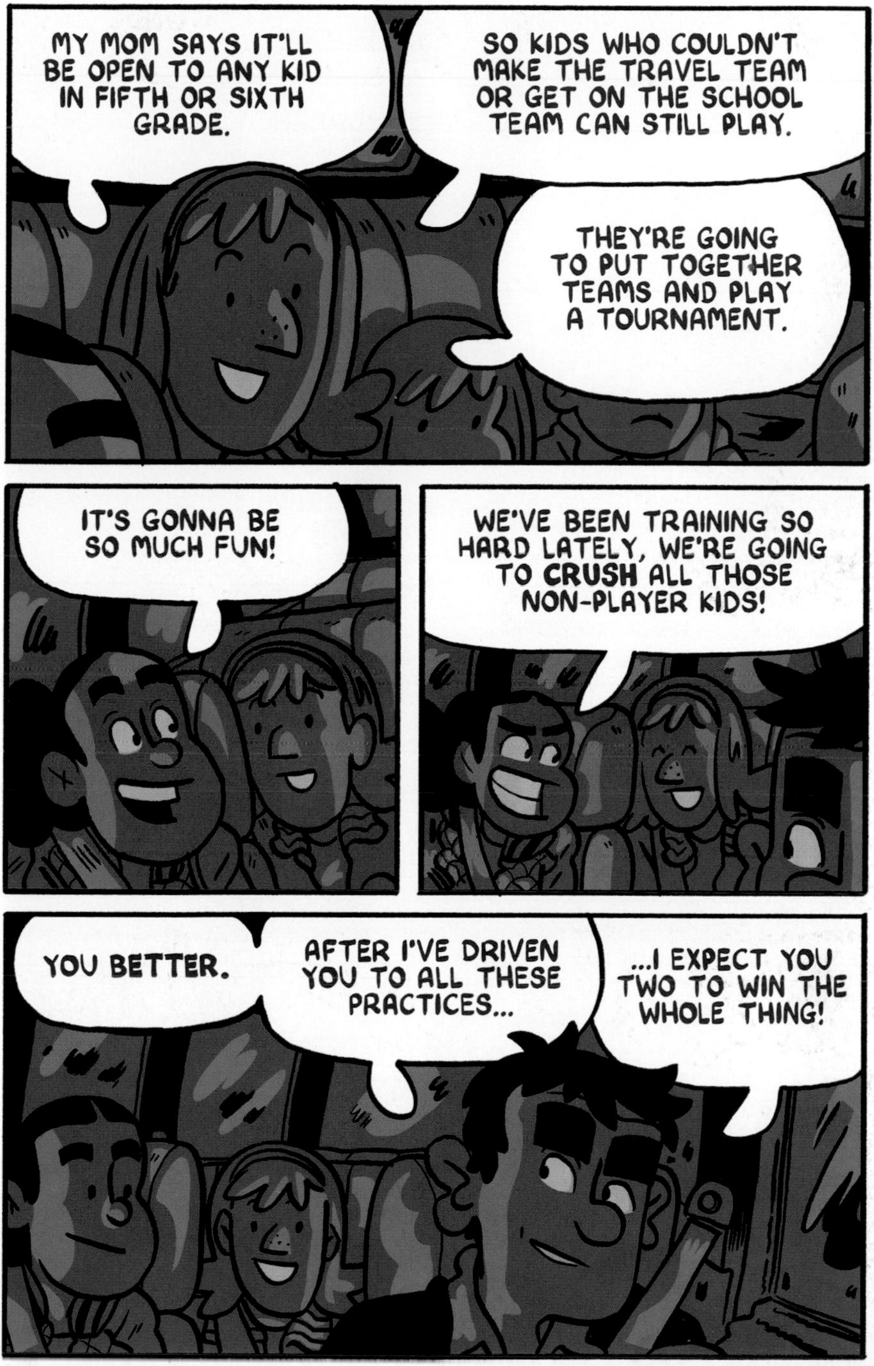
MY MOM SAYS IT'LL BE OPEN TO ANY KID IN FIFTH OR SIXTH GRADE.
SO KIDS WHO COULDN'T MAKE THE TRAVEL TEAM OR GET ON THE SCHOOL TEAM CAN STILL PLAY.
THEY'RE GOING TO PUT TOGETHER TEAMS AND PLAY A TOURNAMENT.
IT'S GONNA BE SO MUCH FUN!
WE'VE BEEN TRAINING SO HARD LATELY, WE'RE GOING TO **CRUSH** ALL THOSE NON-PLAYER KIDS!
YOU **BETTER.**
AFTER I'VE DRIVEN YOU TO ALL THESE PRACTICES...
...I EXPECT YOU TWO TO WIN THE WHOLE THING!

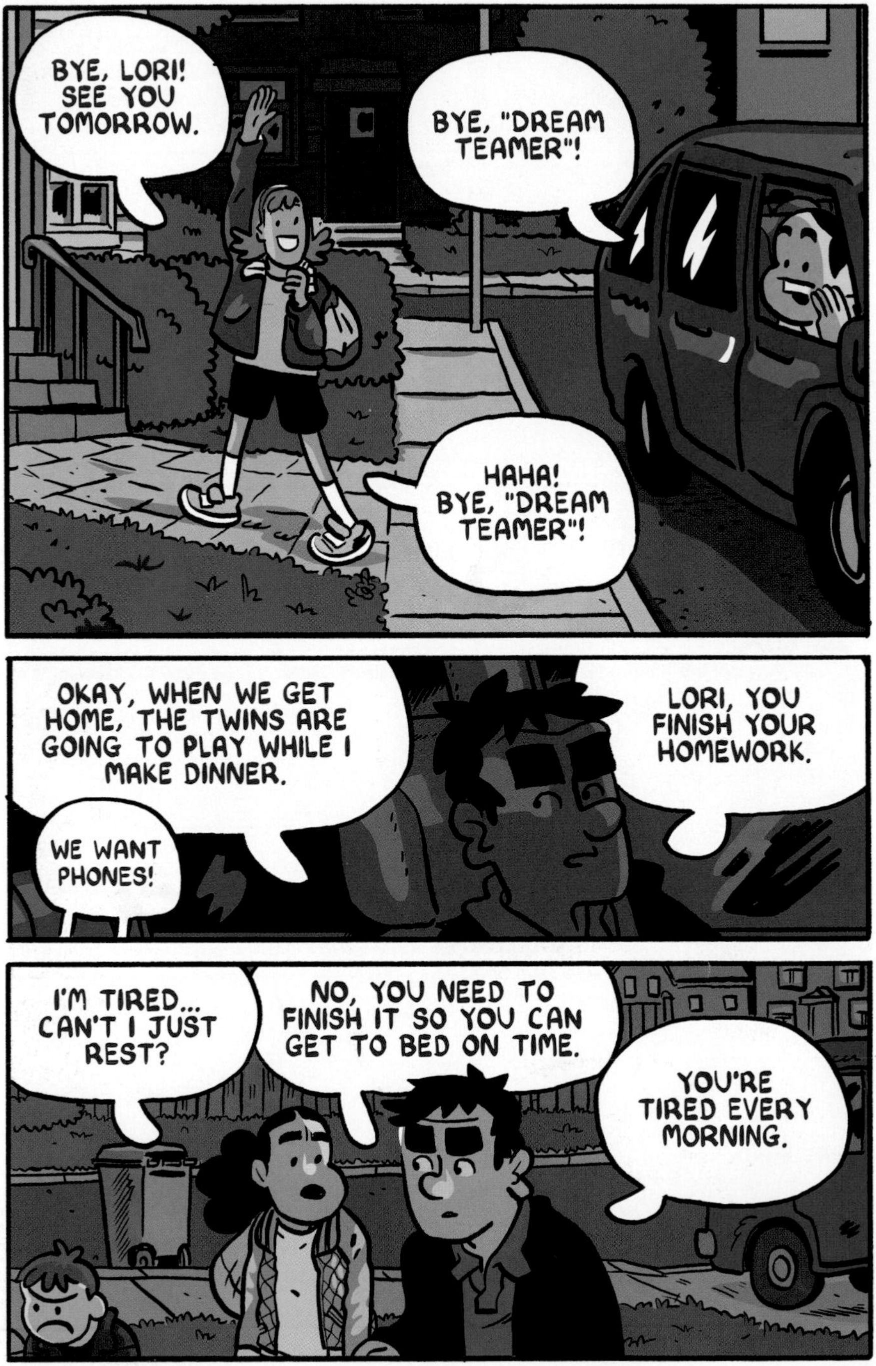
BYE, LORI! SEE YOU TOMORROW.
BYE, "DREAM TEAMER"!
HAHA! BYE, "DREAM TEAMER"!
OKAY, WHEN WE GET HOME, THE TWINS ARE GOING TO PLAY WHILE I MAKE DINNER.
LORI, YOU FINISH YOUR HOMEWORK.
WE WANT PHONES!
I'M TIRED... CAN'T I JUST REST?
NO, YOU NEED TO FINISH IT SO YOU CAN GET TO BED ON TIME.
YOU'RE TIRED EVERY MORNING.

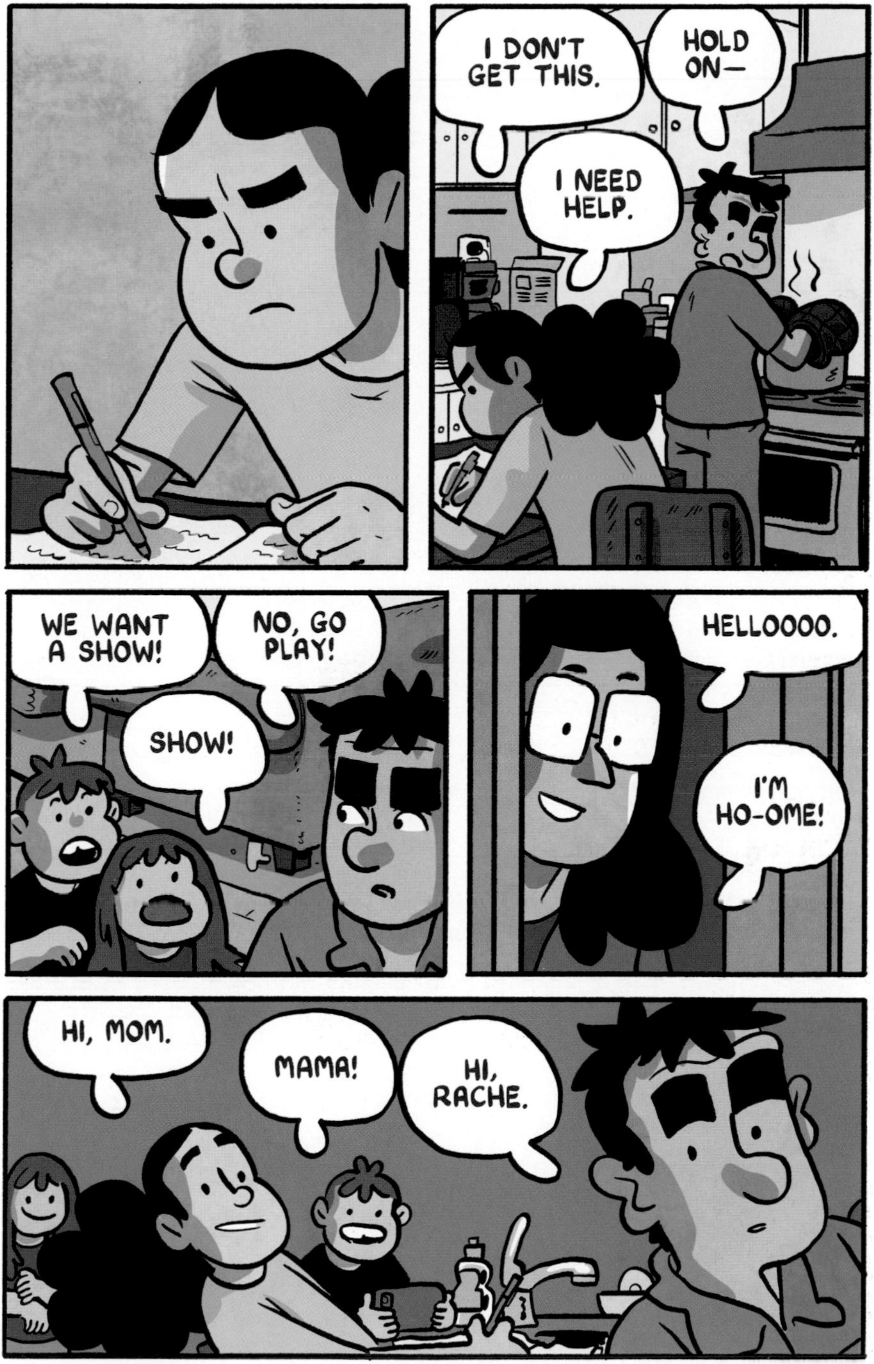
I DON'T GET THIS.
HOLD ON—
I NEED HELP.
WE WANT A SHOW!
NO, GO PLAY!
SHOW!
HELLOOOO.
I'M HO-OME!
HI, MOM.
MAMA!
HI, RACHE.

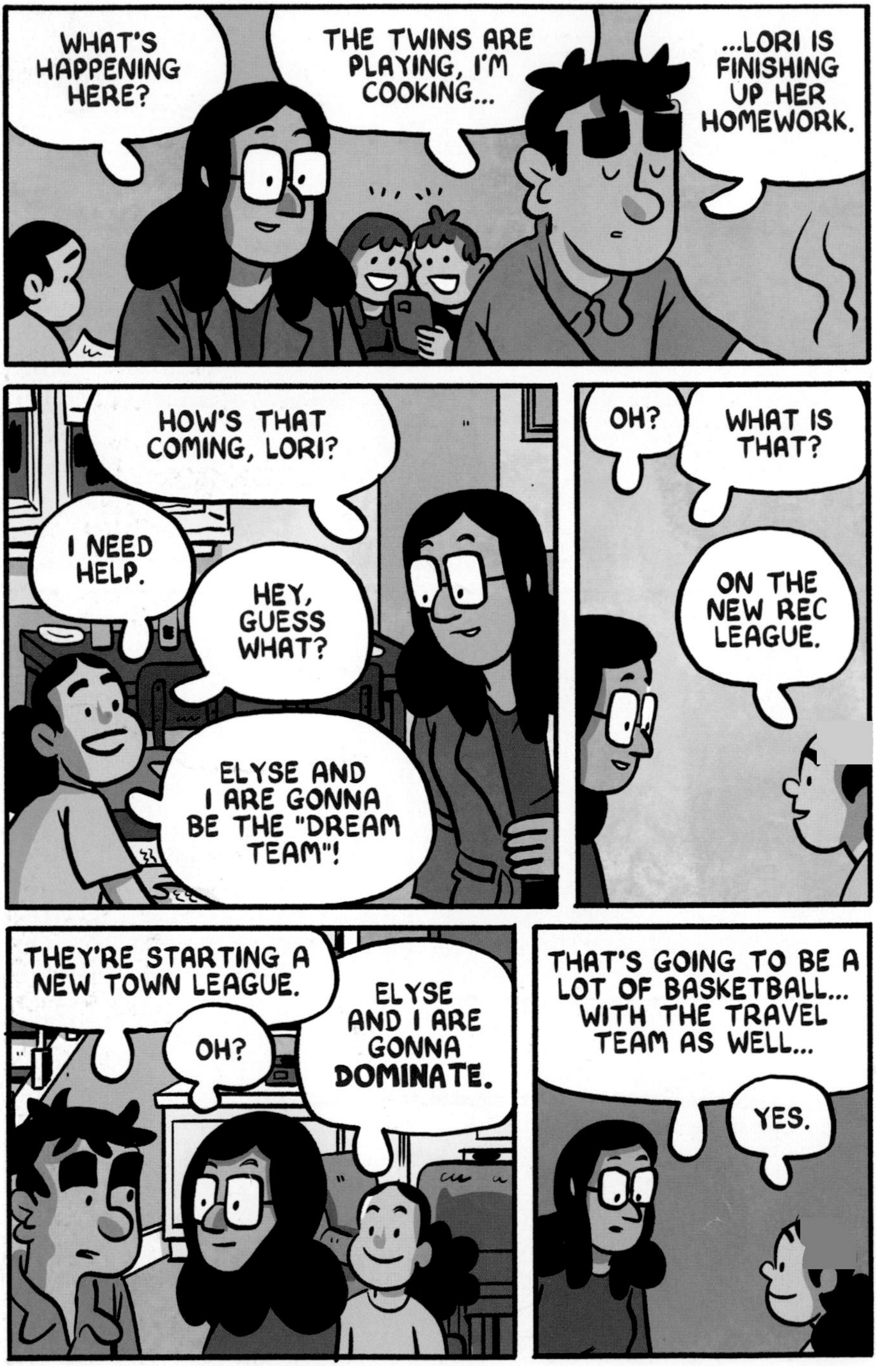
WHAT'S HAPPENING HERE?
THE TWINS ARE PLAYING, I'M COOKING...
...LORI IS FINISHING UP HER HOMEWORK.
HOW'S THAT COMING, LORI?
I NEED HELP.
HEY, GUESS WHAT?
ELYSE AND I ARE GONNA BE THE "DREAM TEAM"!
OH?
WHAT IS THAT?
ON THE NEW REC LEAGUE.
THEY'RE STARTING A NEW TOWN LEAGUE.
OH?
ELYSE AND I ARE GONNA **DOMINATE.**
THAT'S GOING TO BE A LOT OF BASKETBALL... WITH THE TRAVEL TEAM AS WELL...
YES.

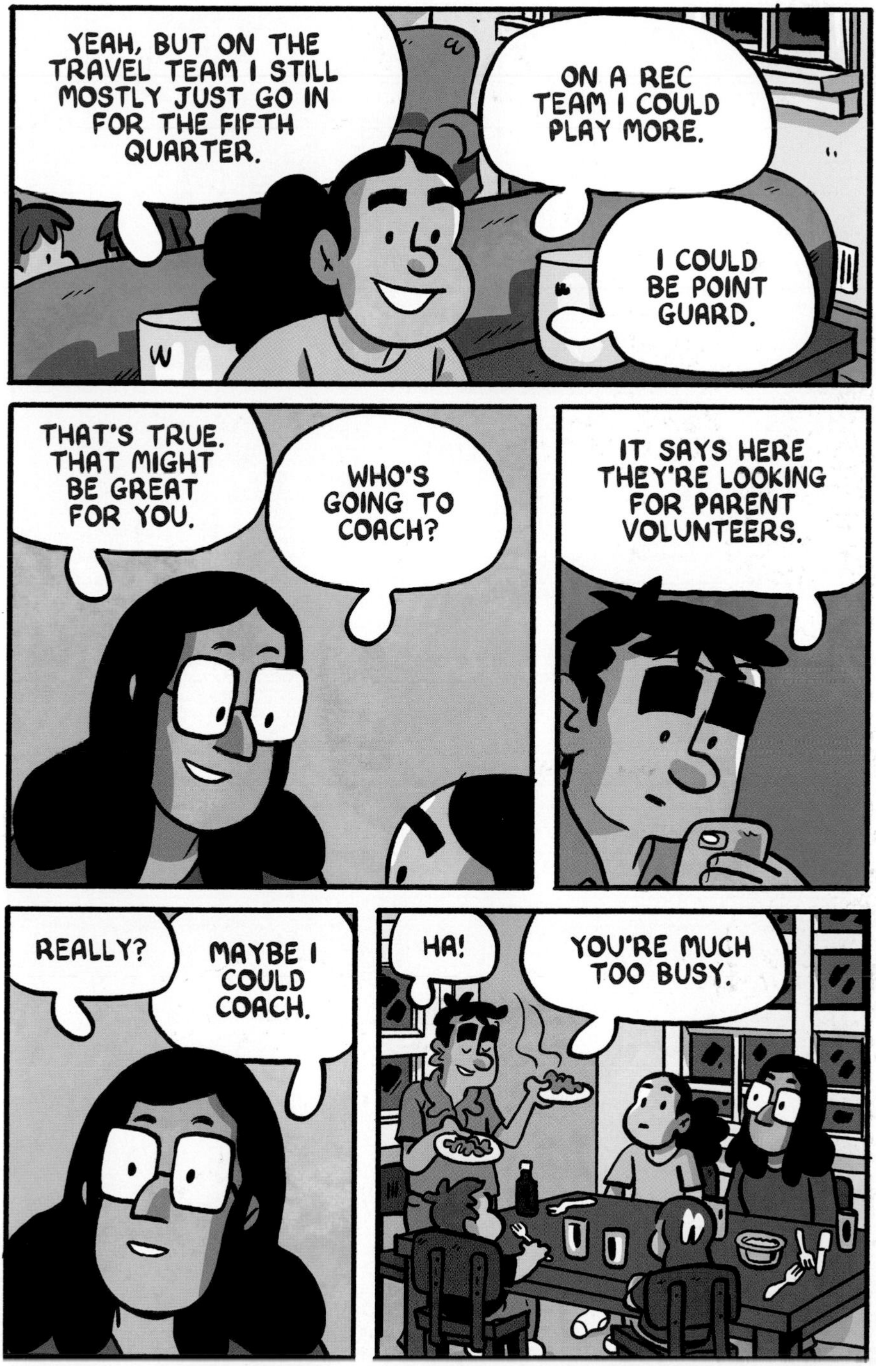
YEAH, BUT ON THE TRAVEL TEAM I STILL MOSTLY JUST GO IN FOR THE FIFTH QUARTER.
ON A REC TEAM I COULD PLAY MORE.
I COULD BE POINT GUARD.
THAT'S TRUE. THAT MIGHT BE GREAT FOR YOU.
WHO'S GOING TO COACH?
IT SAYS HERE THEY'RE LOOKING FOR PARENT VOLUNTEERS.
REALLY?
MAYBE I COULD COACH.
HA!
YOU'RE MUCH TOO BUSY.

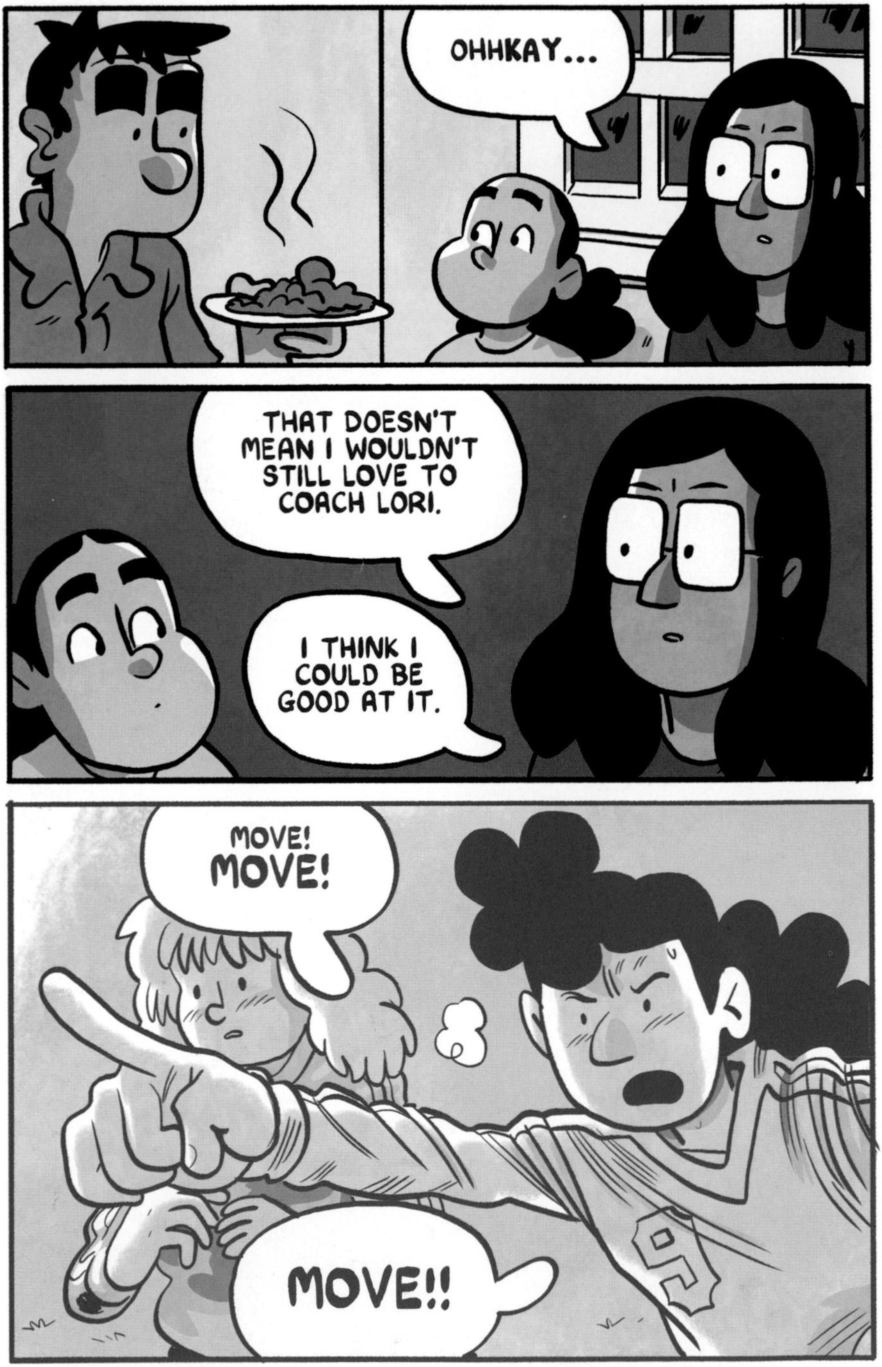
OHHKAY...
THAT DOESN'T MEAN I WOULDN'T STILL LOVE TO COACH LORI.
I THINK I COULD BE GOOD AT IT.
MOVE! MOVE!
MOVE!!

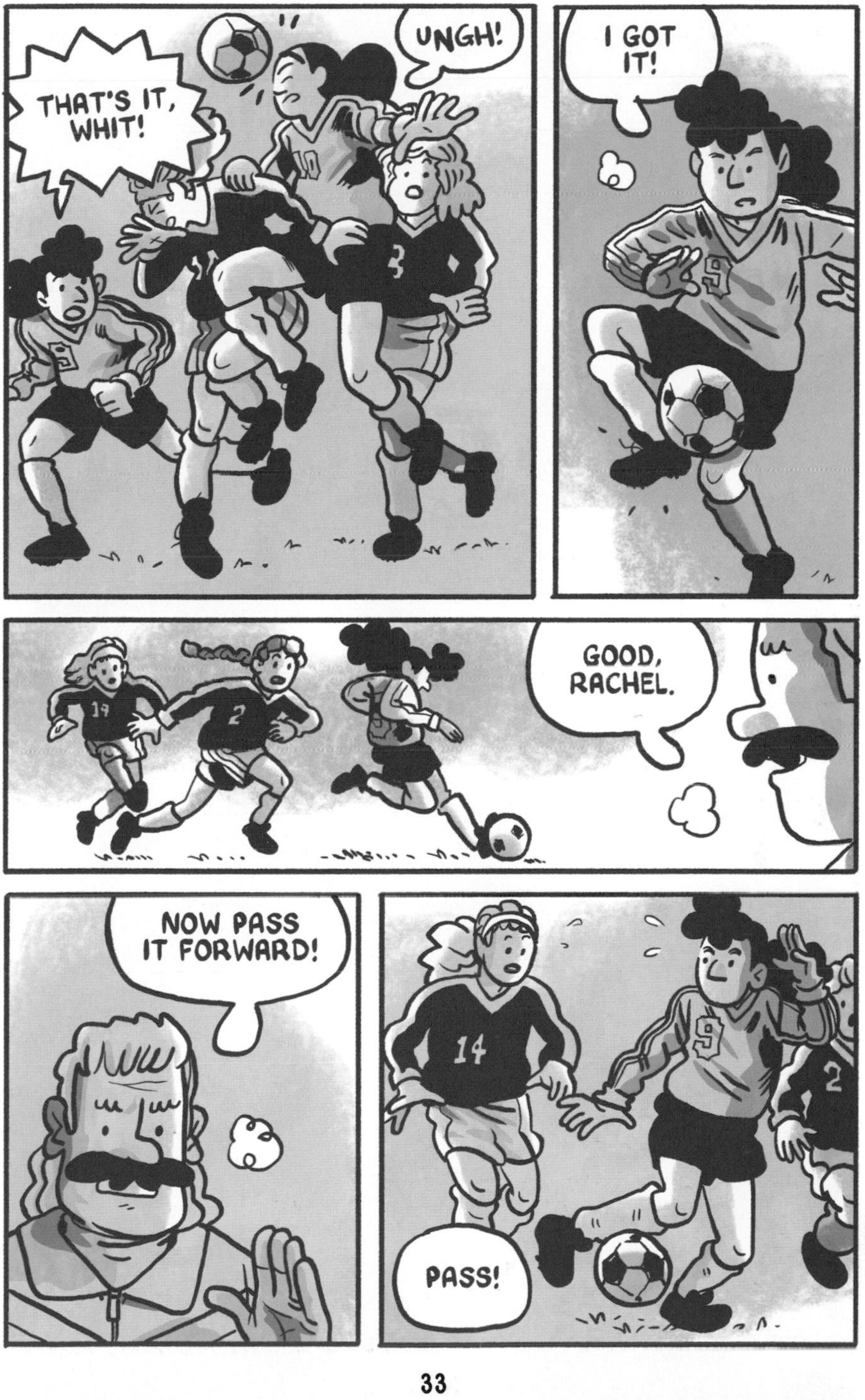
THAT'S IT, WHIT!
UNGH!
I GOT IT!
GOOD, RACHEL.
NOW PASS IT FORWARD!
PASS!

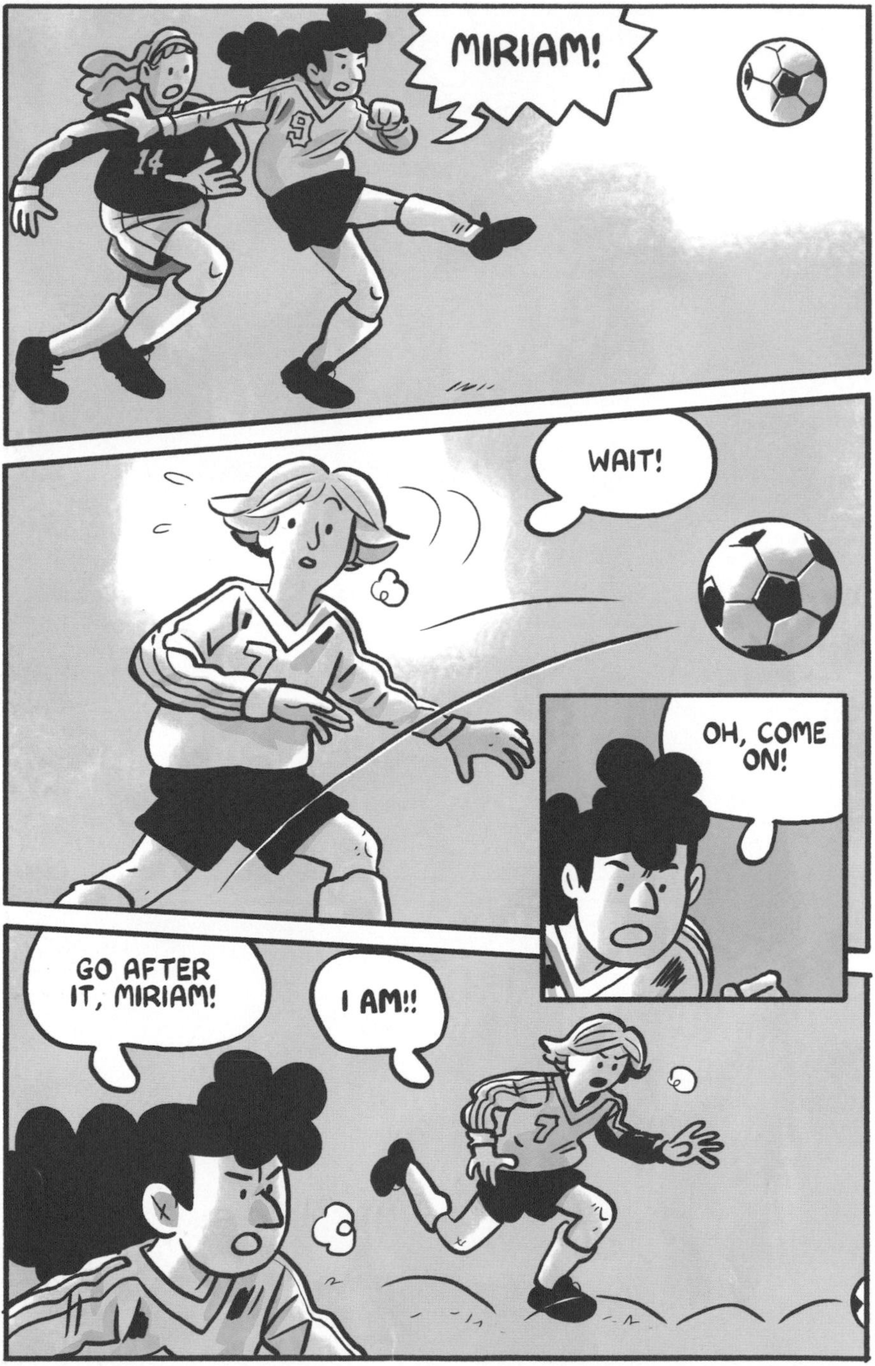
MIRIAM!
WAIT!
OH, COME ON!
GO AFTER IT, MIRIAM!
I AM!!

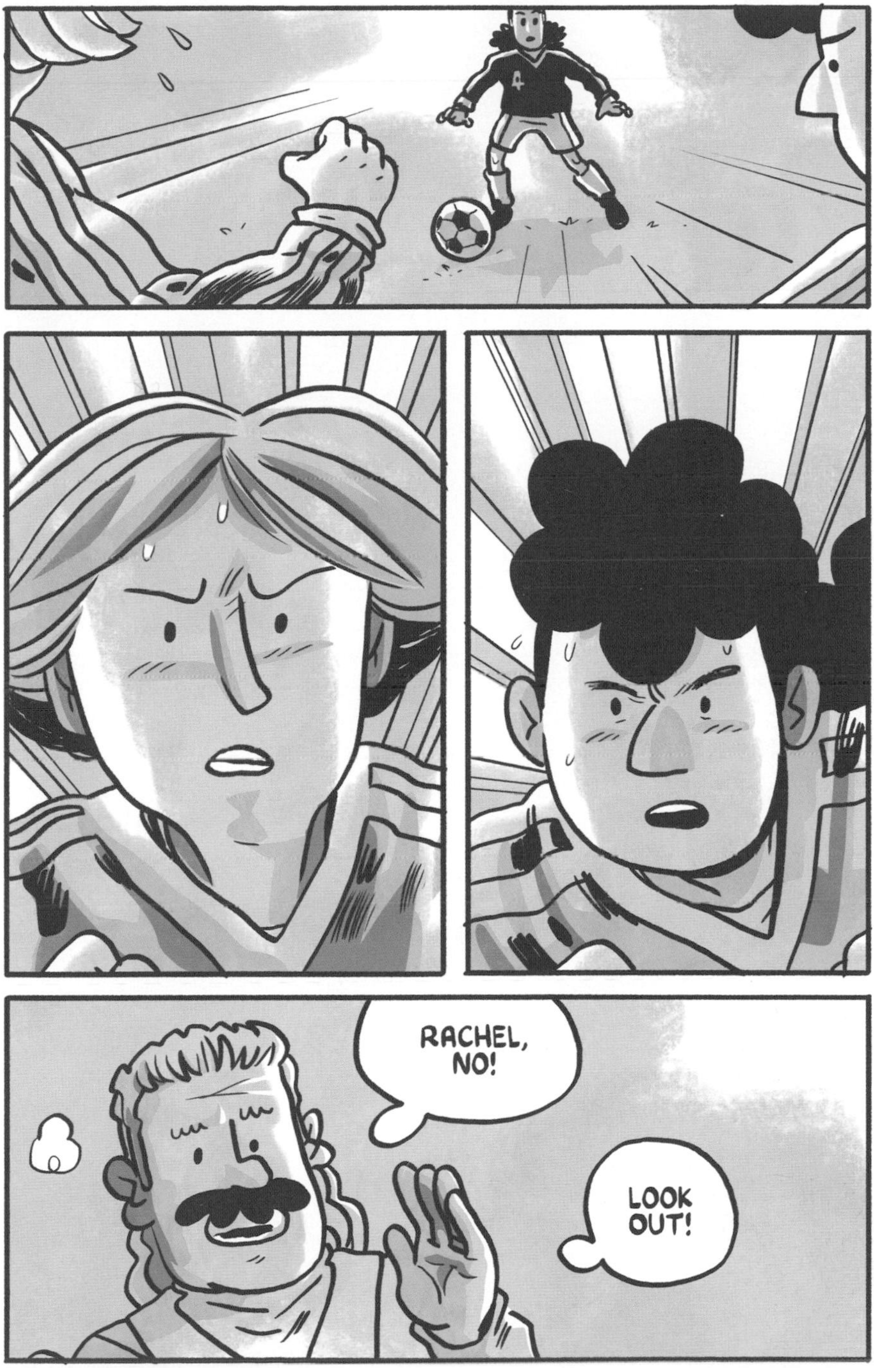
RACHEL, NO!
LOOK OUT!

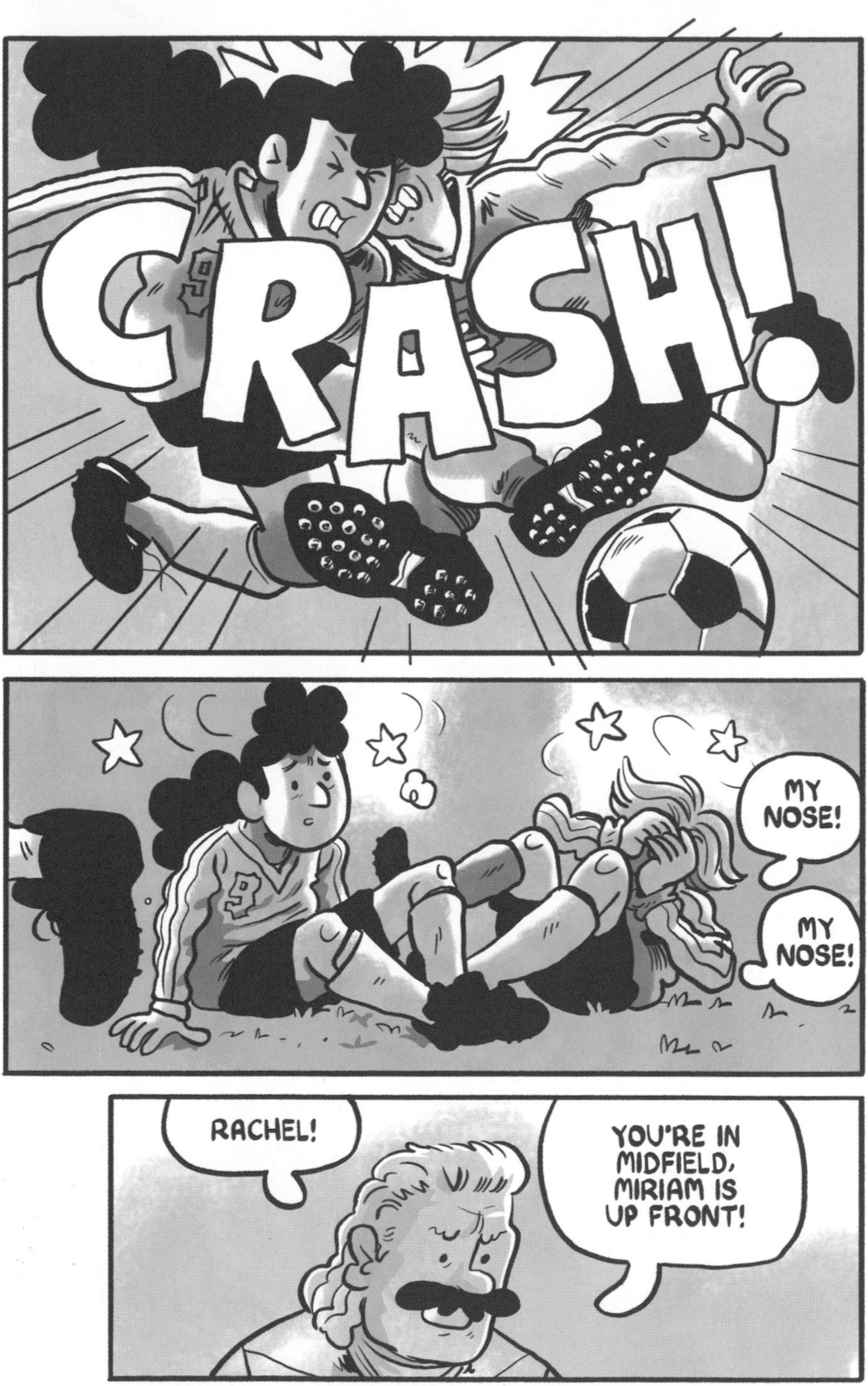
CRASH!
MY NOSE!
MY NOSE!
RACHEL!
YOU'RE IN MIDFIELD, MIRIAM IS UP FRONT!

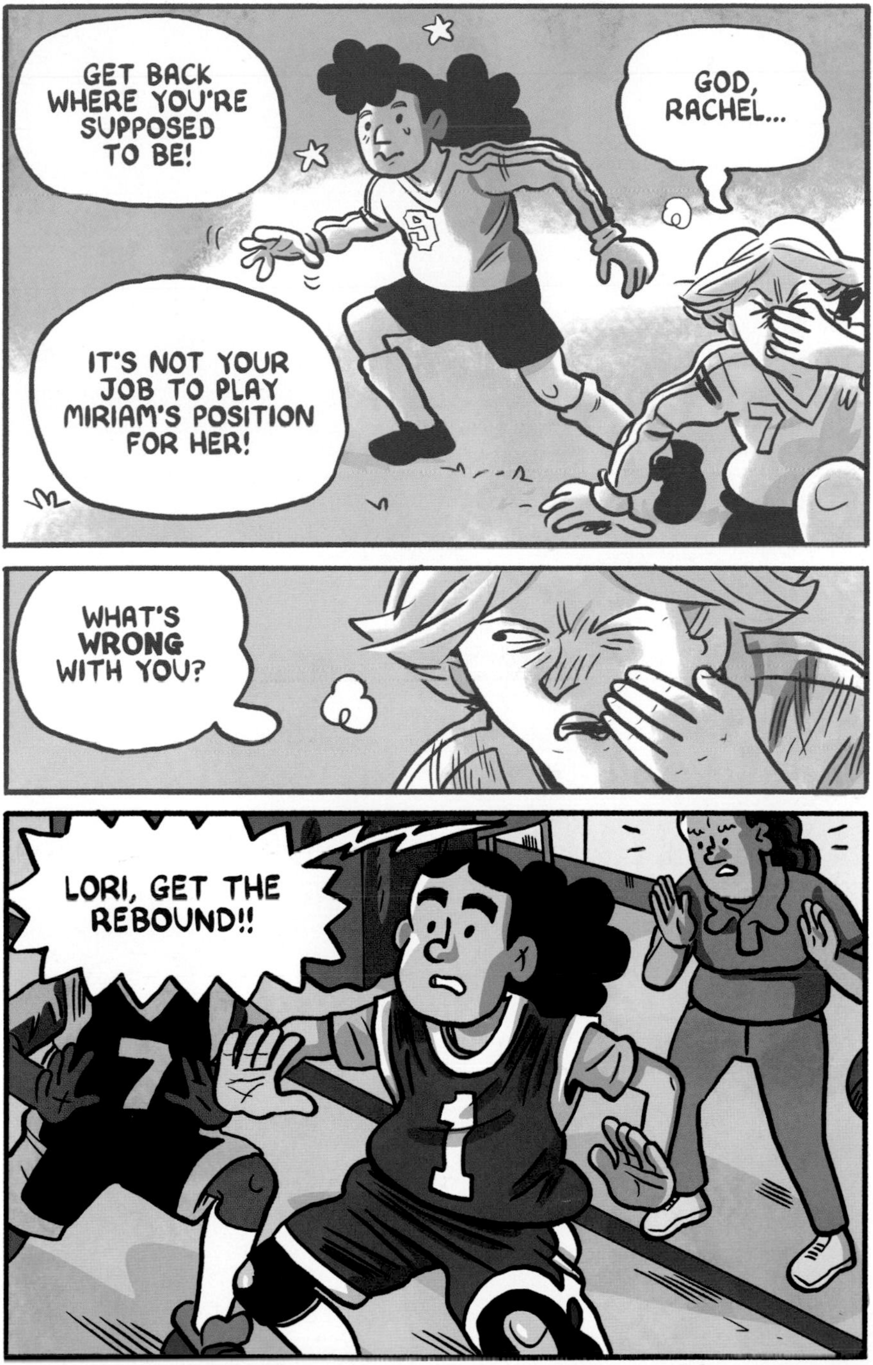
GET BACK WHERE YOU'RE SUPPOSED TO BE!
GOD, RACHEL...
IT'S NOT YOUR JOB TO PLAY MIRIAM'S POSITION FOR HER!
WHAT'S **WRONG** WITH YOU?
LORI, GET THE REBOUND!!

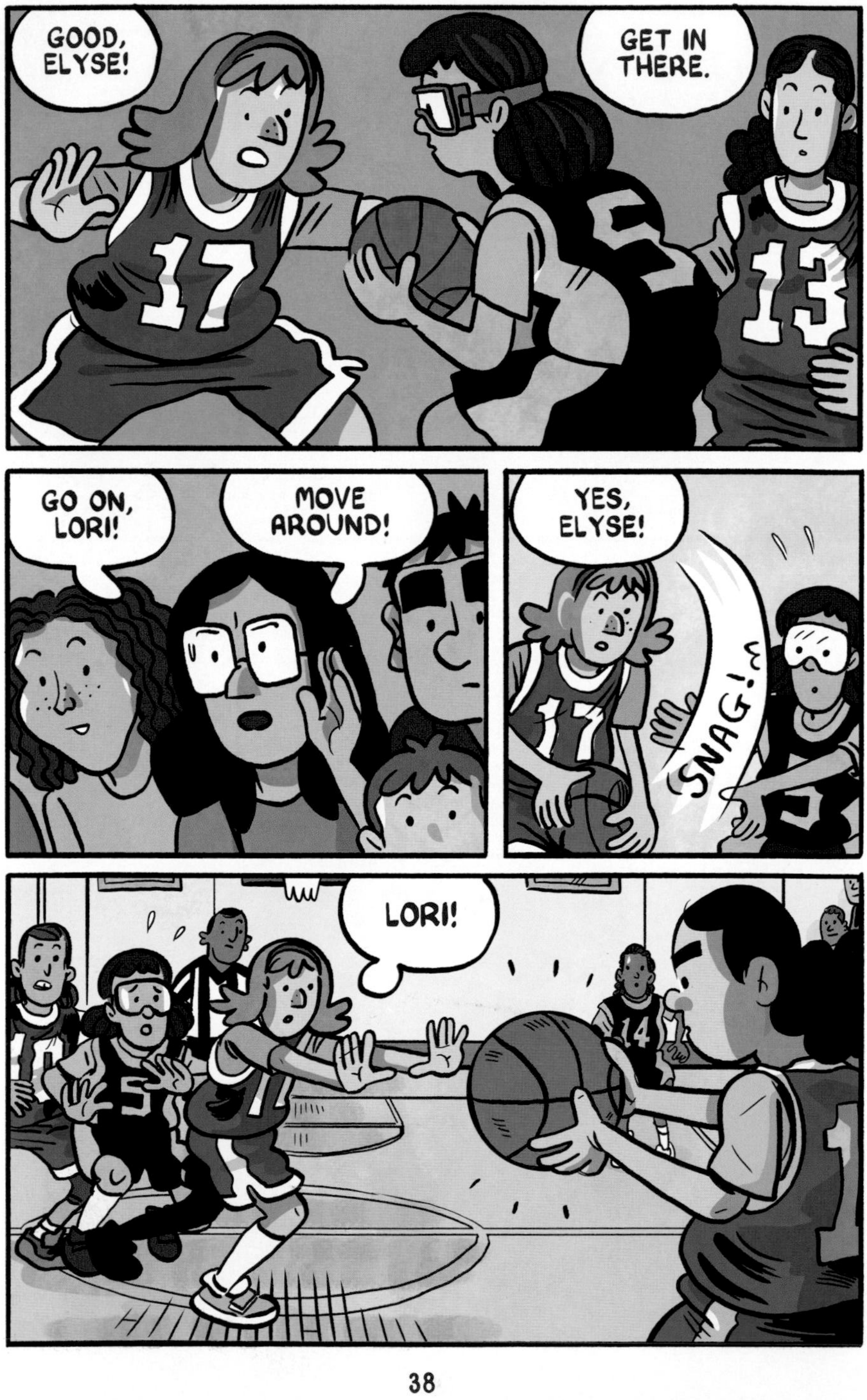
GOOD, ELYSE!
GET IN THERE.
GO ON, LORI!
MOVE AROUND!
YES, ELYSE!
SNAG!
LORI!

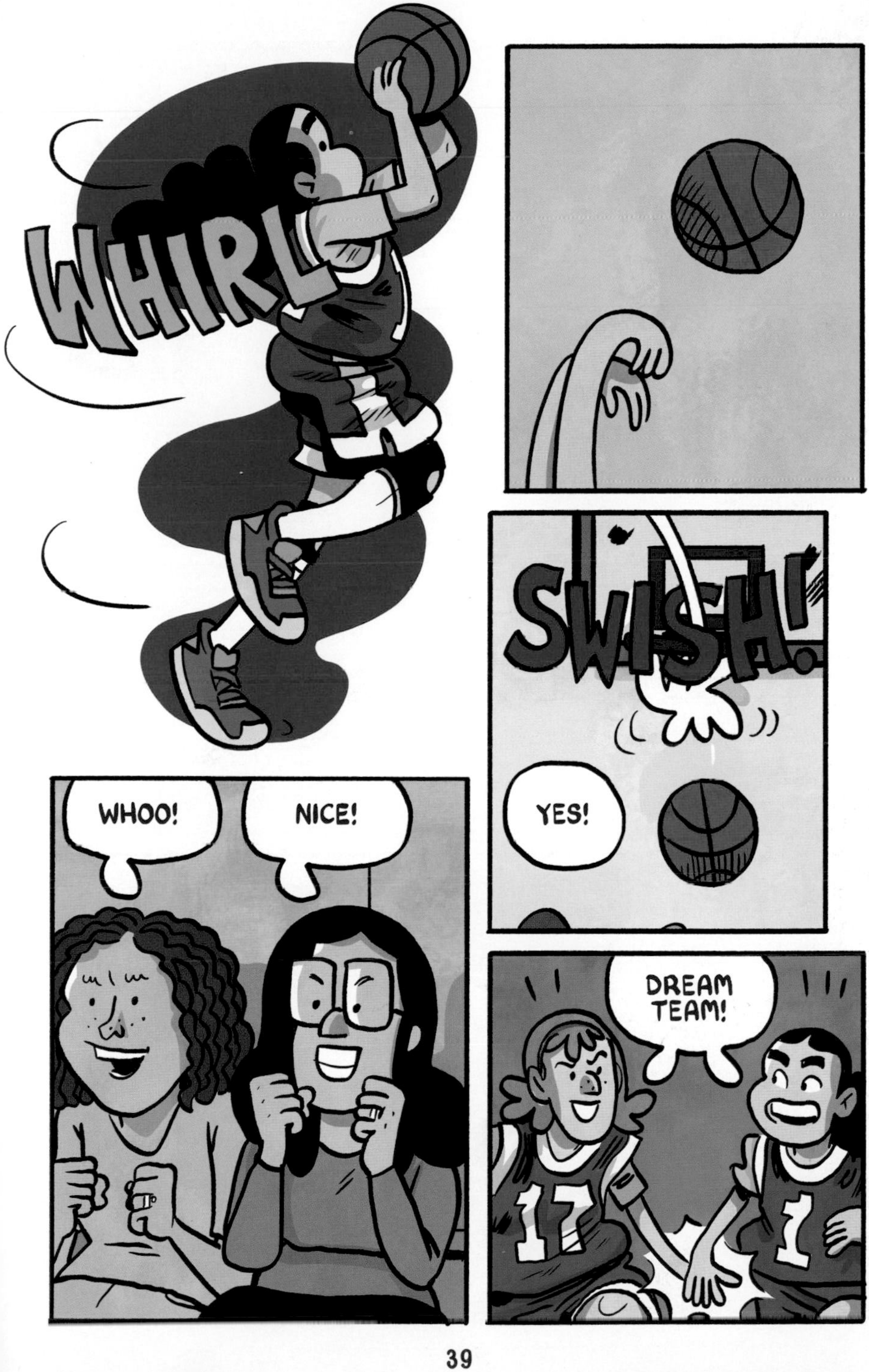
WHIRL
SWISH!
YES!
WHOO!
NICE!
DREAM TEAM!

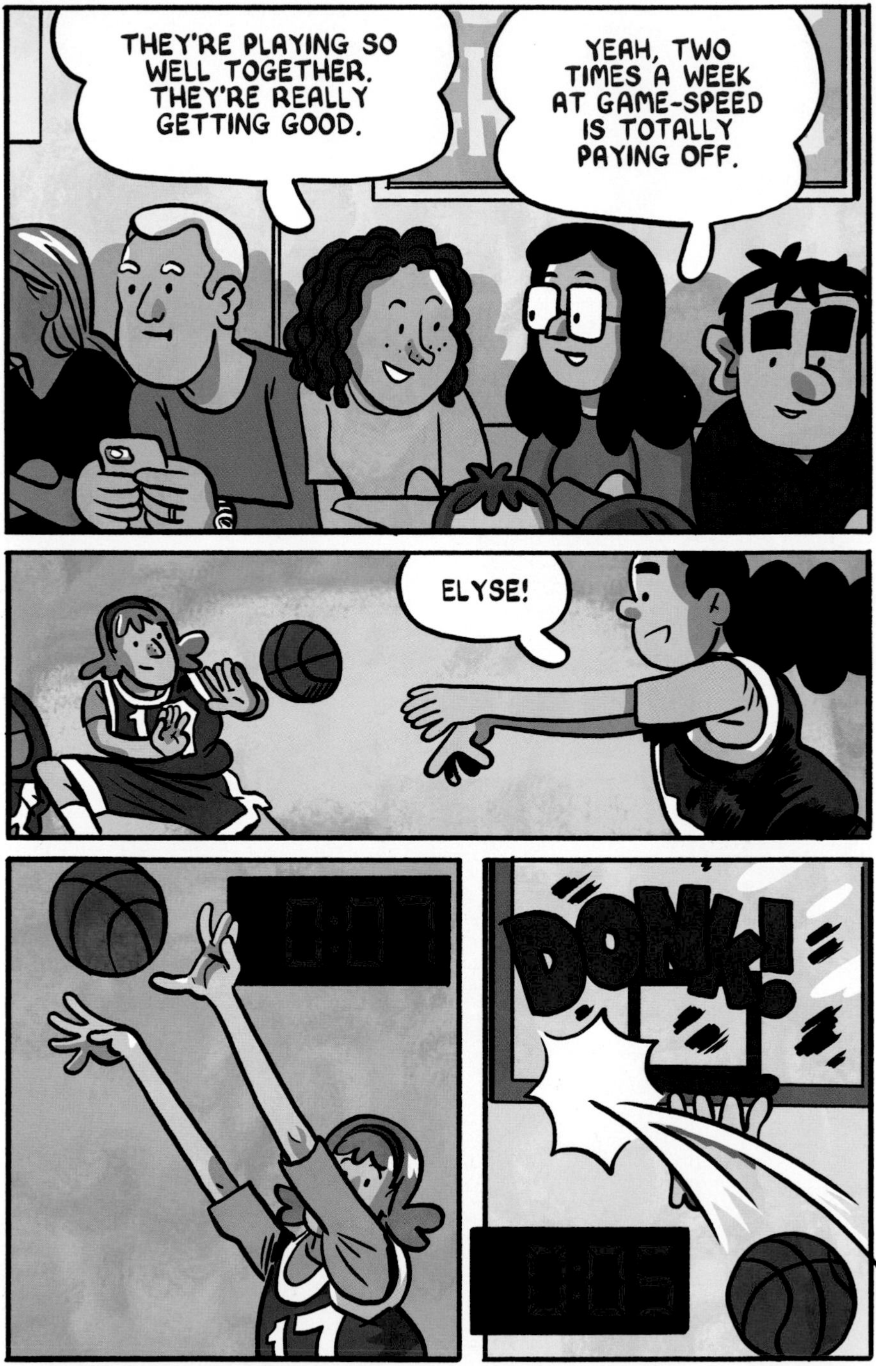
THEY'RE PLAYING SO WELL TOGETHER. THEY'RE REALLY GETTING GOOD.
YEAH, TWO TIMES A WEEK AT GAME-SPEED IS TOTALLY PAYING OFF.
ELYSE!
DONK!

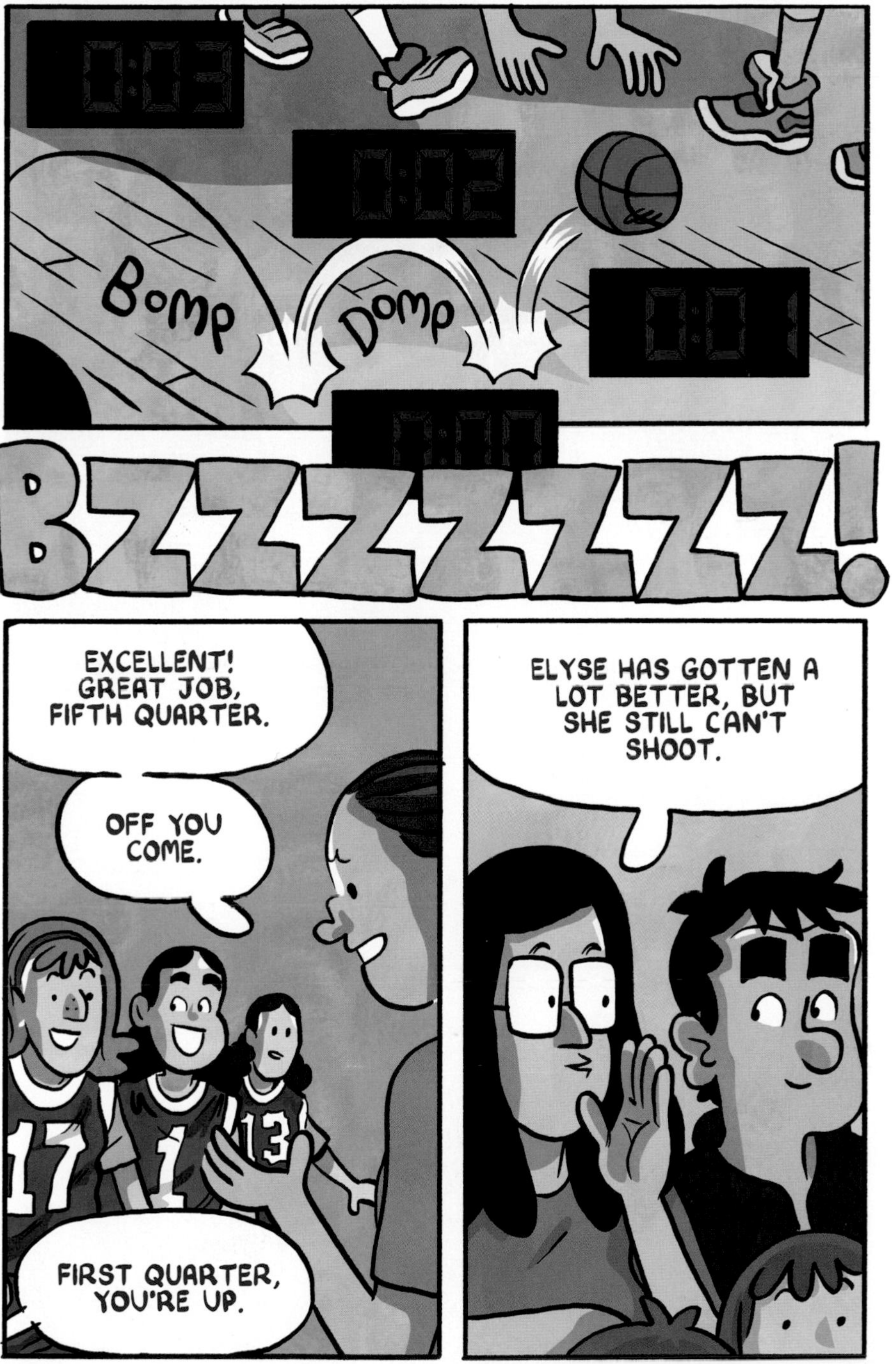
0:03
0:02
BOMP
DOMP
0:01
0:00
BZZZZZZZZZ!
EXCELLENT! GREAT JOB, FIFTH QUARTER.
OFF YOU COME.
FIRST QUARTER, YOU'RE UP.
17
1
13
ELYSE HAS GOTTEN A LOT BETTER, BUT SHE STILL CAN'T SHOOT.

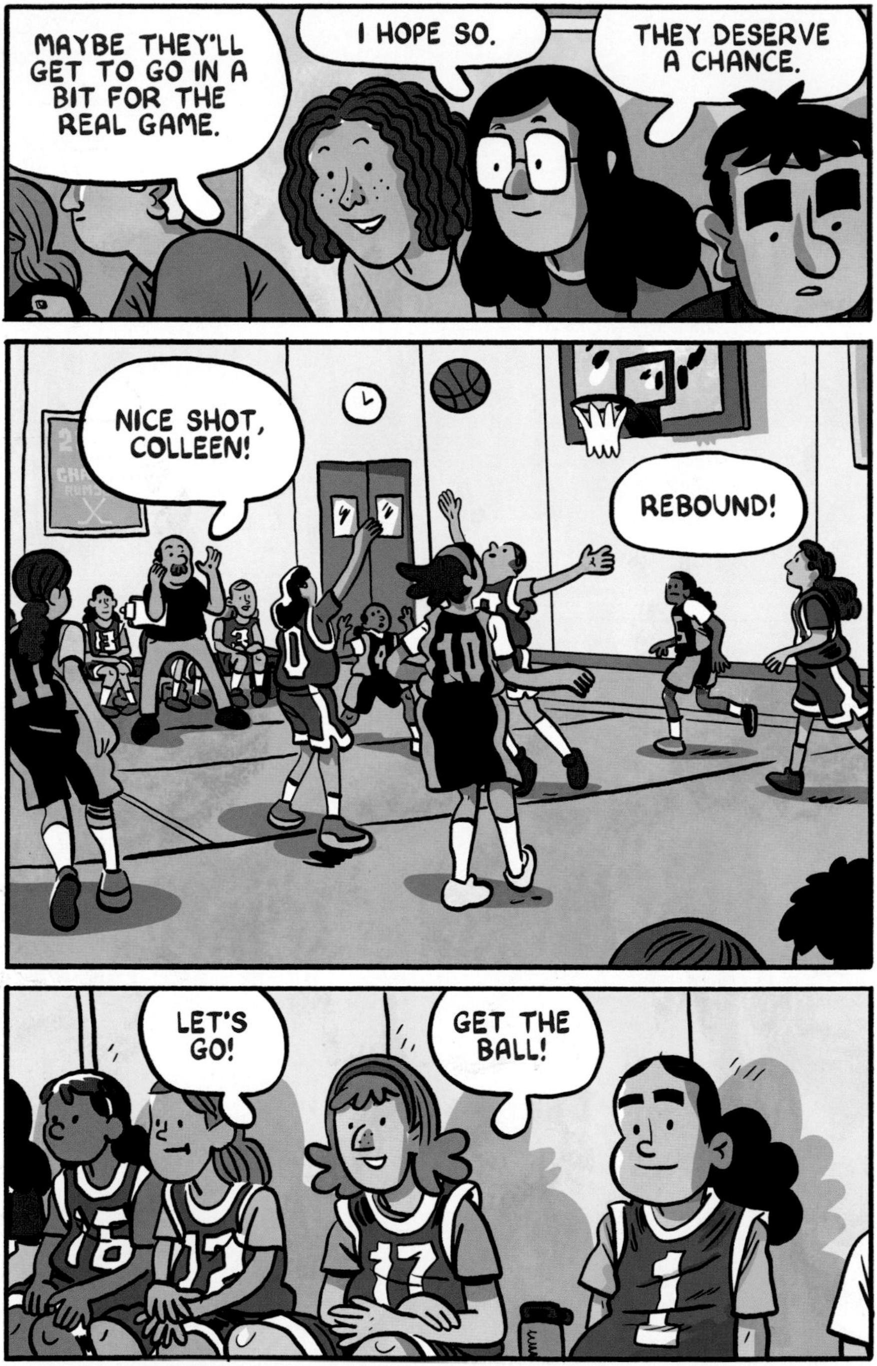
MAYBE THEY'LL GET TO GO IN A BIT FOR THE REAL GAME.
I HOPE SO.
THEY DESERVE A CHANCE.
NICE SHOT, COLLEEN!
REBOUND!
LET'S GO!
GET THE BALL!

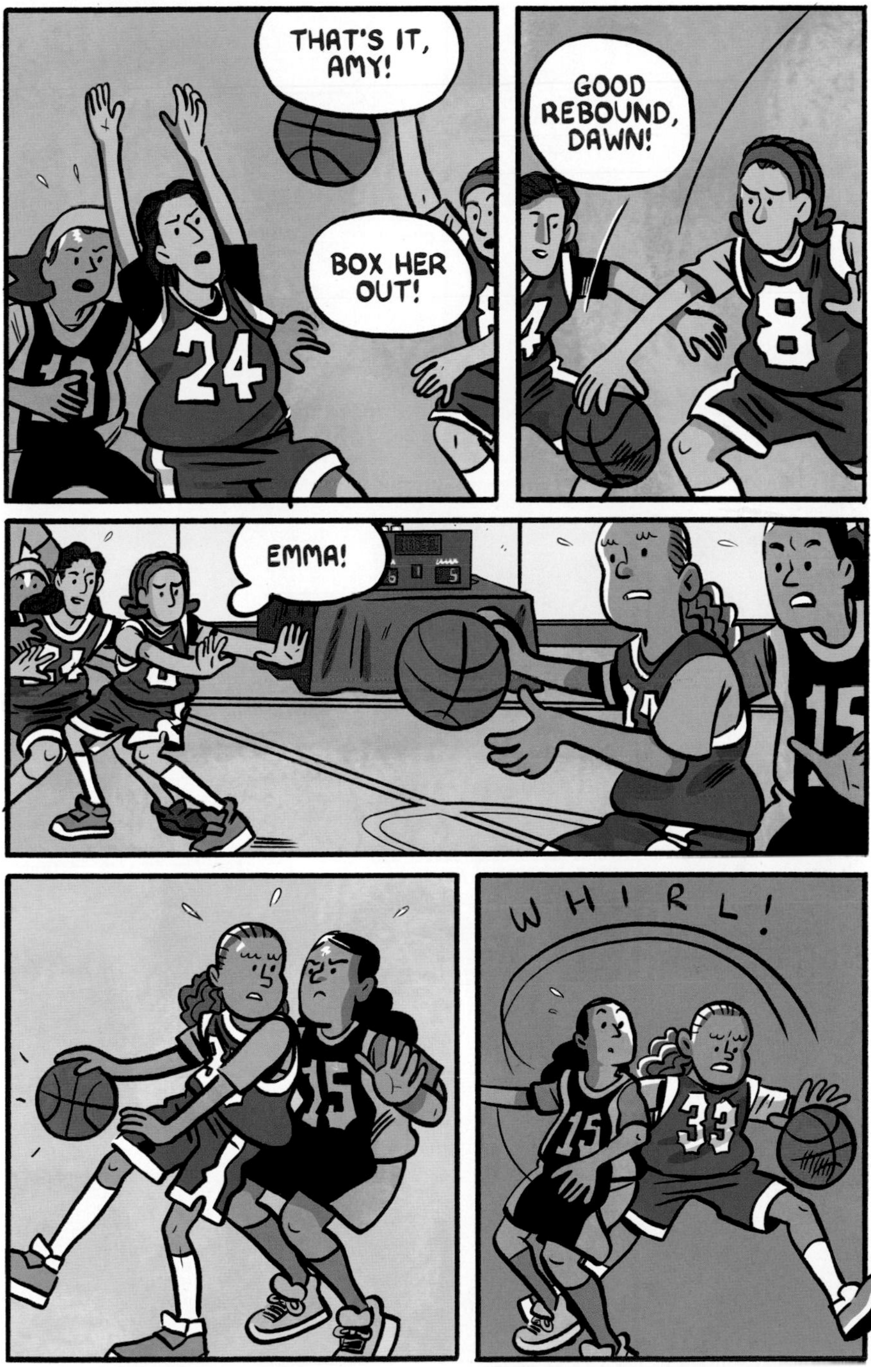
THAT'S IT, AMY!
BOX HER OUT!
GOOD REBOUND, DAWN!
EMMA!
WHIRL!

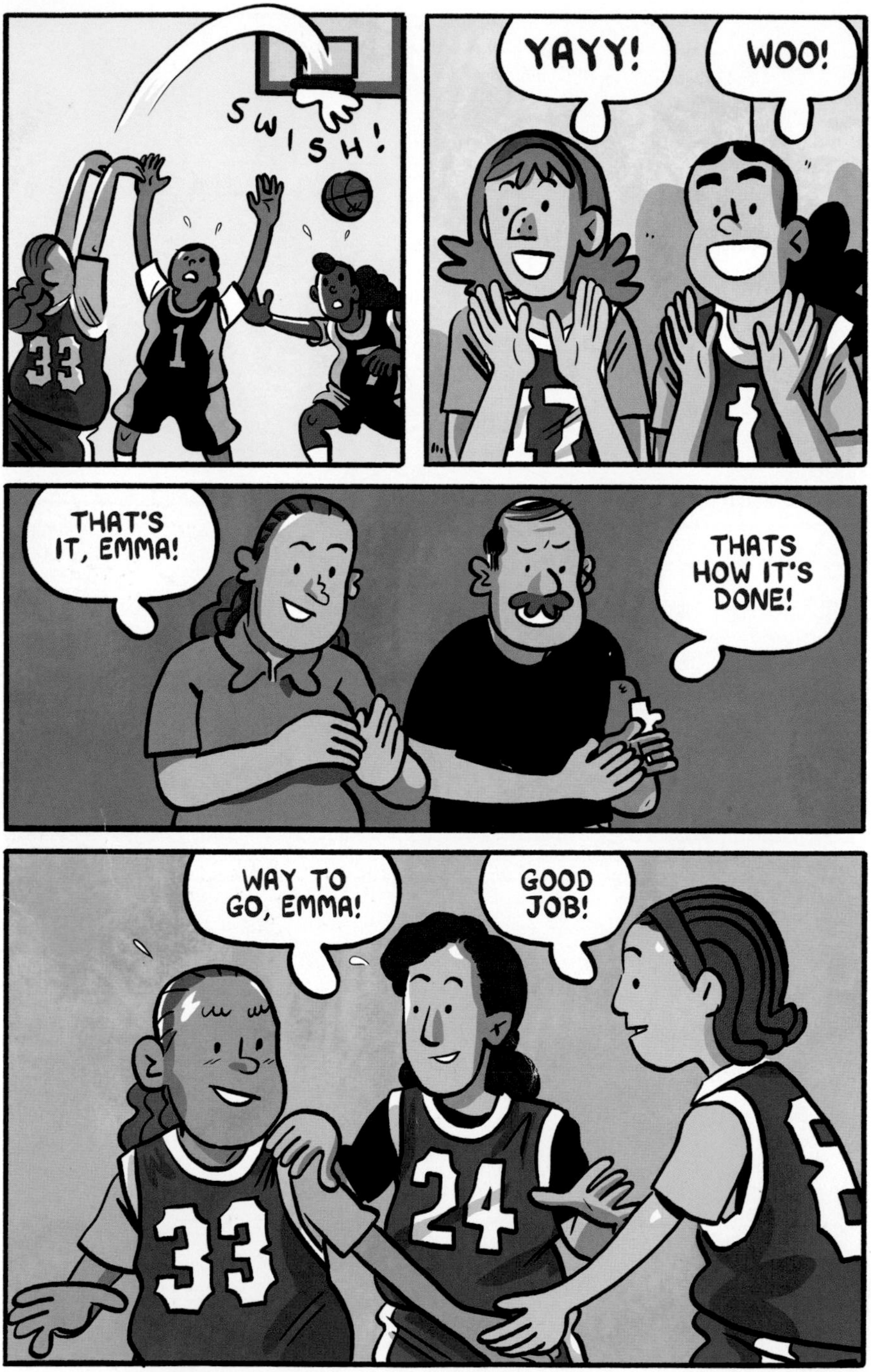
SWISH!
YAYY!
WOO!
THAT'S IT, EMMA!
THATS HOW IT'S DONE!
WAY TO GO, EMMA!
GOOD JOB!

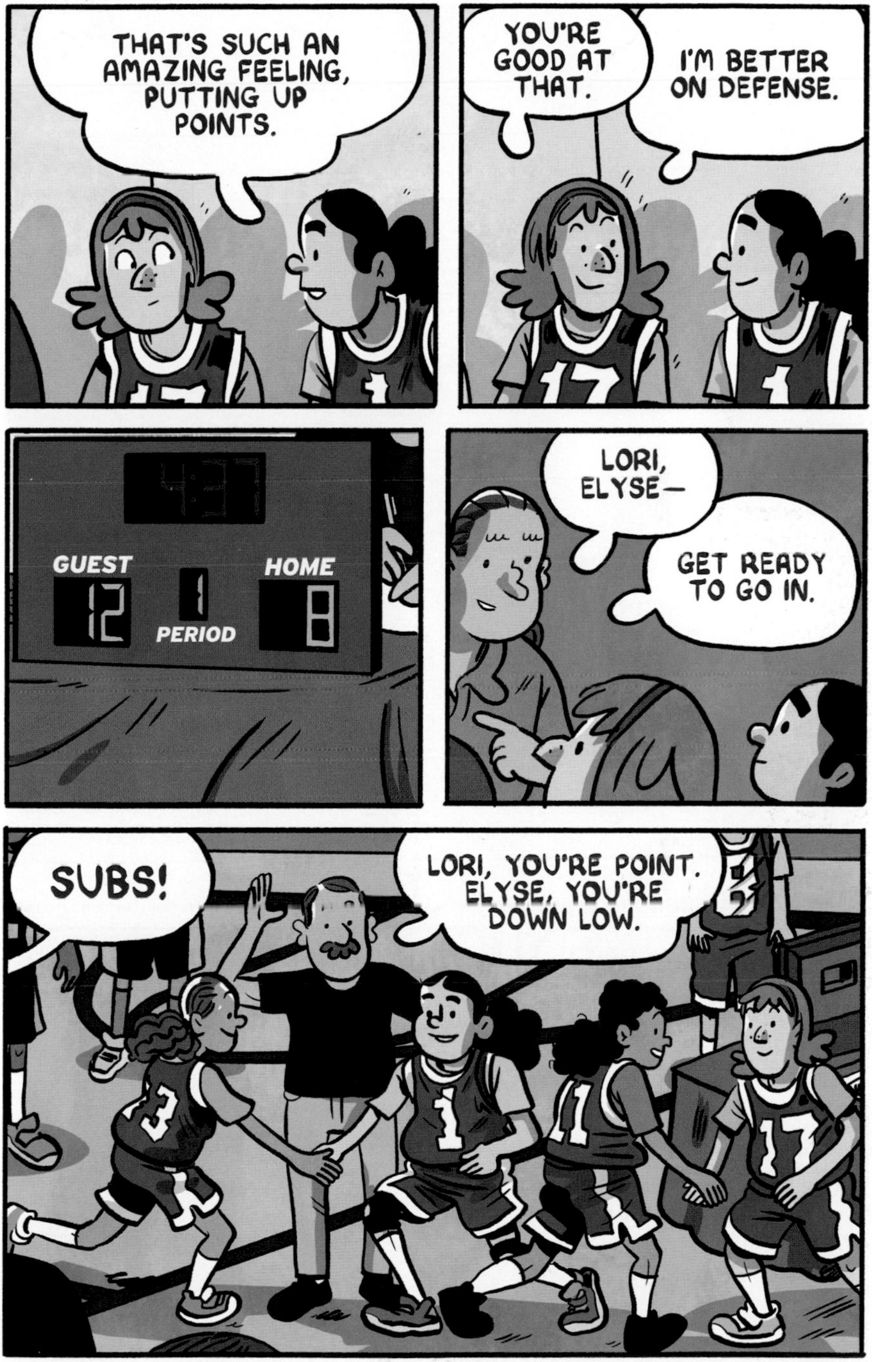
THAT'S SUCH AN AMAZING FEELING, PUTTING UP POINTS.
YOU'RE GOOD AT THAT.
I'M BETTER ON DEFENSE.
GUEST
HOME
12
1
8
PERIOD
LORI, ELYSE—
GET READY TO GO IN.
SUBS!
LORI, YOU'RE POINT. ELYSE, YOU'RE DOWN LOW.

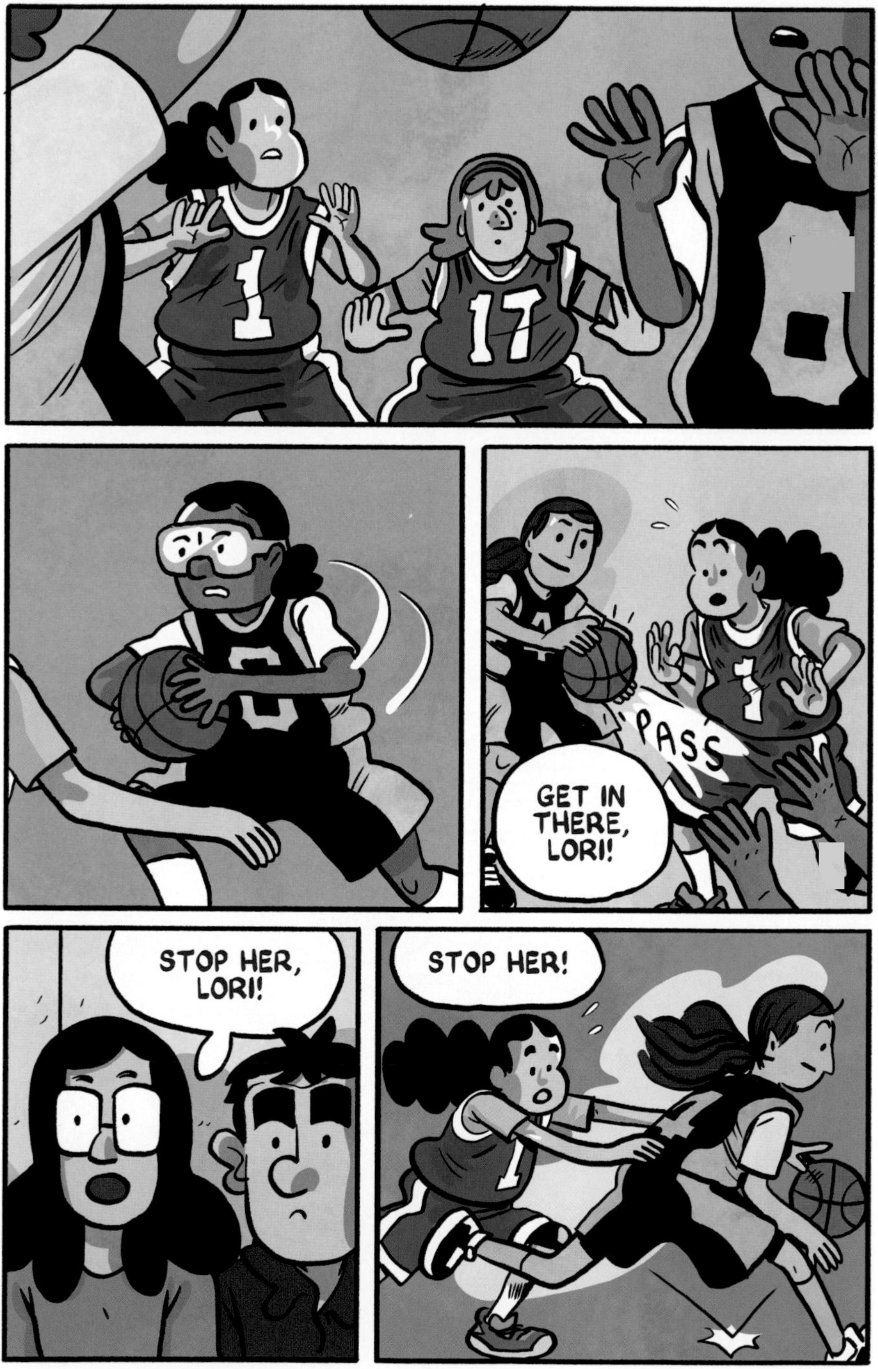
PASS
GET IN THERE, LORI!
STOP HER, LORI!
STOP HER!

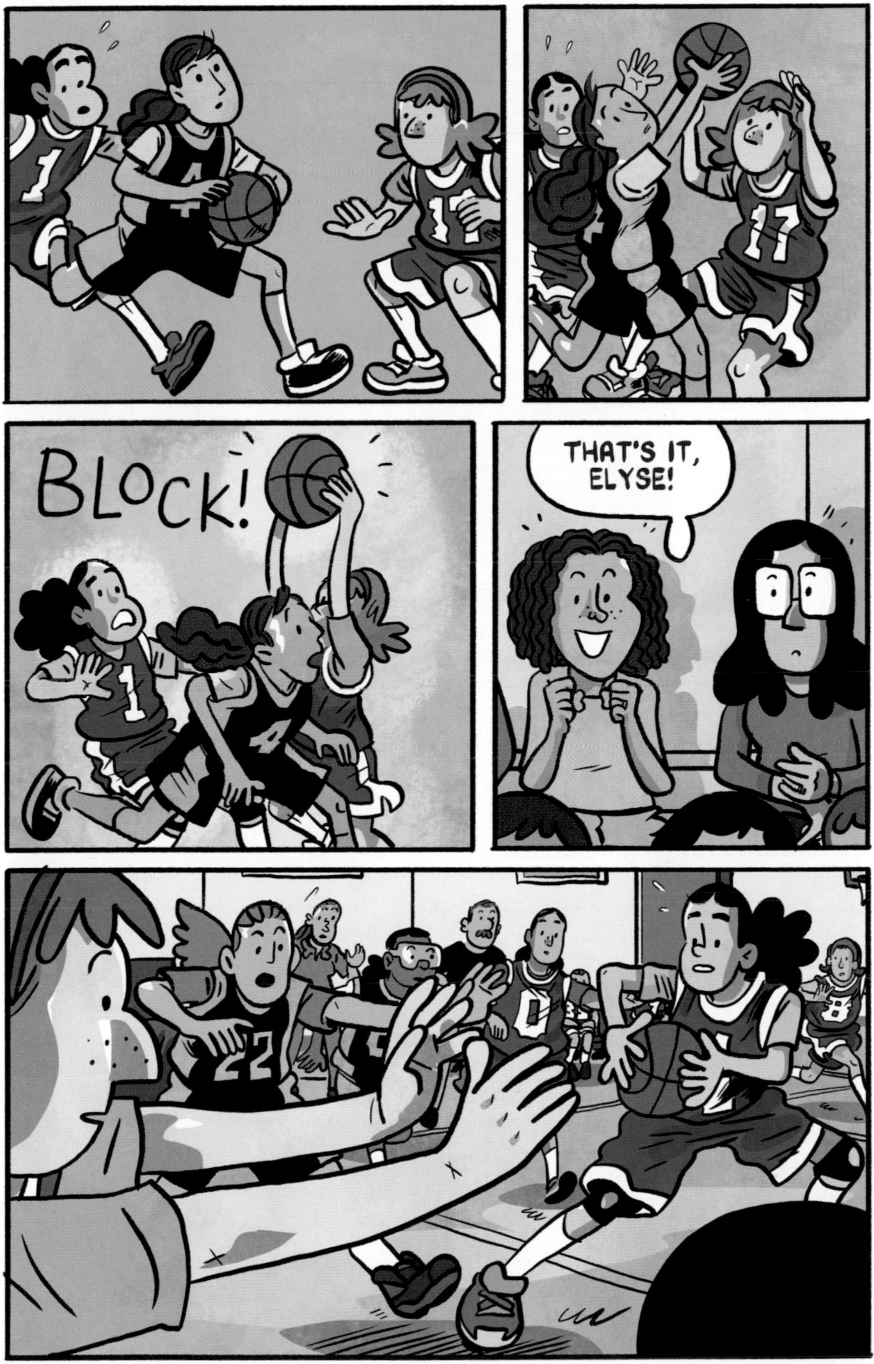
BLOCK!
THAT'S IT, ELYSE!

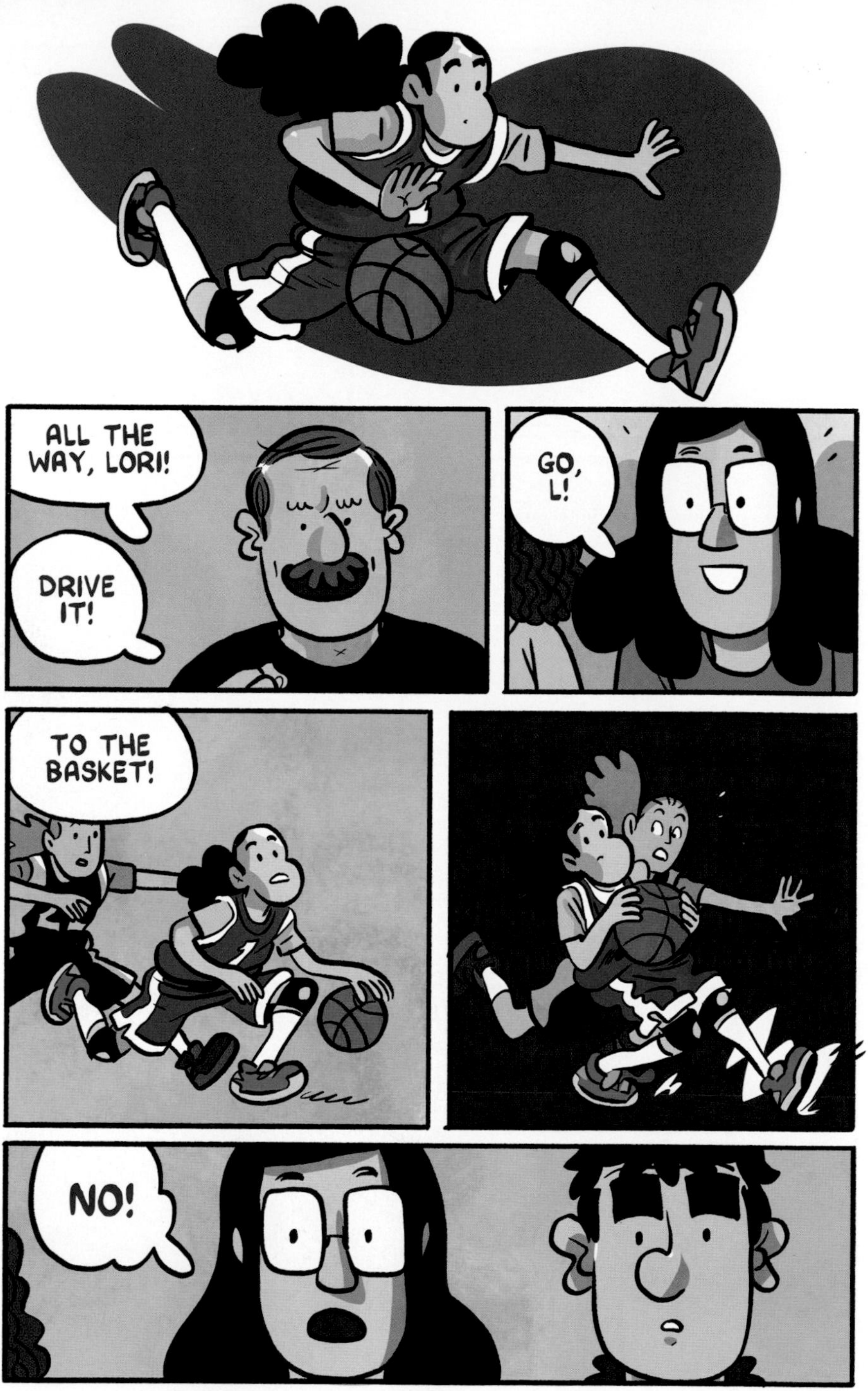
ALL THE WAY, LORI!
DRIVE IT!
GO, L!
TO THE BASKET!
NO!

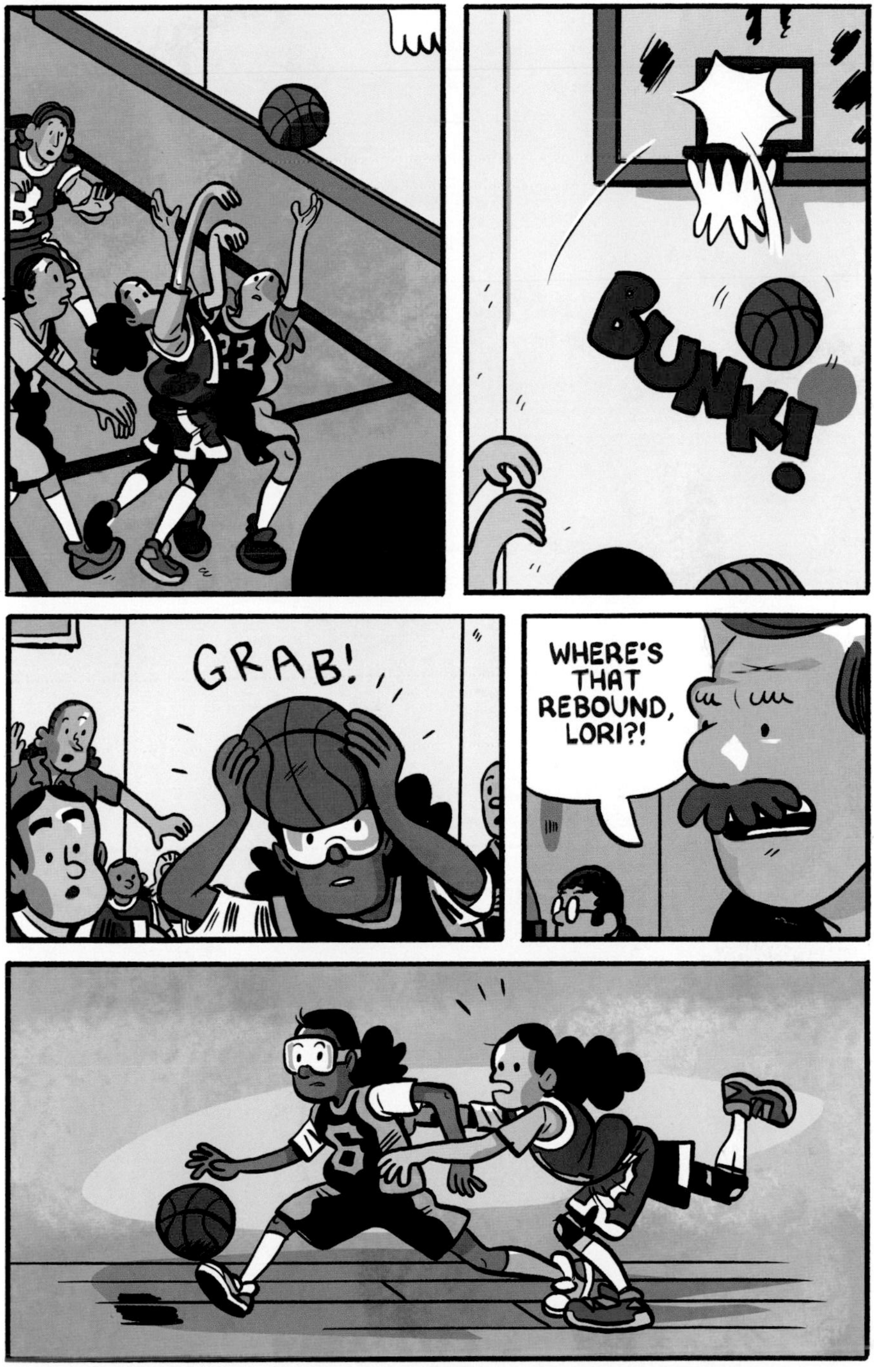
BUNK!
GRAB!
WHERE'S THAT REBOUND, LORI?!

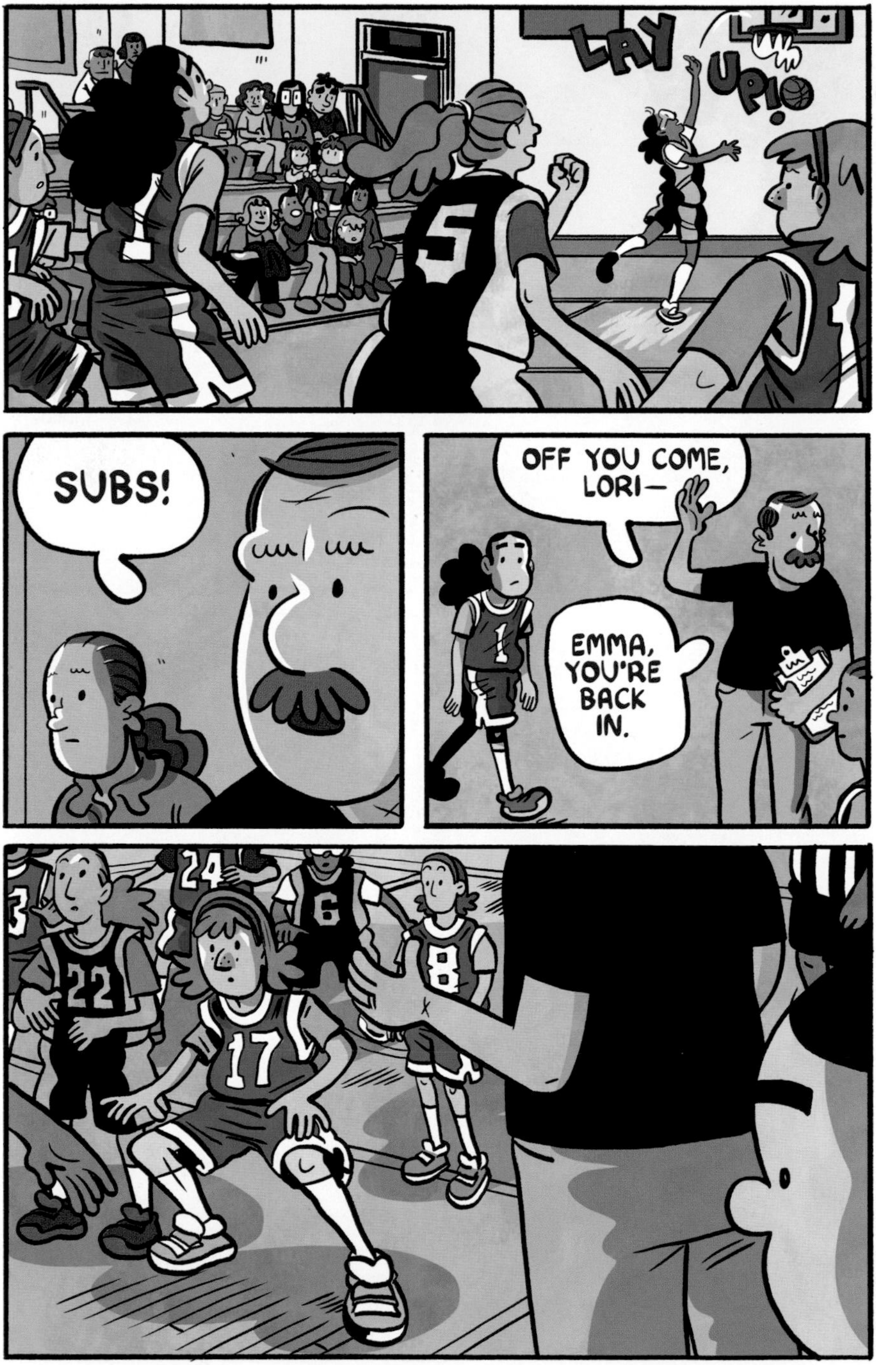
LAY UP!
SUBS!
OFF YOU COME, LORI—
EMMA, YOU'RE BACK IN.

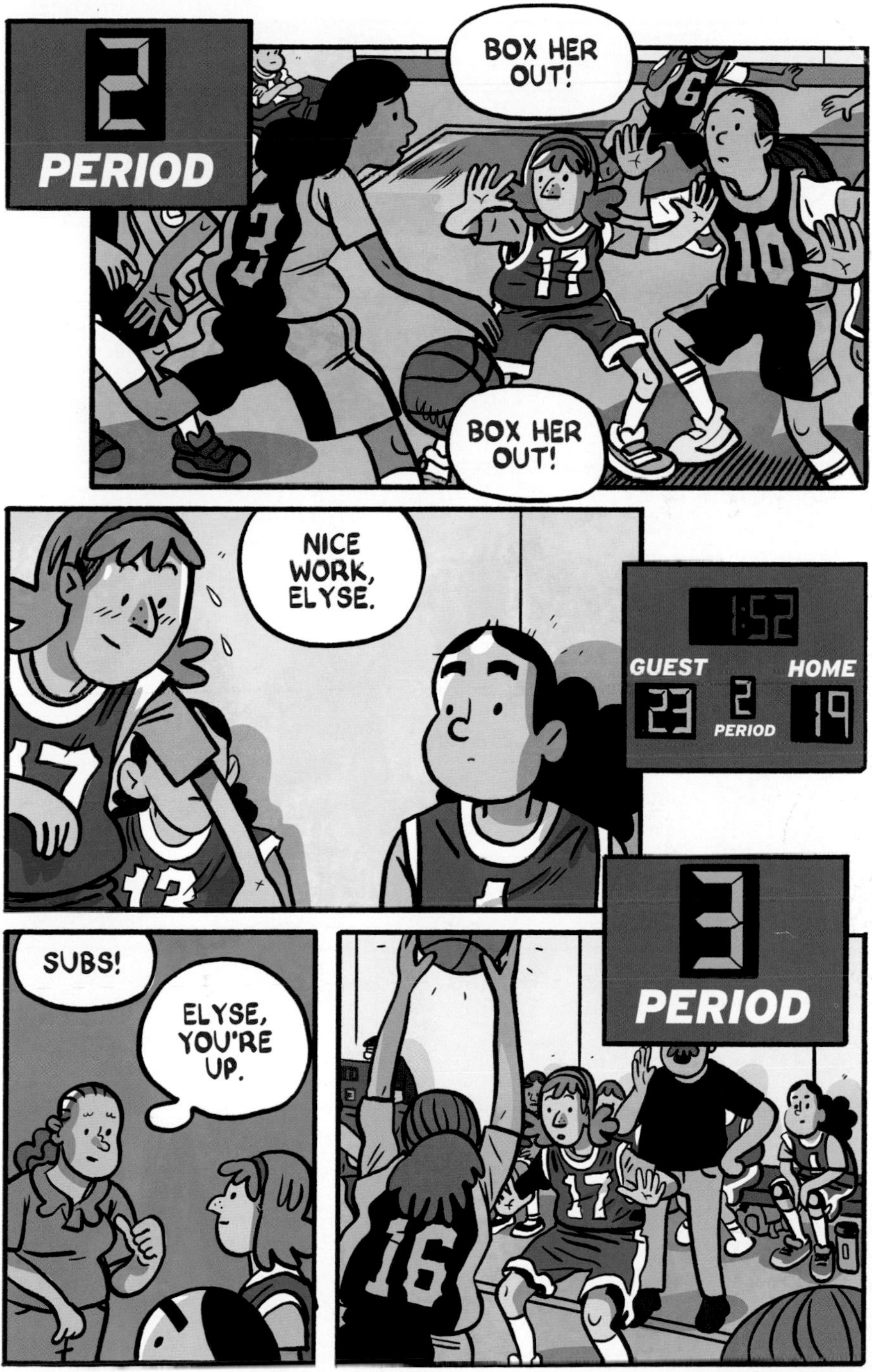
2
PERIOD
BOX HER OUT!
BOX HER OUT!
NICE WORK, ELYSE.
1:52
GUEST
HOME
23
2
PERIOD
19
3
PERIOD
SUBS!
ELYSE, YOU'RE UP.

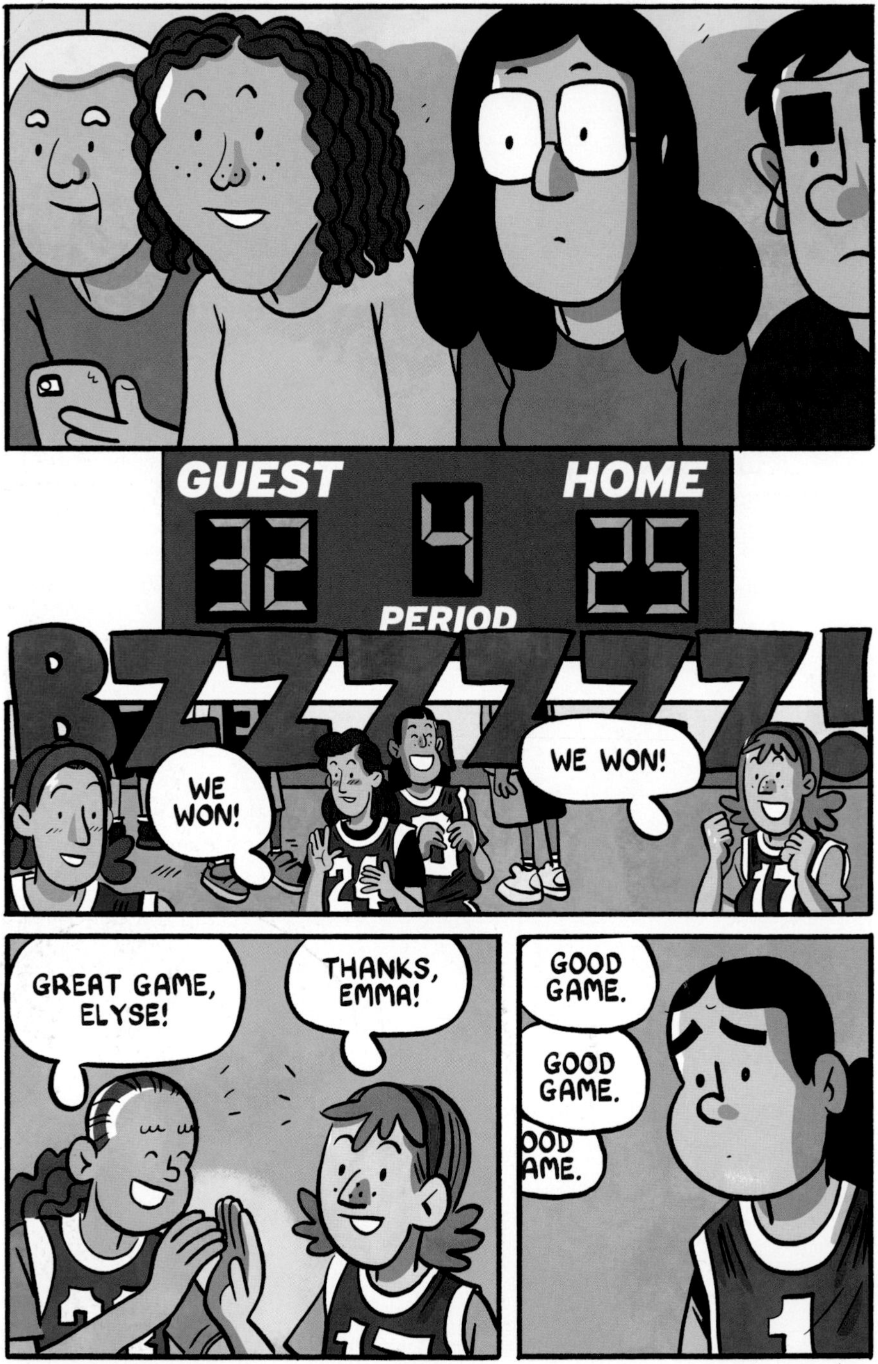
GUEST
HOME
32
4
25
PERIOD
BZZZZZZ!
WE WON!
WE WON!
GREAT GAME, ELYSE!
THANKS, EMMA!
GOOD GAME.
GOOD GAME.
OOD AME.

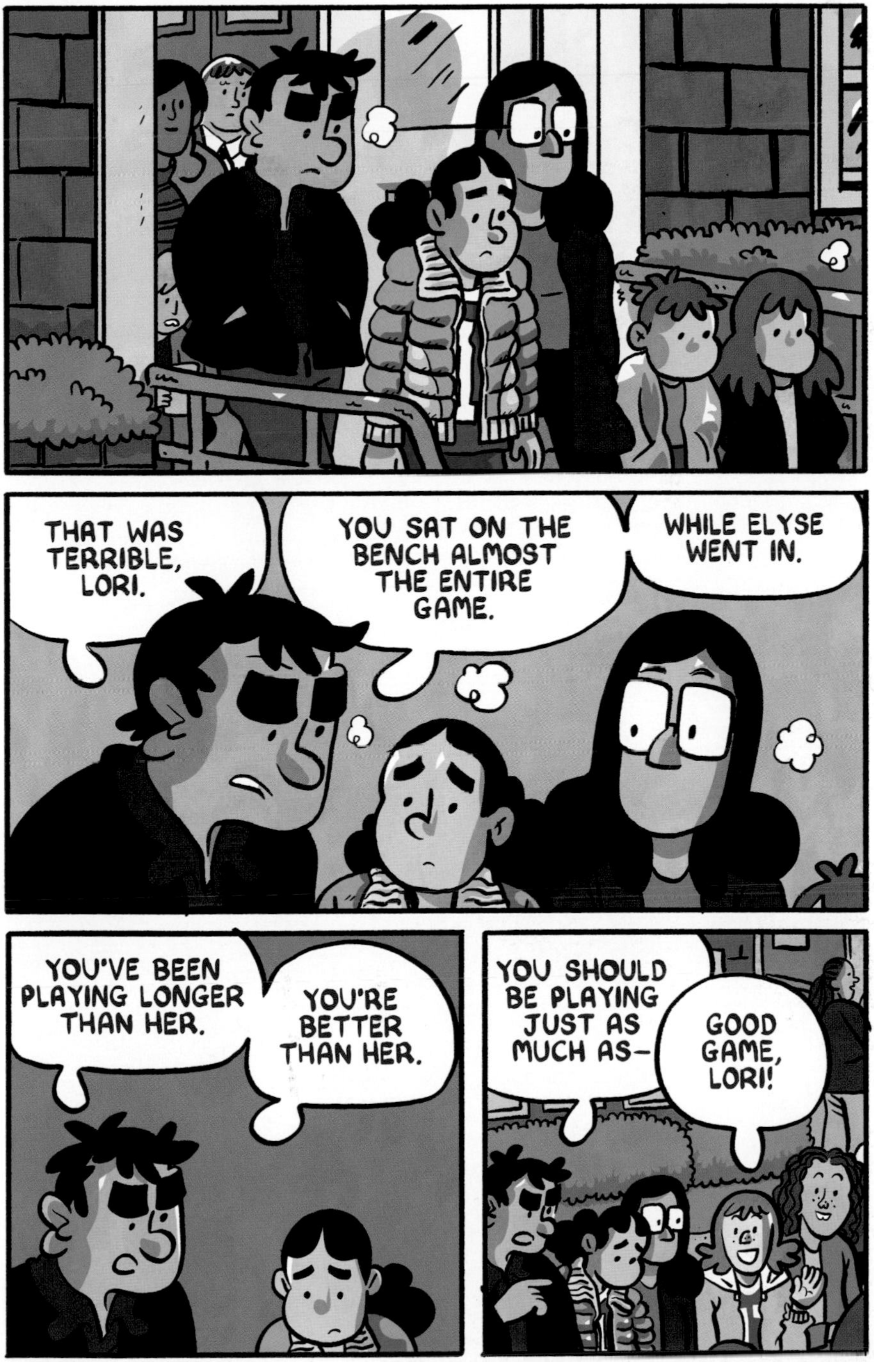
THAT WAS TERRIBLE, LORI.
YOU SAT ON THE BENCH ALMOST THE ENTIRE GAME.
WHILE ELYSE WENT IN.
YOU'VE BEEN PLAYING LONGER THAN HER.
YOU'RE BETTER THAN HER.
YOU SHOULD BE PLAYING JUST AS MUCH AS—
GOOD GAME, LORI!

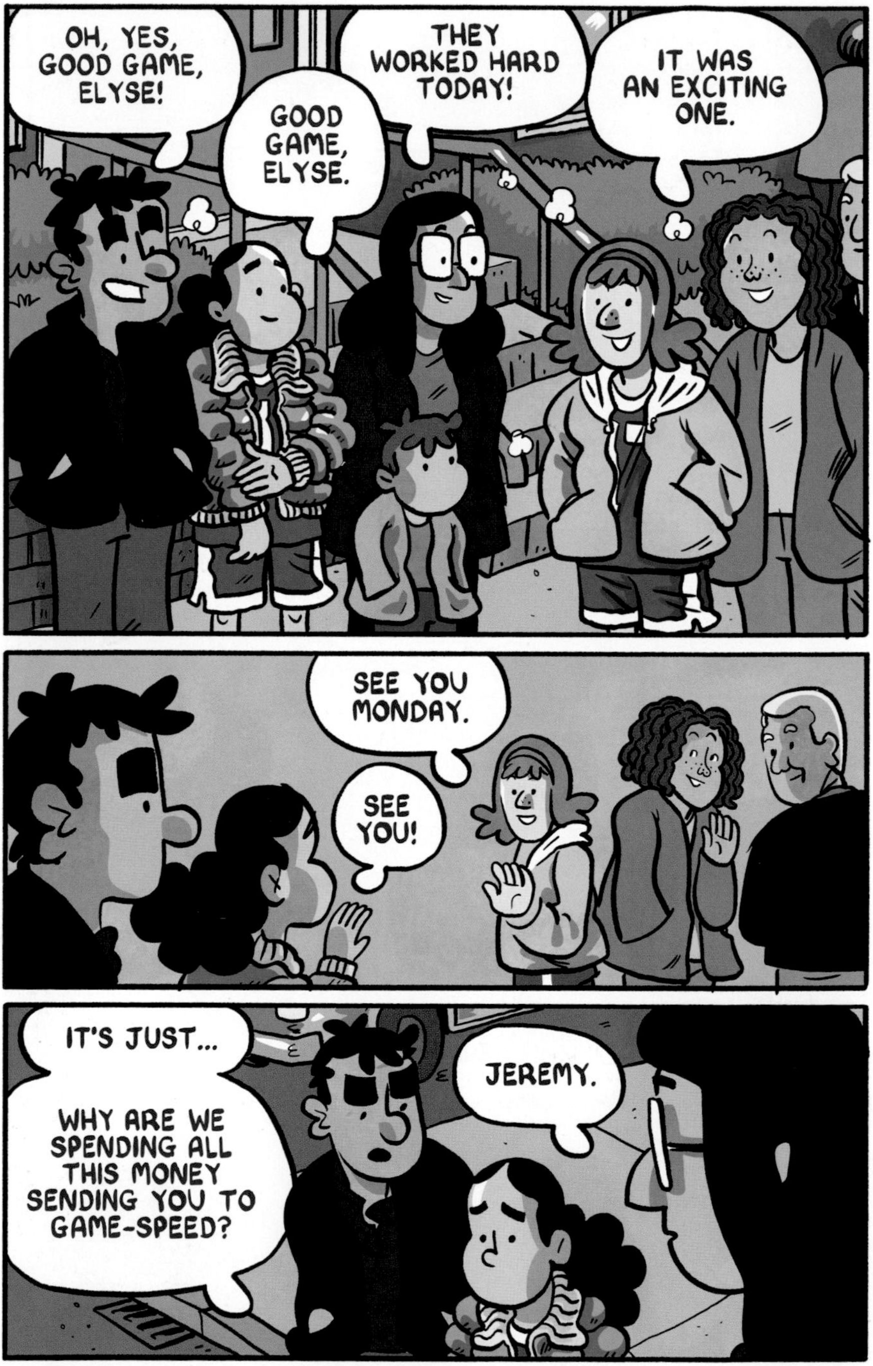
OH, YES, GOOD GAME, ELYSE!
GOOD GAME, ELYSE.
THEY WORKED HARD TODAY!
IT WAS AN EXCITING ONE.
SEE YOU MONDAY.
SEE YOU!
IT'S JUST...
WHY ARE WE SPENDING ALL THIS MONEY SENDING YOU TO GAME-SPEED?
JEREMY.

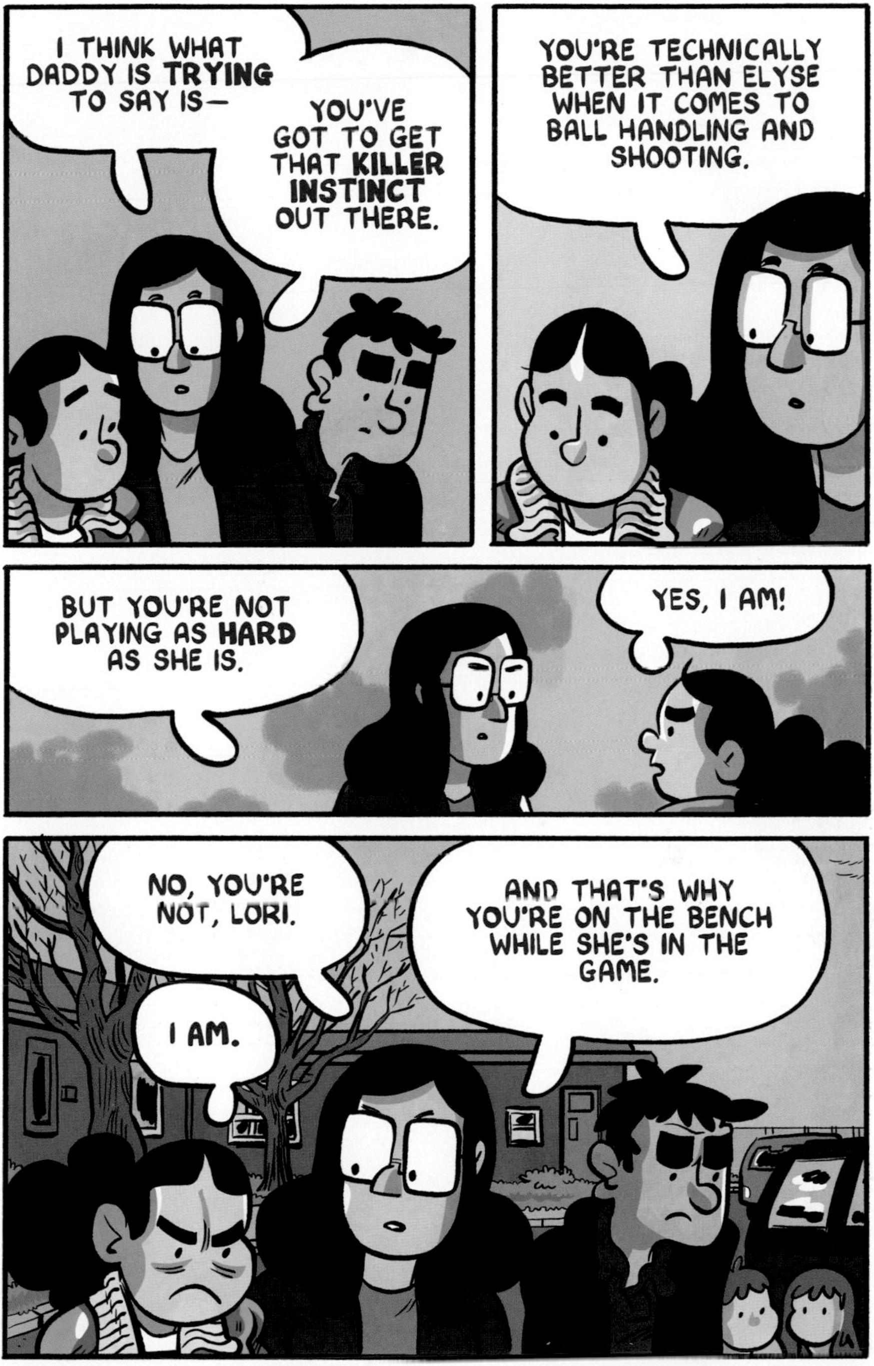
I THINK WHAT DADDY IS TRYING TO SAY IS—
YOU'VE GOT TO GET THAT KILLER INSTINCT OUT THERE.
YOU'RE TECHNICALLY BETTER THAN ELYSE WHEN IT COMES TO BALL HANDLING AND SHOOTING.
BUT YOU'RE NOT PLAYING AS HARD AS SHE IS.
YES, I AM!
NO, YOU'RE NOT, LORI.
I AM.
AND THAT'S WHY YOU'RE ON THE BENCH WHILE SHE'S IN THE GAME.

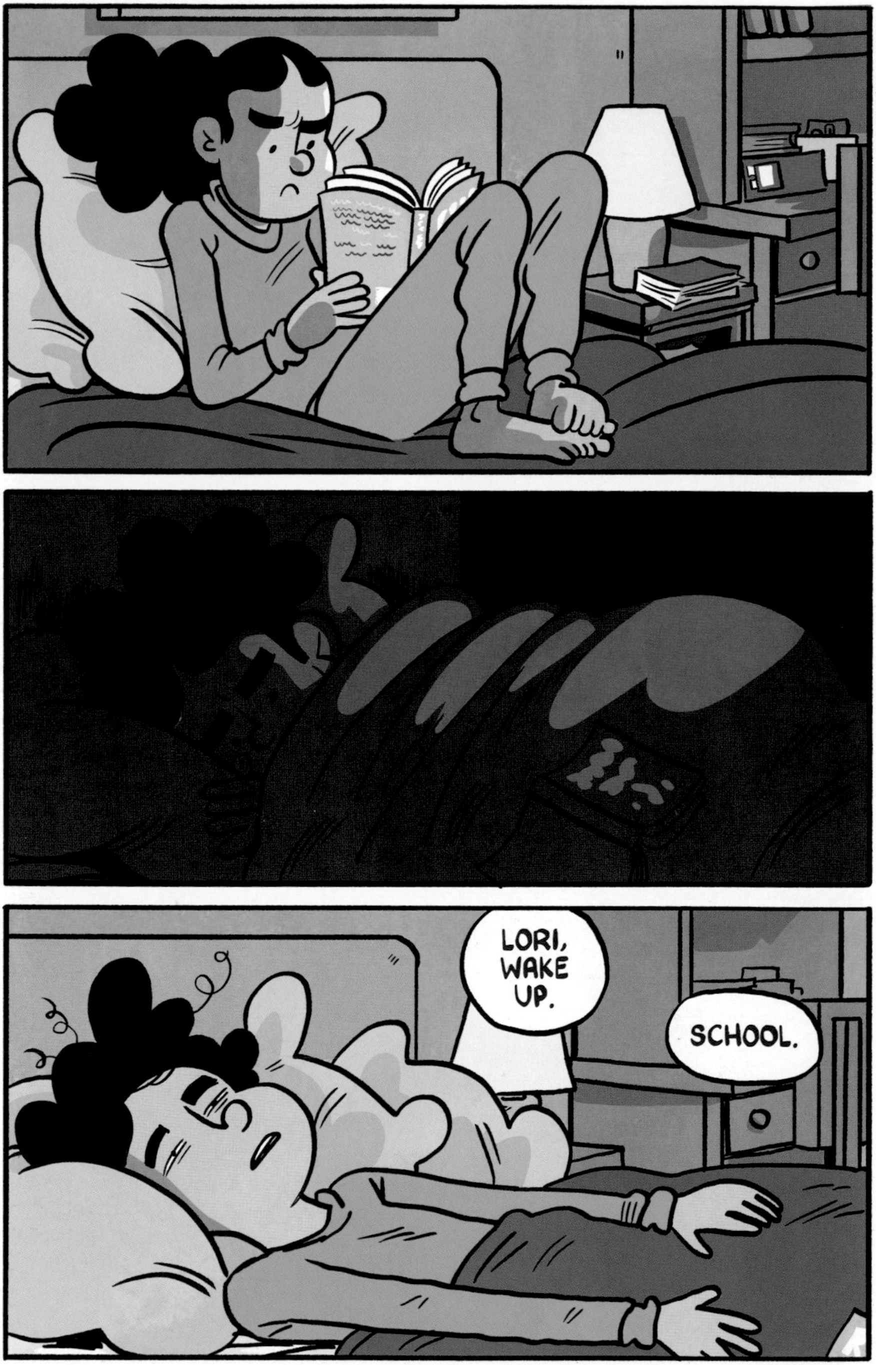
LORI, WAKE UP.
SCHOOL.

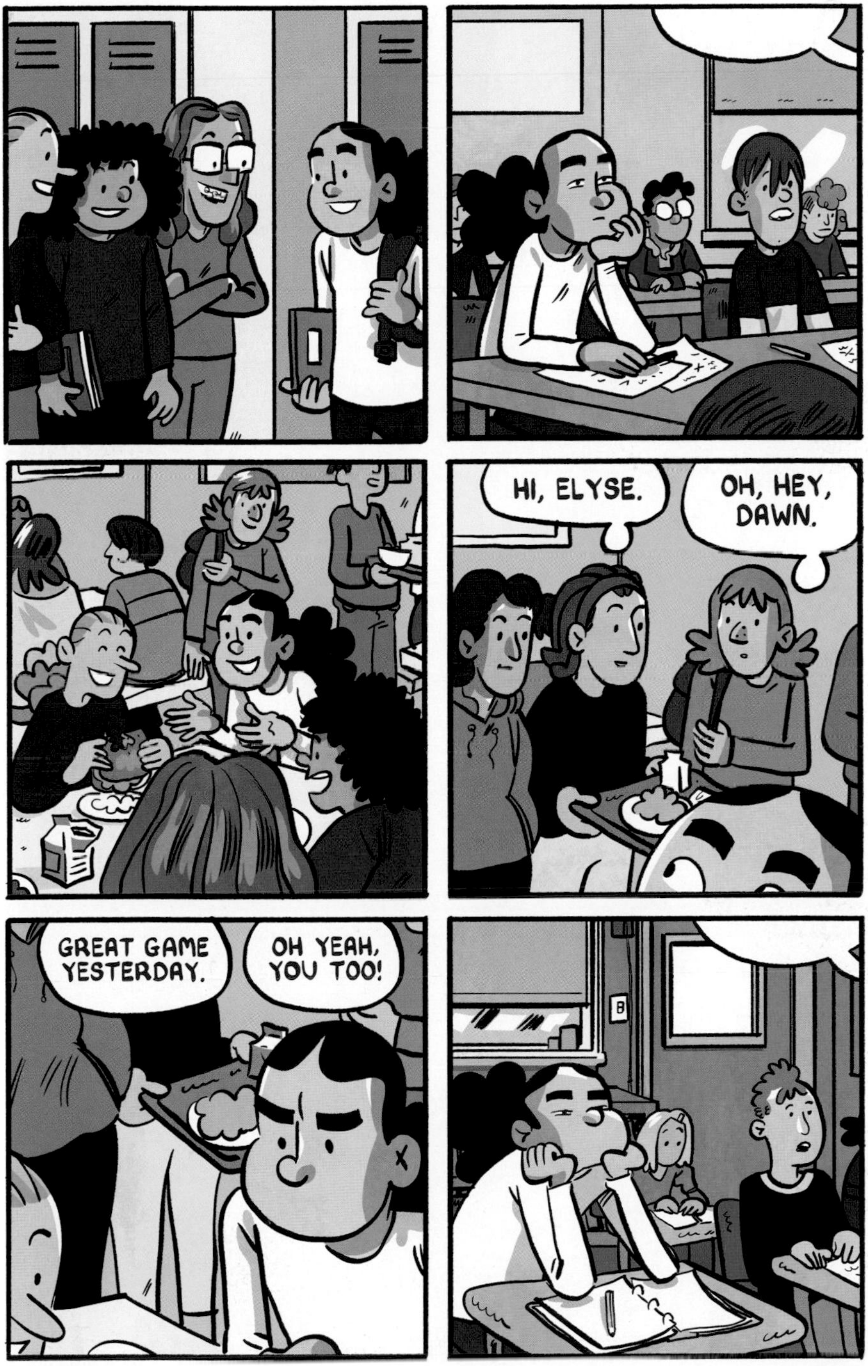
HI, ELYSE.
OH, HEY, DAWN.
GREAT GAME YESTERDAY.
OH YEAH, YOU TOO!

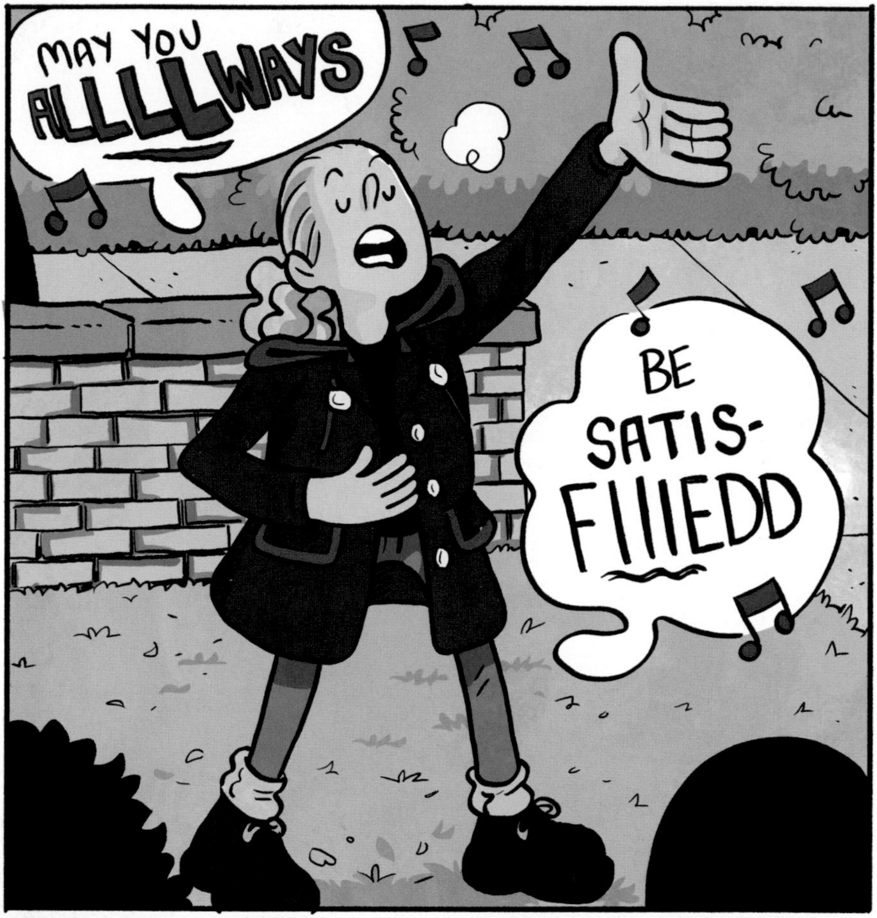
MAY YOU ALLLLWAYS
BE SATIS-FIIIEDD
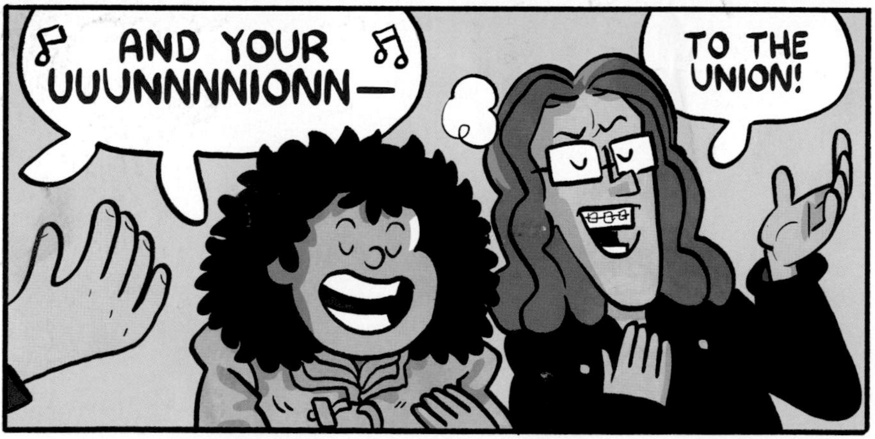
AND YOUR UUUNNNNIONN—
TO THE UNION!

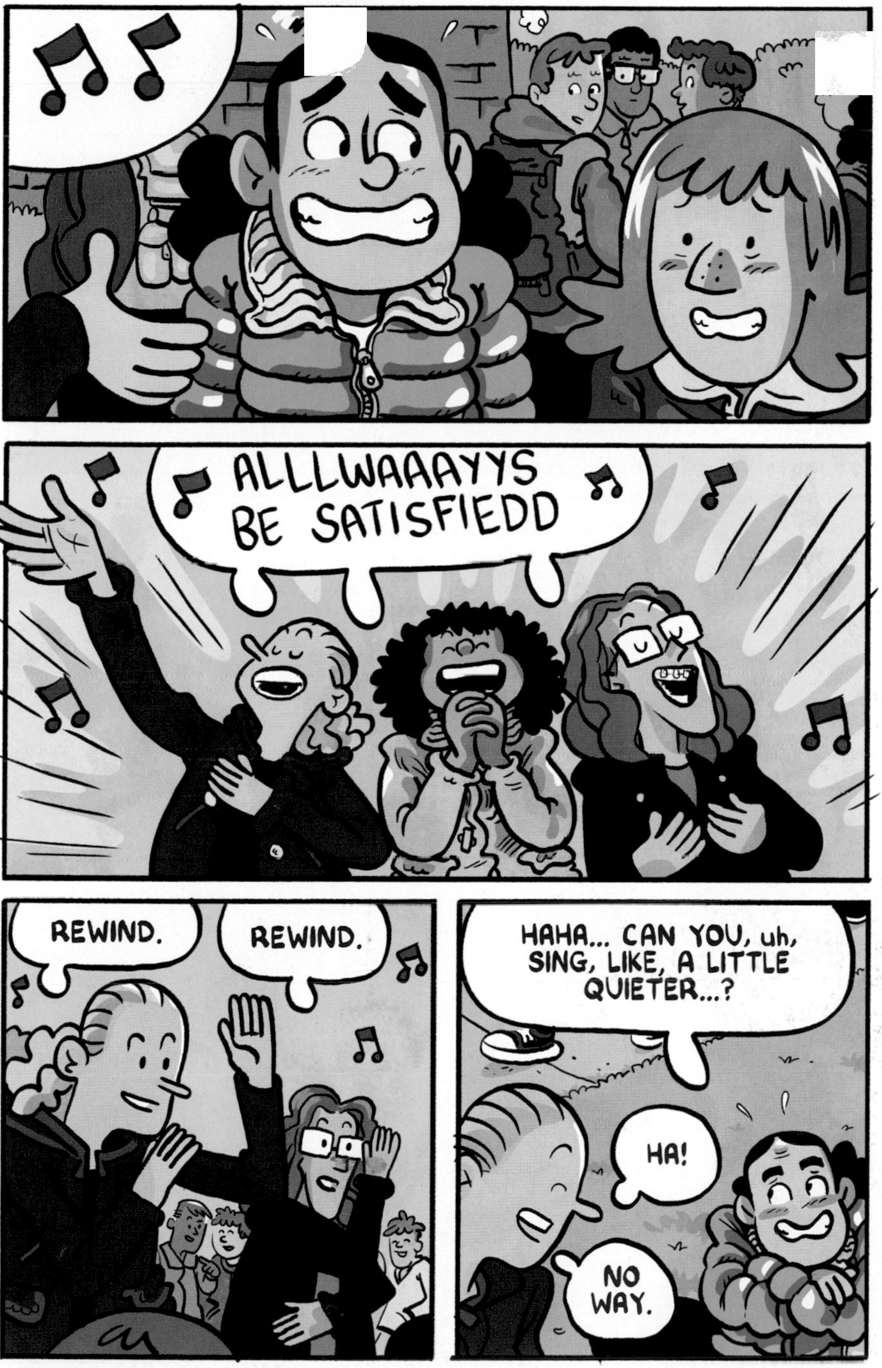
ALLLWAAAYYS BE SATISFIEDD
REWIND.
REWIND.
HAHA... CAN YOU, uh, SING, LIKE, A LITTLE QUIETER...?
HA!
NO WAY.

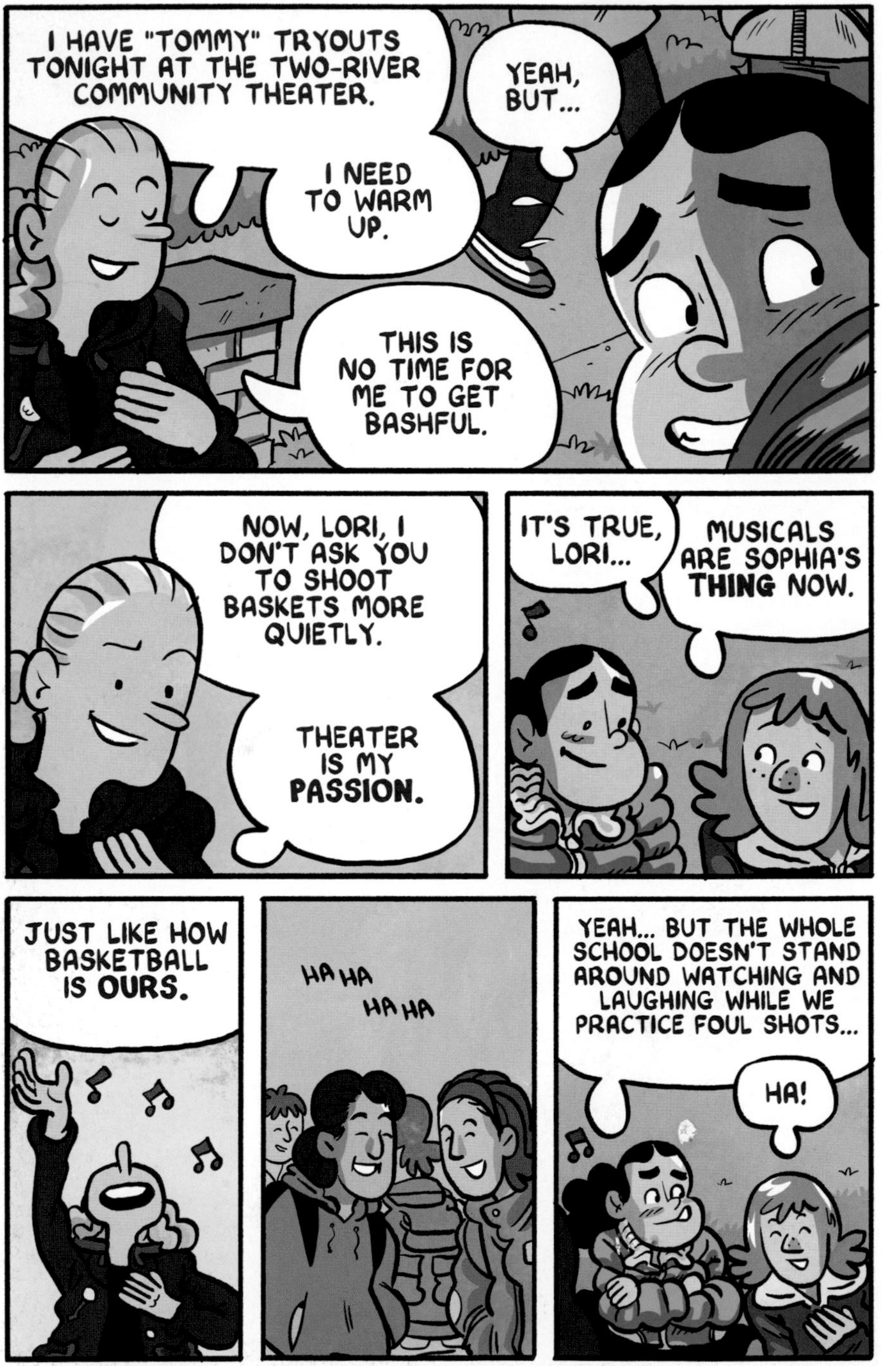
I HAVE "TOMMY" TRYOUTS TONIGHT AT THE TWO-RIVER COMMUNITY THEATER.
I NEED TO WARM UP.
YEAH, BUT...
THIS IS NO TIME FOR ME TO GET BASHFUL.
NOW, LORI, I DON'T ASK YOU TO SHOOT BASKETS MORE QUIETLY.
THEATER IS MY PASSION.
IT'S TRUE, LORI...
MUSICALS ARE SOPHIA'S THING NOW.
JUST LIKE HOW BASKETBALL IS OURS.
HA HA
HA HA
YEAH... BUT THE WHOLE SCHOOL DOESN'T STAND AROUND WATCHING AND LAUGHING WHILE WE PRACTICE FOUL SHOTS...
HA!

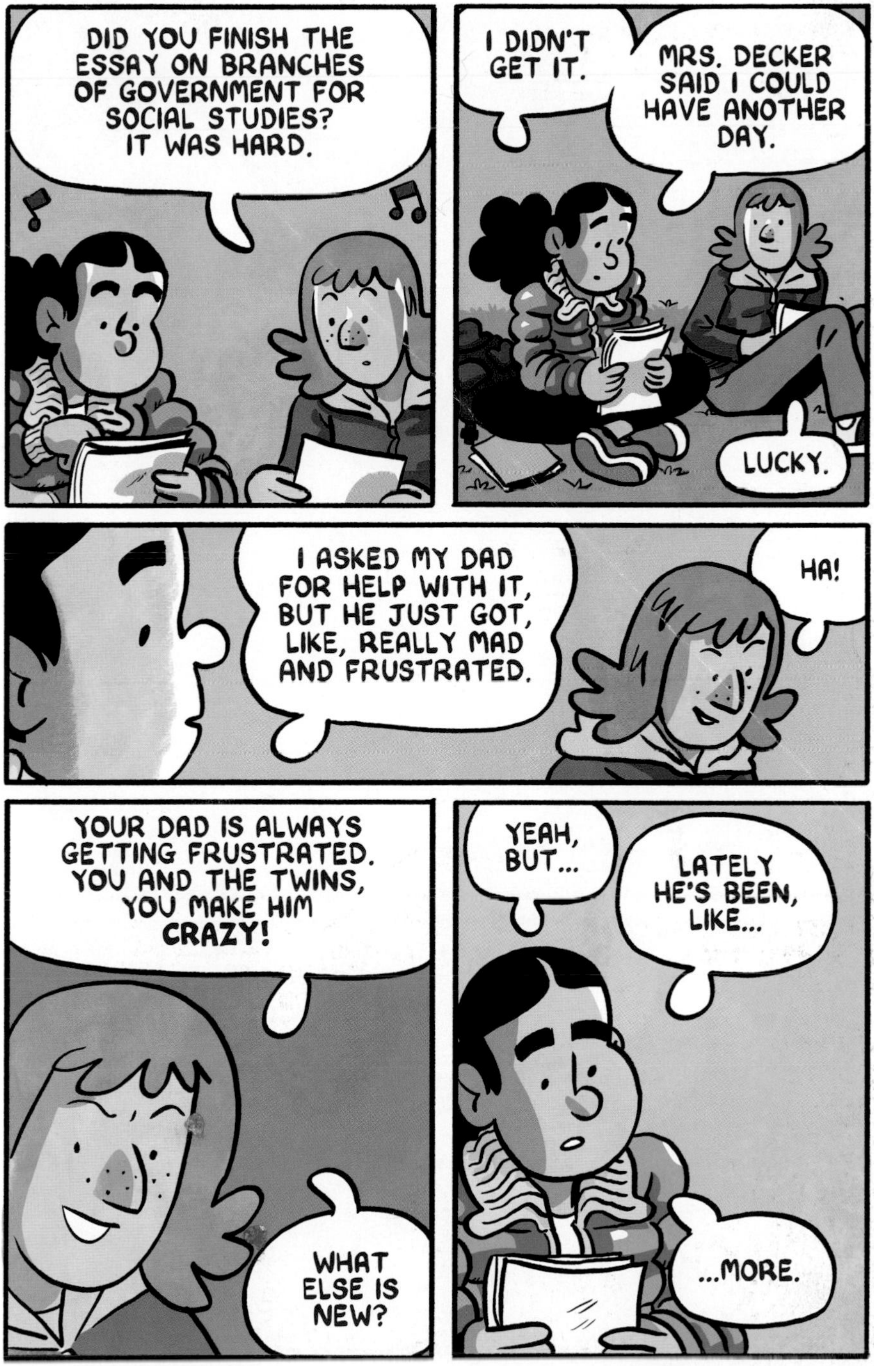
DID YOU FINISH THE ESSAY ON BRANCHES OF GOVERNMENT FOR SOCIAL STUDIES? IT WAS HARD.
I DIDN'T GET IT.
MRS. DECKER SAID I COULD HAVE ANOTHER DAY.
LUCKY.
I ASKED MY DAD FOR HELP WITH IT, BUT HE JUST GOT, LIKE, REALLY MAD AND FRUSTRATED.
HA!
YOUR DAD IS ALWAYS GETTING FRUSTRATED. YOU AND THE TWINS, YOU MAKE HIM **CRAZY!**
WHAT ELSE IS NEW?
YEAH, BUT...
LATELY HE'S BEEN, LIKE...
...MORE.

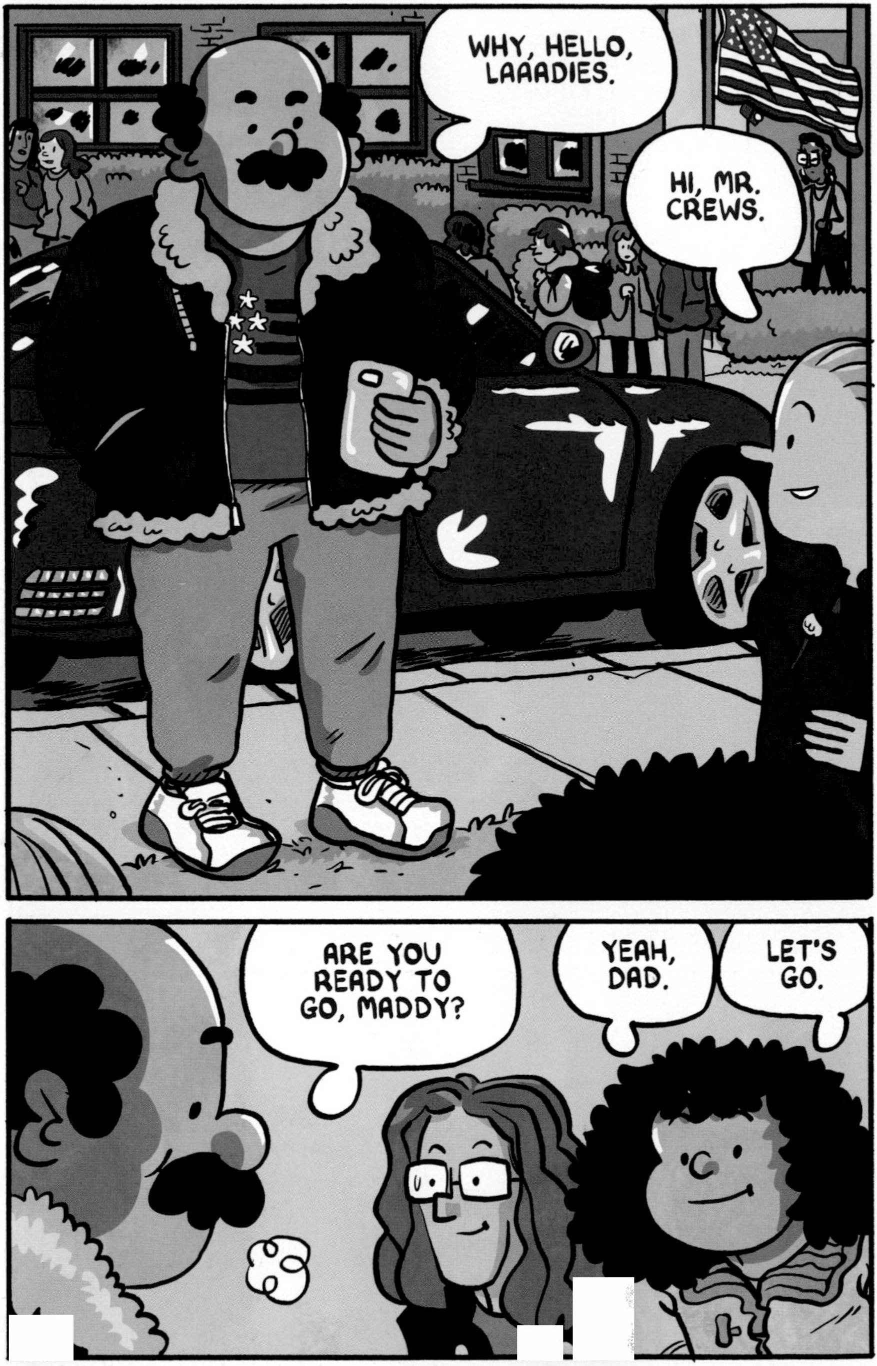
WHY, HELLO, LAAADIES.
HI, MR. CREWS.
ARE YOU READY TO GO, MADDY?
YEAH, DAD.
LET'S GO.

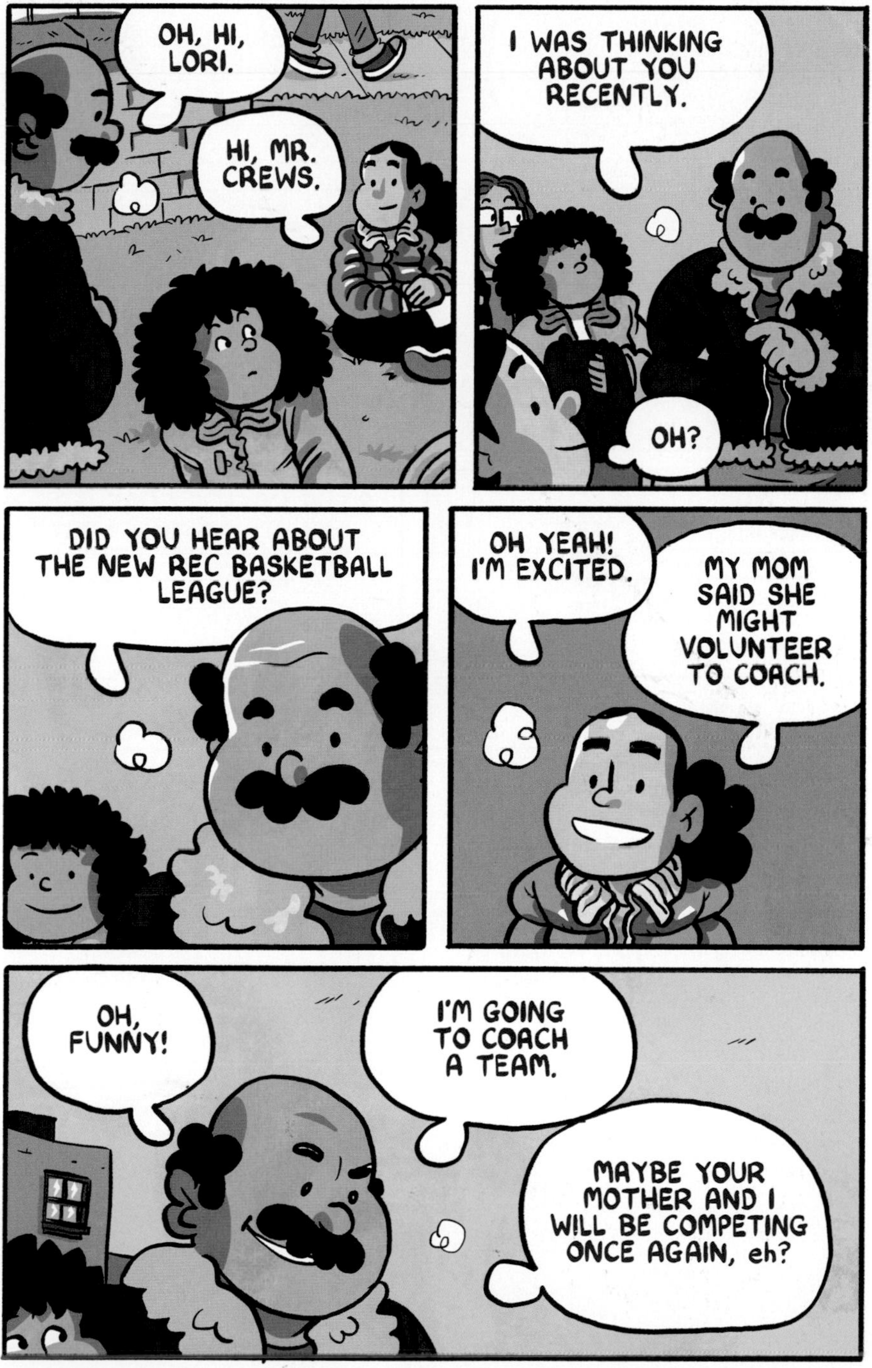
OH, HI, LORI.
HI, MR. CREWS.
I WAS THINKING ABOUT YOU RECENTLY.
OH?
DID YOU HEAR ABOUT THE NEW REC BASKETBALL LEAGUE?
OH YEAH! I'M EXCITED.
MY MOM SAID SHE MIGHT VOLUNTEER TO COACH.
OH, FUNNY!
I'M GOING TO COACH A TEAM.
MAYBE YOUR MOTHER AND I WILL BE COMPETING ONCE AGAIN, eh?

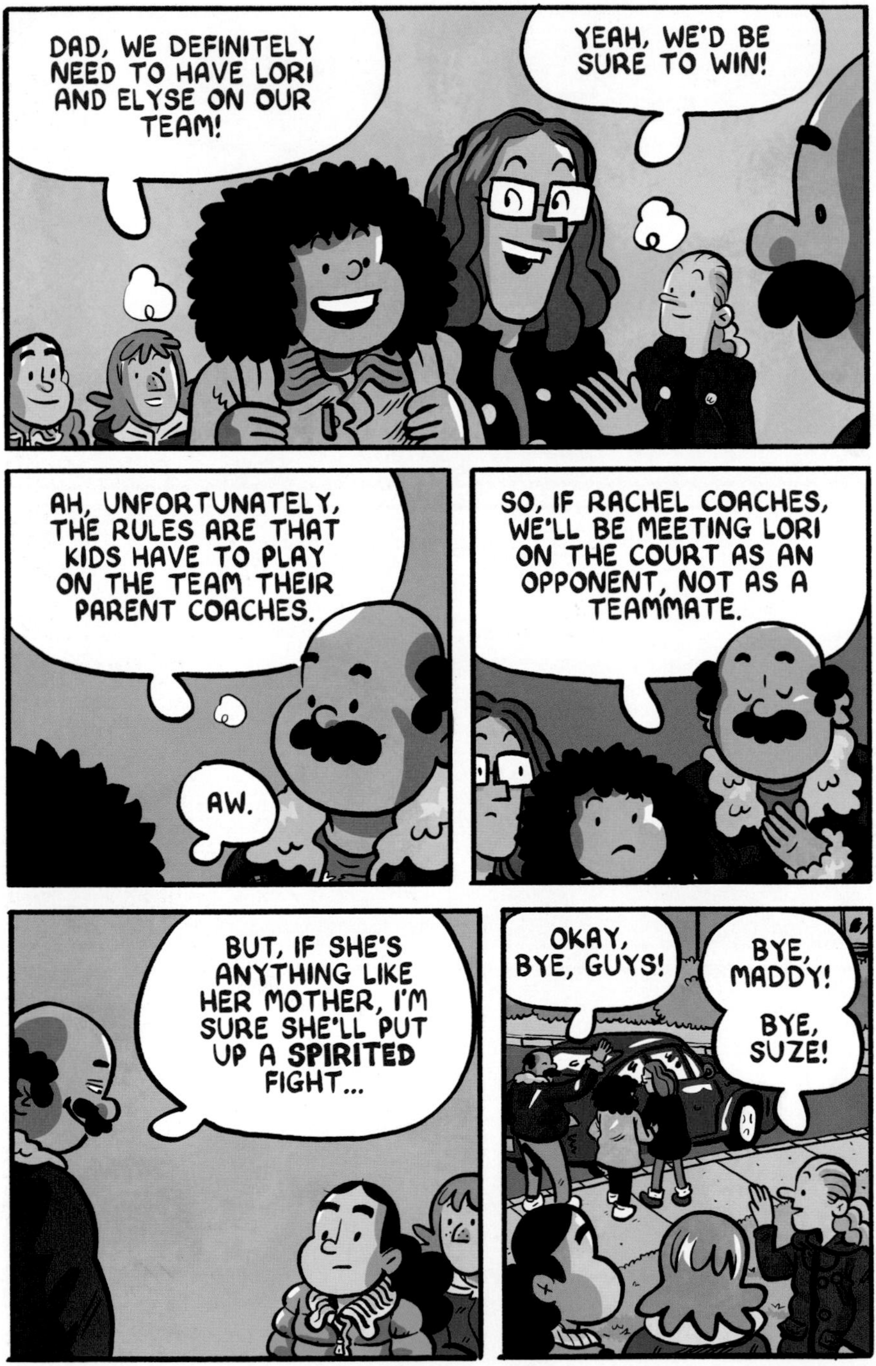
DAD, WE DEFINITELY NEED TO HAVE LORI AND ELYSE ON OUR TEAM!
YEAH, WE'D BE SURE TO WIN!
AH, UNFORTUNATELY, THE RULES ARE THAT KIDS HAVE TO PLAY ON THE TEAM THEIR PARENT COACHES.
AW.
SO, IF RACHEL COACHES, WE'LL BE MEETING LORI ON THE COURT AS AN OPPONENT, NOT AS A TEAMMATE.
BUT, IF SHE'S ANYTHING LIKE HER MOTHER, I'M SURE SHE'LL PUT UP A **SPIRITED** FIGHT...
OKAY, BYE, GUYS!
BYE, MADDY!
BYE, SUZE!

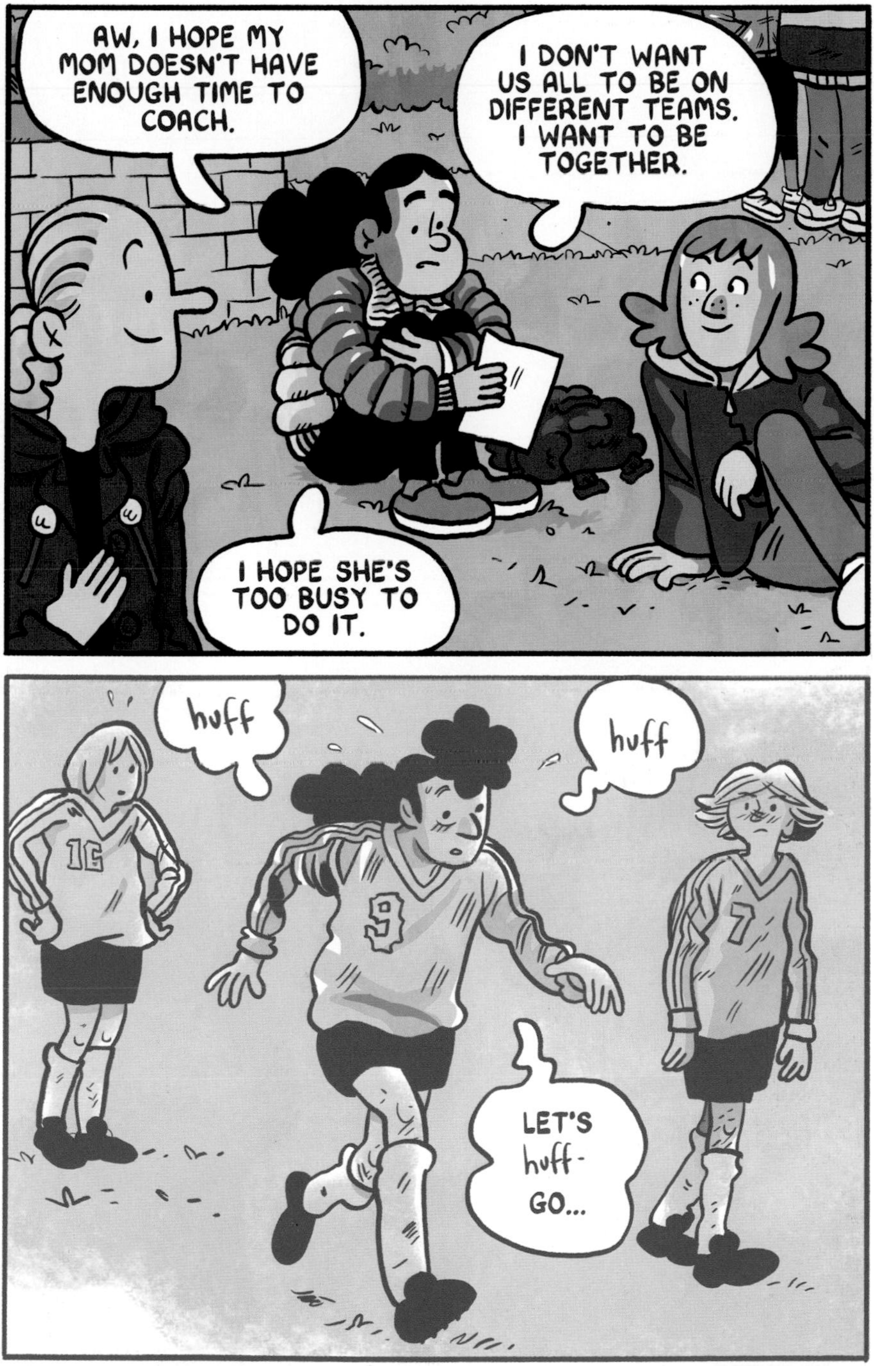
AW, I HOPE MY MOM DOESN'T HAVE ENOUGH TIME TO COACH.
I DON'T WANT US ALL TO BE ON DIFFERENT TEAMS. I WANT TO BE TOGETHER.
I HOPE SHE'S TOO BUSY TO DO IT.
huff
huff
LET'S huff-GO...

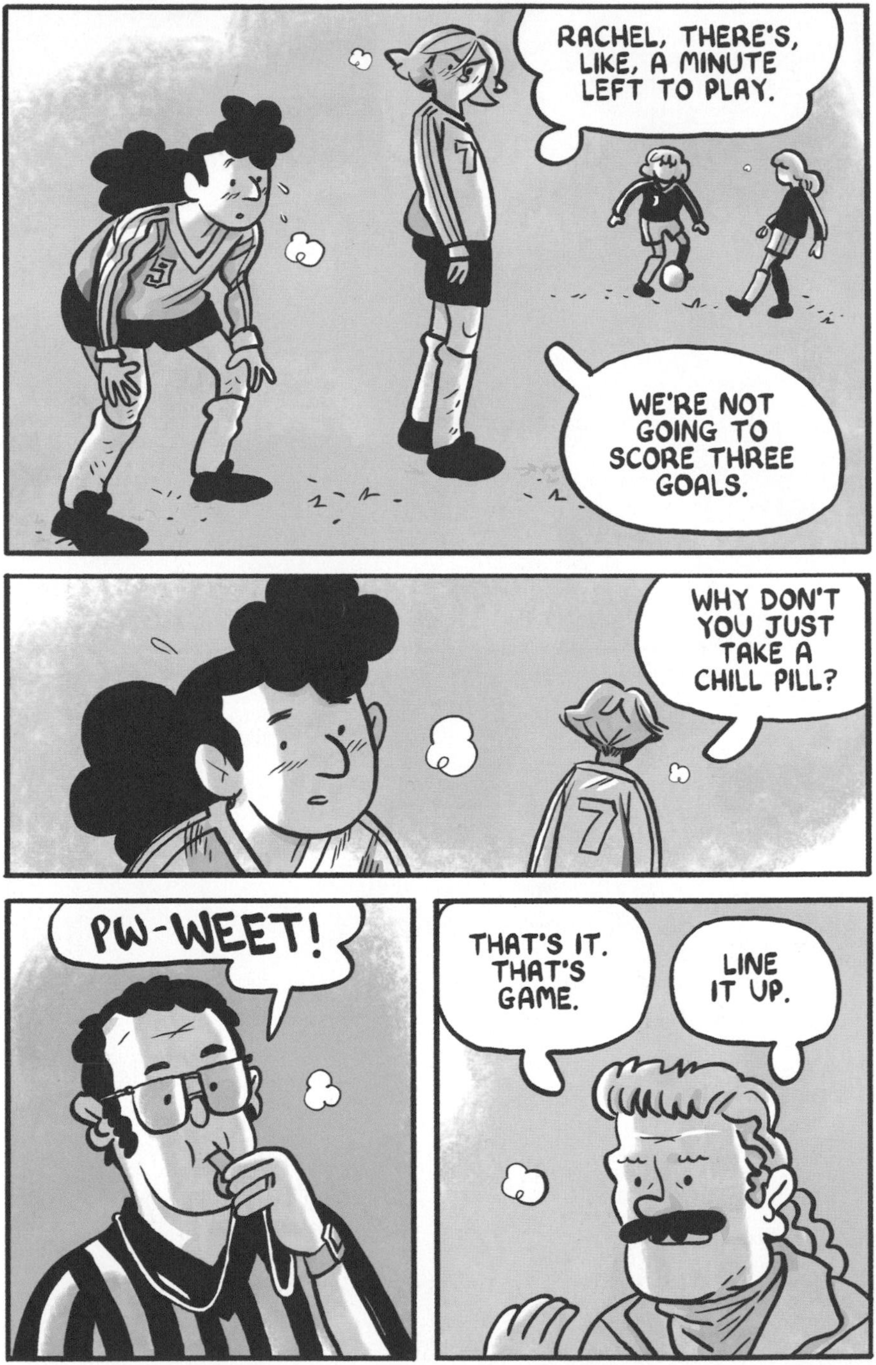
RACHEL, THERE'S, LIKE, A MINUTE LEFT TO PLAY.
WE'RE NOT GOING TO SCORE THREE GOALS.
WHY DON'T YOU JUST TAKE A CHILL PILL?
PW-WEET!
THAT'S IT. THAT'S GAME.
LINE IT UP.

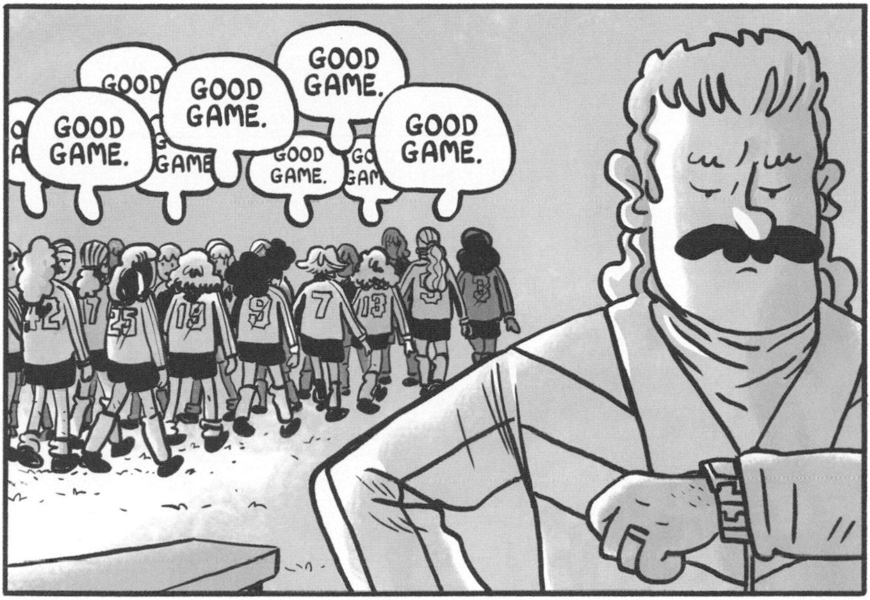
GOOD GAME.
GOOD GAME.
GOOD GAME.
GOOD GAME.
GOOD GAME.

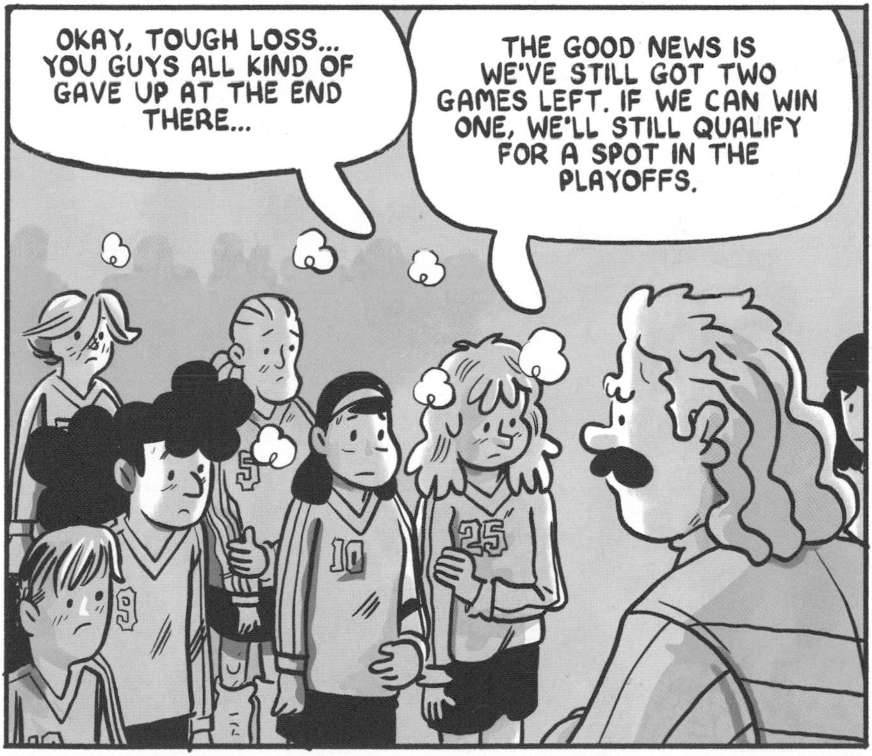
OKAY, TOUGH LOSS... YOU GUYS ALL KIND OF GAVE UP AT THE END THERE...
THE GOOD NEWS IS WE'VE STILL GOT TWO GAMES LEFT. IF WE CAN WIN ONE, WE'LL STILL QUALIFY FOR A SPOT IN THE PLAYOFFS.

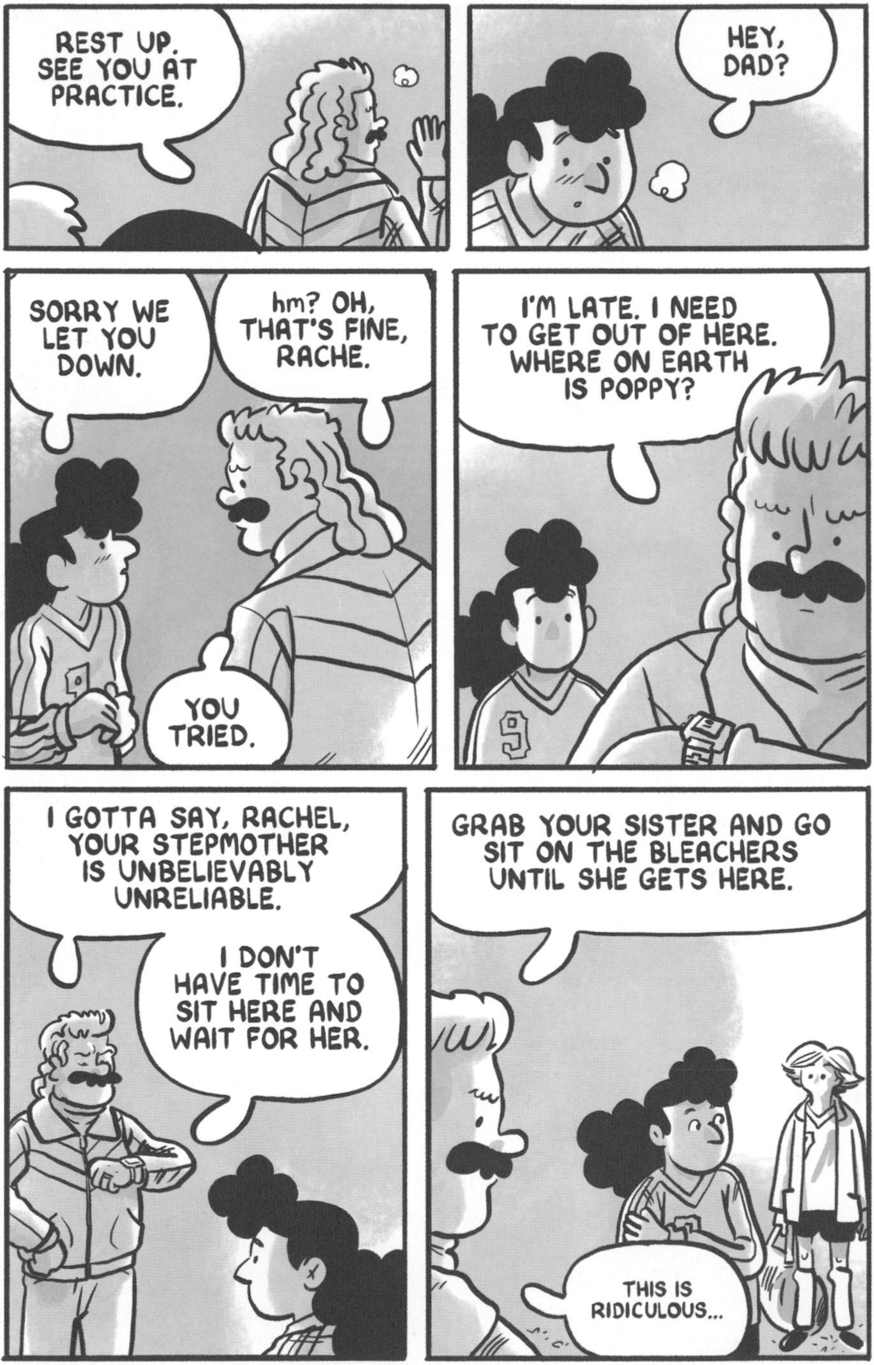
REST UP. SEE YOU AT PRACTICE.
HEY, DAD?
SORRY WE LET YOU DOWN.
hm? OH, THAT'S FINE, RACHE.
YOU TRIED.
I'M LATE. I NEED TO GET OUT OF HERE. WHERE ON EARTH IS POPPY?
I GOTTA SAY, RACHEL, YOUR STEPMOTHER IS UNBELIEVABLY UNRELIABLE.
I DON'T HAVE TIME TO SIT HERE AND WAIT FOR HER.
GRAB YOUR SISTER AND GO SIT ON THE BLEACHERS UNTIL SHE GETS HERE.
THIS IS RIDICULOUS...

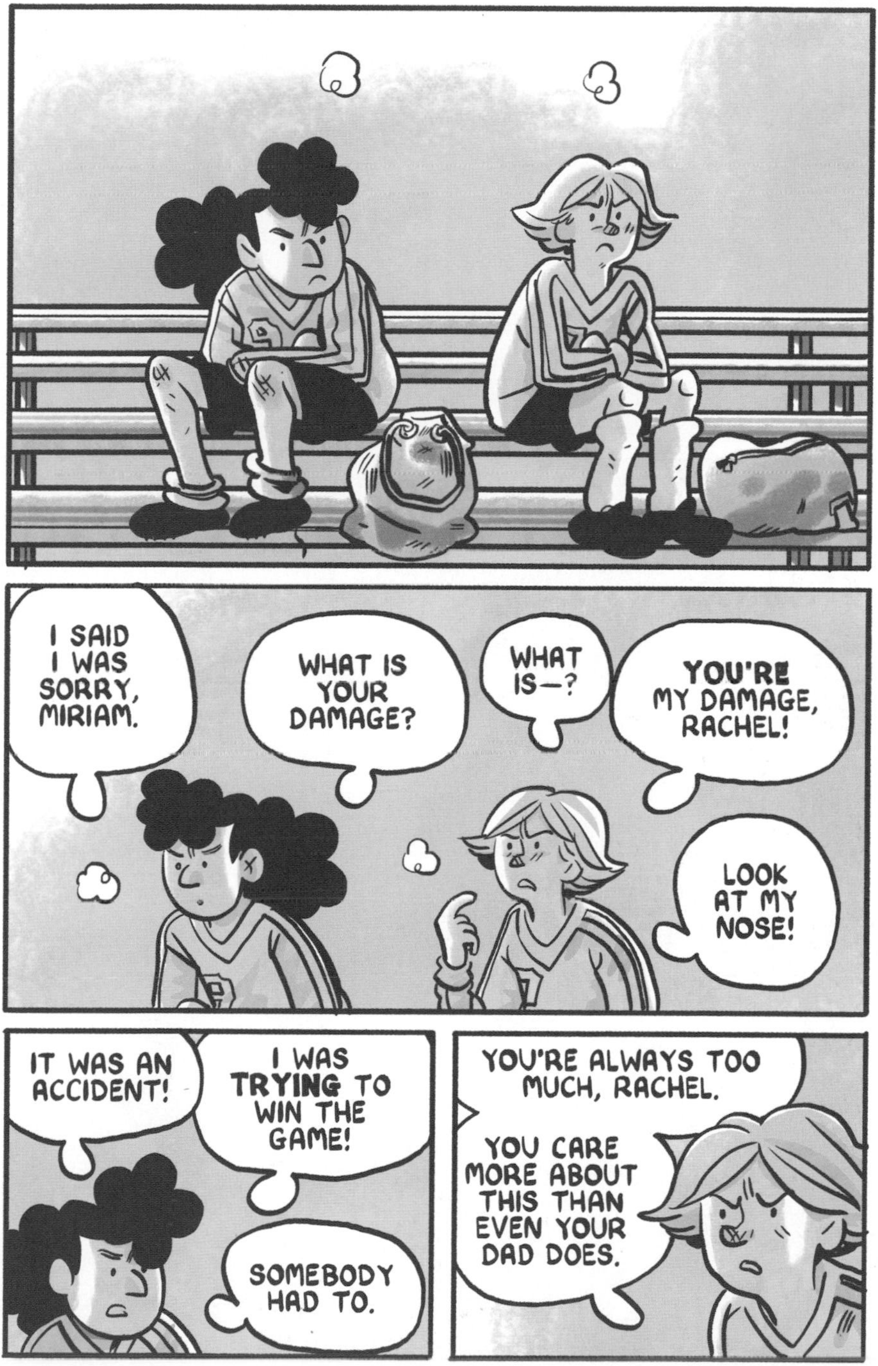
I SAID I WAS SORRY, MIRIAM.
WHAT IS YOUR DAMAGE?
WHAT IS—?
YOU'RE MY DAMAGE, RACHEL!
LOOK AT MY NOSE!
IT WAS AN ACCIDENT!
I WAS TRYING TO WIN THE GAME!
SOMEBODY HAD TO.
YOU'RE ALWAYS TOO MUCH, RACHEL.
YOU CARE MORE ABOUT THIS THAN EVEN YOUR DAD DOES.

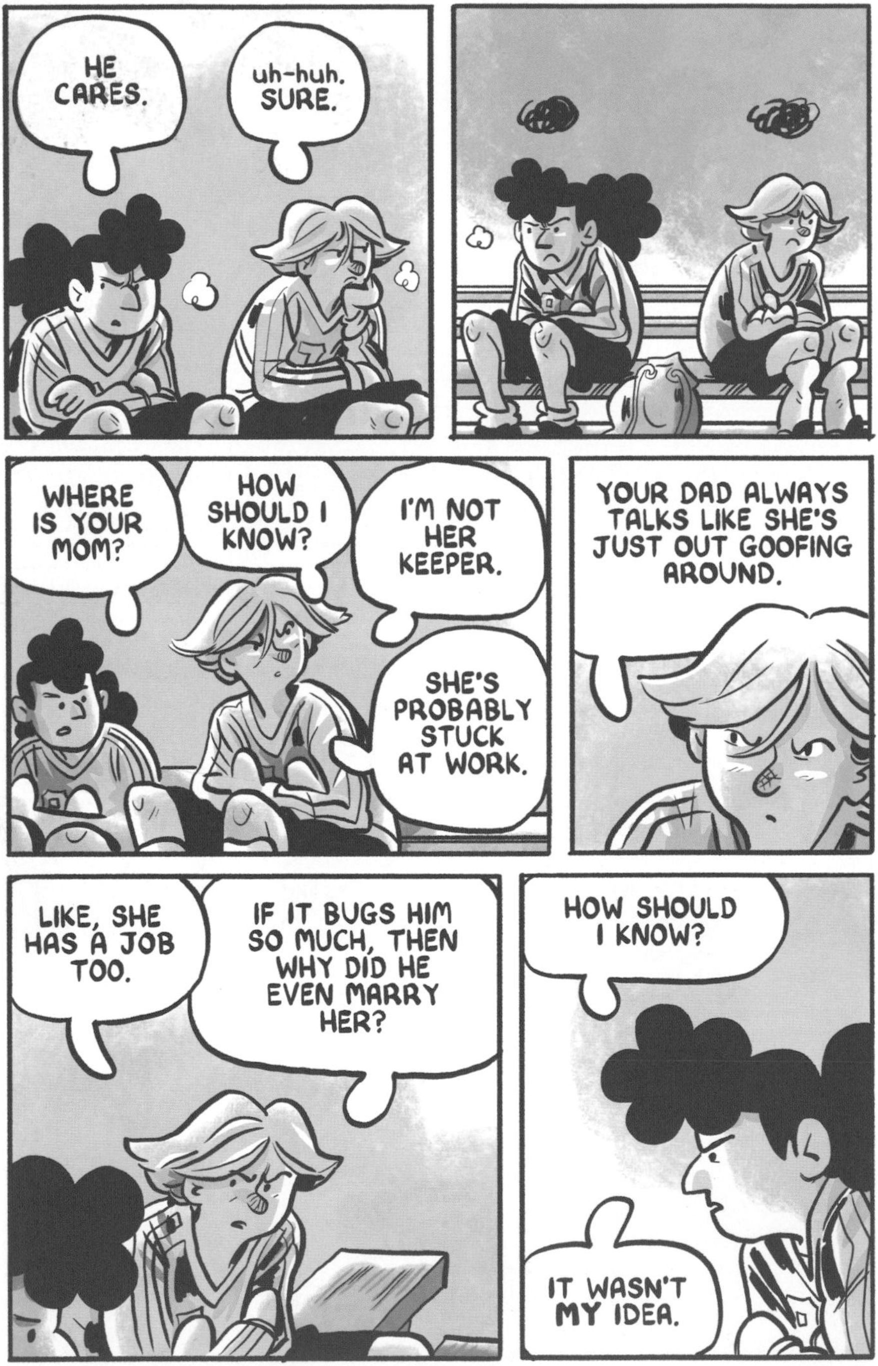
HE CARES.
uh-huh. SURE.
WHERE IS YOUR MOM?
HOW SHOULD I KNOW?
I'M NOT HER KEEPER.
SHE'S PROBABLY STUCK AT WORK.
YOUR DAD ALWAYS TALKS LIKE SHE'S JUST OUT GOOFING AROUND.
LIKE, SHE HAS A JOB TOO.
IF IT BUGS HIM SO MUCH, THEN WHY DID HE EVEN MARRY HER?
HOW SHOULD I KNOW?
IT WASN'T MY IDEA.

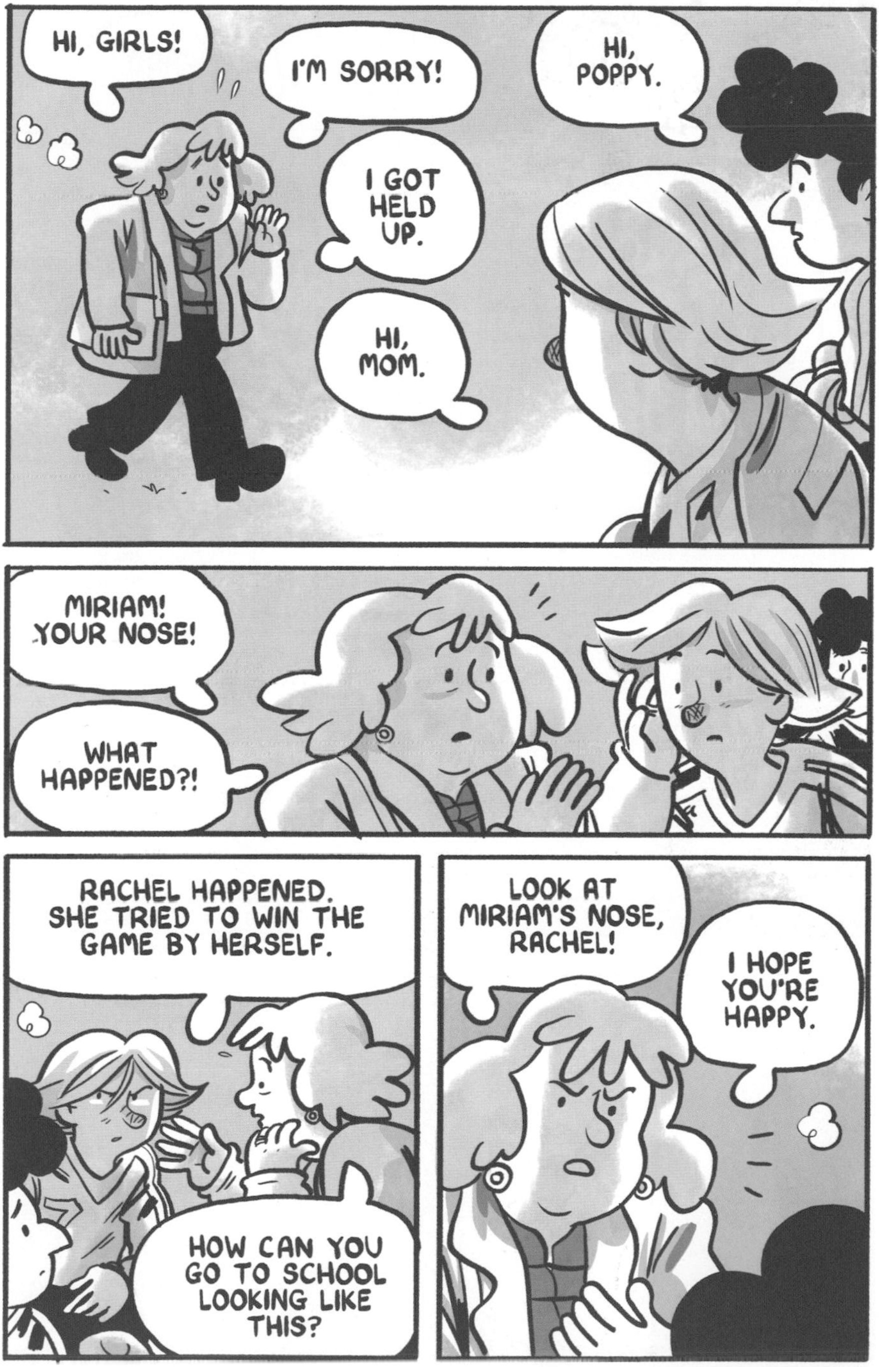
HI, GIRLS!
I'M SORRY!
I GOT HELD UP.
HI, POPPY.
HI, MOM.
MIRIAM! YOUR NOSE!
WHAT HAPPENED?!
RACHEL HAPPENED. SHE TRIED TO WIN THE GAME BY HERSELF.
HOW CAN YOU GO TO SCHOOL LOOKING LIKE THIS?
LOOK AT MIRIAM'S NOSE, RACHEL!
I HOPE YOU'RE HAPPY.

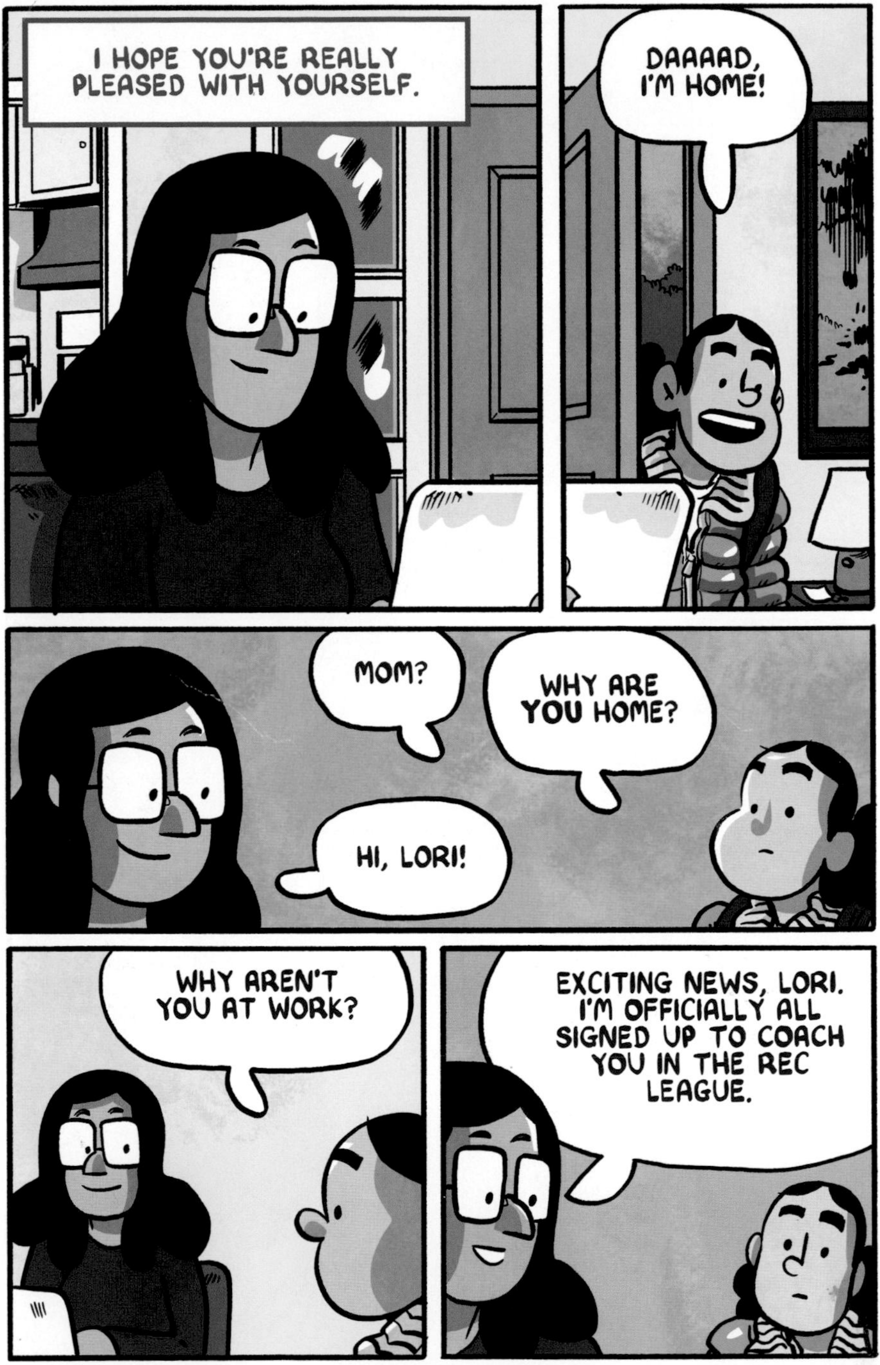
I HOPE YOU'RE REALLY PLEASED WITH YOURSELF.
DAAAAD, I'M HOME!
MOM?
WHY ARE YOU HOME?
HI, LORI!
WHY AREN'T YOU AT WORK?
EXCITING NEWS, LORI. I'M OFFICIALLY ALL SIGNED UP TO COACH YOU IN THE REC LEAGUE.

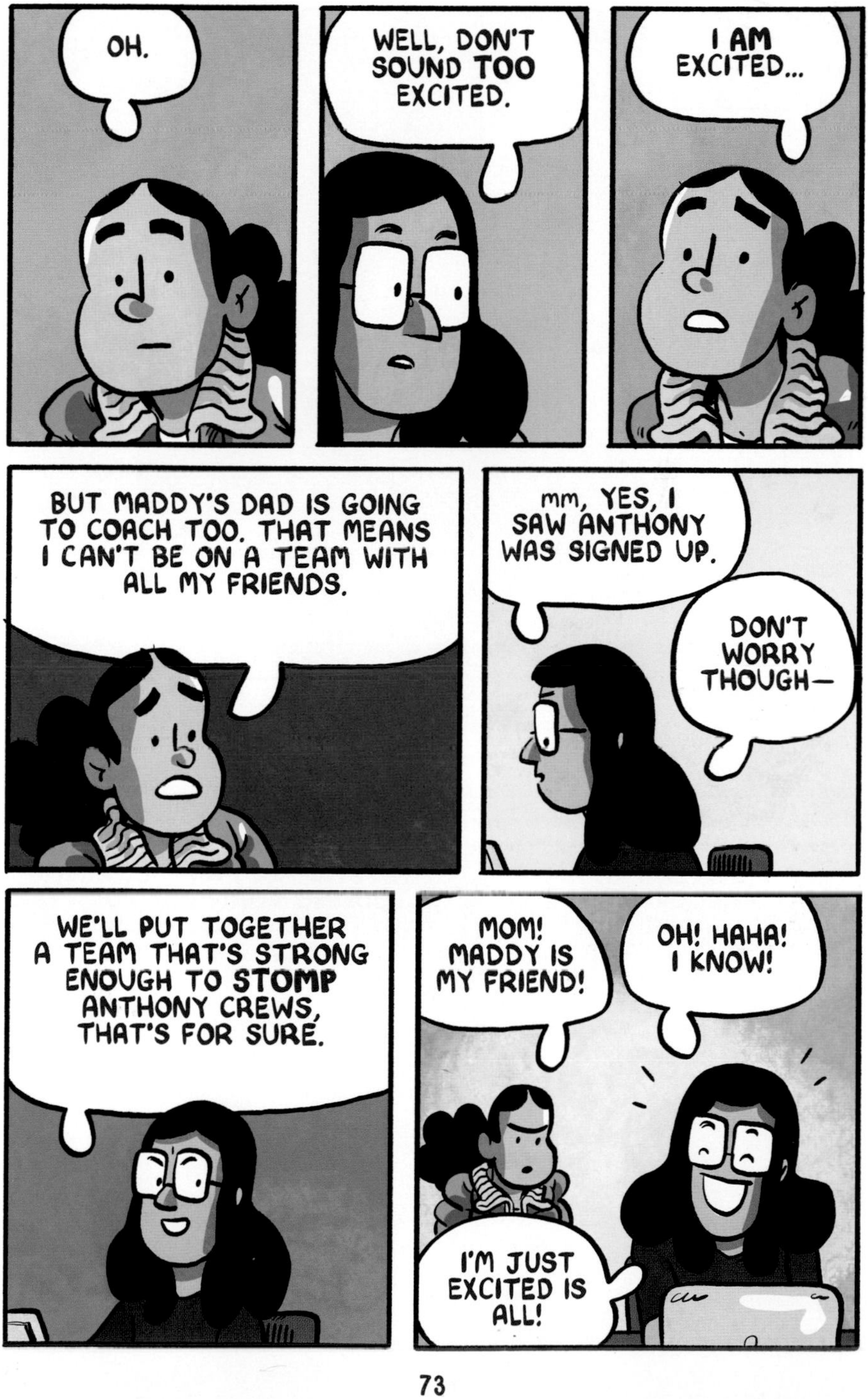
OH.
WELL, DON'T SOUND **TOO** EXCITED.
I **AM** EXCITED...
BUT MADDY'S DAD IS GOING TO COACH TOO. THAT MEANS I CAN'T BE ON A TEAM WITH ALL MY FRIENDS.
mm, YES, I SAW ANTHONY WAS SIGNED UP.
DON'T WORRY THOUGH—
WE'LL PUT TOGETHER A TEAM THAT'S STRONG ENOUGH TO **STOMP** ANTHONY CREWS, THAT'S FOR SURE.
MOM! MADDY IS MY FRIEND!
OH! HAHA! I KNOW!
I'M JUST EXCITED IS ALL!

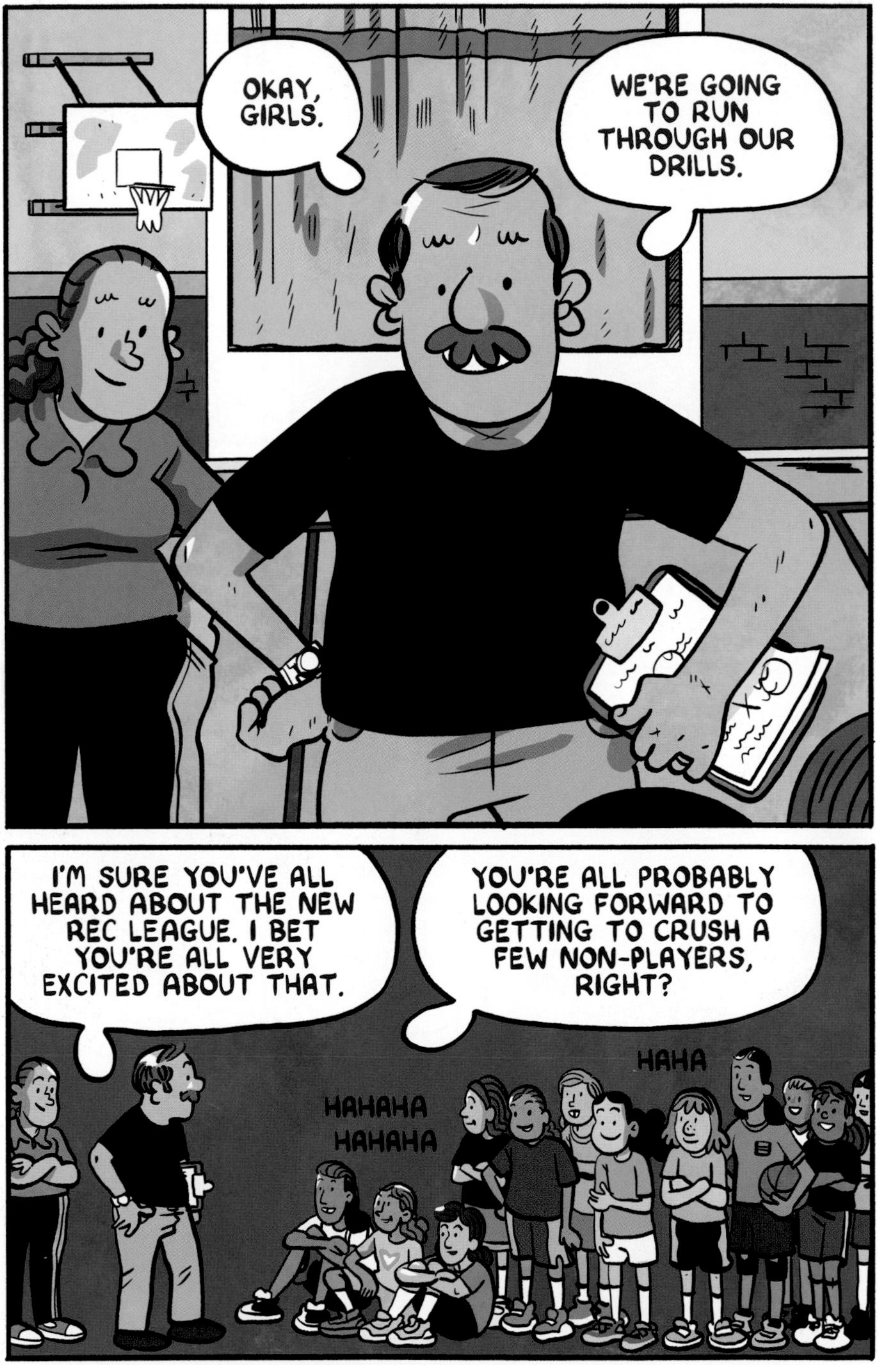
OKAY, GIRLS.
WE'RE GOING TO RUN THROUGH OUR DRILLS.
I'M SURE YOU'VE ALL HEARD ABOUT THE NEW REC LEAGUE. I BET YOU'RE ALL VERY EXCITED ABOUT THAT.
YOU'RE ALL PROBABLY LOOKING FORWARD TO GETTING TO CRUSH A FEW NON-PLAYERS, RIGHT?
HAHAHA HAHAHA
HAHA

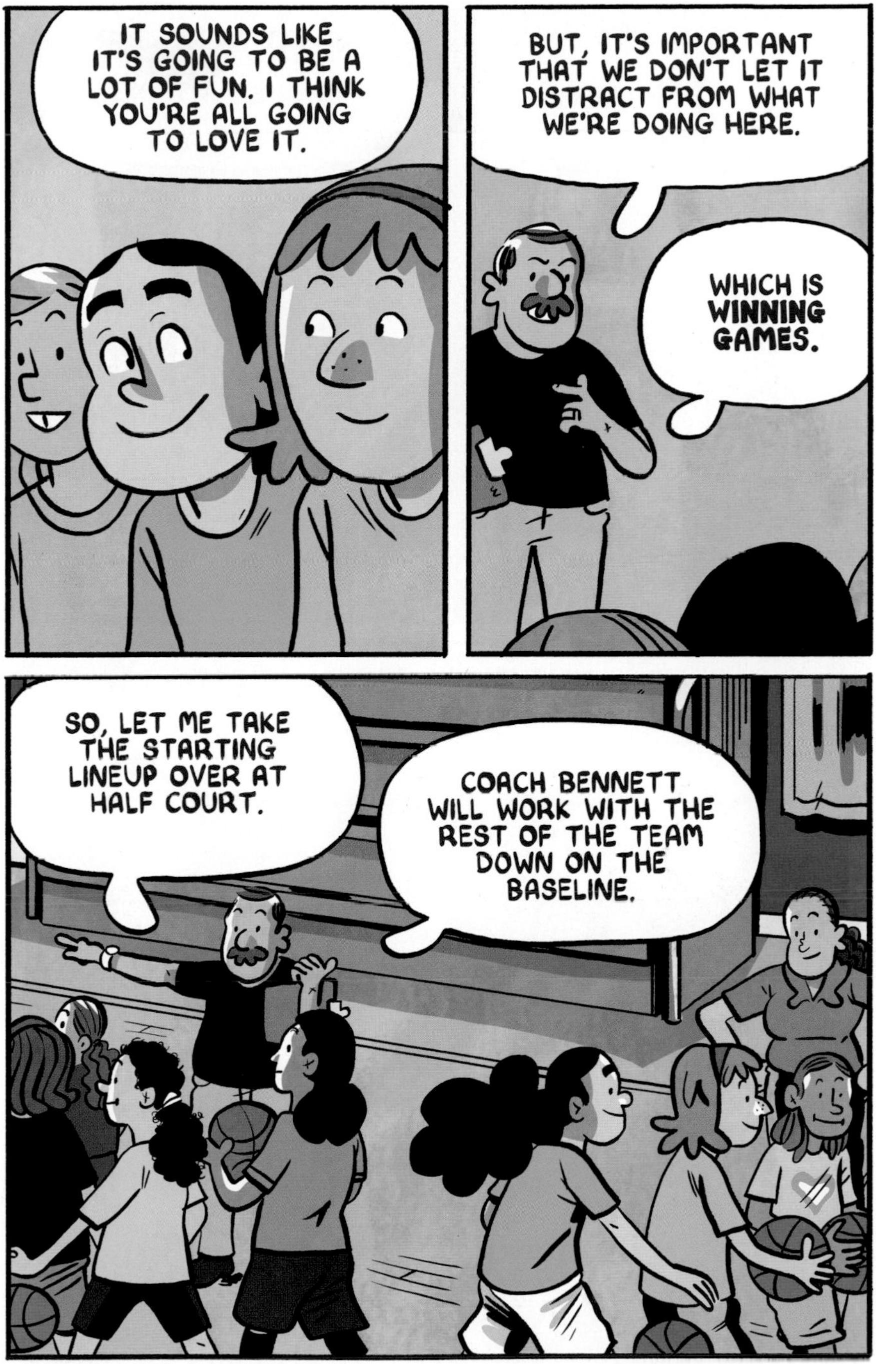
IT SOUNDS LIKE IT'S GOING TO BE A LOT OF FUN. I THINK YOU'RE ALL GOING TO LOVE IT.
BUT, IT'S IMPORTANT THAT WE DON'T LET IT DISTRACT FROM WHAT WE'RE DOING HERE.
WHICH IS **WINNING** GAMES.
SO, LET ME TAKE THE STARTING LINEUP OVER AT HALF COURT.
COACH BENNETT WILL WORK WITH THE REST OF THE TEAM DOWN ON THE BASELINE.

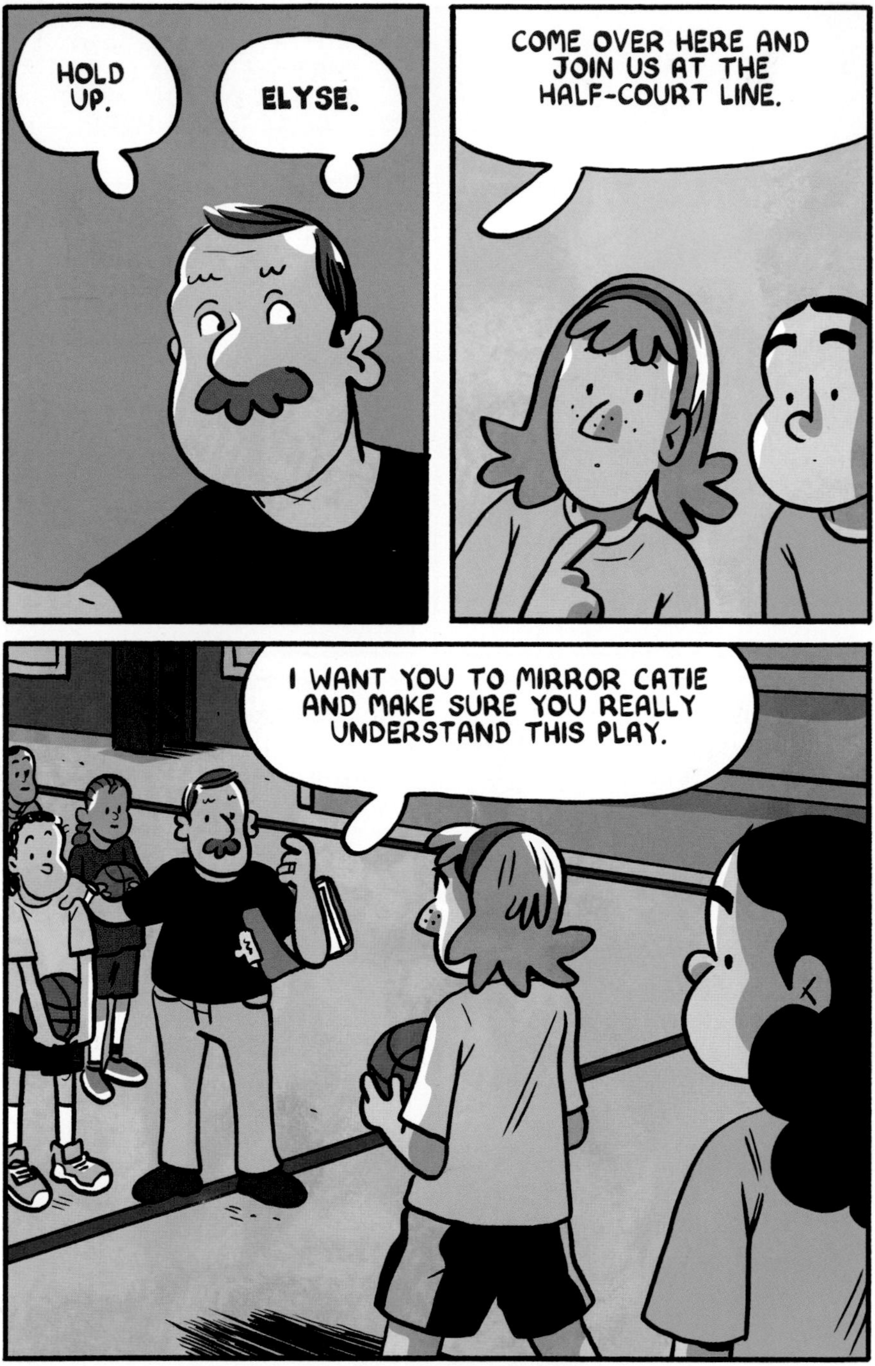
HOLD UP.
ELYSE.
COME OVER HERE AND JOIN US AT THE HALF-COURT LINE.
I WANT YOU TO MIRROR CATIE AND MAKE SURE YOU REALLY UNDERSTAND THIS PLAY.

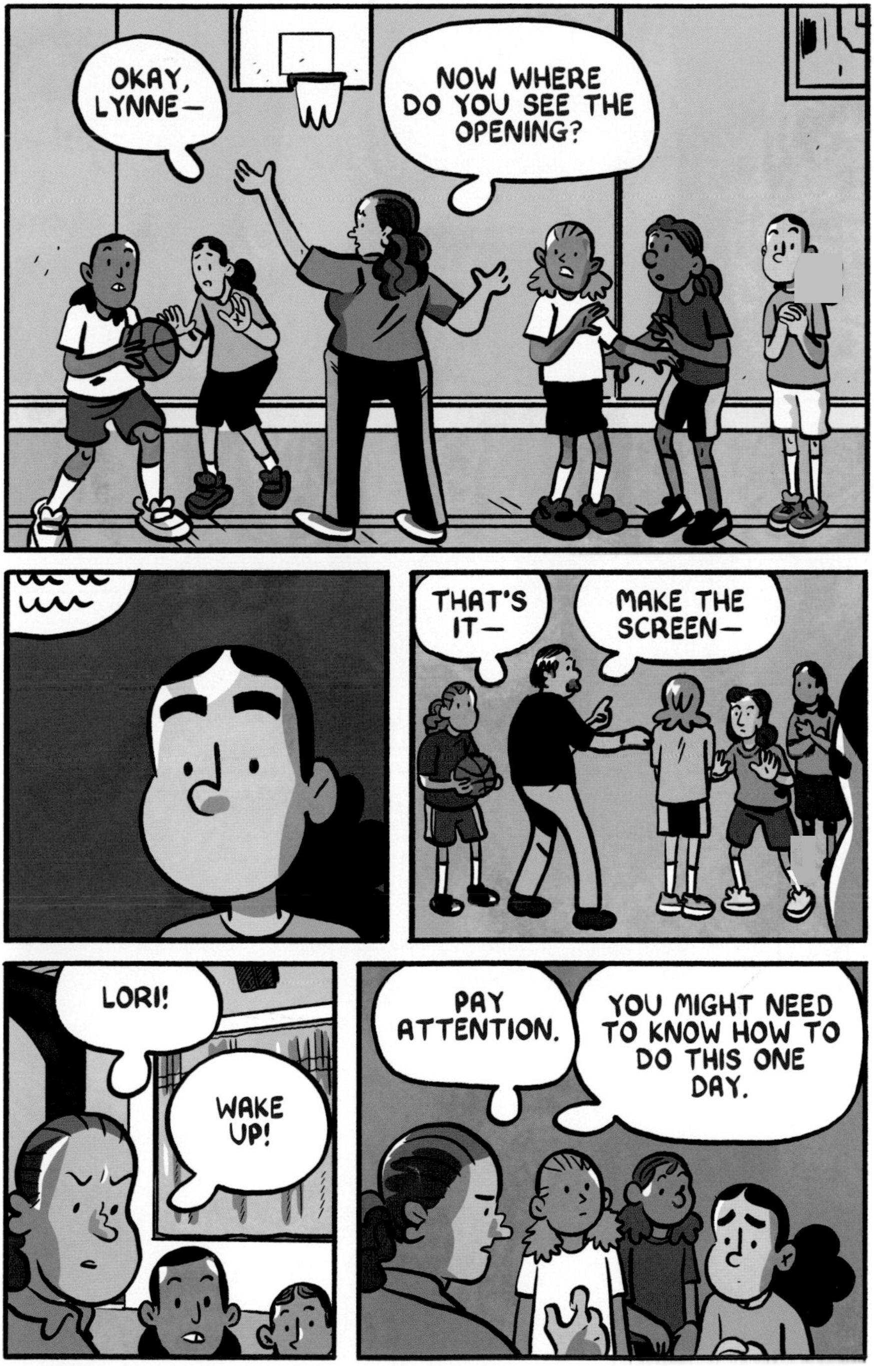
OKAY, LYNNE—
NOW WHERE DO YOU SEE THE OPENING?
THAT'S IT—
MAKE THE SCREEN—
LORI!
WAKE UP!
PAY ATTENTION.
YOU MIGHT NEED TO KNOW HOW TO DO THIS ONE DAY.

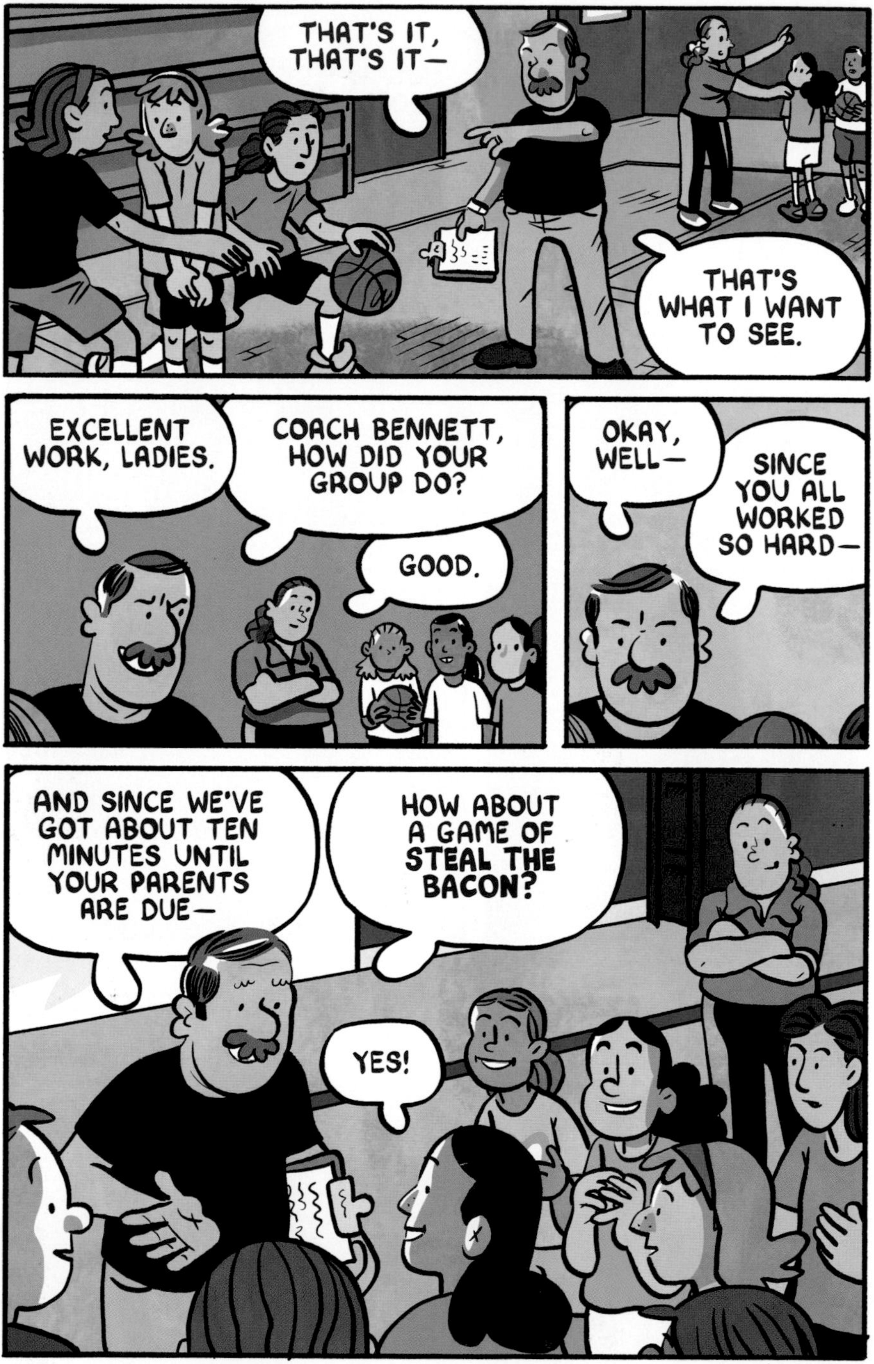
THAT'S IT, THAT'S IT—
THAT'S WHAT I WANT TO SEE.
EXCELLENT WORK, LADIES.
COACH BENNETT, HOW DID YOUR GROUP DO?
GOOD.
OKAY, WELL—
SINCE YOU ALL WORKED SO HARD—
AND SINCE WE'VE GOT ABOUT TEN MINUTES UNTIL YOUR PARENTS ARE DUE—
HOW ABOUT A GAME OF **STEAL THE BACON?**
YES!

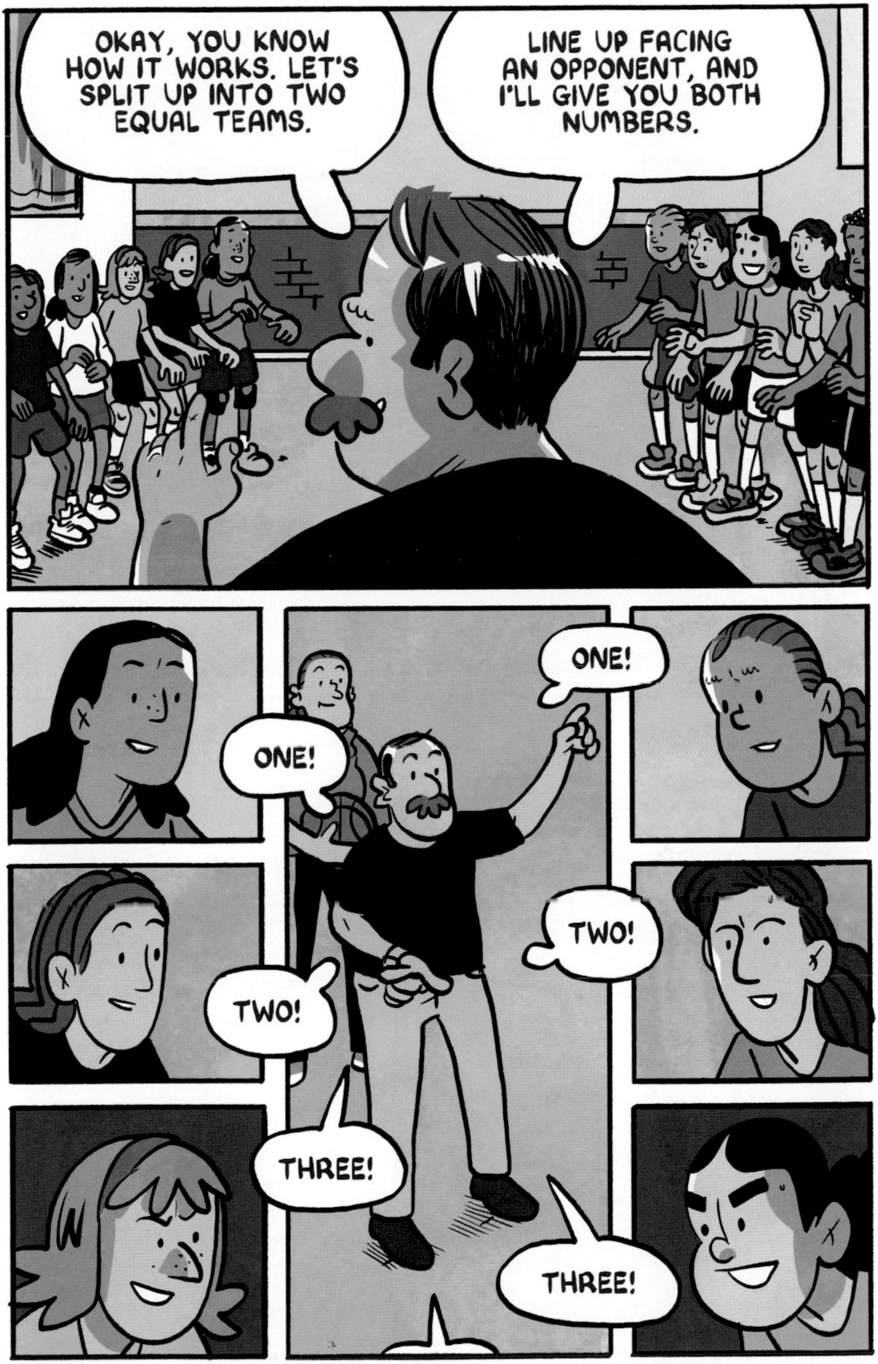
OKAY, YOU KNOW HOW IT WORKS. LET'S SPLIT UP INTO TWO EQUAL TEAMS.
LINE UP FACING AN OPPONENT, AND I'LL GIVE YOU BOTH NUMBERS.
ONE!
ONE!
TWO!
TWO!
THREE!
THREE!

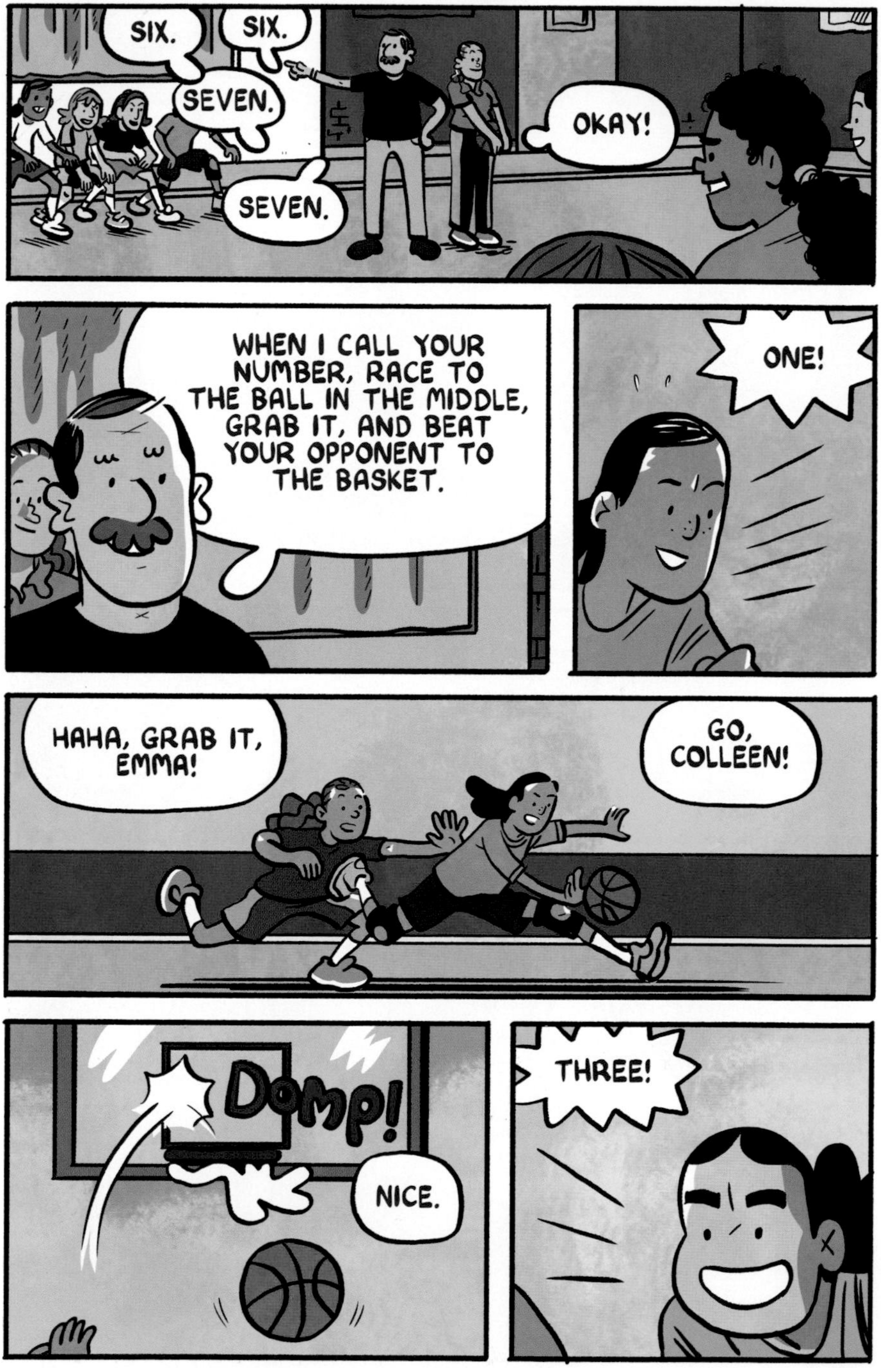
SIX.
SIX.
SEVEN.
SEVEN.
OKAY!
WHEN I CALL YOUR NUMBER, RACE TO THE BALL IN THE MIDDLE, GRAB IT, AND BEAT YOUR OPPONENT TO THE BASKET.
ONE!
HAHA, GRAB IT, EMMA!
GO, COLLEEN!
DOMP!
NICE.
THREE!

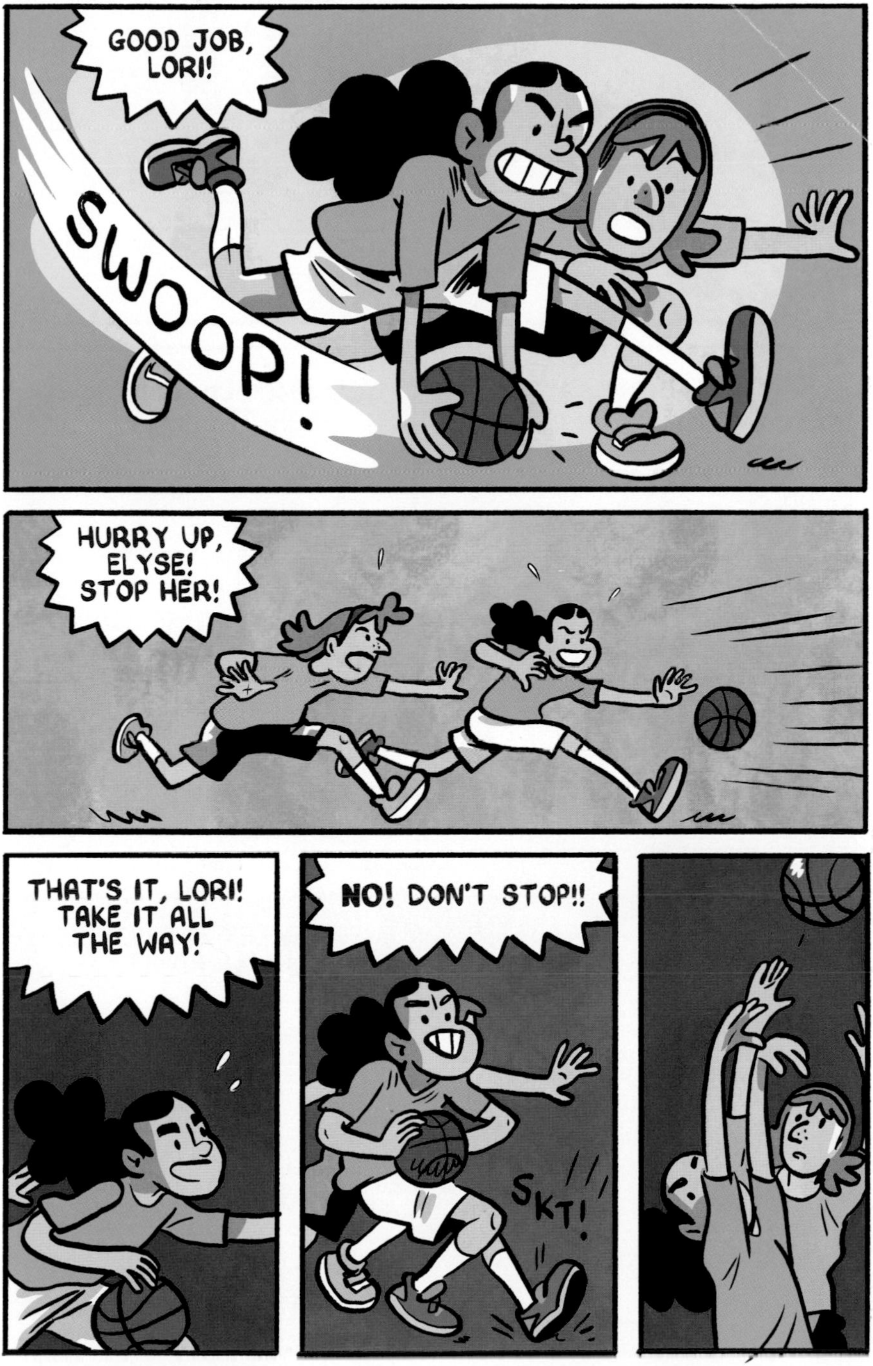
GOOD JOB, LORI!
SWOOP!
HURRY UP, ELYSE! STOP HER!
THAT'S IT, LORI! TAKE IT ALL THE WAY!
NO! DON'T STOP!!
SKT!

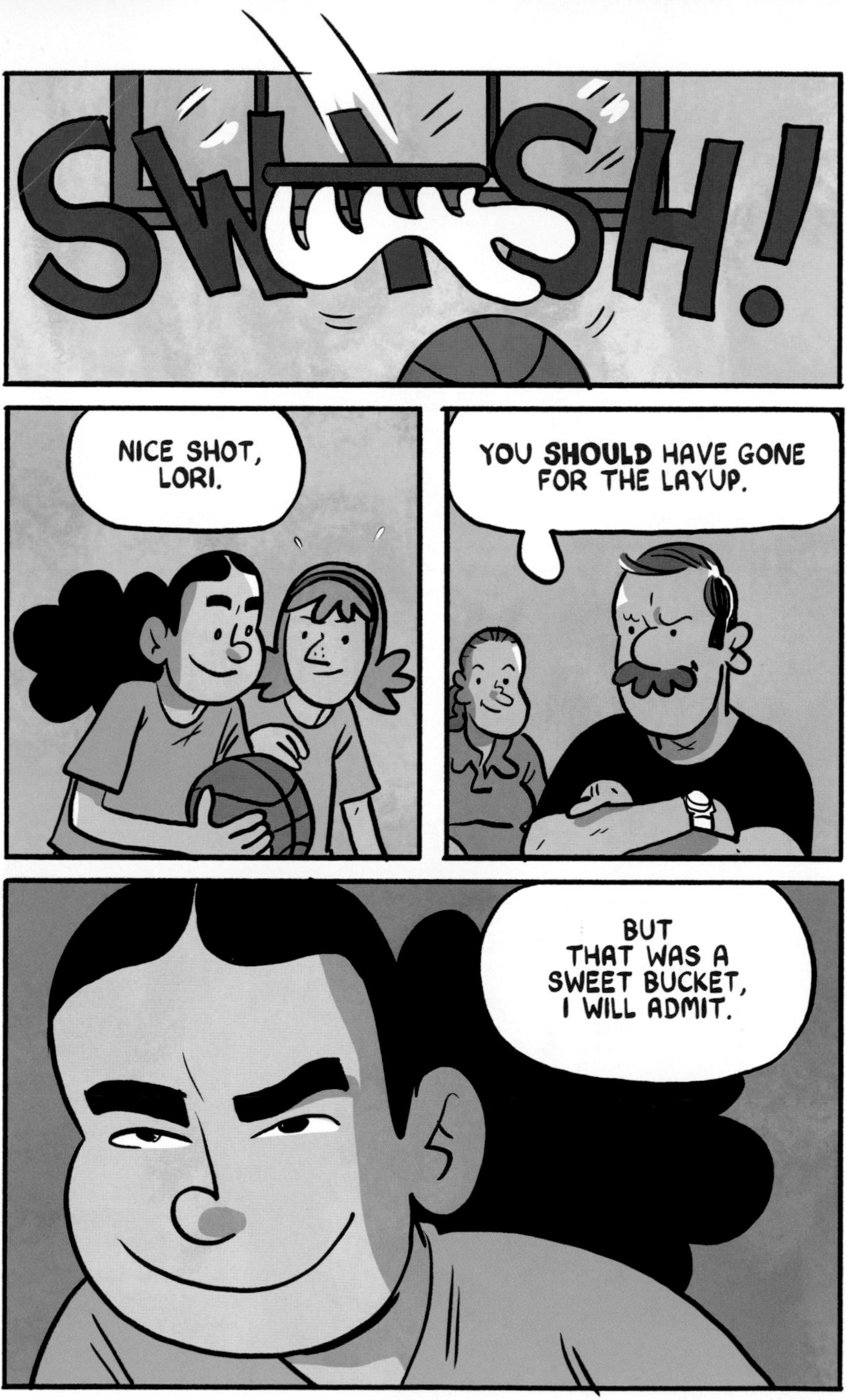
SWISH!
NICE SHOT, LORI.
YOU **SHOULD** HAVE GONE FOR THE LAYUP.
BUT THAT WAS A SWEET BUCKET, I WILL ADMIT.

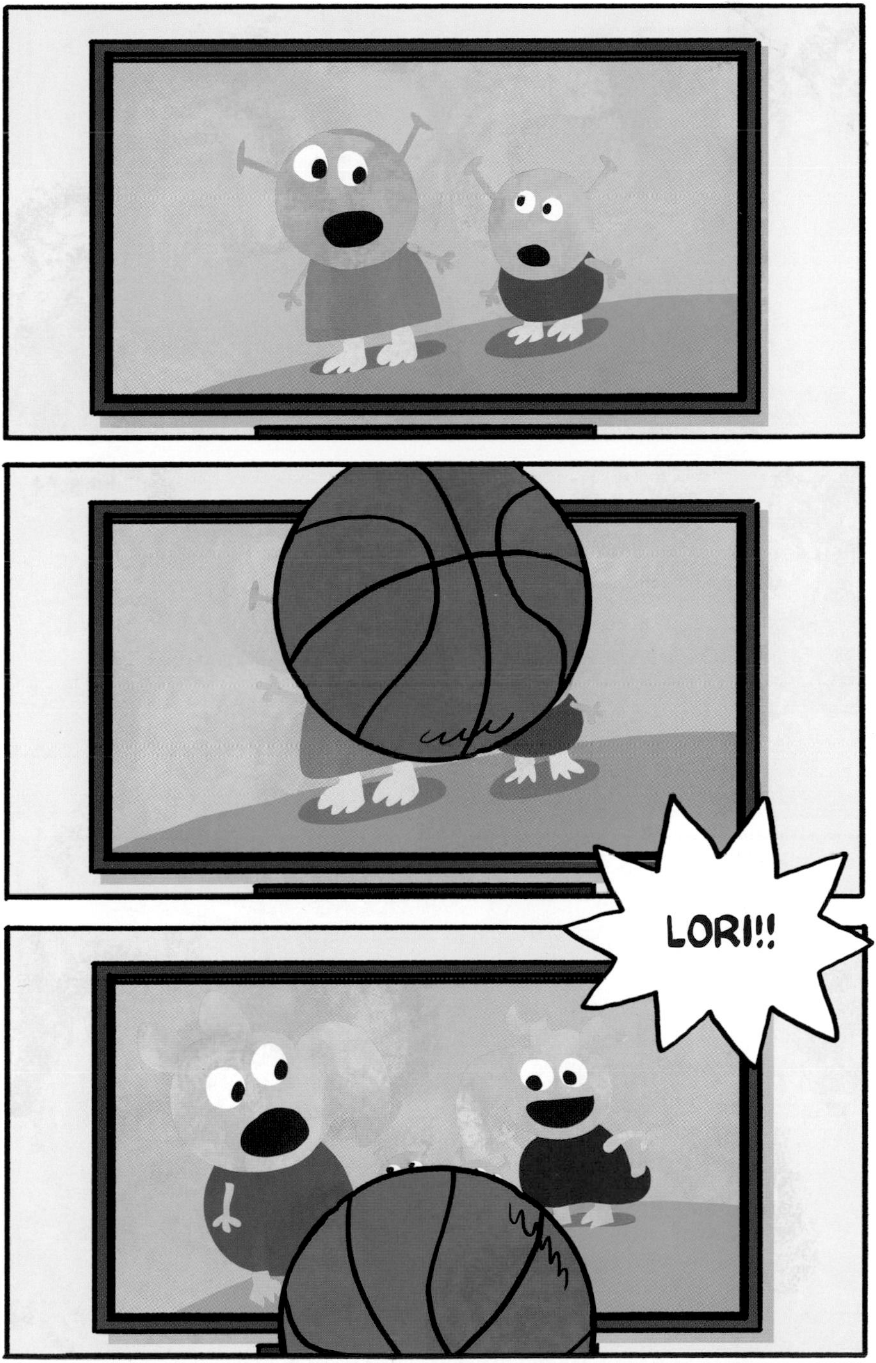
LORI!!

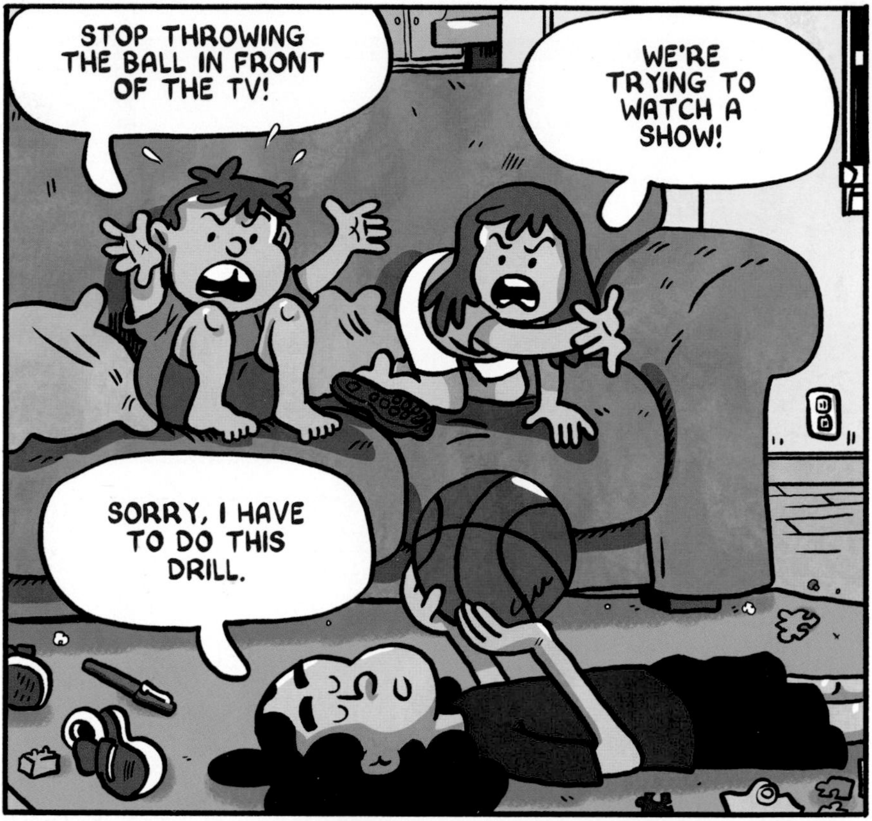
STOP THROWING THE BALL IN FRONT OF THE TV!
WE'RE TRYING TO WATCH A SHOW!
SORRY, I HAVE TO DO THIS DRILL.

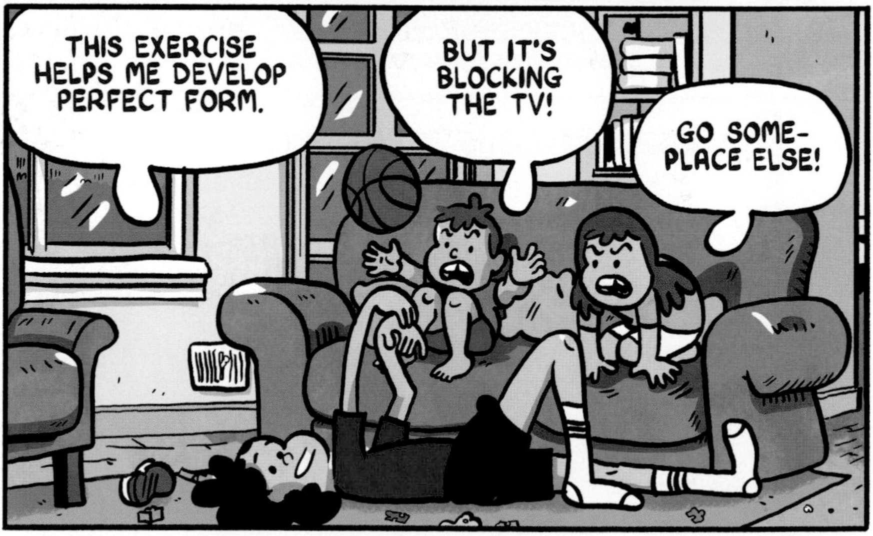
THIS EXERCISE HELPS ME DEVELOP PERFECT FORM.
BUT IT'S BLOCKING THE TV!
GO SOME-PLACE ELSE!

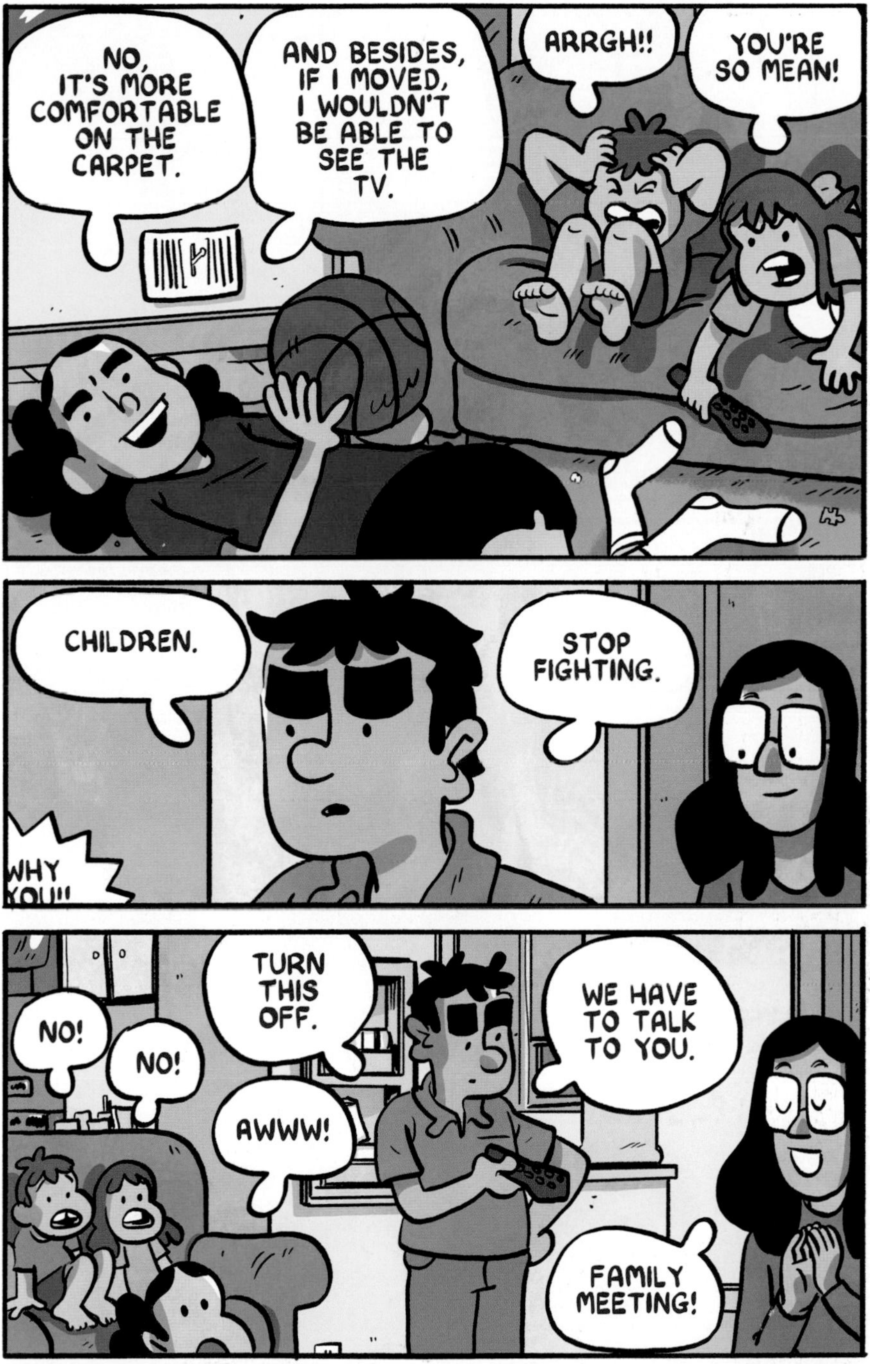
NO, IT'S MORE COMFORTABLE ON THE CARPET.
AND BESIDES, IF I MOVED, I WOULDN'T BE ABLE TO SEE THE TV.
ARRGH!!
YOU'RE SO MEAN!
CHILDREN.
STOP FIGHTING.
WHY YOU!!
NO!
NO!
TURN THIS OFF.
AWWW!
WE HAVE TO TALK TO YOU.
FAMILY MEETING!

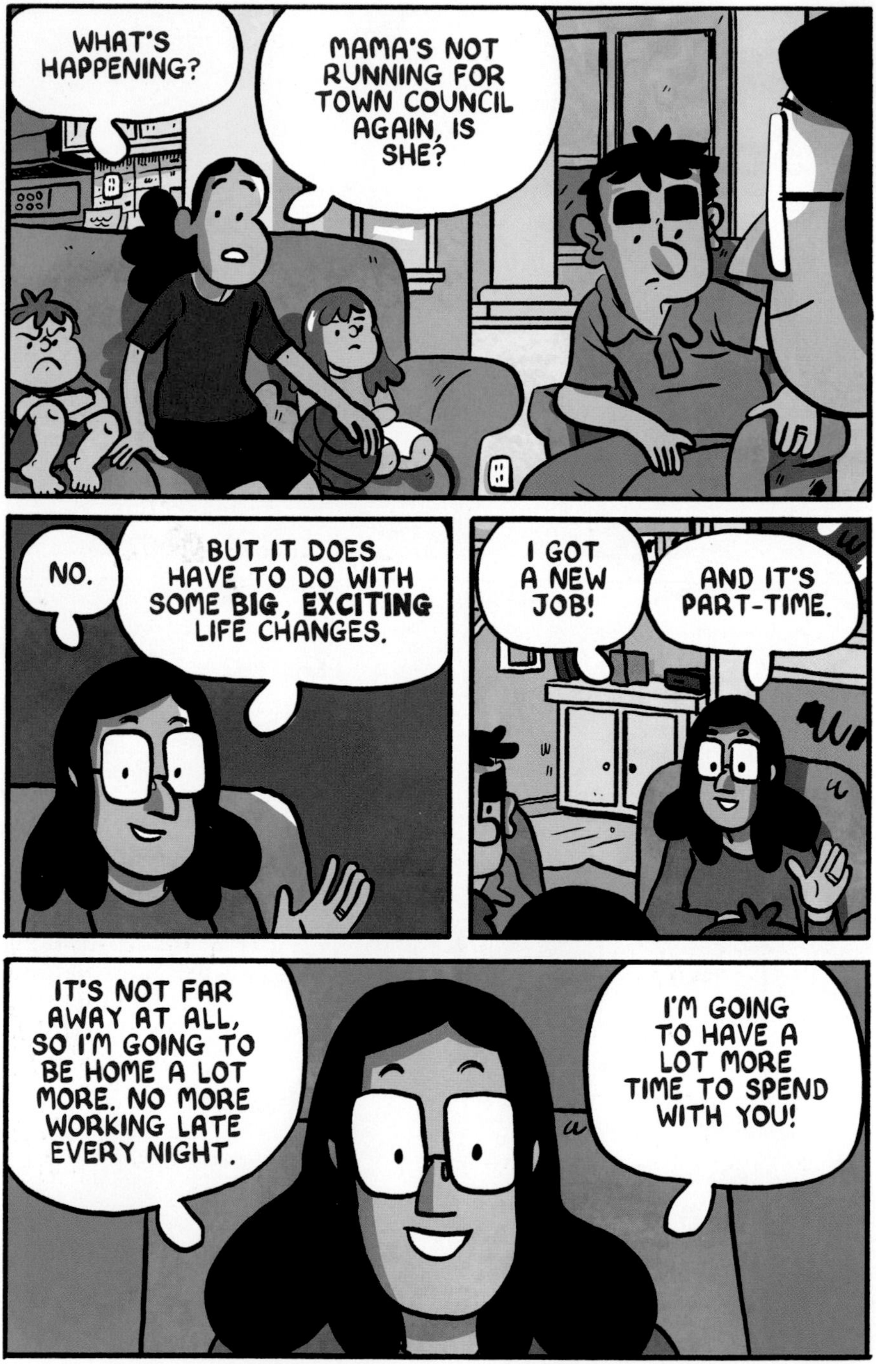
WHAT'S HAPPENING?
MAMA'S NOT RUNNING FOR TOWN COUNCIL AGAIN, IS SHE?
NO.
BUT IT DOES HAVE TO DO WITH SOME **BIG, EXCITING** LIFE CHANGES.
I GOT A NEW JOB!
AND IT'S PART-TIME.
IT'S NOT FAR AWAY AT ALL, SO I'M GOING TO BE HOME A LOT MORE. NO MORE WORKING LATE EVERY NIGHT.
I'M GOING TO HAVE A LOT MORE TIME TO SPEND WITH YOU!

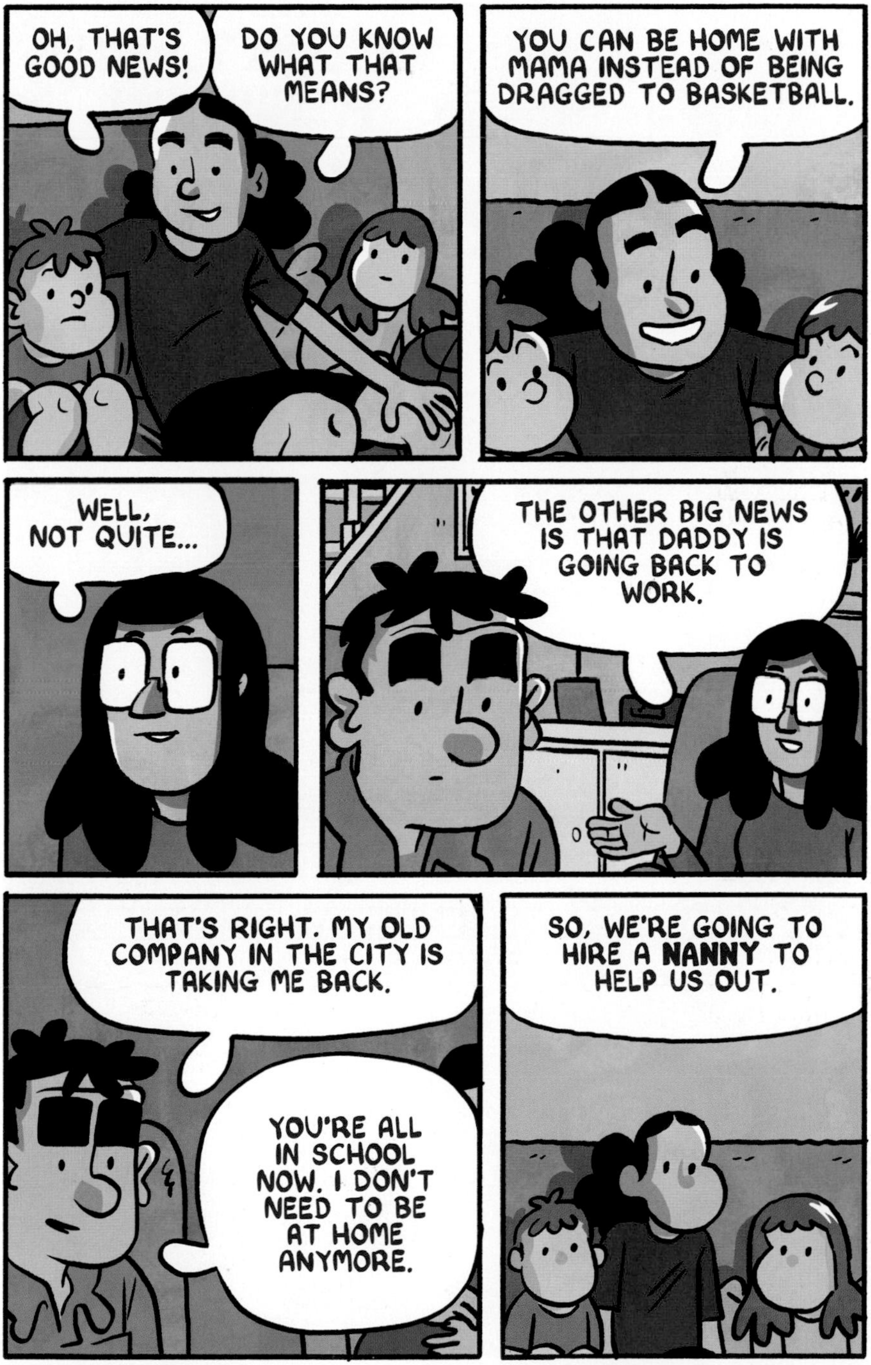
OH, THAT'S GOOD NEWS!
DO YOU KNOW WHAT THAT MEANS?
YOU CAN BE HOME WITH MAMA INSTEAD OF BEING DRAGGED TO BASKETBALL.
WELL, NOT QUITE...
THE OTHER BIG NEWS IS THAT DADDY IS GOING BACK TO WORK.
THAT'S RIGHT. MY OLD COMPANY IN THE CITY IS TAKING ME BACK.
YOU'RE ALL IN SCHOOL NOW. I DON'T NEED TO BE AT HOME ANYMORE.
SO, WE'RE GOING TO HIRE A **NANNY** TO HELP US OUT.

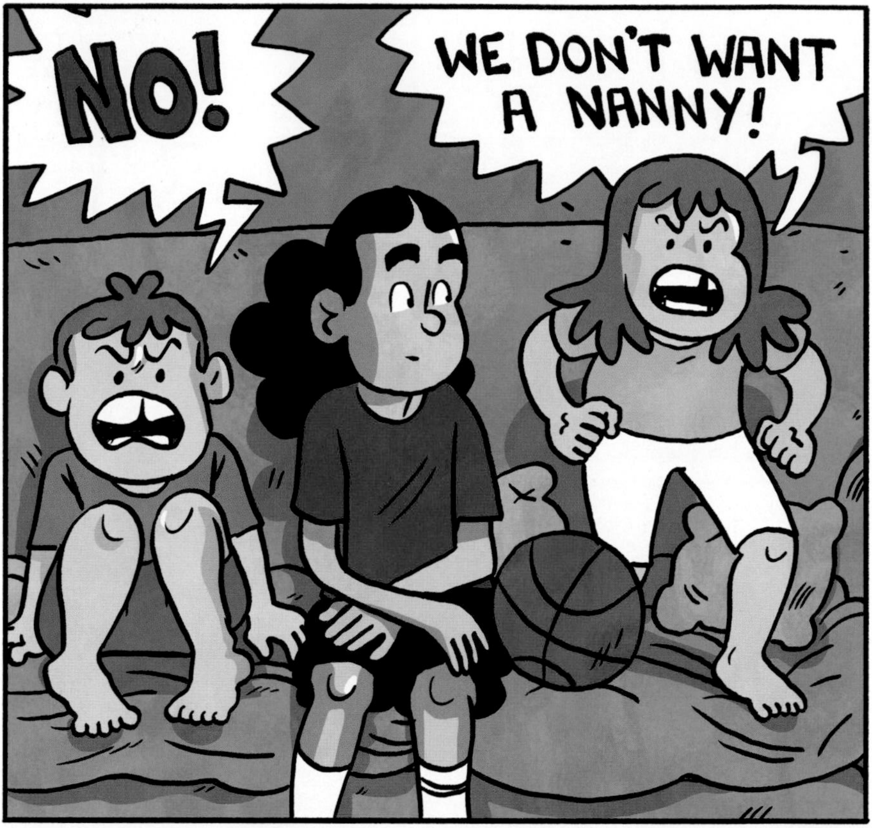
NO!
WE DON'T WANT A NANNY!

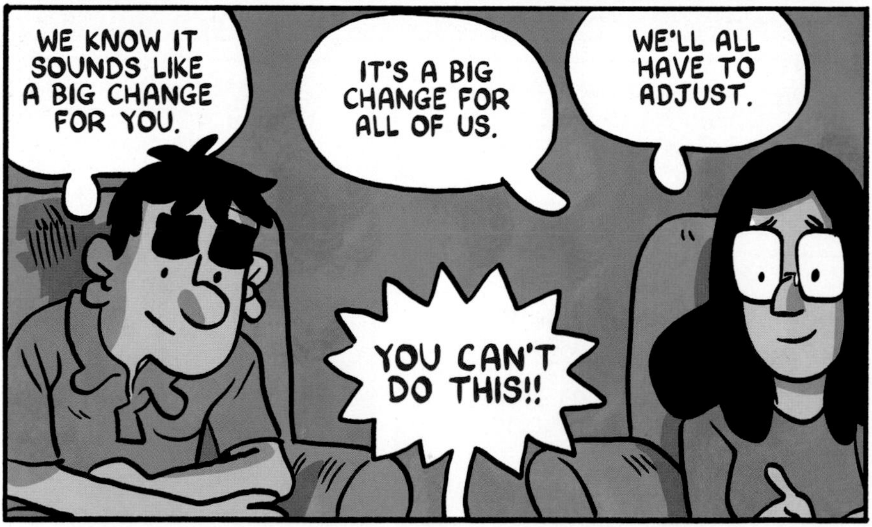
WE KNOW IT SOUNDS LIKE A BIG CHANGE FOR YOU.
IT'S A BIG CHANGE FOR ALL OF US.
WE'LL ALL HAVE TO ADJUST.
YOU CAN'T DO THIS!!

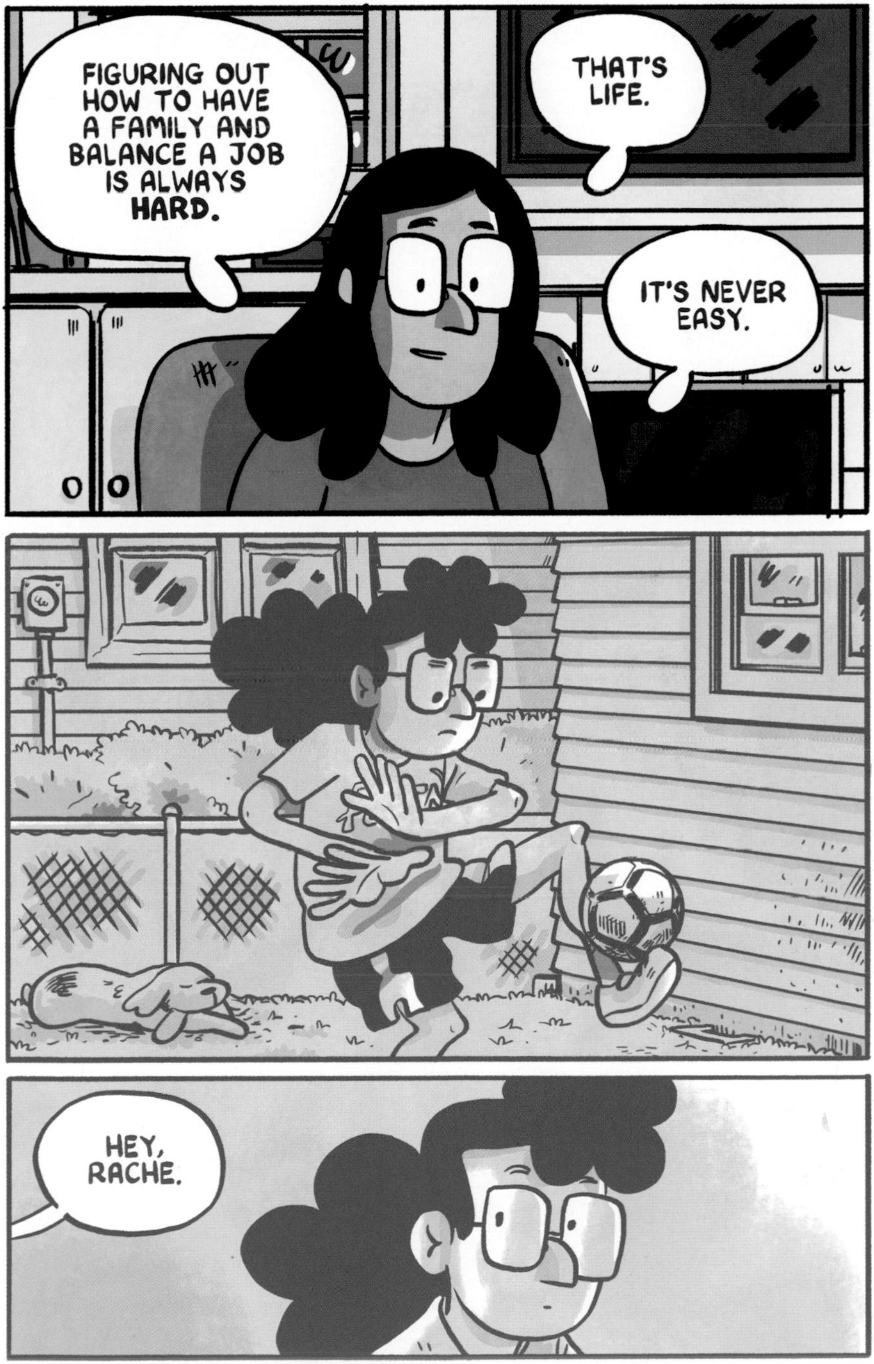
FIGURING OUT HOW TO HAVE A FAMILY AND BALANCE A JOB IS ALWAYS **HARD**.
THAT'S LIFE.
IT'S NEVER EASY.
HEY, RACHE.

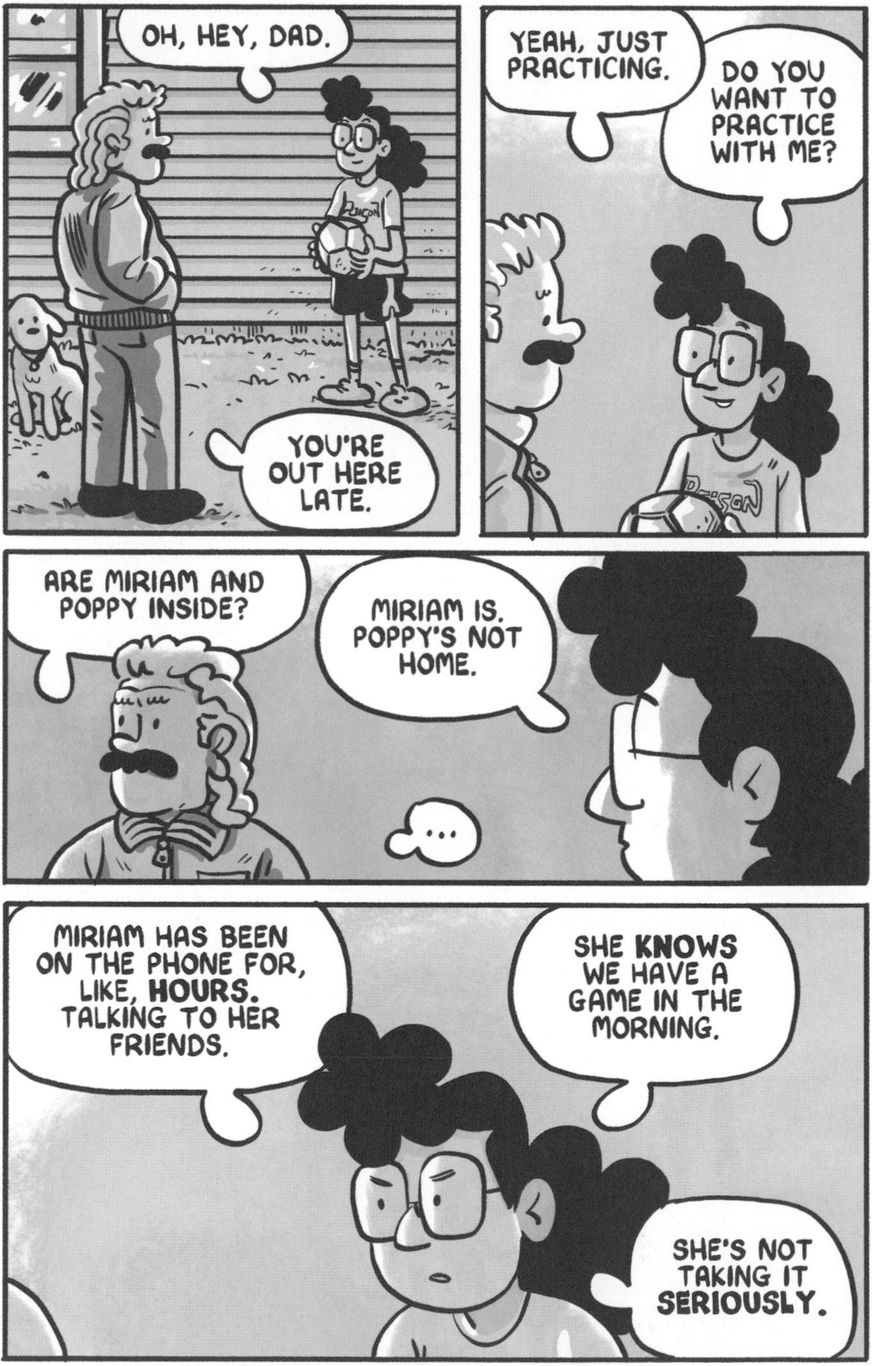
OH, HEY, DAD.
YOU'RE OUT HERE LATE.
YEAH, JUST PRACTICING.
DO YOU WANT TO PRACTICE WITH ME?
ARE MIRIAM AND POPPY INSIDE?
MIRIAM IS. POPPY'S NOT HOME.
...
MIRIAM HAS BEEN ON THE PHONE FOR, LIKE, **HOURS.** TALKING TO HER FRIENDS.
SHE **KNOWS** WE HAVE A GAME IN THE MORNING.
SHE'S NOT TAKING IT **SERIOUSLY.**

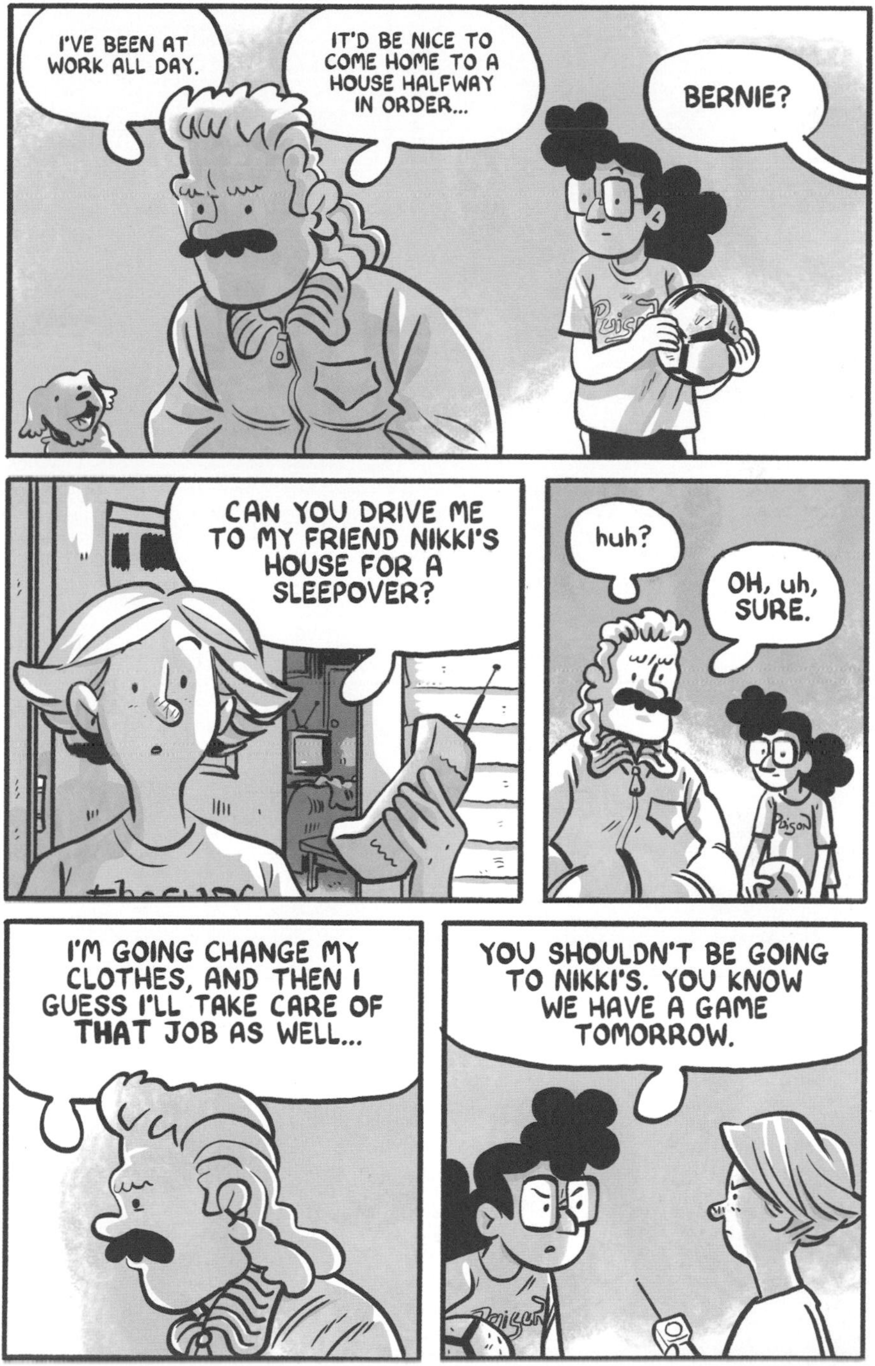
I'VE BEEN AT WORK ALL DAY.
IT'D BE NICE TO COME HOME TO A HOUSE HALFWAY IN ORDER...
BERNIE?
CAN YOU DRIVE ME TO MY FRIEND NIKKI'S HOUSE FOR A SLEEPOVER?
huh?
OH, uh, SURE.
I'M GOING CHANGE MY CLOTHES, AND THEN I GUESS I'LL TAKE CARE OF THAT JOB AS WELL...
YOU SHOULDN'T BE GOING TO NIKKI'S. YOU KNOW WE HAVE A GAME TOMORROW.

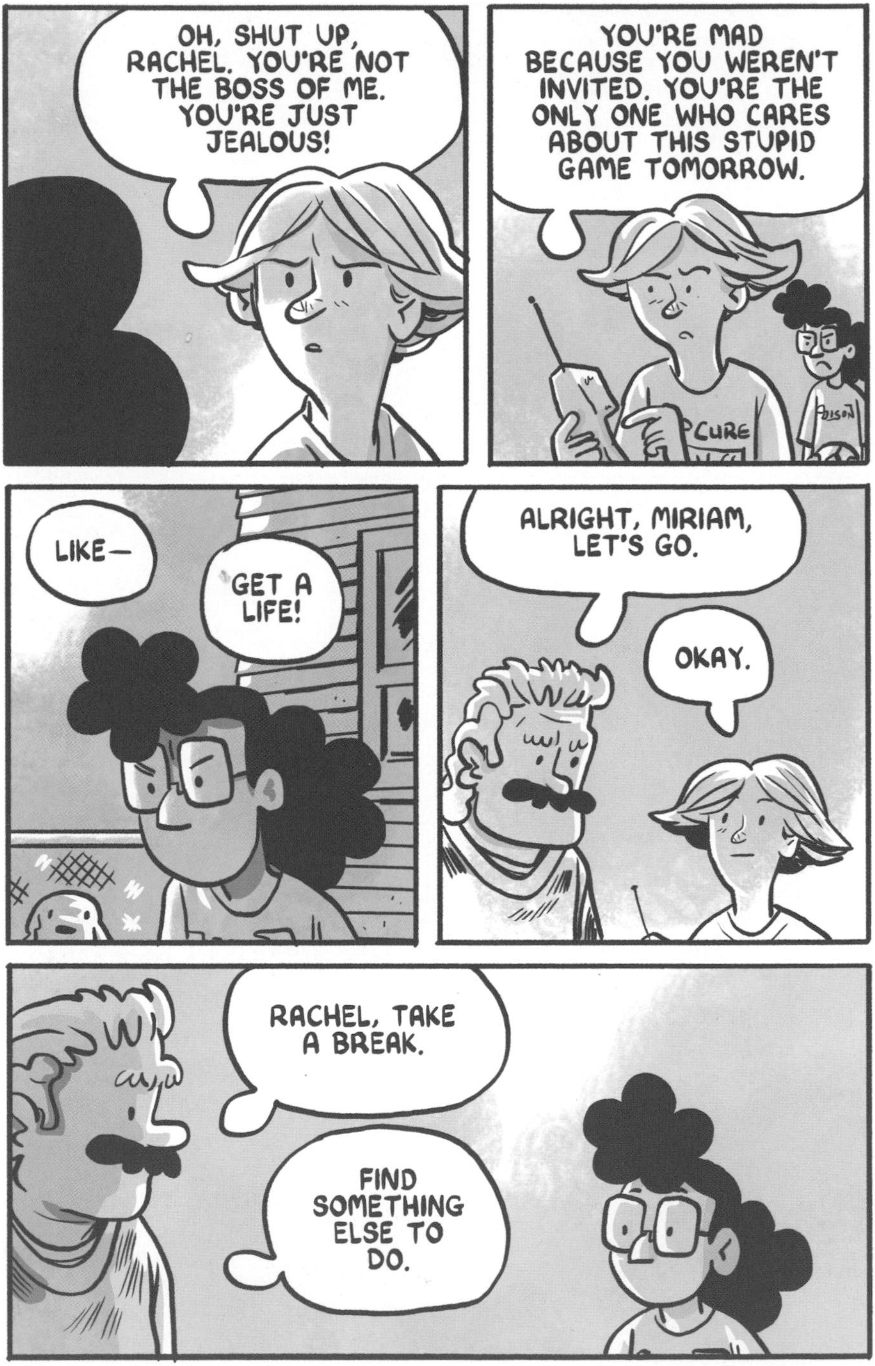

OH, SHUT UP, RACHEL. YOU'RE NOT THE BOSS OF ME. YOU'RE JUST JEALOUS!
YOU'RE MAD BECAUSE YOU WEREN'T INVITED. YOU'RE THE ONLY ONE WHO CARES ABOUT THIS STUPID GAME TOMORROW.
CURE
LIKE—
GET A LIFE!
ALRIGHT, MIRIAM, LET'S GO.
OKAY.
RACHEL, TAKE A BREAK.
FIND SOMETHING ELSE TO DO.

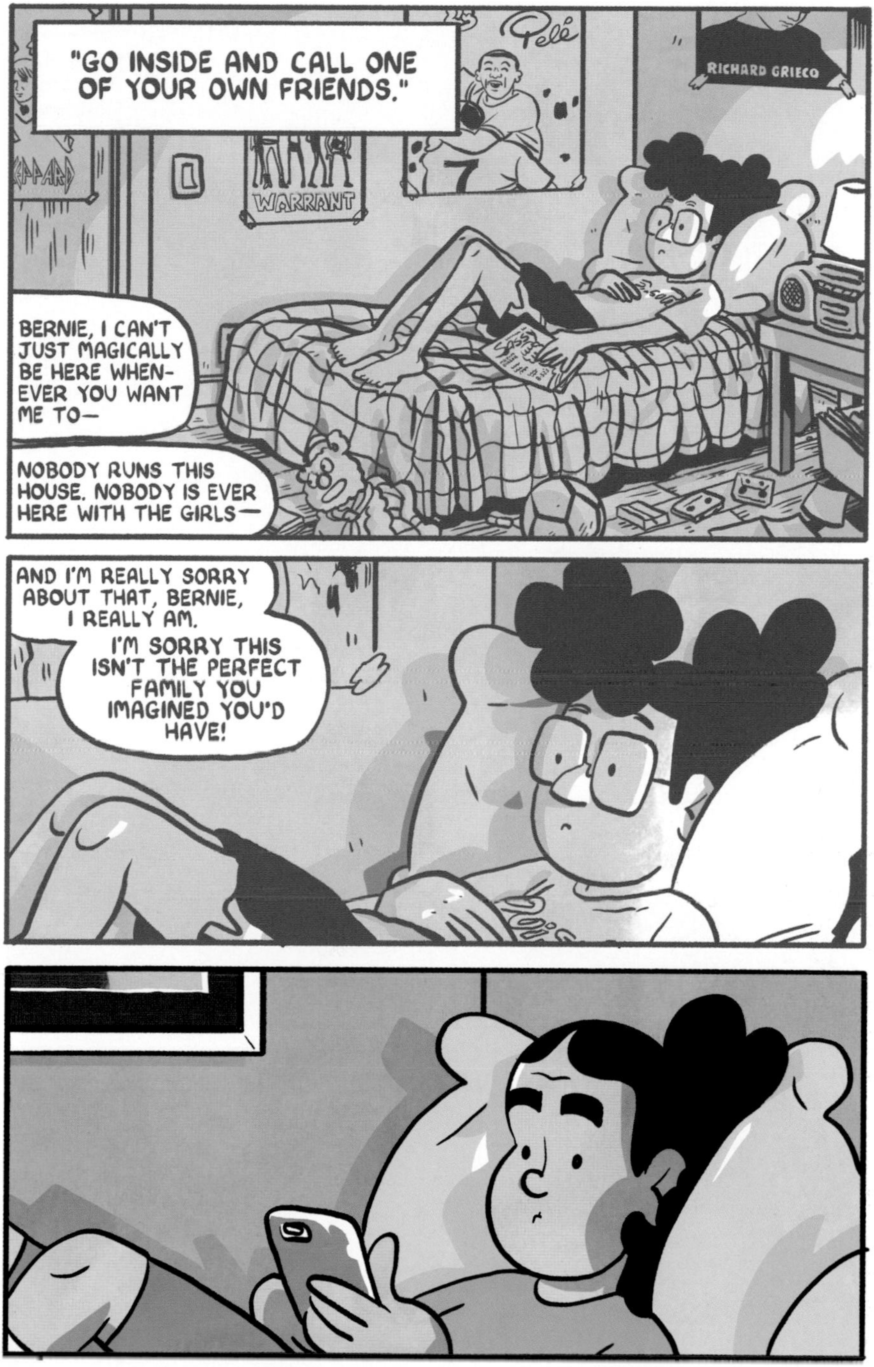
"GO INSIDE AND CALL ONE OF YOUR OWN FRIENDS."
RICHARD GRIECO
WARRANT
BERNIE, I CAN'T JUST MAGICALLY BE HERE WHEN-EVER YOU WANT ME TO—
NOBODY RUNS THIS HOUSE. NOBODY IS EVER HERE WITH THE GIRLS—
AND I'M REALLY SORRY ABOUT THAT, BERNIE, I REALLY AM.
I'M SORRY THIS ISN'T THE PERFECT FAMILY YOU IMAGINED YOU'D HAVE!

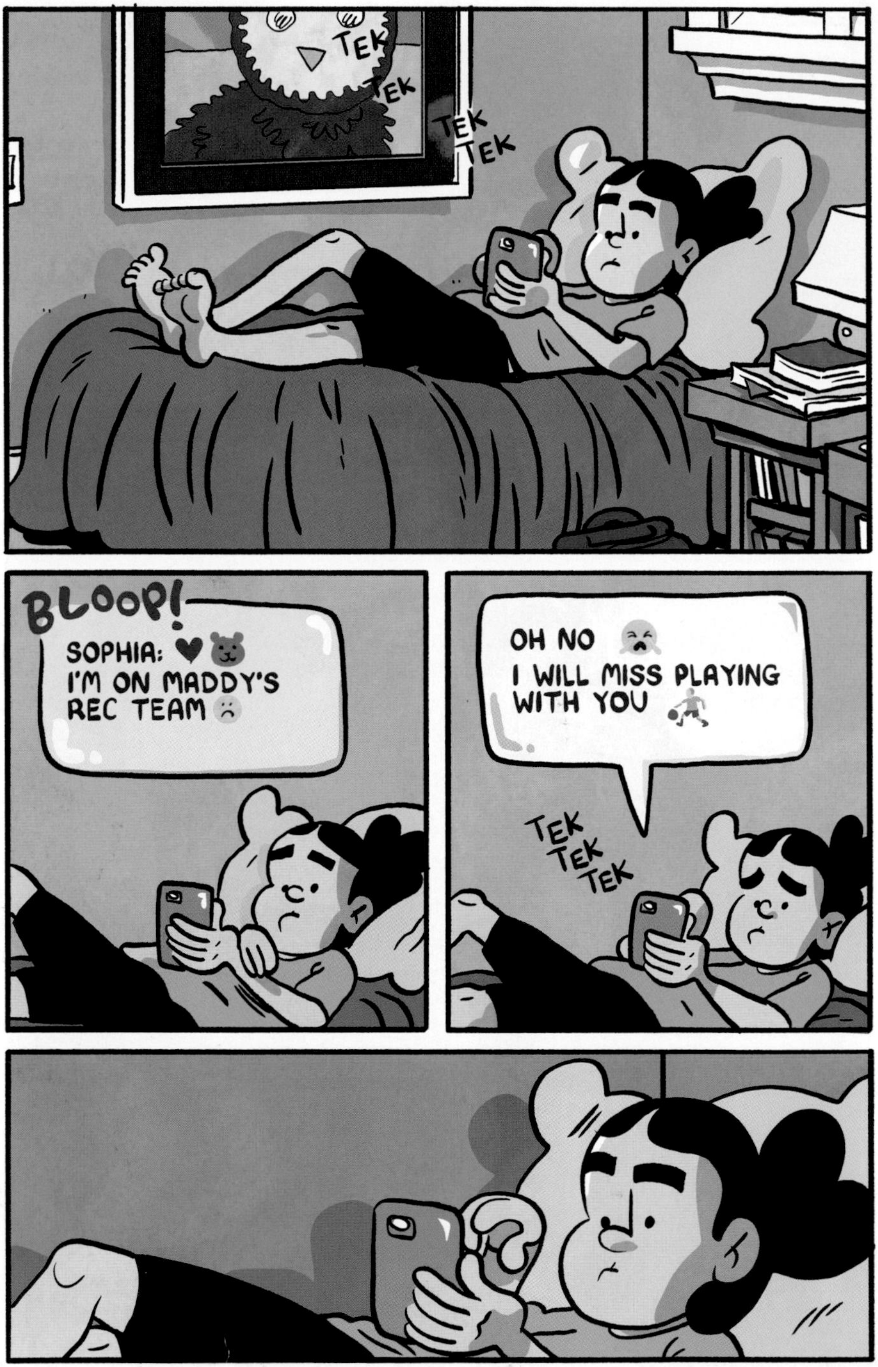
TEK
TEK
TEK
TEK
BLOOP!
SOPHIA:
I'M ON MADDY'S
REC TEAM
OH NO
I WILL MISS PLAYING
WITH YOU
TEK
TEK
TEK

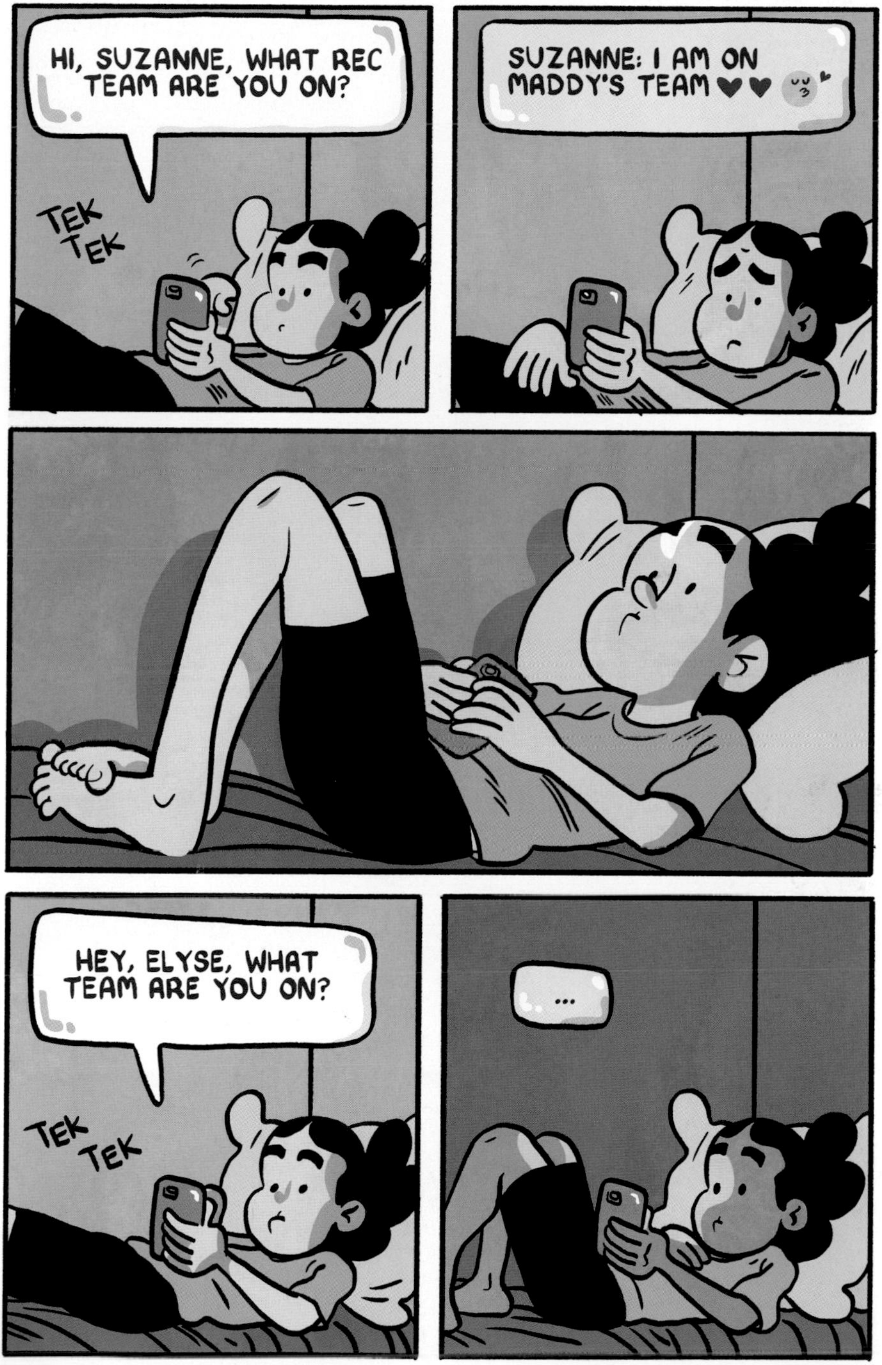
HI, SUZANNE, WHAT REC TEAM ARE YOU ON?
TEK TEK
SUZANNE: I AM ON MADDY'S TEAM ♥♥
HEY, ELYSE, WHAT TEAM ARE YOU ON?
TEK TEK
...

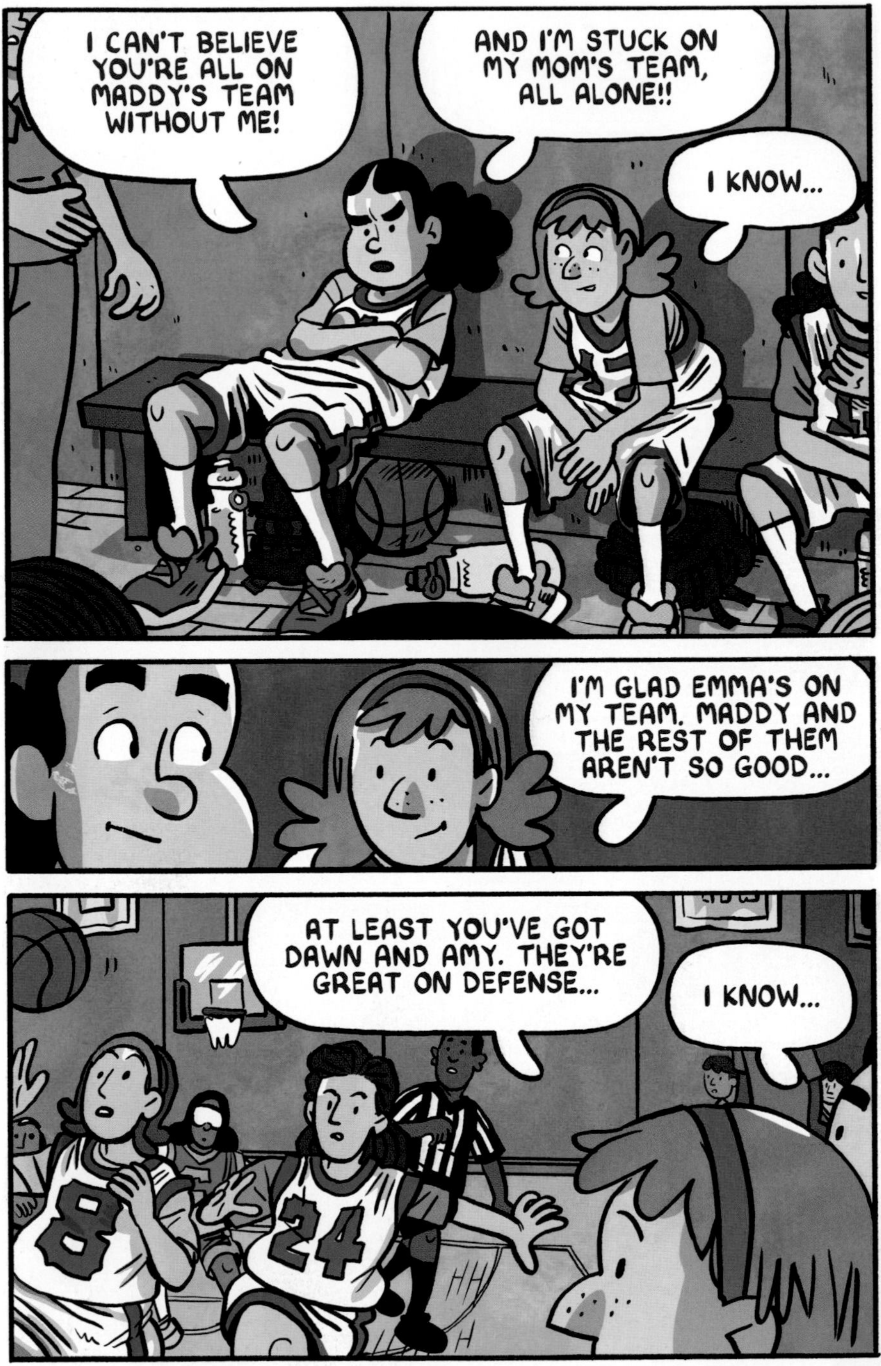
I CAN'T BELIEVE YOU'RE ALL ON MADDY'S TEAM WITHOUT ME!
AND I'M STUCK ON MY MOM'S TEAM, ALL ALONE!!
I KNOW...
I'M GLAD EMMA'S ON MY TEAM. MADDY AND THE REST OF THEM AREN'T SO GOOD...
AT LEAST YOU'VE GOT DAWN AND AMY. THEY'RE GREAT ON DEFENSE...
I KNOW...
8
24

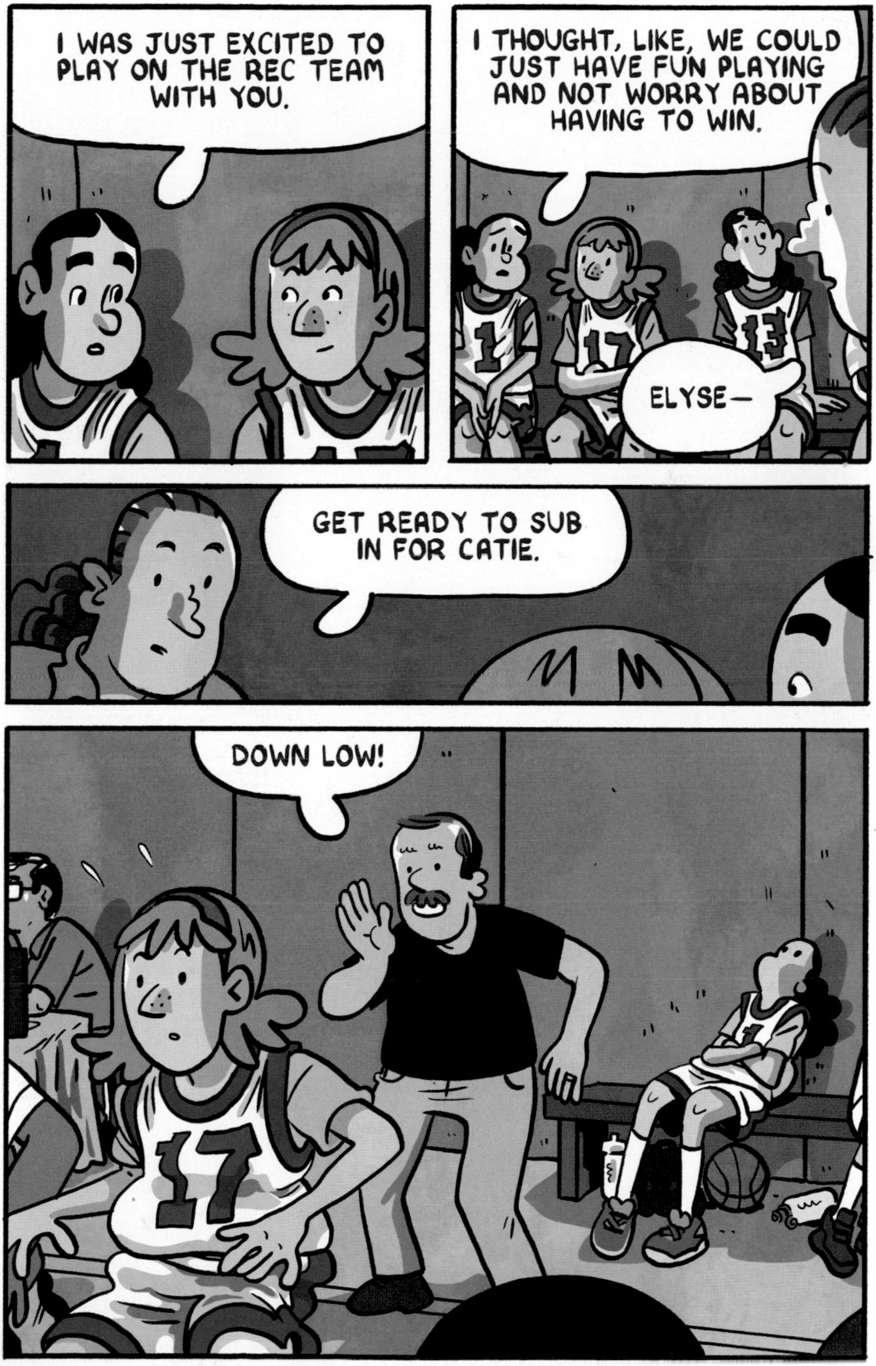
I WAS JUST EXCITED TO PLAY ON THE REC TEAM WITH YOU.
I THOUGHT, LIKE, WE COULD JUST HAVE FUN PLAYING AND NOT WORRY ABOUT HAVING TO WIN.
ELYSE—
GET READY TO SUB IN FOR CATIE.
DOWN LOW!

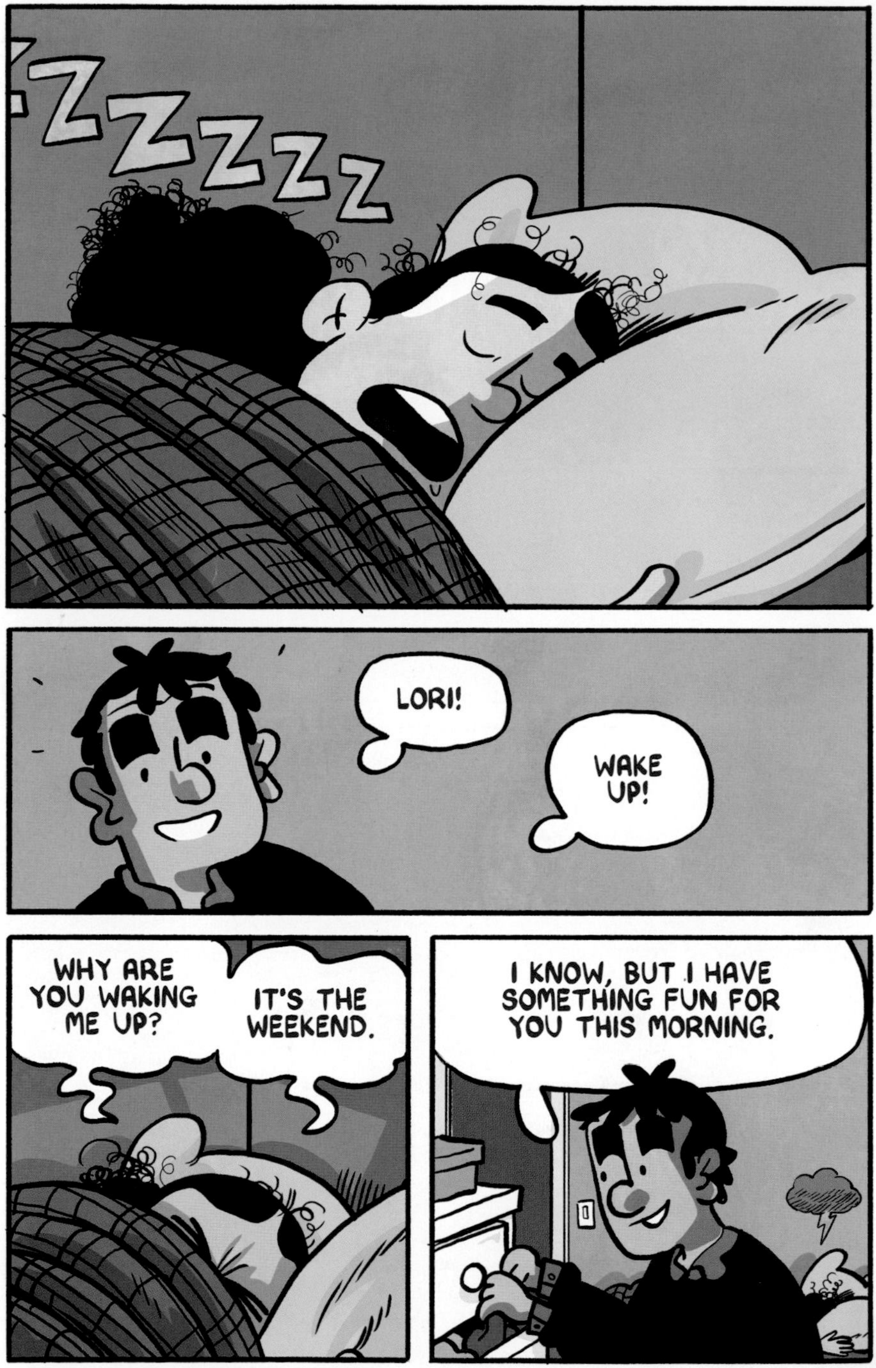
ZZZZZZZ
LORI!
WAKE UP!
WHY ARE YOU WAKING ME UP?
IT'S THE WEEKEND.
I KNOW, BUT I HAVE SOMETHING FUN FOR YOU THIS MORNING.

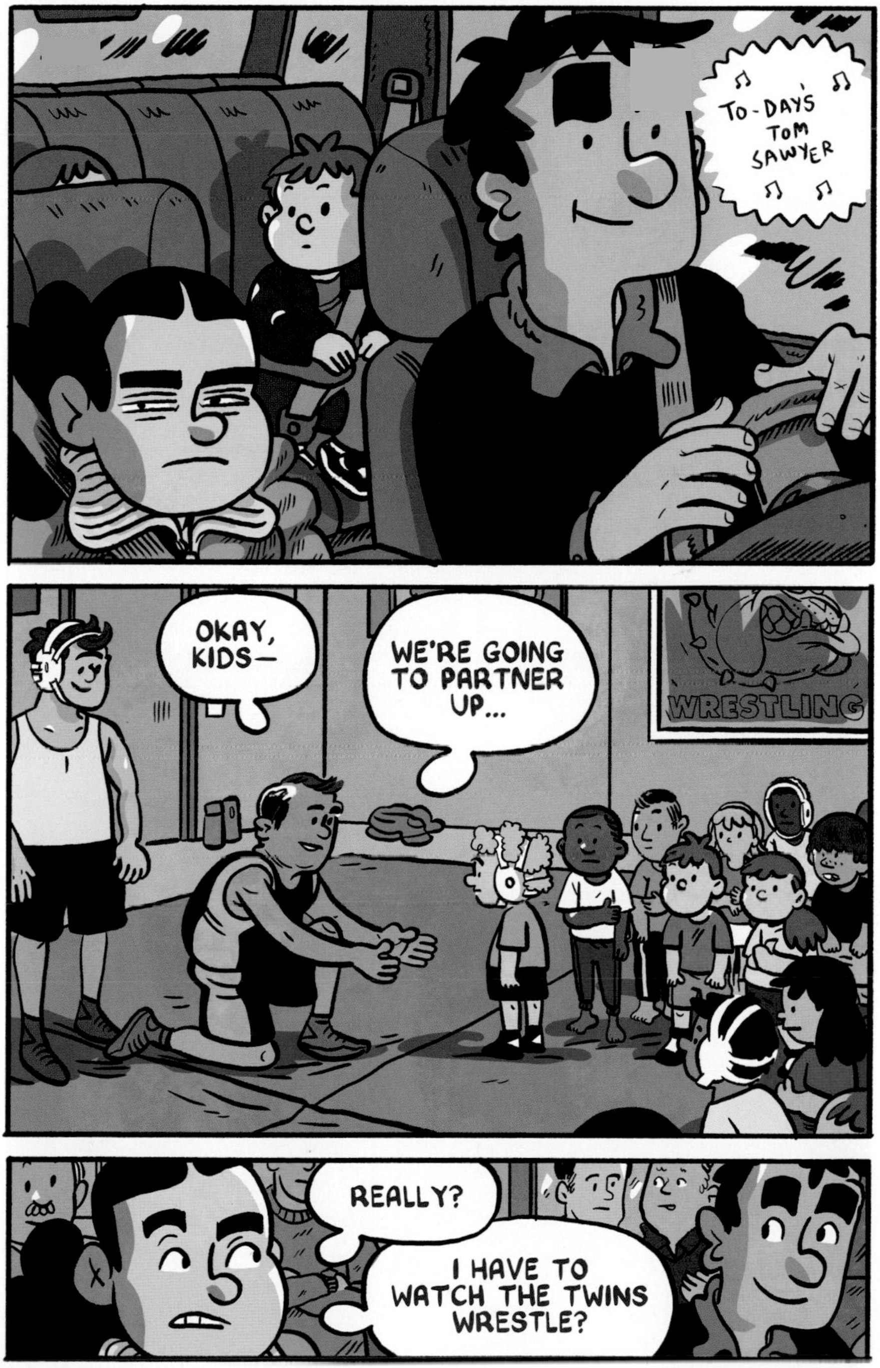
TO-DAYS TOM SAWYER
OKAY, KIDS—
WE'RE GOING TO PARTNER UP...
WRESTLING
REALLY?
I HAVE TO WATCH THE TWINS WRESTLE?

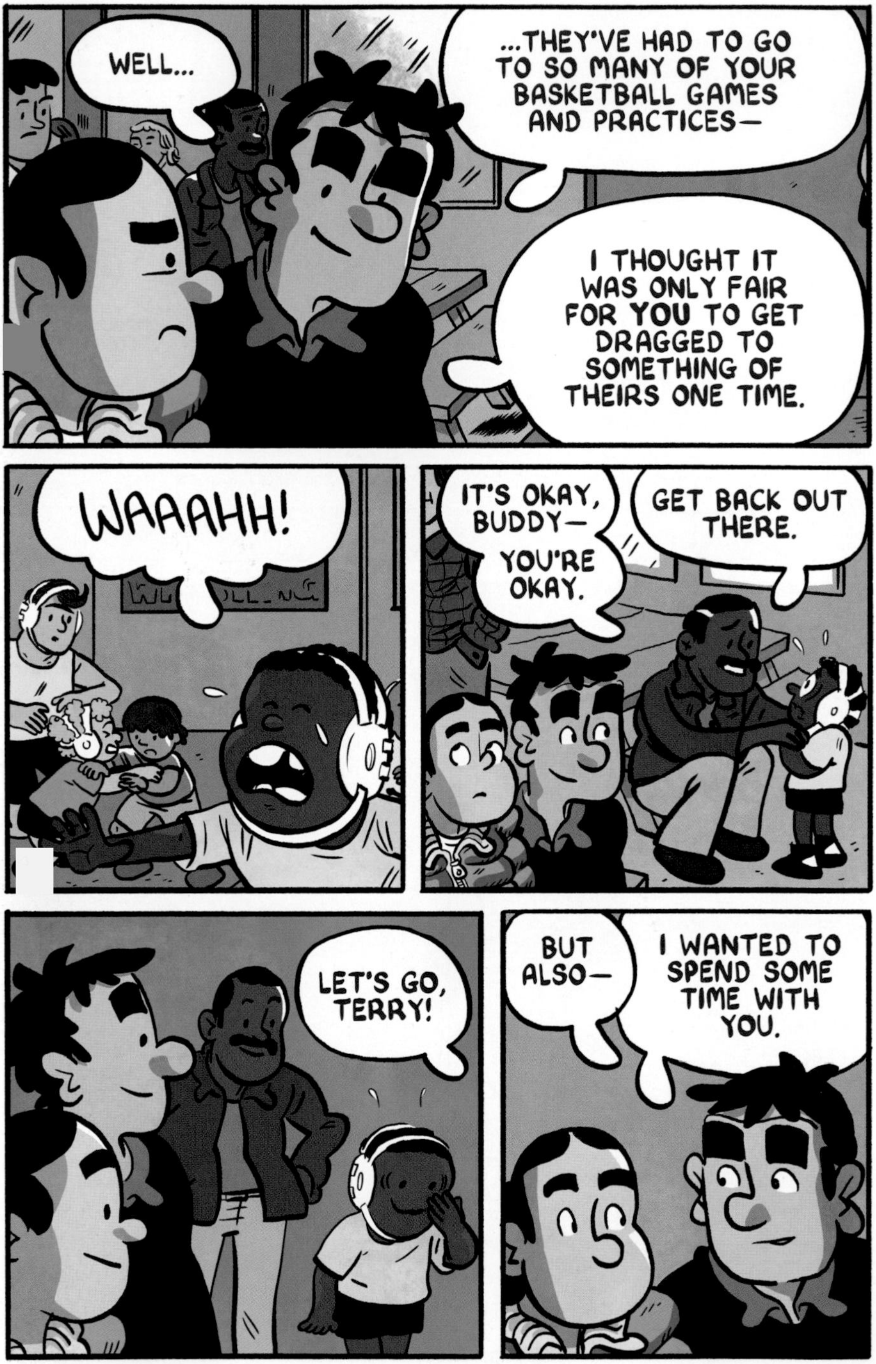
WELL...
...THEY'VE HAD TO GO TO SO MANY OF YOUR BASKETBALL GAMES AND PRACTICES—
I THOUGHT IT WAS ONLY FAIR FOR YOU TO GET DRAGGED TO SOMETHING OF THEIRS ONE TIME.
WAAAHH!
IT'S OKAY, BUDDY—
YOU'RE OKAY.
GET BACK OUT THERE.
LET'S GO, TERRY!
BUT ALSO—
I WANTED TO SPEND SOME TIME WITH YOU.

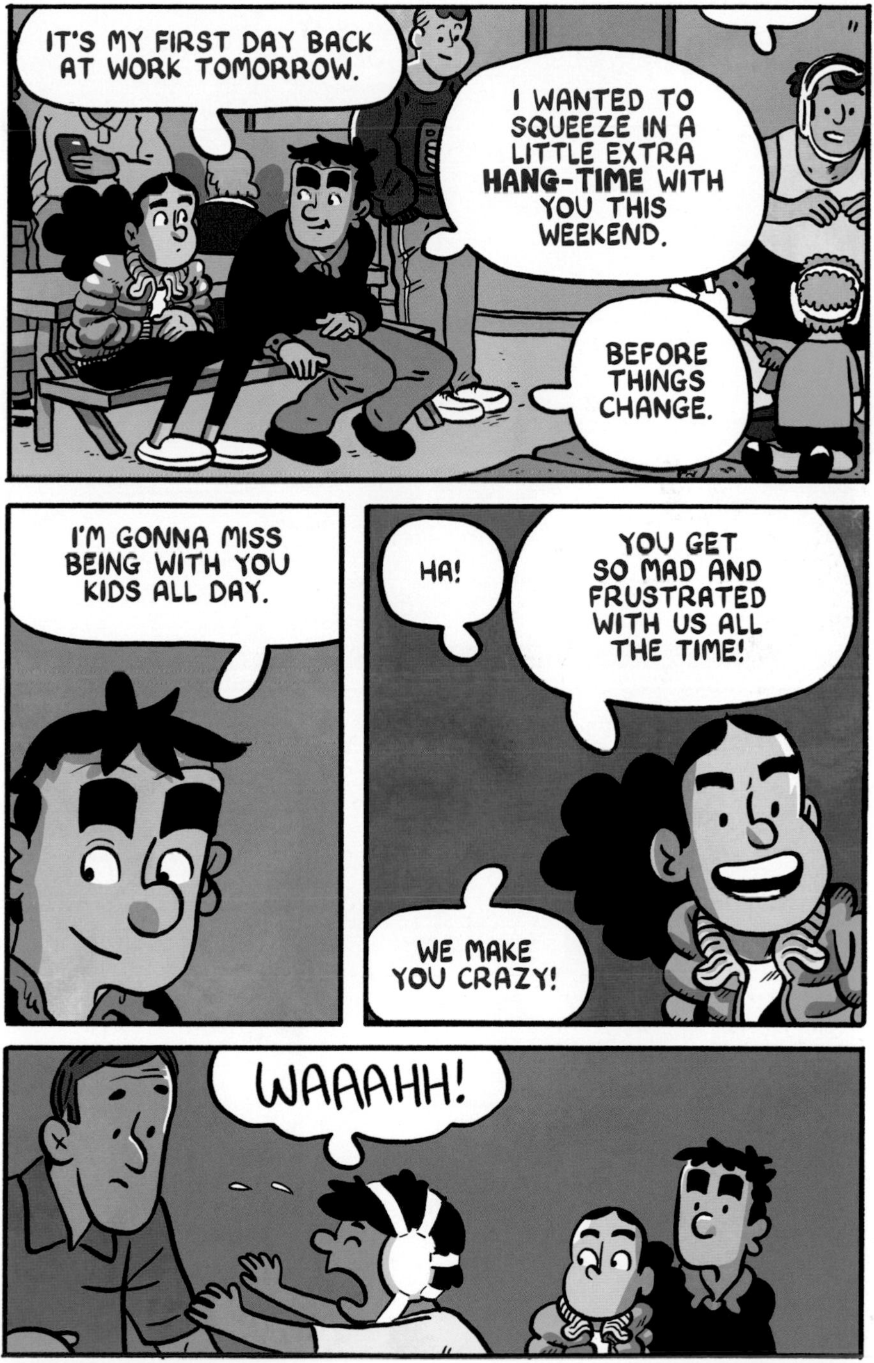
IT'S MY FIRST DAY BACK AT WORK TOMORROW.
I WANTED TO SQUEEZE IN A LITTLE EXTRA **HANG-TIME** WITH YOU THIS WEEKEND.
BEFORE THINGS CHANGE.
I'M GONNA MISS BEING WITH YOU KIDS ALL DAY.
HA!
YOU GET SO MAD AND FRUSTRATED WITH US ALL THE TIME!
WE MAKE YOU CRAZY!
WAAAHH!

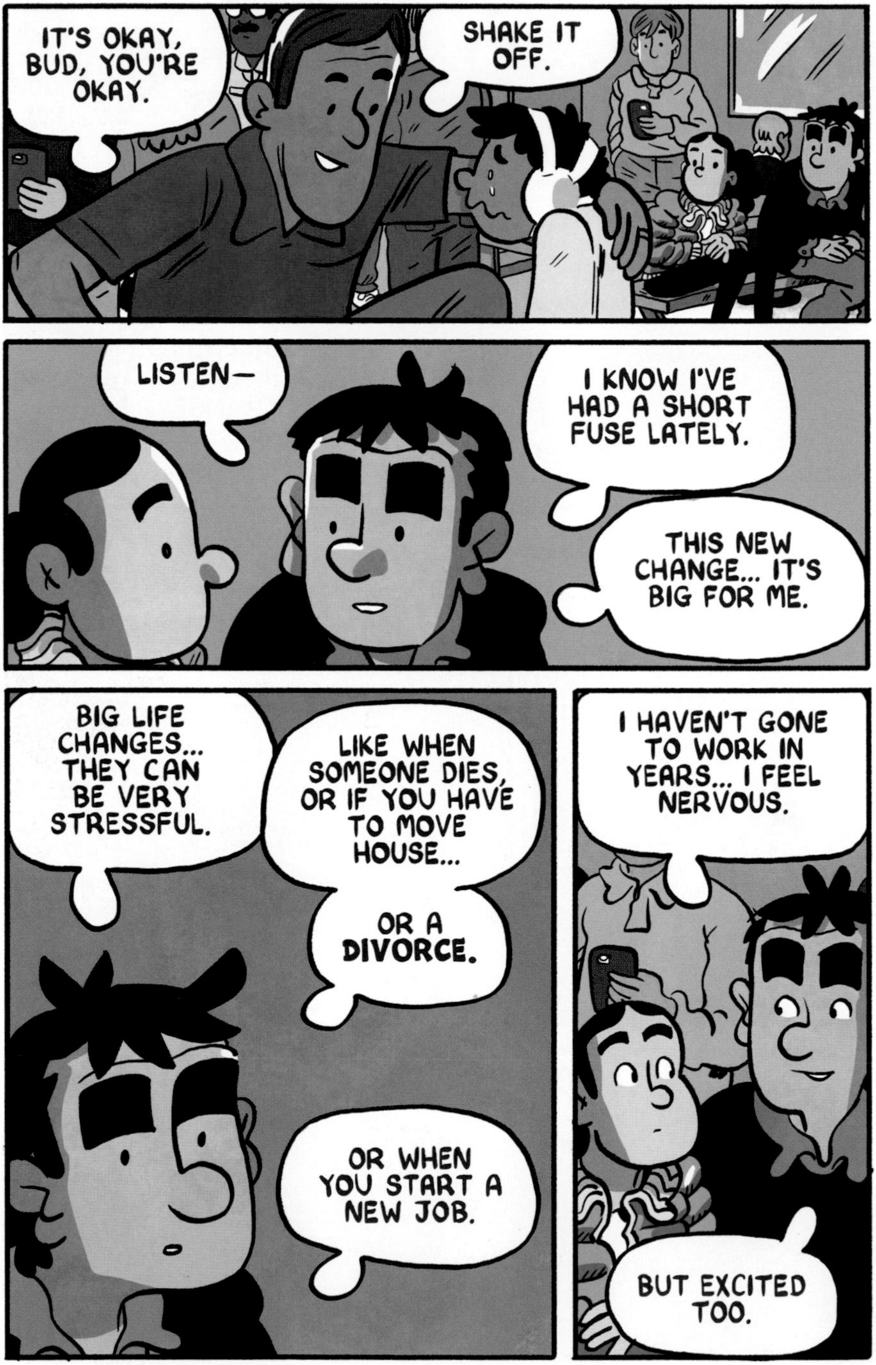
IT'S OKAY, BUD, YOU'RE OKAY.
SHAKE IT OFF.
LISTEN—
I KNOW I'VE HAD A SHORT FUSE LATELY.
THIS NEW CHANGE... IT'S BIG FOR ME.
BIG LIFE CHANGES... THEY CAN BE VERY STRESSFUL.
LIKE WHEN SOMEONE DIES, OR IF YOU HAVE TO MOVE HOUSE...
OR A **DIVORCE.**
OR WHEN YOU START A NEW JOB.
I HAVEN'T GONE TO WORK IN YEARS... I FEEL NERVOUS.
BUT EXCITED TOO.

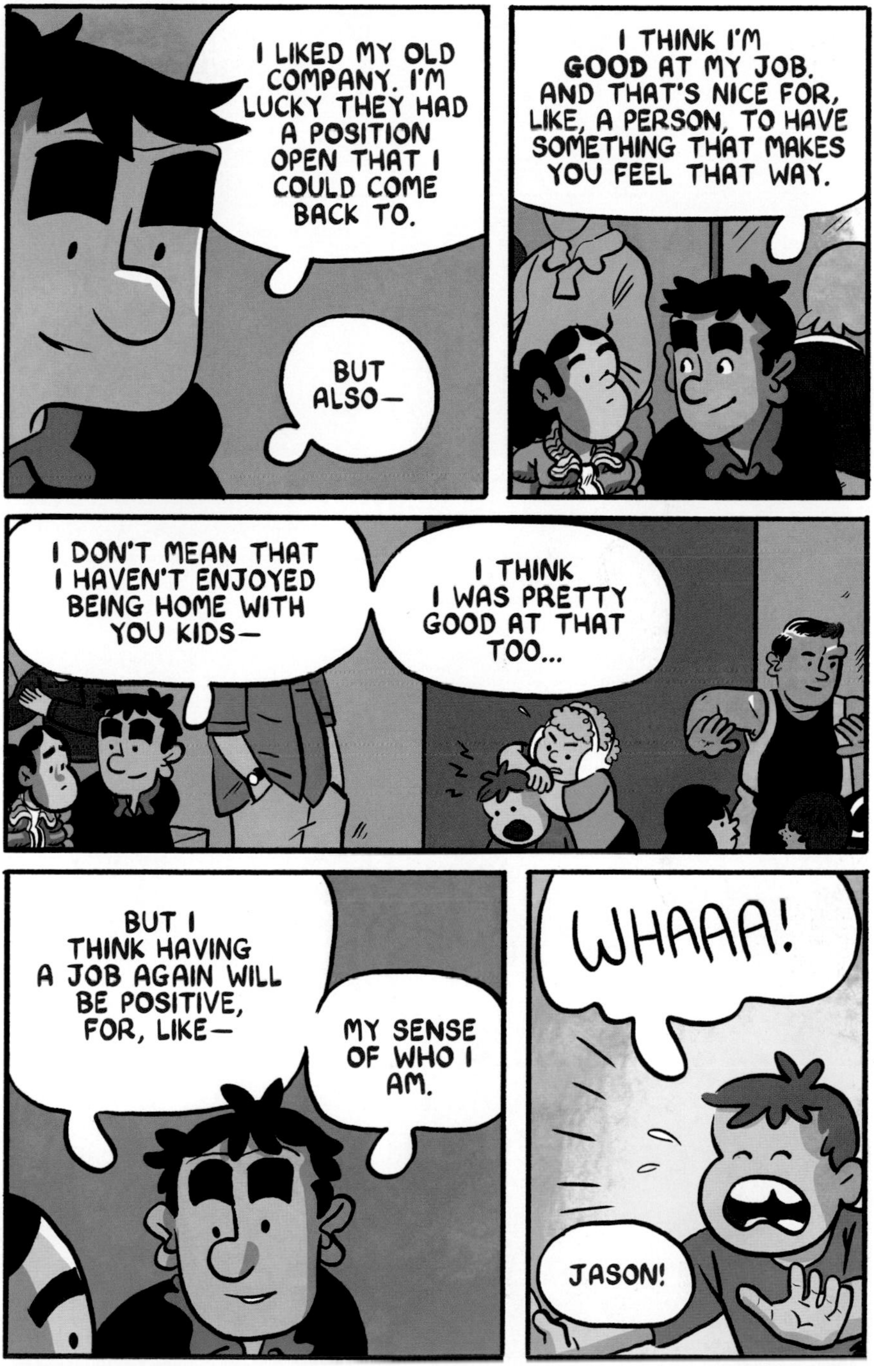
I LIKED MY OLD COMPANY. I'M LUCKY THEY HAD A POSITION OPEN THAT I COULD COME BACK TO.
BUT ALSO—
I THINK I'M **GOOD** AT MY JOB. AND THAT'S NICE FOR, LIKE, A PERSON, TO HAVE SOMETHING THAT MAKES YOU FEEL THAT WAY.
I DON'T MEAN THAT I HAVEN'T ENJOYED BEING HOME WITH YOU KIDS—
I THINK I WAS PRETTY GOOD AT THAT TOO...
BUT I THINK HAVING A JOB AGAIN WILL BE POSITIVE, FOR, LIKE—
MY SENSE OF WHO I AM.
WHAAA!
JASON!

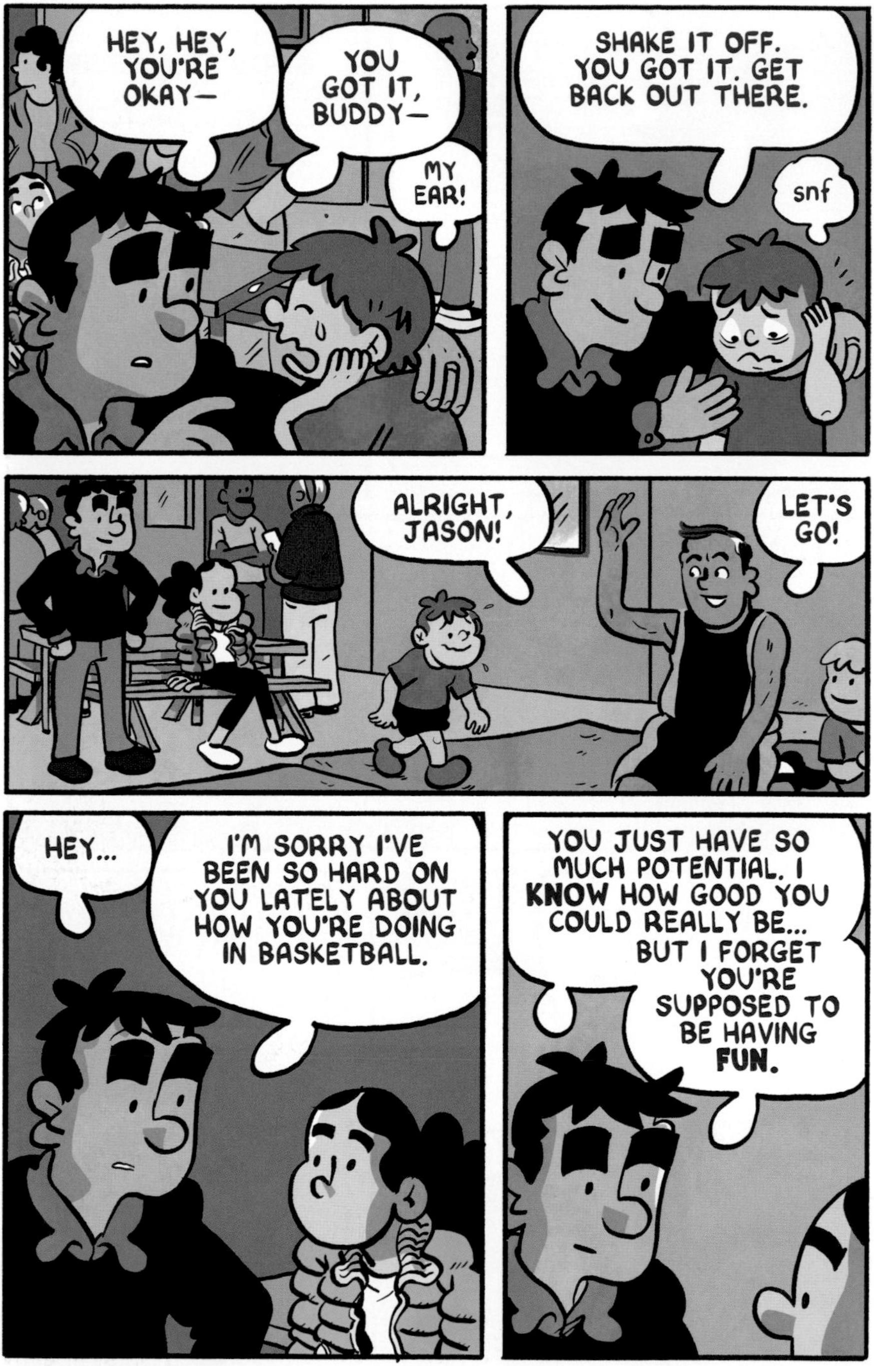
HEY, HEY, YOU'RE OKAY—
YOU GOT IT, BUDDY—
MY EAR!
SHAKE IT OFF. YOU GOT IT. GET BACK OUT THERE.
snf
ALRIGHT, JASON!
LET'S GO!
HEY...
I'M SORRY I'VE BEEN SO HARD ON YOU LATELY ABOUT HOW YOU'RE DOING IN BASKETBALL.
YOU JUST HAVE SO MUCH POTENTIAL. I **KNOW** HOW GOOD YOU COULD REALLY BE... BUT I FORGET YOU'RE SUPPOSED TO BE HAVING **FUN**.

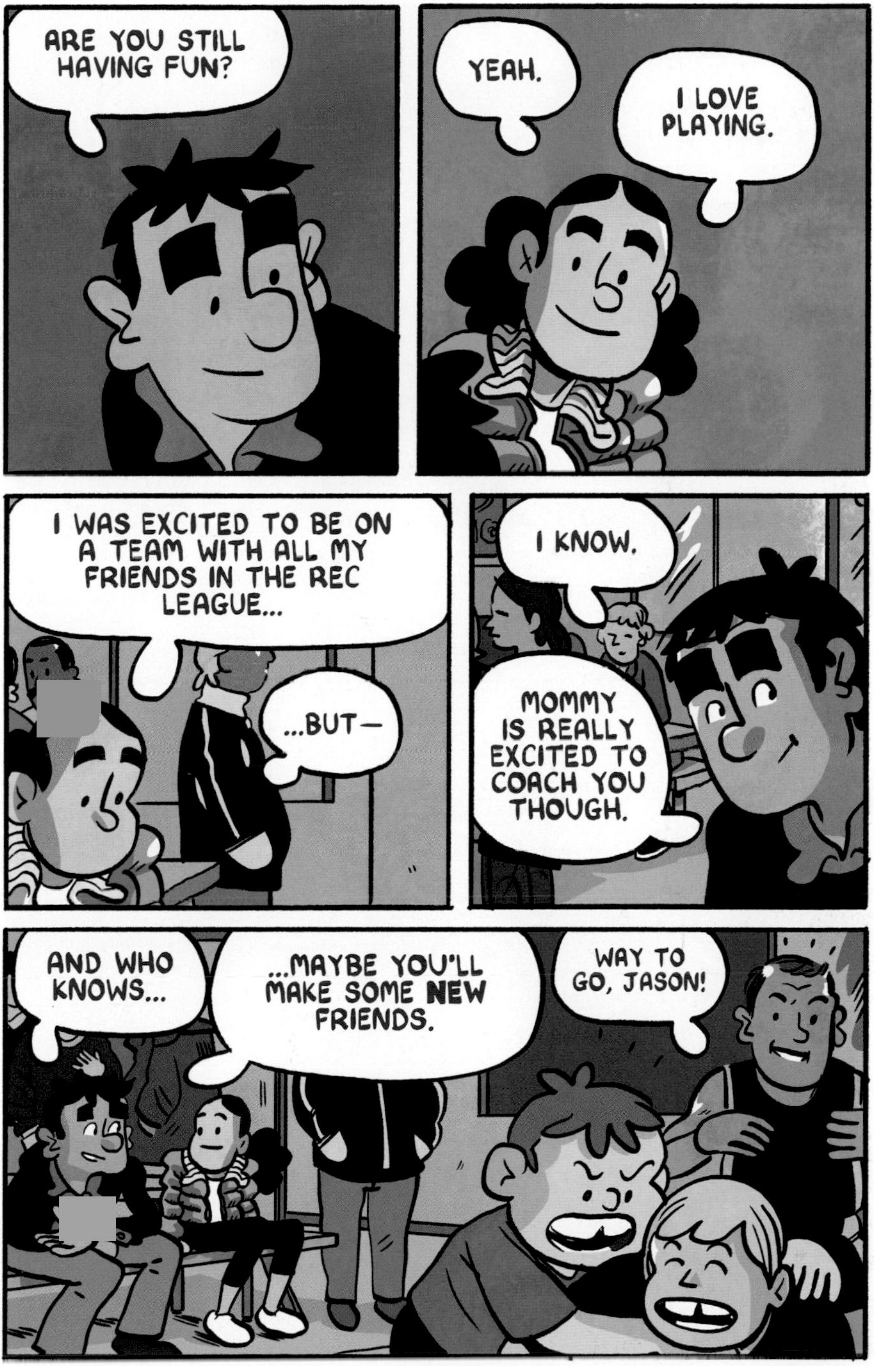
ARE YOU STILL HAVING FUN?
YEAH.
I LOVE PLAYING.
I WAS EXCITED TO BE ON A TEAM WITH ALL MY FRIENDS IN THE REC LEAGUE...
...BUT—
I KNOW.
MOMMY IS REALLY EXCITED TO COACH YOU THOUGH.
AND WHO KNOWS...
...MAYBE YOU'LL MAKE SOME **NEW** FRIENDS.
WAY TO GO, JASON!

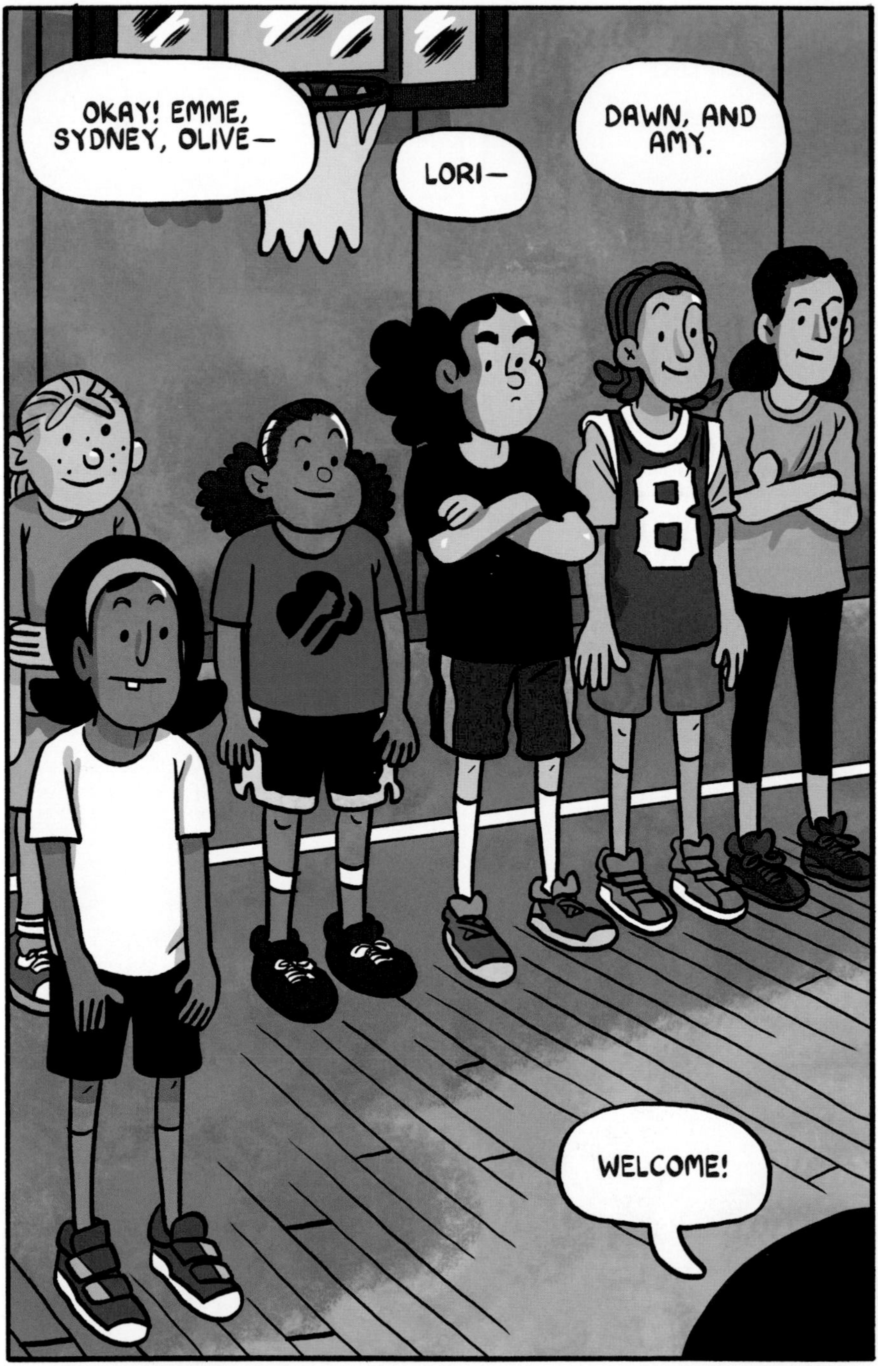
OKAY! EMME, SYDNEY, OLIVE—
LORI—
DAWN, AND AMY.
WELCOME!

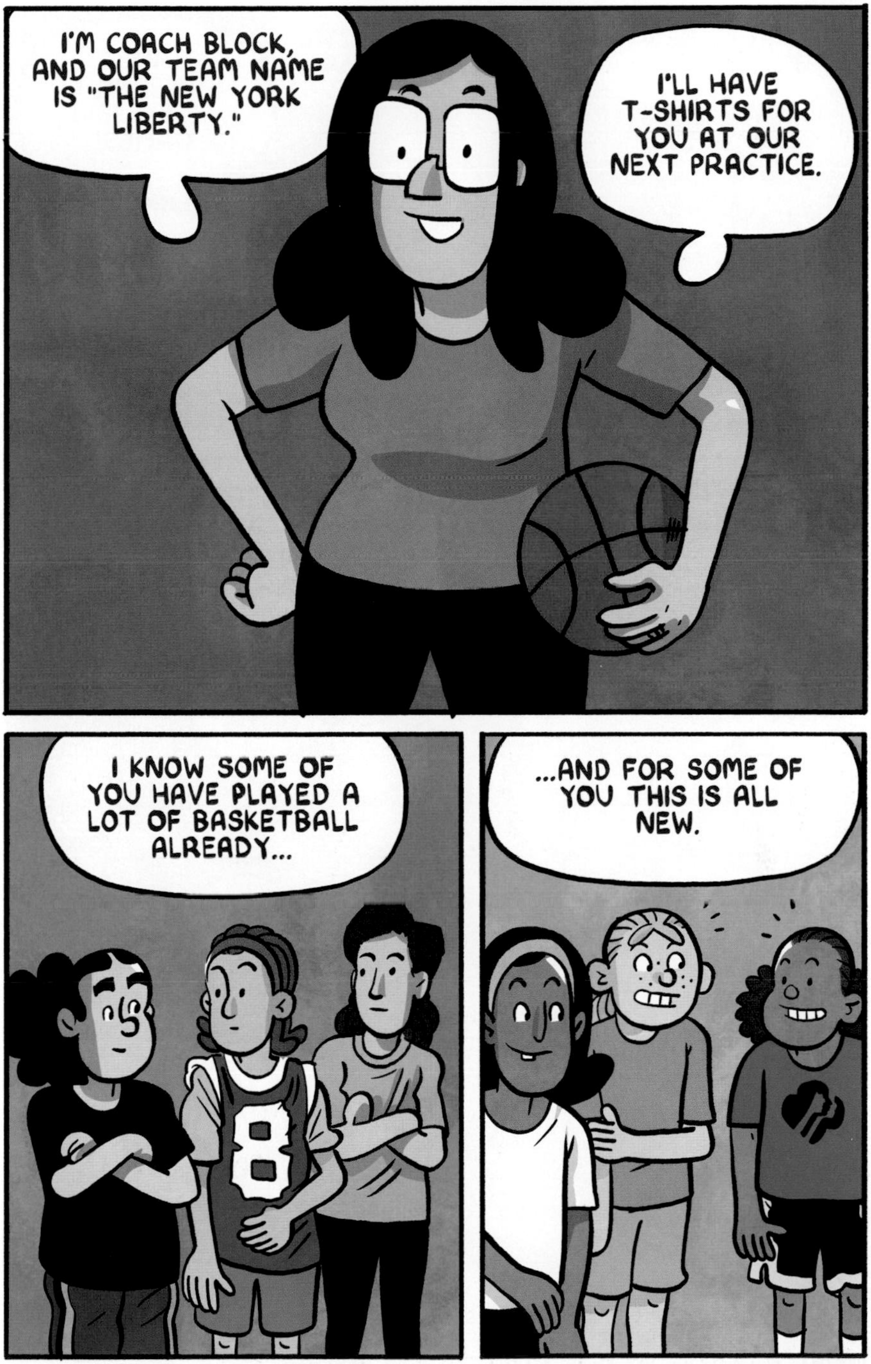
I'M COACH BLOCK, AND OUR TEAM NAME IS "THE NEW YORK LIBERTY."
I'LL HAVE T-SHIRTS FOR YOU AT OUR NEXT PRACTICE.
I KNOW SOME OF YOU HAVE PLAYED A LOT OF BASKETBALL ALREADY...
...AND FOR SOME OF YOU THIS IS ALL NEW.

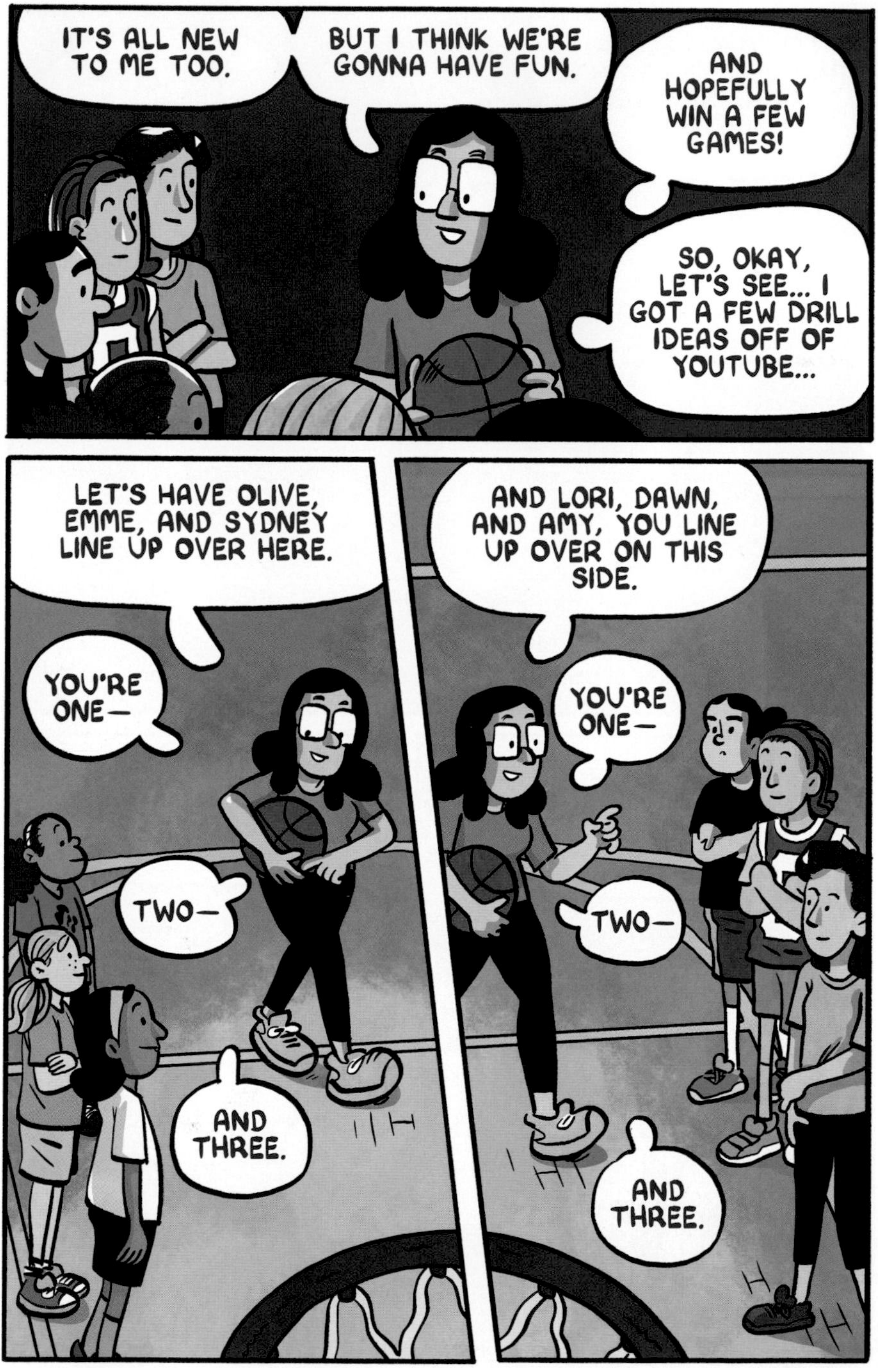
IT'S ALL NEW TO ME TOO.
BUT I THINK WE'RE GONNA HAVE FUN.
AND HOPEFULLY WIN A FEW GAMES!
SO, OKAY, LET'S SEE... I GOT A FEW DRILL IDEAS OFF OF YOUTUBE...
LET'S HAVE OLIVE, EMME, AND SYDNEY LINE UP OVER HERE.
YOU'RE ONE—
TWO—
AND THREE.
AND LORI, DAWN, AND AMY, YOU LINE UP OVER ON THIS SIDE.
YOU'RE ONE—
TWO—
AND THREE.

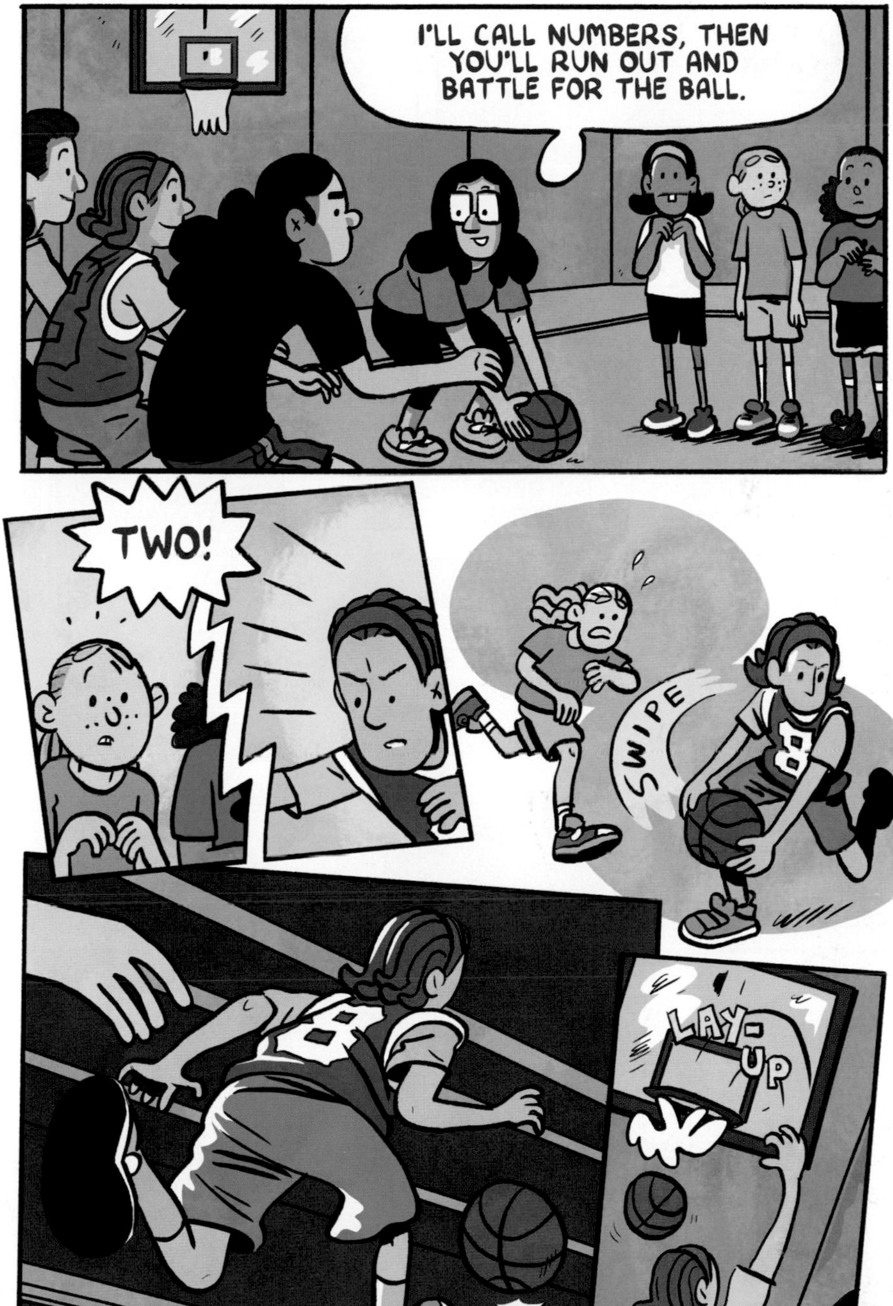
I'LL CALL NUMBERS, THEN YOU'LL RUN OUT AND BATTLE FOR THE BALL.
TWO!
SWIPE
LAY-UP

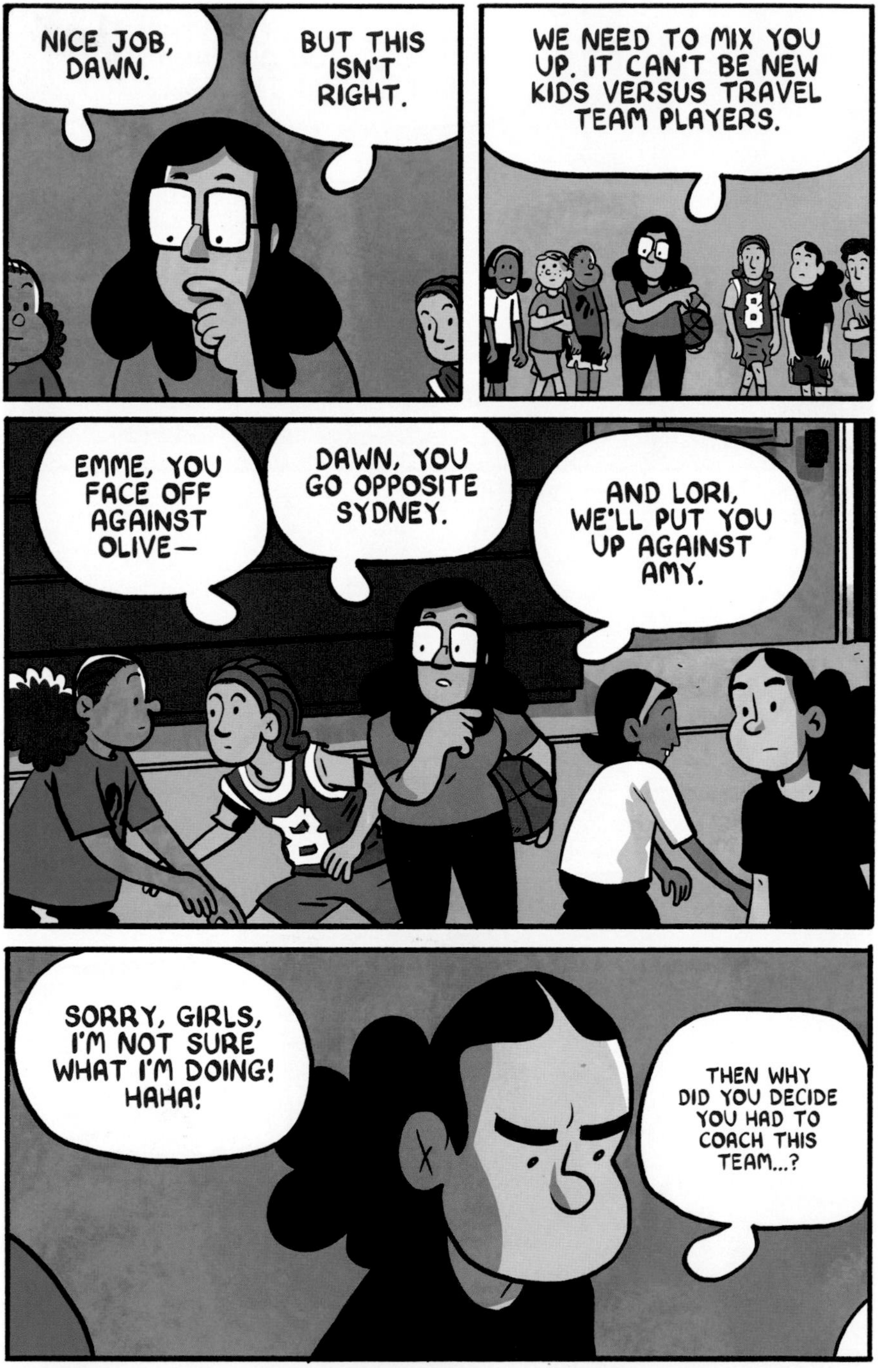
NICE JOB, DAWN.
BUT THIS ISN'T RIGHT.
WE NEED TO MIX YOU UP. IT CAN'T BE NEW KIDS VERSUS TRAVEL TEAM PLAYERS.
EMME, YOU FACE OFF AGAINST OLIVE—
DAWN, YOU GO OPPOSITE SYDNEY.
AND LORI, WE'LL PUT YOU UP AGAINST AMY.
SORRY, GIRLS, I'M NOT SURE WHAT I'M DOING! HAHA!
THEN WHY DID YOU DECIDE YOU HAD TO COACH THIS TEAM...?

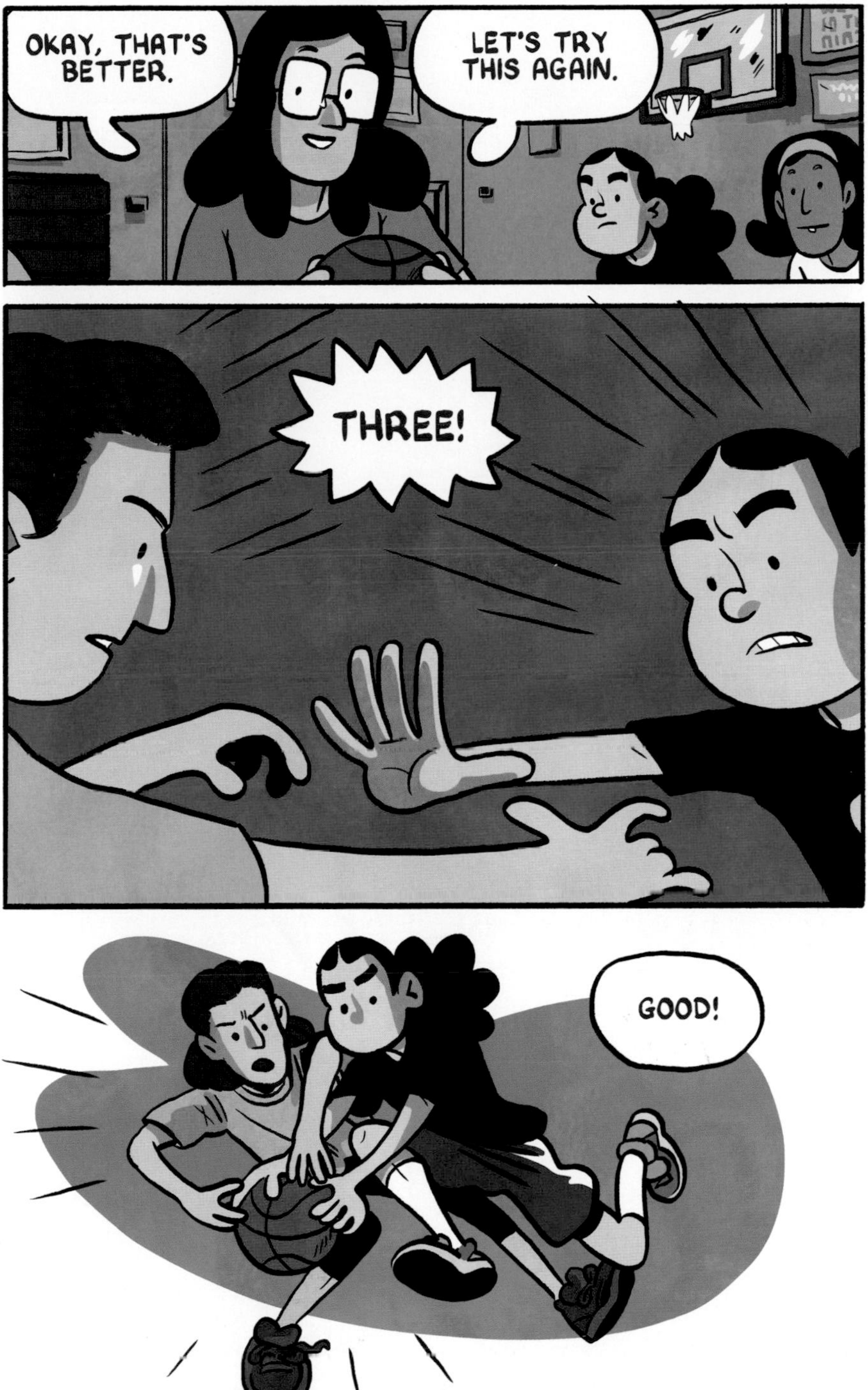
OKAY, THAT'S BETTER.
LET'S TRY THIS AGAIN.
THREE!
GOOD!

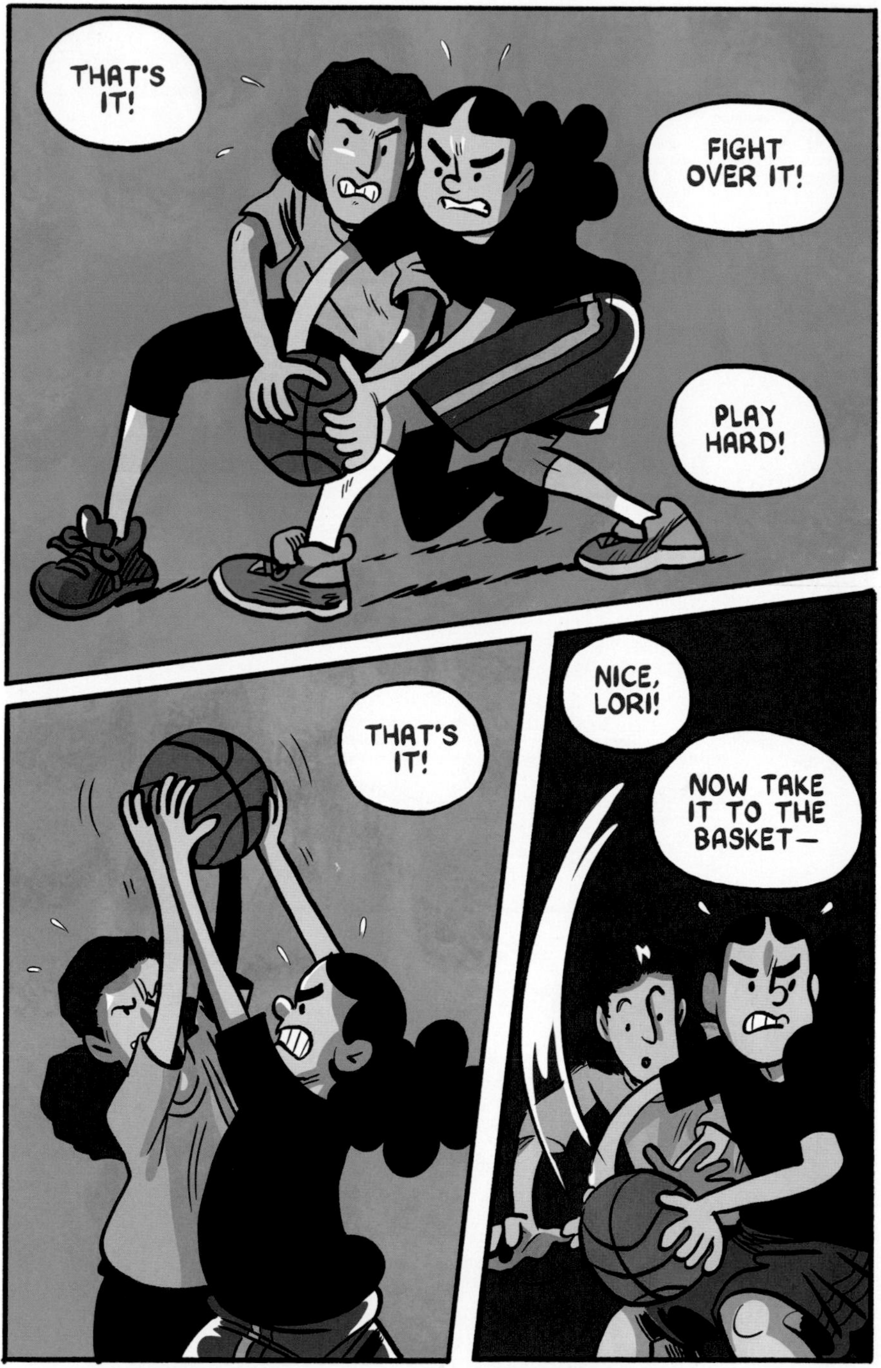
THAT'S IT!
FIGHT OVER IT!
PLAY HARD!
THAT'S IT!
NICE, LORI!
NOW TAKE IT TO THE BASKET—

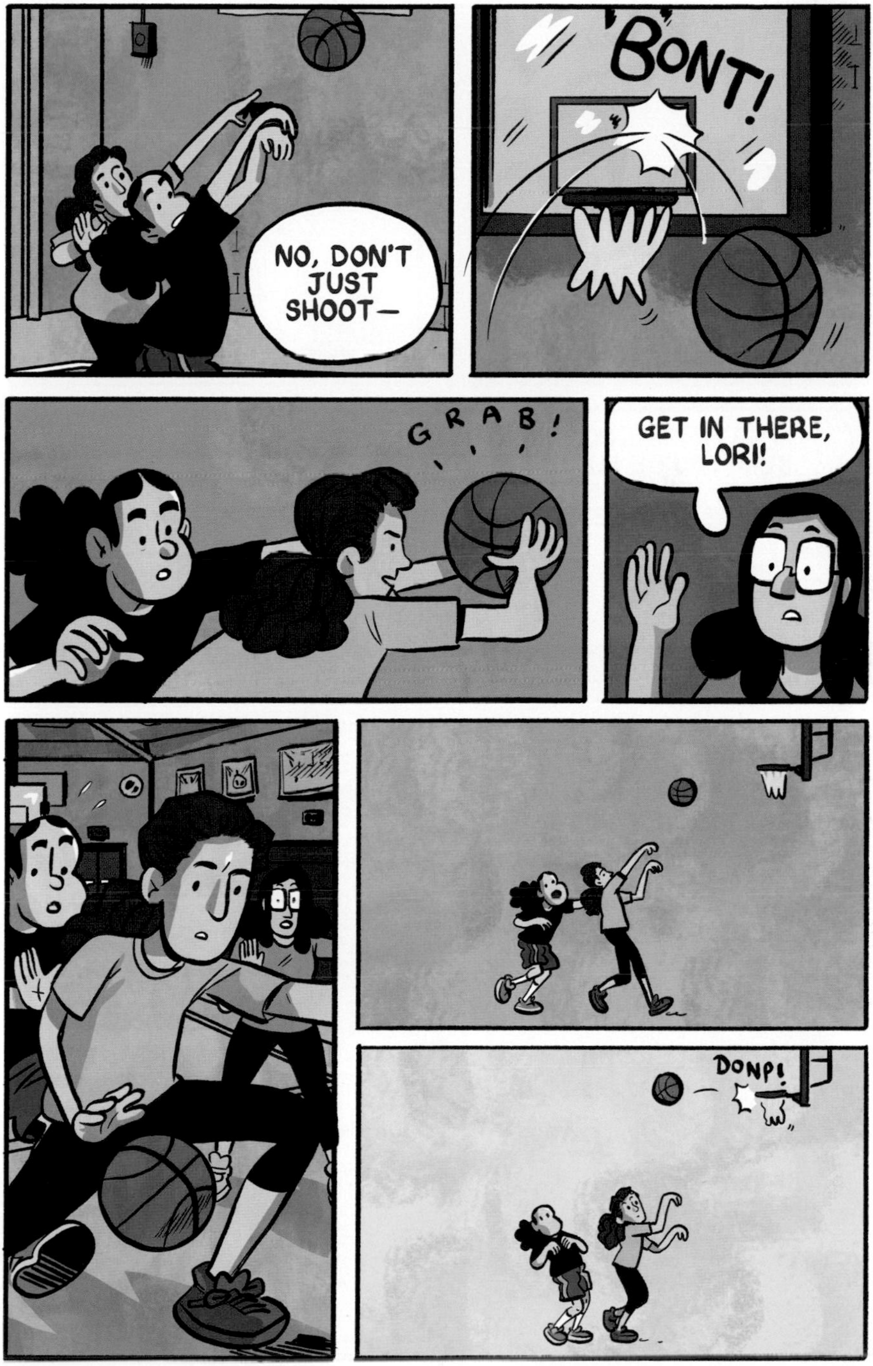
NO, DON'T JUST SHOOT—
BONT!
GRAB!
GET IN THERE, LORI!
DONP!

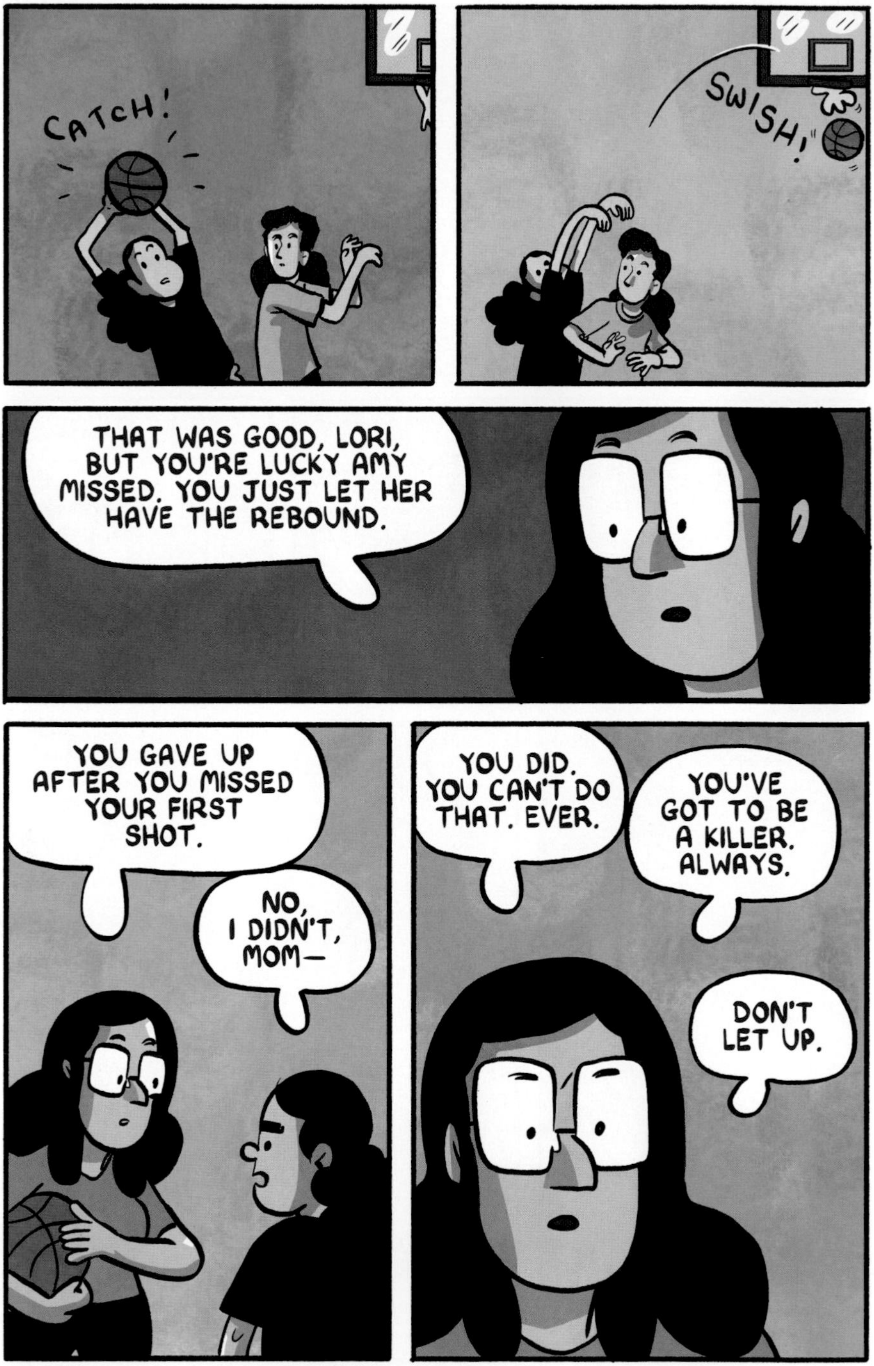
CATCH!
SWISH!
THAT WAS GOOD, LORI, BUT YOU'RE LUCKY AMY MISSED. YOU JUST LET HER HAVE THE REBOUND.
YOU GAVE UP AFTER YOU MISSED YOUR FIRST SHOT.
NO, I DIDN'T, MOM—
YOU DID. YOU CAN'T DO THAT. EVER.
YOU'VE GOT TO BE A KILLER. ALWAYS.
DON'T LET UP.

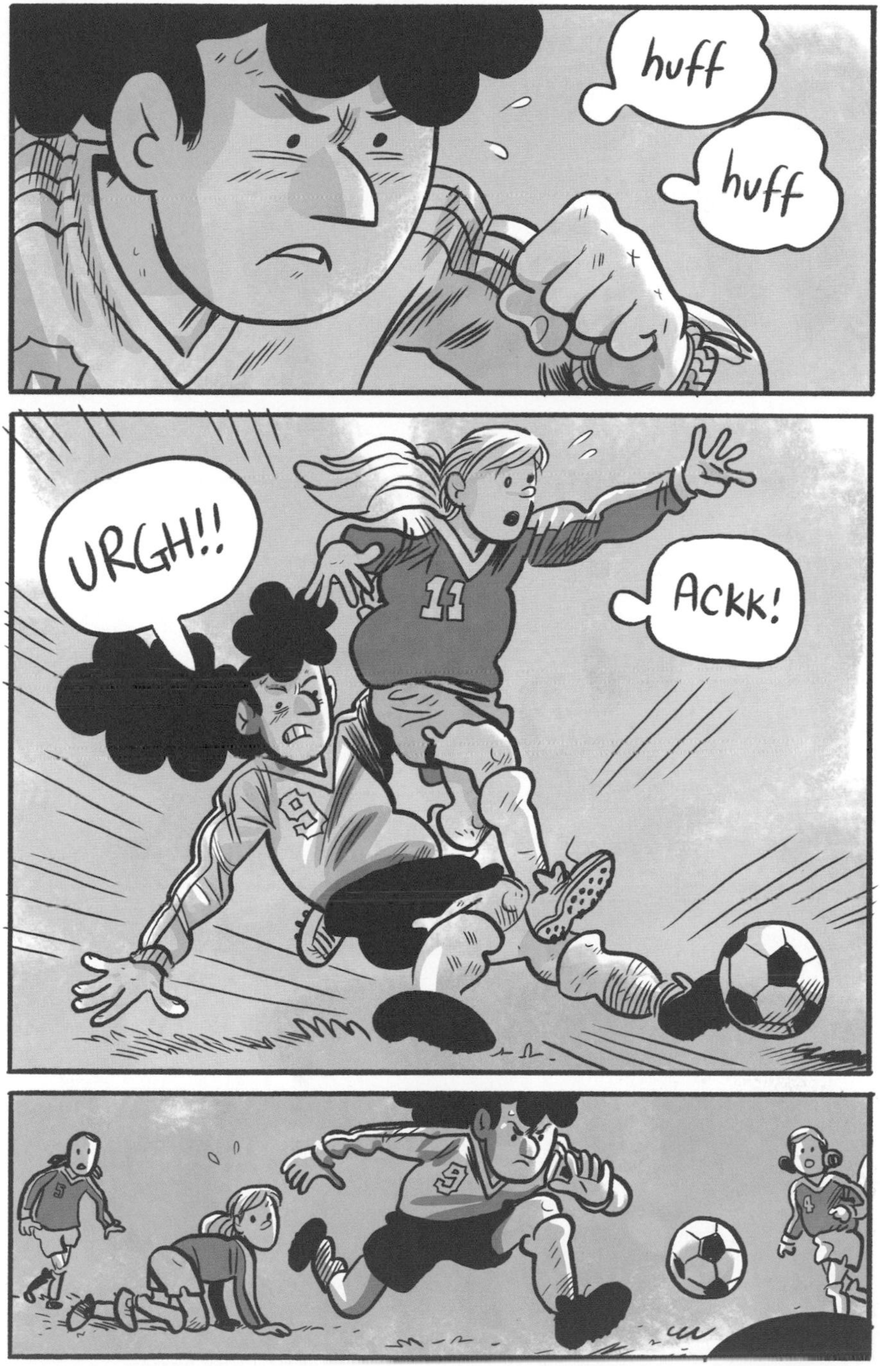
huff
huff
URGH!!
ACKK!

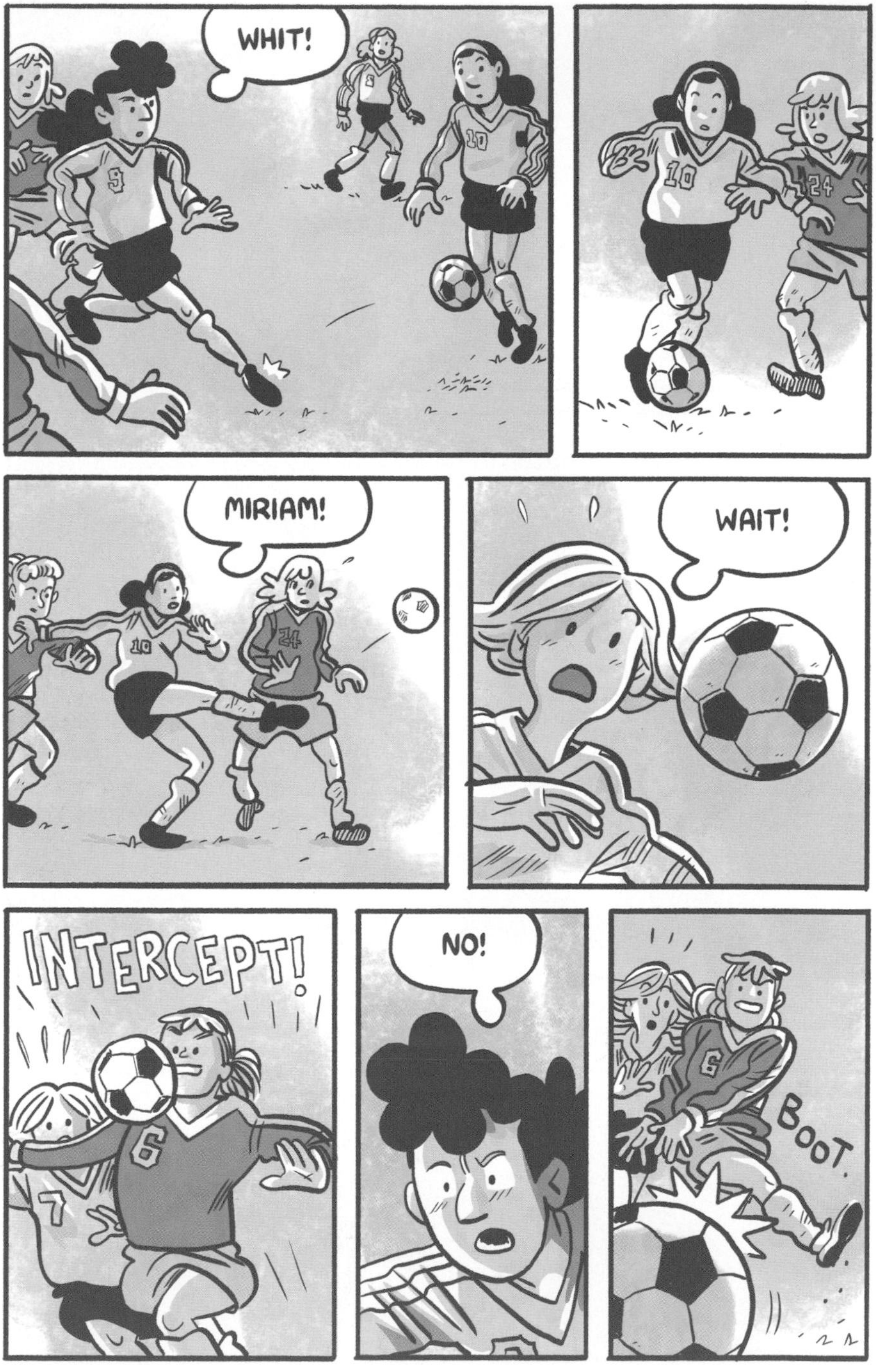
WHIT!
MIRIAM!
WAIT!
INTERCEPT!
NO!
BOOT.

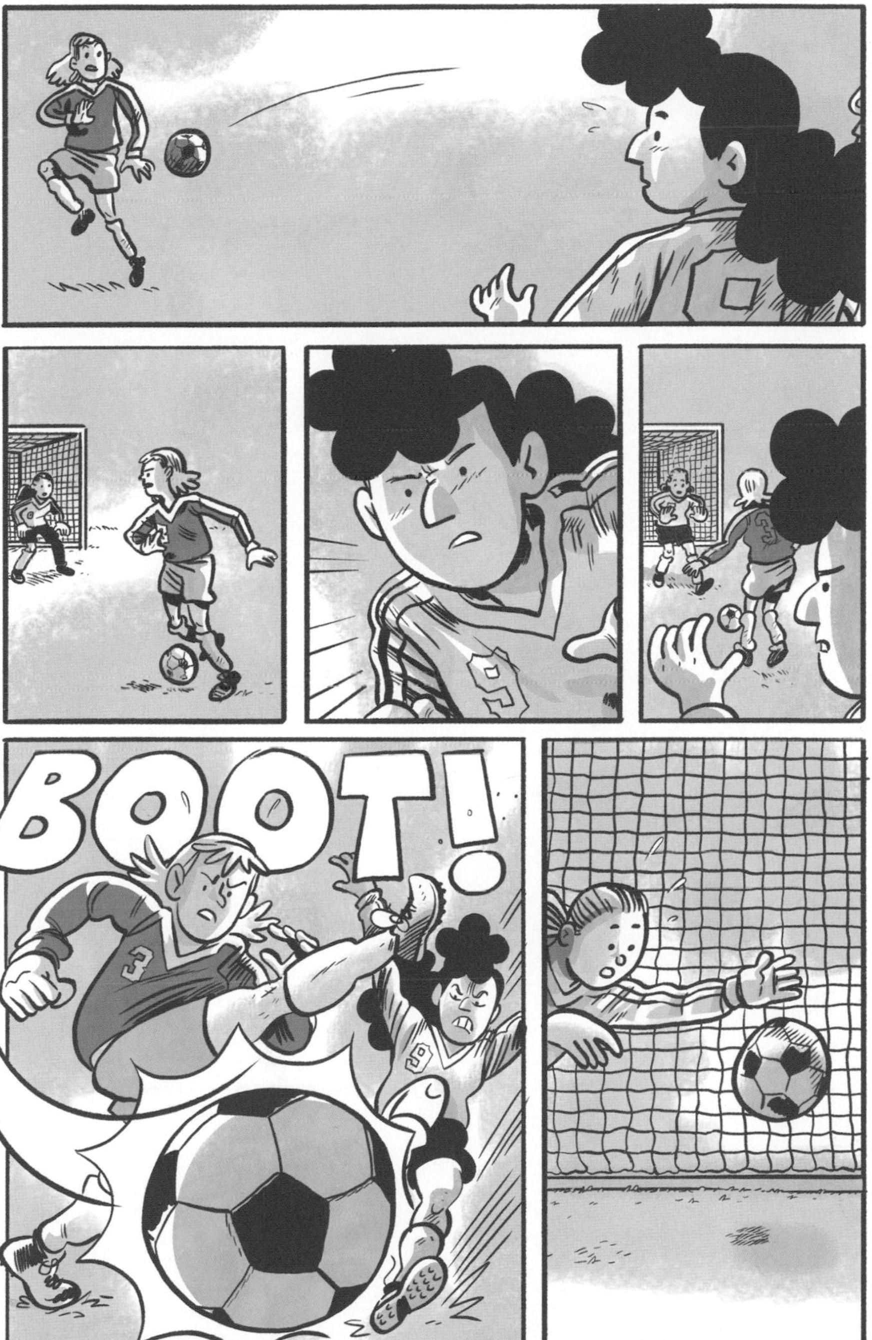
BOOT!

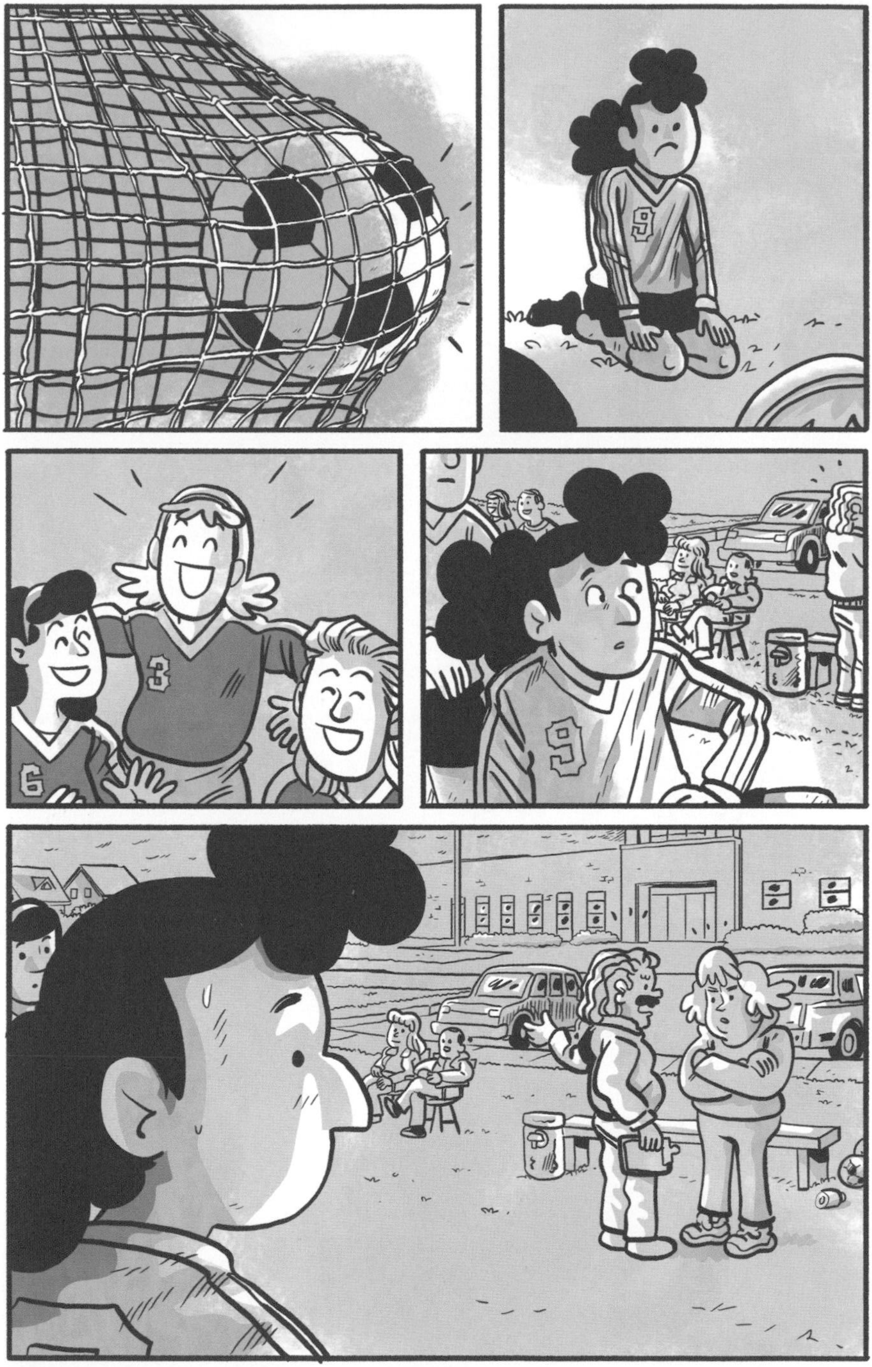

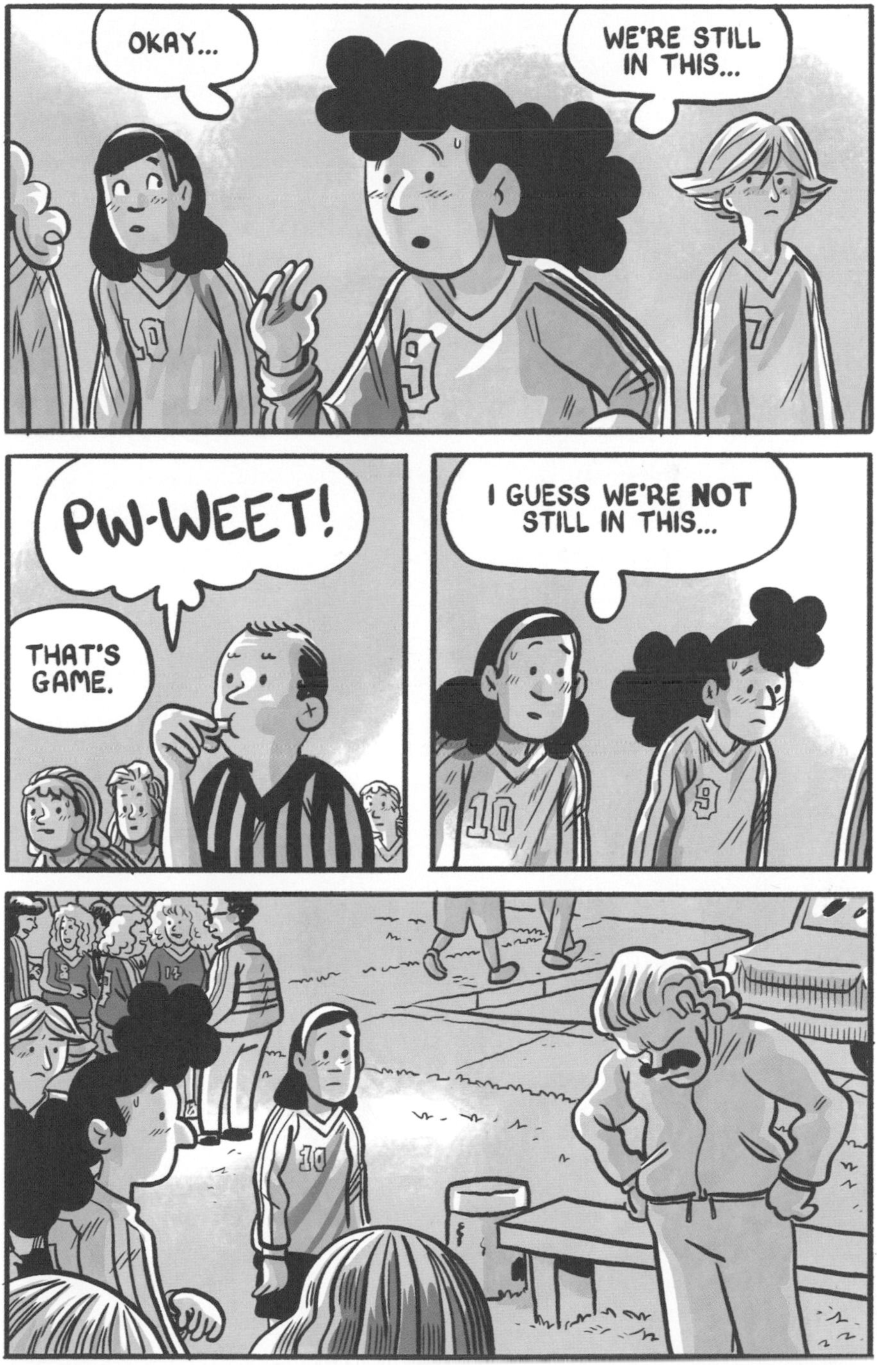
OKAY...
WE'RE STILL IN THIS...
PW-WEET!
THAT'S GAME.
I GUESS WE'RE NOT STILL IN THIS...

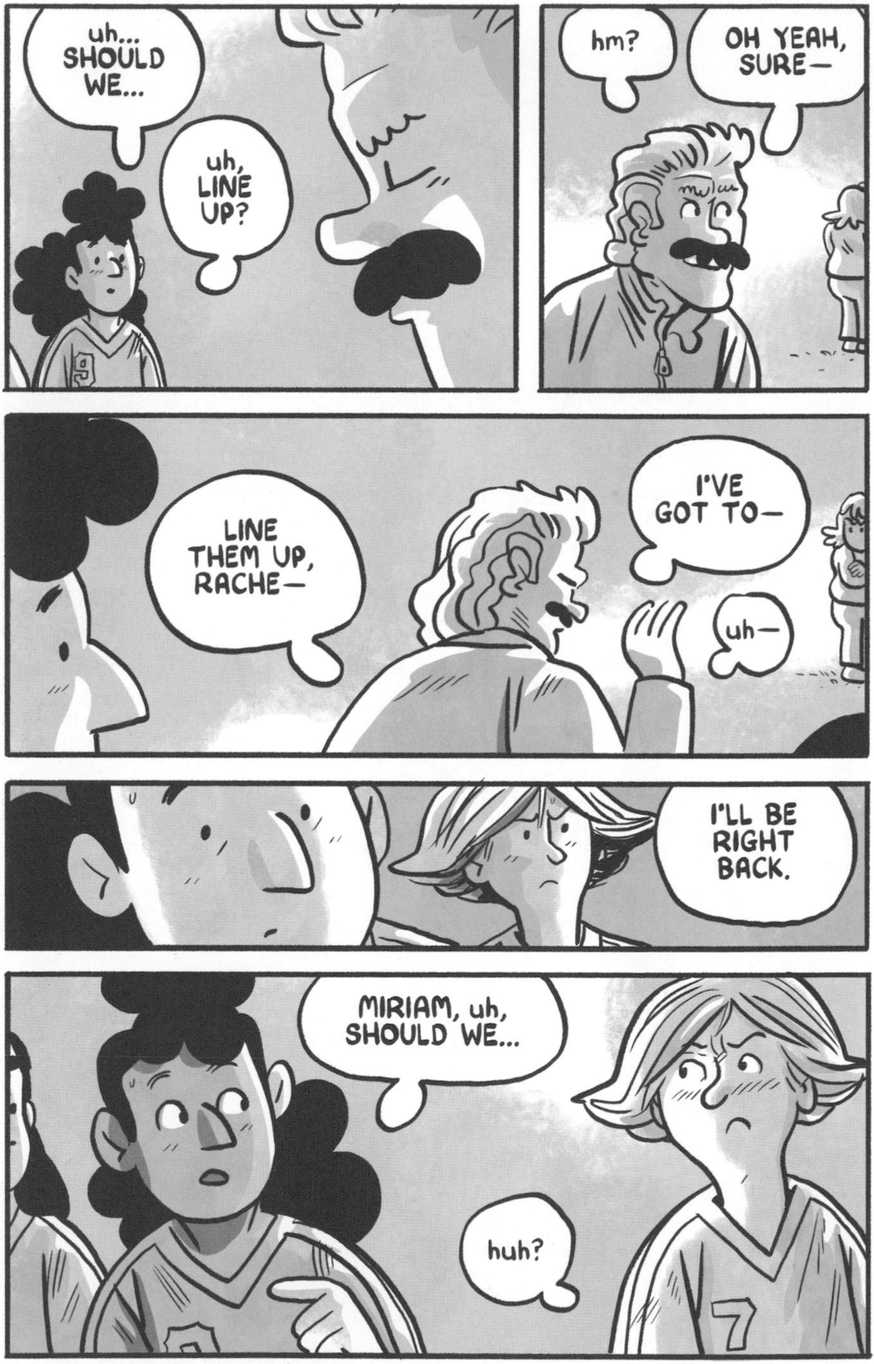
uh... SHOULD WE...
uh, LINE UP?
hm?
OH YEAH, SURE—
LINE THEM UP, RACHE—
I'VE GOT TO—
uh—
I'LL BE RIGHT BACK.
MIRIAM, uh, SHOULD WE...
huh?

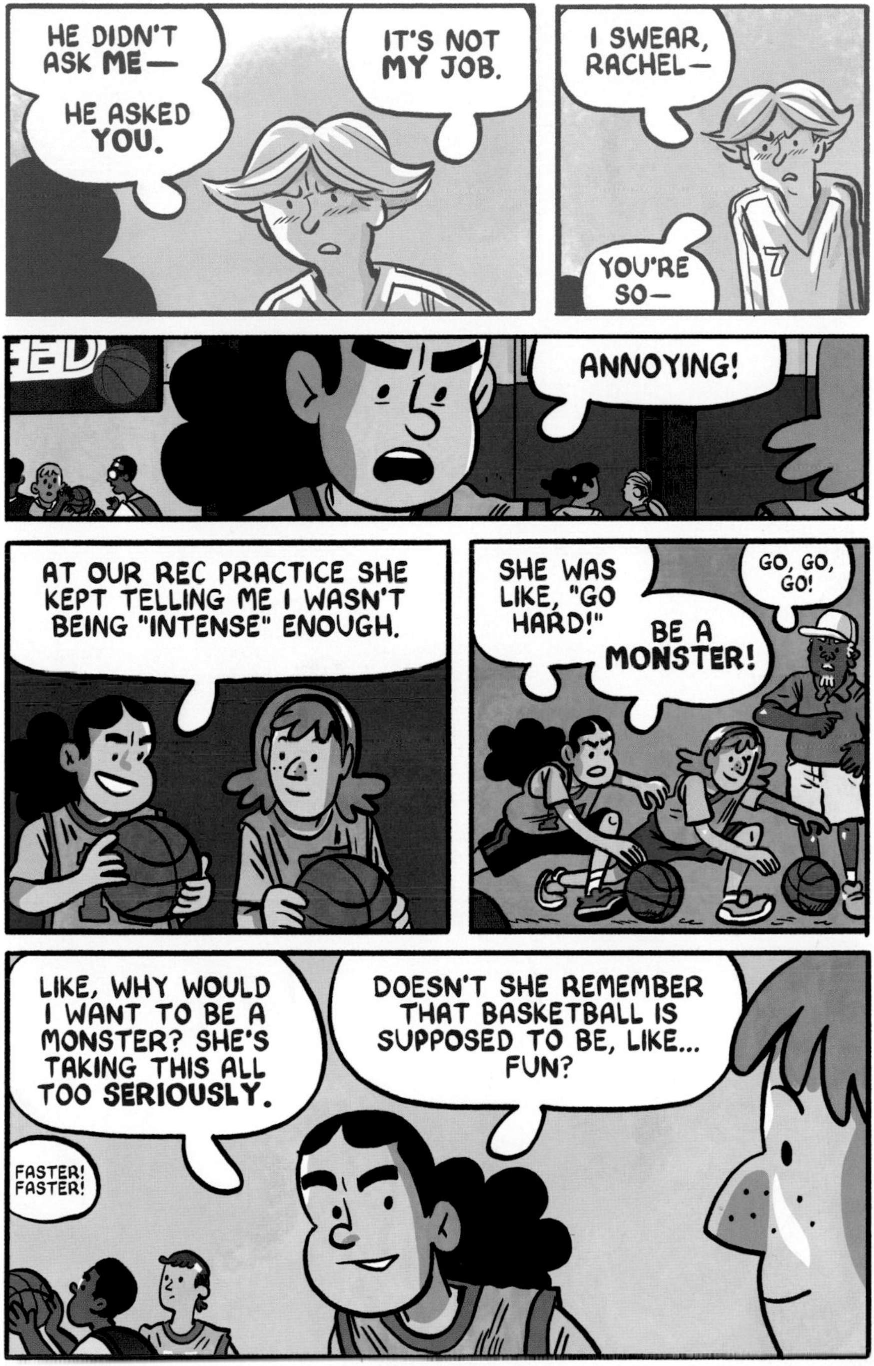
HE DIDN'T ASK **ME**—
HE ASKED **YOU**.
IT'S NOT **MY** JOB.
I SWEAR, RACHEL—
YOU'RE SO—
ANNOYING!
AT OUR REC PRACTICE SHE KEPT TELLING ME I WASN'T BEING "INTENSE" ENOUGH.
SHE WAS LIKE, "GO HARD!"
GO, GO, GO!
BE A **MONSTER!**
LIKE, WHY WOULD I WANT TO BE A MONSTER? SHE'S TAKING THIS ALL TOO **SERIOUSLY**.
DOESN'T SHE REMEMBER THAT BASKETBALL IS SUPPOSED TO BE, LIKE... FUN?
FASTER! FASTER!

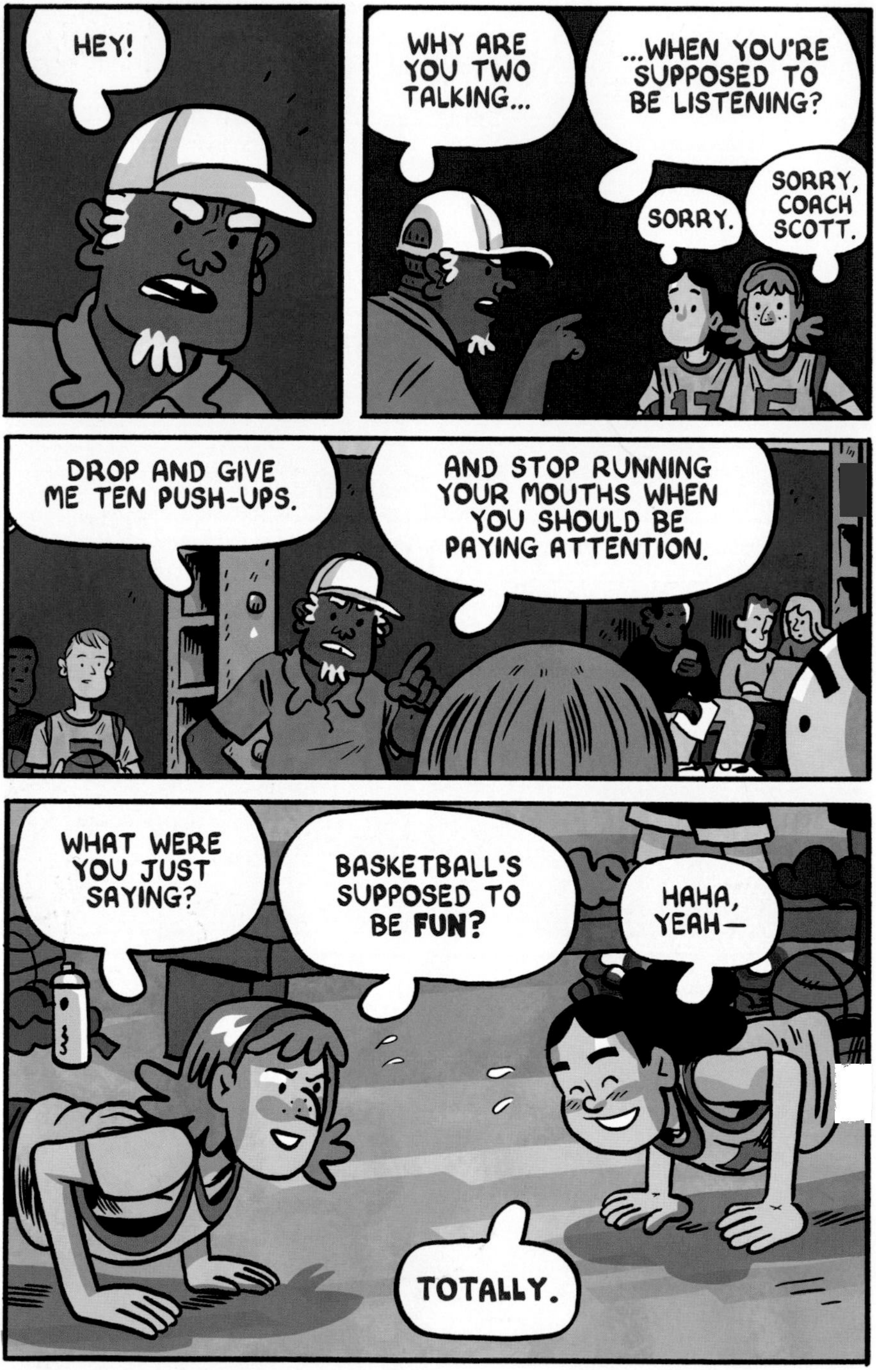
HEY!
WHY ARE YOU TWO TALKING...
...WHEN YOU'RE SUPPOSED TO BE LISTENING?
SORRY.
SORRY, COACH SCOTT.
DROP AND GIVE ME TEN PUSH-UPS.
AND STOP RUNNING YOUR MOUTHS WHEN YOU SHOULD BE PAYING ATTENTION.
WHAT WERE YOU JUST SAYING?
BASKETBALL'S SUPPOSED TO BE **FUN?**
HAHA, YEAH—
TOTALLY.

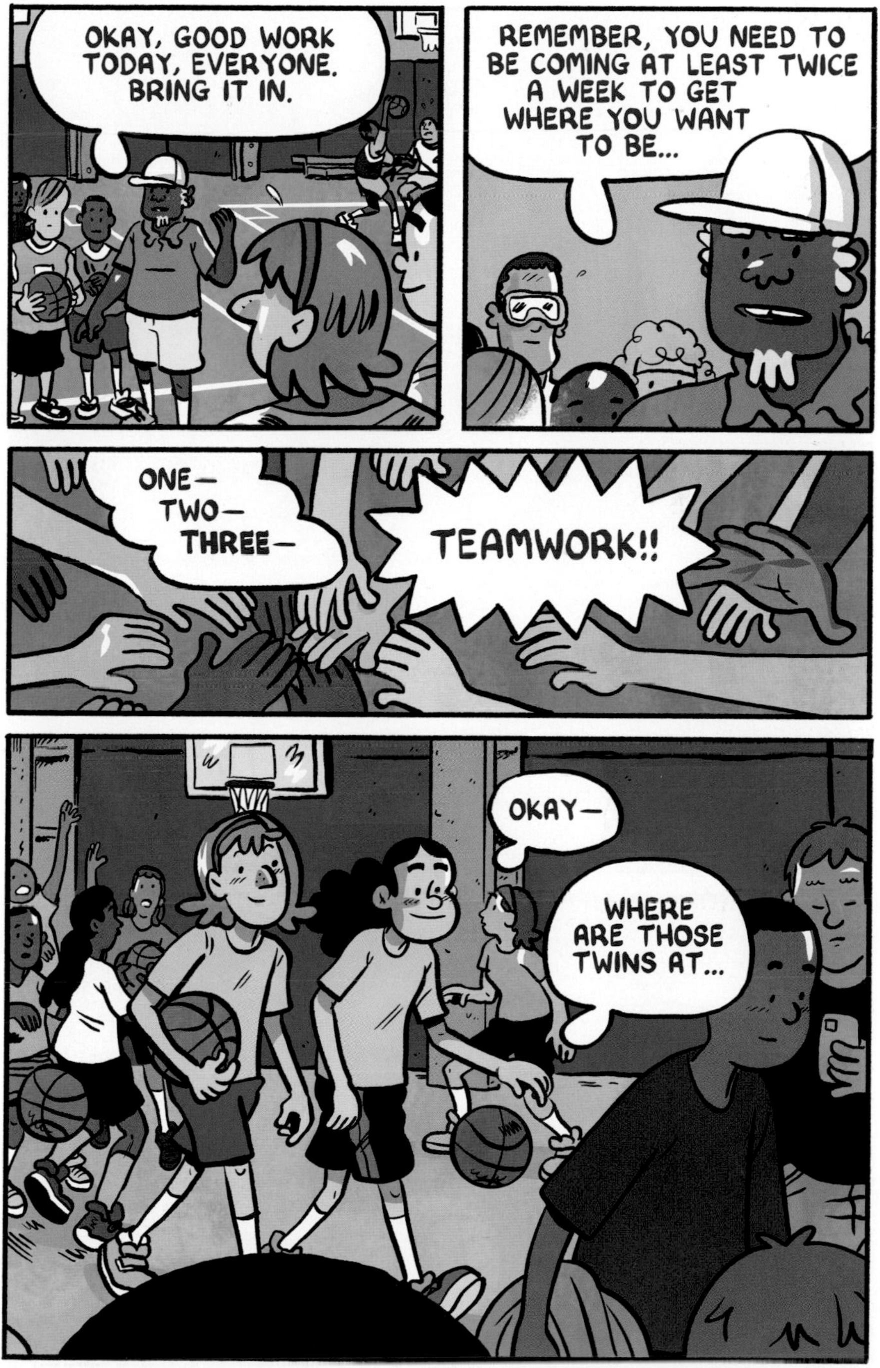
OKAY, GOOD WORK TODAY, EVERYONE. BRING IT IN.
REMEMBER, YOU NEED TO BE COMING AT LEAST TWICE A WEEK TO GET WHERE YOU WANT TO BE...
ONE— TWO— THREE—
TEAMWORK!!
OKAY—
WHERE ARE THOSE TWINS AT...

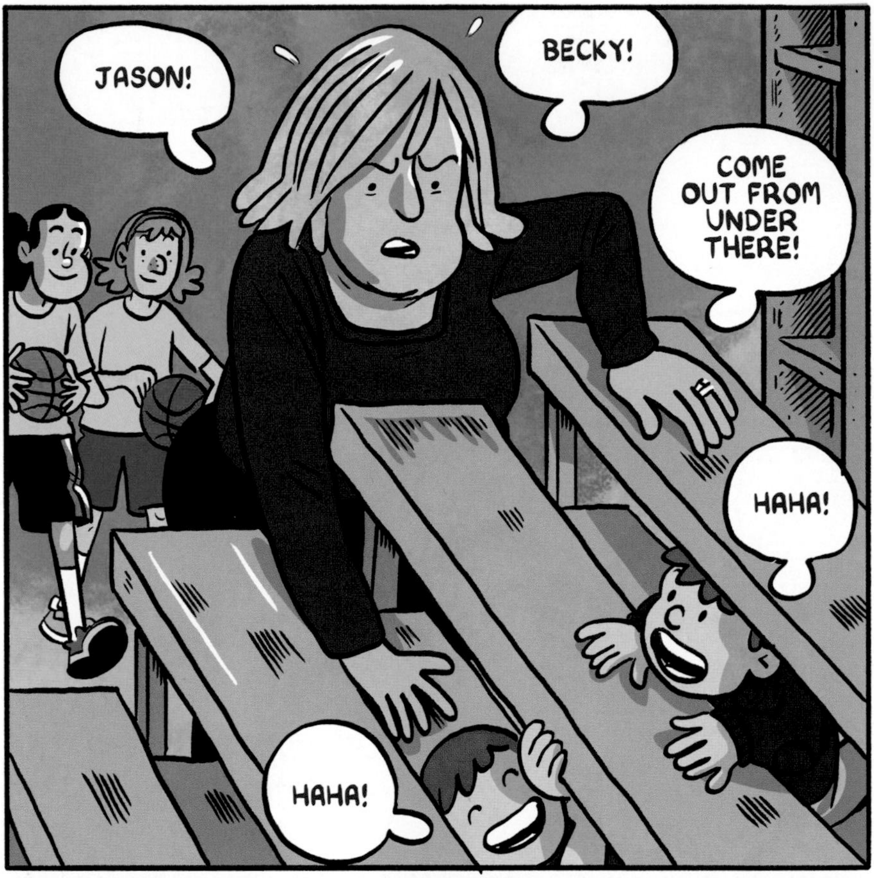
JASON!
BECKY!
COME OUT FROM UNDER THERE!
HAHA!
HAHA!

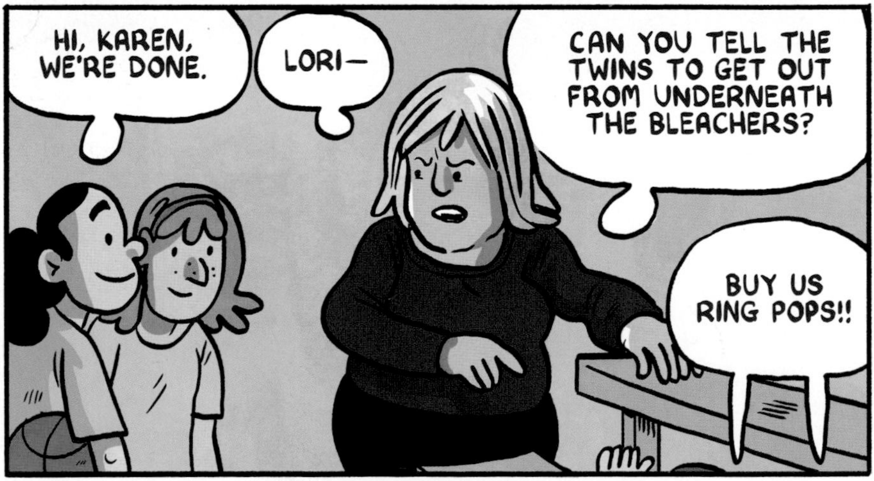
HI, KAREN, WE'RE DONE.
LORI—
CAN YOU TELL THE TWINS TO GET OUT FROM UNDERNEATH THE BLEACHERS?
BUY US RING POPS!!

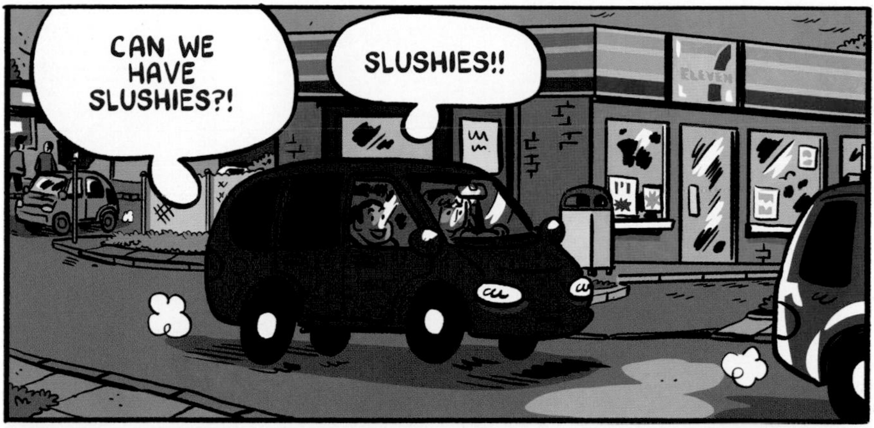
CAN WE HAVE SLUSHIES?!
SLUSHIES!!
ELEVEN

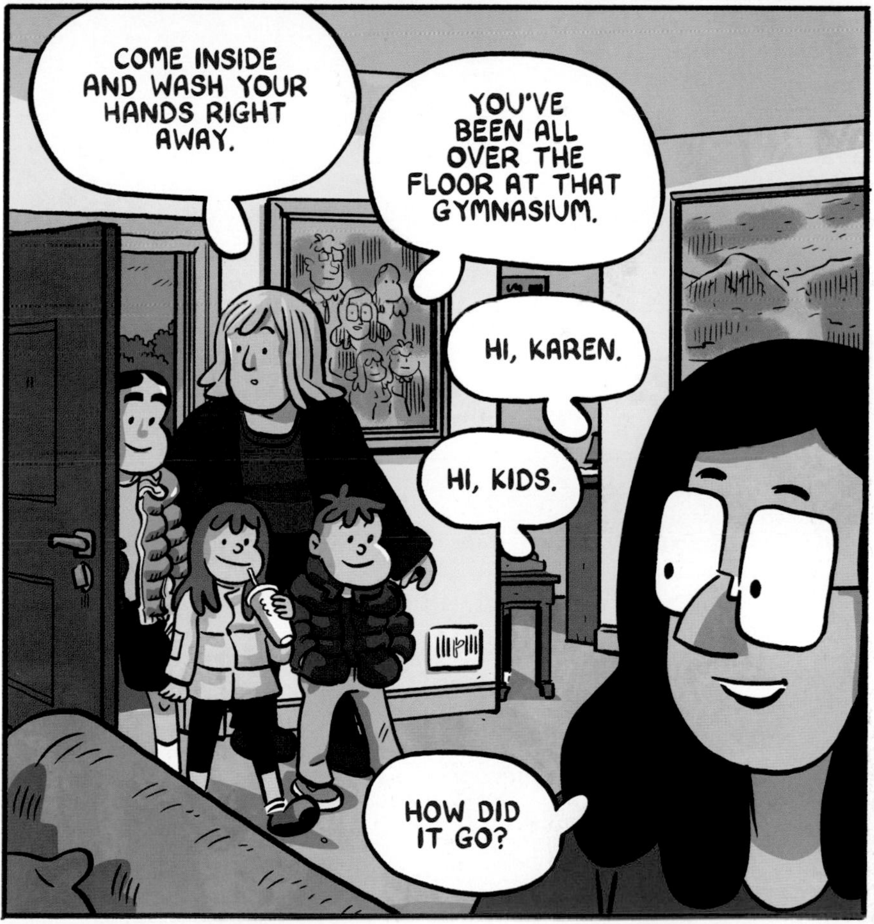
COME INSIDE AND WASH YOUR HANDS RIGHT AWAY.
YOU'VE BEEN ALL OVER THE FLOOR AT THAT GYMNASIUM.
HI, KAREN.
HI, KIDS.
HOW DID IT GO?

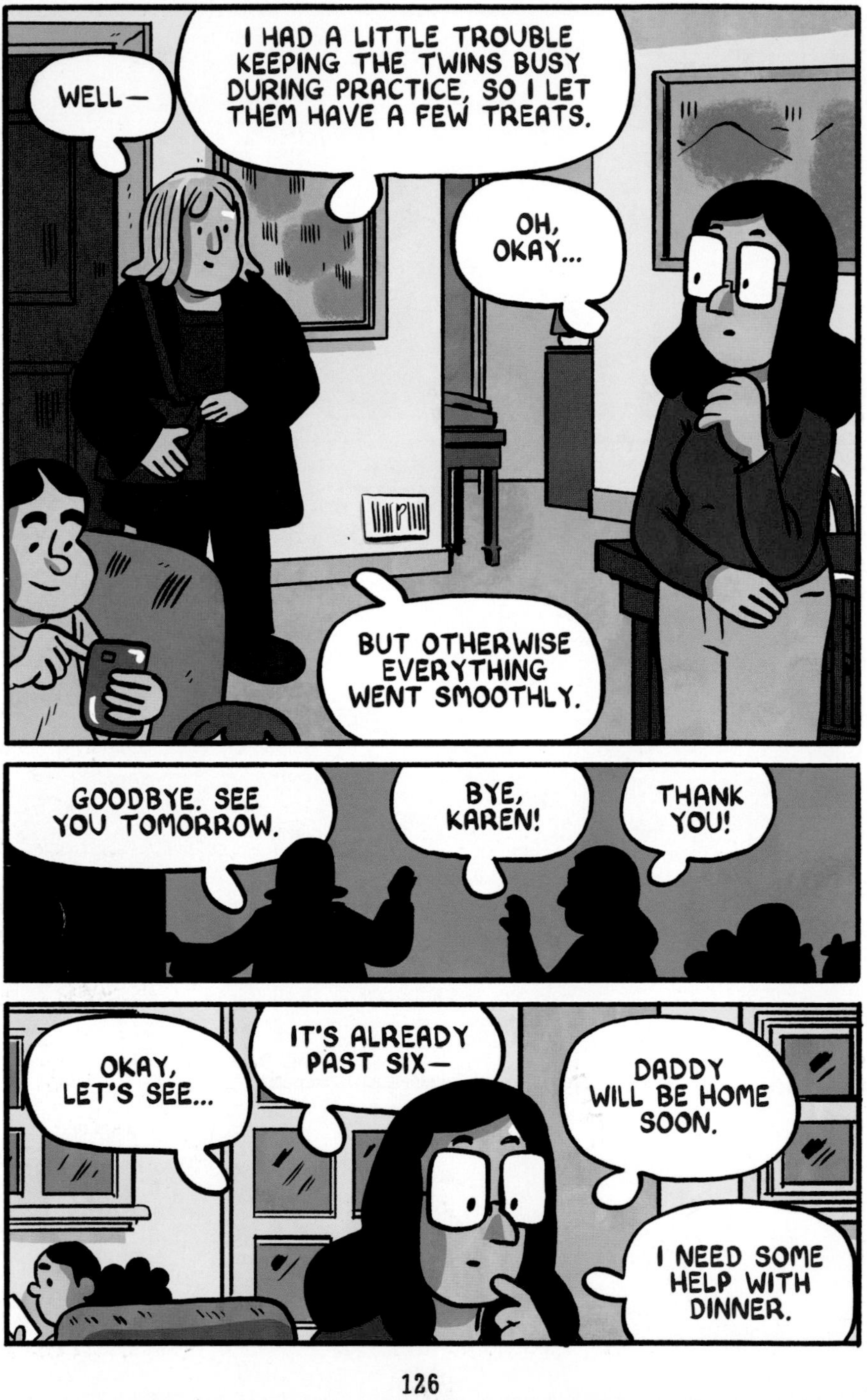
WELL—
I HAD A LITTLE TROUBLE KEEPING THE TWINS BUSY DURING PRACTICE, SO I LET THEM HAVE A FEW TREATS.
OH, OKAY...
BUT OTHERWISE EVERYTHING WENT SMOOTHLY.
GOODBYE. SEE YOU TOMORROW.
BYE, KAREN!
THANK YOU!
OKAY, LET'S SEE...
IT'S ALREADY PAST SIX—
DADDY WILL BE HOME SOON.
I NEED SOME HELP WITH DINNER.

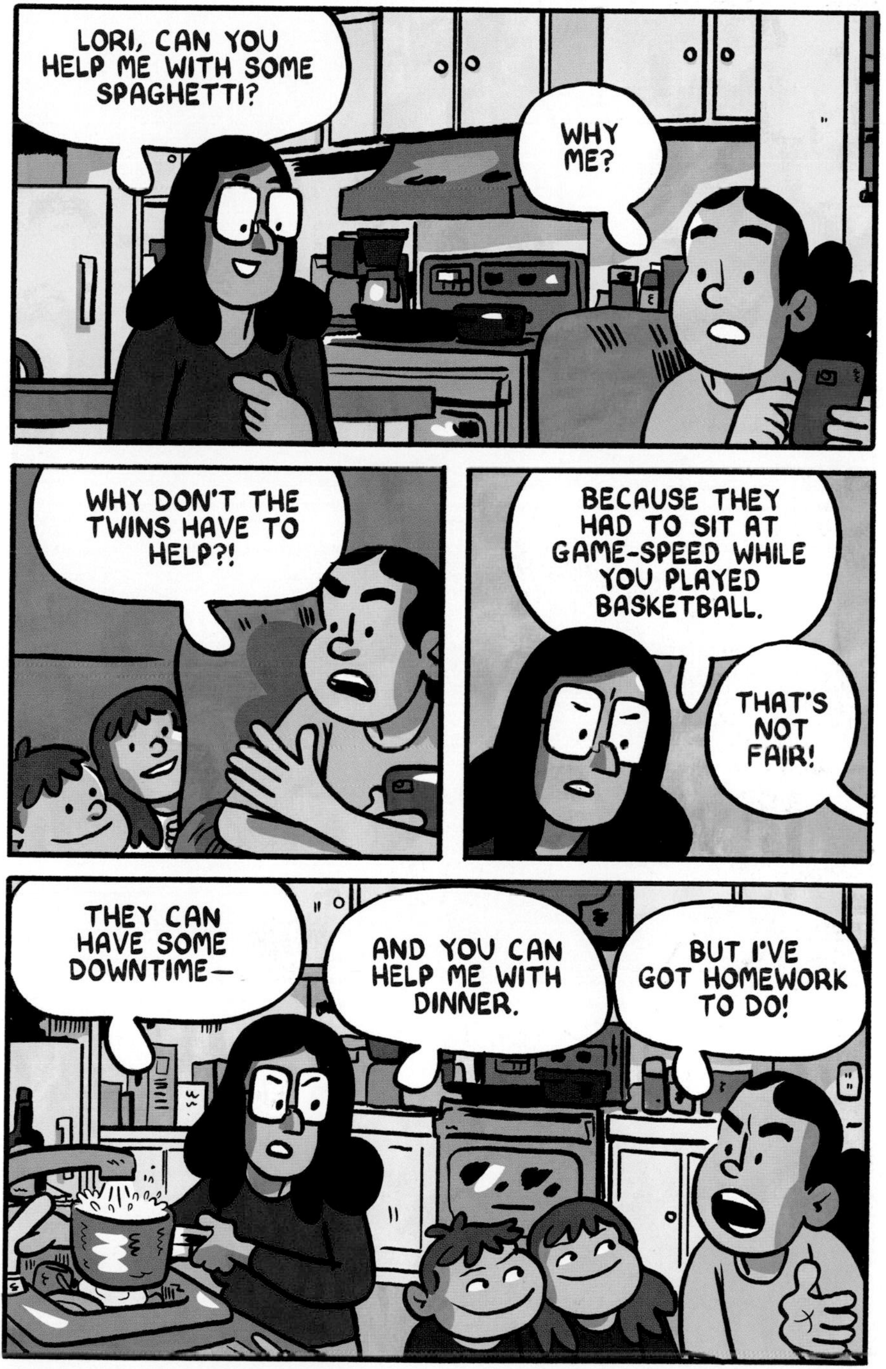
LORI, CAN YOU HELP ME WITH SOME SPAGHETTI?
WHY ME?
WHY DON'T THE TWINS HAVE TO HELP?!
BECAUSE THEY HAD TO SIT AT GAME-SPEED WHILE YOU PLAYED BASKETBALL.
THAT'S NOT FAIR!
THEY CAN HAVE SOME DOWNTIME—
AND YOU CAN HELP ME WITH DINNER.
BUT I'VE GOT HOMEWORK TO DO!

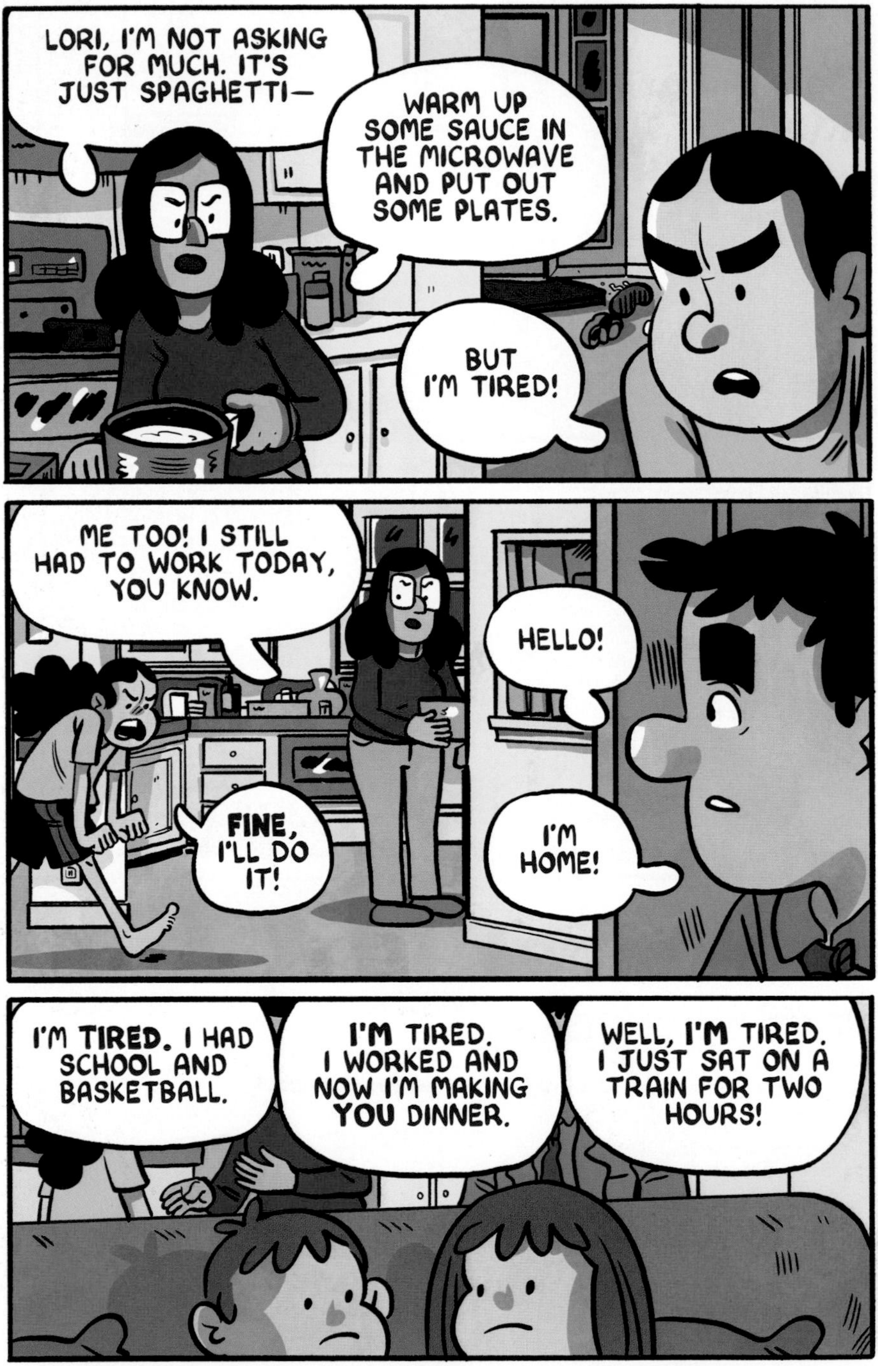
LORI, I'M NOT ASKING FOR MUCH. IT'S JUST SPAGHETTI—
WARM UP SOME SAUCE IN THE MICROWAVE AND PUT OUT SOME PLATES.
BUT I'M TIRED!
ME TOO! I STILL HAD TO WORK TODAY, YOU KNOW.
FINE, I'LL DO IT!
HELLO!
I'M HOME!
I'M TIRED. I HAD SCHOOL AND BASKETBALL.
I'M TIRED. I WORKED AND NOW I'M MAKING YOU DINNER.
WELL, I'M TIRED. I JUST SAT ON A TRAIN FOR TWO HOURS!

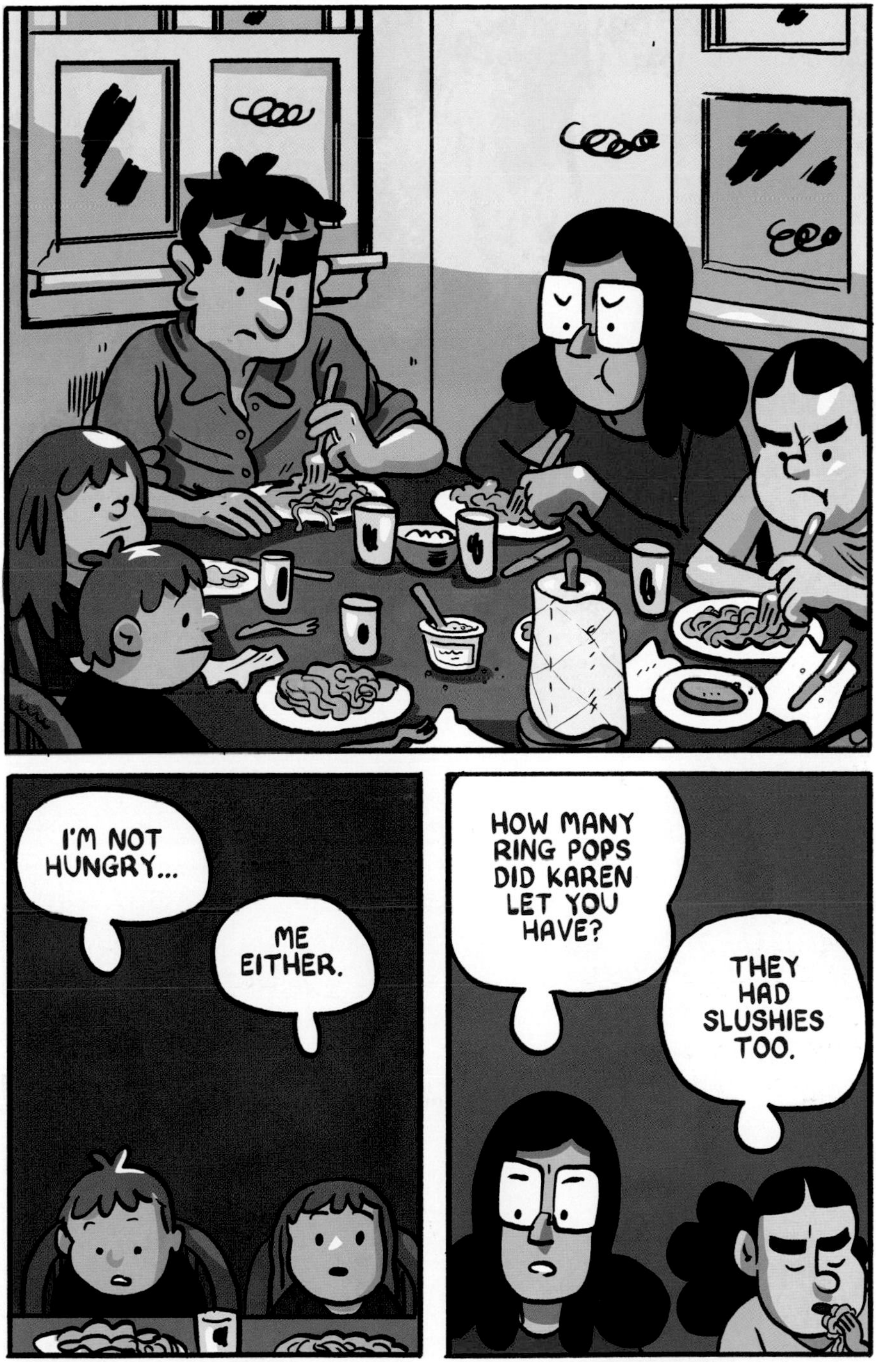
I'M NOT HUNGRY...
ME EITHER.
HOW MANY RING POPS DID KAREN LET YOU HAVE?
THEY HAD SLUSHIES TOO.

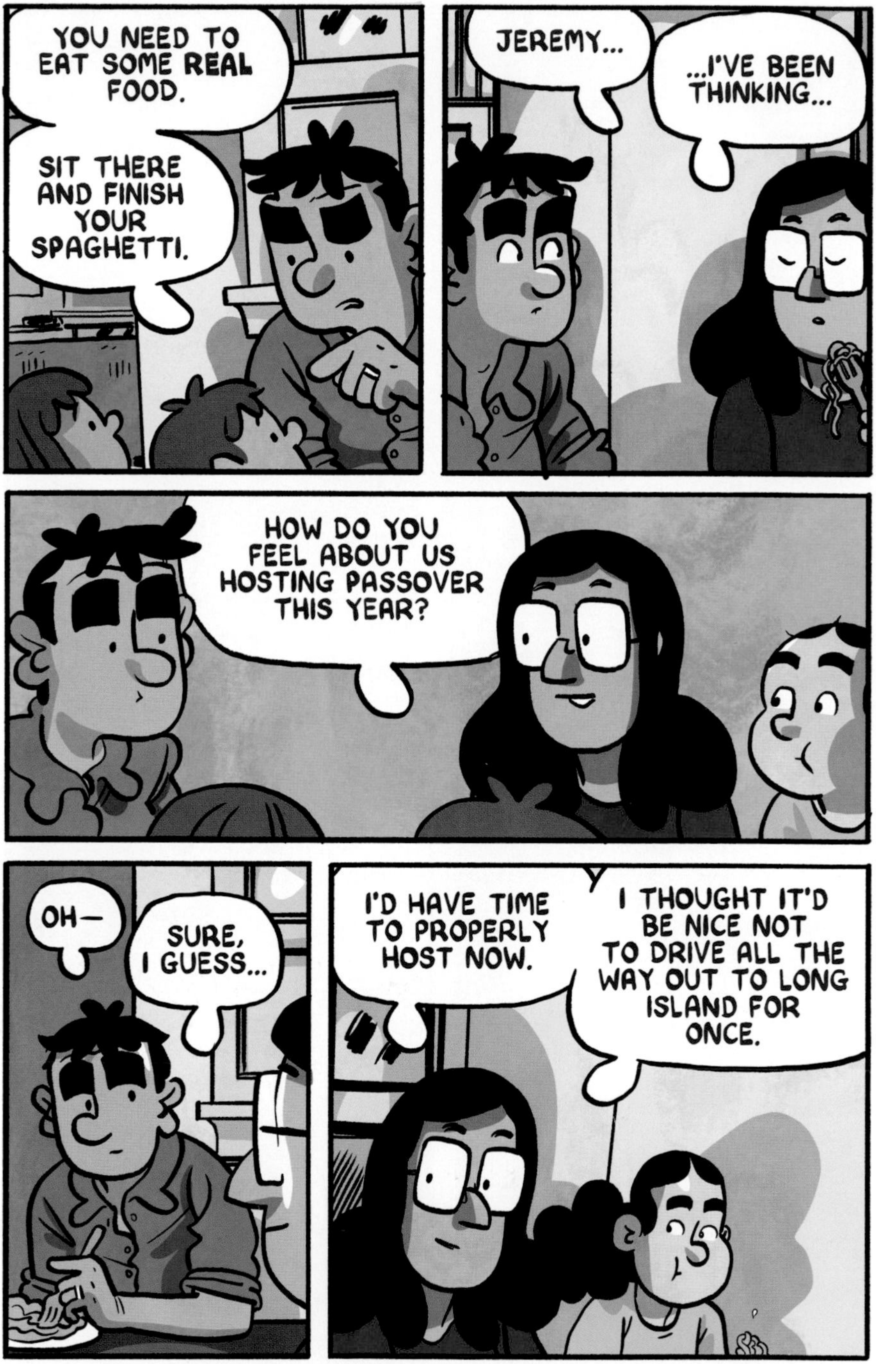
YOU NEED TO EAT SOME REAL FOOD.
SIT THERE AND FINISH YOUR SPAGHETTI.
JEREMY...
...I'VE BEEN THINKING...
HOW DO YOU FEEL ABOUT US HOSTING PASSOVER THIS YEAR?
OH—
SURE, I GUESS...
I'D HAVE TIME TO PROPERLY HOST NOW.
I THOUGHT IT'D BE NICE NOT TO DRIVE ALL THE WAY OUT TO LONG ISLAND FOR ONCE.

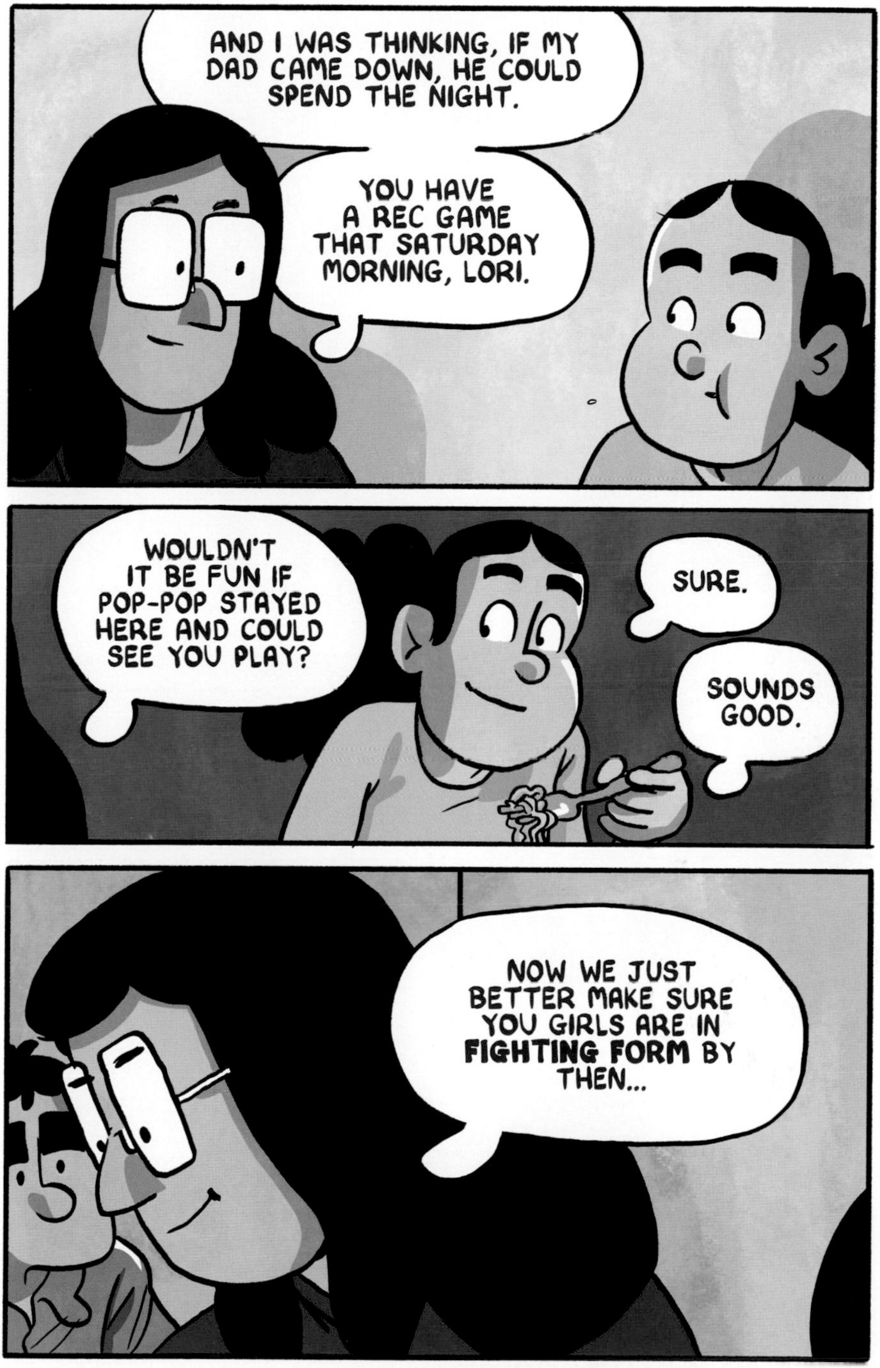
AND I WAS THINKING, IF MY DAD CAME DOWN, HE COULD SPEND THE NIGHT.
YOU HAVE A REC GAME THAT SATURDAY MORNING, LORI.
WOULDN'T IT BE FUN IF POP-POP STAYED HERE AND COULD SEE YOU PLAY?
SURE.
SOUNDS GOOD.
NOW WE JUST BETTER MAKE SURE YOU GIRLS ARE IN **FIGHTING FORM** BY THEN...

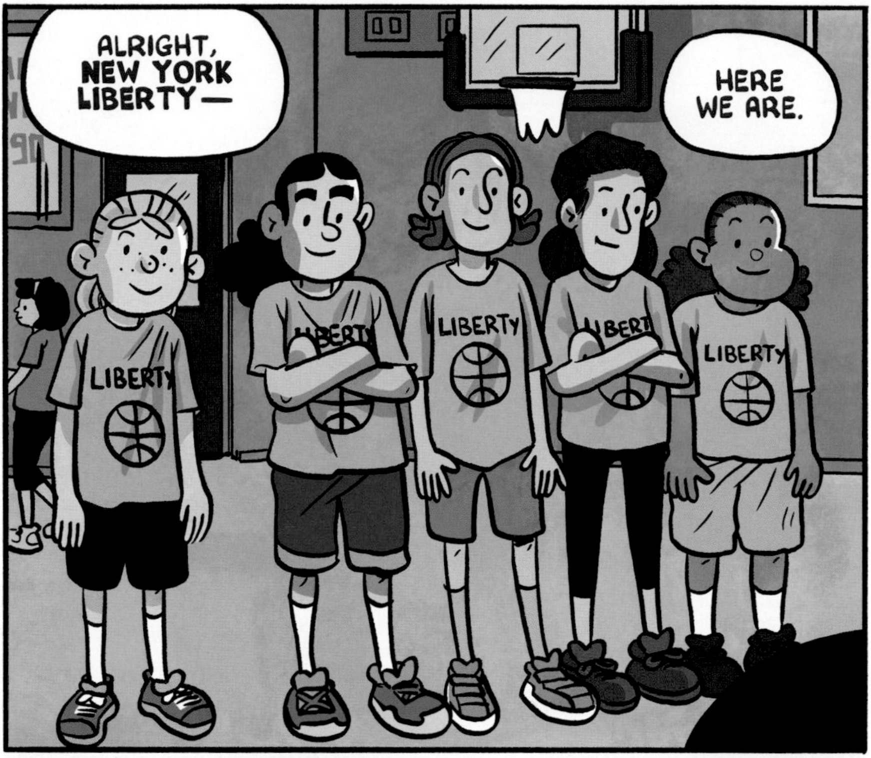
ALRIGHT, NEW YORK LIBERTY—
HERE WE ARE.
LIBERTY
LIBERTY
LIBERTY
LIBERTY
LIBERTY

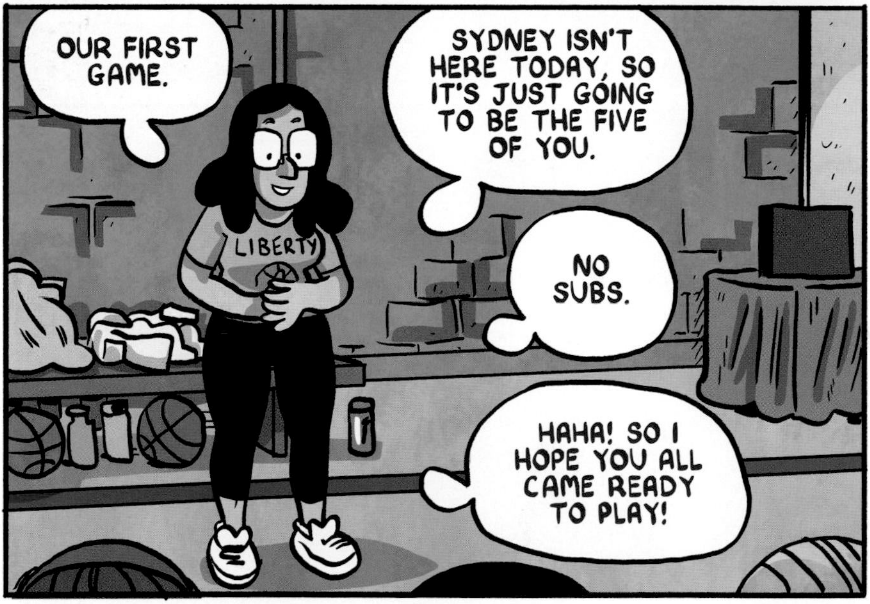
OUR FIRST GAME.
SYDNEY ISN'T HERE TODAY, SO IT'S JUST GOING TO BE THE FIVE OF YOU.
NO SUBS.
HAHA! SO I HOPE YOU ALL CAME READY TO PLAY!
LIBERTY

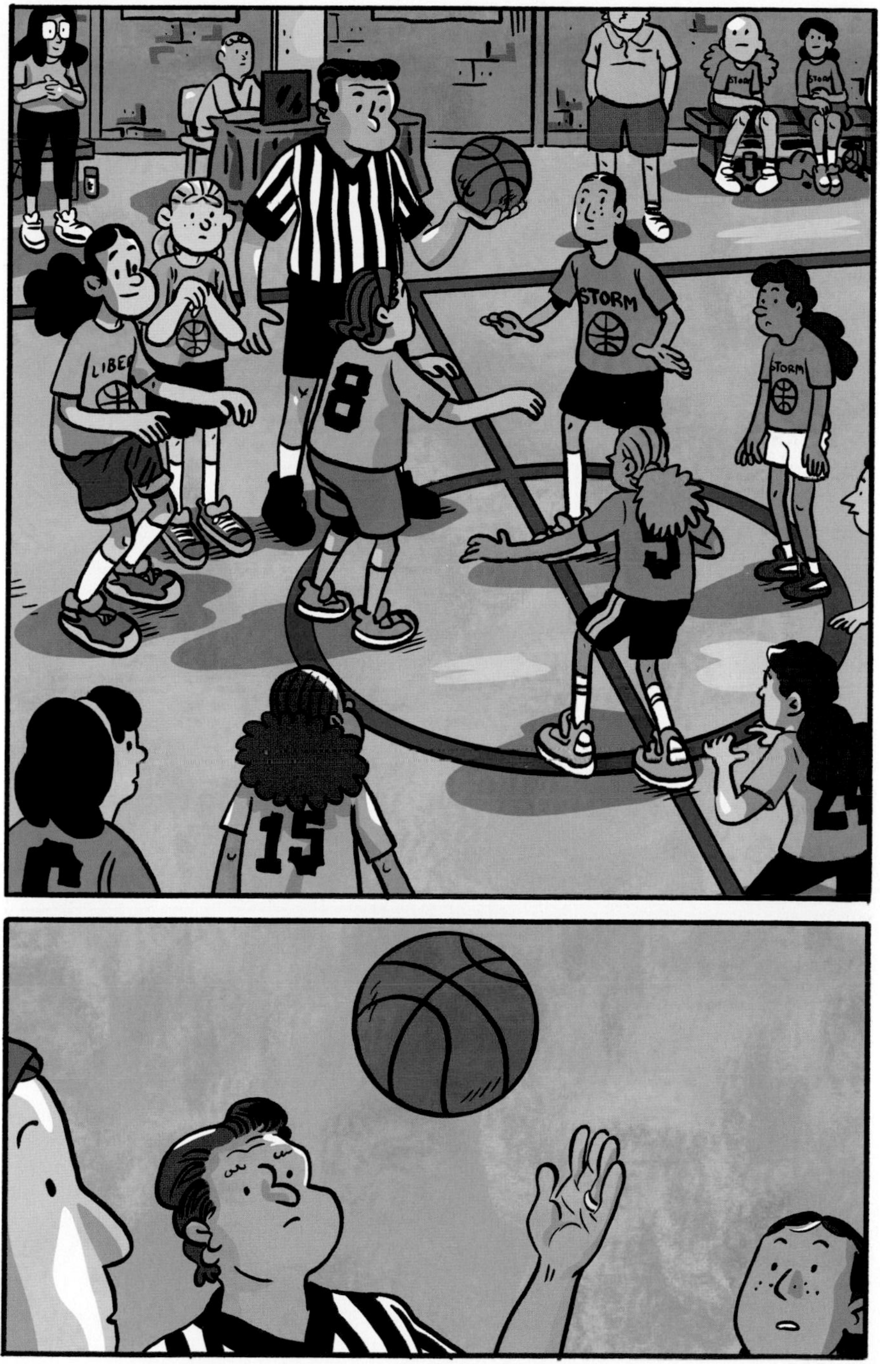
STORM
STORM
STORM
STORM
8
15

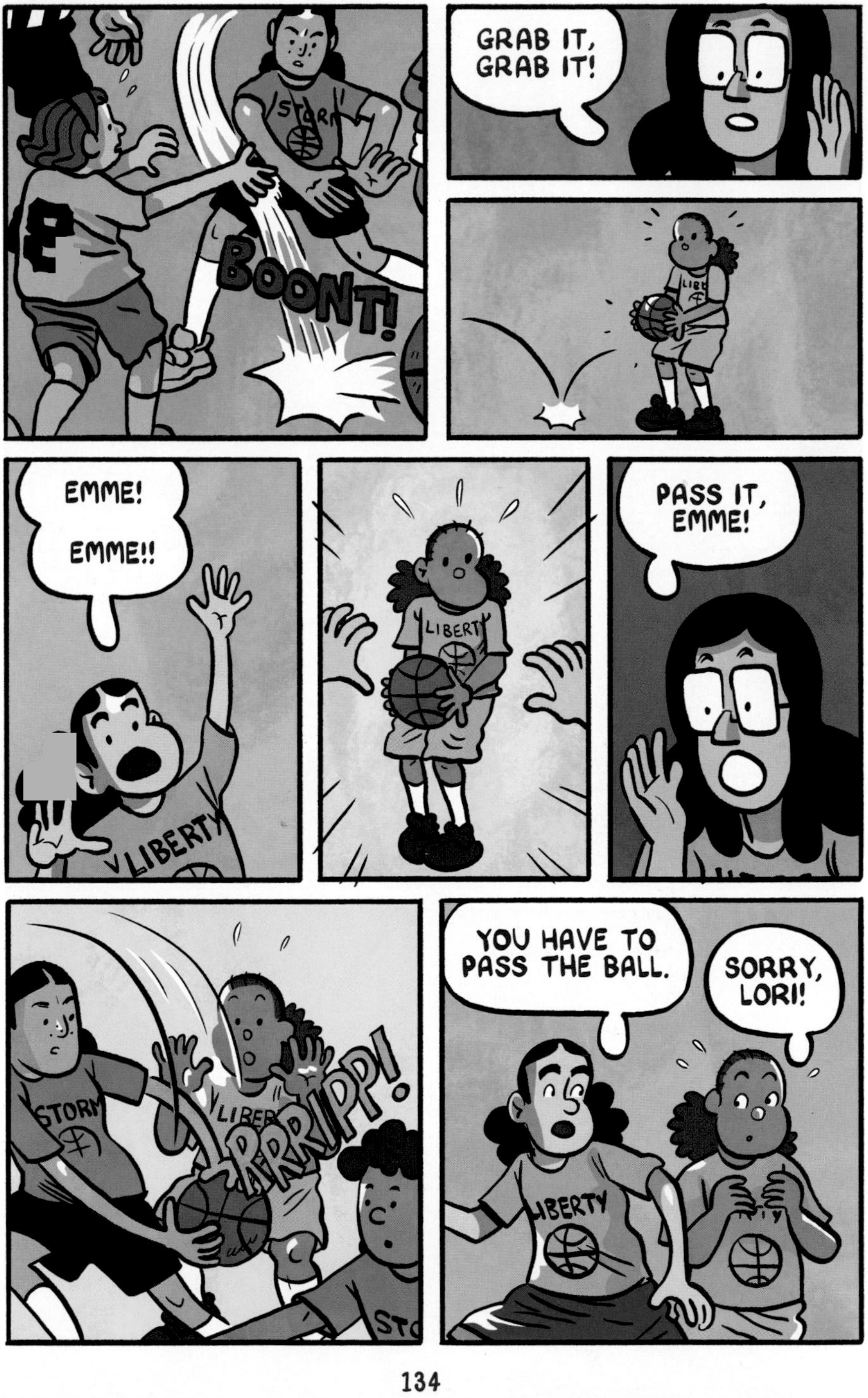
BOONT!
GRAB IT, GRAB IT!
EMME!
EMME!!
PASS IT, EMME!
RRRIPP!
YOU HAVE TO PASS THE BALL.
SORRY, LORI!

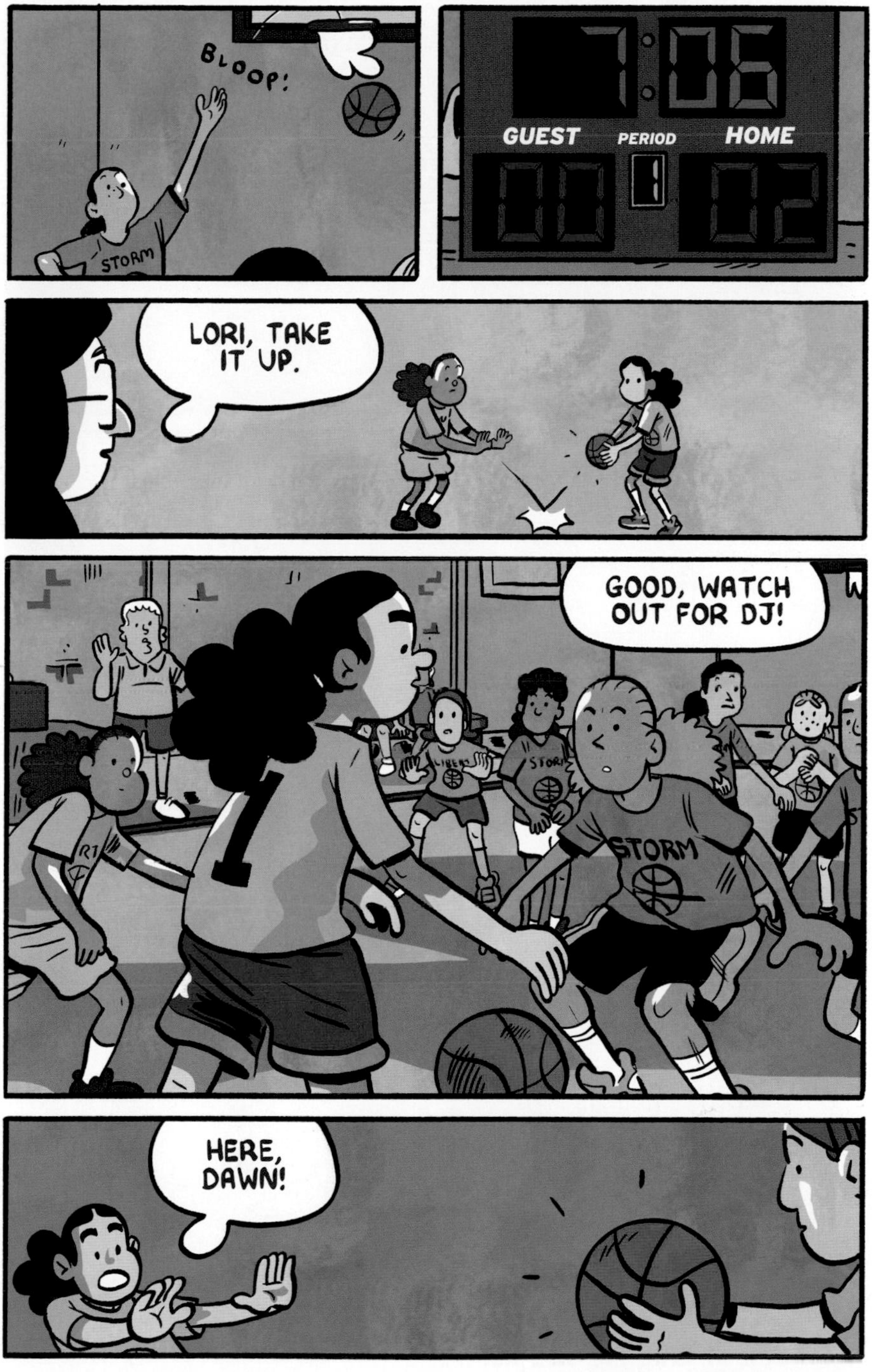
BLOOP!
STORM
7:06
GUEST
PERIOD
HOME
00
1
02
LORI, TAKE IT UP.
GOOD, WATCH OUT FOR DJ!
STORM
HERE, DAWN!

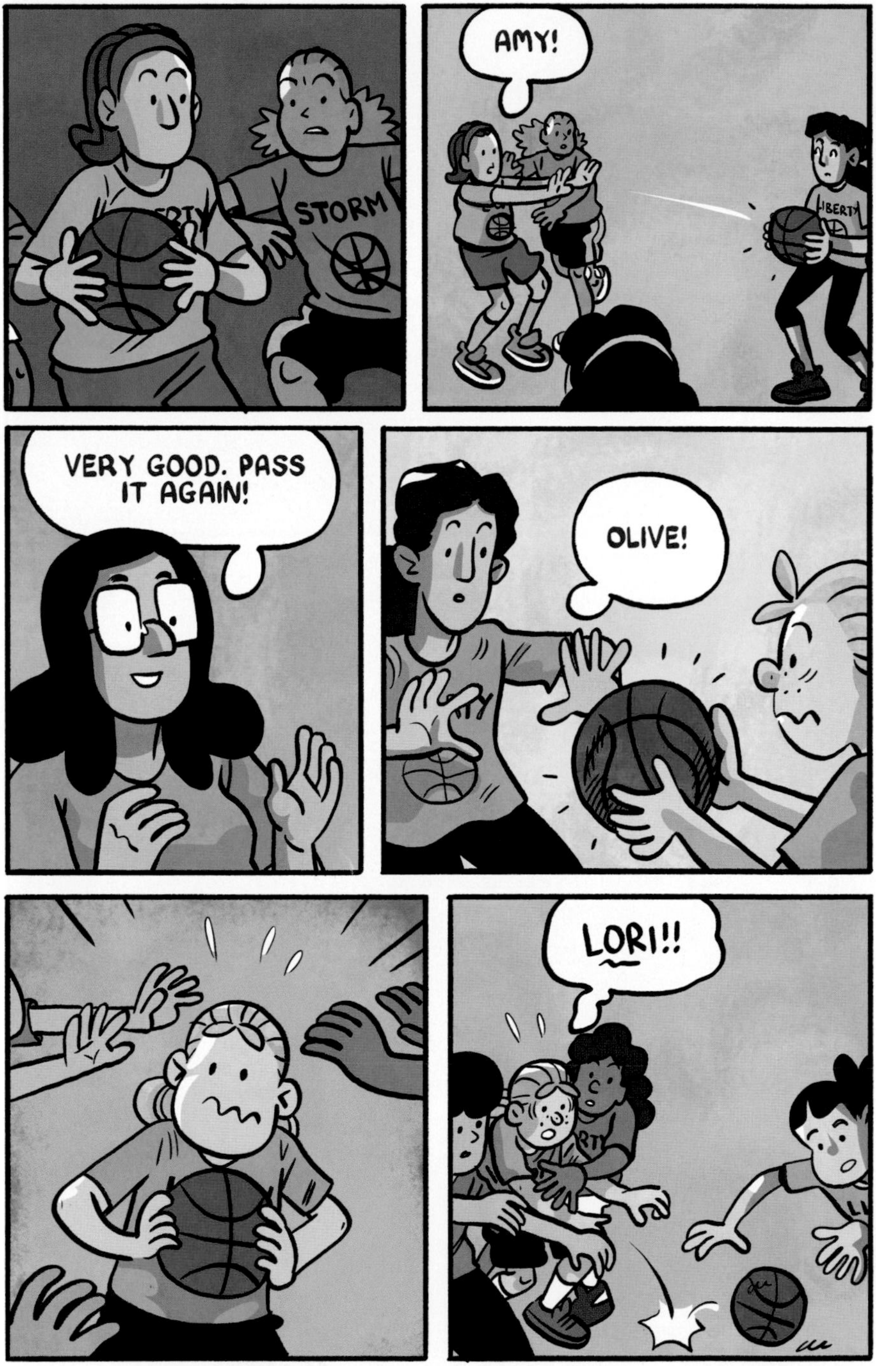
STORM
AMY!
LIBERTY
VERY GOOD. PASS IT AGAIN!
OLIVE!
LORI!!

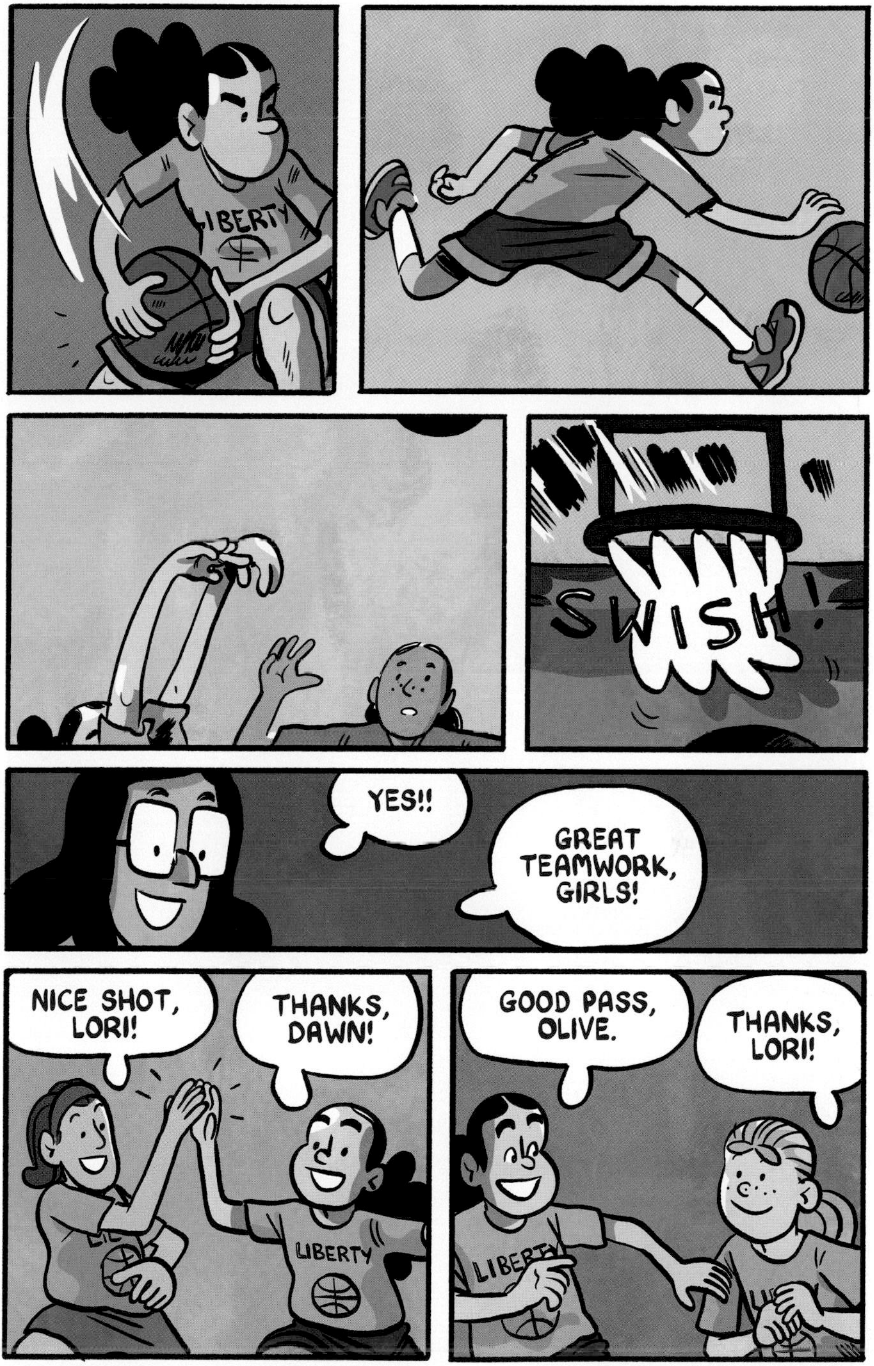
LIBERTY
SWISH!
YES!!
GREAT TEAMWORK, GIRLS!
NICE SHOT, LORI!
THANKS, DAWN!
LIBERTY
GOOD PASS, OLIVE.
THANKS, LORI!
LIBERTY

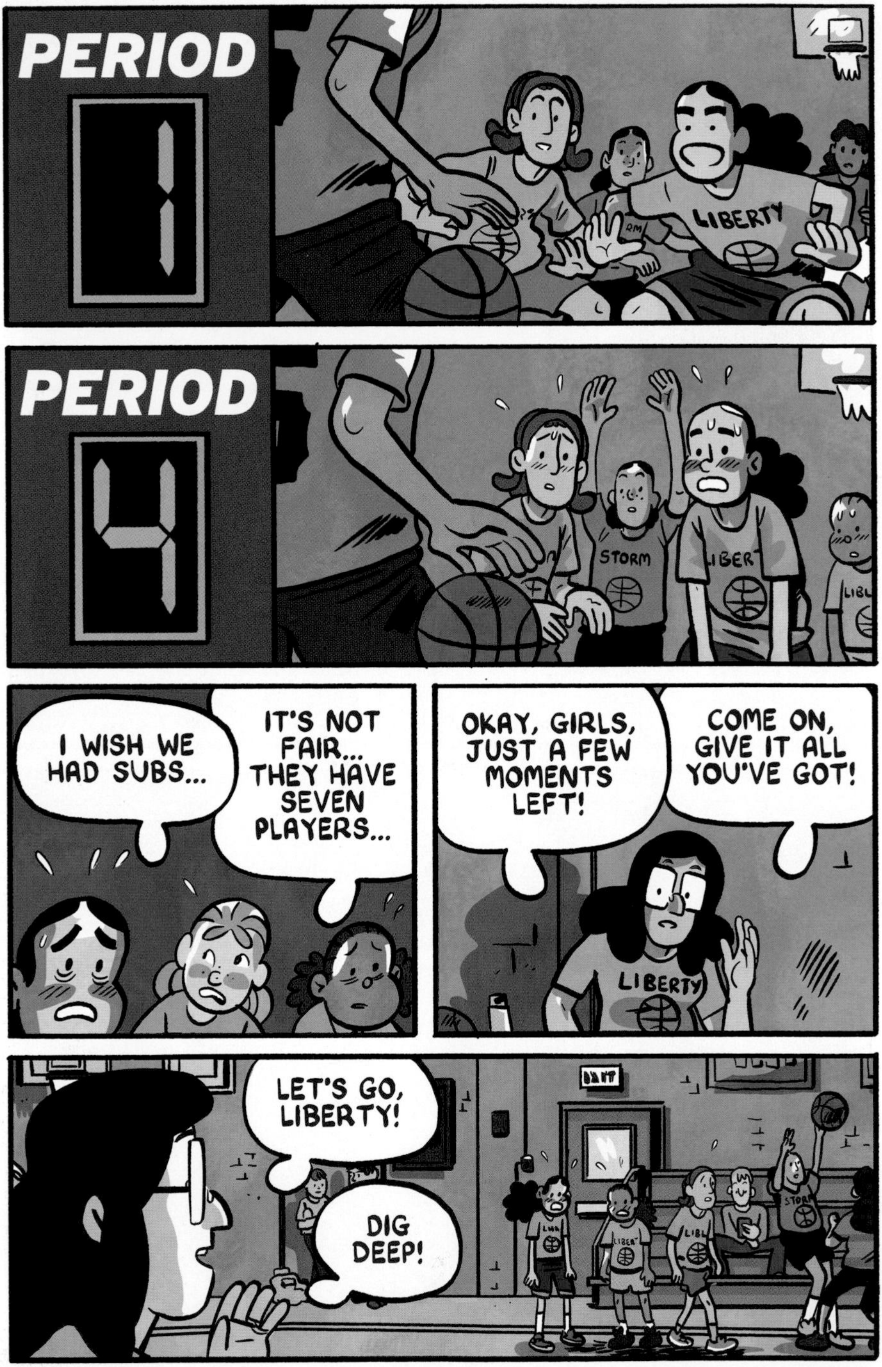

PERIOD
1
LIBERTY
PERIOD
4
STORM
I WISH WE HAD SUBS...
IT'S NOT FAIR... THEY HAVE SEVEN PLAYERS...
OKAY, GIRLS, JUST A FEW MOMENTS LEFT!
COME ON, GIVE IT ALL YOU'VE GOT!
LIBERTY
LET'S GO, LIBERTY!
DIG DEEP!

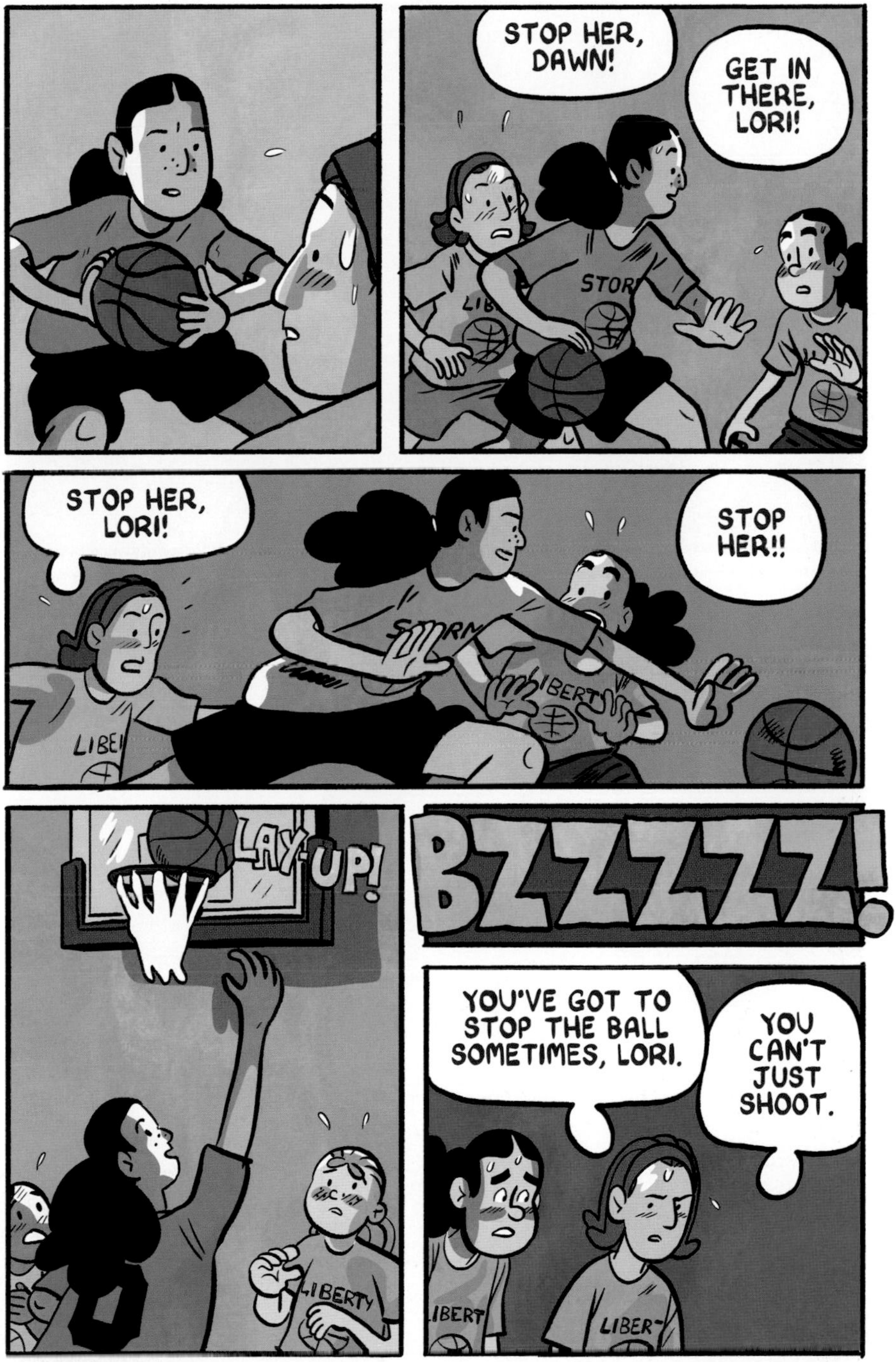
STOP HER, DAWN!
GET IN THERE, LORI!
STOR
LIB
STOP HER, LORI!
STOP HER!!
STORM
LIBERTY
LIBE
LAY-UP!
BZZZZZZ!
LIBERTY
YOU'VE GOT TO STOP THE BALL SOMETIMES, LORI.
YOU CAN'T JUST SHOOT.
LIBERT
LIBER

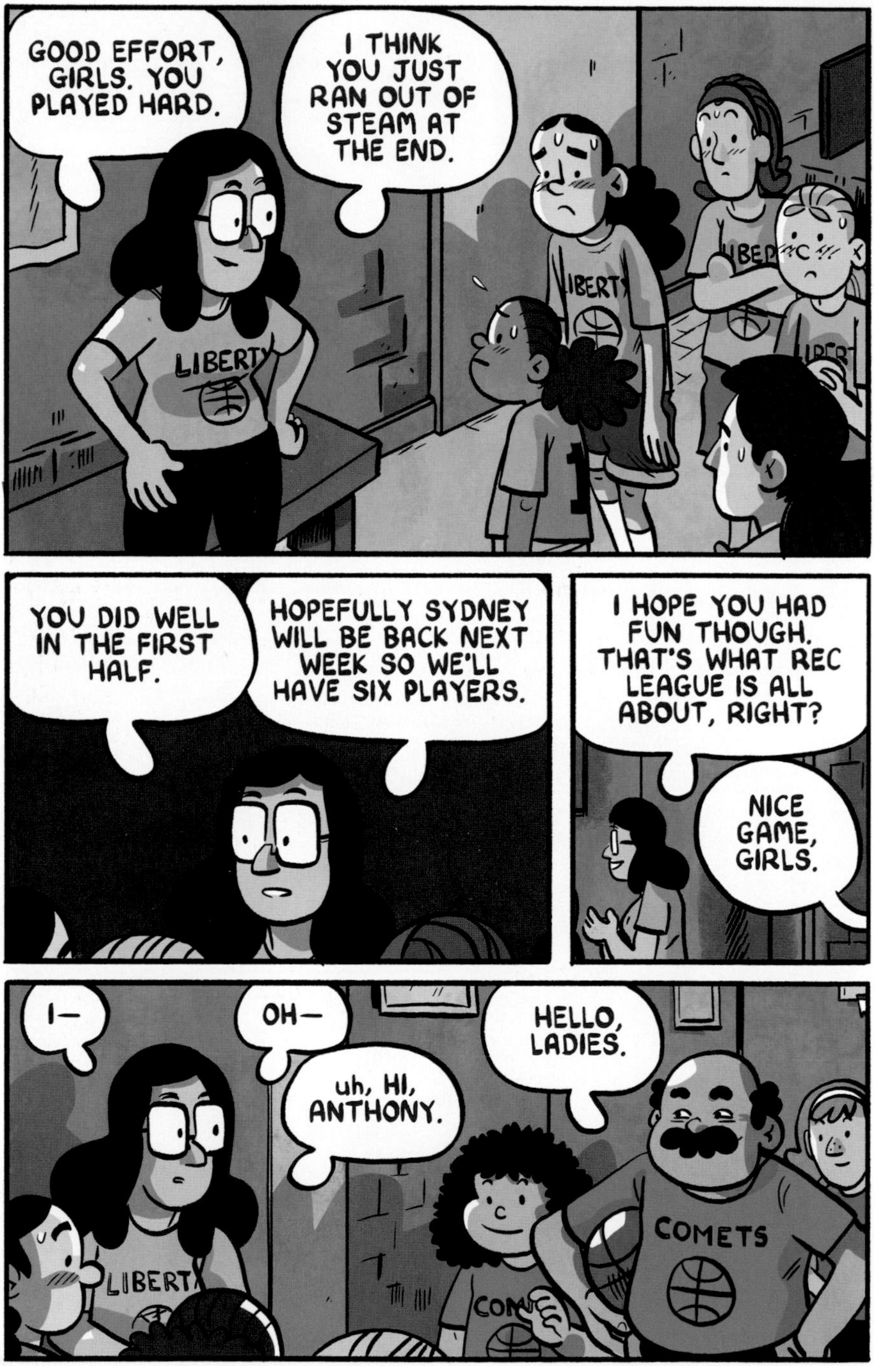
GOOD EFFORT, GIRLS. YOU PLAYED HARD.
I THINK YOU JUST RAN OUT OF STEAM AT THE END.
LIBERTY
YOU DID WELL IN THE FIRST HALF.
HOPEFULLY SYDNEY WILL BE BACK NEXT WEEK SO WE'LL HAVE SIX PLAYERS.
I HOPE YOU HAD FUN THOUGH. THAT'S WHAT REC LEAGUE IS ALL ABOUT, RIGHT?
NICE GAME, GIRLS.
I—
OH—
uh, HI, ANTHONY.
HELLO, LADIES.
COMETS

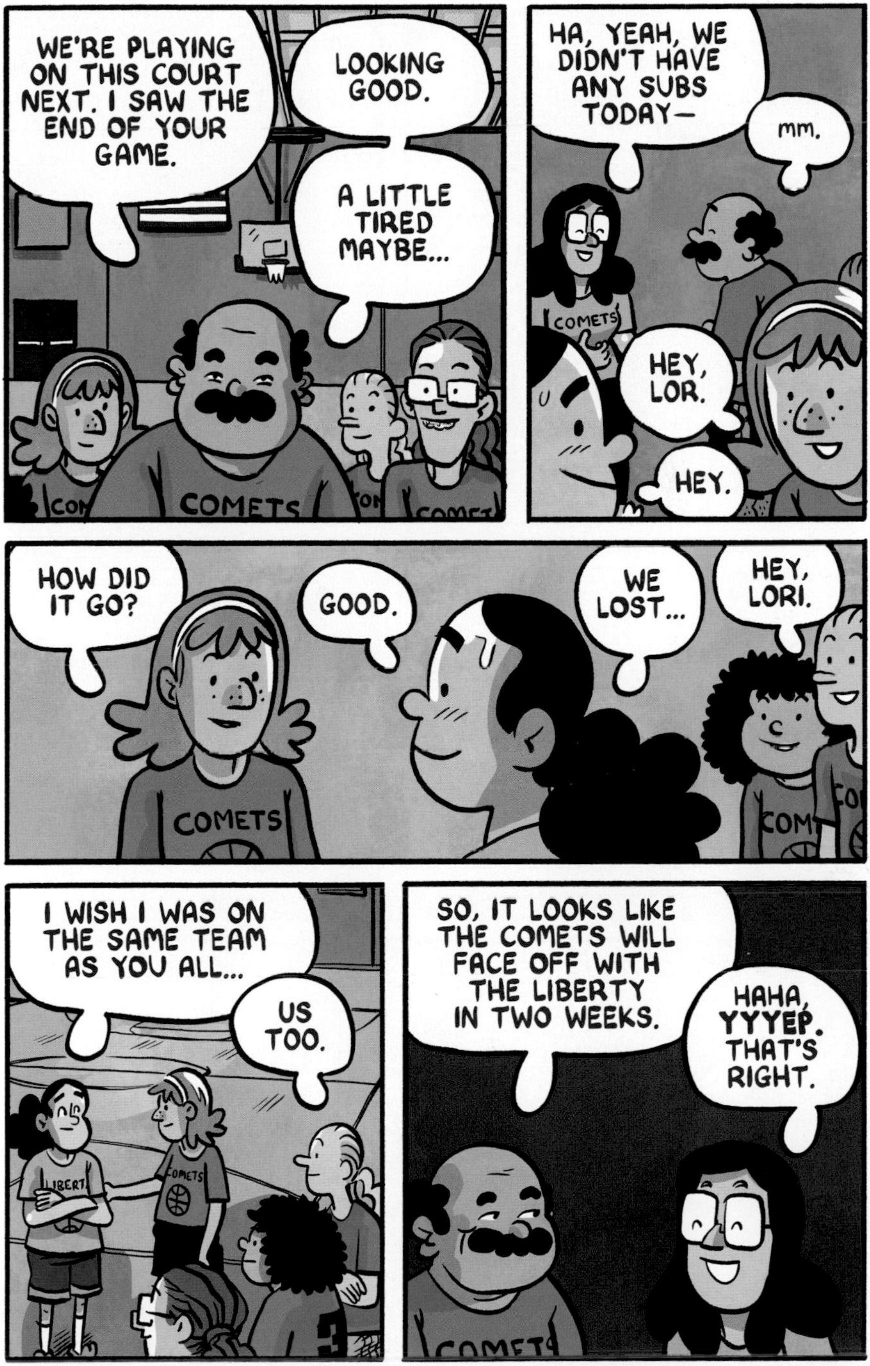
WE'RE PLAYING ON THIS COURT NEXT. I SAW THE END OF YOUR GAME.
LOOKING GOOD.
A LITTLE TIRED MAYBE...
HA, YEAH, WE DIDN'T HAVE ANY SUBS TODAY—
mm.
HEY, LOR.
HEY.
HOW DID IT GO?
GOOD.
WE LOST...
HEY, LORI.
I WISH I WAS ON THE SAME TEAM AS YOU ALL...
US TOO.
SO, IT LOOKS LIKE THE COMETS WILL FACE OFF WITH THE LIBERTY IN TWO WEEKS.
HAHA, **YYYEP**. THAT'S RIGHT.

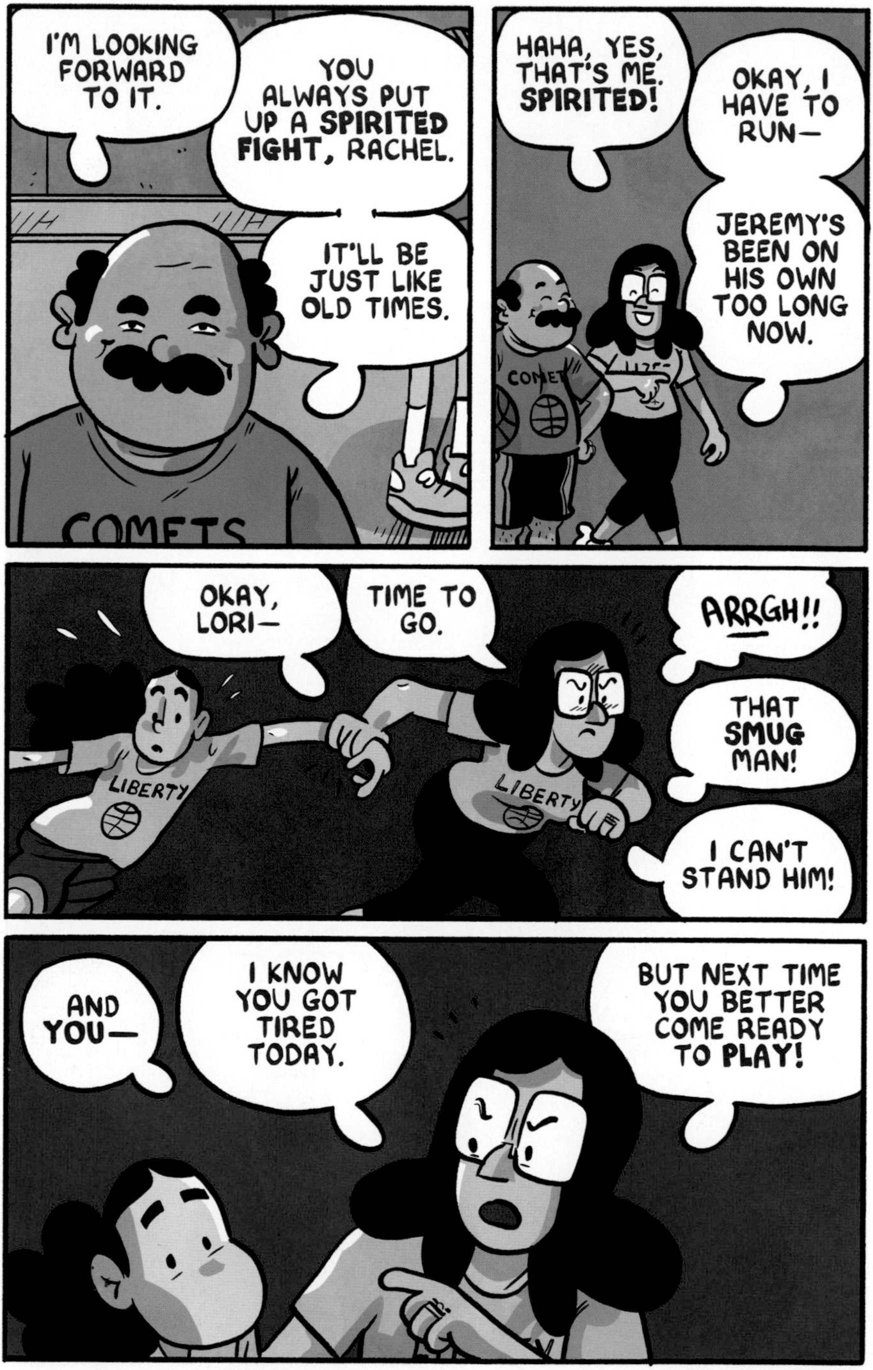
I'M LOOKING FORWARD TO IT.
YOU ALWAYS PUT UP A **SPIRITED FIGHT**, RACHEL.
IT'LL BE JUST LIKE OLD TIMES.
COMETS
HAHA, YES, THAT'S ME. **SPIRITED!**
OKAY, I HAVE TO RUN—
JEREMY'S BEEN ON HIS OWN TOO LONG NOW.
OKAY, LORI—
TIME TO GO.
ARRGH!!
THAT **SMUG** MAN!
I CAN'T STAND HIM!
LIBERTY
LIBERTY
AND **YOU**—
I KNOW YOU GOT TIRED TODAY.
BUT NEXT TIME YOU BETTER COME READY TO **PLAY!**

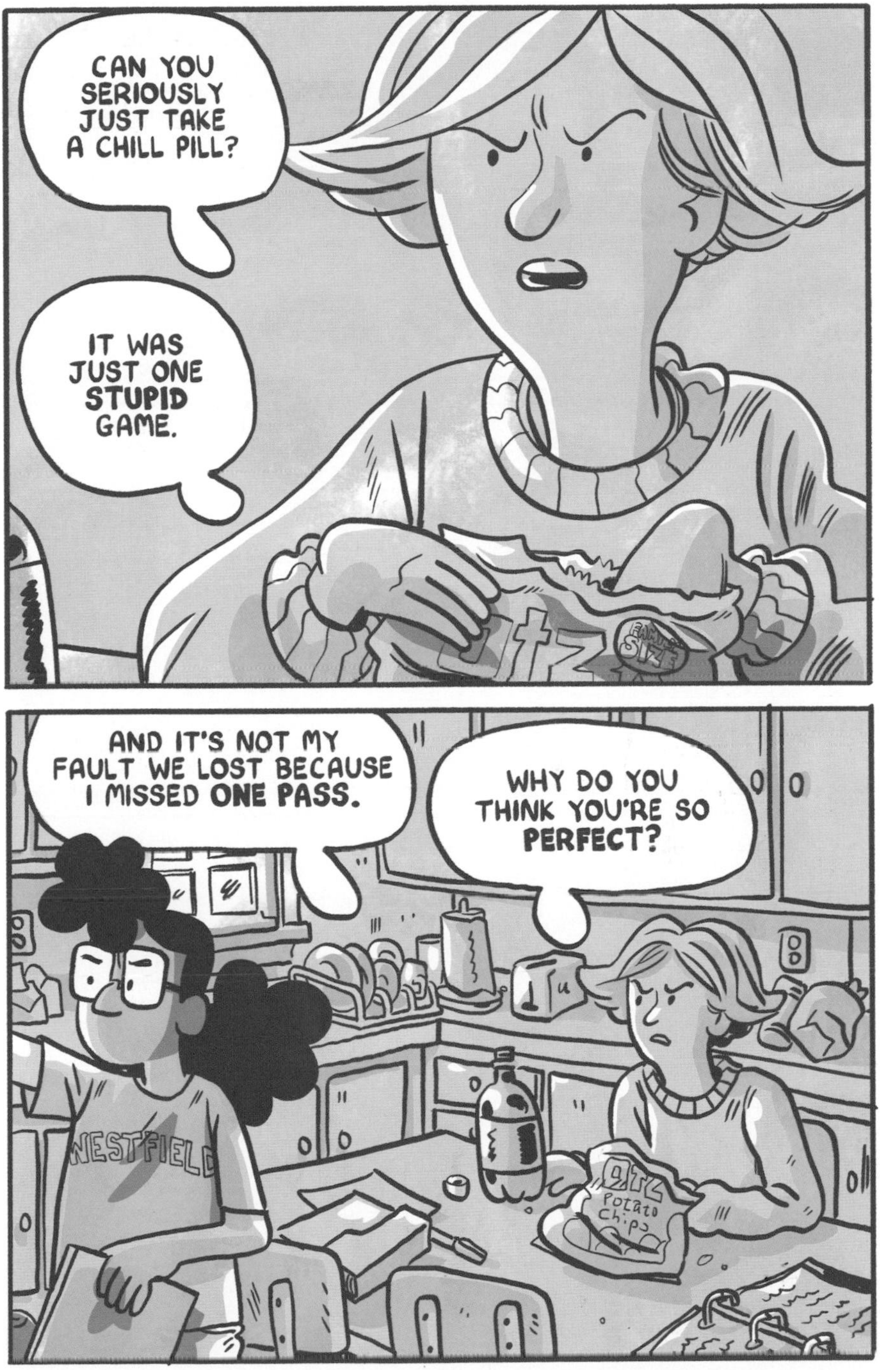
CAN YOU SERIOUSLY JUST TAKE A CHILL PILL?
IT WAS JUST ONE **STUPID** GAME.
AND IT'S NOT MY FAULT WE LOST BECAUSE I MISSED **ONE PASS.**
WHY DO YOU THINK YOU'RE SO **PERFECT?**
WESTFIELD
QTZ
Potato Chips

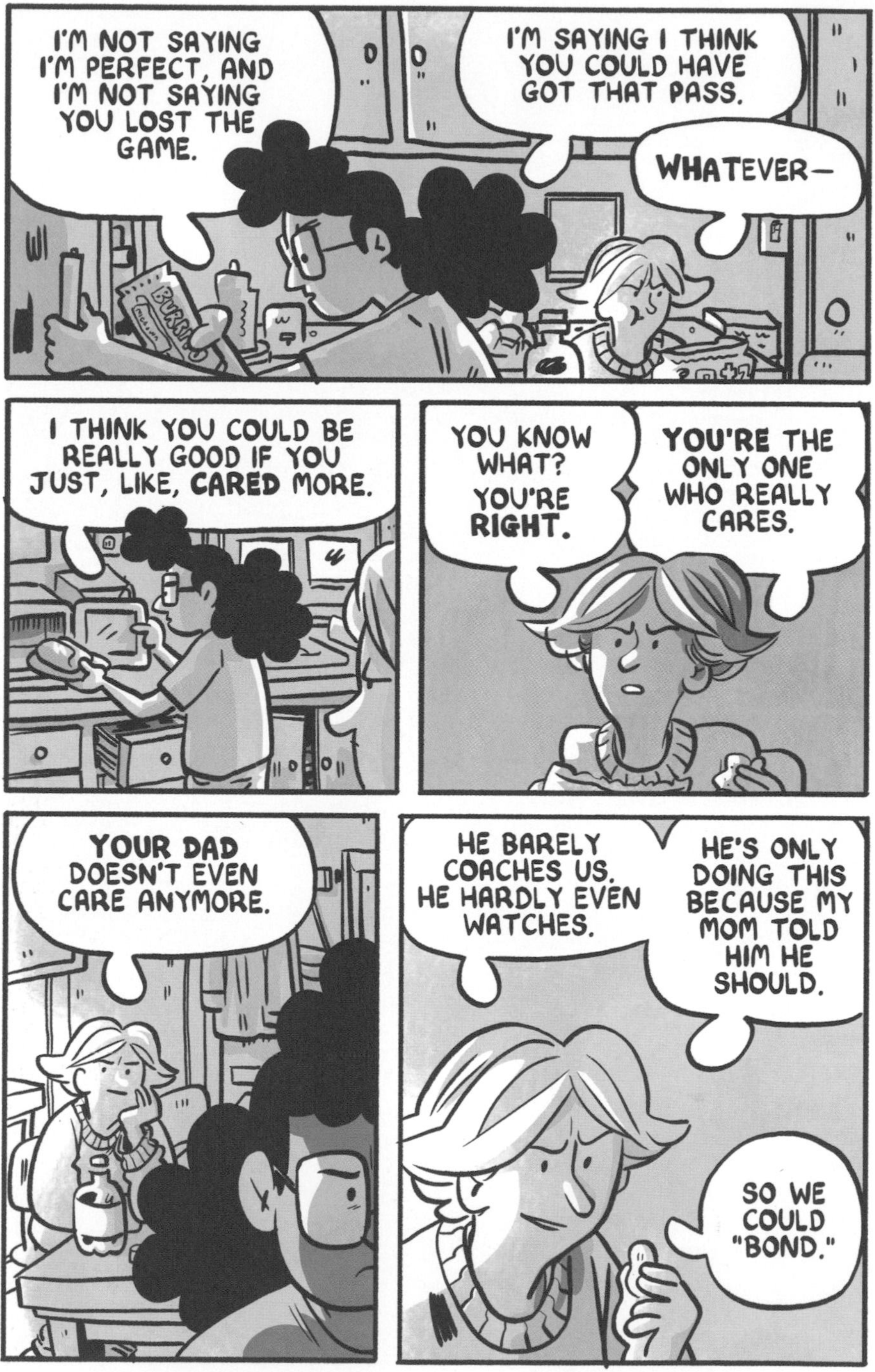
I'M NOT SAYING I'M PERFECT, AND I'M NOT SAYING YOU LOST THE GAME.
I'M SAYING I THINK YOU COULD HAVE GOT THAT PASS.
WHATEVER—
I THINK YOU COULD BE REALLY GOOD IF YOU JUST, LIKE, CARED MORE.
YOU KNOW WHAT? YOU'RE RIGHT.
YOU'RE THE ONLY ONE WHO REALLY CARES.
YOUR DAD DOESN'T EVEN CARE ANYMORE.
HE BARELY COACHES US. HE HARDLY EVEN WATCHES.
HE'S ONLY DOING THIS BECAUSE MY MOM TOLD HIM HE SHOULD.
SO WE COULD "BOND."

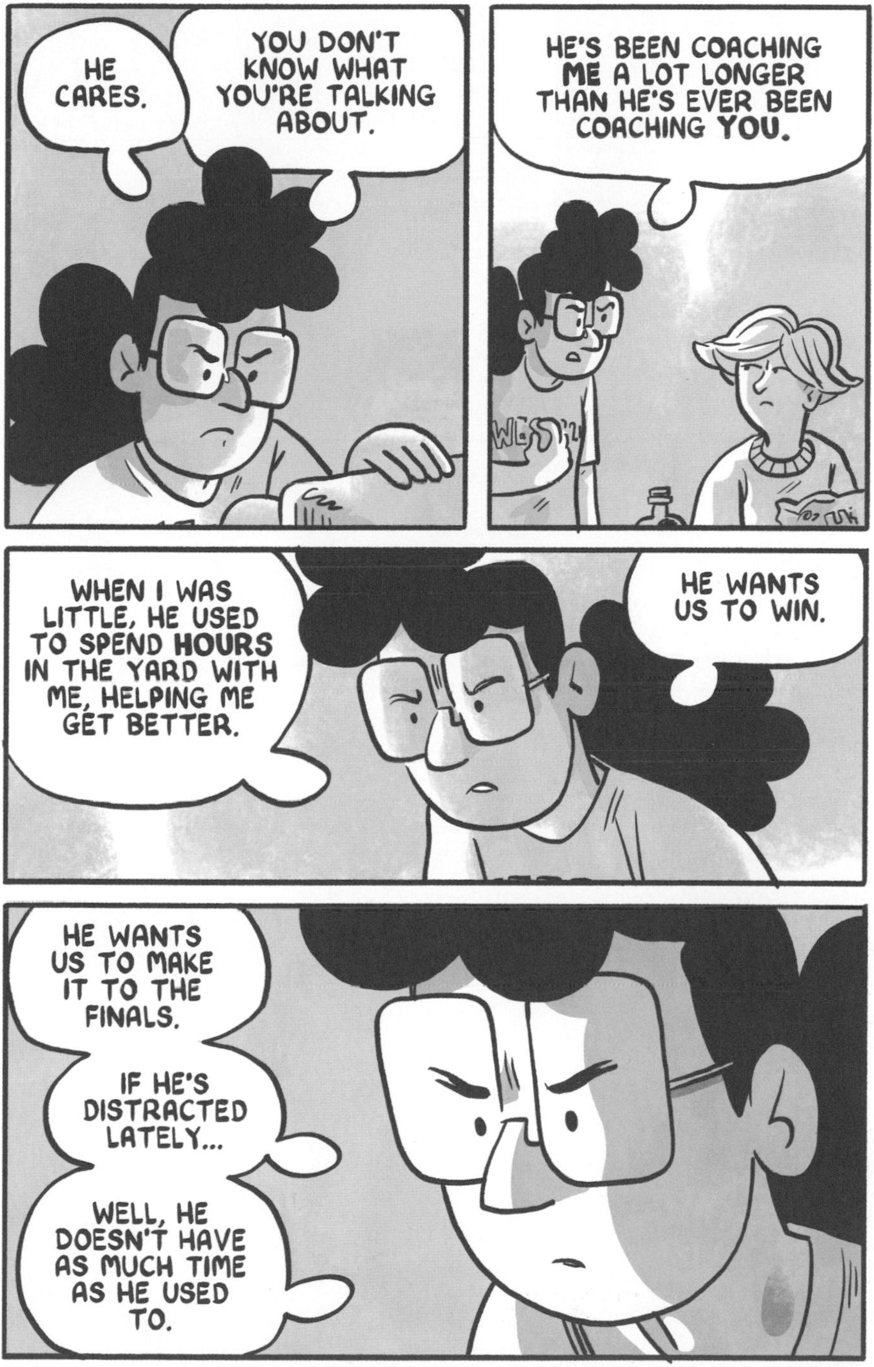
HE CARES.
YOU DON'T KNOW WHAT YOU'RE TALKING ABOUT.
HE'S BEEN COACHING **ME** A LOT LONGER THAN HE'S EVER BEEN COACHING **YOU.**
WHEN I WAS LITTLE, HE USED TO SPEND **HOURS** IN THE YARD WITH ME, HELPING ME GET BETTER.
HE WANTS US TO WIN.
HE WANTS US TO MAKE IT TO THE FINALS.
IF HE'S DISTRACTED LATELY...
WELL, HE DOESN'T HAVE AS MUCH TIME AS HE USED TO.

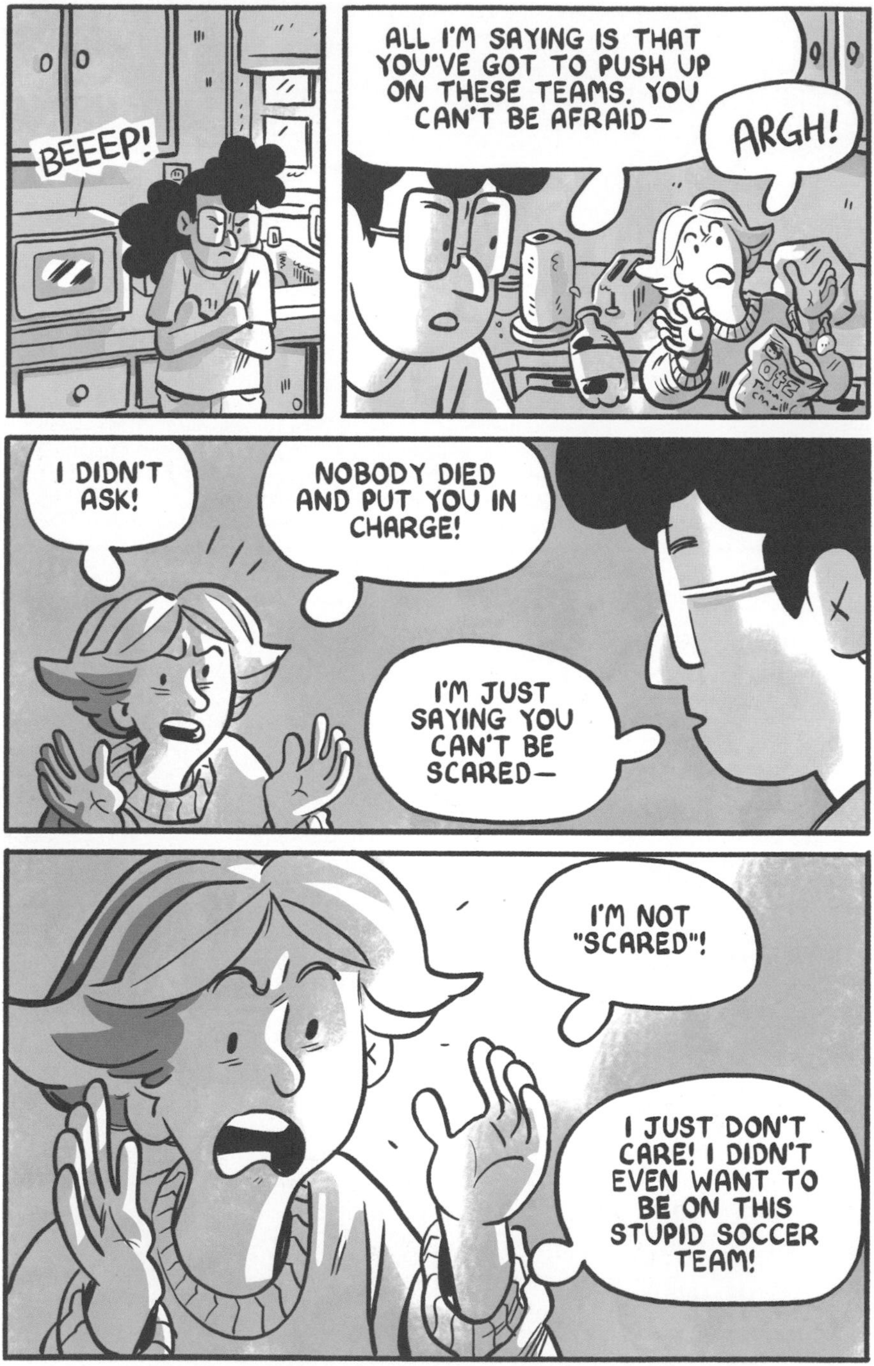
BEEEP!
ALL I'M SAYING IS THAT YOU'VE GOT TO PUSH UP ON THESE TEAMS. YOU CAN'T BE AFRAID—
ARGH!
I DIDN'T ASK!
NOBODY DIED AND PUT YOU IN CHARGE!
I'M JUST SAYING YOU CAN'T BE SCARED—
I'M NOT "SCARED"!
I JUST DON'T CARE! I DIDN'T EVEN WANT TO BE ON THIS STUPID SOCCER TEAM!

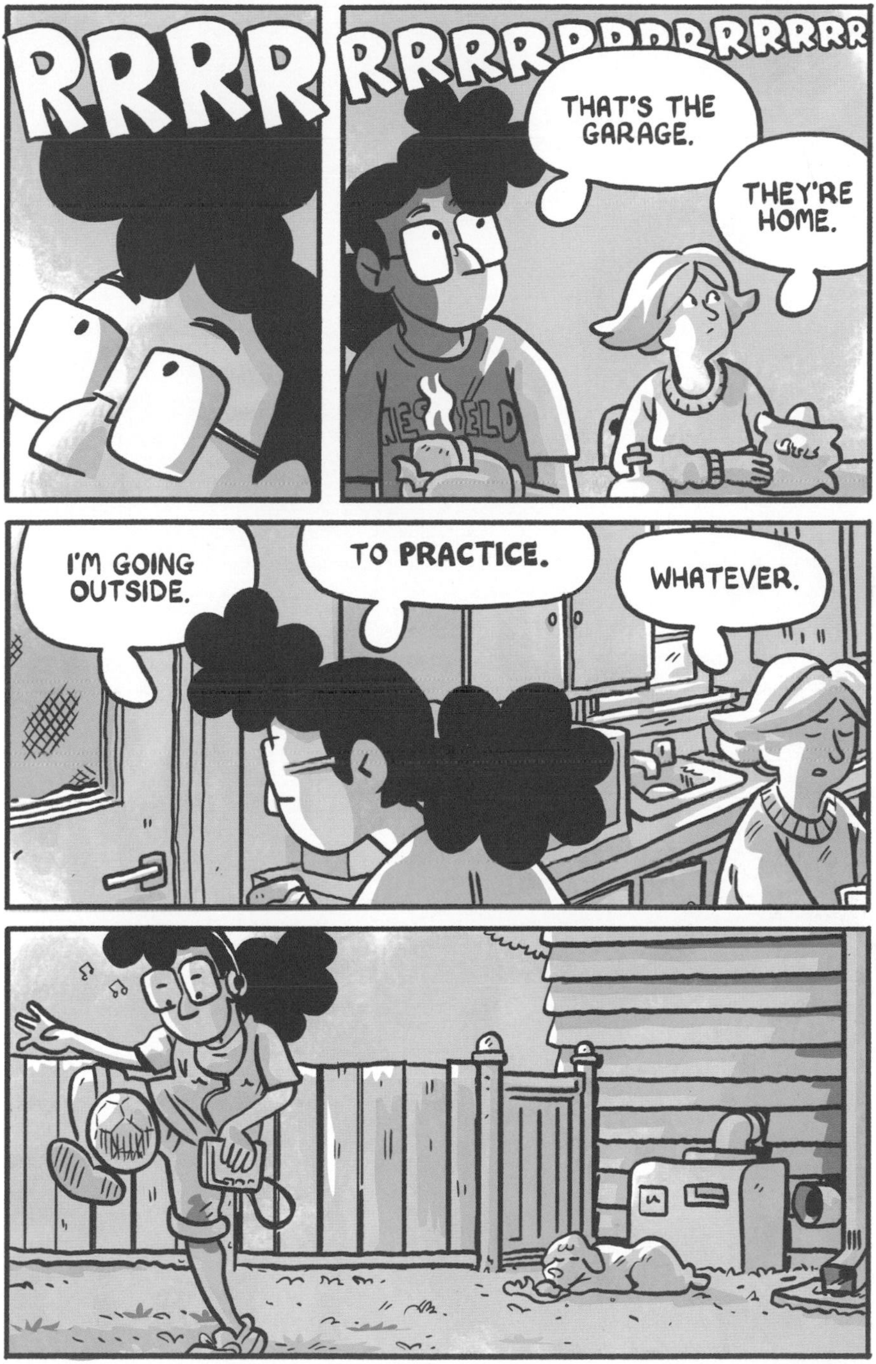
RRRRRRRRRRRRRRR
THAT'S THE GARAGE.
THEY'RE HOME.
I'M GOING OUTSIDE.
TO PRACTICE.
WHATEVER.

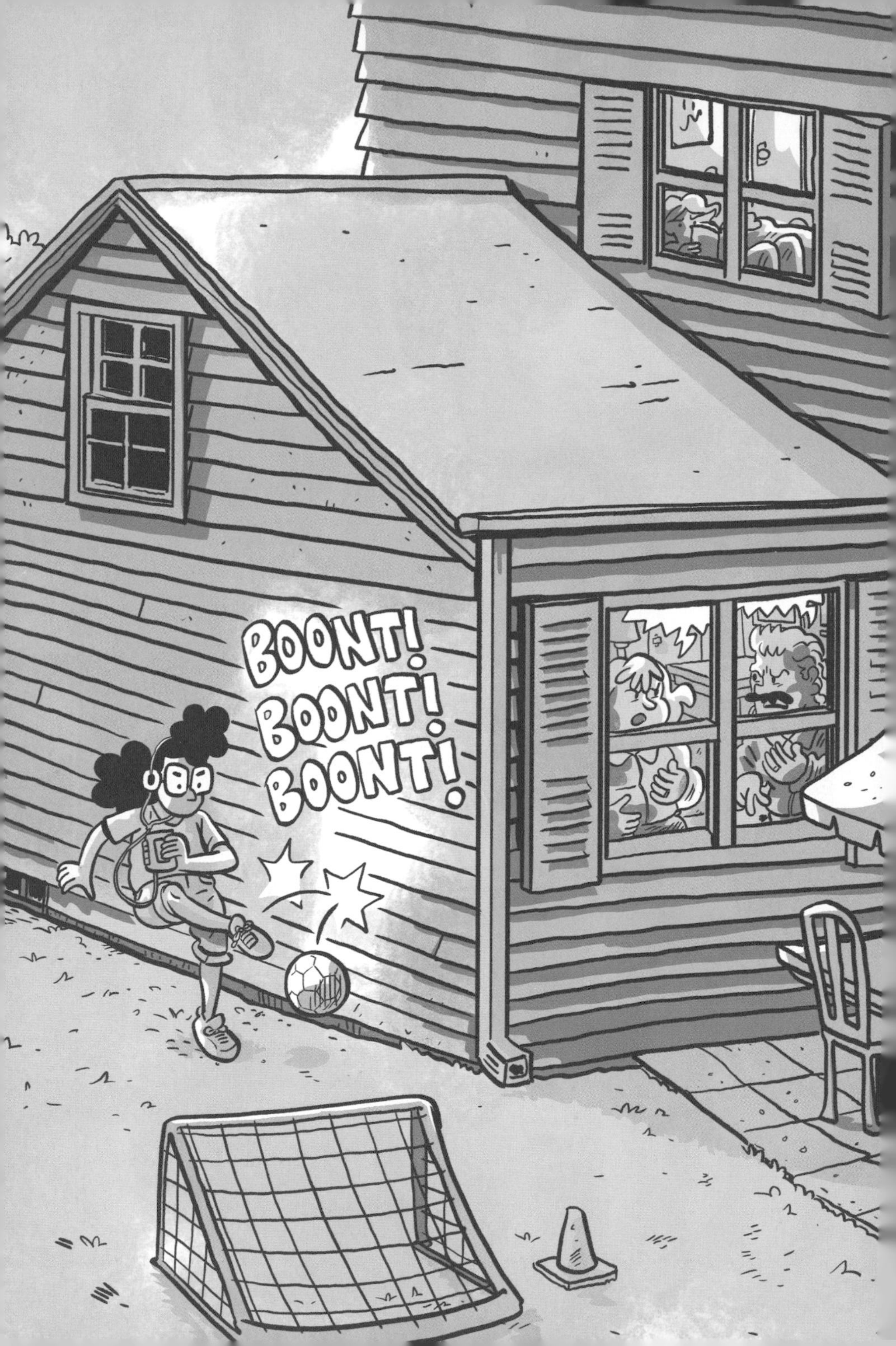
BOONT!
BOONT!
BOONT!

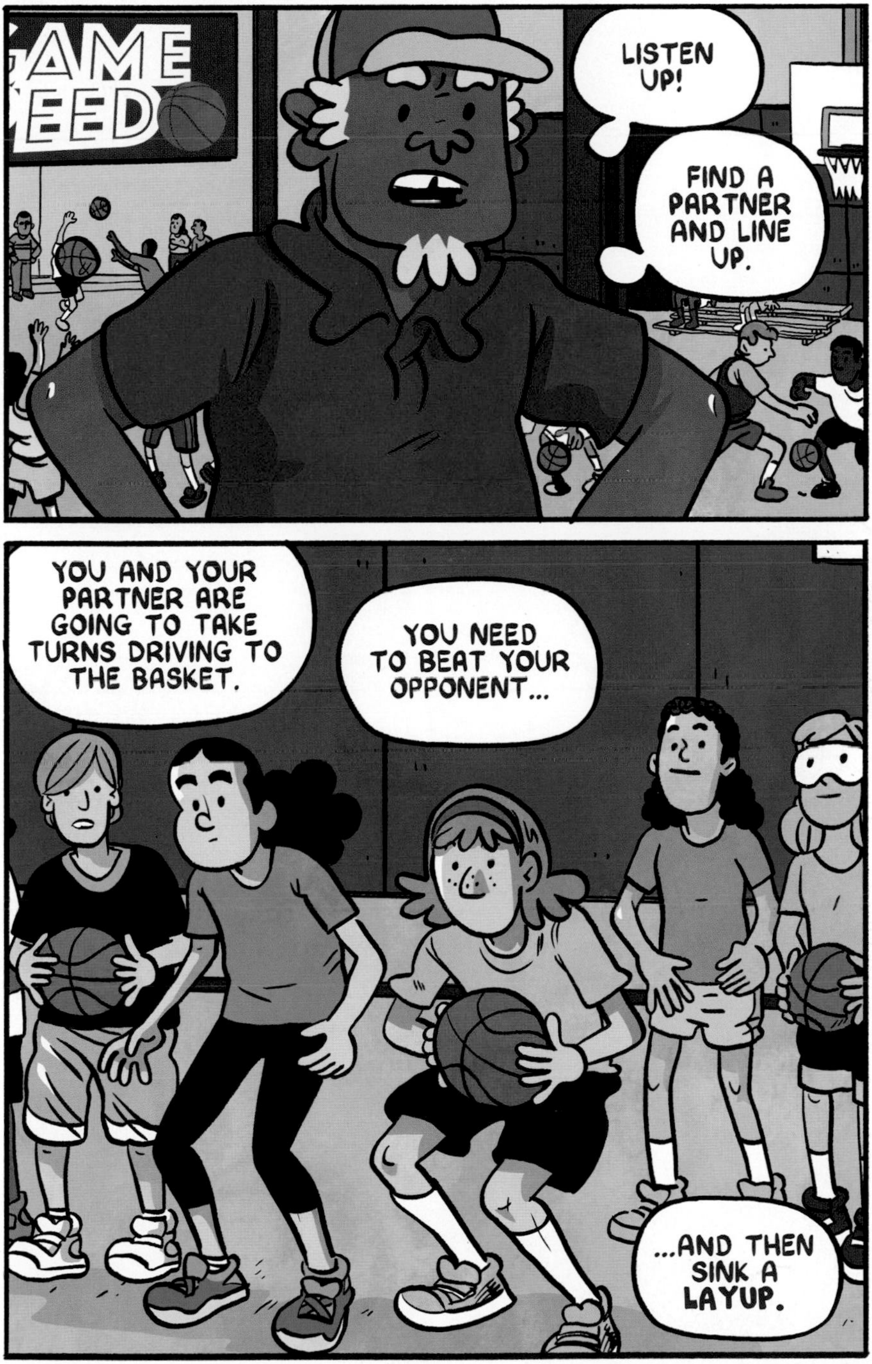
GAME
EED
LISTEN UP!
FIND A PARTNER AND LINE UP.
YOU AND YOUR PARTNER ARE GOING TO TAKE TURNS DRIVING TO THE BASKET.
YOU NEED TO BEAT YOUR OPPONENT...
...AND THEN SINK A **LAYUP.**

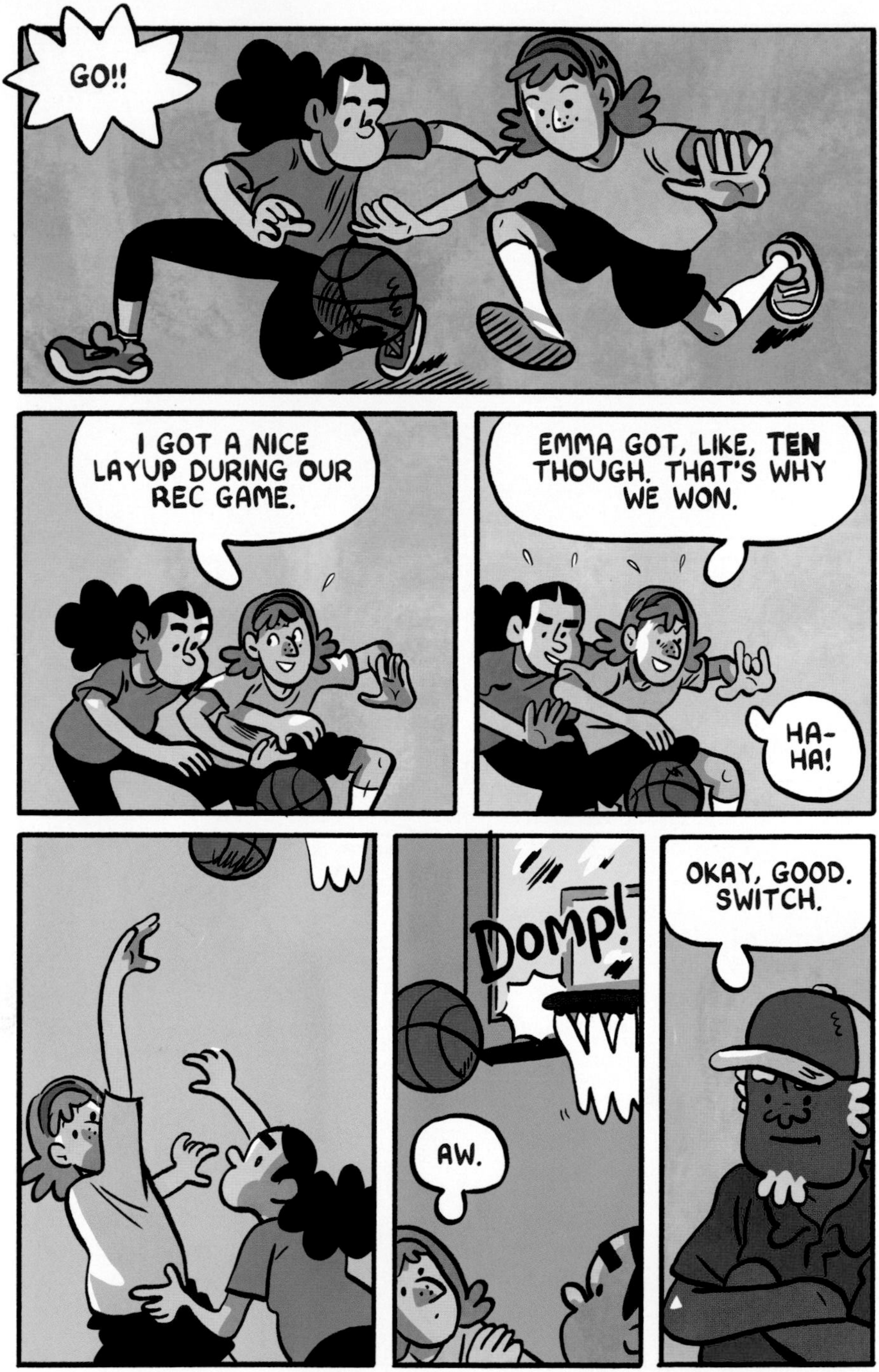
GO!!
I GOT A NICE LAYUP DURING OUR REC GAME.
EMMA GOT, LIKE, TEN THOUGH. THAT'S WHY WE WON.
HA-HA!
DOMP!
AW.
OKAY, GOOD. SWITCH.

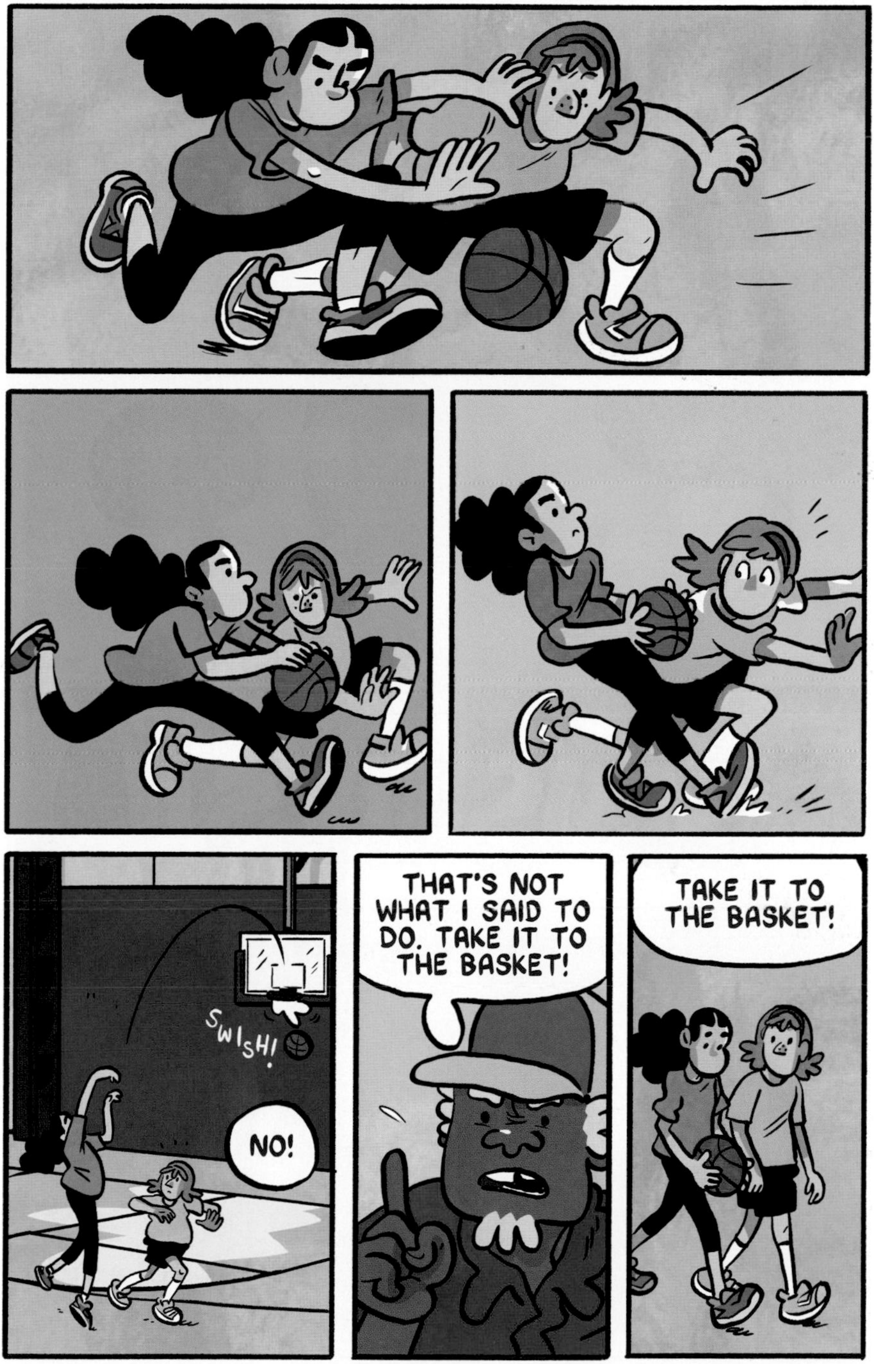
SWISH!
NO!
THAT'S NOT WHAT I SAID TO DO. TAKE IT TO THE BASKET!
TAKE IT TO THE BASKET!

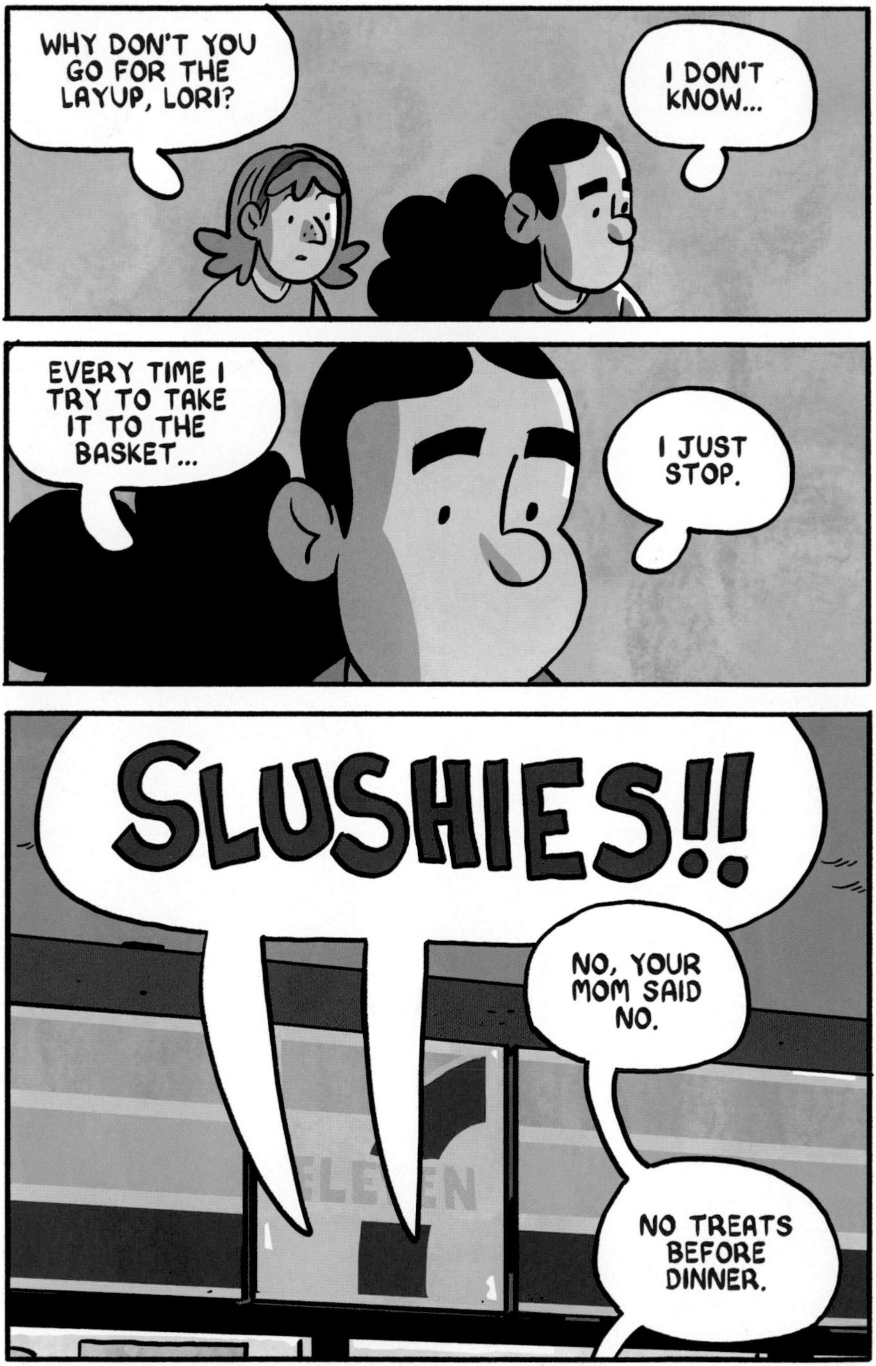
WHY DON'T YOU GO FOR THE LAYUP, LORI?
I DON'T KNOW...
EVERY TIME I TRY TO TAKE IT TO THE BASKET...
I JUST STOP.
SLUSHIES!!
NO, YOUR MOM SAID NO.
NO TREATS BEFORE DINNER.

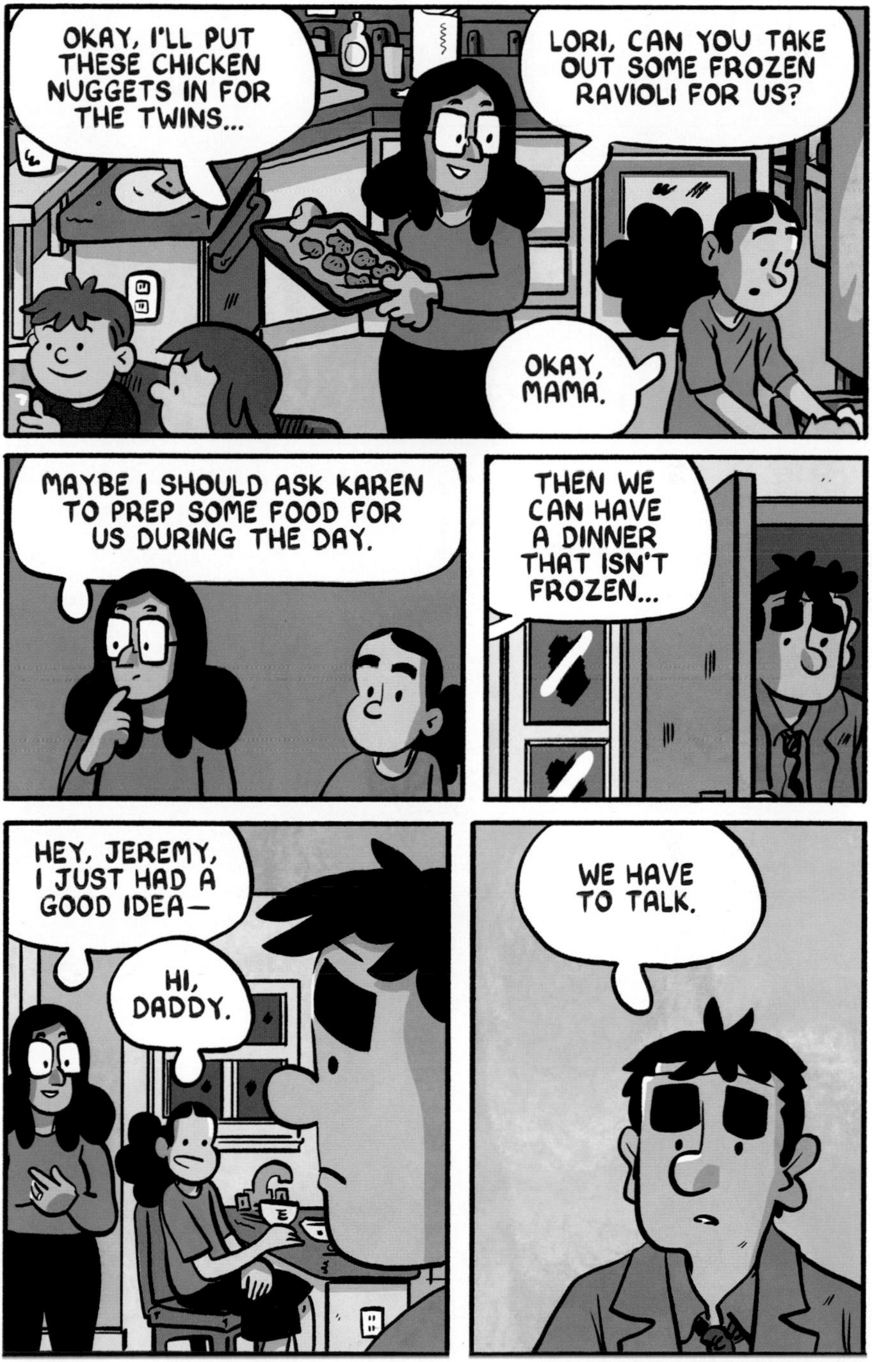
OKAY, I'LL PUT THESE CHICKEN NUGGETS IN FOR THE TWINS...
LORI, CAN YOU TAKE OUT SOME FROZEN RAVIOLI FOR US?
OKAY, MAMA.
MAYBE I SHOULD ASK KAREN TO PREP SOME FOOD FOR US DURING THE DAY.
THEN WE CAN HAVE A DINNER THAT ISN'T FROZEN...
HEY, JEREMY, I JUST HAD A GOOD IDEA—
HI, DADDY.
WE HAVE TO TALK.

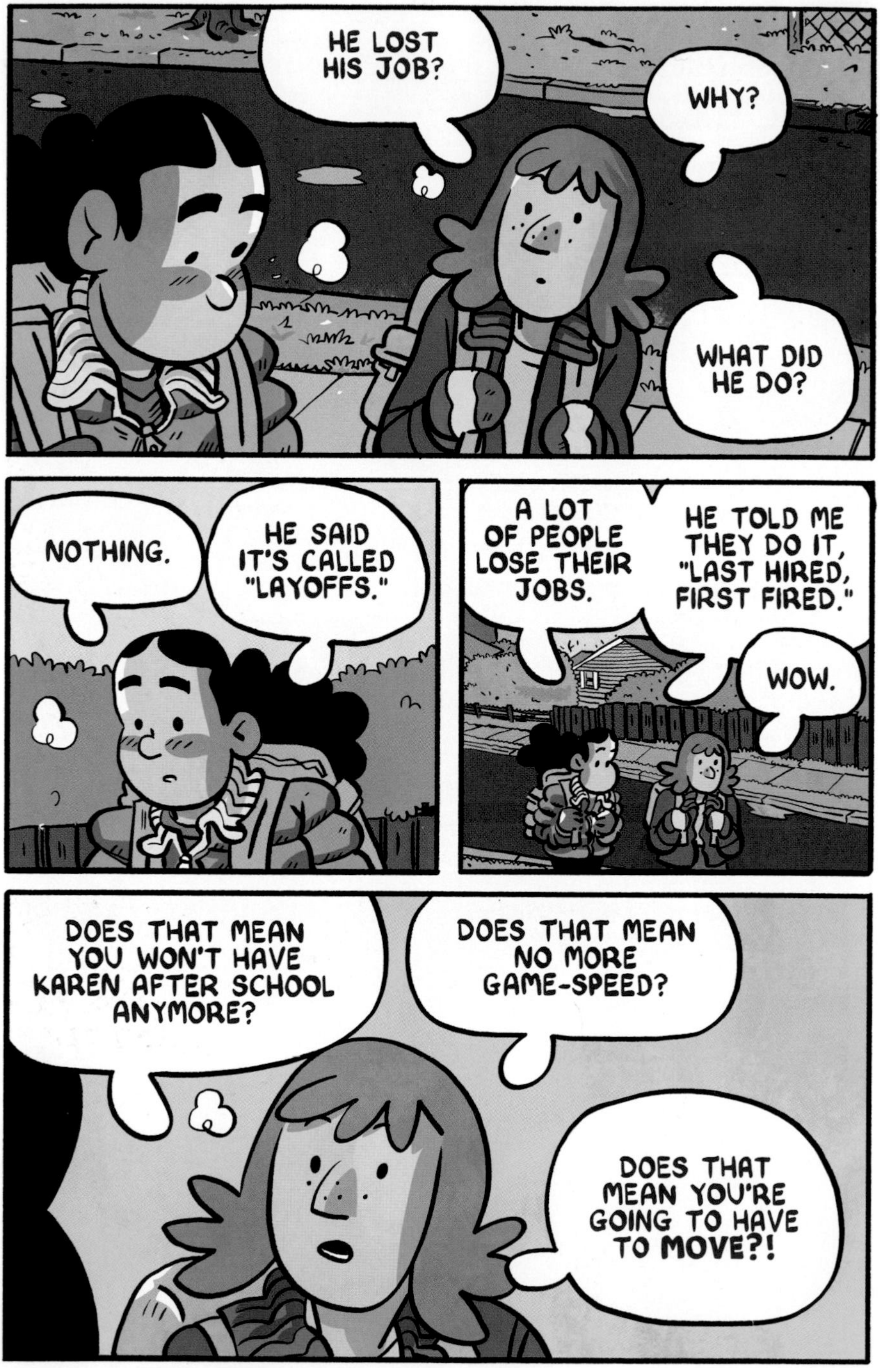
HE LOST HIS JOB?
WHY?
WHAT DID HE DO?
NOTHING.
HE SAID IT'S CALLED "LAYOFFS."
A LOT OF PEOPLE LOSE THEIR JOBS.
HE TOLD ME THEY DO IT, "LAST HIRED, FIRST FIRED."
WOW.
DOES THAT MEAN YOU WON'T HAVE KAREN AFTER SCHOOL ANYMORE?
DOES THAT MEAN NO MORE GAME-SPEED?
DOES THAT MEAN YOU'RE GOING TO HAVE TO **MOVE**?!

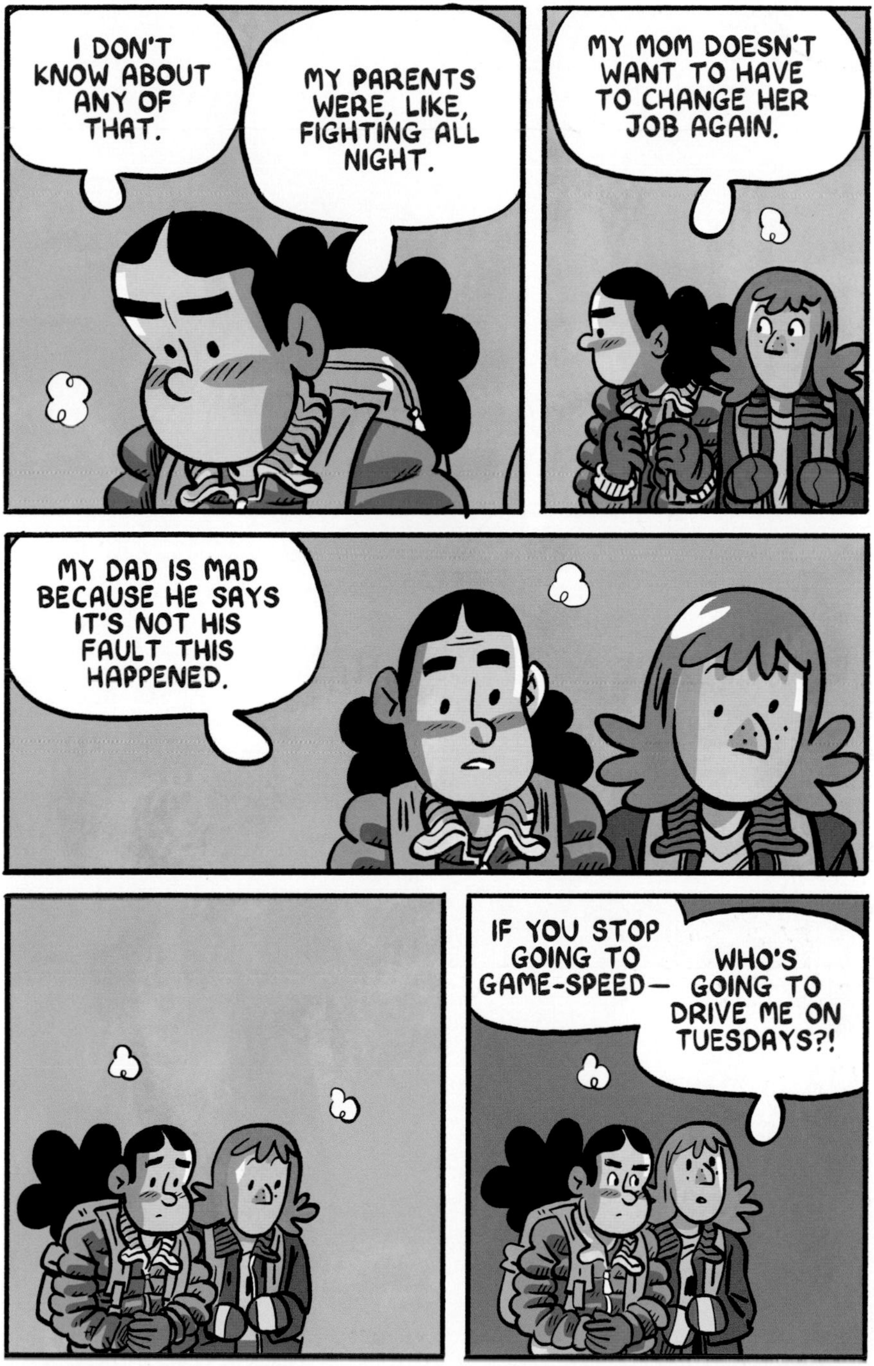
I DON'T KNOW ABOUT ANY OF THAT.
MY PARENTS WERE, LIKE, FIGHTING ALL NIGHT.
MY MOM DOESN'T WANT TO HAVE TO CHANGE HER JOB AGAIN.
MY DAD IS MAD BECAUSE HE SAYS IT'S NOT HIS FAULT THIS HAPPENED.
IF YOU STOP GOING TO GAME-SPEED—
WHO'S GOING TO DRIVE ME ON TUESDAYS?!

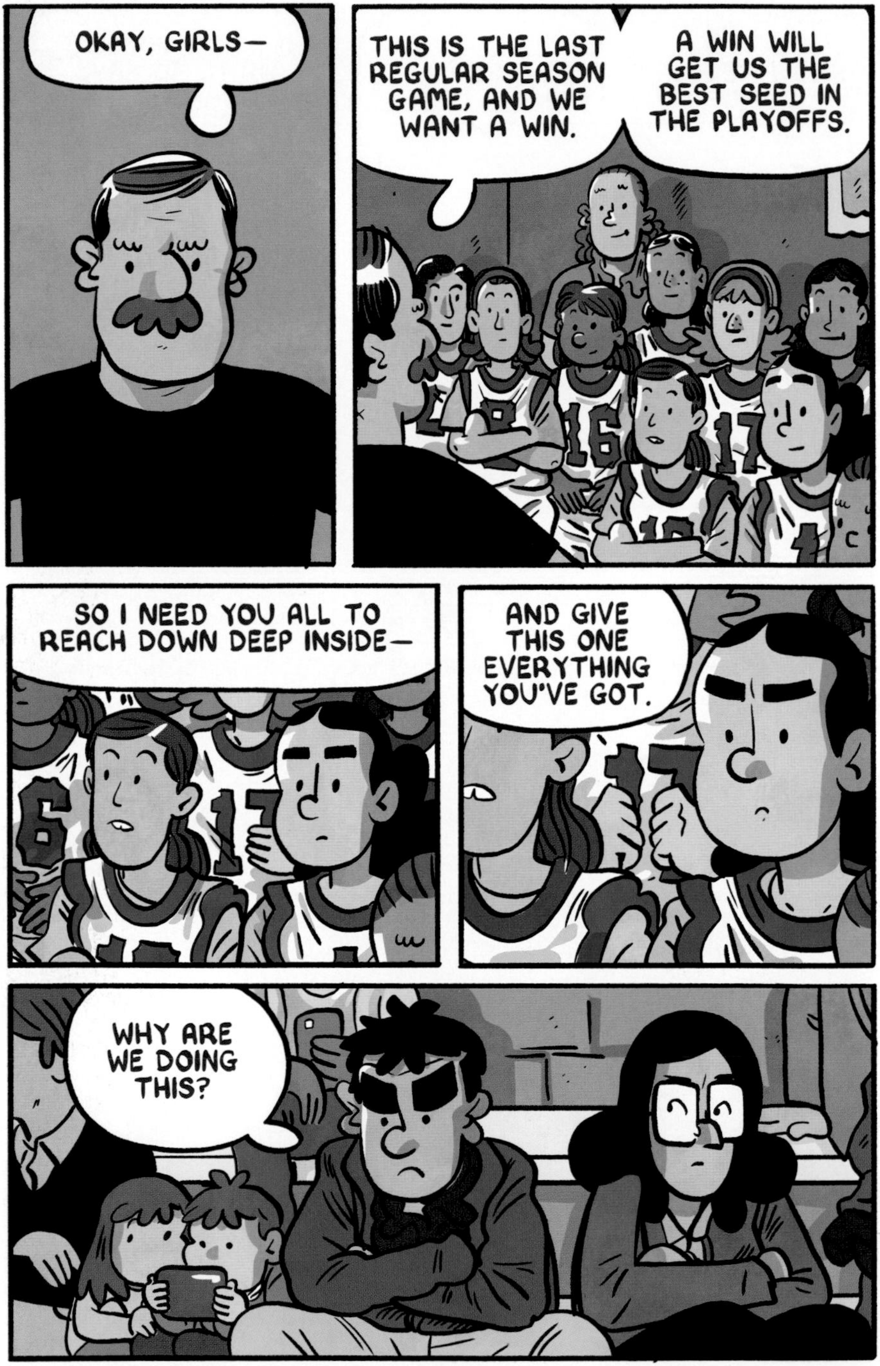
OKAY, GIRLS—
THIS IS THE LAST REGULAR SEASON GAME, AND WE WANT A WIN.
A WIN WILL GET US THE BEST SEED IN THE PLAYOFFS.
SO I NEED YOU ALL TO REACH DOWN DEEP INSIDE—
AND GIVE THIS ONE EVERYTHING YOU'VE GOT.
WHY ARE WE DOING THIS?

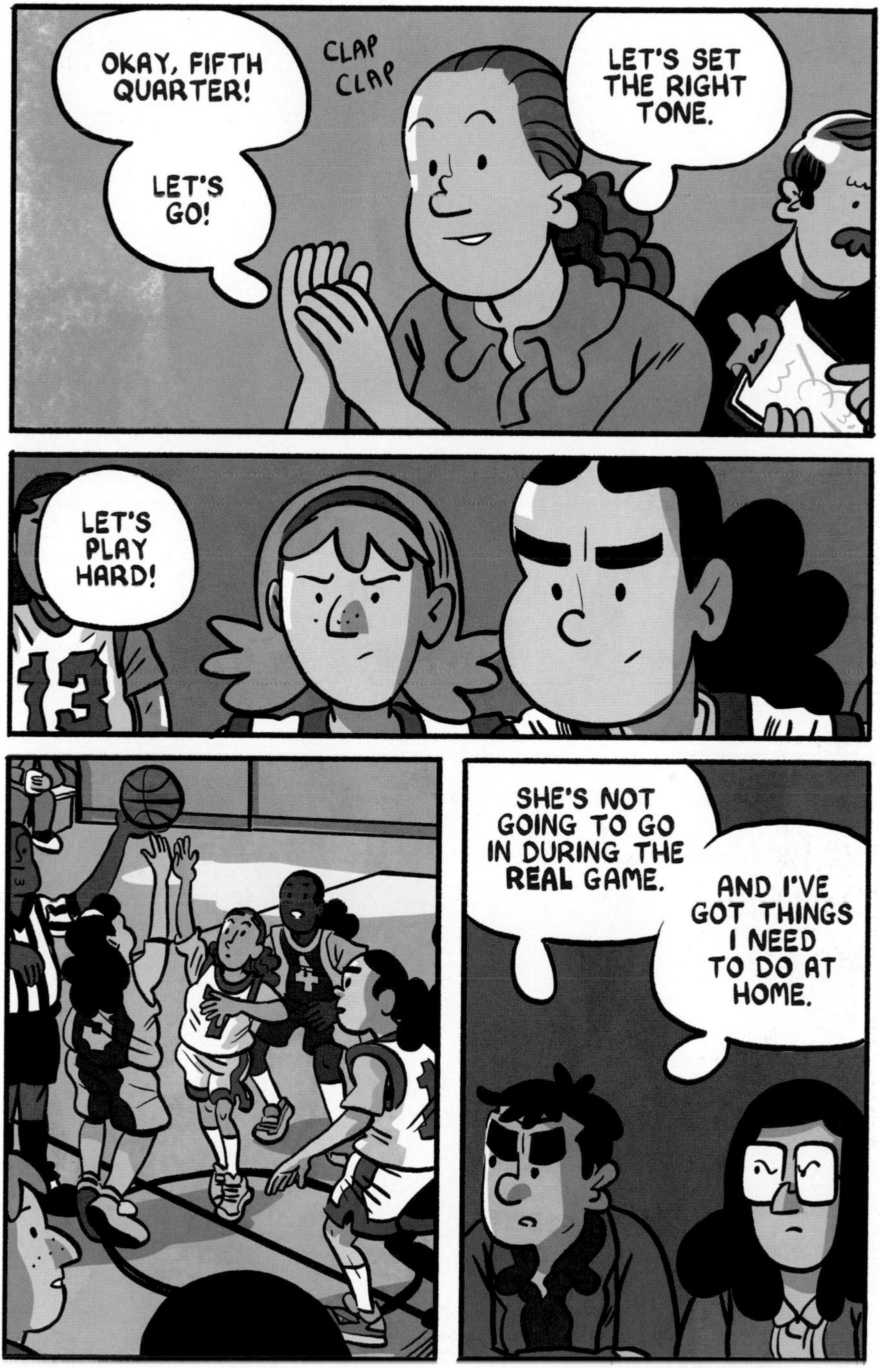

OKAY, FIFTH QUARTER!
LET'S GO!
CLAP CLAP
LET'S SET THE RIGHT TONE.
LET'S PLAY HARD!
SHE'S NOT GOING TO GO IN DURING THE **REAL** GAME.
AND I'VE GOT THINGS I NEED TO DO AT HOME.

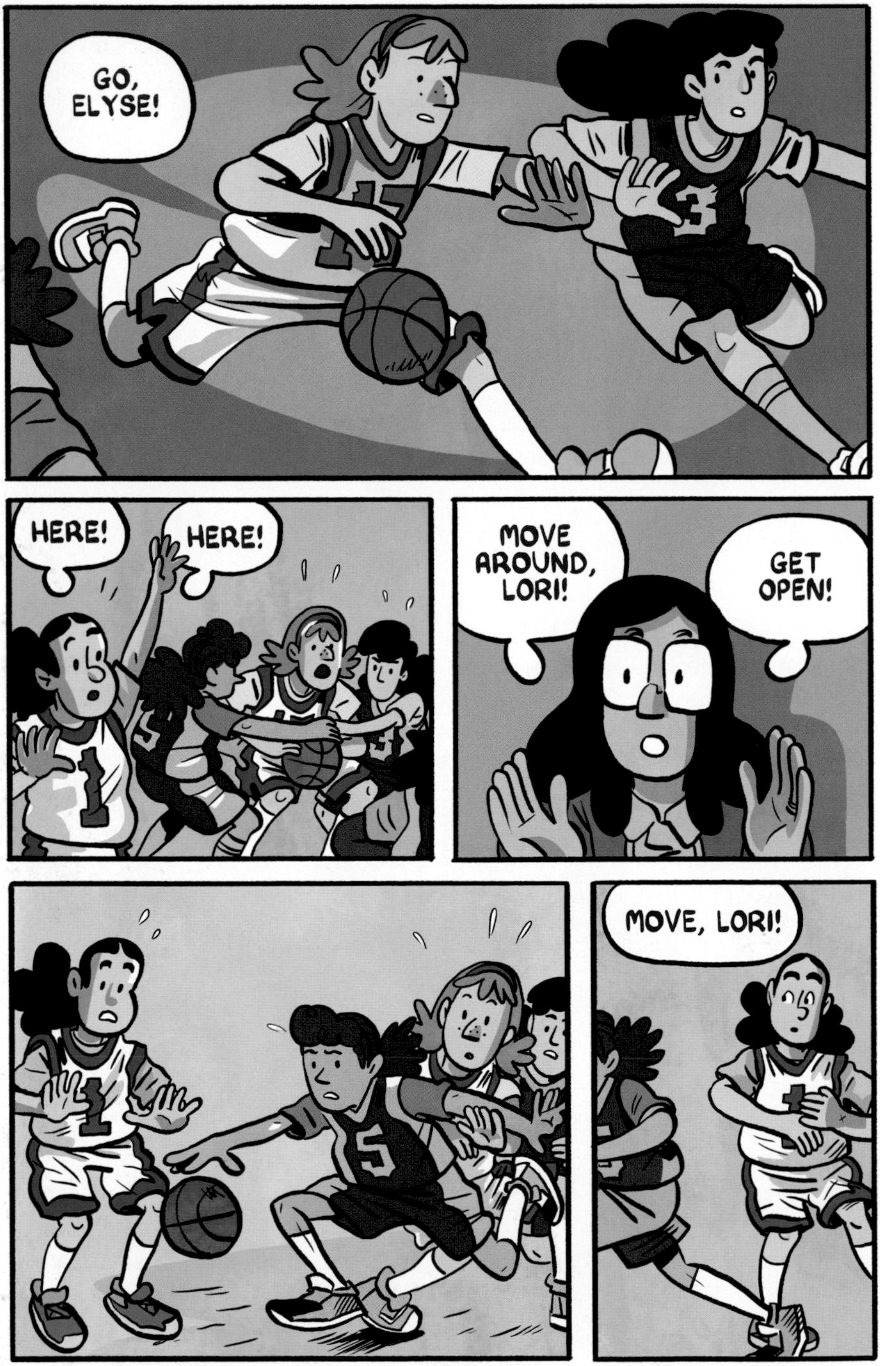
GO, ELYSE!
HERE!
HERE!
MOVE AROUND, LORI!
GET OPEN!
MOVE, LORI!

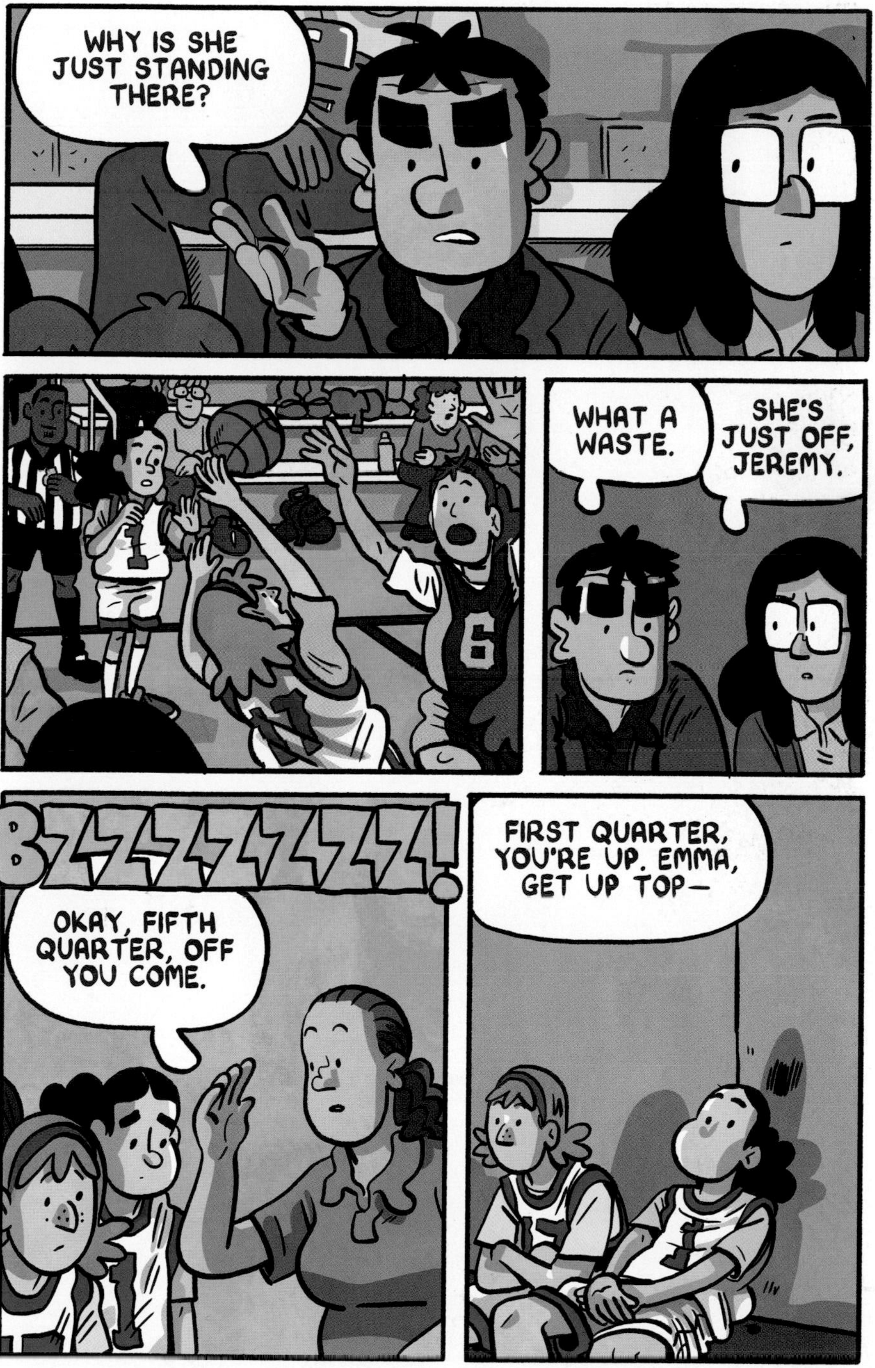
WHY IS SHE JUST STANDING THERE?
WHAT A WASTE.
SHE'S JUST OFF, JEREMY.
BZZZZZZZZZZ!
OKAY, FIFTH QUARTER, OFF YOU COME.
FIRST QUARTER, YOU'RE UP. EMMA, GET UP TOP—

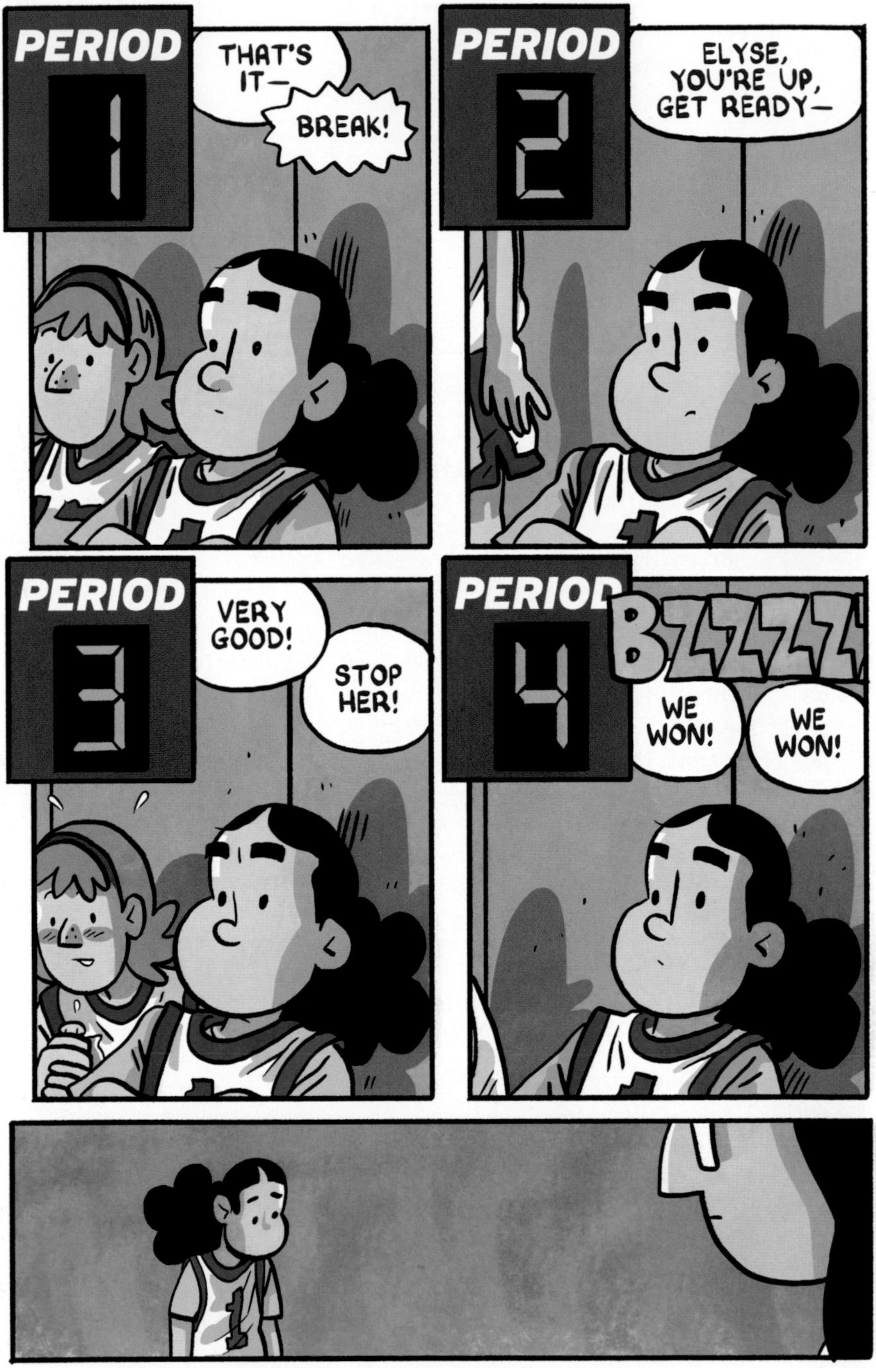
PERIOD
1
THAT'S IT—
BREAK!
PERIOD
2
ELYSE, YOU'RE UP, GET READY—
PERIOD
3
VERY GOOD!
STOP HER!
PERIOD
4
BZZZZZ
WE WON!
WE WON!

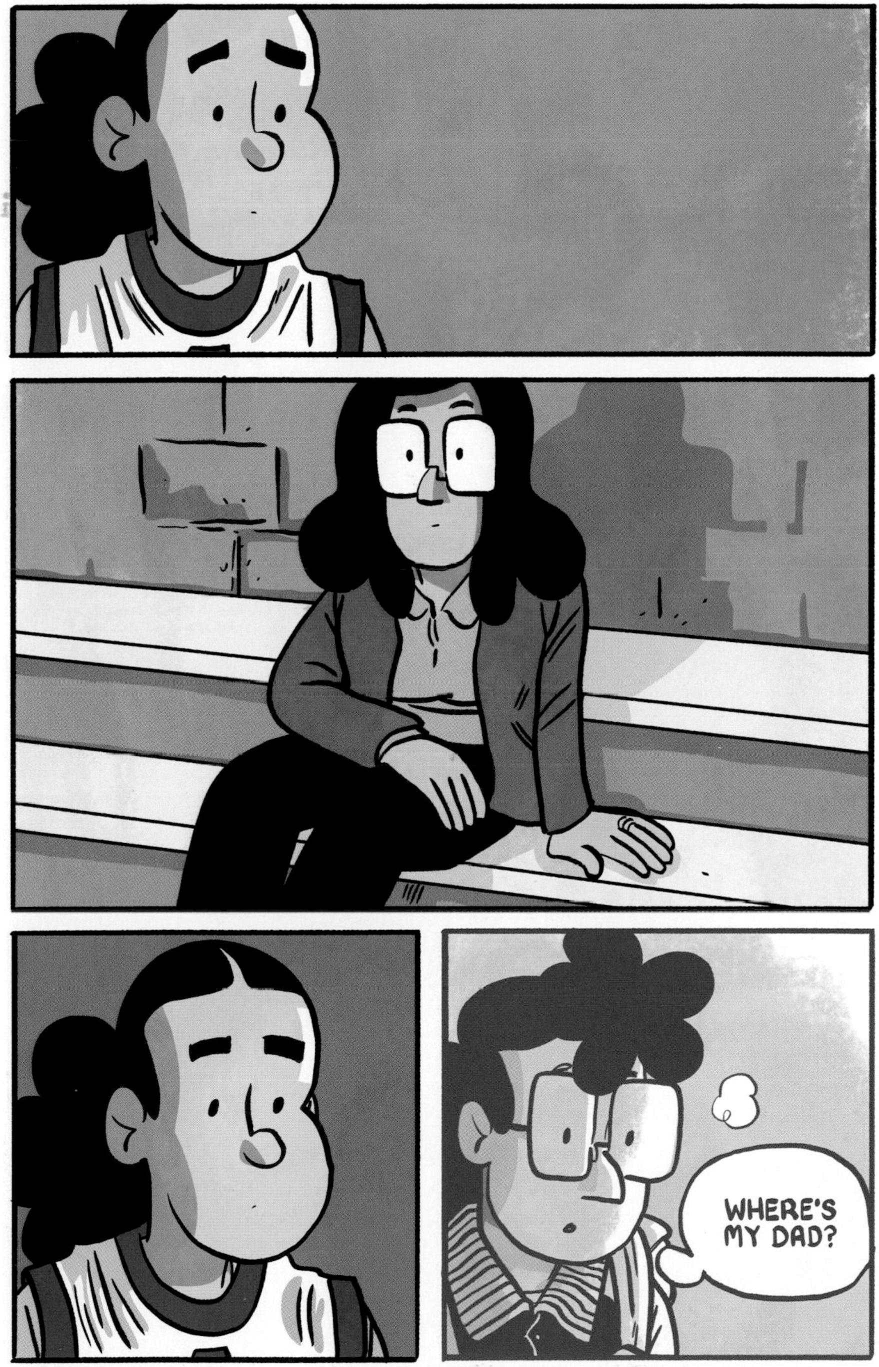
WHERE'S
MY DAD?

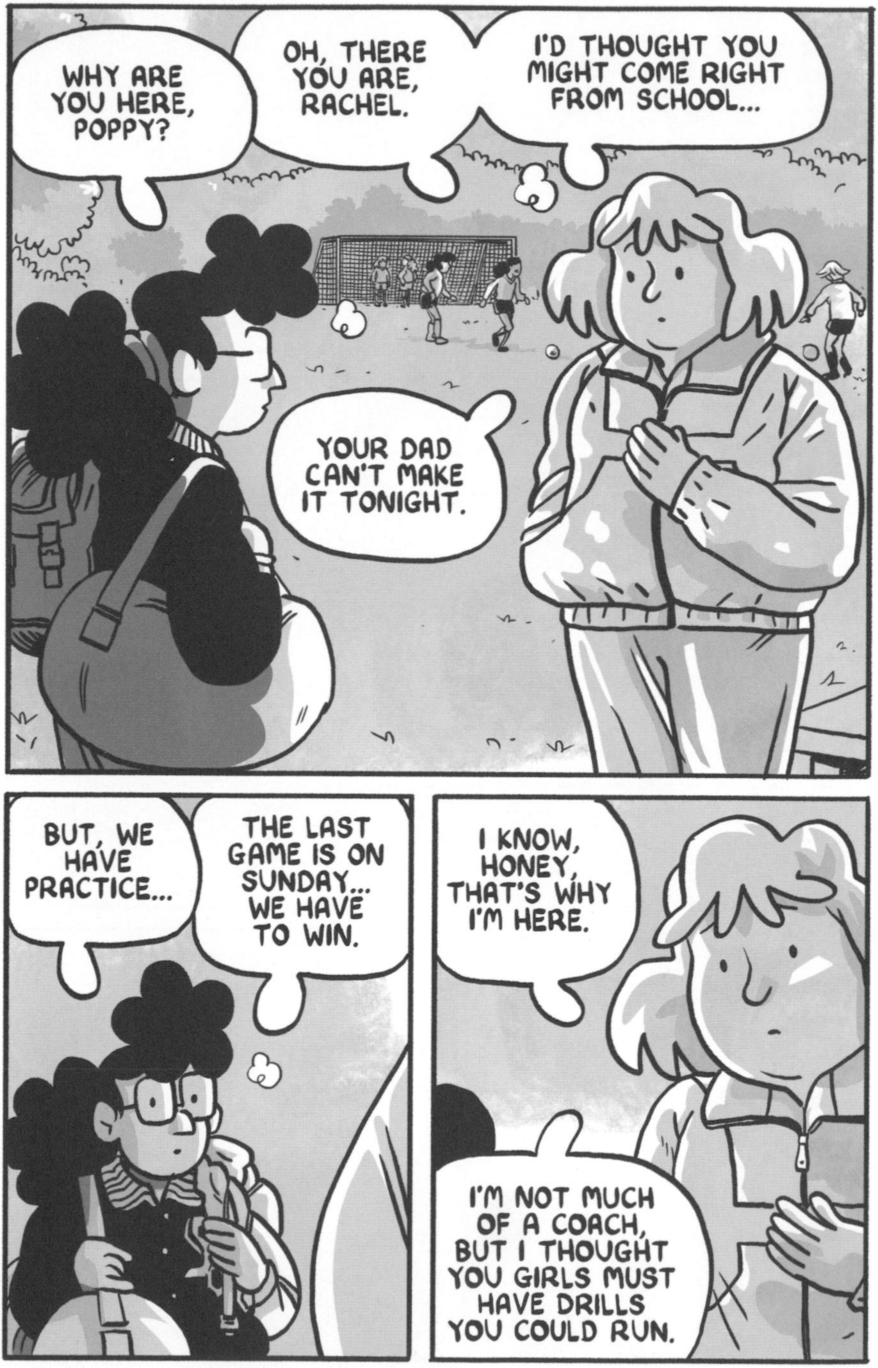
WHY ARE YOU HERE, POPPY?
OH, THERE YOU ARE, RACHEL.
I'D THOUGHT YOU MIGHT COME RIGHT FROM SCHOOL...
YOUR DAD CAN'T MAKE IT TONIGHT.
BUT, WE HAVE PRACTICE...
THE LAST GAME IS ON SUNDAY... WE HAVE TO WIN.
I KNOW, HONEY, THAT'S WHY I'M HERE.
I'M NOT MUCH OF A COACH, BUT I THOUGHT YOU GIRLS MUST HAVE DRILLS YOU COULD RUN.

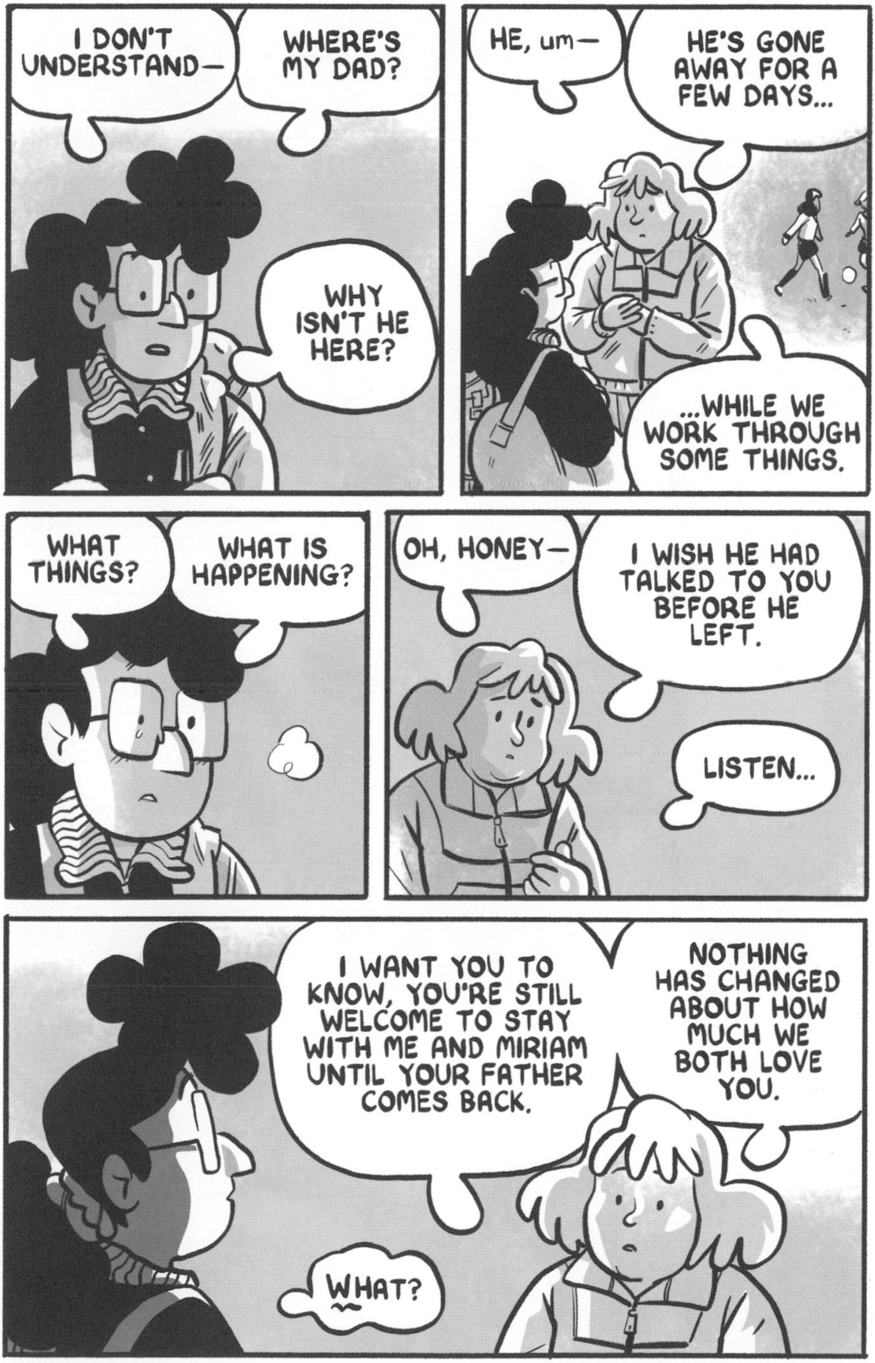
I DON'T UNDERSTAND—
WHERE'S MY DAD?
WHY ISN'T HE HERE?
HE, um—
HE'S GONE AWAY FOR A FEW DAYS...
...WHILE WE WORK THROUGH SOME THINGS.
WHAT THINGS?
WHAT IS HAPPENING?
OH, HONEY—
I WISH HE HAD TALKED TO YOU BEFORE HE LEFT.
LISTEN...
I WANT YOU TO KNOW, YOU'RE STILL WELCOME TO STAY WITH ME AND MIRIAM UNTIL YOUR FATHER COMES BACK.
NOTHING HAS CHANGED ABOUT HOW MUCH WE BOTH LOVE YOU.
WHAT?

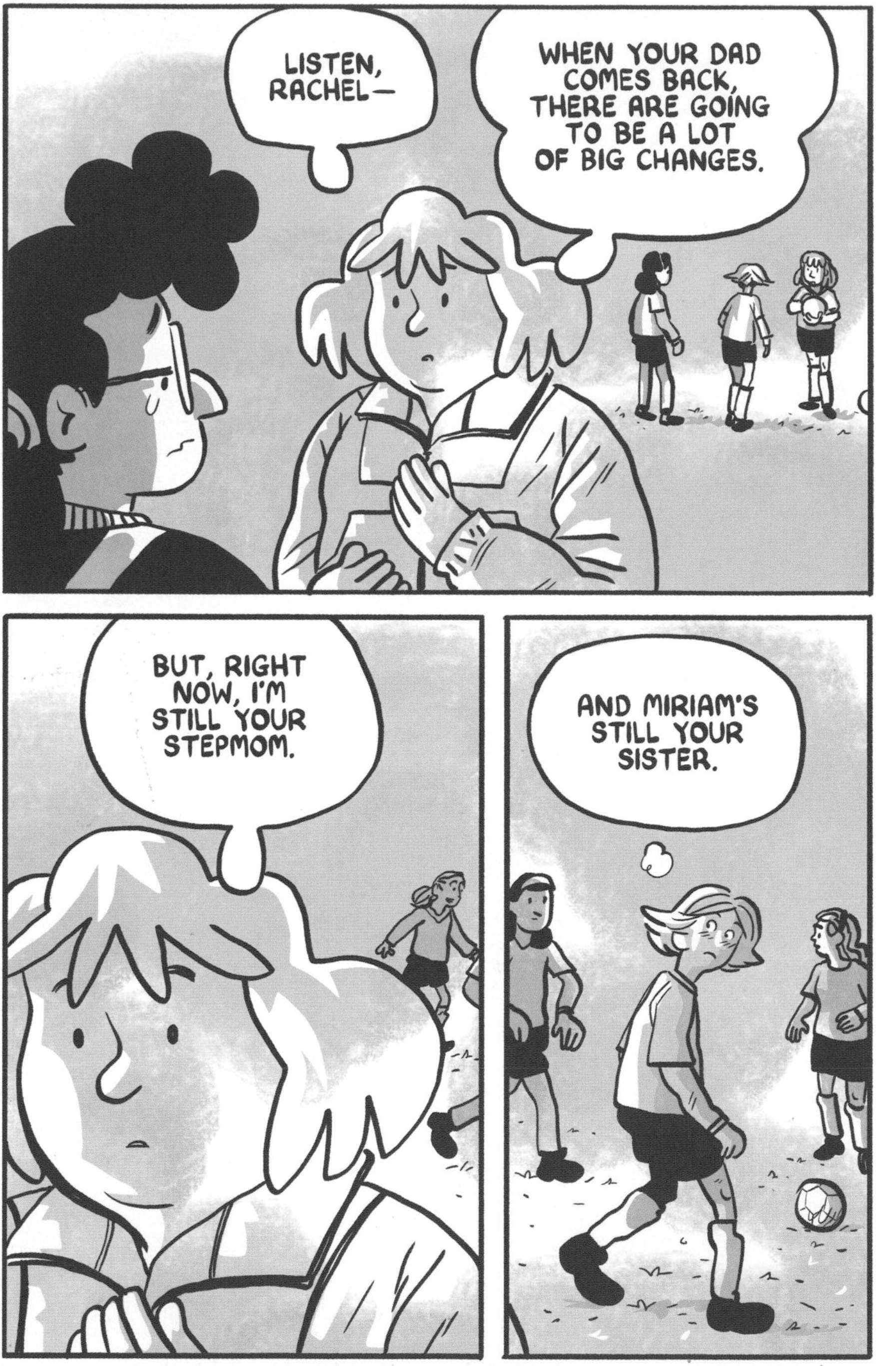
LISTEN, RACHEL—
WHEN YOUR DAD COMES BACK, THERE ARE GOING TO BE A LOT OF BIG CHANGES.
BUT, RIGHT NOW, I'M STILL YOUR STEPMOM.
AND MIRIAM'S STILL YOUR SISTER.

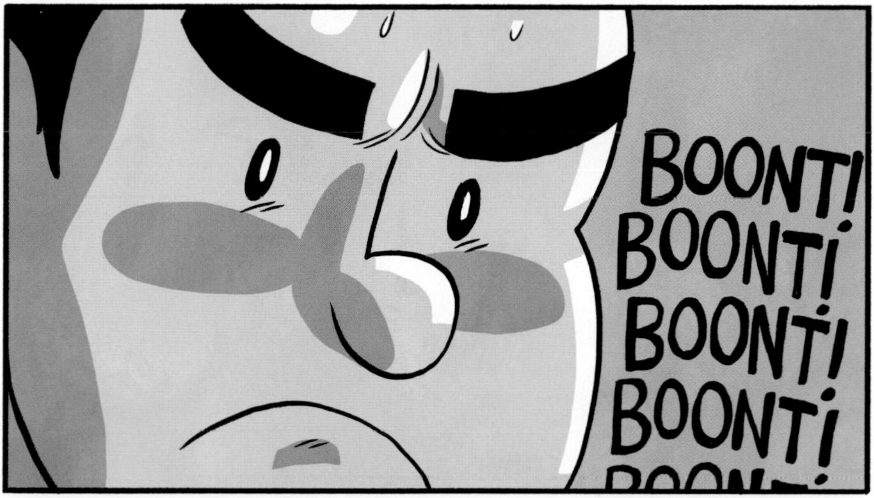
BOONT!
BOONT!
BOONT!
BOONT!

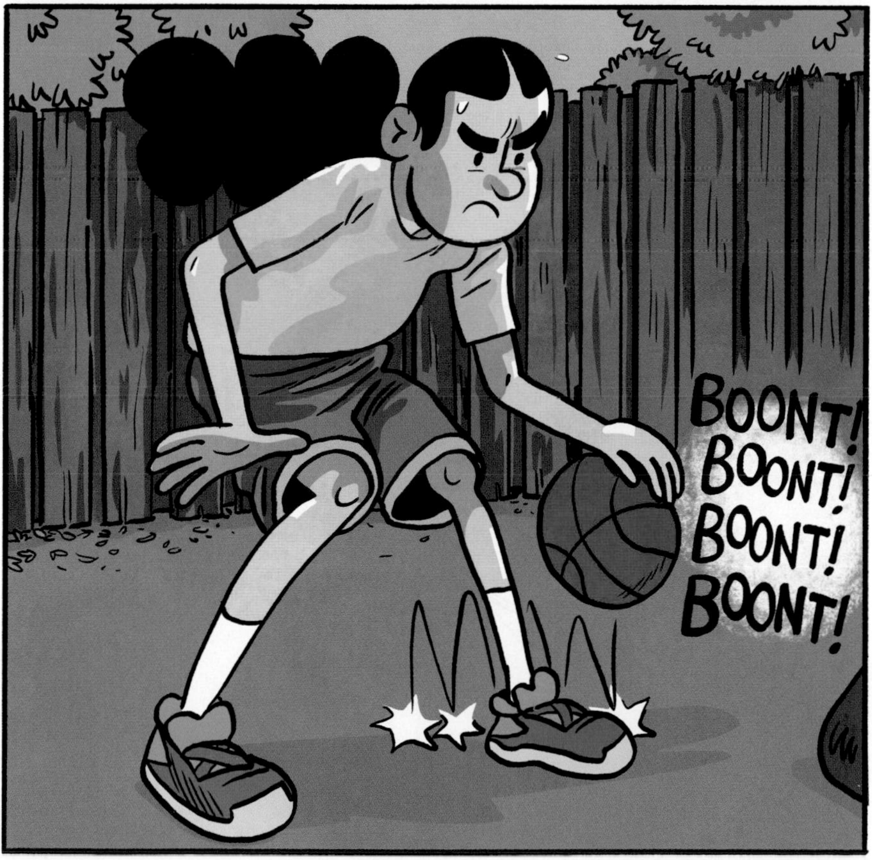
BOONT!
BOONT!
BOONT!
BOONT!

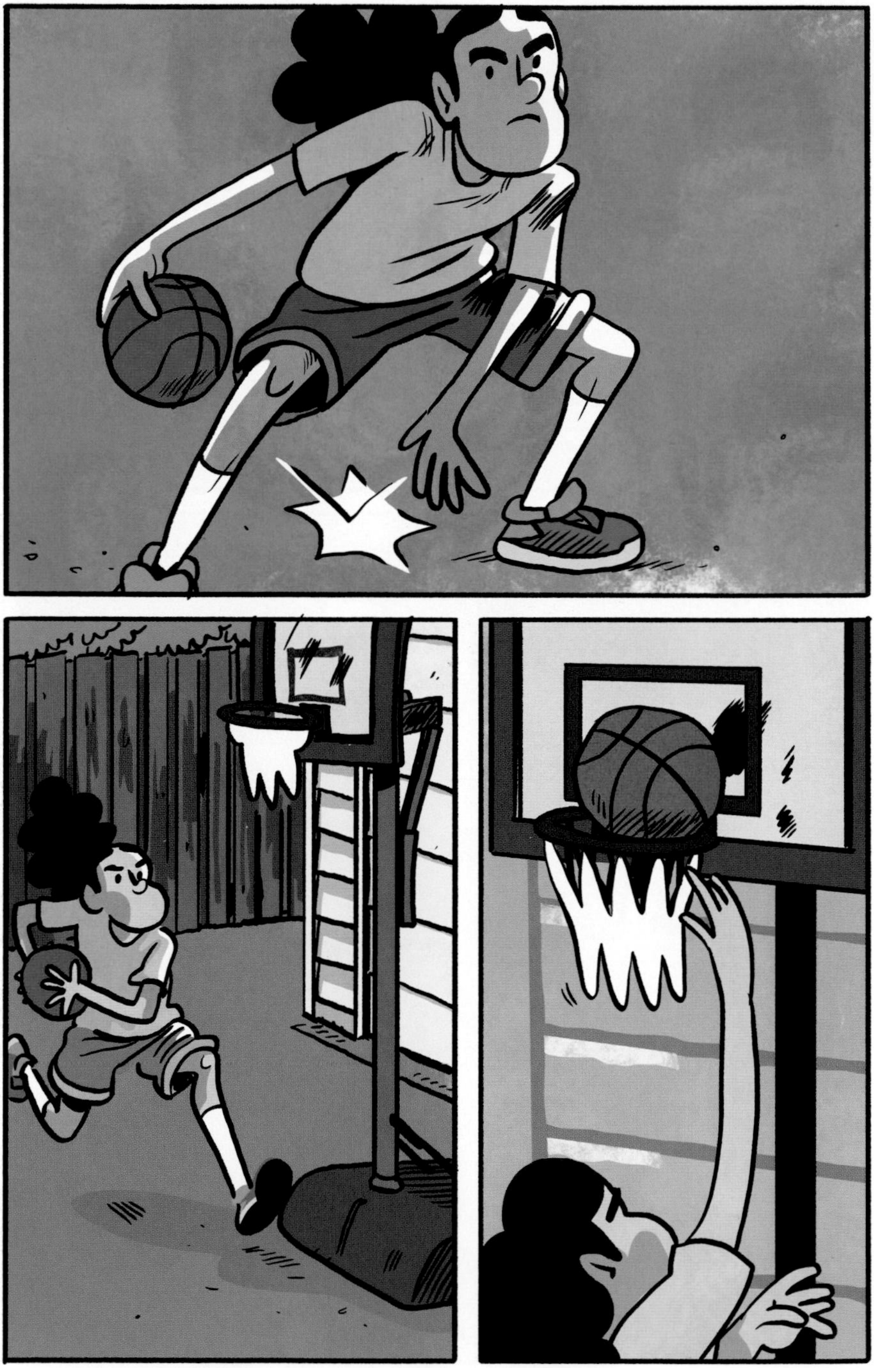

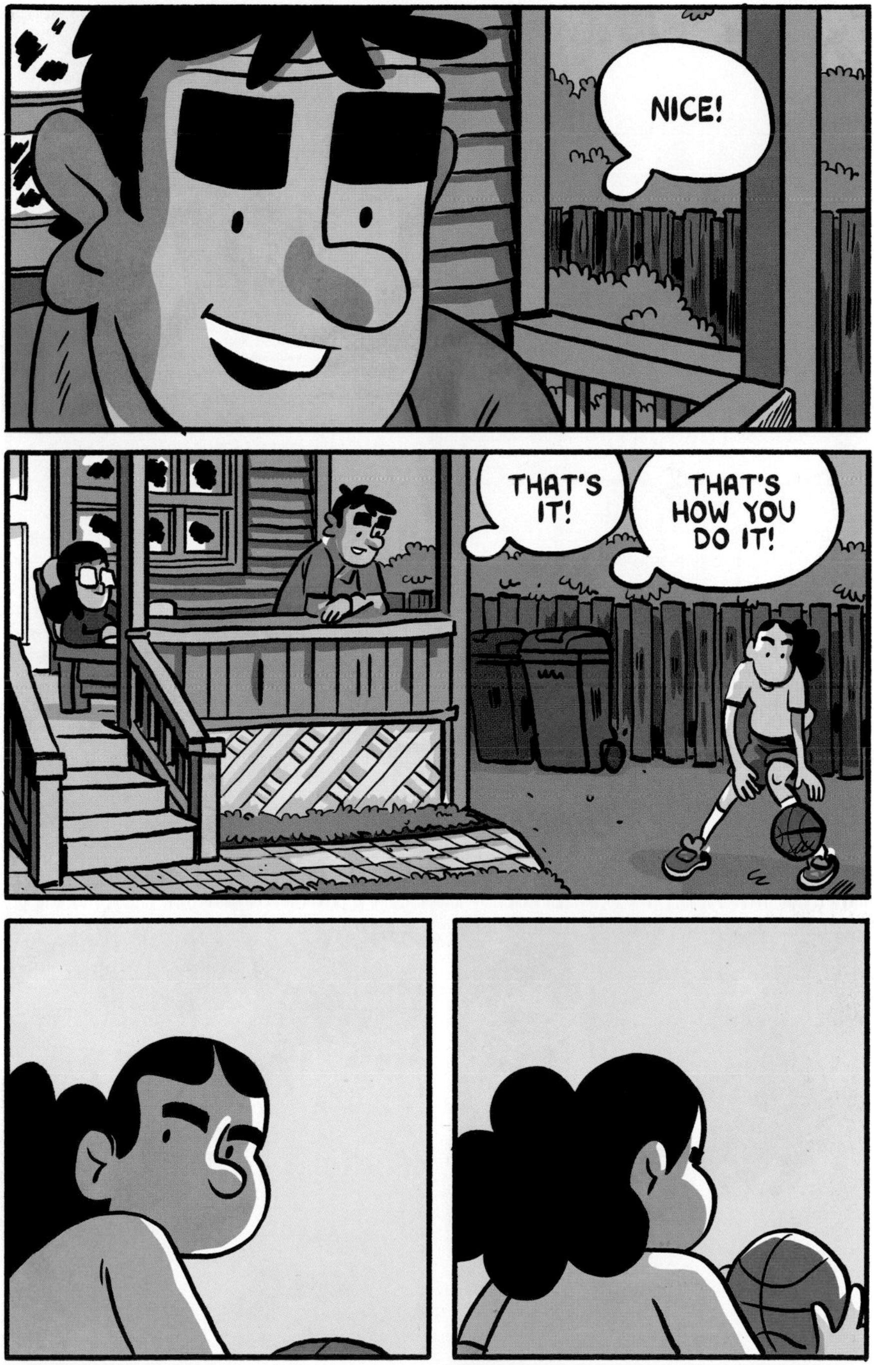
NICE!
THAT'S IT!
THAT'S HOW YOU DO IT!

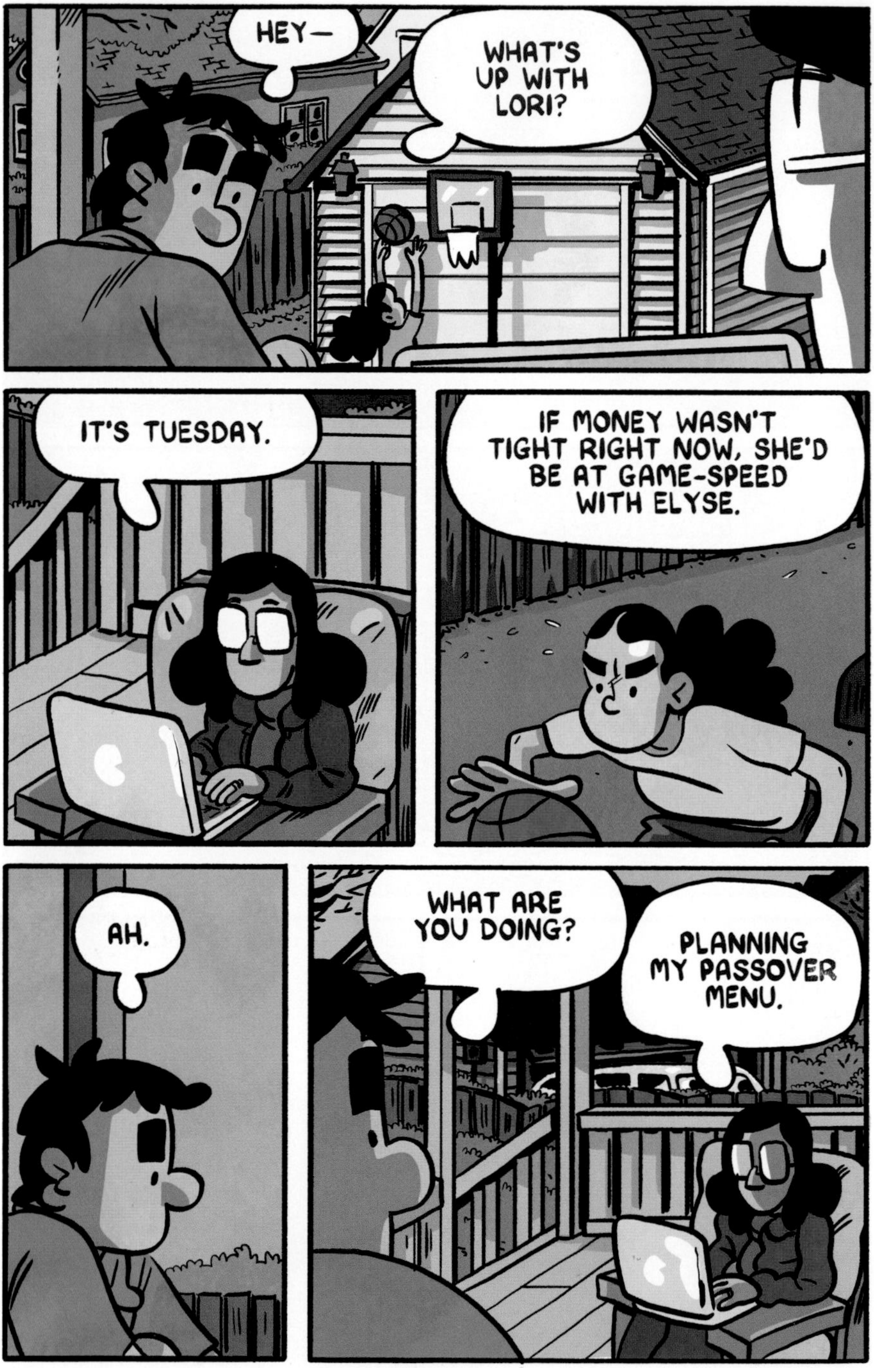
HEY—
WHAT'S UP WITH LORI?
IT'S TUESDAY.
IF MONEY WASN'T TIGHT RIGHT NOW, SHE'D BE AT GAME-SPEED WITH ELYSE.
AH.
WHAT ARE YOU DOING?
PLANNING MY PASSOVER MENU.

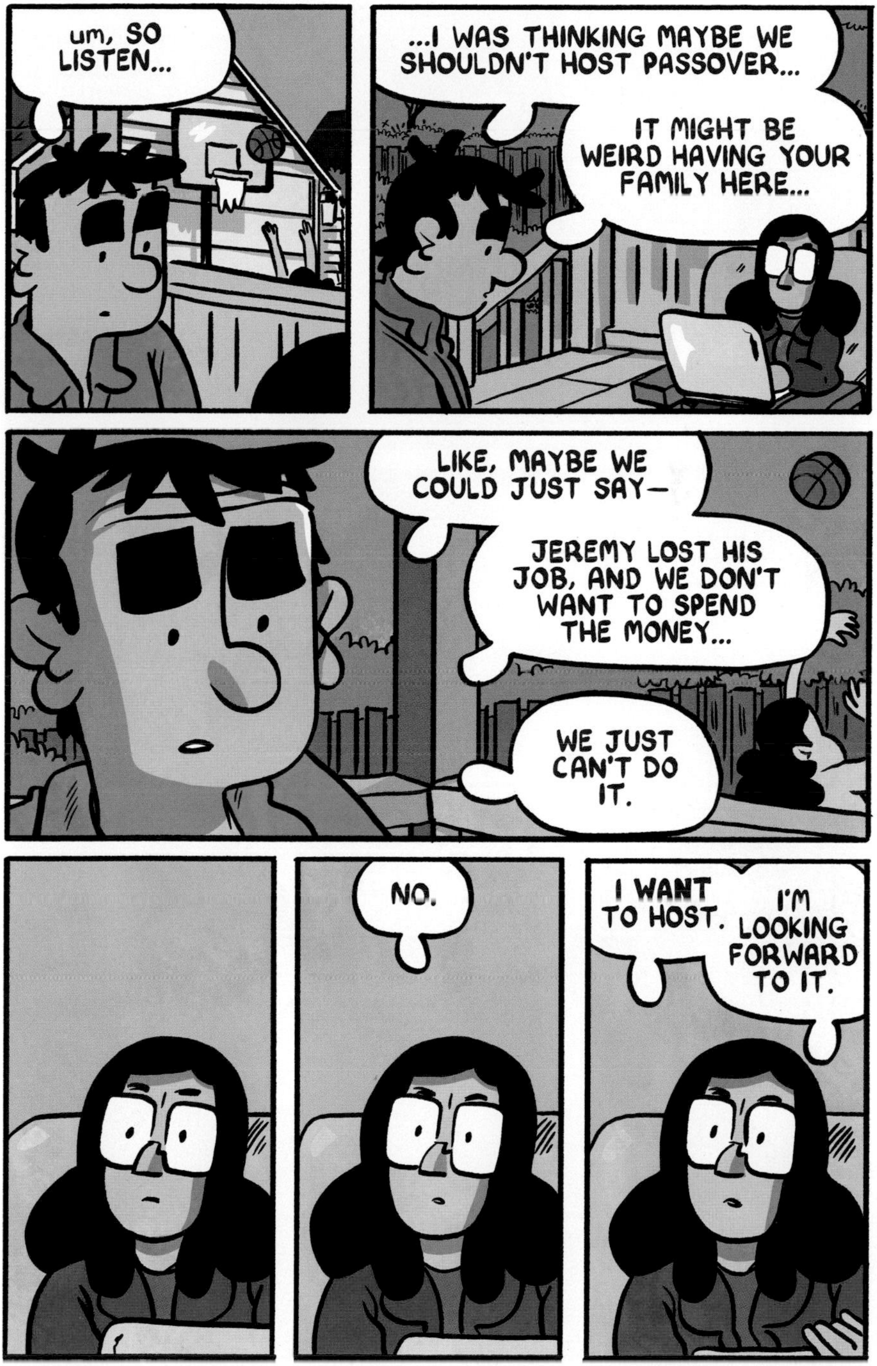
um, SO LISTEN...
...I WAS THINKING MAYBE WE SHOULDN'T HOST PASSOVER...
IT MIGHT BE WEIRD HAVING YOUR FAMILY HERE...
LIKE, MAYBE WE COULD JUST SAY—
JEREMY LOST HIS JOB, AND WE DON'T WANT TO SPEND THE MONEY...
WE JUST CAN'T DO IT.
NO.
I WANT TO HOST.
I'M LOOKING FORWARD TO IT.

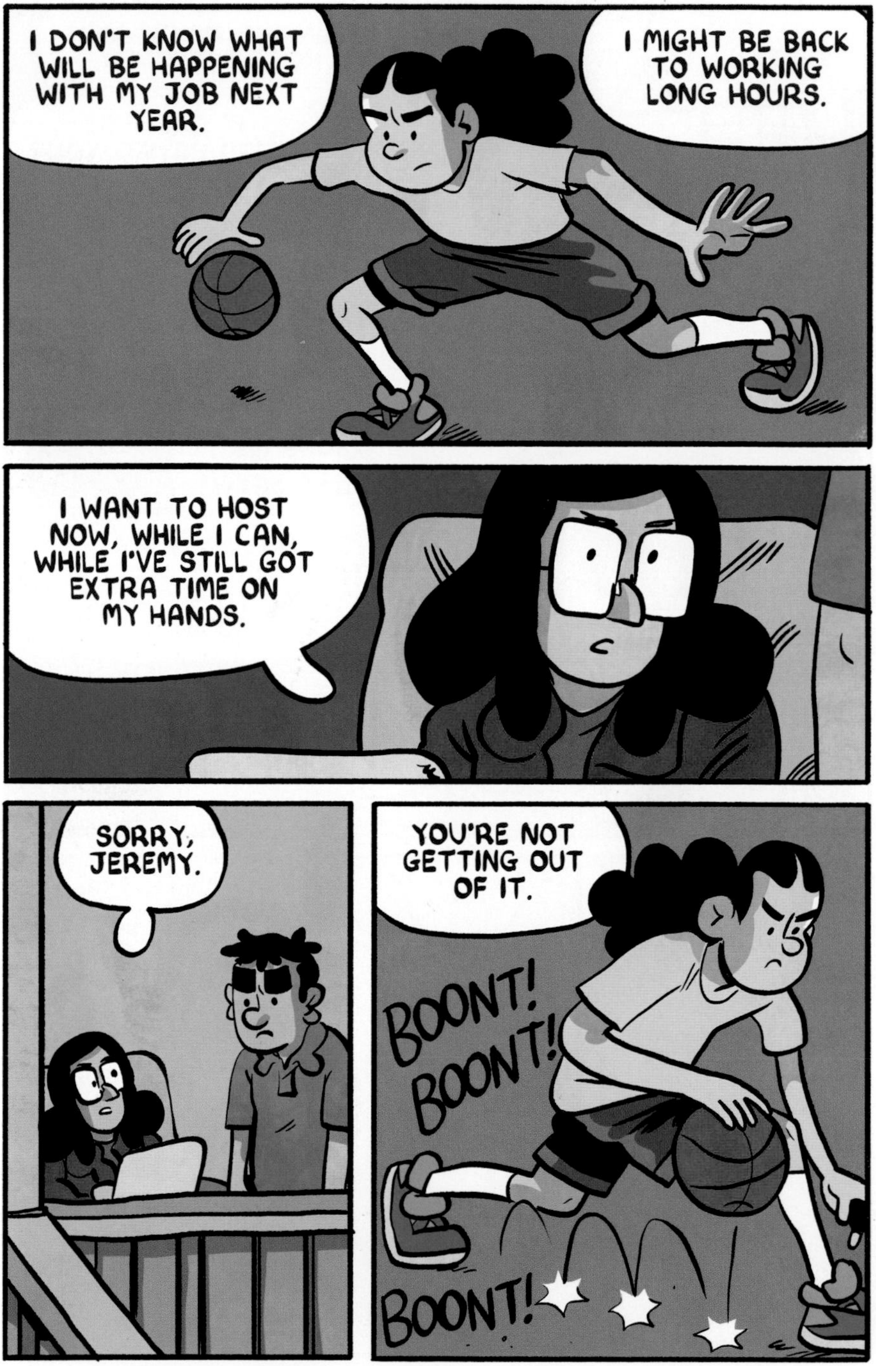
I DON'T KNOW WHAT WILL BE HAPPENING WITH MY JOB NEXT YEAR.
I MIGHT BE BACK TO WORKING LONG HOURS.
I WANT TO HOST NOW, WHILE I CAN, WHILE I'VE STILL GOT EXTRA TIME ON MY HANDS.
SORRY, JEREMY.
YOU'RE NOT GETTING OUT OF IT.
BOONT! BOONT!
BOONT!

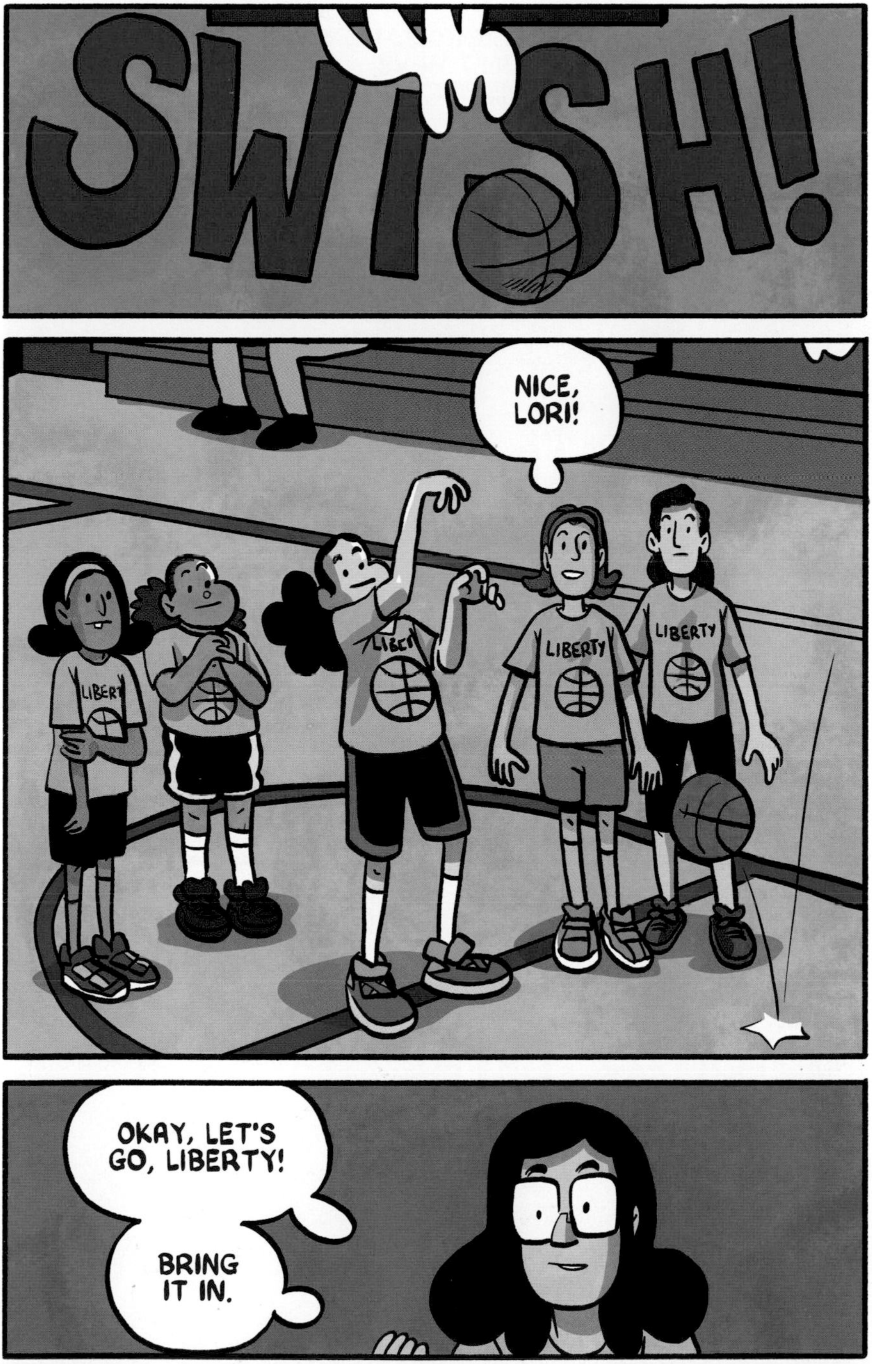
SWISH!
NICE, LORI!
LIBERTY
LIBERTY
LIBERTY
OKAY, LET'S GO, LIBERTY!
BRING IT IN.

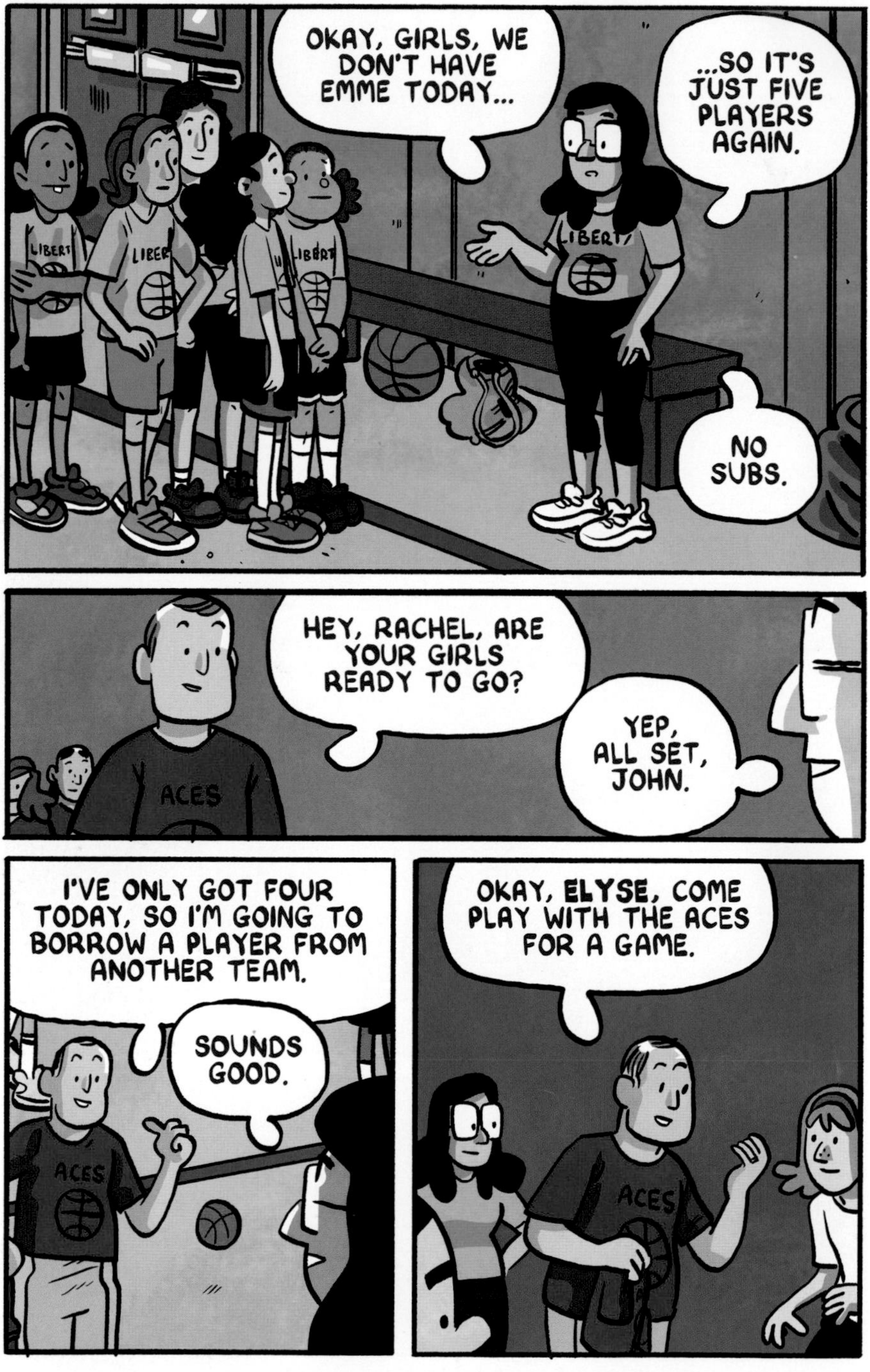
OKAY, GIRLS, WE DON'T HAVE EMME TODAY...
...SO IT'S JUST FIVE PLAYERS AGAIN.
NO SUBS.
HEY, RACHEL, ARE YOUR GIRLS READY TO GO?
YEP, ALL SET, JOHN.
I'VE ONLY GOT FOUR TODAY, SO I'M GOING TO BORROW A PLAYER FROM ANOTHER TEAM.
SOUNDS GOOD.
OKAY, **ELYSE**, COME PLAY WITH THE ACES FOR A GAME.

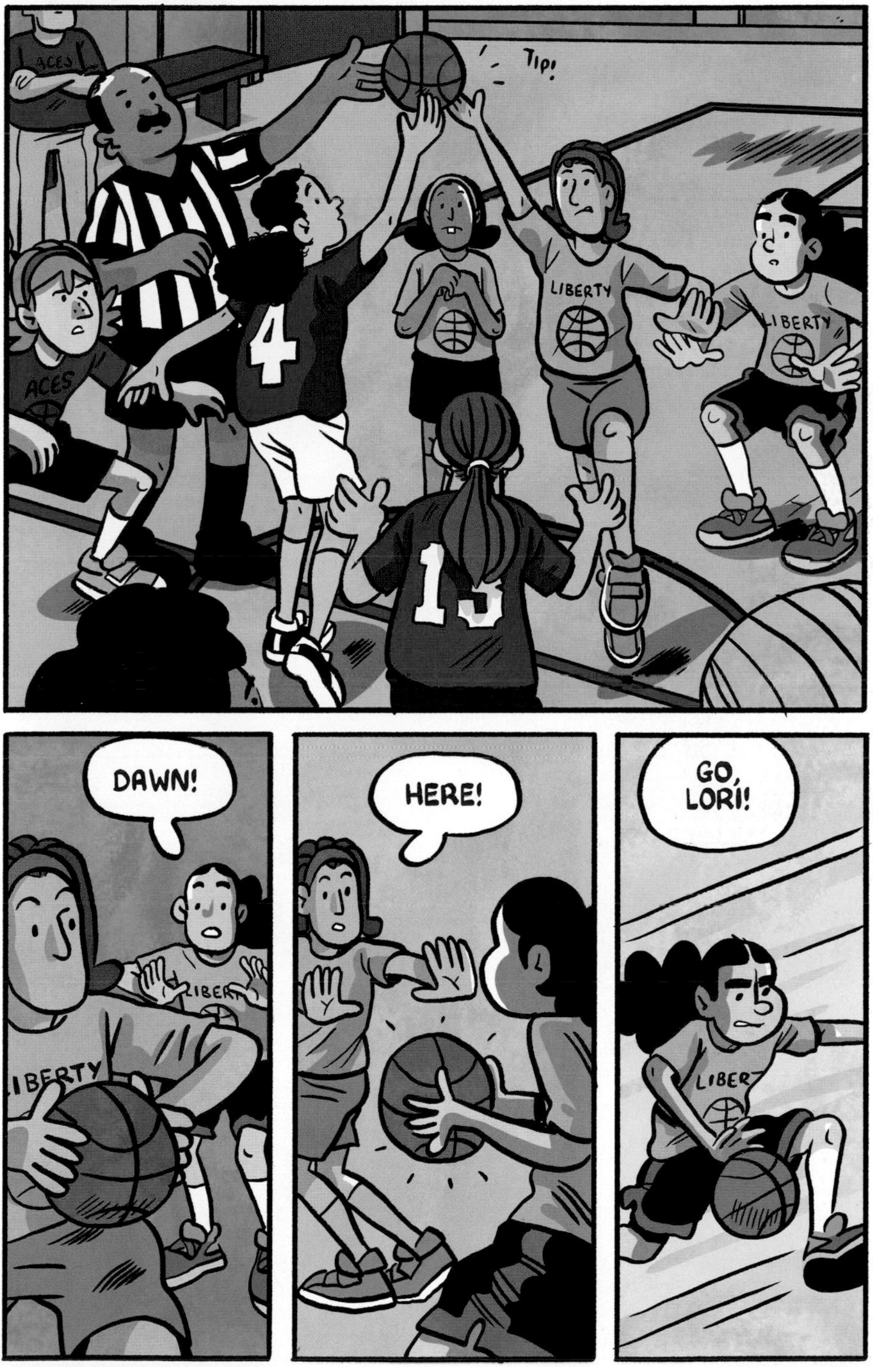
TIP!
DAWN!
HERE!
GO, LORI!

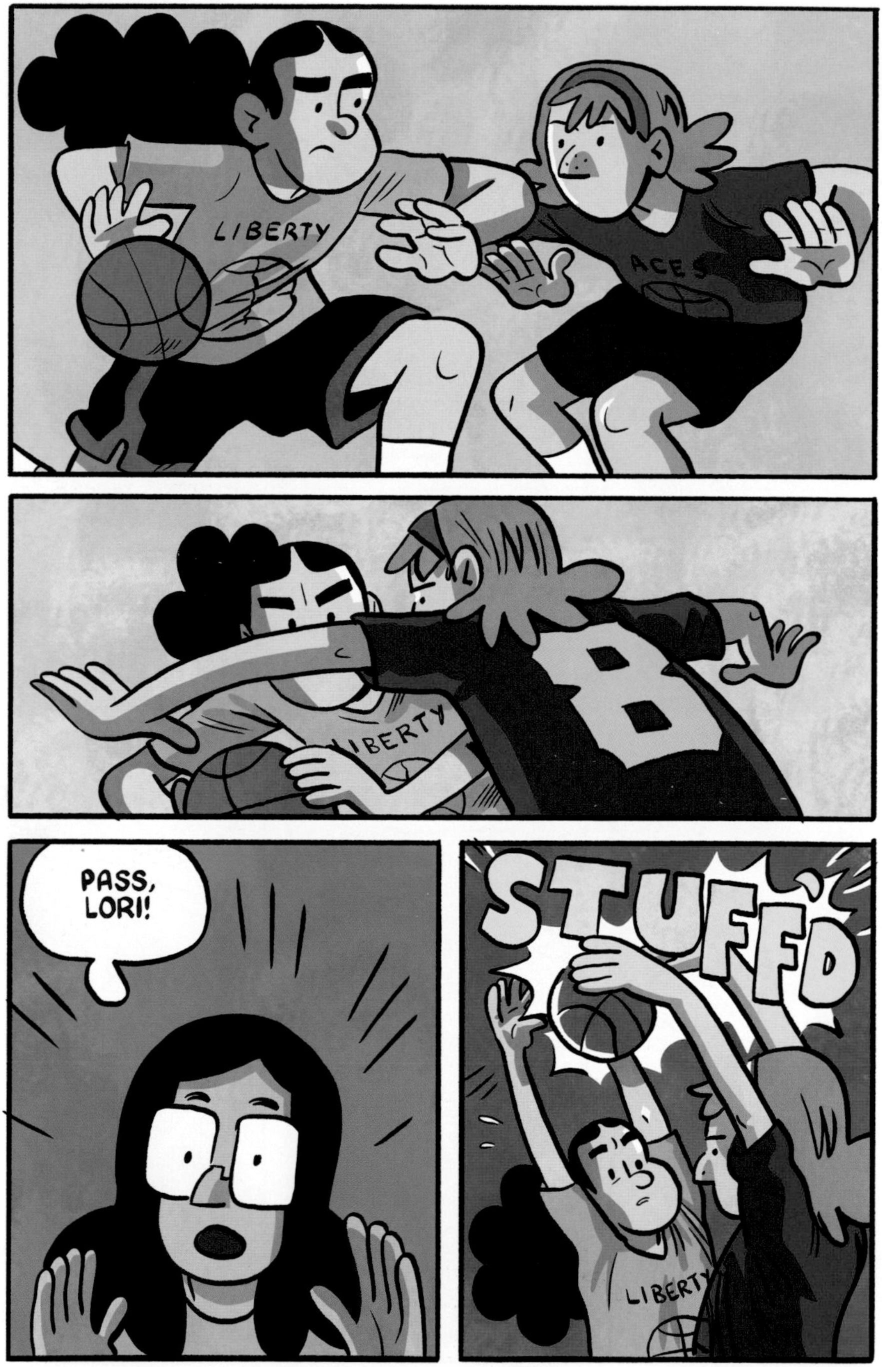

LIBERTY
ACES
LIBERTY
PASS, LORI!
STUFF'D
LIBERTY

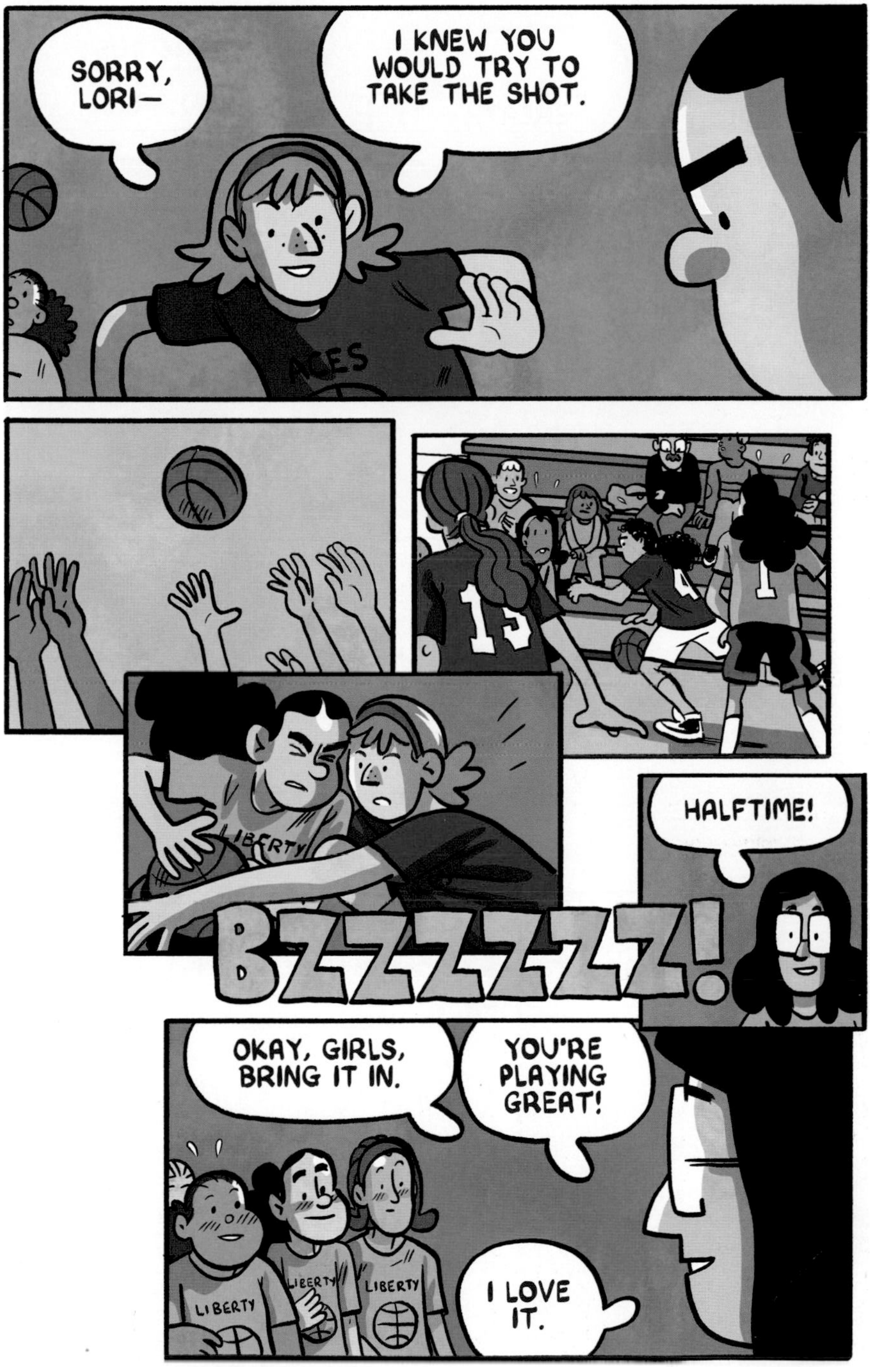
SORRY, LORI—
I KNEW YOU WOULD TRY TO TAKE THE SHOT.
ACES
LIBERTY
BZZZZZZZ!
HALFTIME!
OKAY, GIRLS, BRING IT IN.
YOU'RE PLAYING GREAT!
LIBERTY
LIBERTY
LIBERTY
I LOVE IT.

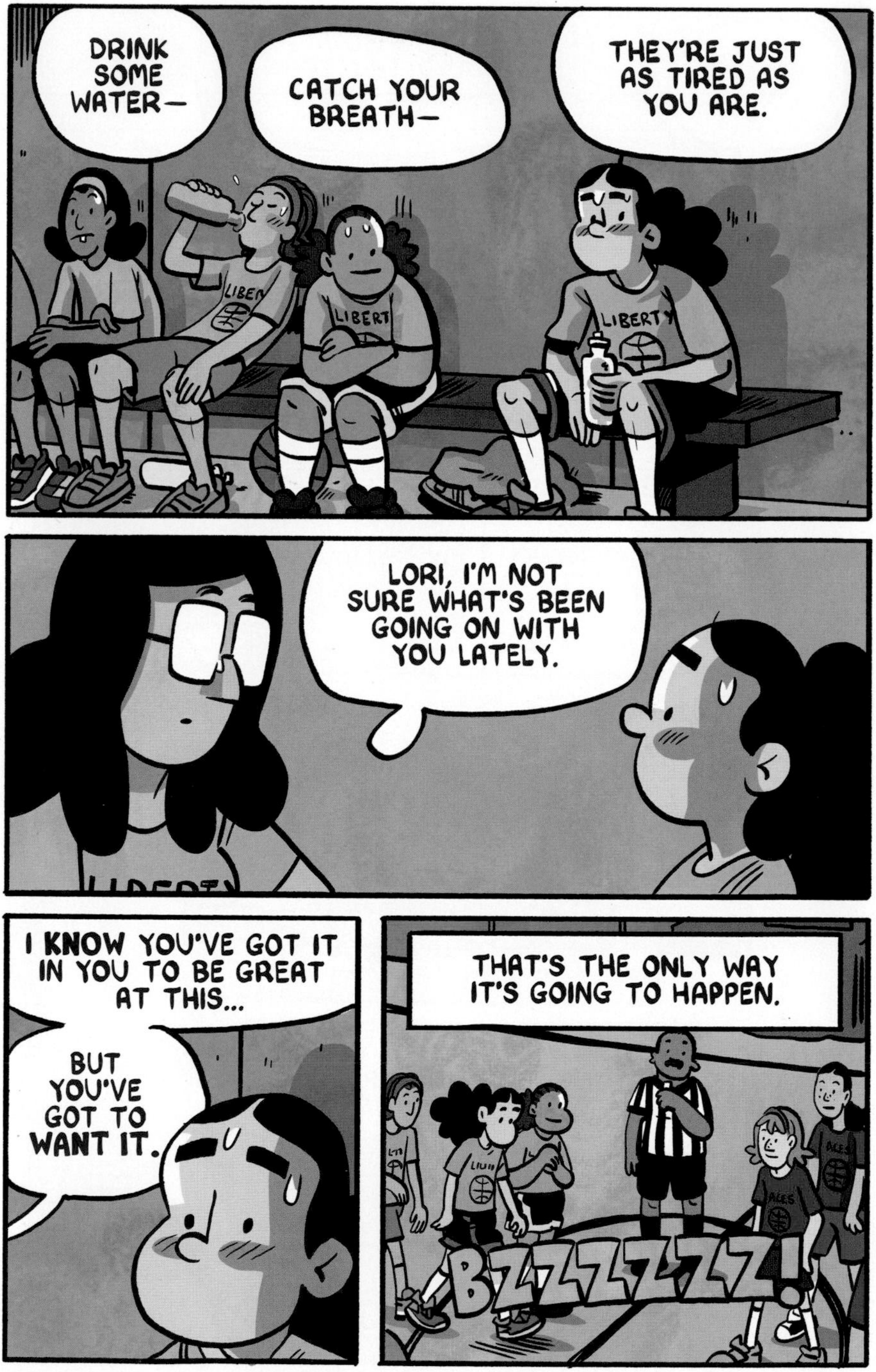
DRINK SOME WATER—
CATCH YOUR BREATH—
THEY'RE JUST AS TIRED AS YOU ARE.
LIBERTY
LORI, I'M NOT SURE WHAT'S BEEN GOING ON WITH YOU LATELY.
I **KNOW** YOU'VE GOT IT IN YOU TO BE GREAT AT THIS...
BUT YOU'VE GOT TO **WANT IT**.
THAT'S THE ONLY WAY IT'S GOING TO HAPPEN.
BZZZZZZZZ!

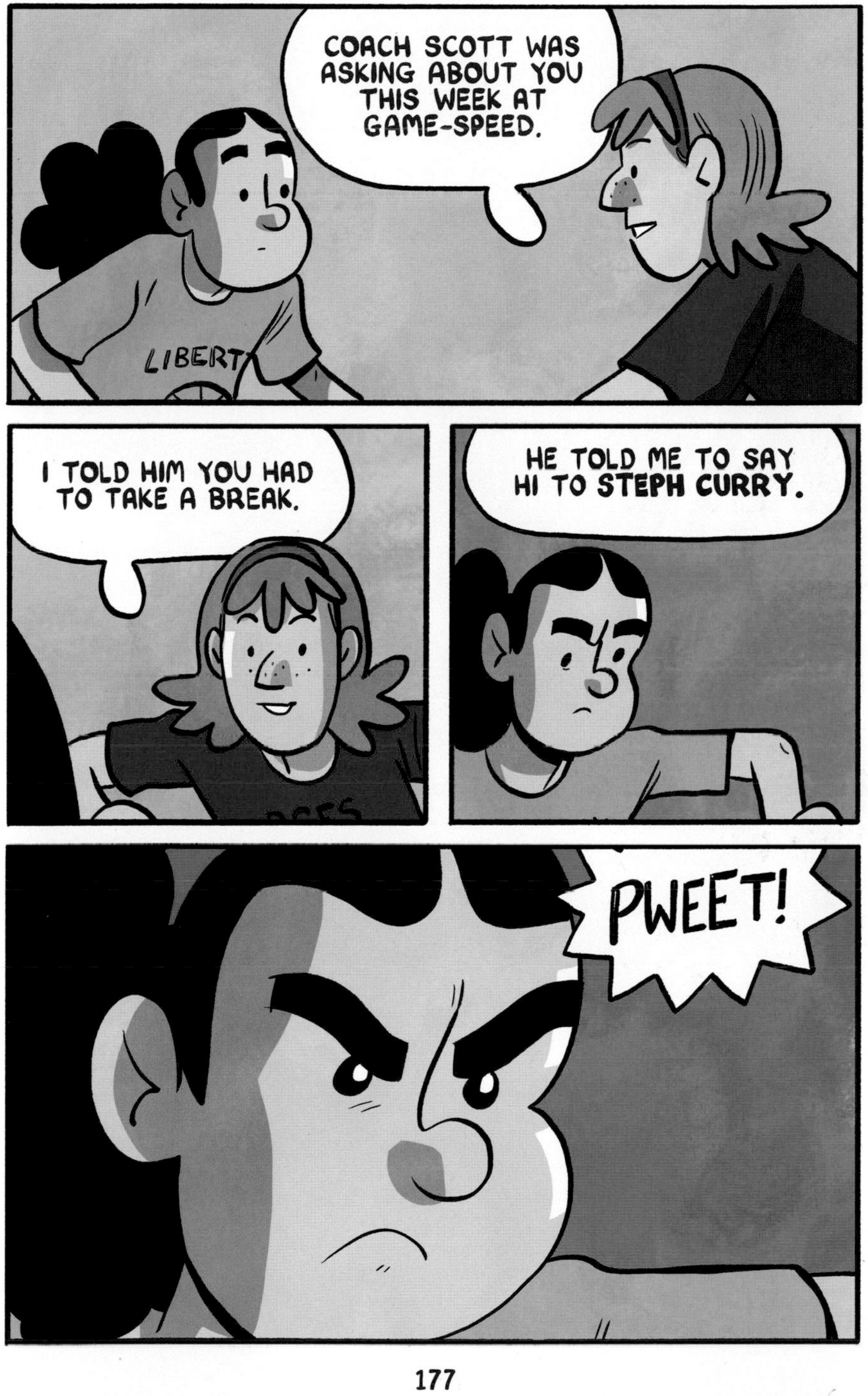
COACH SCOTT WAS ASKING ABOUT YOU THIS WEEK AT GAME-SPEED.
LIBERTY
I TOLD HIM YOU HAD TO TAKE A BREAK.
HE TOLD ME TO SAY HI TO **STEPH CURRY**.
PWEET!

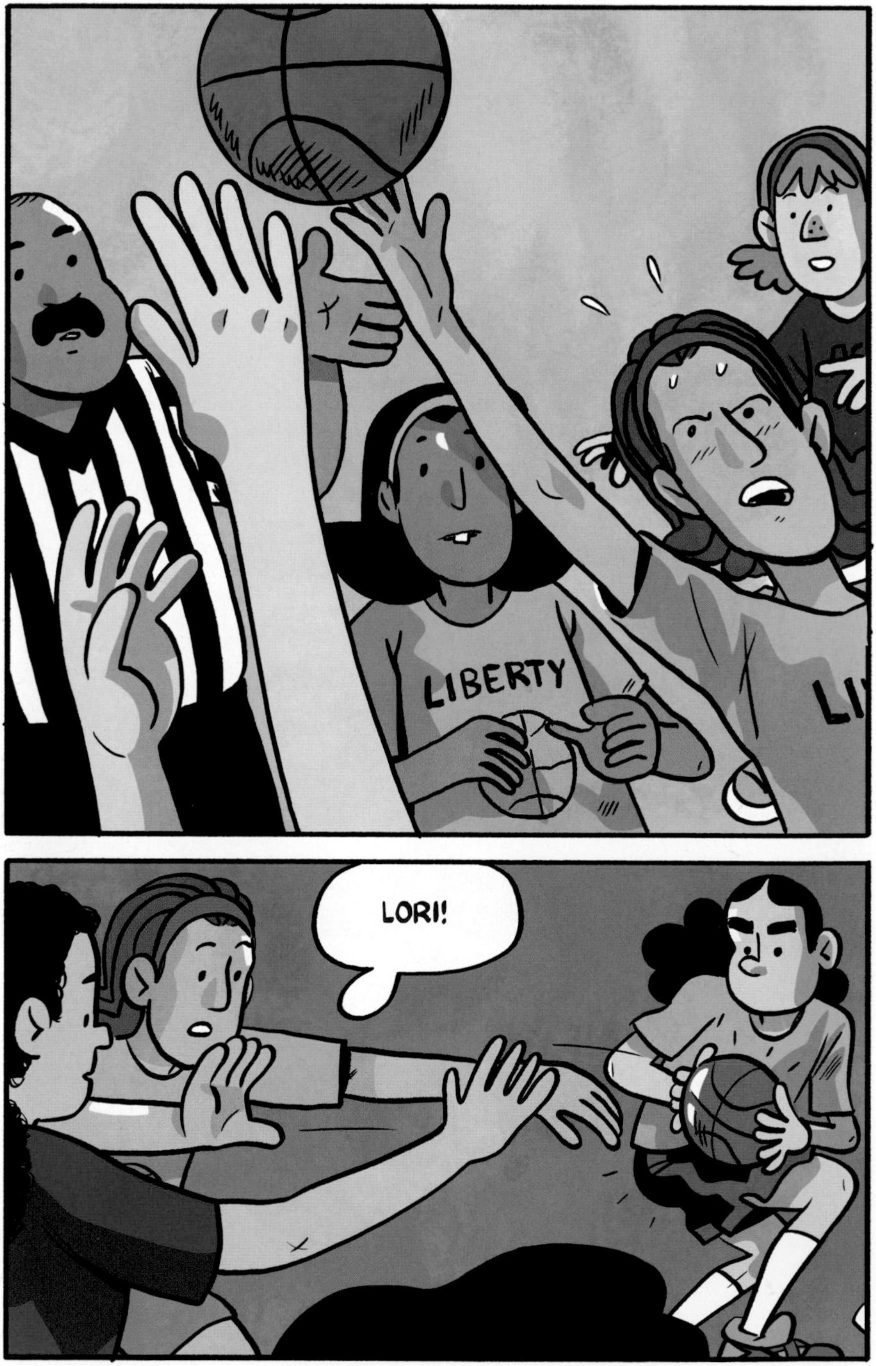
LIBERTY
LORI!

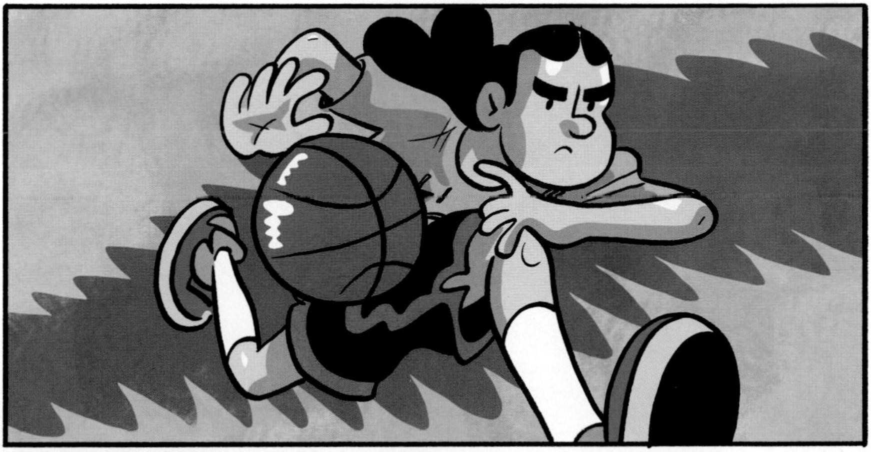

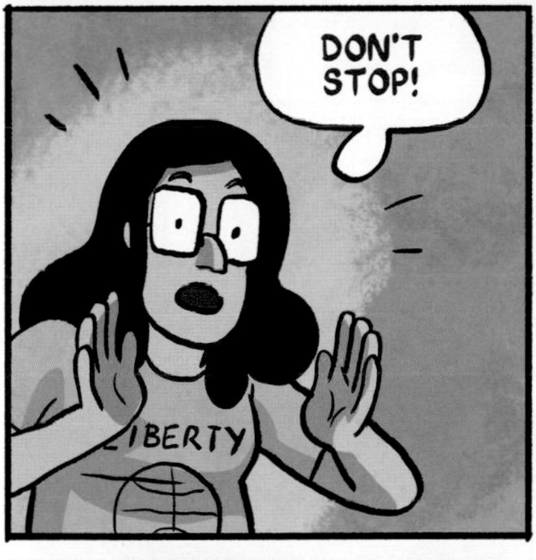
DON'T STOP!
LIBERTY

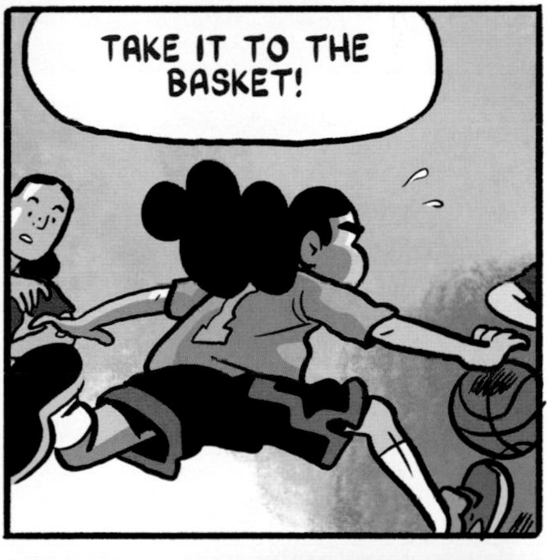
TAKE IT TO THE BASKET!

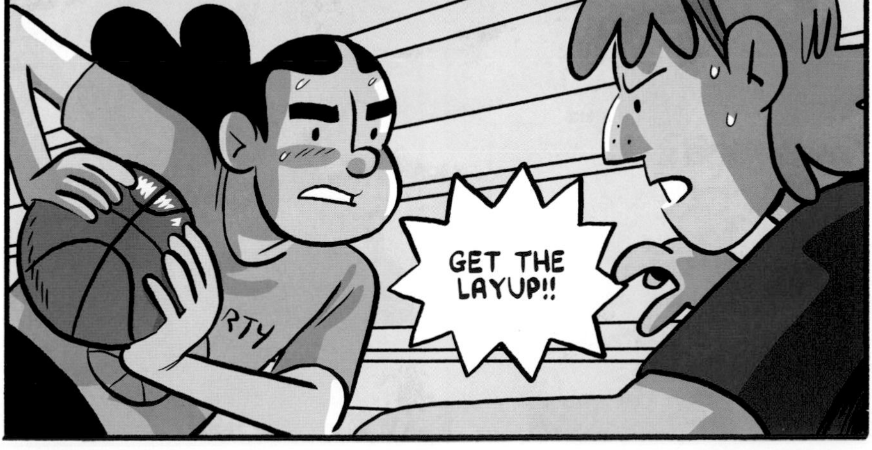
RTY
GET THE LAYUP!!

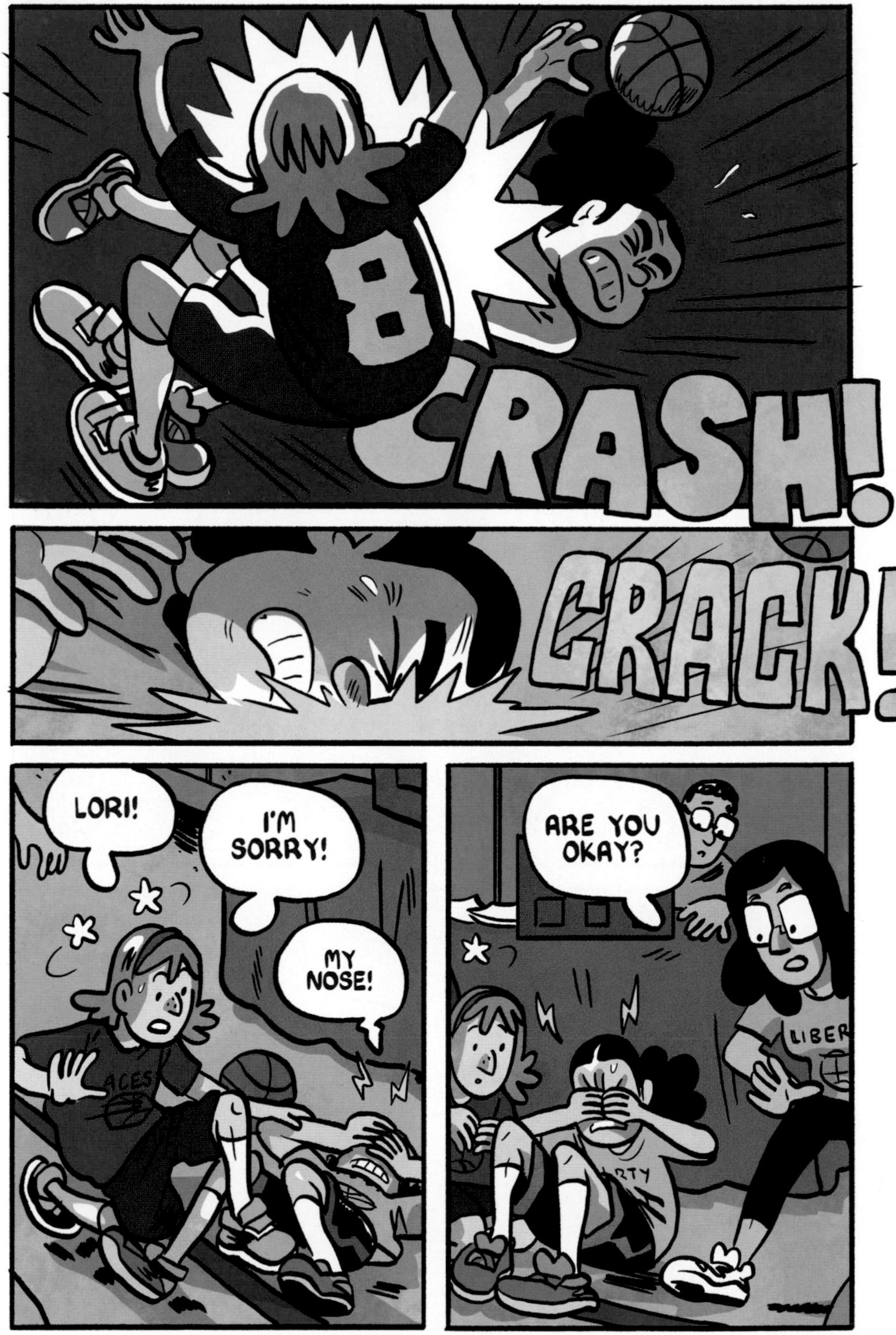
CRASH!
CRACK!
LORI!
I'M SORRY!
MY NOSE!
ACES
ARE YOU OKAY?
LIBER
RTY

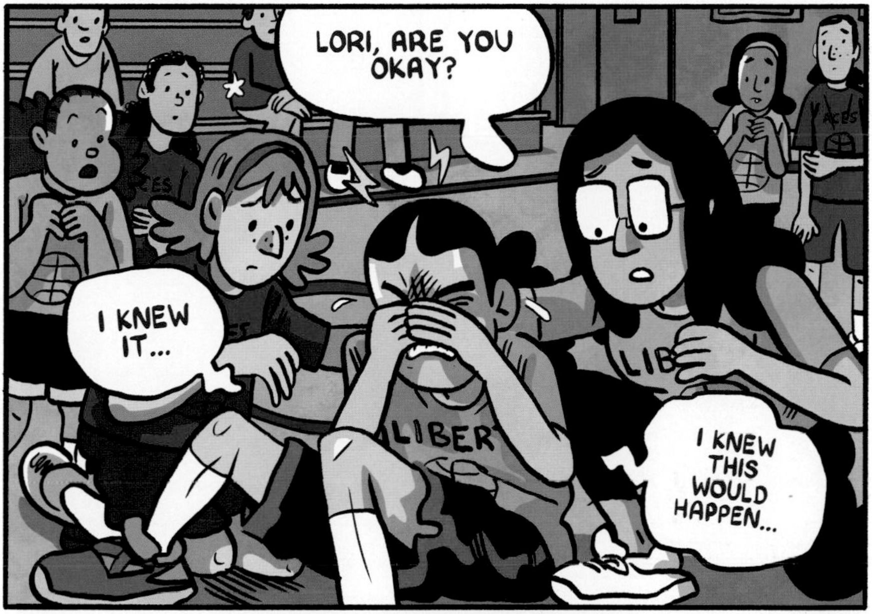
LORI, ARE YOU OKAY?
I KNEW IT...
I KNEW THIS WOULD HAPPEN...

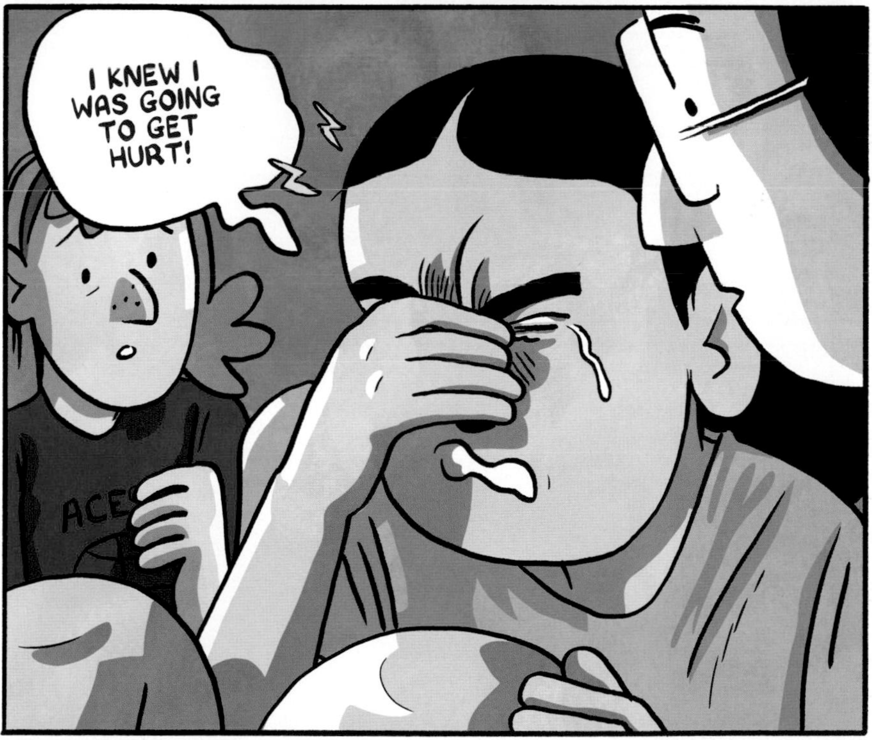
I KNEW I WAS GOING TO GET HURT!

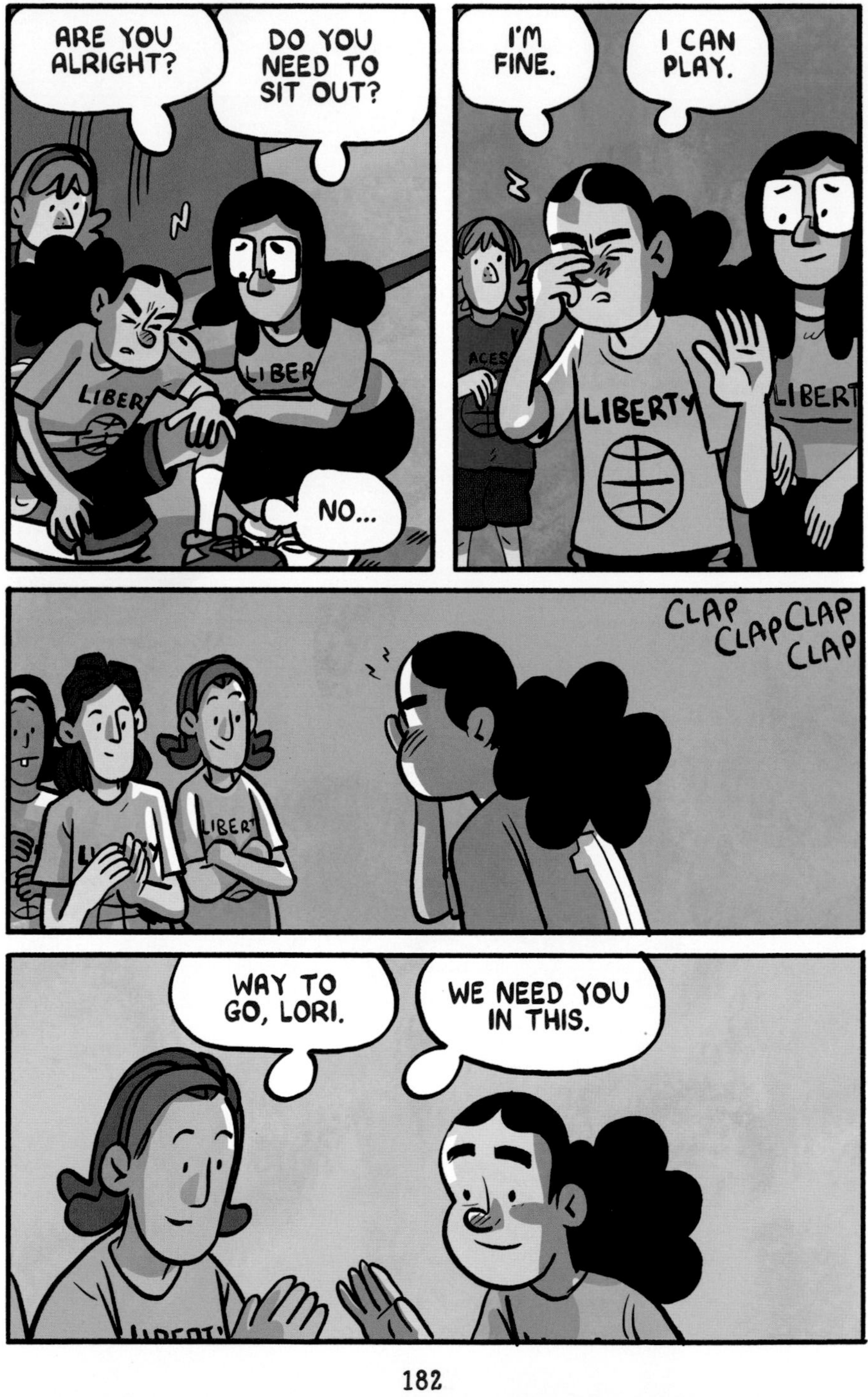
ARE YOU ALRIGHT?
DO YOU NEED TO SIT OUT?
LIBERTY
LIBER
NO...
I'M FINE.
I CAN PLAY.
ACES
LIBERTY
LIBERT
CLAP CLAP CLAP CLAP
LIBERT
WAY TO GO, LORI.
WE NEED YOU IN THIS.

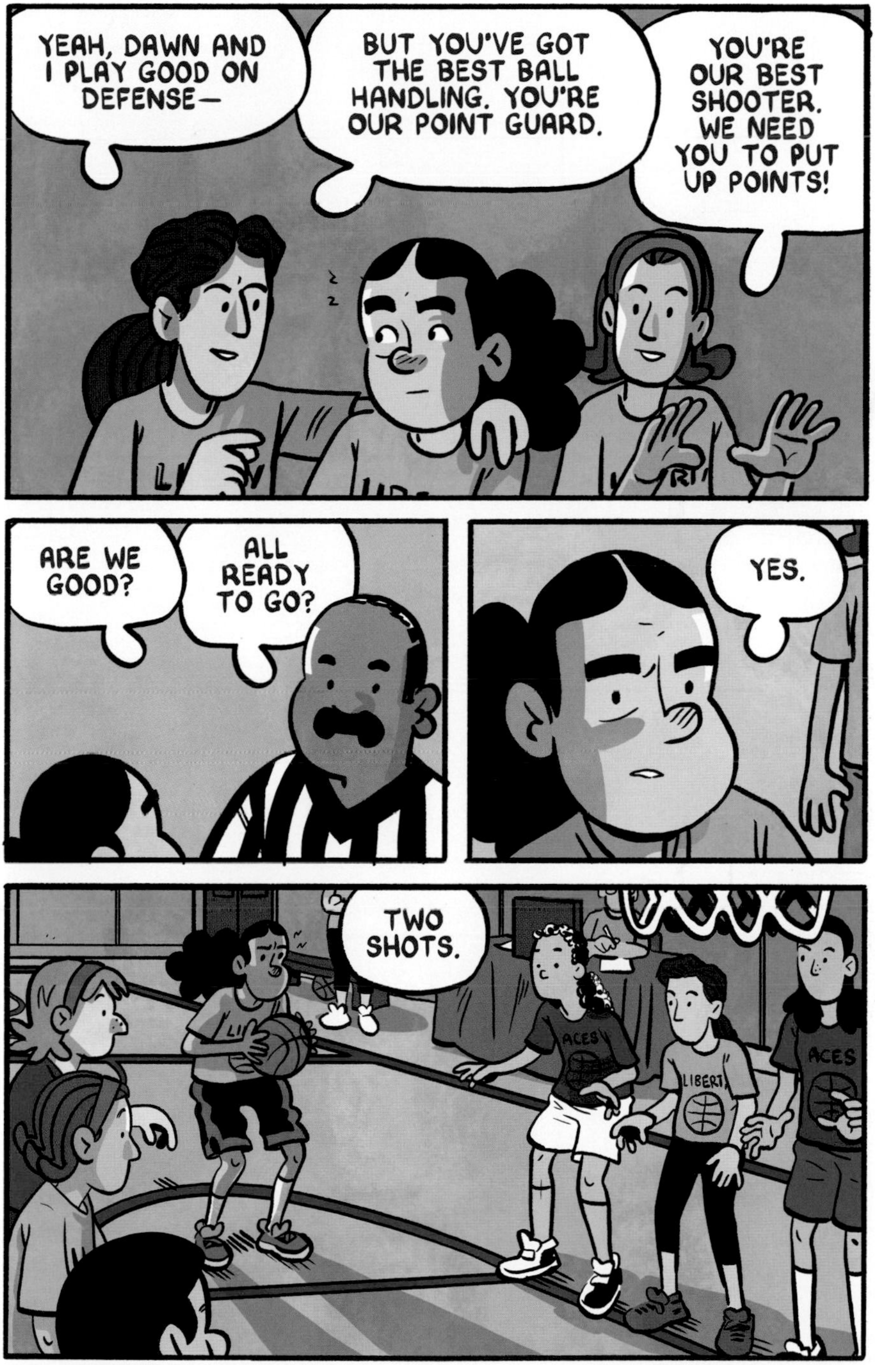
YEAH, DAWN AND I PLAY GOOD ON DEFENSE—
BUT YOU'VE GOT THE BEST BALL HANDLING. YOU'RE OUR POINT GUARD.
YOU'RE OUR BEST SHOOTER. WE NEED YOU TO PUT UP POINTS!
ARE WE GOOD?
ALL READY TO GO?
YES.
TWO SHOTS.
ACES
LIBERTY
ACES

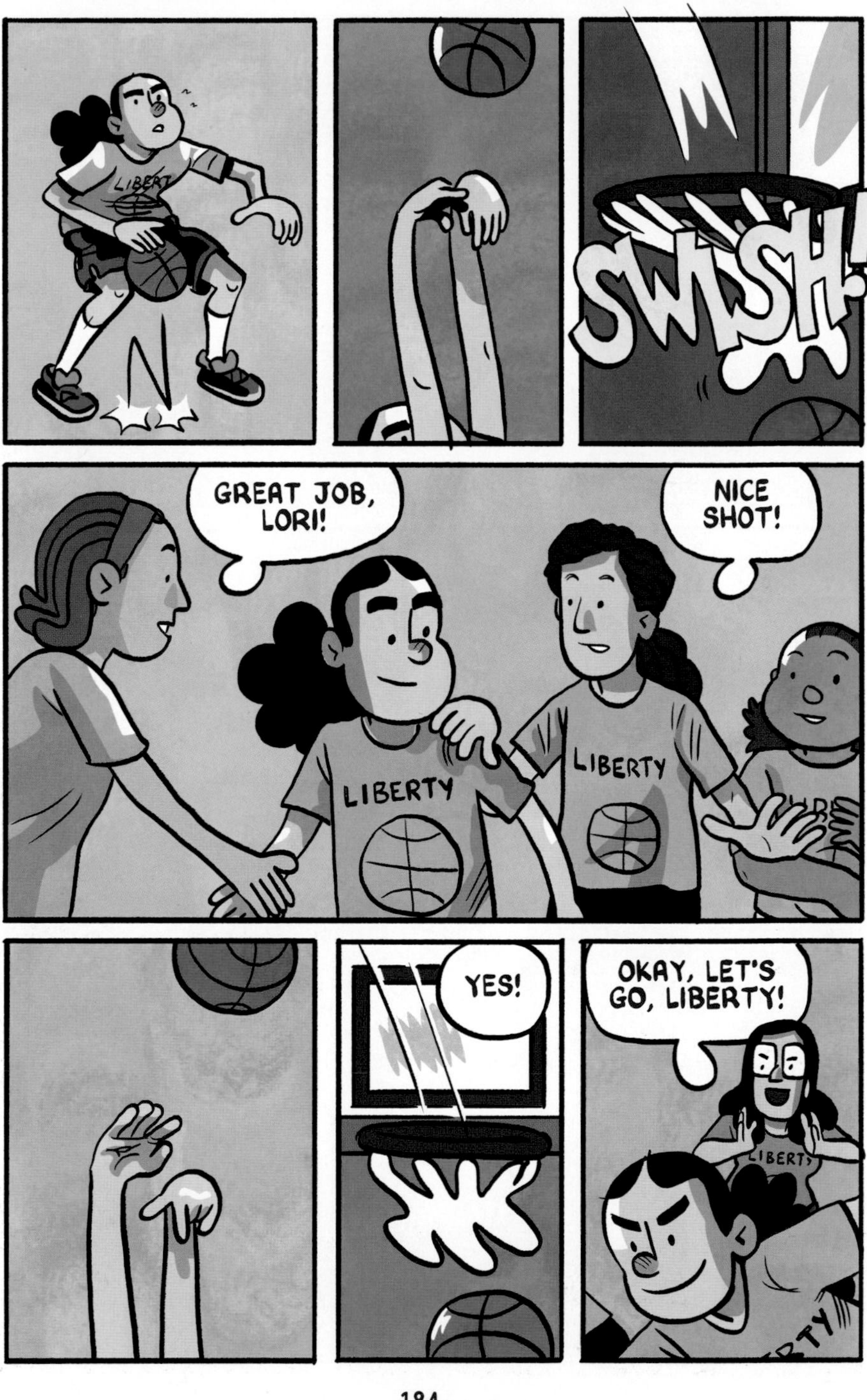
SWISH!
GREAT JOB, LORI!
NICE SHOT!
LIBERTY
LIBERTY
YES!
OKAY, LET'S GO, LIBERTY!

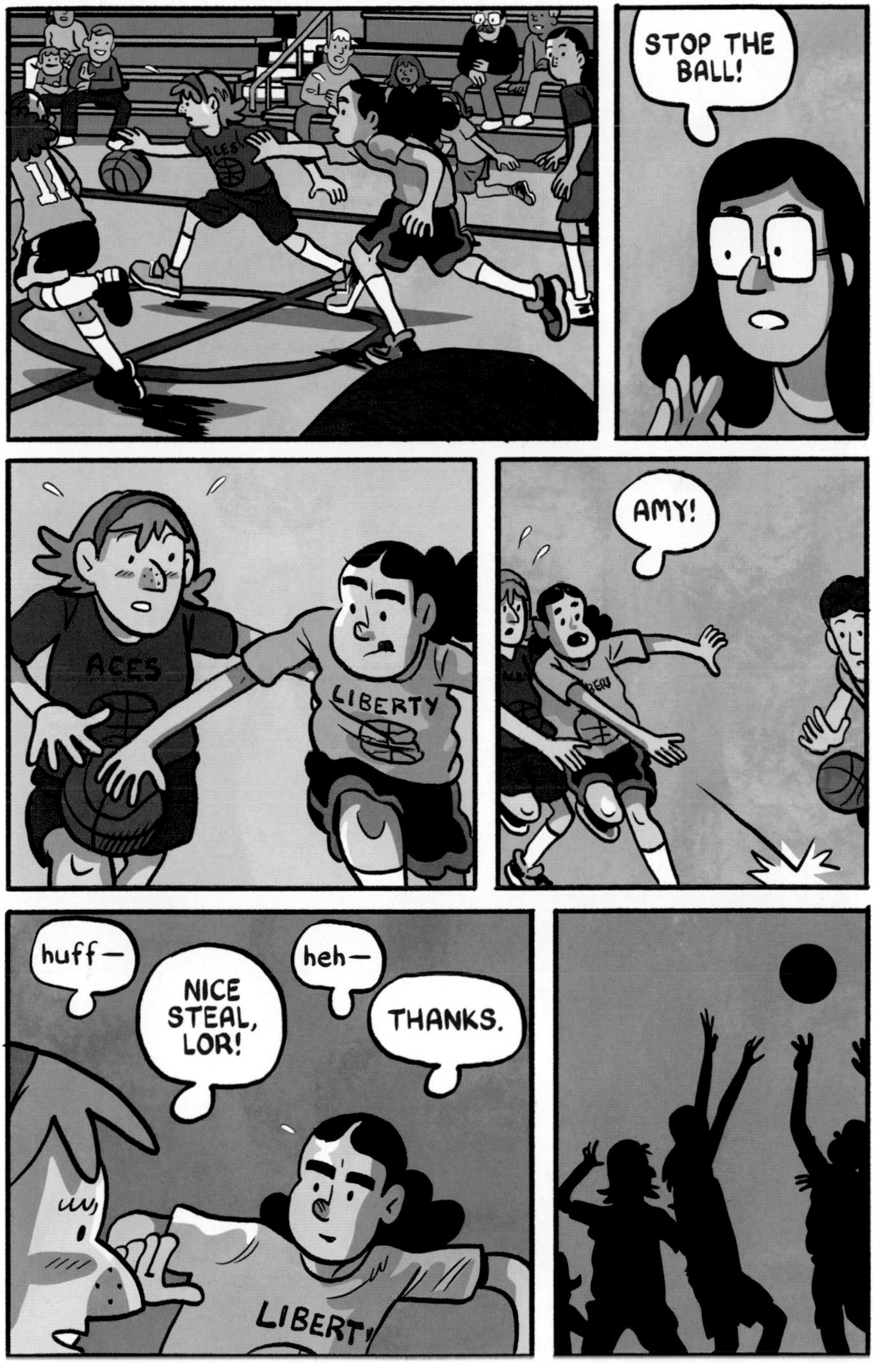
STOP THE BALL!
AMY!
huff—
NICE STEAL, LOR!
heh—
THANKS.

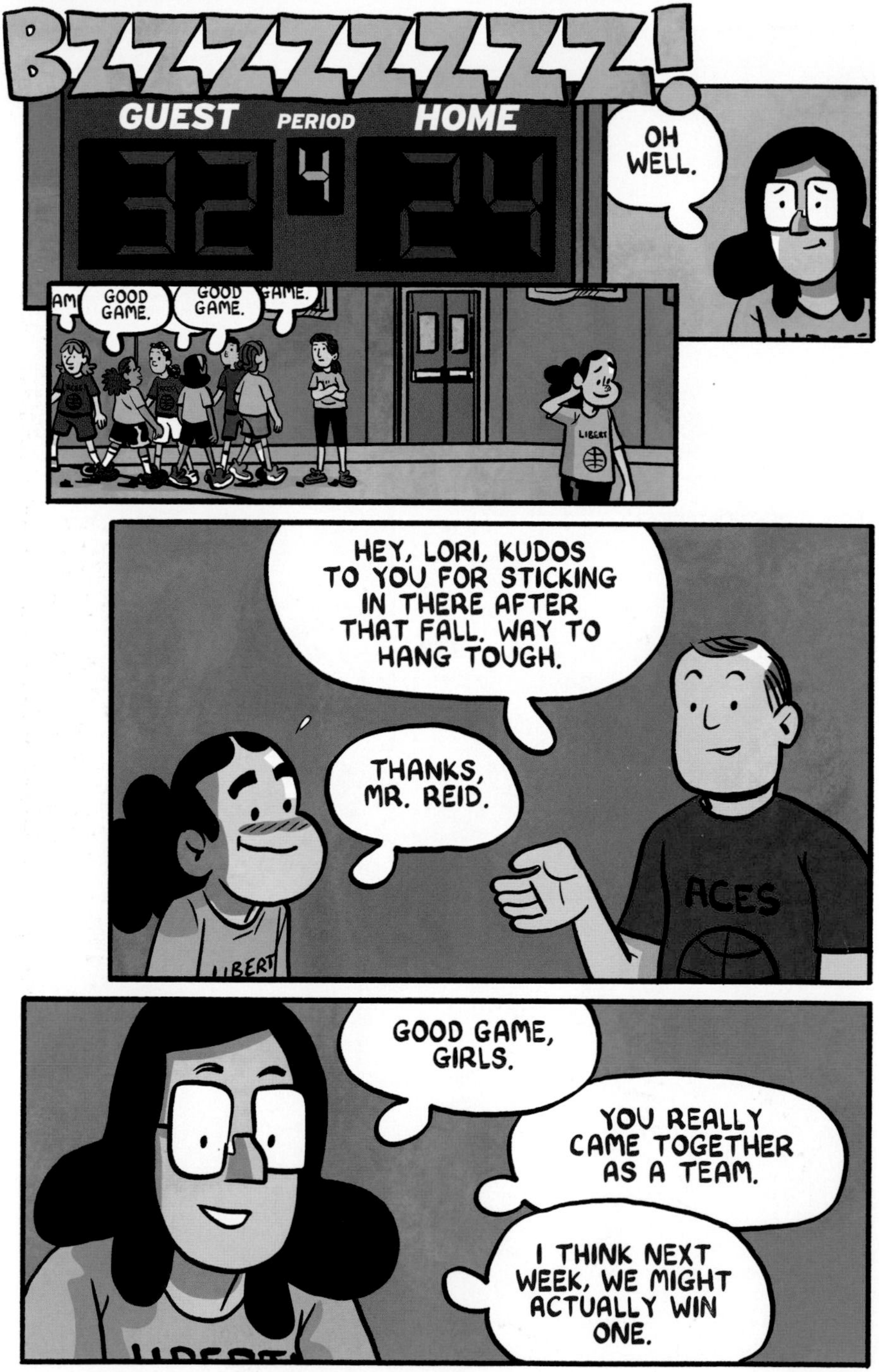
BZZZZZZZZZZZZ!
GUEST
PERIOD
HOME
32
4
24
OH WELL.
GOOD GAME.
GOOD GAME.
HEY, LORI, KUDOS TO YOU FOR STICKING IN THERE AFTER THAT FALL. WAY TO HANG TOUGH.
THANKS, MR. REID.
ACES
GOOD GAME, GIRLS.
YOU REALLY CAME TOGETHER AS A TEAM.
I THINK NEXT WEEK, WE MIGHT ACTUALLY WIN ONE.

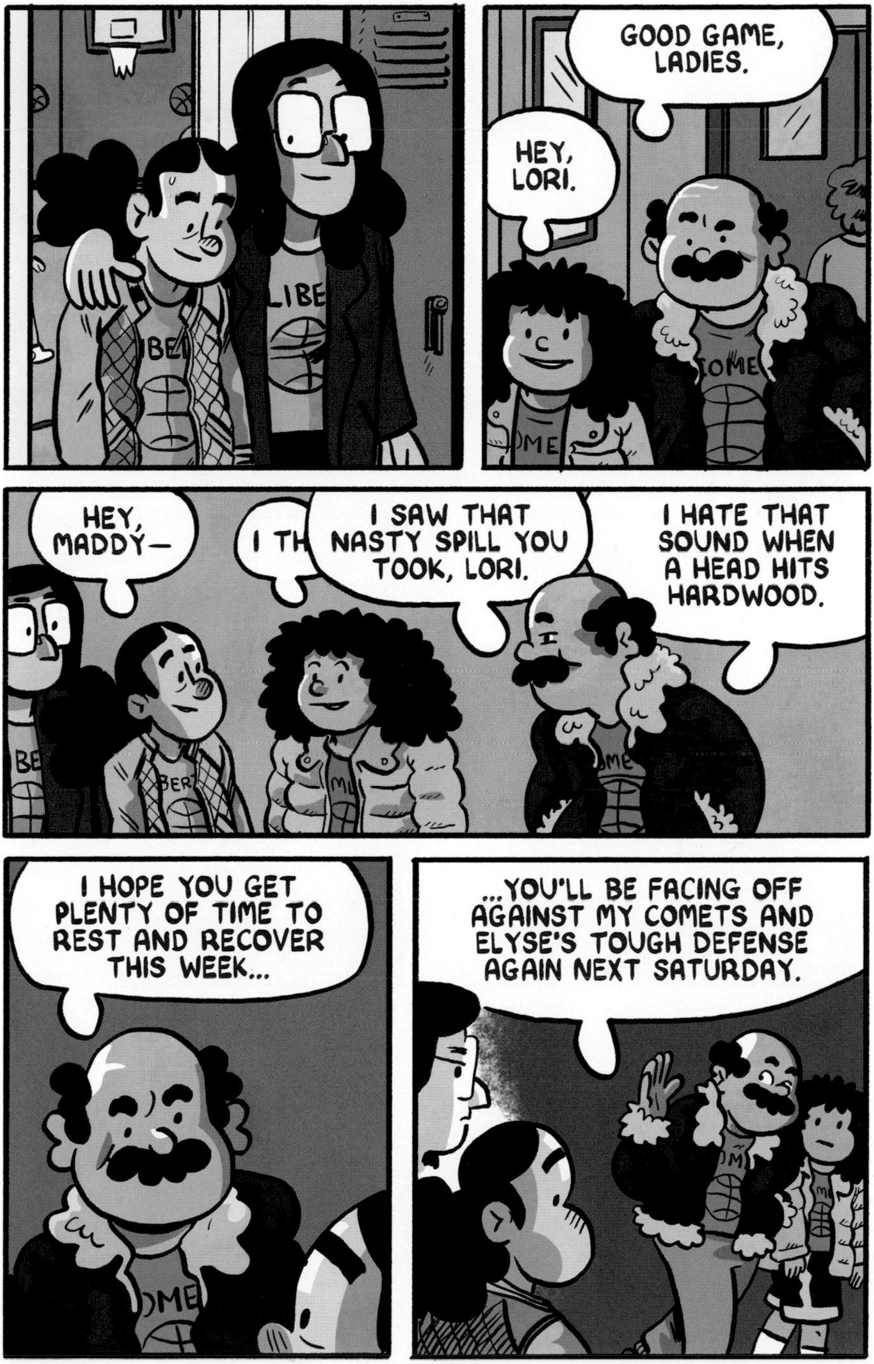

GOOD GAME, LADIES.
HEY, LORI.
HEY, MADDY—
I TH
I SAW THAT NASTY SPILL YOU TOOK, LORI.
I HATE THAT SOUND WHEN A HEAD HITS HARDWOOD.
I HOPE YOU GET PLENTY OF TIME TO REST AND RECOVER THIS WEEK...
...YOU'LL BE FACING OFF AGAINST MY COMETS AND ELYSE'S TOUGH DEFENSE AGAIN NEXT SATURDAY.

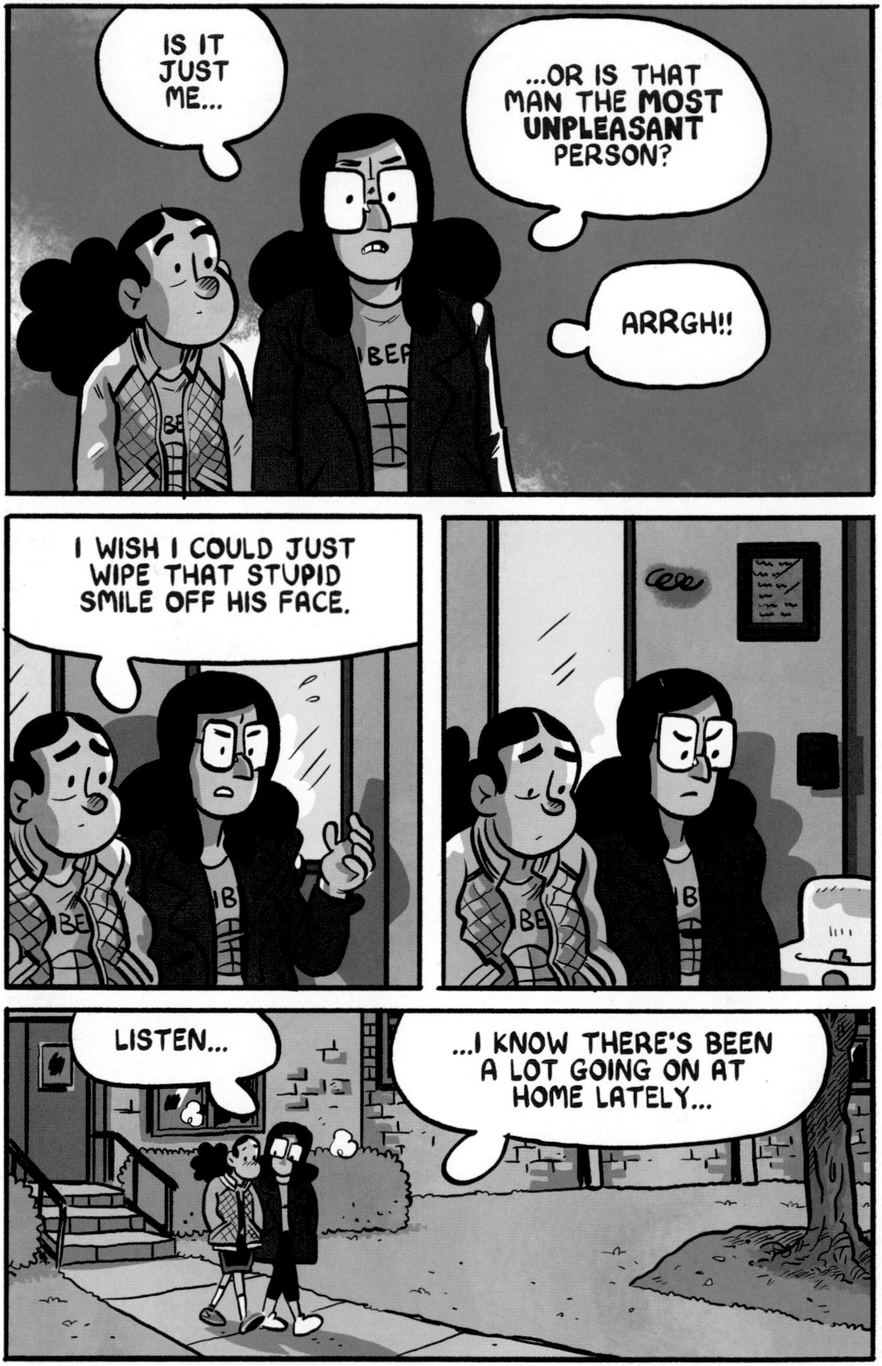
IS IT JUST ME...
...OR IS THAT MAN THE MOST UNPLEASANT PERSON?
ARRGH!!
I WISH I COULD JUST WIPE THAT STUPID SMILE OFF HIS FACE.
LISTEN...
...I KNOW THERE'S BEEN A LOT GOING ON AT HOME LATELY...

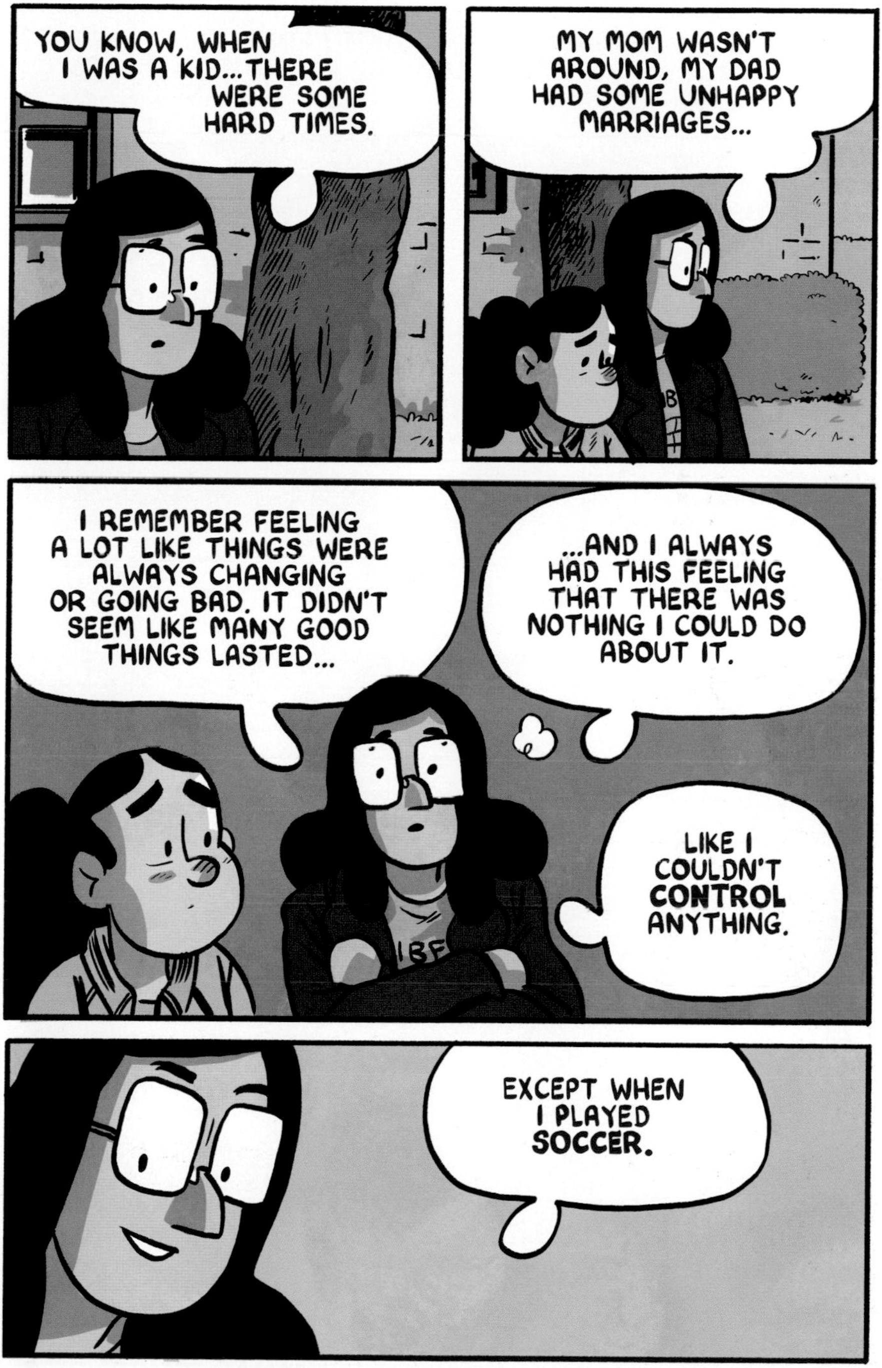
YOU KNOW, WHEN I WAS A KID... THERE WERE SOME HARD TIMES.
MY MOM WASN'T AROUND, MY DAD HAD SOME UNHAPPY MARRIAGES...
I REMEMBER FEELING A LOT LIKE THINGS WERE ALWAYS CHANGING OR GOING BAD. IT DIDN'T SEEM LIKE MANY GOOD THINGS LASTED...
...AND I ALWAYS HAD THIS FEELING THAT THERE WAS NOTHING I COULD DO ABOUT IT.
LIKE I COULDN'T **CONTROL** ANYTHING.
EXCEPT WHEN I PLAYED **SOCCER**.

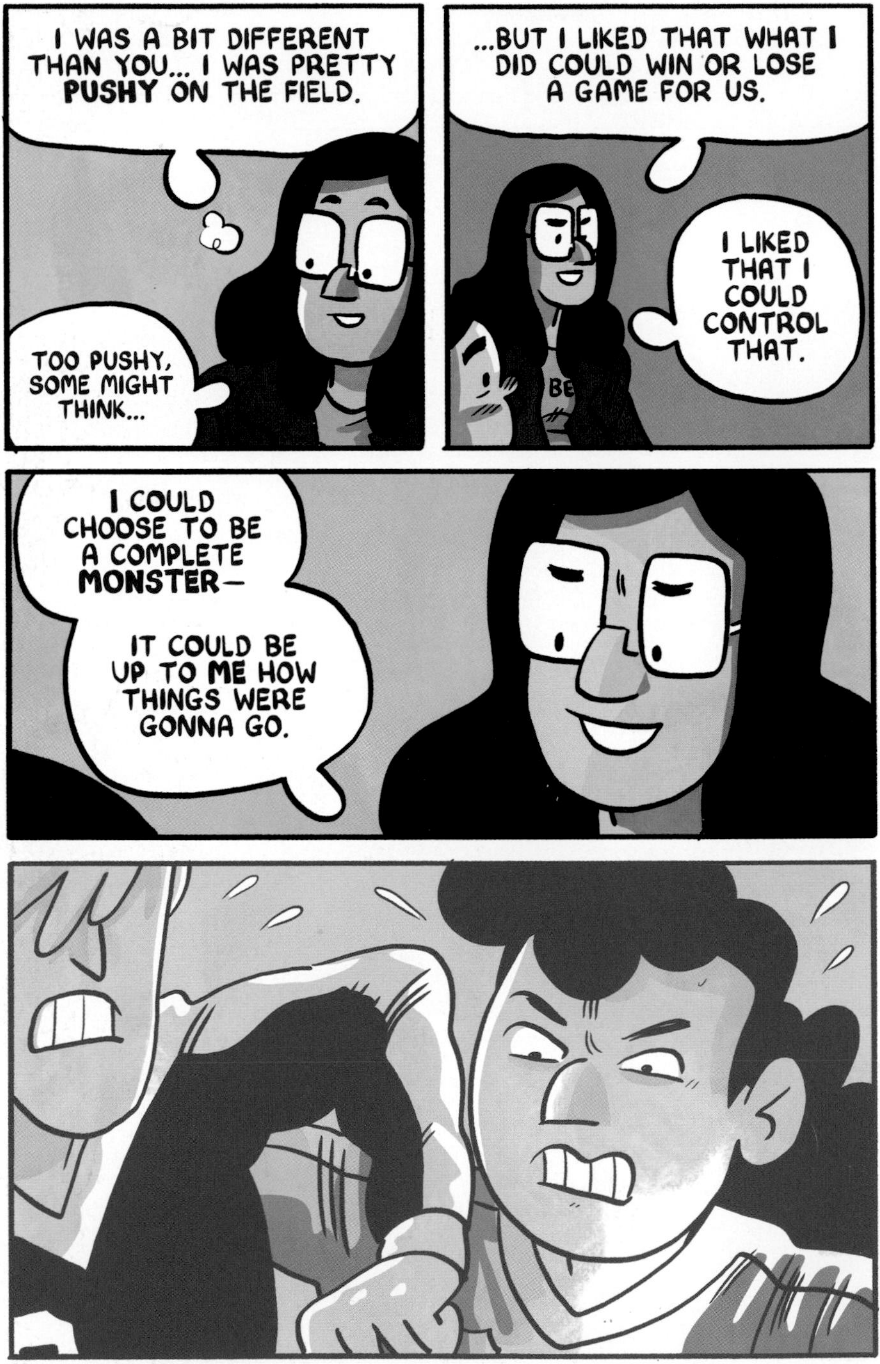
I WAS A BIT DIFFERENT THAN YOU... I WAS PRETTY PUSHY ON THE FIELD.
TOO PUSHY, SOME MIGHT THINK...
...BUT I LIKED THAT WHAT I DID COULD WIN OR LOSE A GAME FOR US.
I LIKED THAT I COULD CONTROL THAT.
I COULD CHOOSE TO BE A COMPLETE MONSTER—
IT COULD BE UP TO ME HOW THINGS WERE GONNA GO.

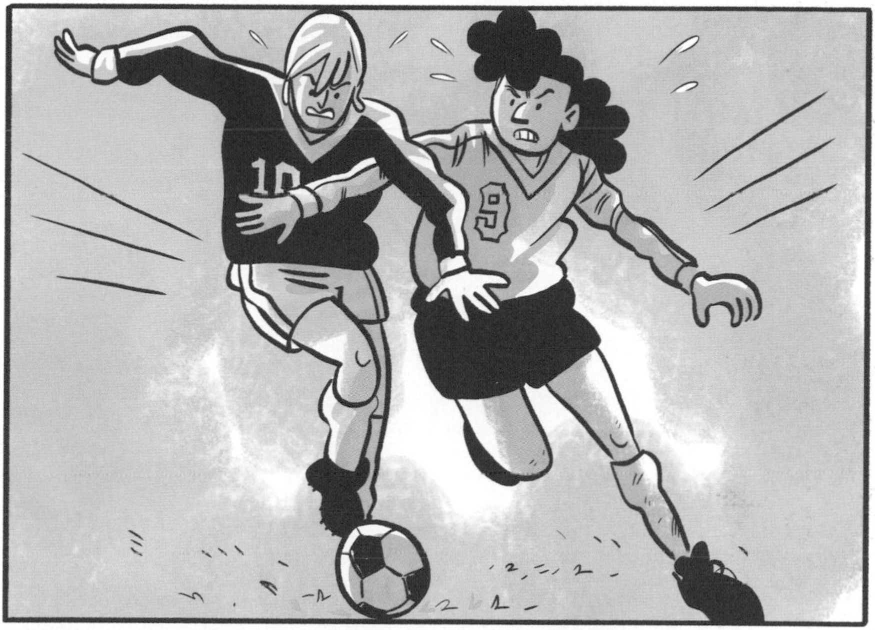
10
9

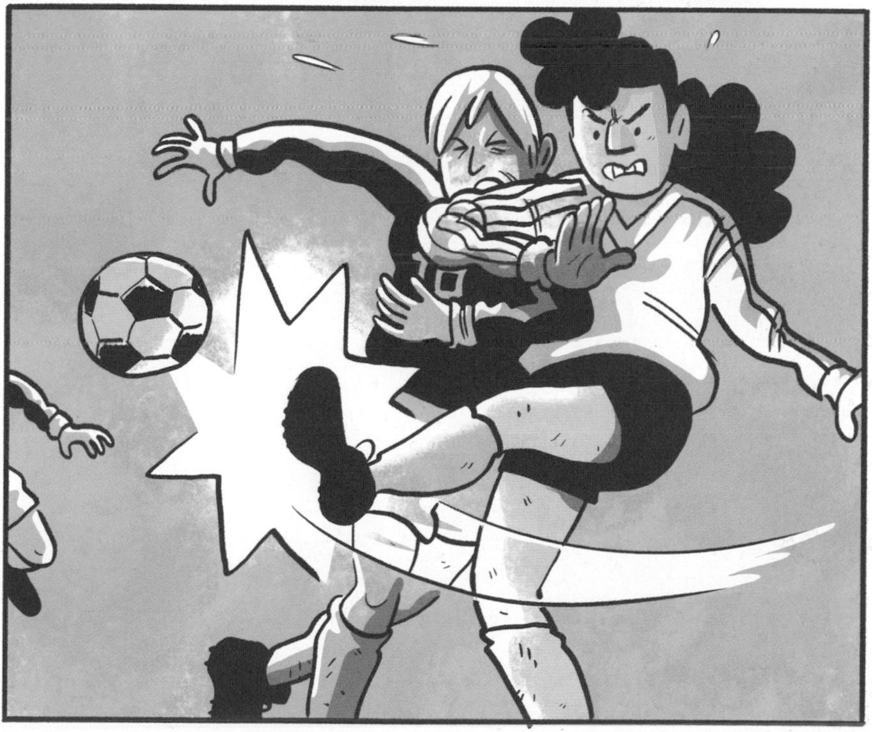

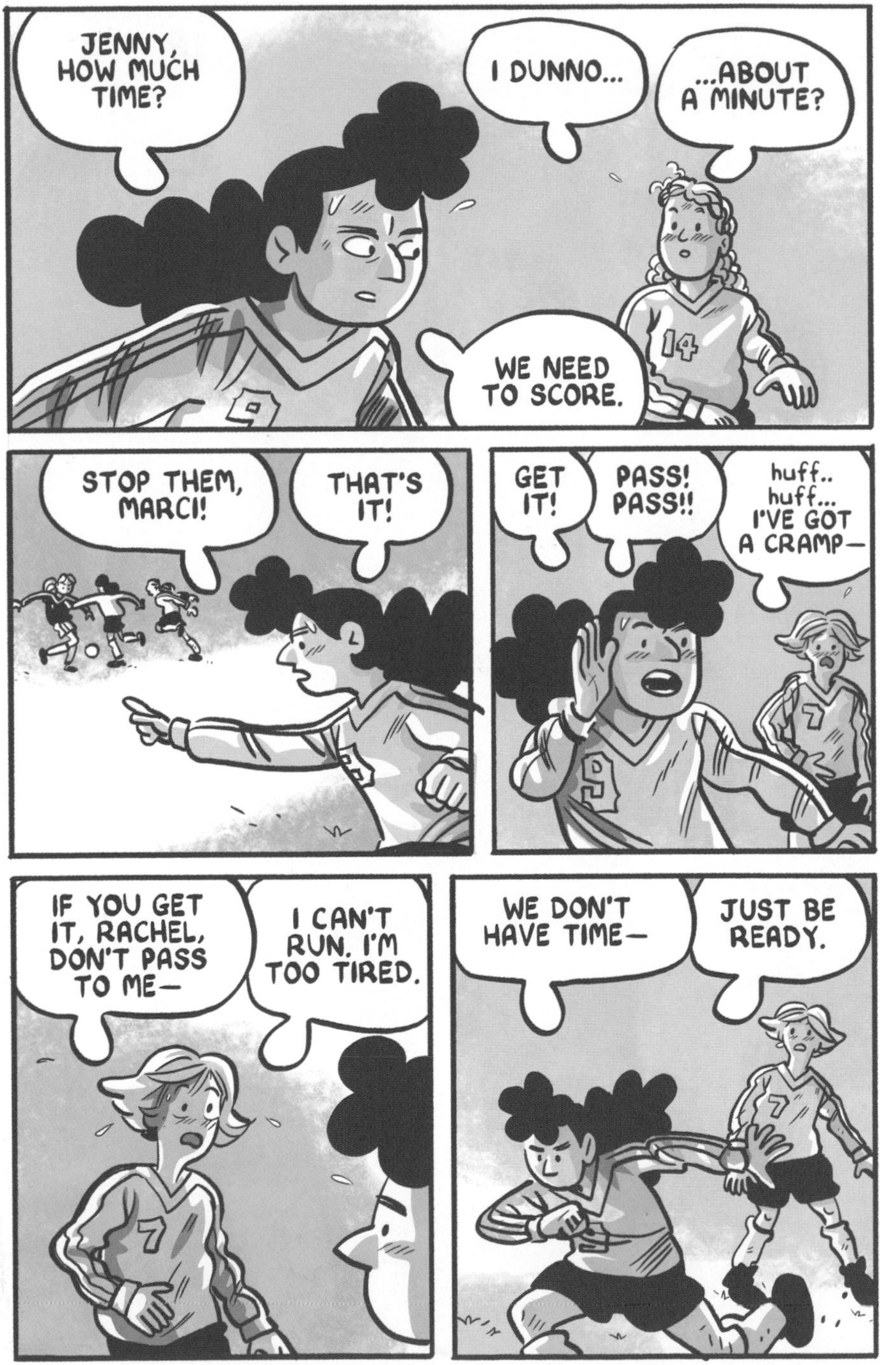

JENNY, HOW MUCH TIME?
I DUNNO...
...ABOUT A MINUTE?
WE NEED TO SCORE.
STOP THEM, MARCI!
THAT'S IT!
GET IT!
PASS! PASS!!
huff.. huff... I'VE GOT A CRAMP—
IF YOU GET IT, RACHEL, DON'T PASS TO ME—
I CAN'T RUN. I'M TOO TIRED.
WE DON'T HAVE TIME—
JUST BE READY.

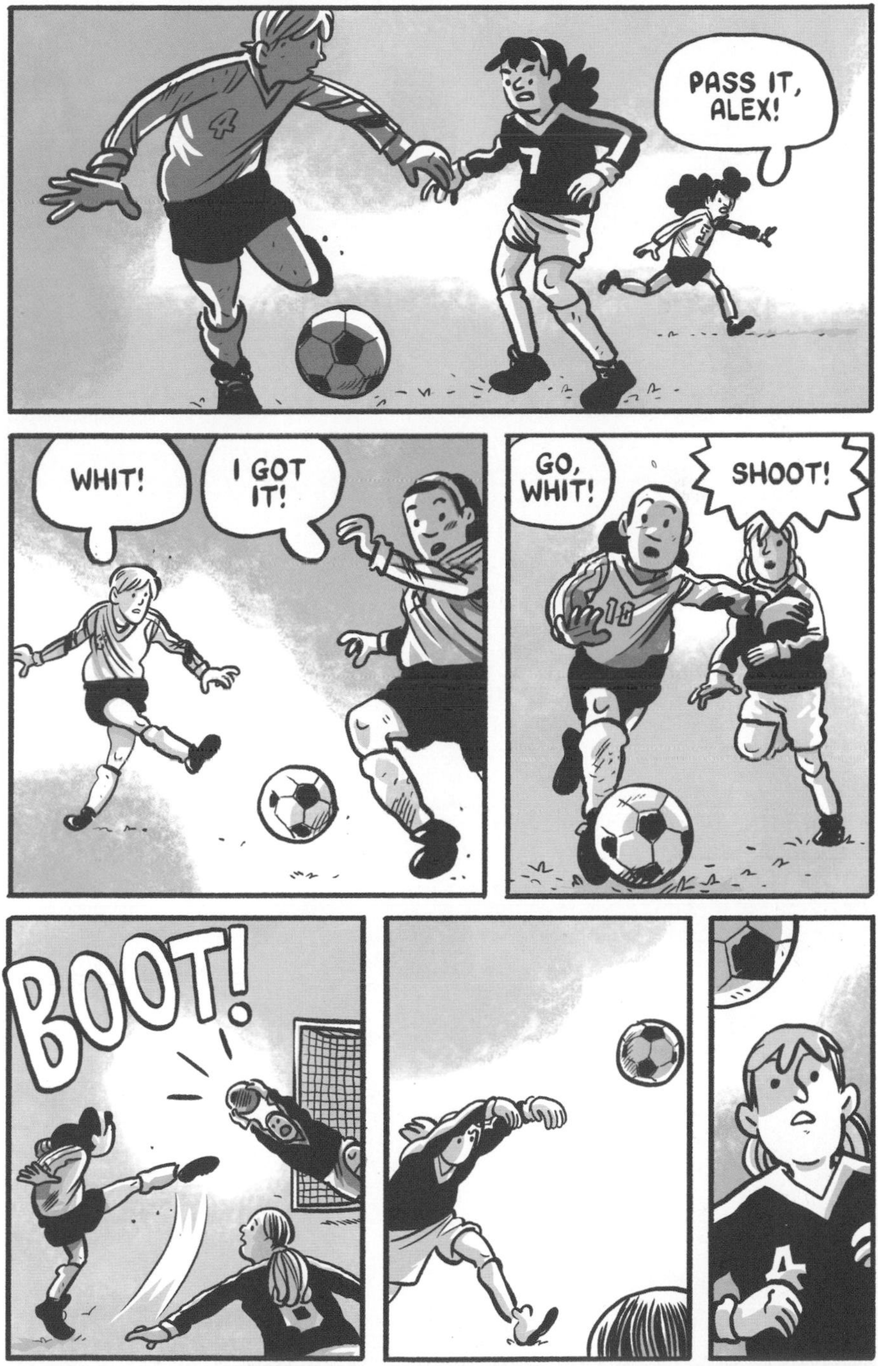
PASS IT, ALEX!
WHIT!
I GOT IT!
GO, WHIT!
SHOOT!
BOOT!

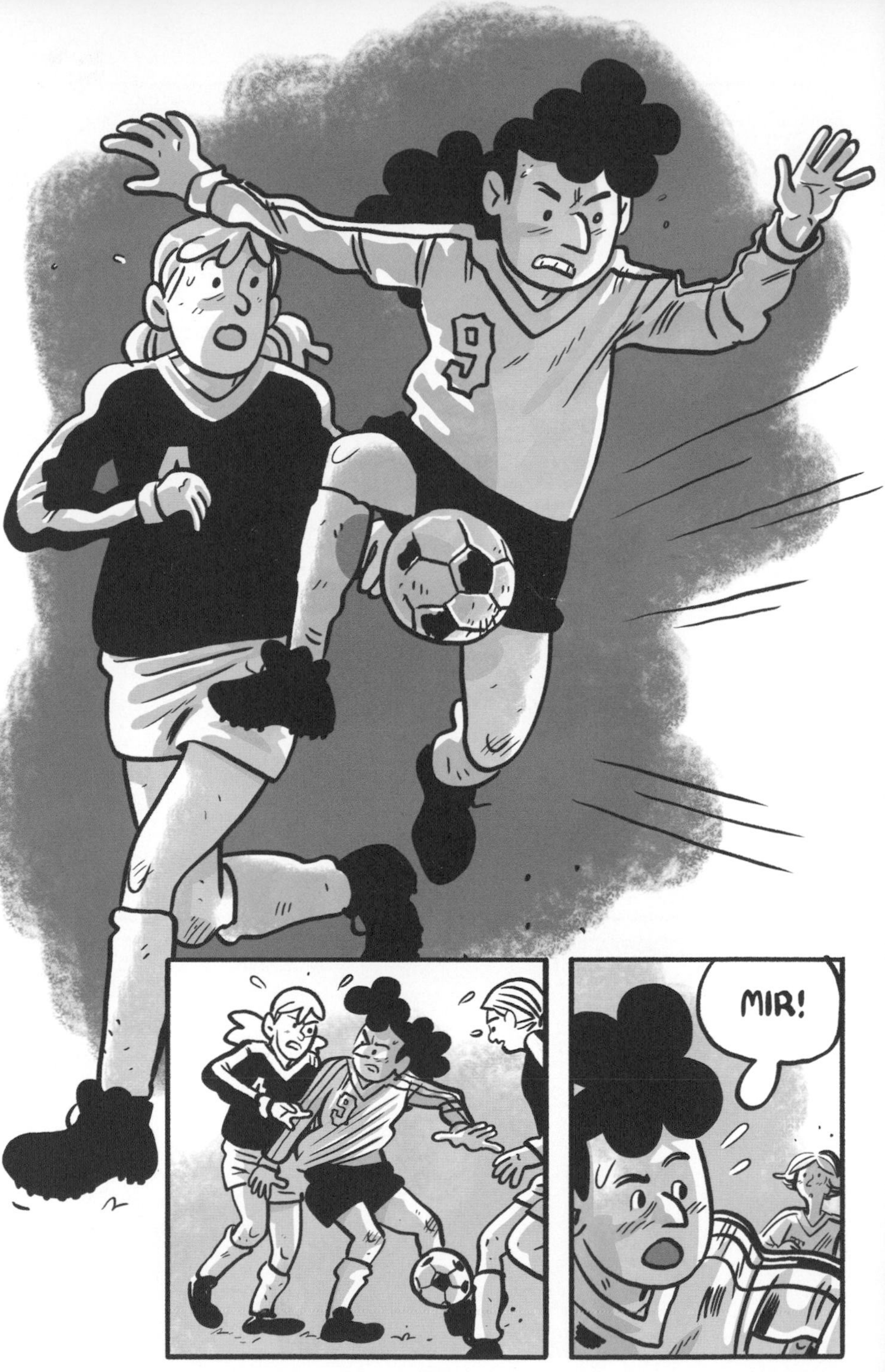
MIR!

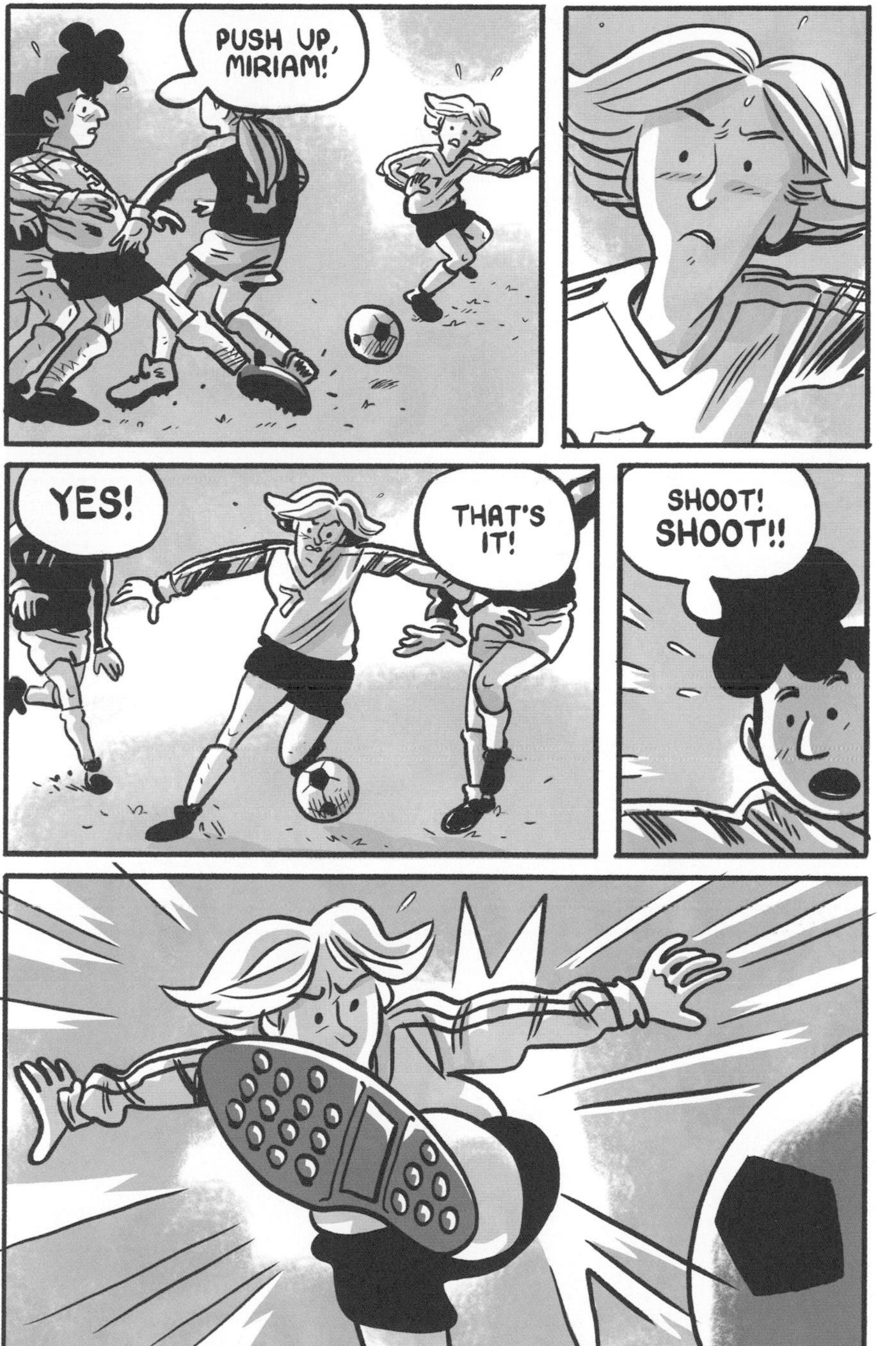
PUSH UP, MIRIAM!
YES!
THAT'S IT!
SHOOT! SHOOT!!

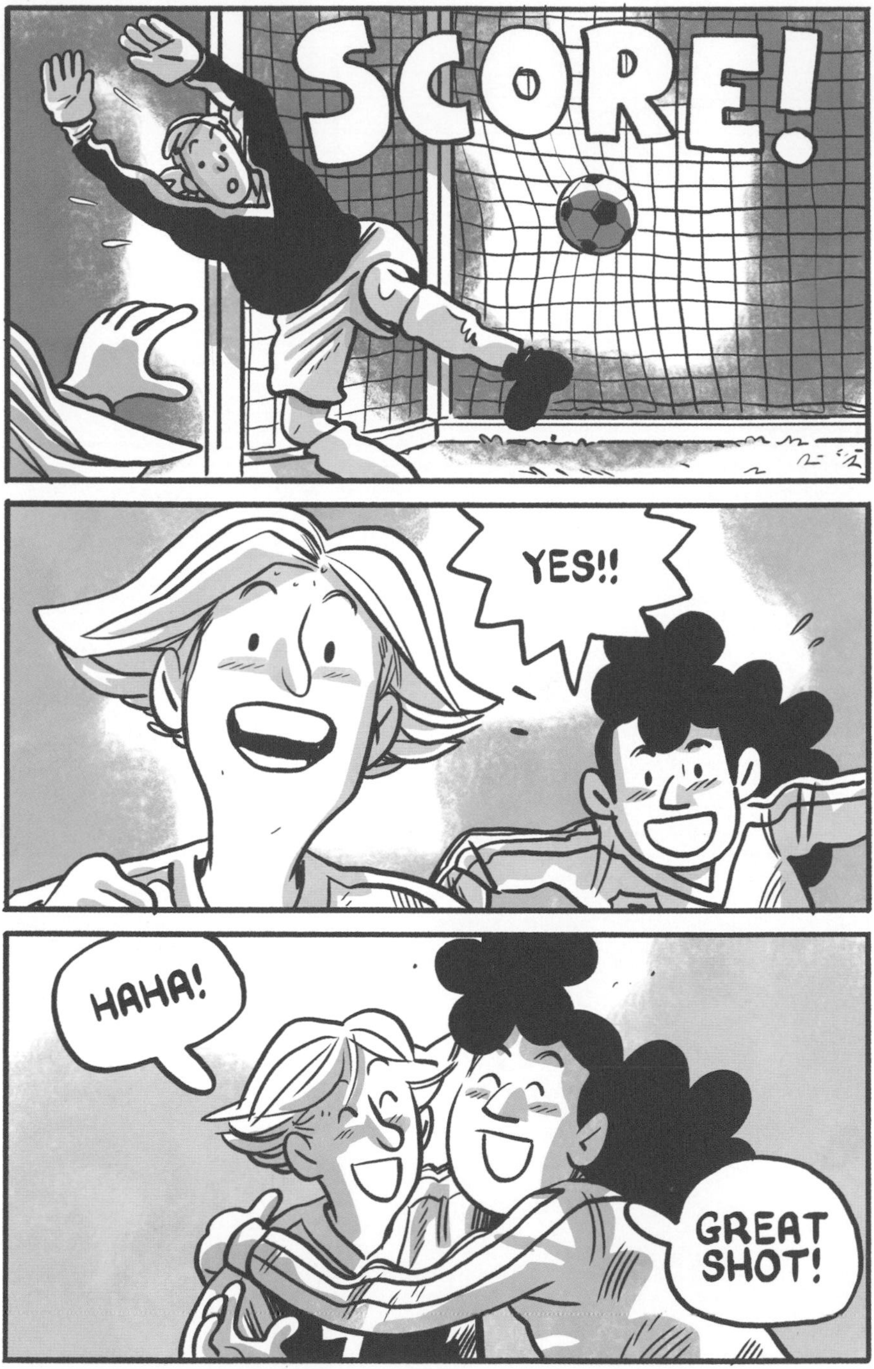
SCORE!
YES!!
HAHA!
GREAT SHOT!

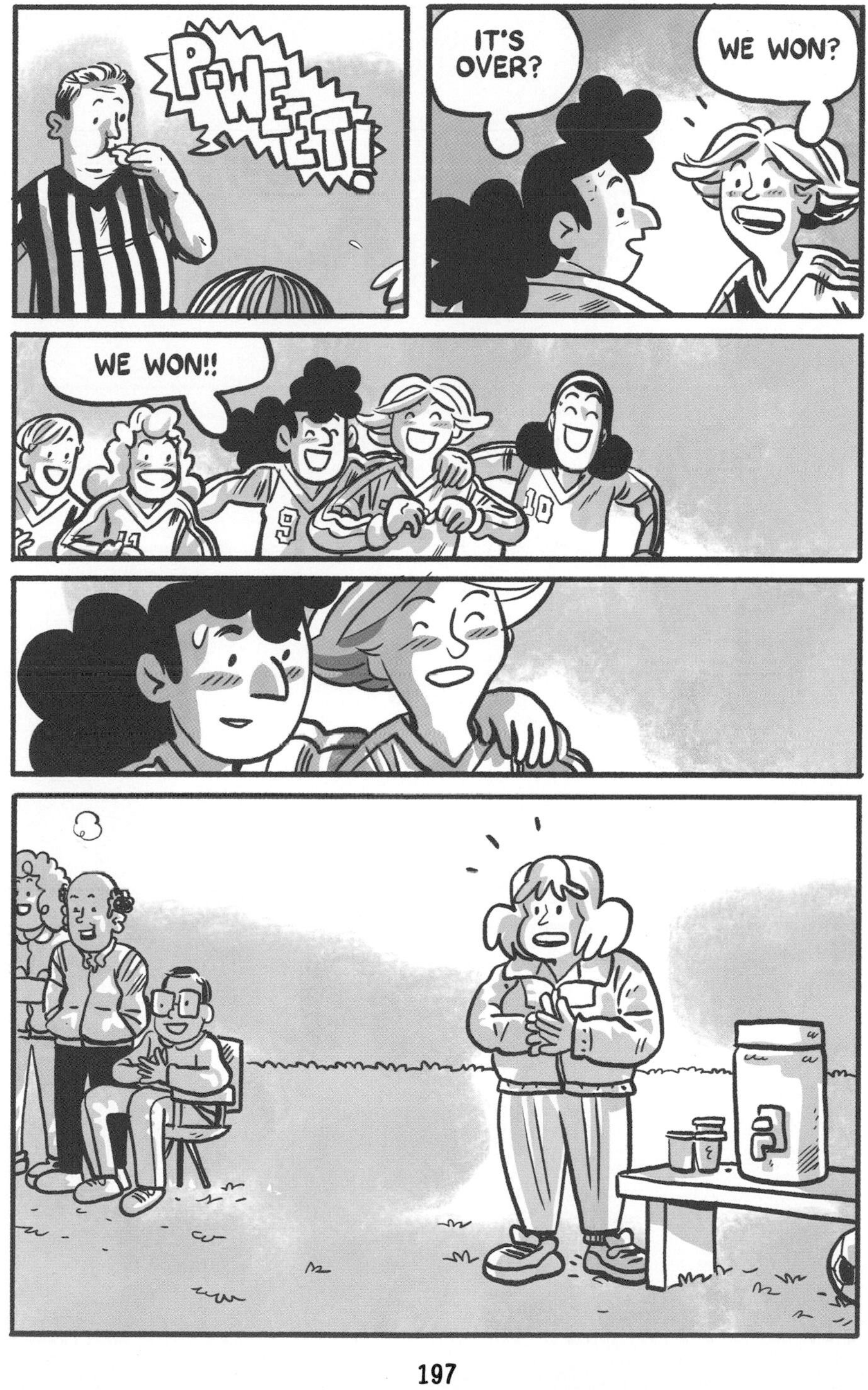
P-WEEET!
IT'S OVER?
WE WON?
WE WON!!

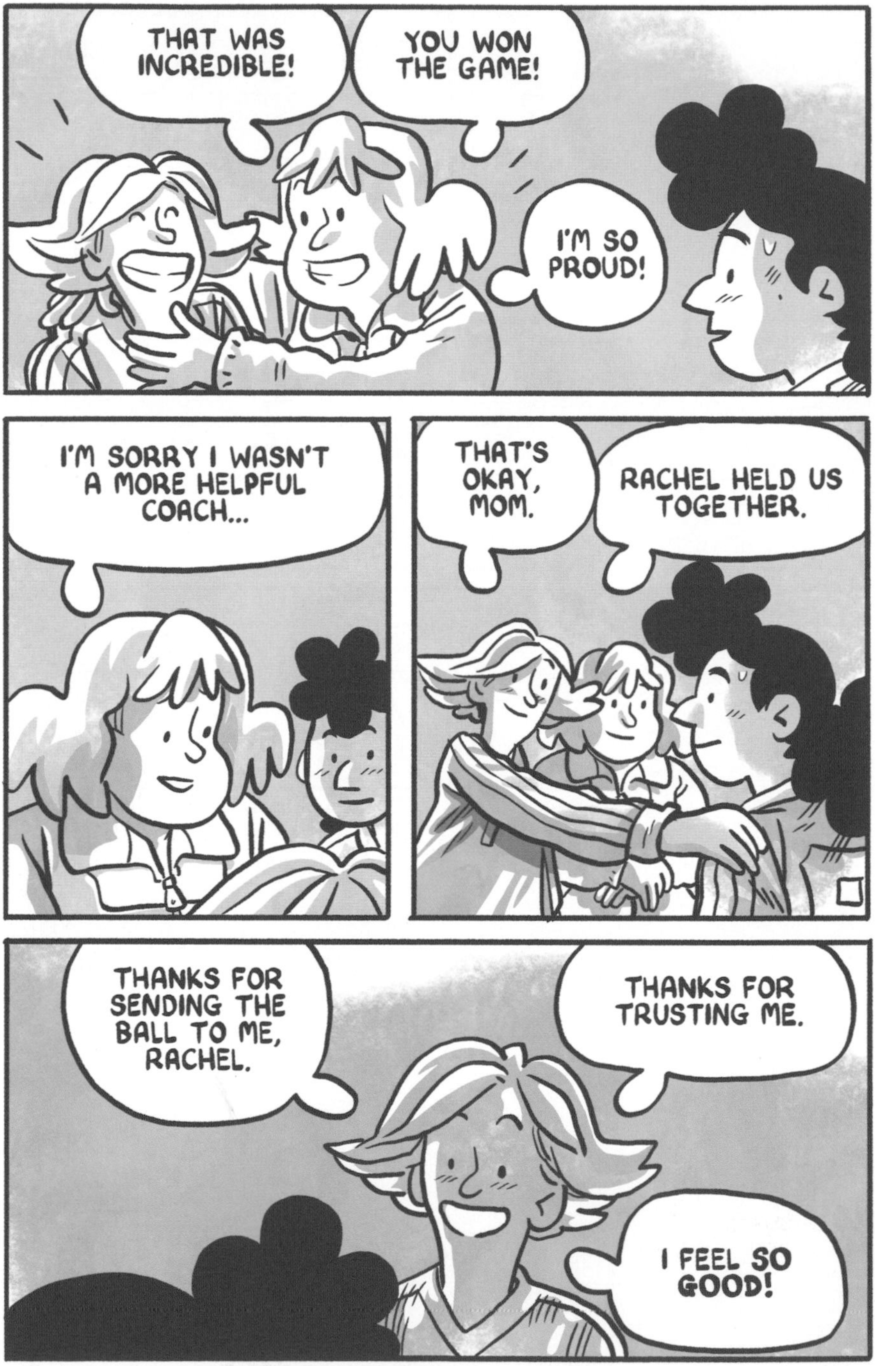
THAT WAS INCREDIBLE!
YOU WON THE GAME!
I'M SO PROUD!
I'M SORRY I WASN'T A MORE HELPFUL COACH...
THAT'S OKAY, MOM.
RACHEL HELD US TOGETHER.
THANKS FOR SENDING THE BALL TO ME, RACHEL.
THANKS FOR TRUSTING ME.
I FEEL SO GOOD!

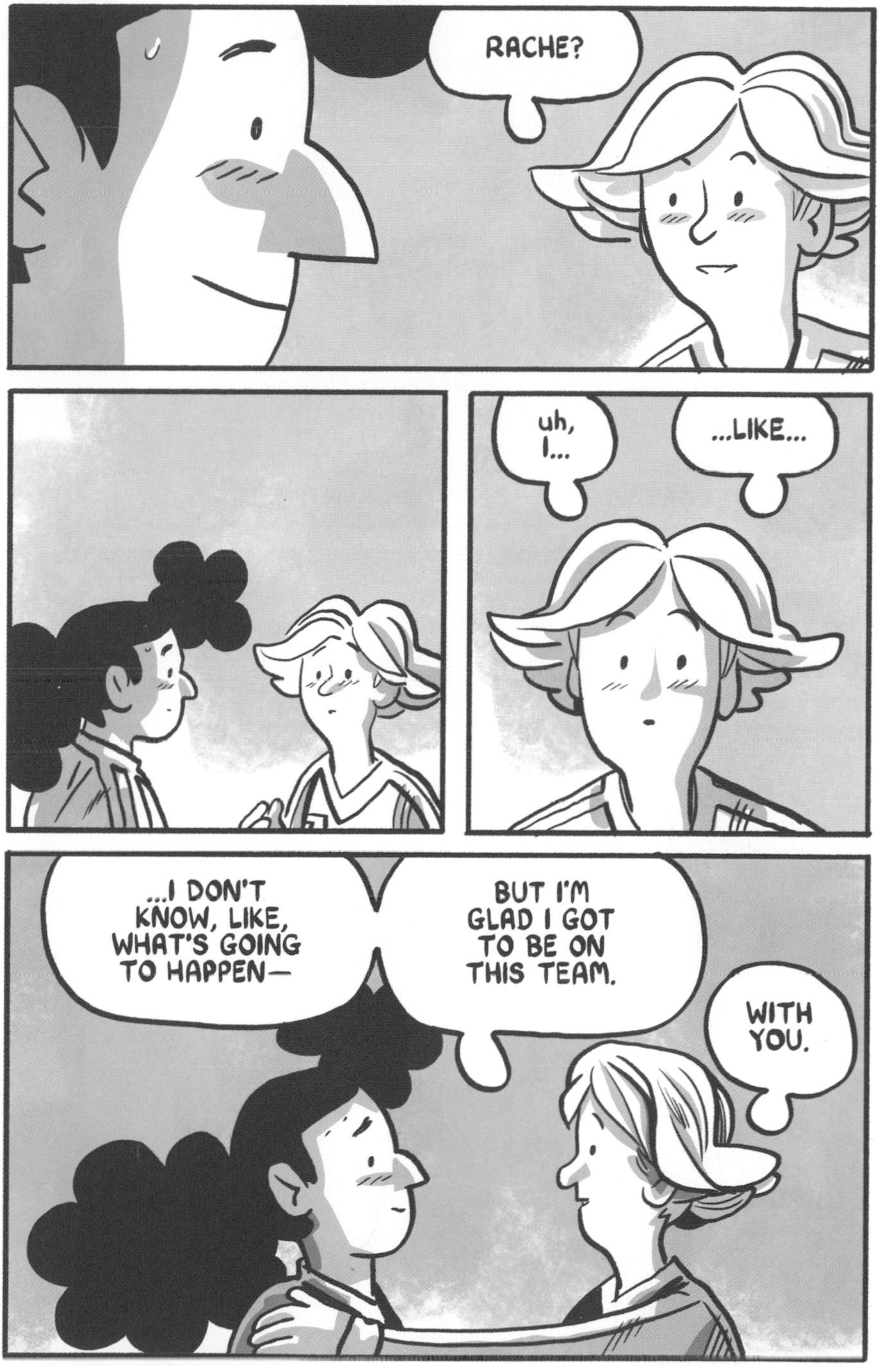
RACHE?
uh, I...
...LIKE...
...I DON'T KNOW, LIKE, WHAT'S GOING TO HAPPEN—
BUT I'M GLAD I GOT TO BE ON THIS TEAM.
WITH YOU.

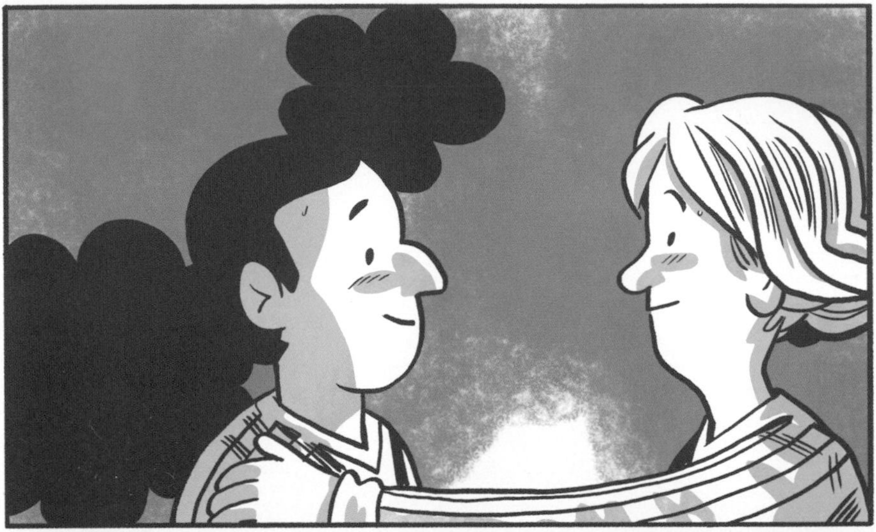

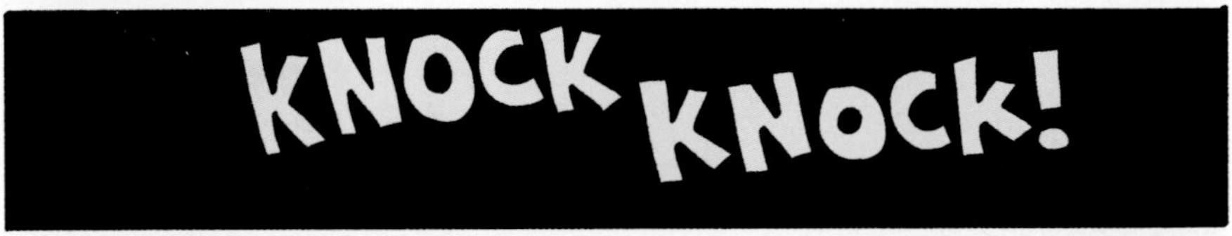
KNOCK KNOCK!

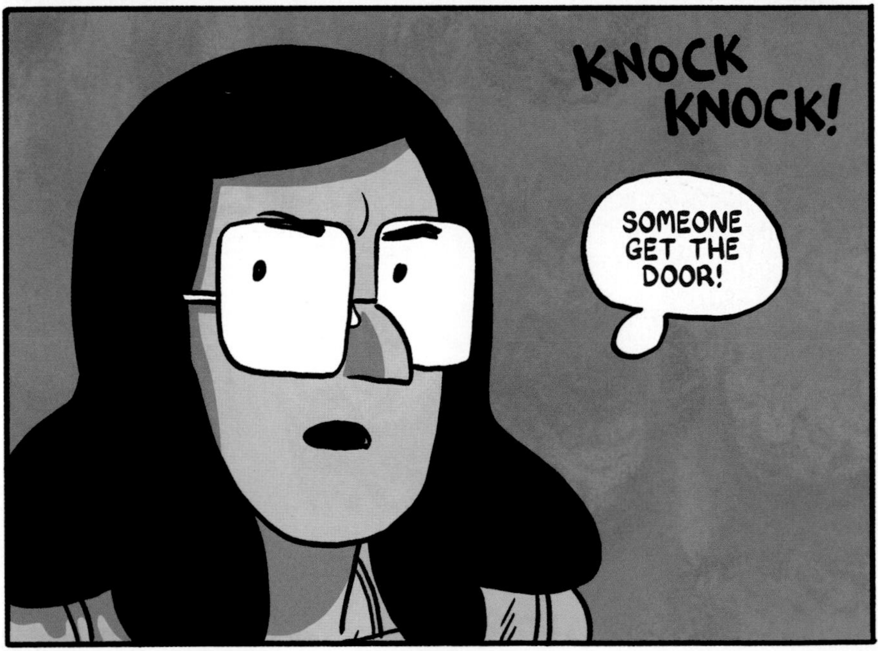
KNOCK KNOCK!
SOMEONE GET THE DOOR!

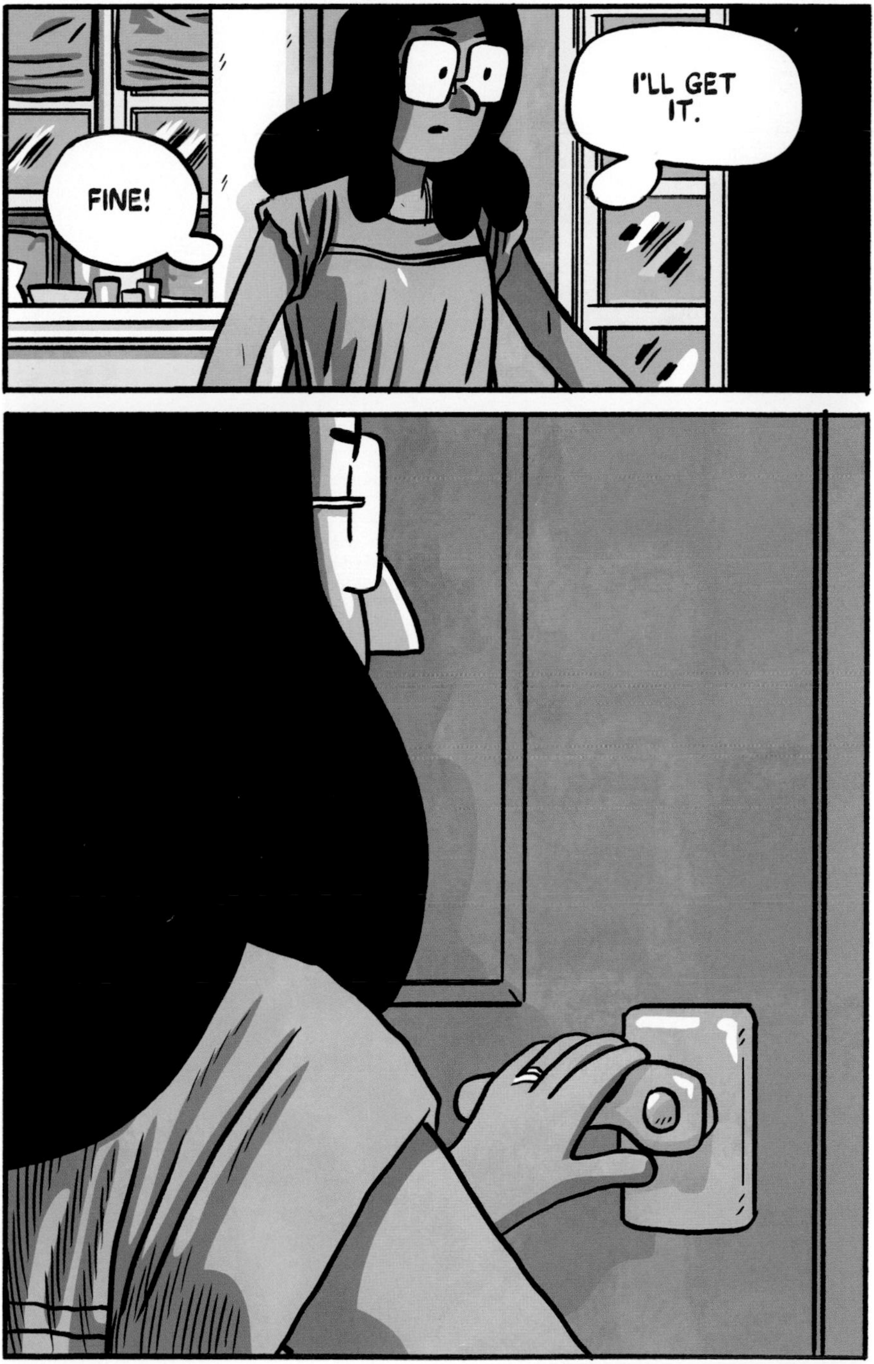
I'LL GET IT.
FINE!

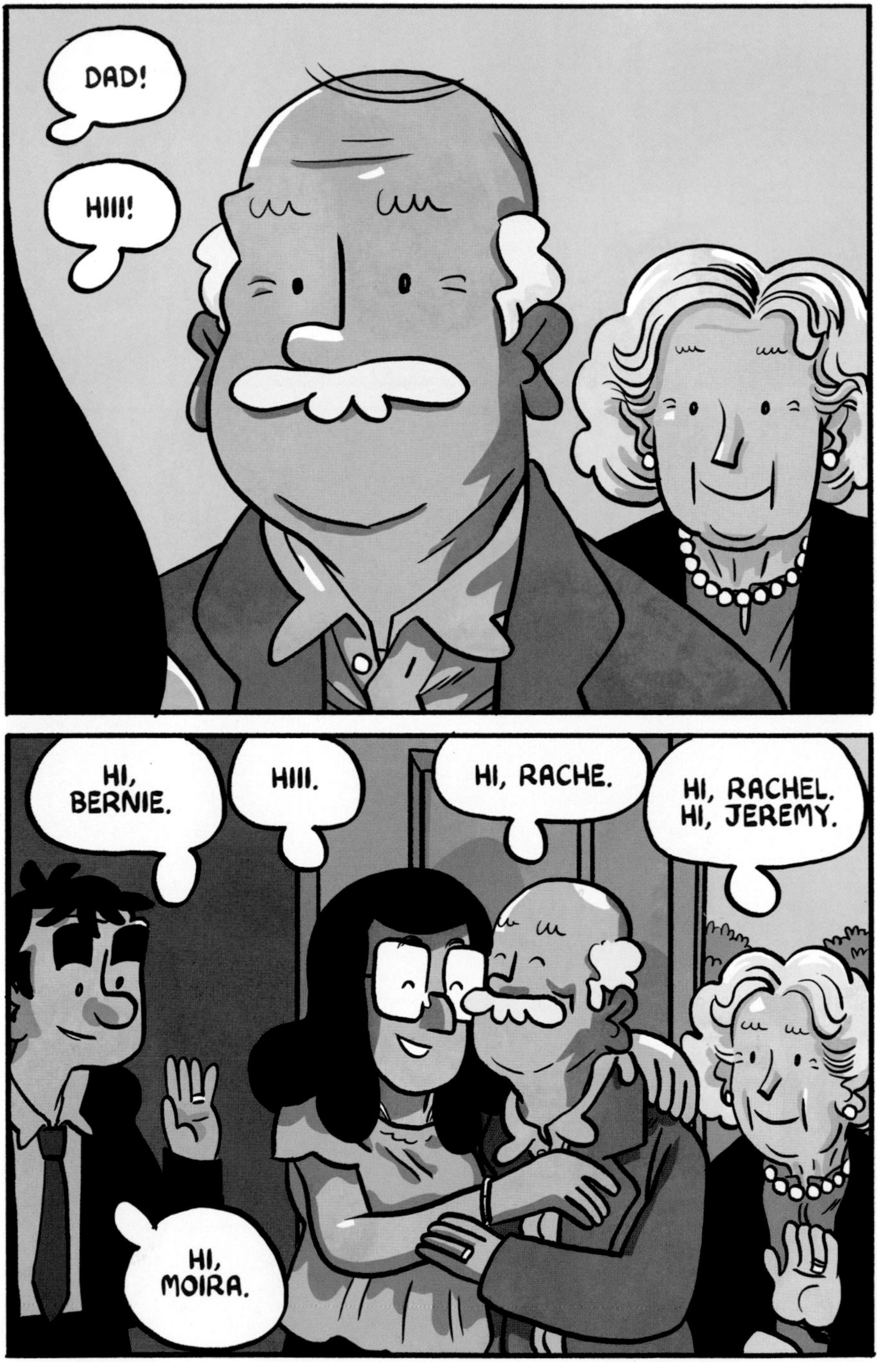
DAD!
HIIII!
HI, BERNIE.
HIII.
HI, RACHE.
HI, RACHEL. HI, JEREMY.
HI, MOIRA.

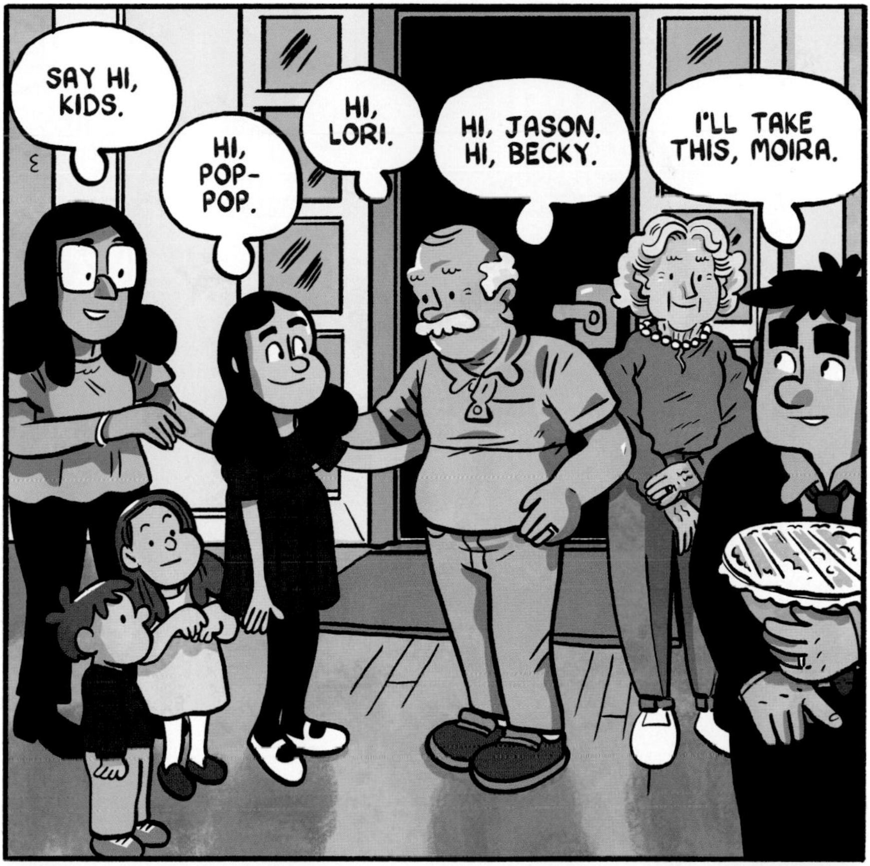
SAY HI, KIDS.
HI, POP-POP.
HI, LORI.
HI, JASON. HI, BECKY.
I'LL TAKE THIS, MOIRA.

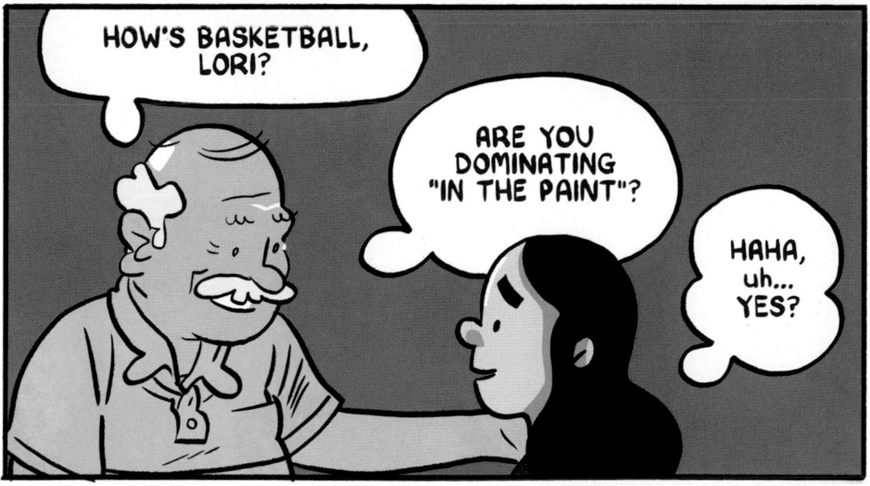
HOW'S BASKETBALL, LORI?
ARE YOU DOMINATING "IN THE PAINT"?
HAHA, uh... YES?

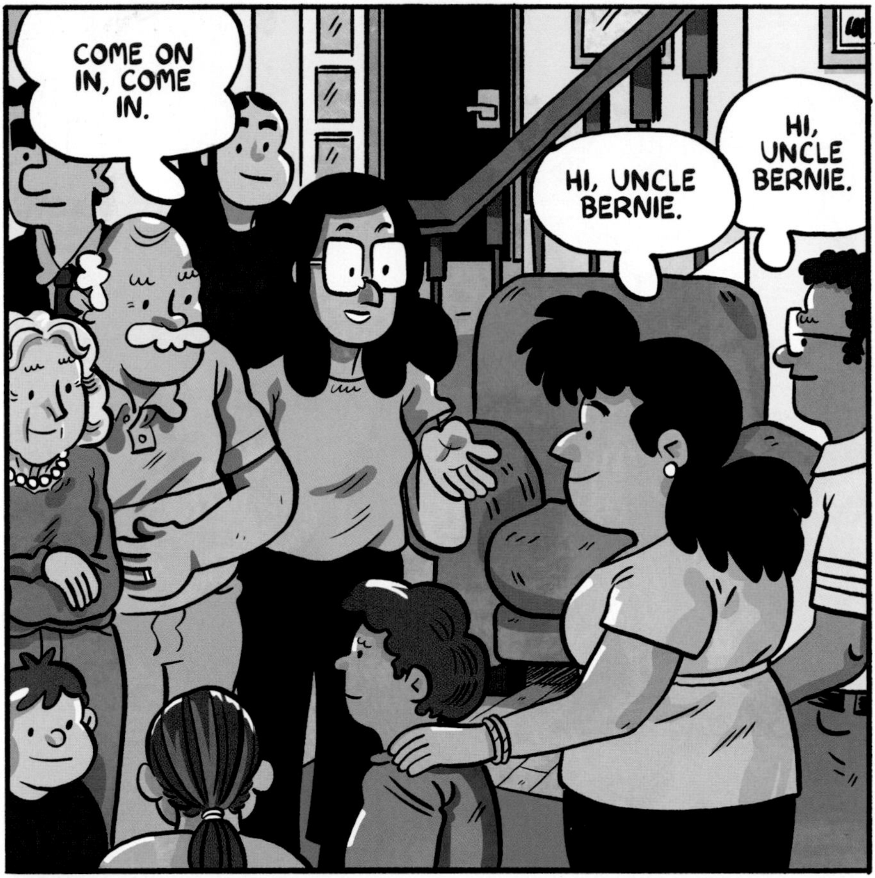
COME ON IN, COME IN.
HI, UNCLE BERNIE.
HI, UNCLE BERNIE.

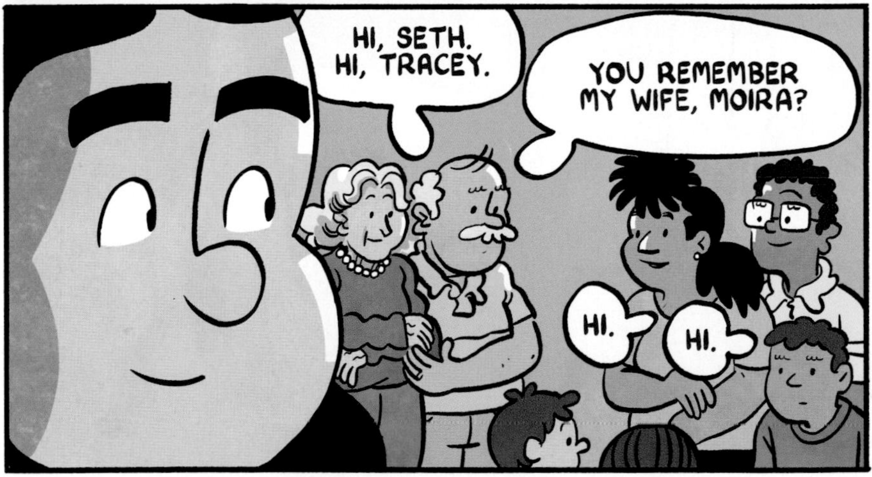
HI, SETH. HI, TRACEY.
YOU REMEMBER MY WIFE, MOIRA?
HI.
HI.

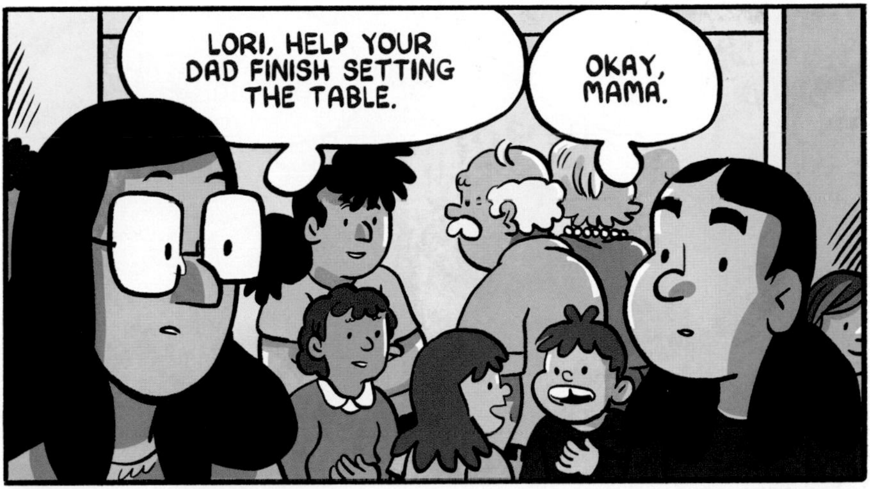
LORI, HELP YOUR DAD FINISH SETTING THE TABLE.
OKAY, MAMA.

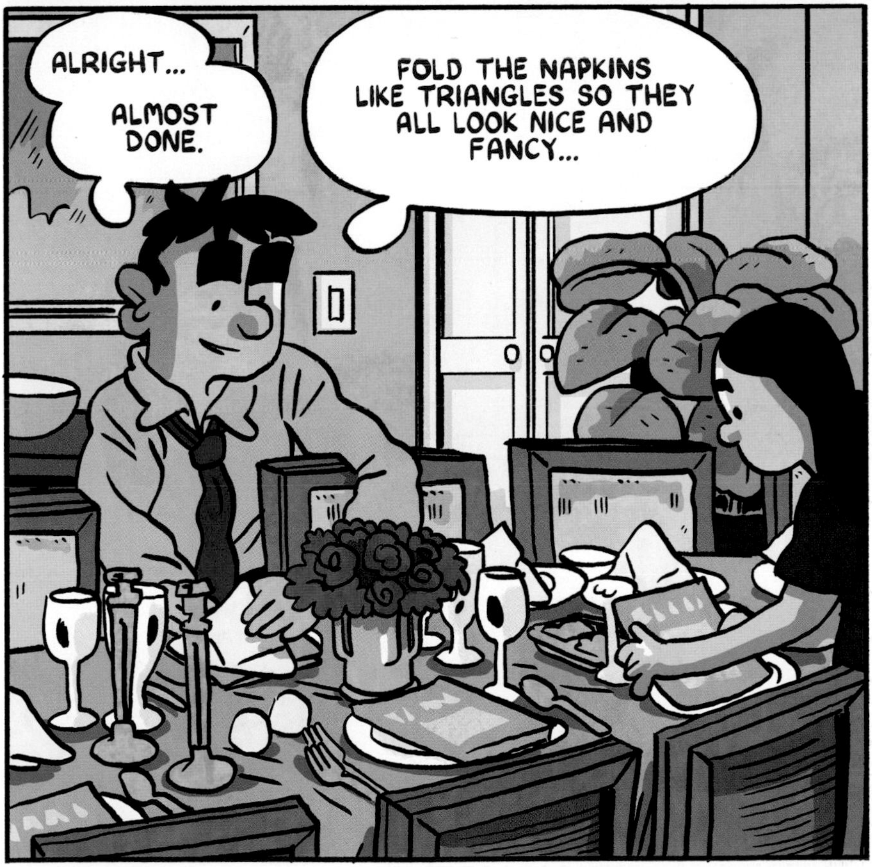
ALRIGHT...
ALMOST DONE.
FOLD THE NAPKINS LIKE TRIANGLES SO THEY ALL LOOK NICE AND FANCY...

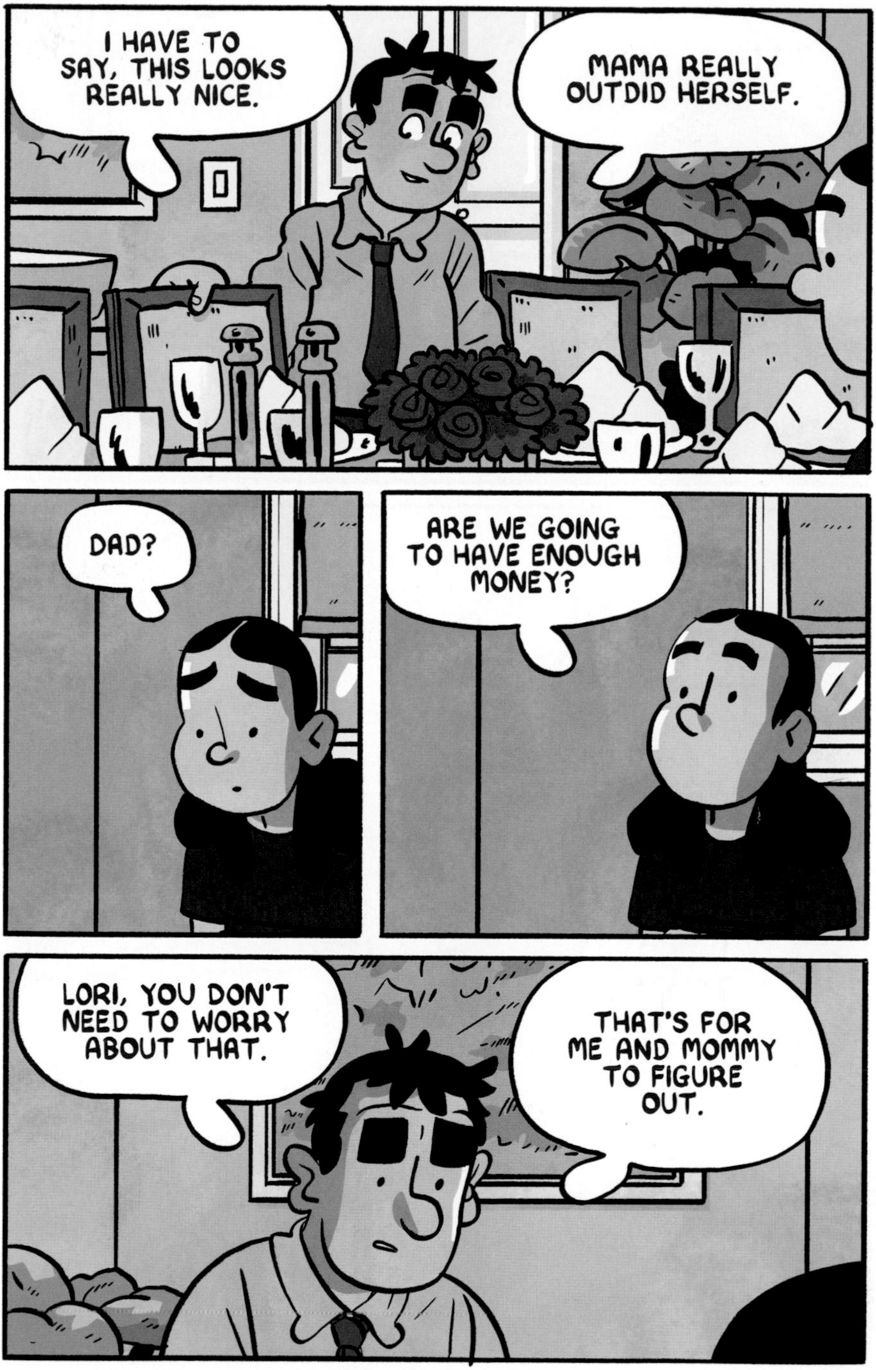
I HAVE TO SAY, THIS LOOKS REALLY NICE.
MAMA REALLY OUTDID HERSELF.
DAD?
ARE WE GOING TO HAVE ENOUGH MONEY?
LORI, YOU DON'T NEED TO WORRY ABOUT THAT.
THAT'S FOR ME AND MOMMY TO FIGURE OUT.

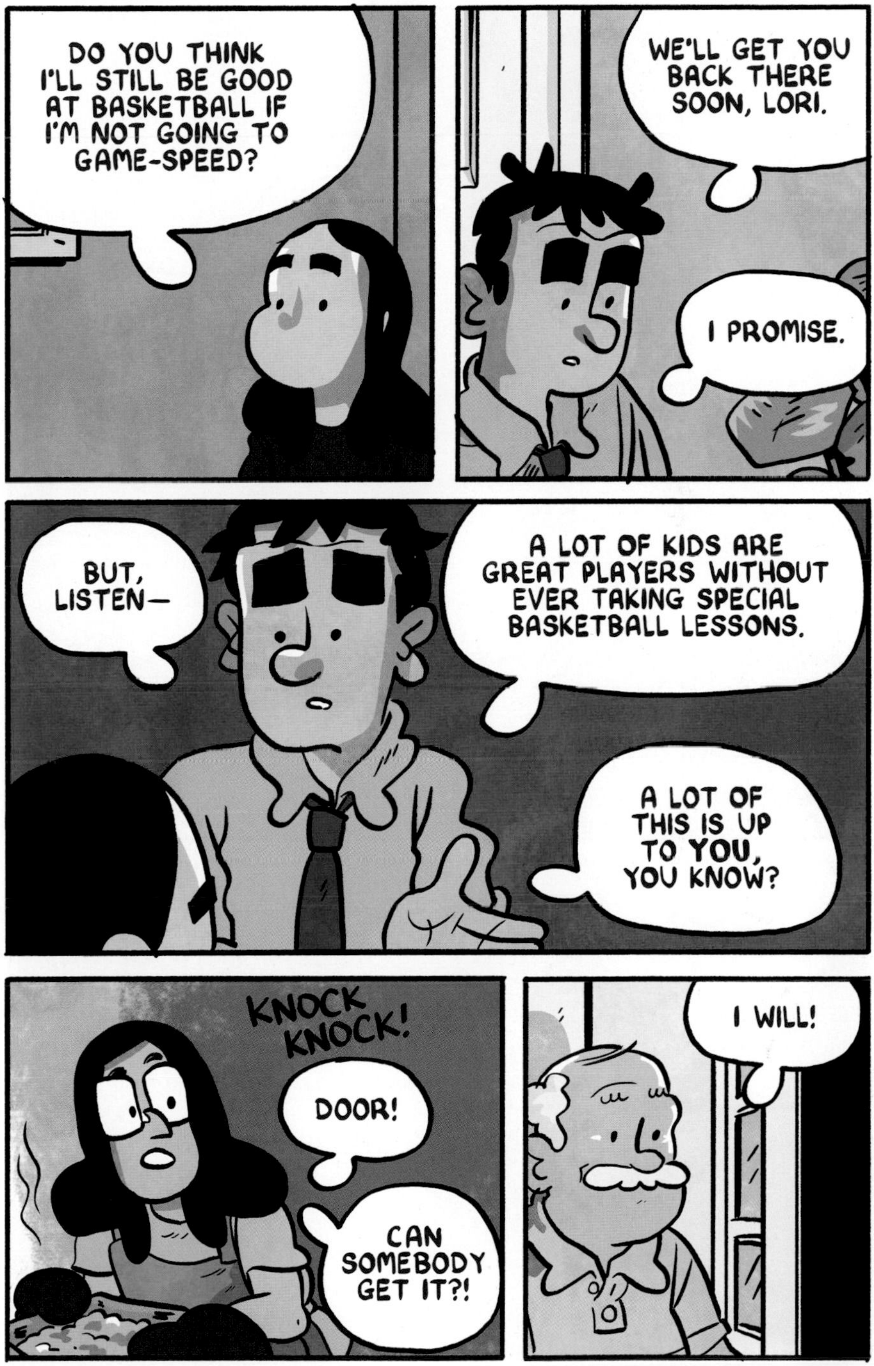
DO YOU THINK I'LL STILL BE GOOD AT BASKETBALL IF I'M NOT GOING TO GAME-SPEED?
WE'LL GET YOU BACK THERE SOON, LORI.
I PROMISE.
BUT, LISTEN—
A LOT OF KIDS ARE GREAT PLAYERS WITHOUT EVER TAKING SPECIAL BASKETBALL LESSONS.
A LOT OF THIS IS UP TO YOU, YOU KNOW?
KNOCK KNOCK!
DOOR!
CAN SOMEBODY GET IT?!
I WILL!

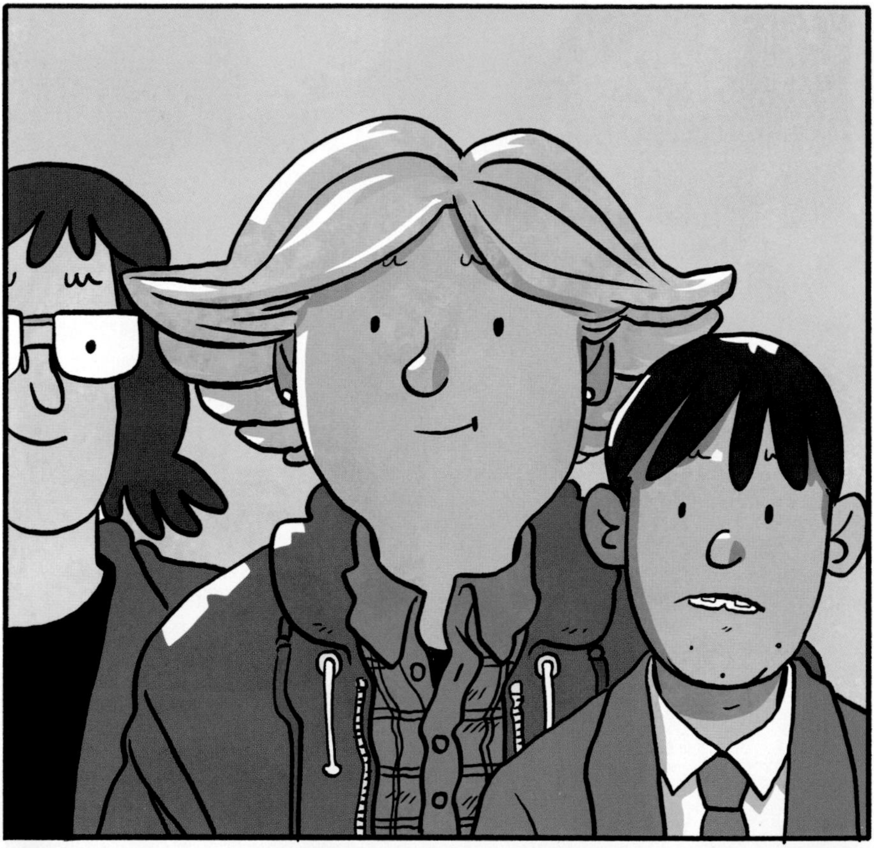

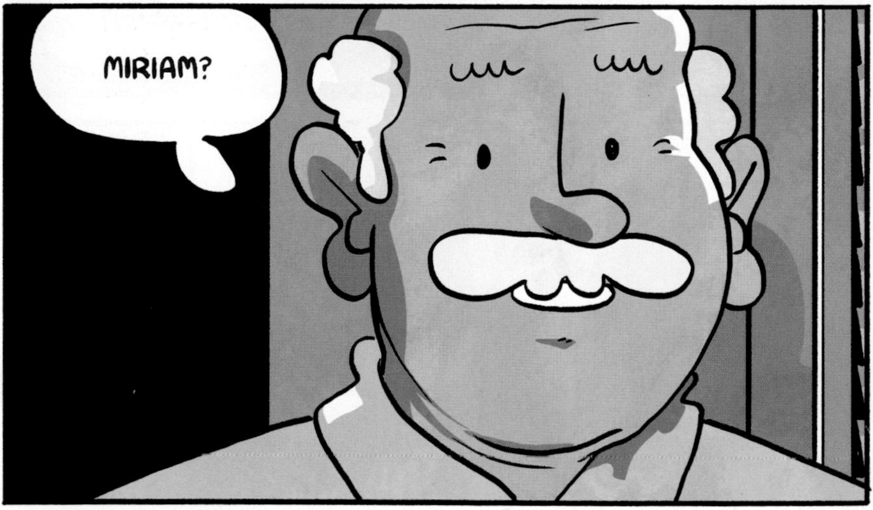
MIRIAM?

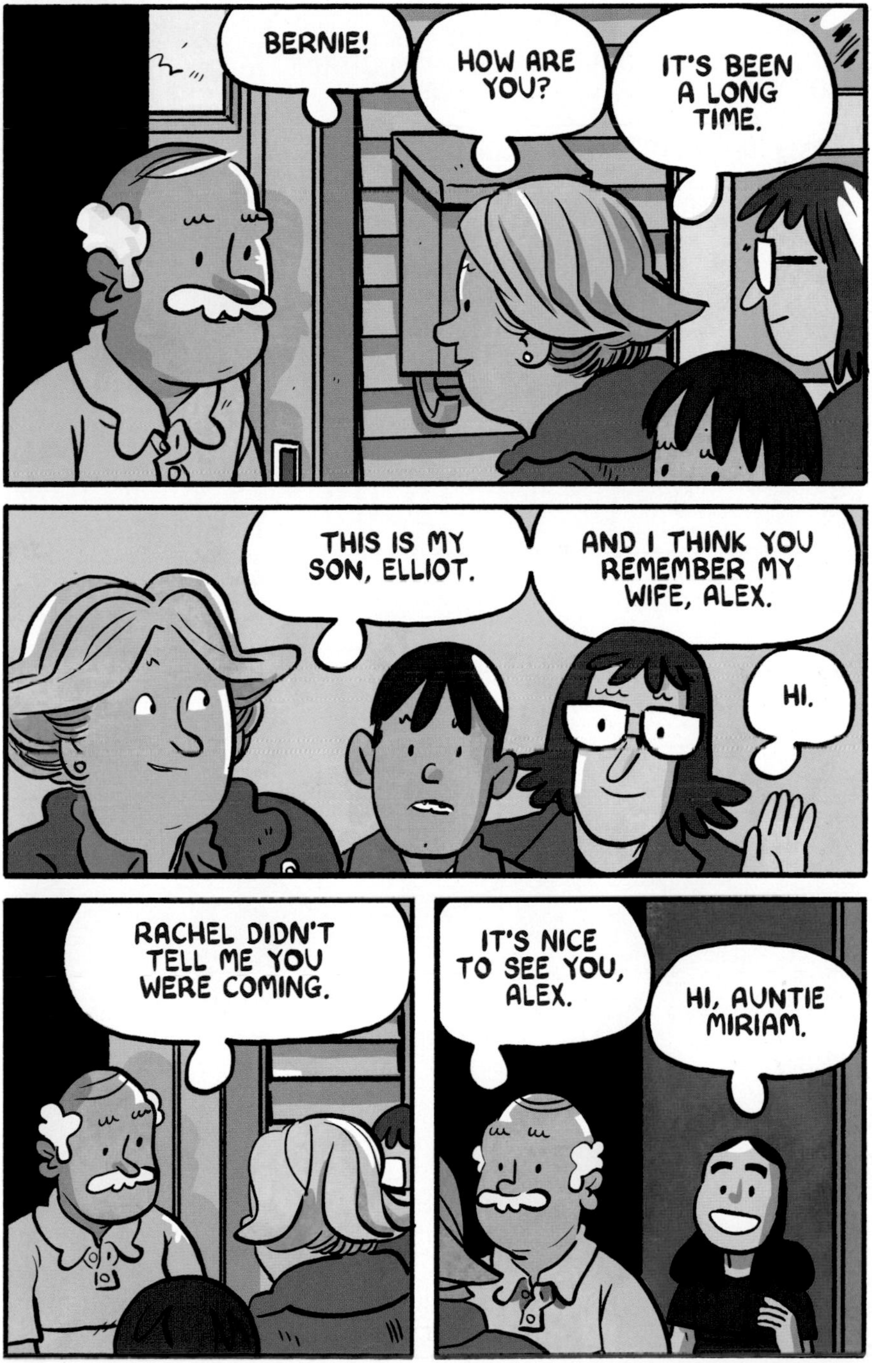
BERNIE!
HOW ARE YOU?
IT'S BEEN A LONG TIME.
THIS IS MY SON, ELLIOT.
AND I THINK YOU REMEMBER MY WIFE, ALEX.
HI.
RACHEL DIDN'T TELL ME YOU WERE COMING.
IT'S NICE TO SEE YOU, ALEX.
HI, AUNTIE MIRIAM.

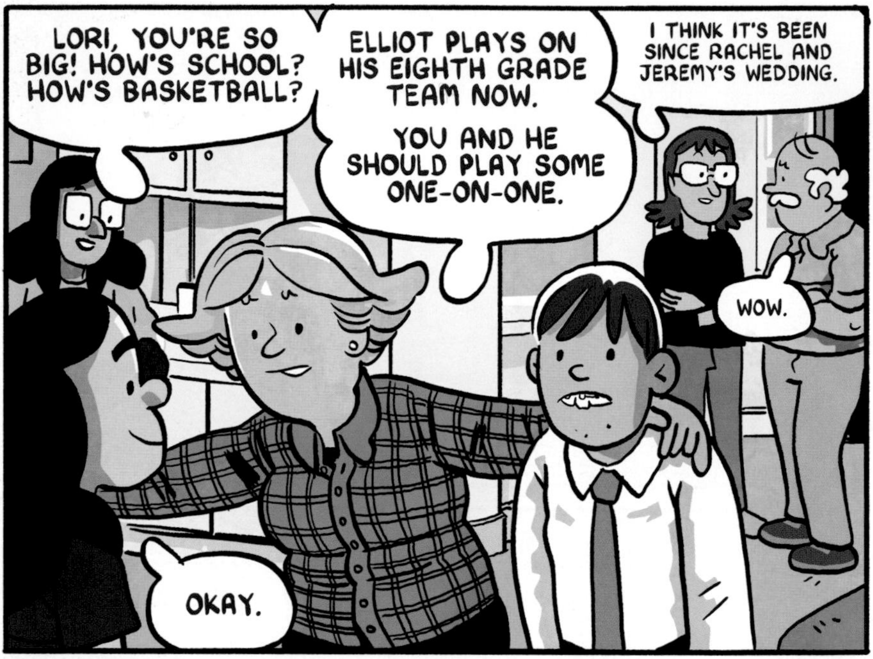
LORI, YOU'RE SO BIG! HOW'S SCHOOL? HOW'S BASKETBALL?
ELLIOT PLAYS ON HIS EIGHTH GRADE TEAM NOW.
YOU AND HE SHOULD PLAY SOME ONE-ON-ONE.
I THINK IT'S BEEN SINCE RACHEL AND JEREMY'S WEDDING.
WOW.
OKAY.

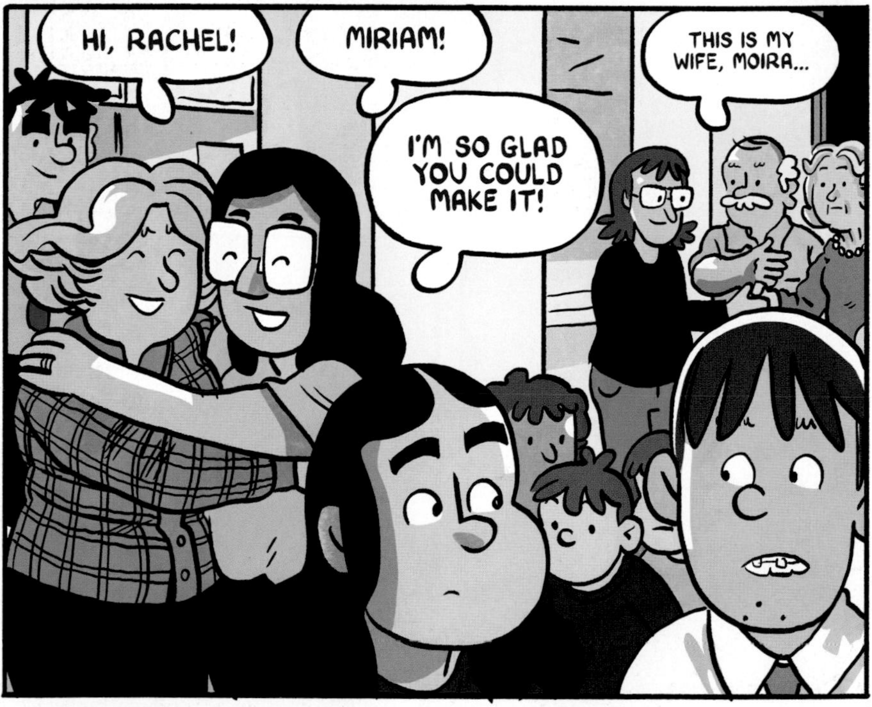
HI, RACHEL!
MIRIAM!
THIS IS MY WIFE, MOIRA...
I'M SO GLAD YOU COULD MAKE IT!

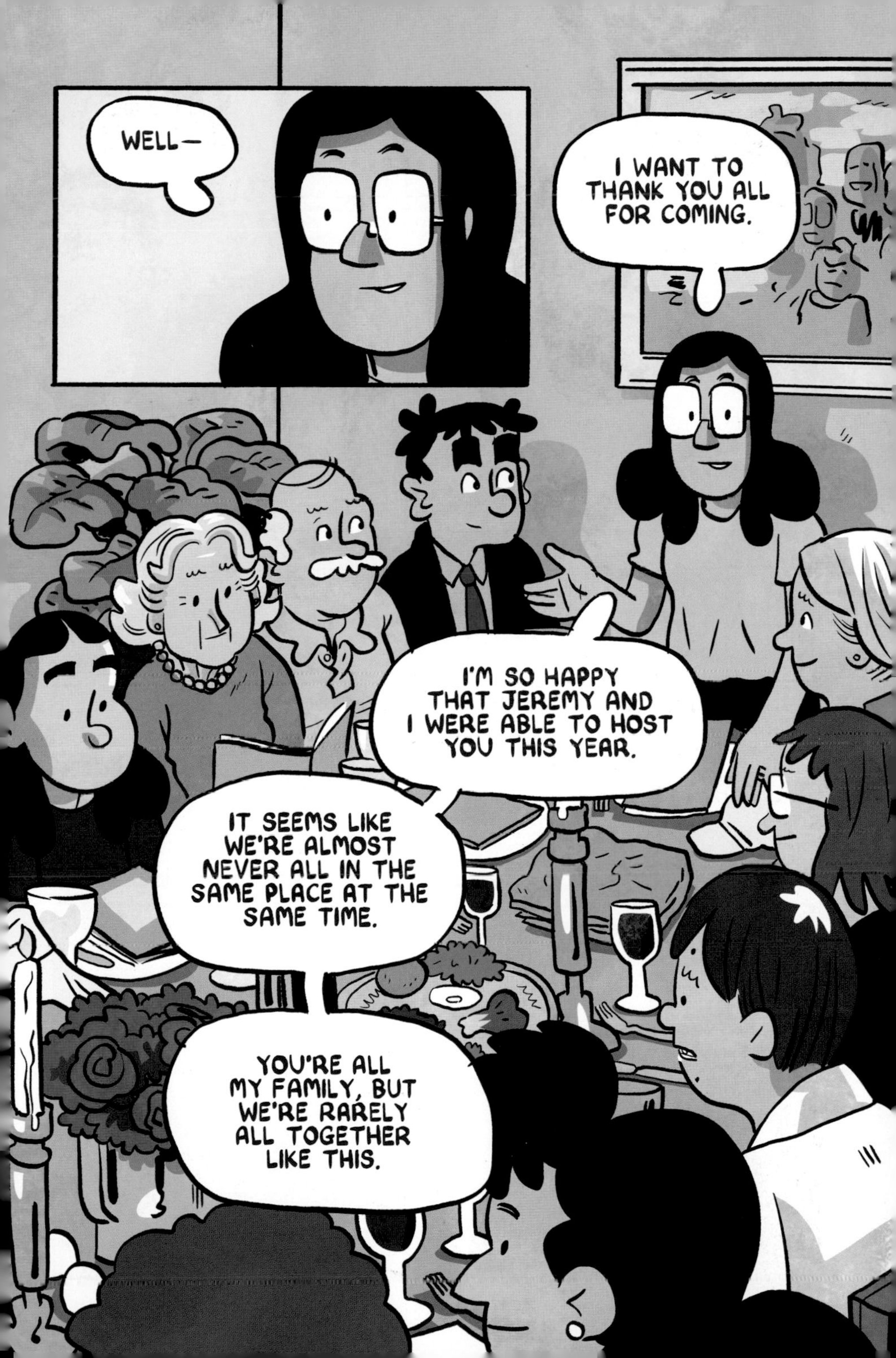
WELL—
I WANT TO THANK YOU ALL FOR COMING.
I'M SO HAPPY THAT JEREMY AND I WERE ABLE TO HOST YOU THIS YEAR.
IT SEEMS LIKE WE'RE ALMOST NEVER ALL IN THE SAME PLACE AT THE SAME TIME.
YOU'RE ALL MY FAMILY, BUT WE'RE RARELY ALL TOGETHER LIKE THIS.

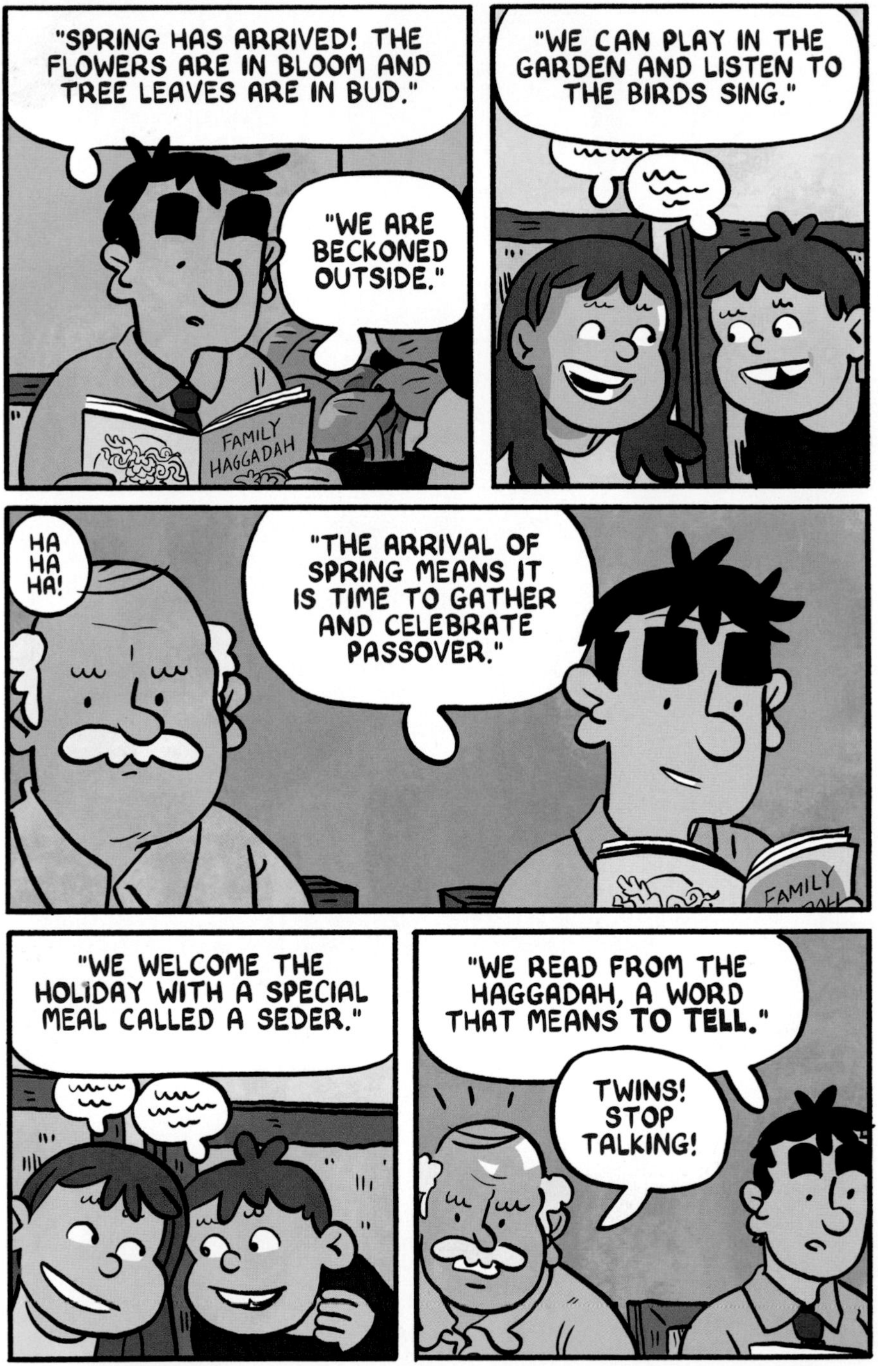
"SPRING HAS ARRIVED! THE FLOWERS ARE IN BLOOM AND TREE LEAVES ARE IN BUD."
"WE ARE BECKONED OUTSIDE."
FAMILY HAGGADAH
"WE CAN PLAY IN THE GARDEN AND LISTEN TO THE BIRDS SING."
HA HA HA!
"THE ARRIVAL OF SPRING MEANS IT IS TIME TO GATHER AND CELEBRATE PASSOVER."
FAMILY
"WE WELCOME THE HOLIDAY WITH A SPECIAL MEAL CALLED A SEDER."
"WE READ FROM THE HAGGADAH, A WORD THAT MEANS **TO TELL.**"
TWINS! STOP TALKING!

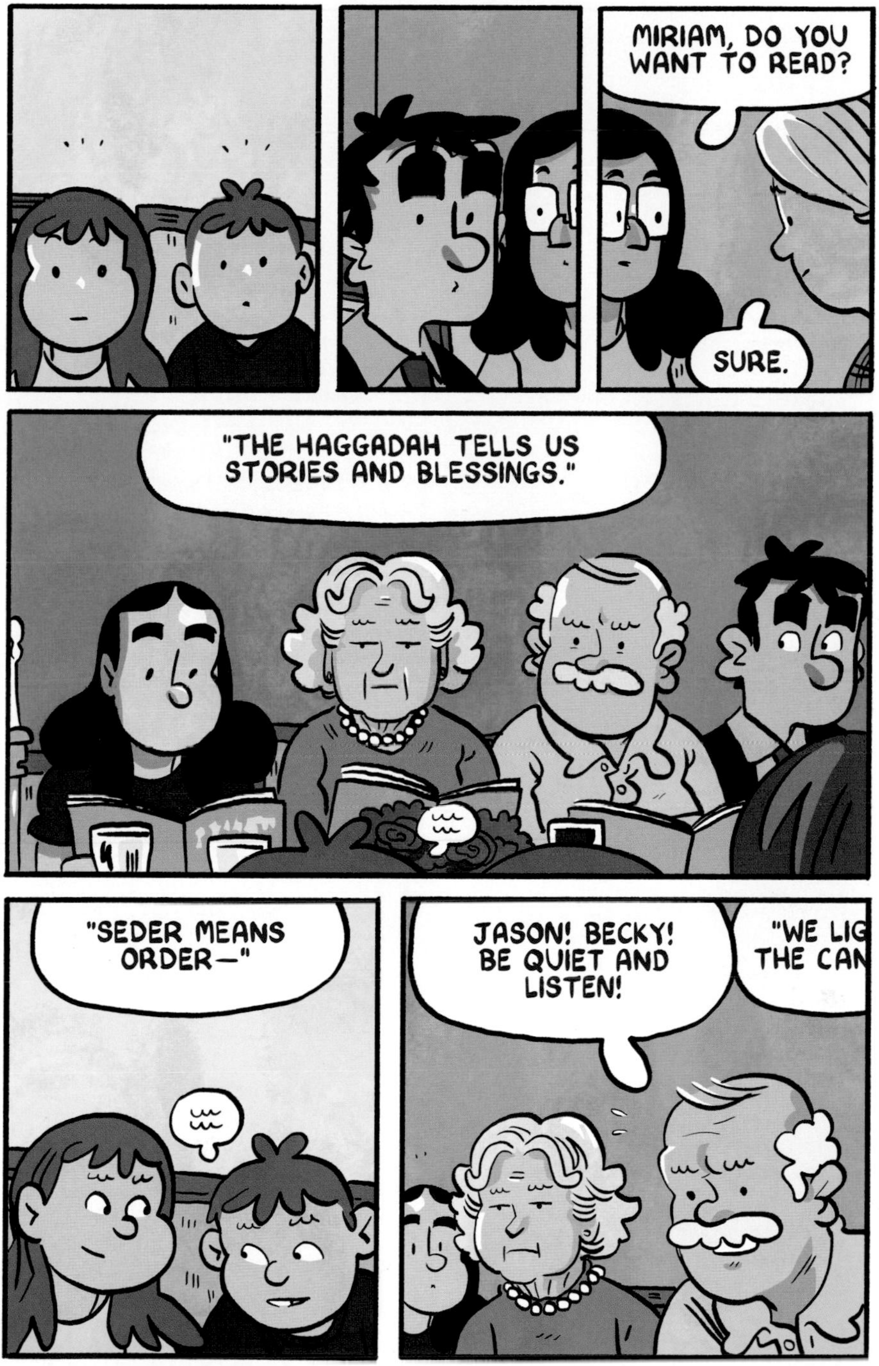
MIRIAM, DO YOU WANT TO READ?
SURE.
"THE HAGGADAH TELLS US STORIES AND BLESSINGS."
"SEDER MEANS ORDER—"
JASON! BECKY! BE QUIET AND LISTEN!
"WE LIG THE CAN

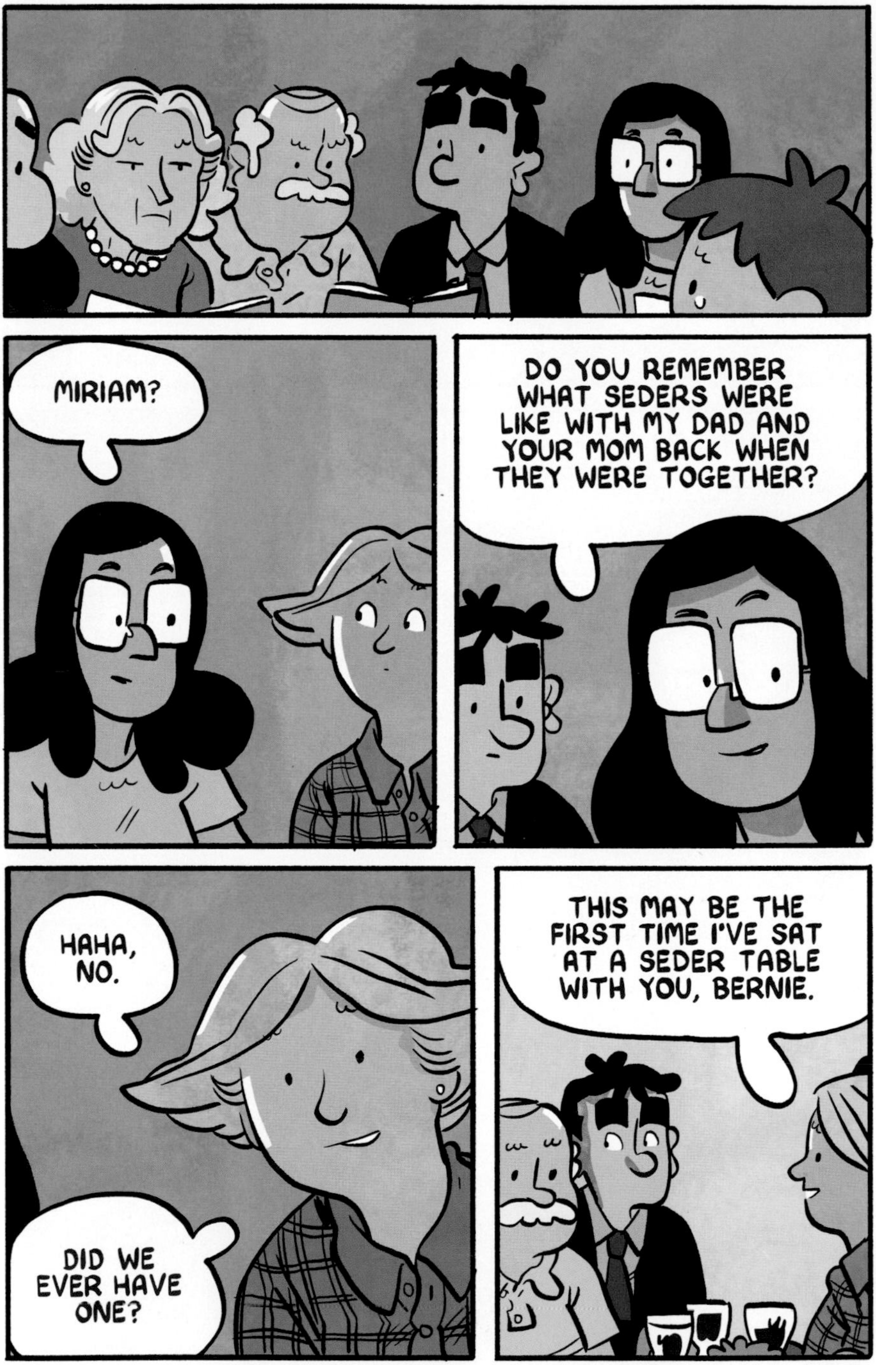
MIRIAM?
DO YOU REMEMBER WHAT SEDERS WERE LIKE WITH MY DAD AND YOUR MOM BACK WHEN THEY WERE TOGETHER?
HAHA, NO.
DID WE EVER HAVE ONE?
THIS MAY BE THE FIRST TIME I'VE SAT AT A SEDER TABLE WITH YOU, BERNIE.

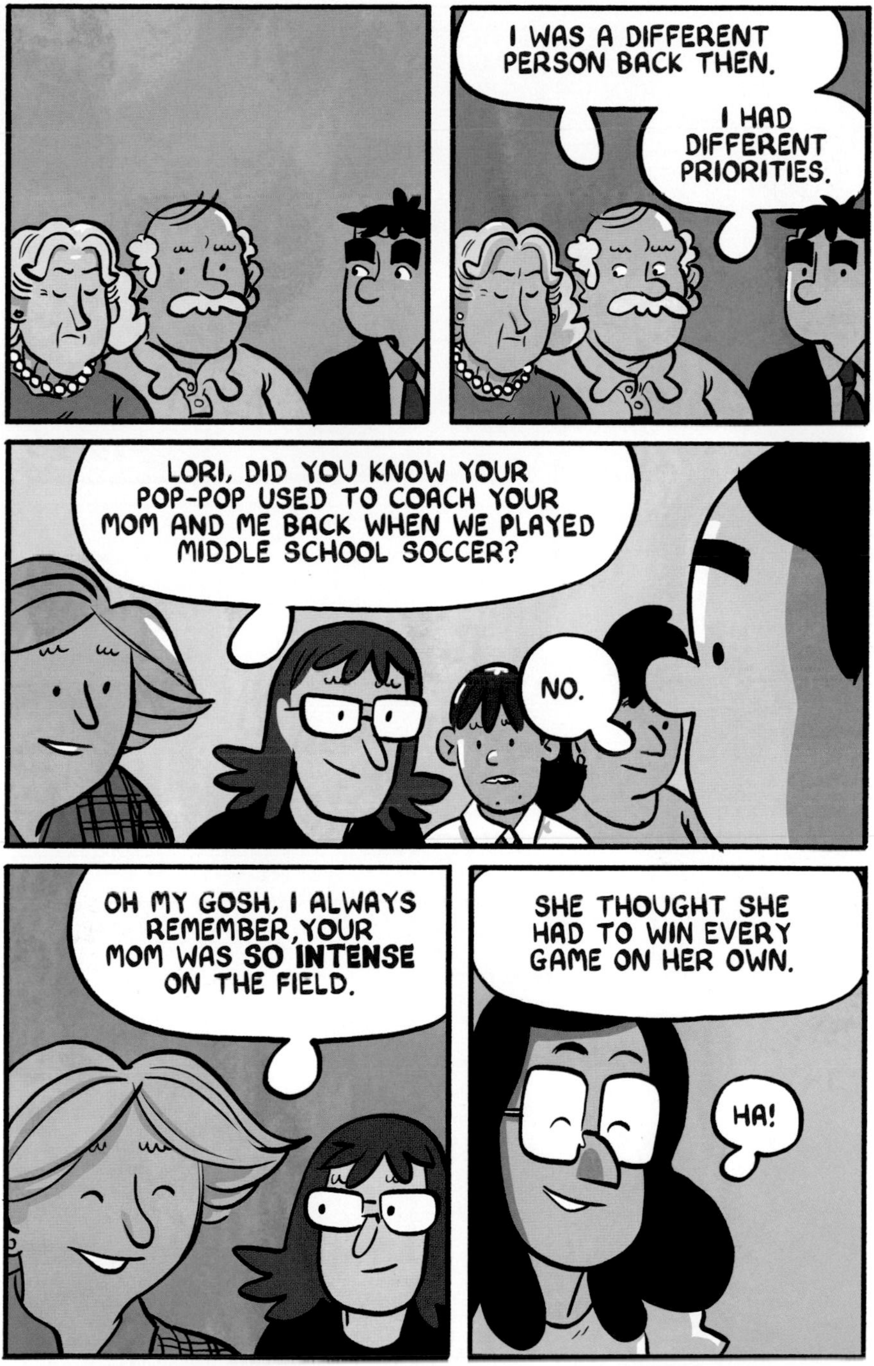
I WAS A DIFFERENT PERSON BACK THEN.
I HAD DIFFERENT PRIORITIES.
LORI, DID YOU KNOW YOUR POP-POP USED TO COACH YOUR MOM AND ME BACK WHEN WE PLAYED MIDDLE SCHOOL SOCCER?
NO.
OH MY GOSH, I ALWAYS REMEMBER, YOUR MOM WAS **SO INTENSE** ON THE FIELD.
SHE THOUGHT SHE HAD TO WIN EVERY GAME ON HER OWN.
HA!

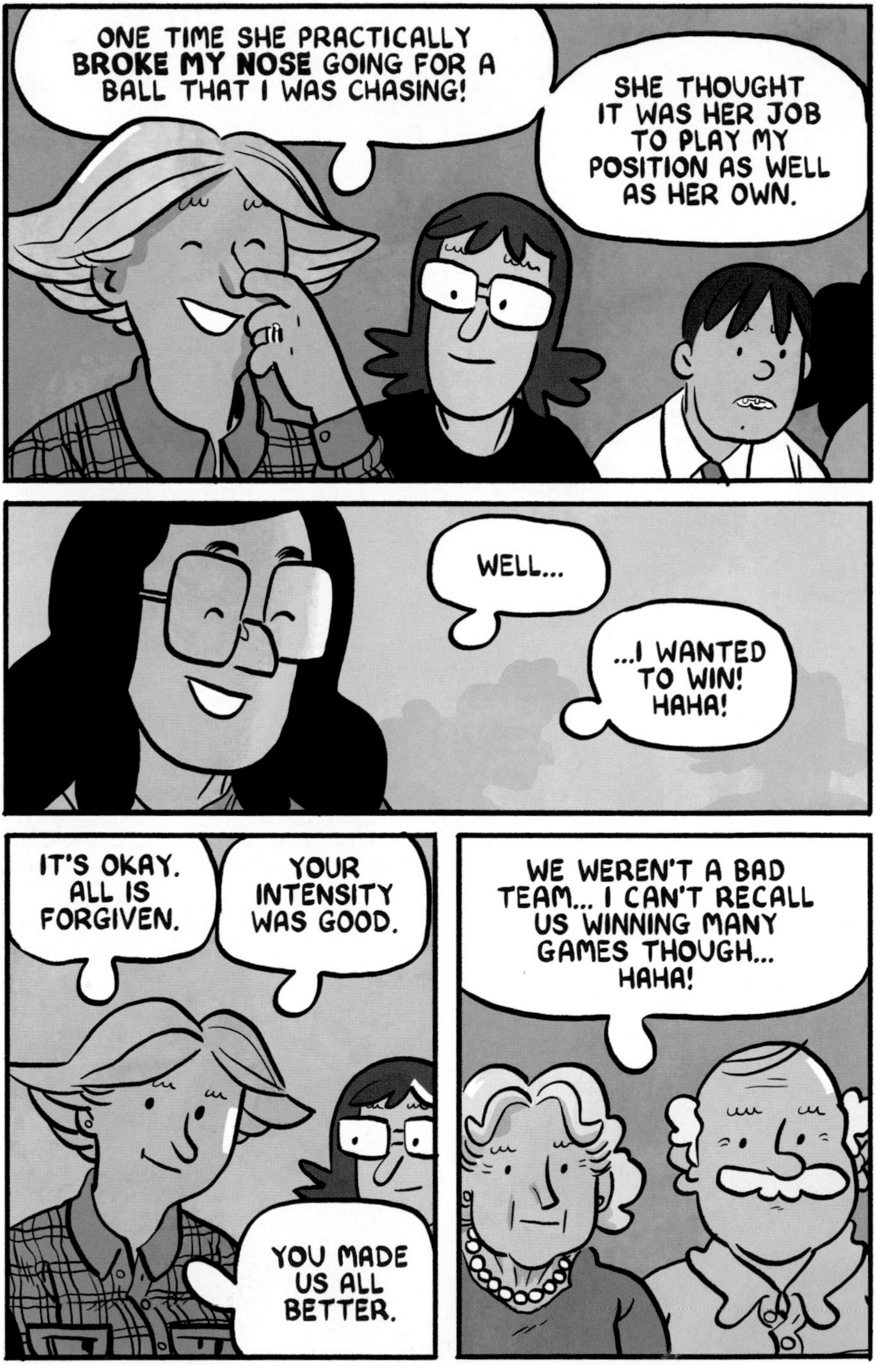
ONE TIME SHE PRACTICALLY BROKE MY NOSE GOING FOR A BALL THAT I WAS CHASING!
SHE THOUGHT IT WAS HER JOB TO PLAY MY POSITION AS WELL AS HER OWN.
WELL...
...I WANTED TO WIN! HAHA!
IT'S OKAY. ALL IS FORGIVEN.
YOUR INTENSITY WAS GOOD.
YOU MADE US ALL BETTER.
WE WEREN'T A BAD TEAM... I CAN'T RECALL US WINNING MANY GAMES THOUGH... HAHA!

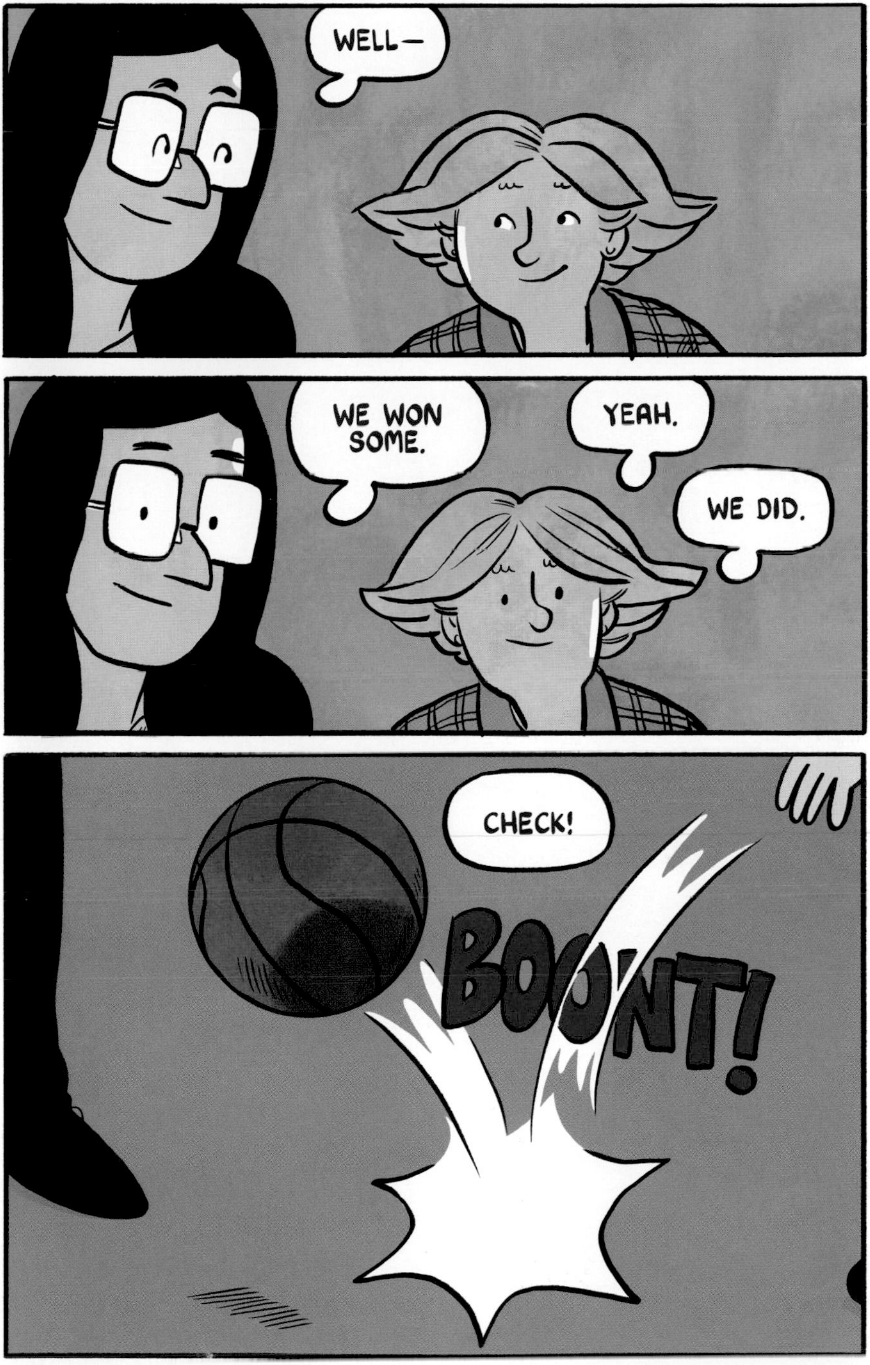
WELL—
WE WON SOME.
YEAH.
WE DID.
CHECK!
BOONT!

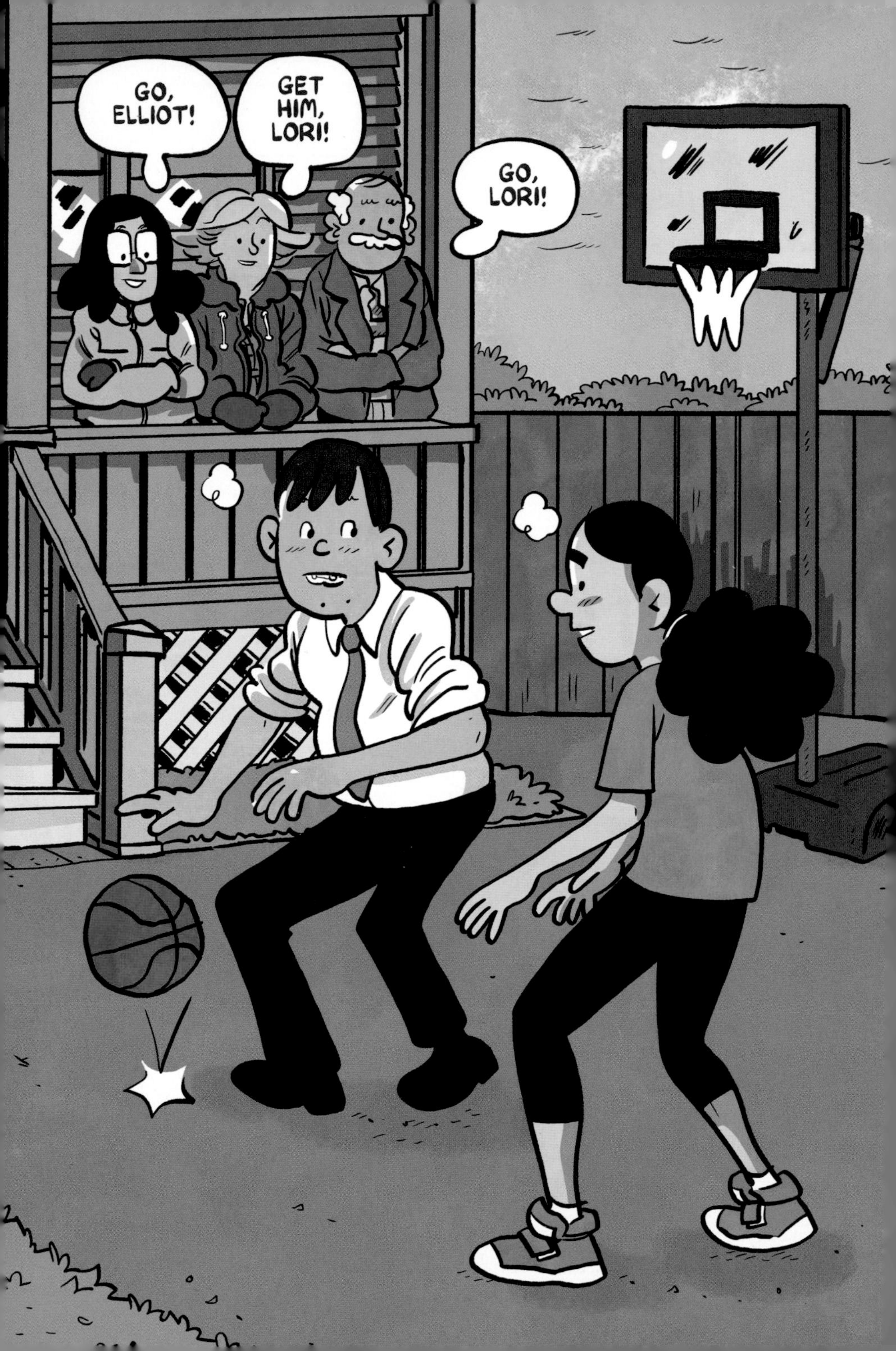
GO, ELLIOT!
GET HIM, LORI!
GO, LORI!

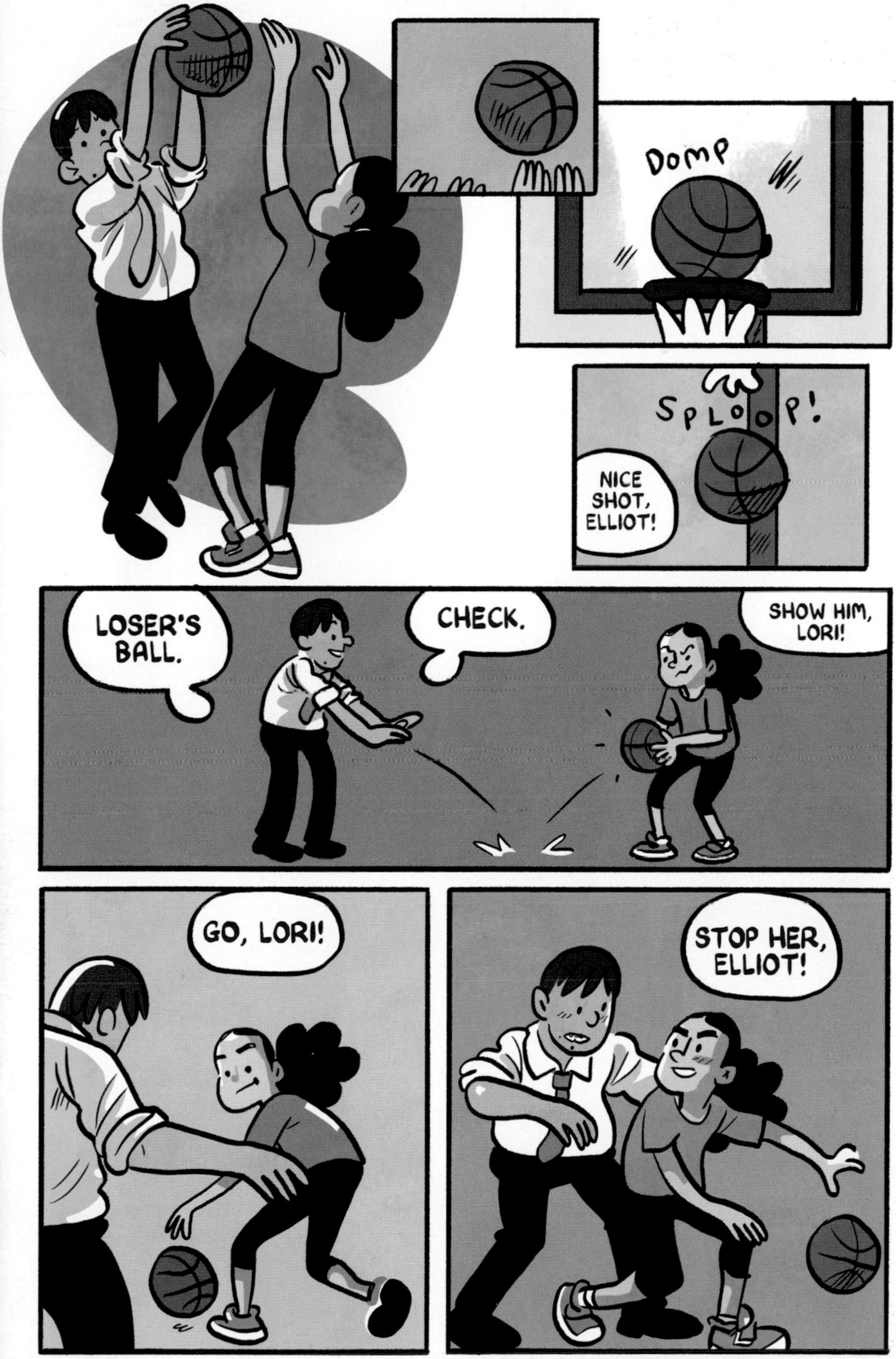

DOMP
SPLOOP!
NICE SHOT, ELLIOT!
LOSER'S BALL.
CHECK.
SHOW HIM, LORI!
GO, LORI!
STOP HER, ELLIOT!

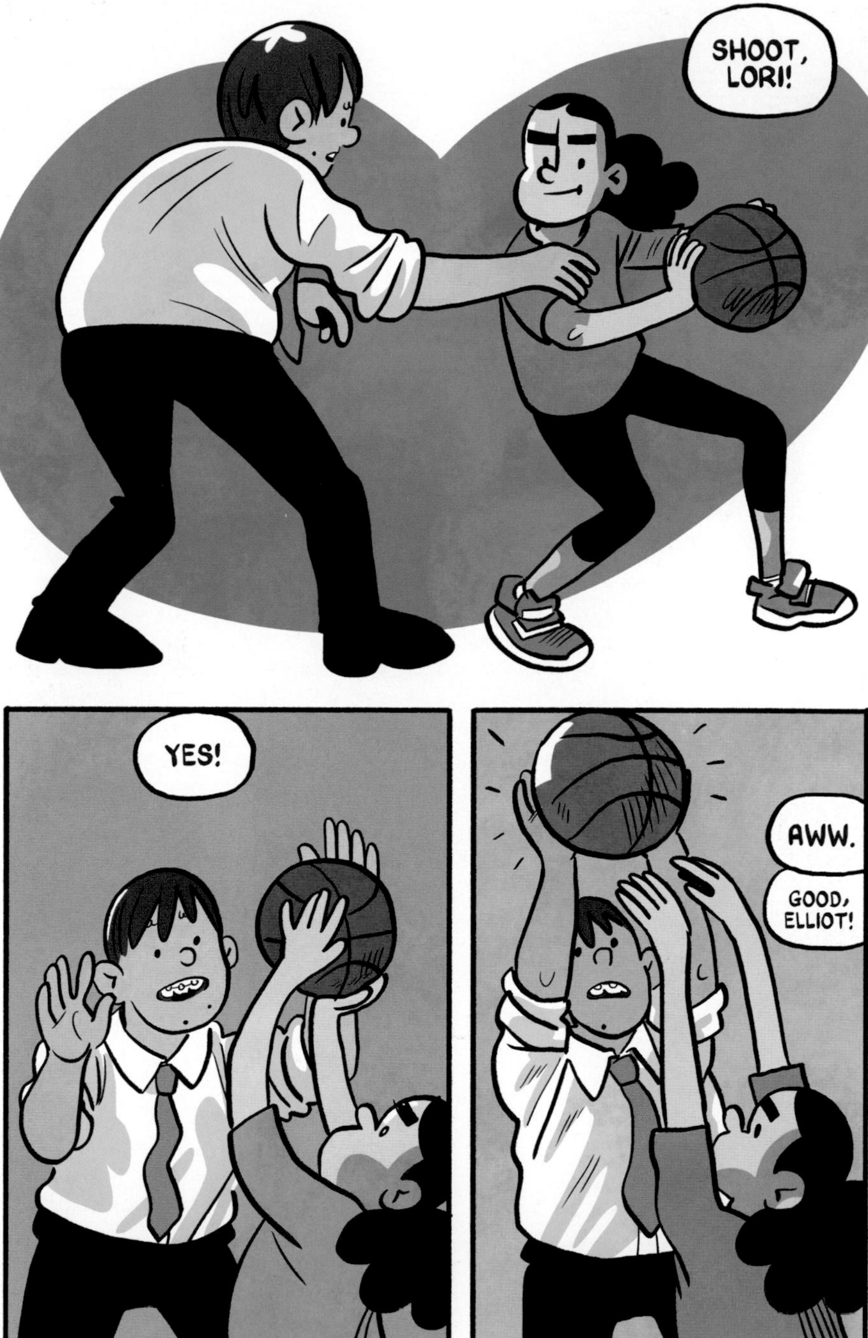
SHOOT, LORI!
YES!
AWW.
GOOD, ELLIOT!

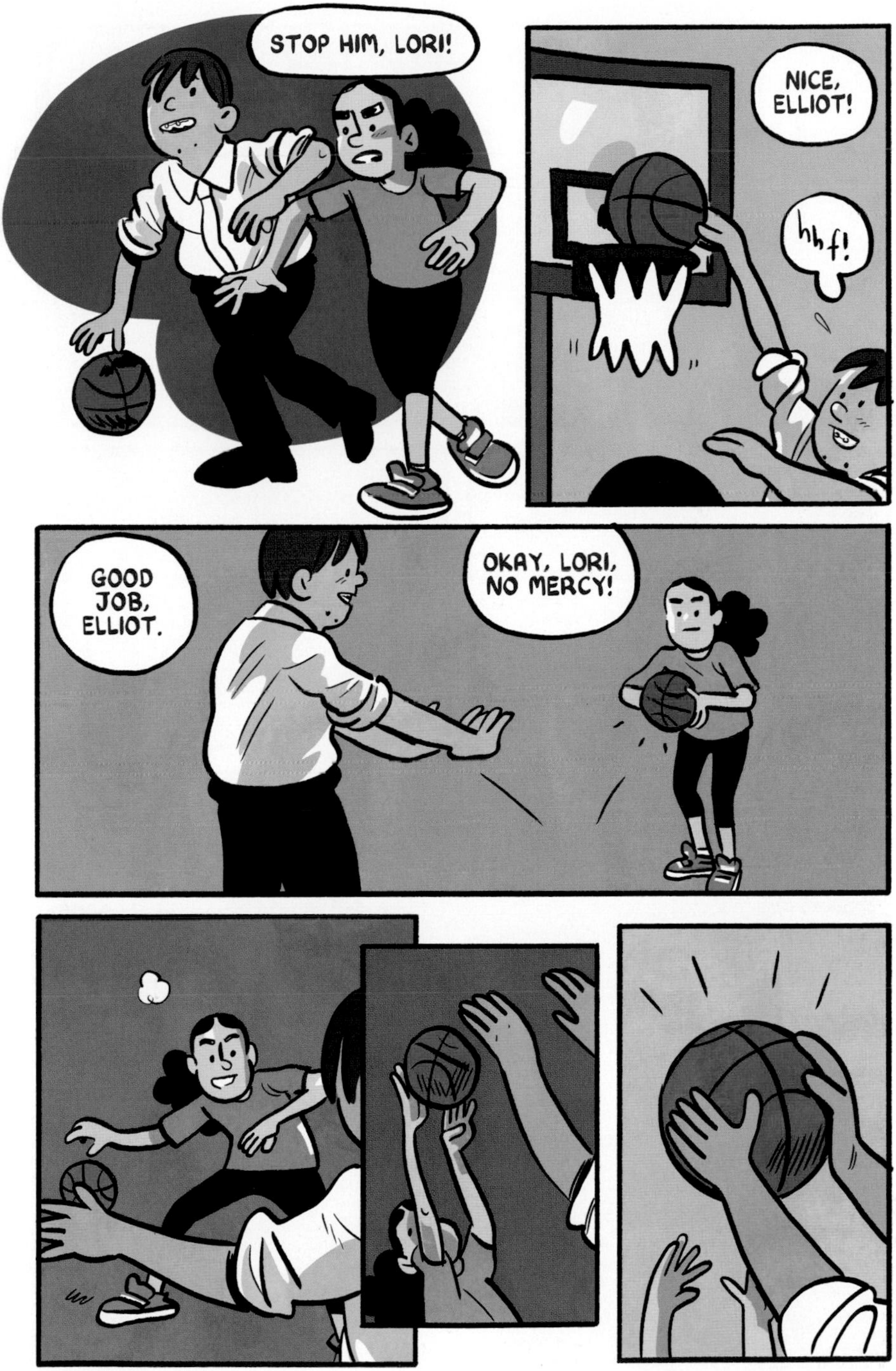
STOP HIM, LORI!
NICE, ELLIOT!
hhf!
GOOD JOB, ELLIOT.
OKAY, LORI, NO MERCY!

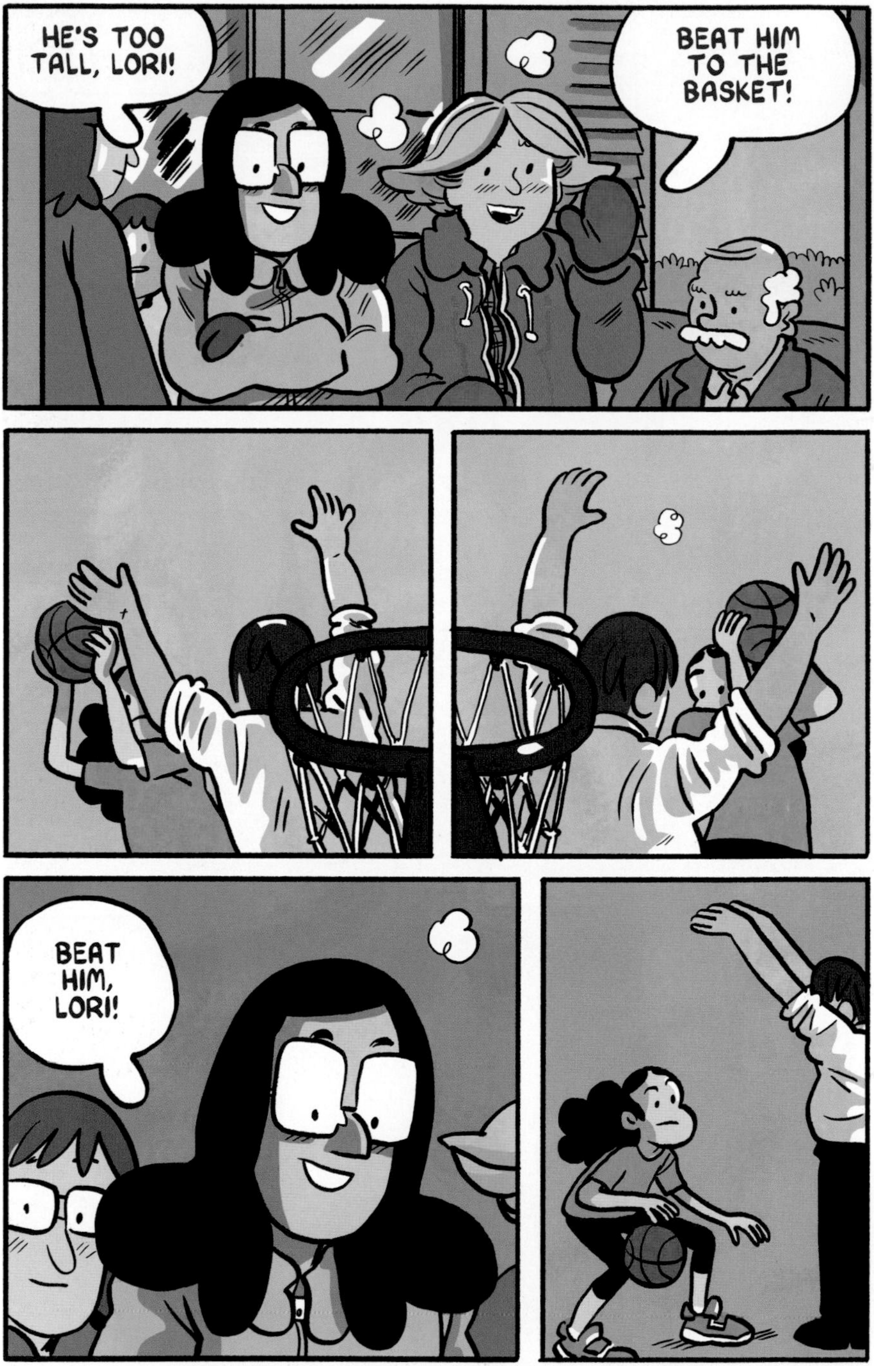
HE'S TOO TALL, LORI!
BEAT HIM TO THE BASKET!
BEAT HIM, LORI!

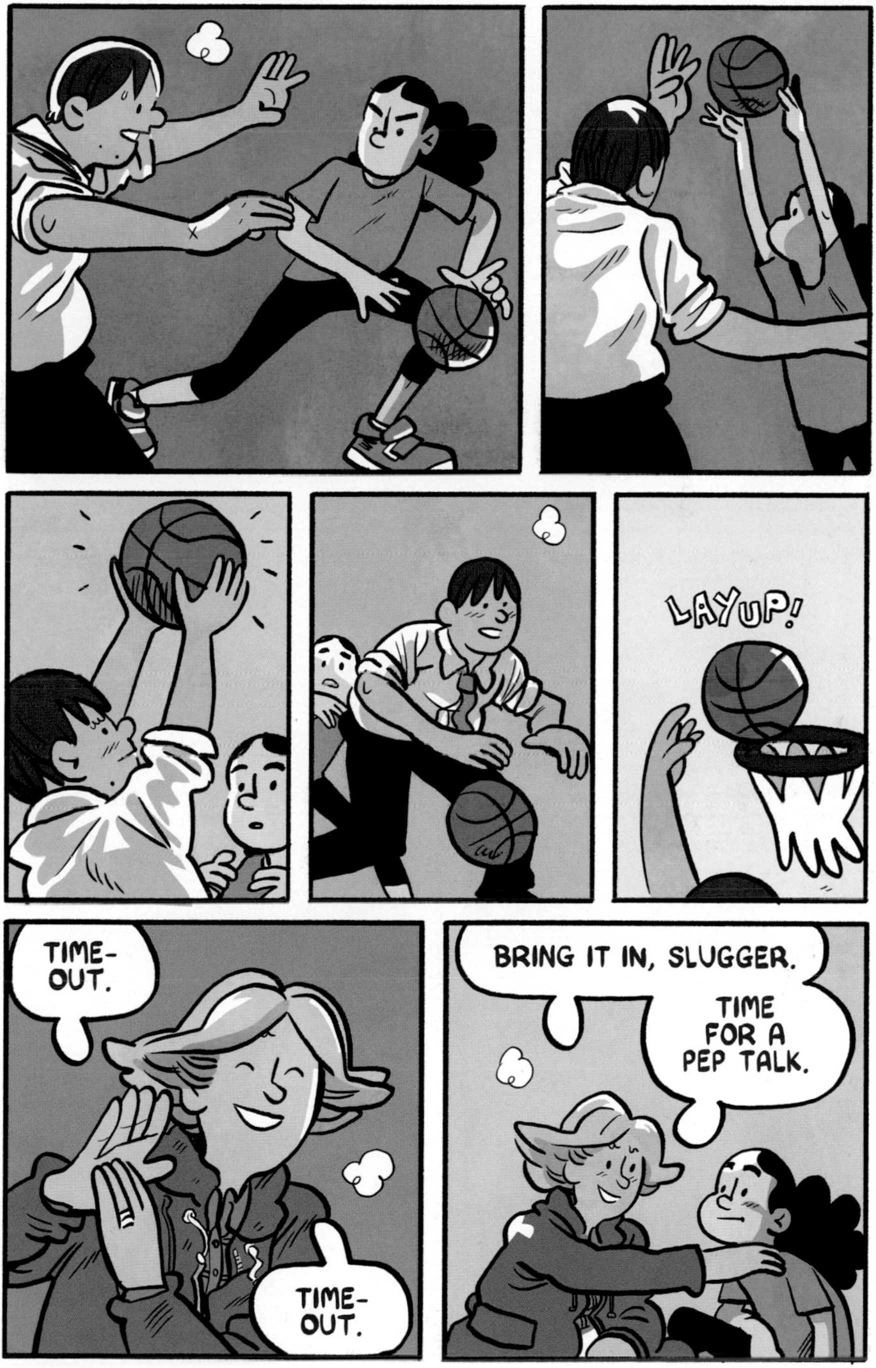
LAYUP!
TIME-OUT.
TIME-OUT.
BRING IT IN, SLUGGER.
TIME FOR A PEP TALK.

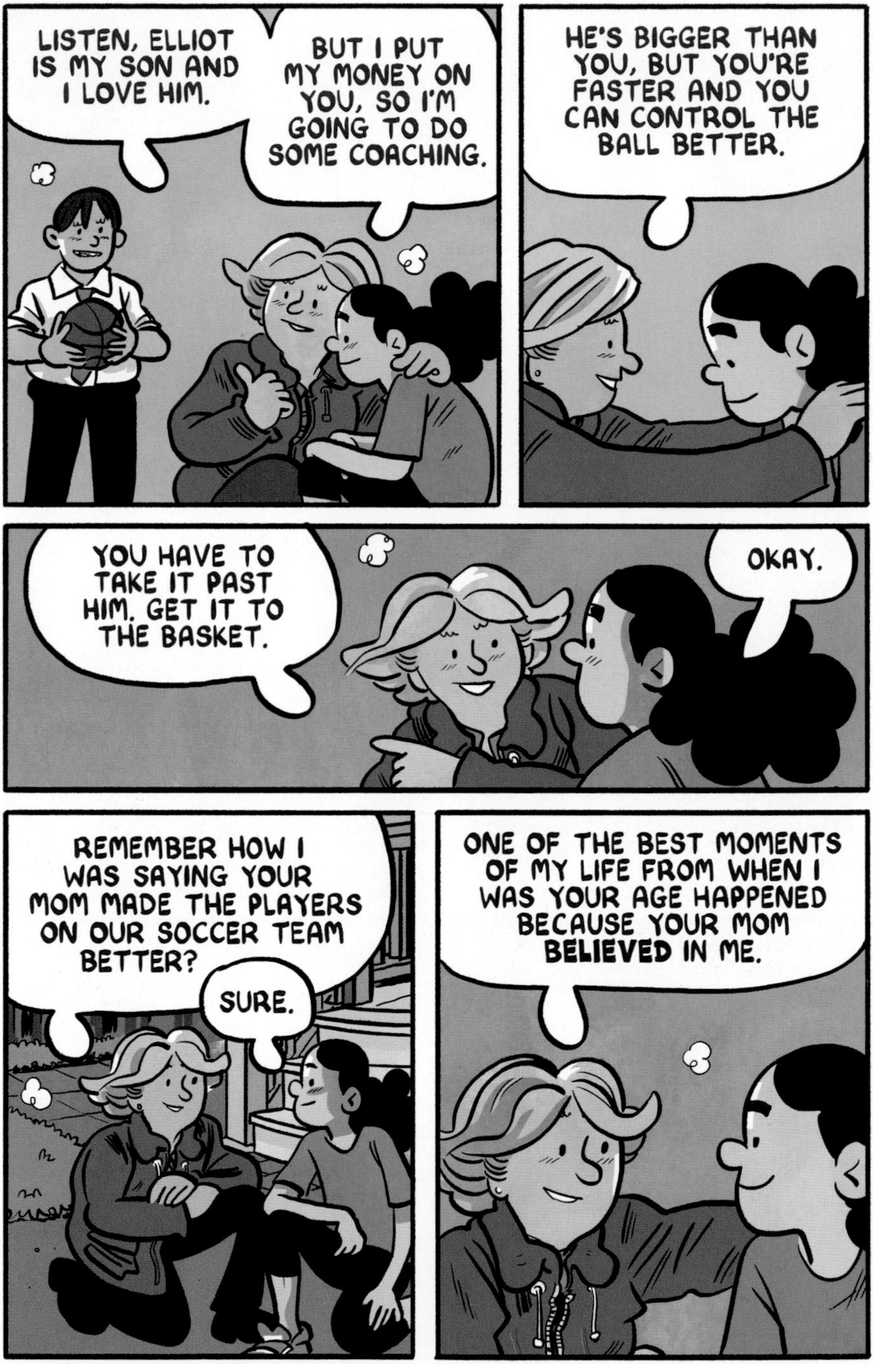
LISTEN, ELLIOT IS MY SON AND I LOVE HIM.
BUT I PUT MY MONEY ON YOU, SO I'M GOING TO DO SOME COACHING.
HE'S BIGGER THAN YOU, BUT YOU'RE FASTER AND YOU CAN CONTROL THE BALL BETTER.
YOU HAVE TO TAKE IT PAST HIM. GET IT TO THE BASKET.
OKAY.
REMEMBER HOW I WAS SAYING YOUR MOM MADE THE PLAYERS ON OUR SOCCER TEAM BETTER?
SURE.
ONE OF THE BEST MOMENTS OF MY LIFE FROM WHEN I WAS YOUR AGE HAPPENED BECAUSE YOUR MOM **BELIEVED** IN ME.

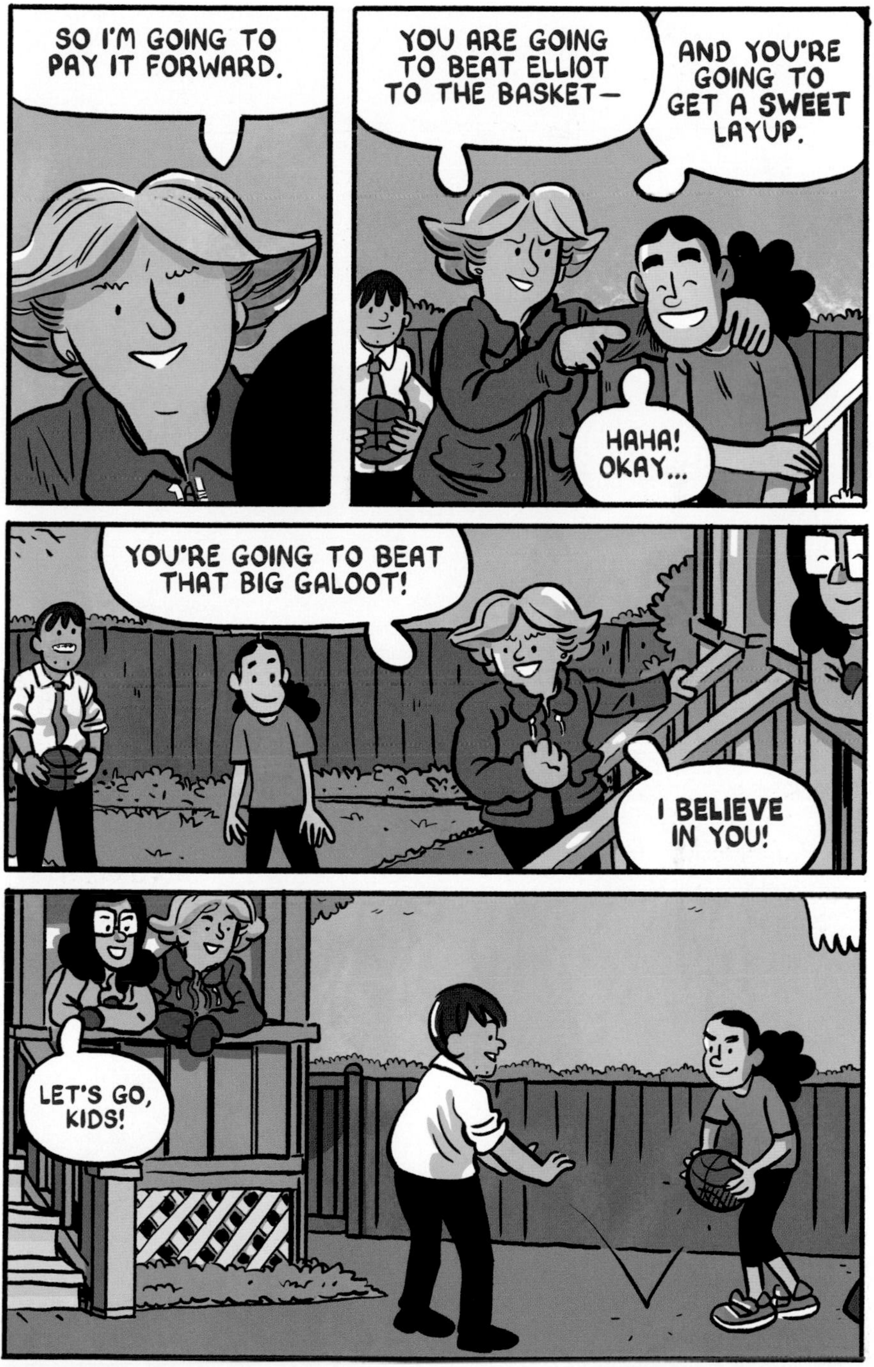
SO I'M GOING TO PAY IT FORWARD.
YOU ARE GOING TO BEAT ELLIOT TO THE BASKET—
AND YOU'RE GOING TO GET A SWEET LAYUP.
HAHA! OKAY...
YOU'RE GOING TO BEAT THAT BIG GALOOT!
I BELIEVE IN YOU!
LET'S GO, KIDS!

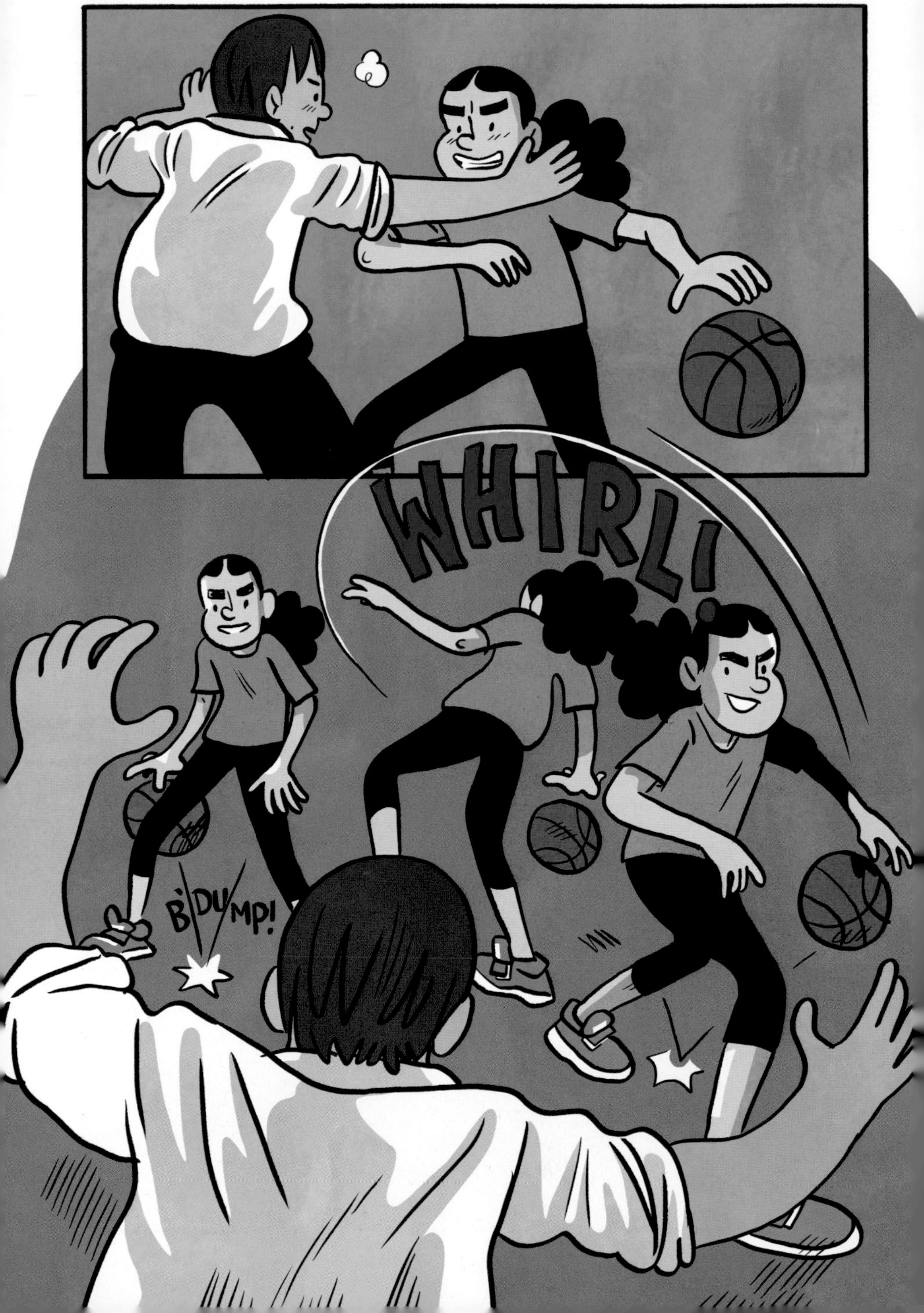
WHIRL!
B'DUMP!

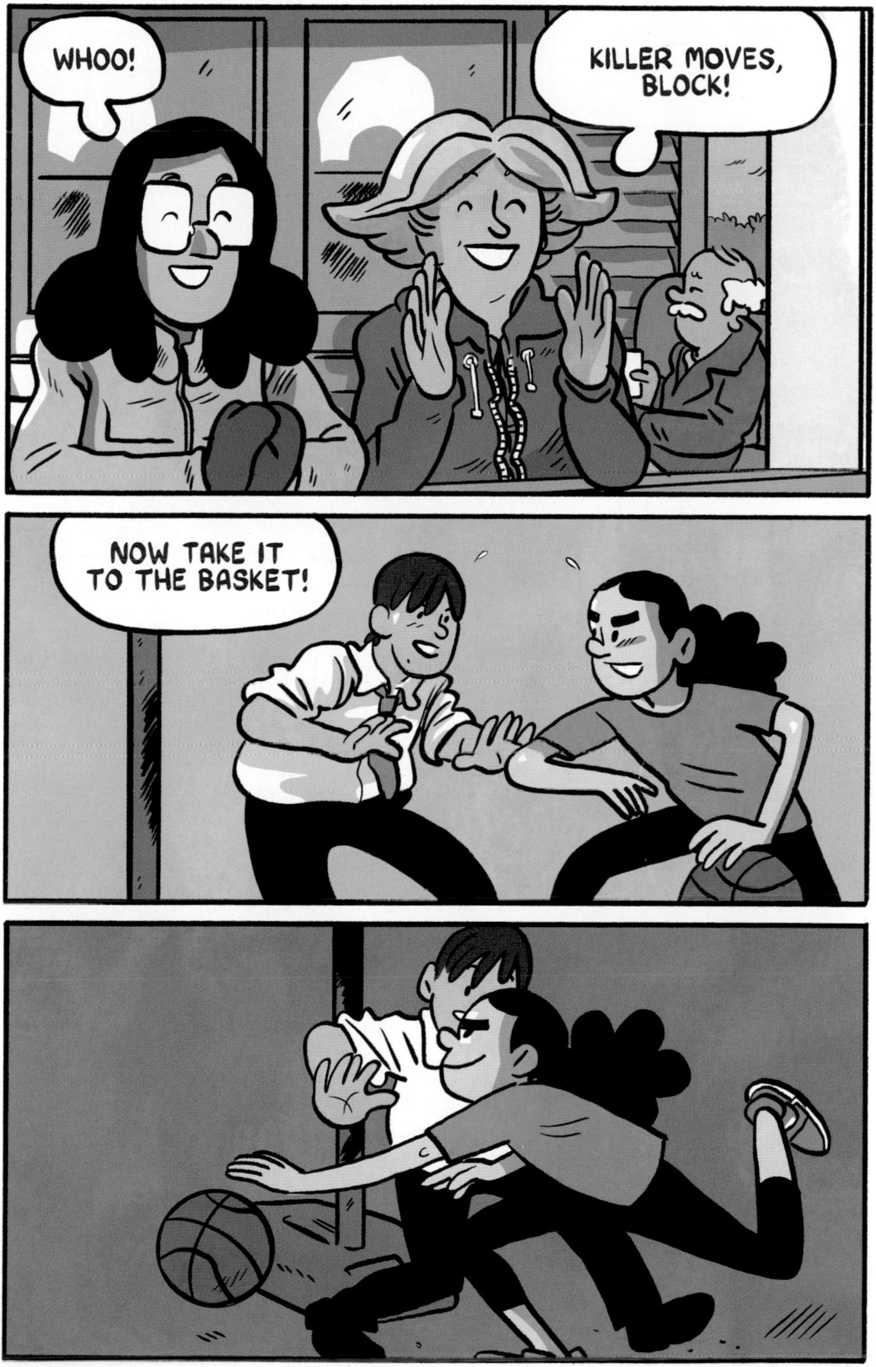
WHOO!
KILLER MOVES, BLOCK!
NOW TAKE IT TO THE BASKET!

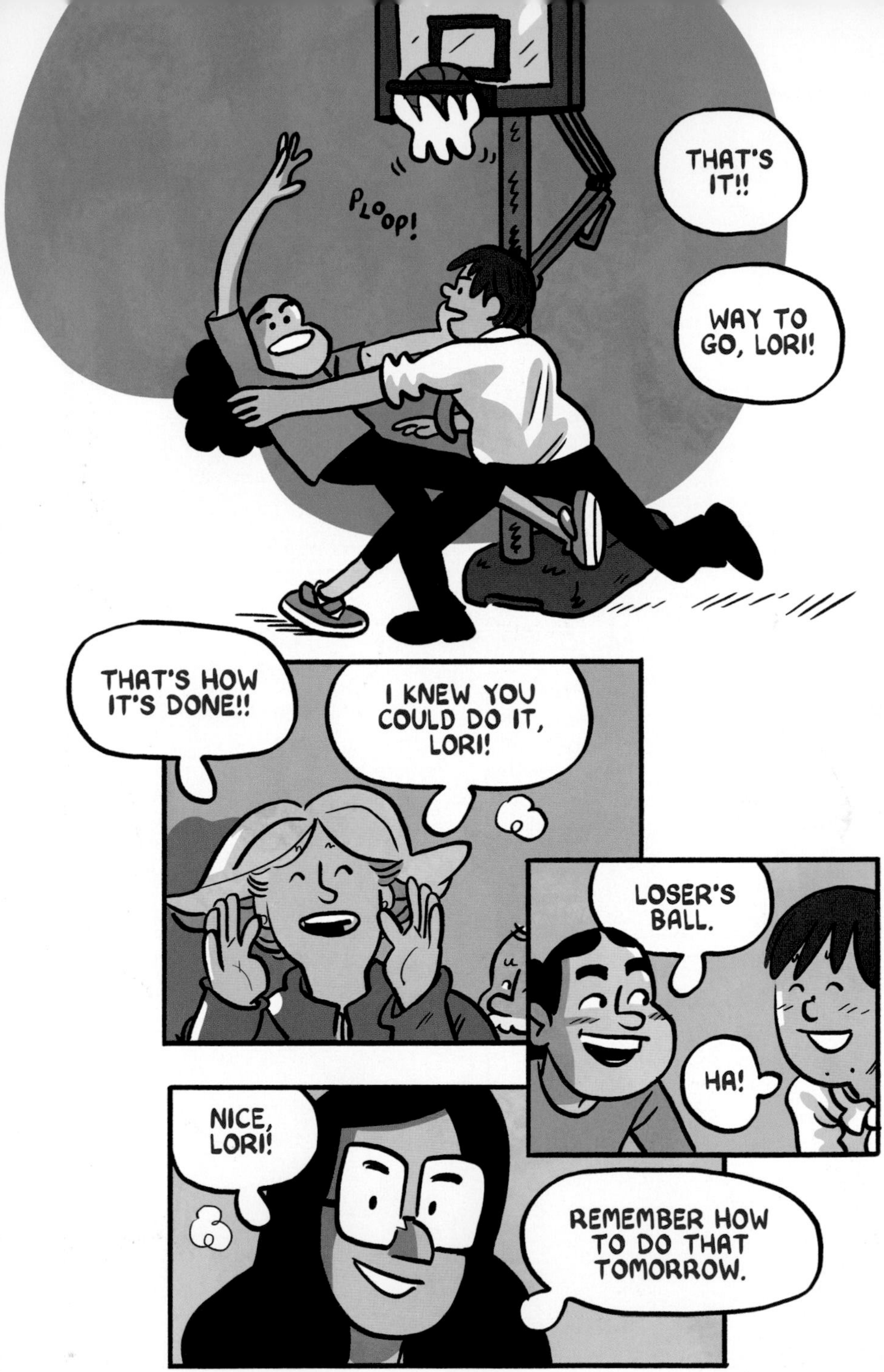
PLOOP!
THAT'S IT!!
WAY TO GO, LORI!
THAT'S HOW IT'S DONE!!
I KNEW YOU COULD DO IT, LORI!
LOSER'S BALL.
HA!
NICE, LORI!
REMEMBER HOW TO DO THAT TOMORROW.

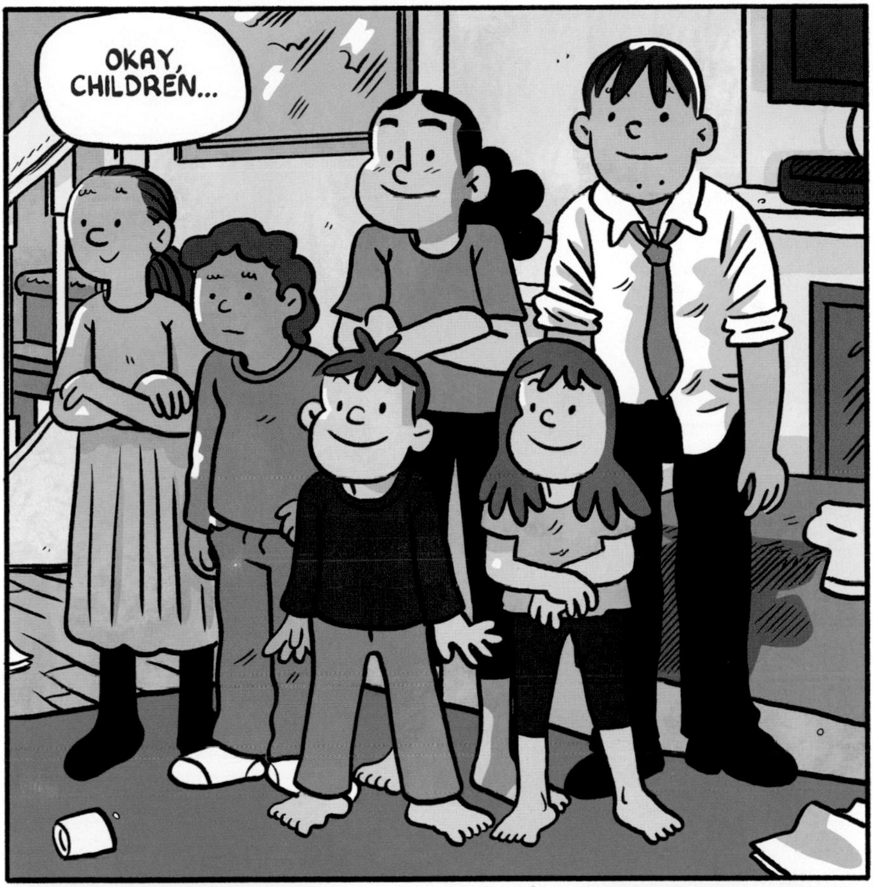
OKAY, CHILDREN...

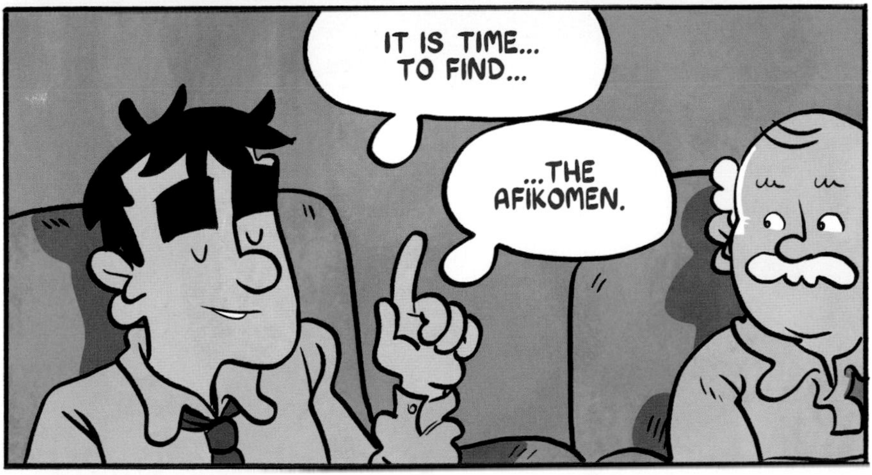
IT IS TIME... TO FIND...
...THE AFIKOMEN.

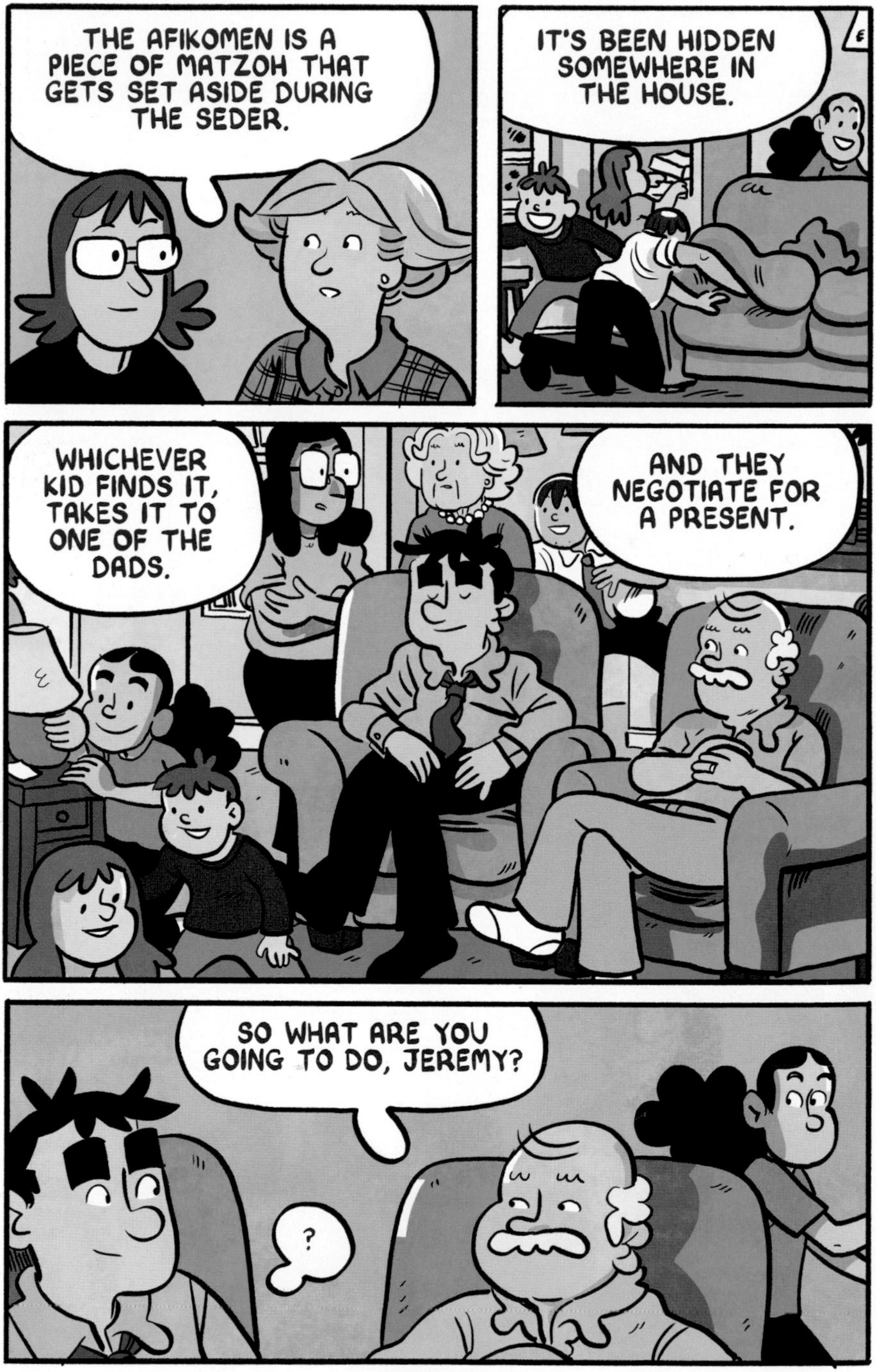
THE AFIKOMEN IS A PIECE OF MATZOH THAT GETS SET ASIDE DURING THE SEDER.
IT'S BEEN HIDDEN SOMEWHERE IN THE HOUSE.
WHICHEVER KID FINDS IT, TAKES IT TO ONE OF THE DADS.
AND THEY NEGOTIATE FOR A PRESENT.
SO WHAT ARE YOU GOING TO DO, JEREMY?
?

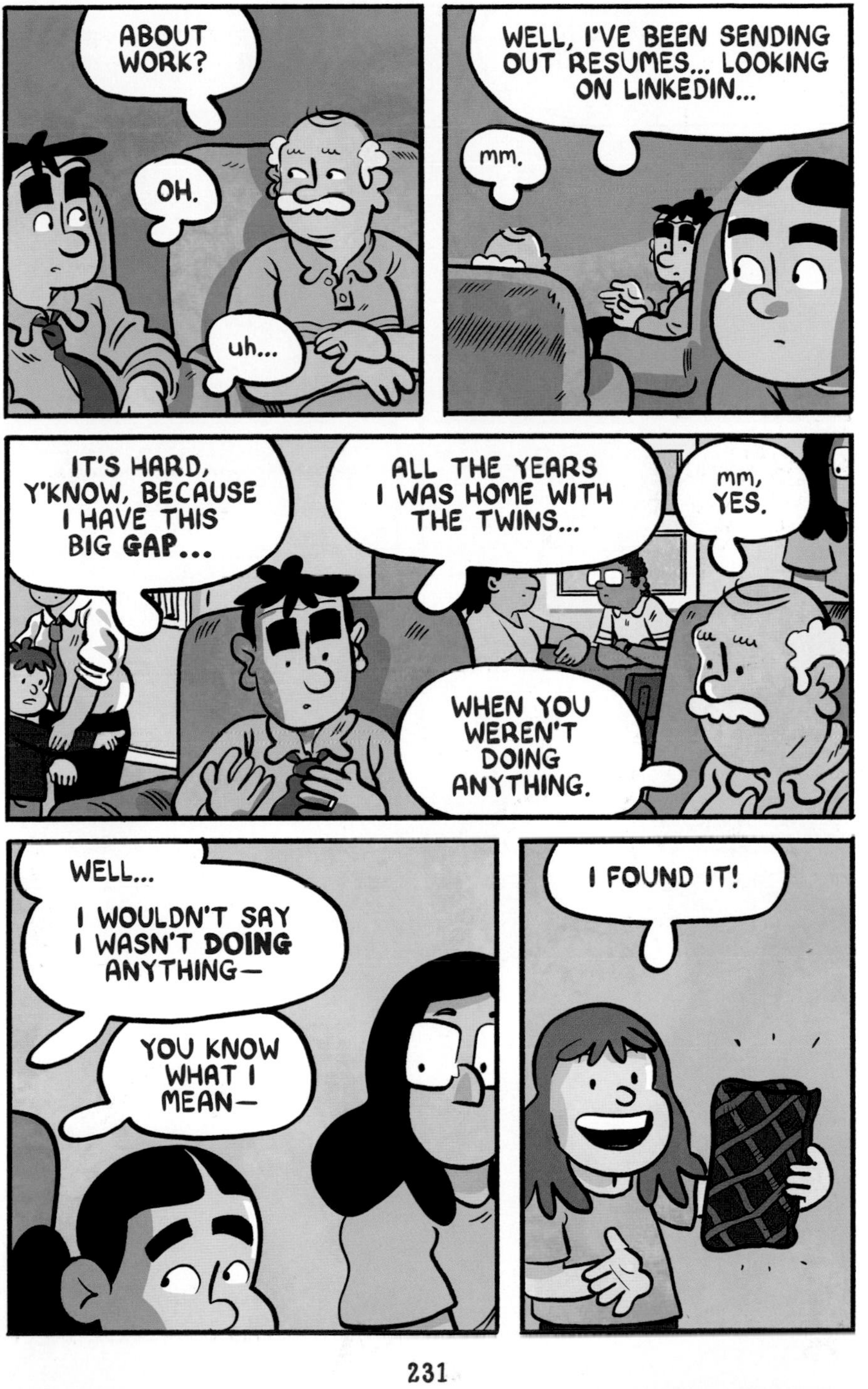
ABOUT WORK?
OH.
uh...
WELL, I'VE BEEN SENDING OUT RESUMES... LOOKING ON LINKEDIN...
mm.
IT'S HARD, Y'KNOW, BECAUSE I HAVE THIS BIG GAP...
ALL THE YEARS I WAS HOME WITH THE TWINS...
mm, YES.
WHEN YOU WEREN'T DOING ANYTHING.
WELL...
I WOULDN'T SAY I WASN'T DOING ANYTHING—
YOU KNOW WHAT I MEAN—
I FOUND IT!

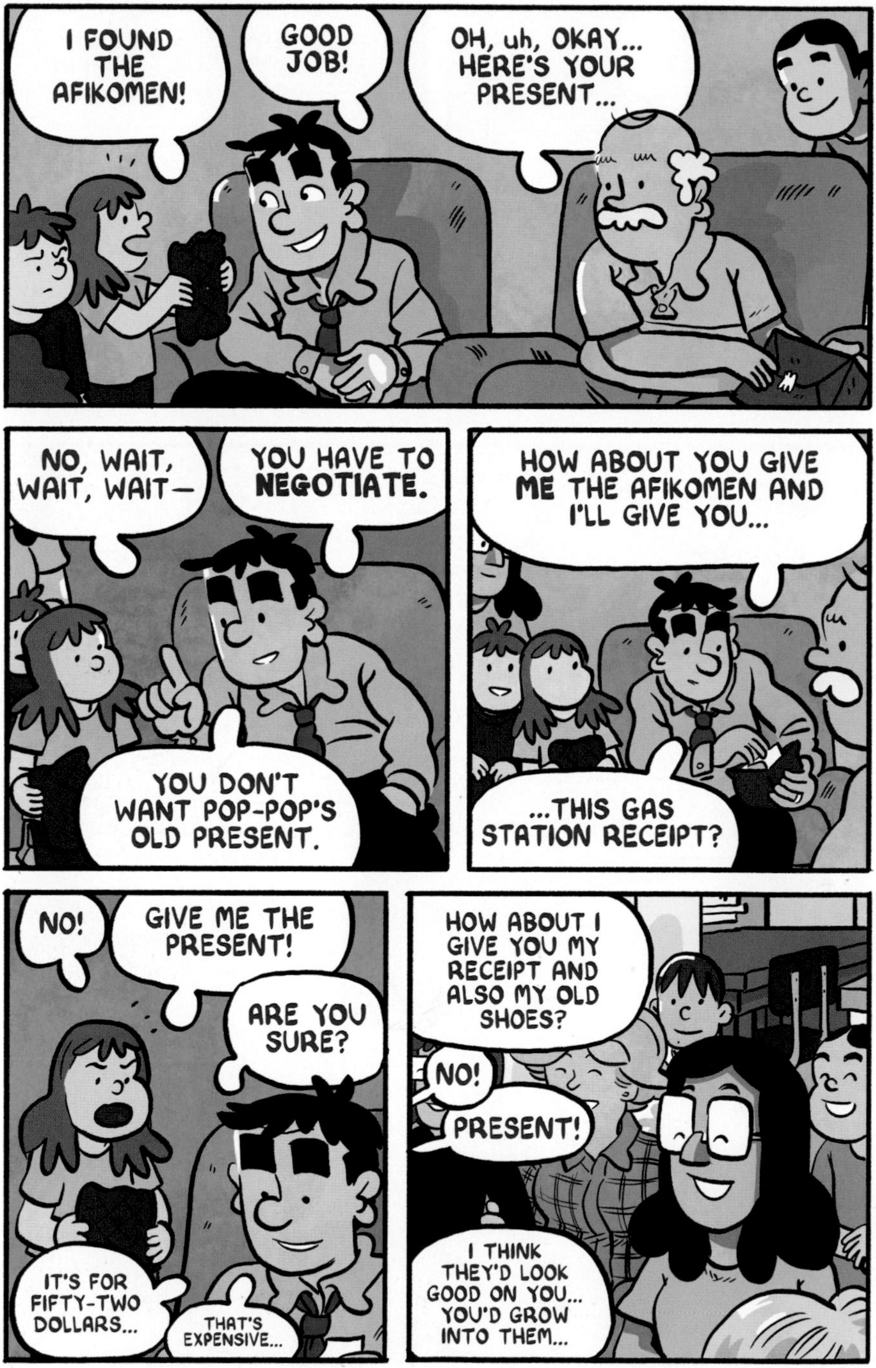
I FOUND THE AFIKOMEN!
GOOD JOB!
OH, uh, OKAY... HERE'S YOUR PRESENT...
NO, WAIT, WAIT, WAIT—
YOU HAVE TO NEGOTIATE.
YOU DON'T WANT POP-POP'S OLD PRESENT.
HOW ABOUT YOU GIVE ME THE AFIKOMEN AND I'LL GIVE YOU...
...THIS GAS STATION RECEIPT?
NO!
GIVE ME THE PRESENT!
ARE YOU SURE?
IT'S FOR FIFTY-TWO DOLLARS...
THAT'S EXPENSIVE...
HOW ABOUT I GIVE YOU MY RECEIPT AND ALSO MY OLD SHOES?
NO!
PRESENT!
I THINK THEY'D LOOK GOOD ON YOU... YOU'D GROW INTO THEM...

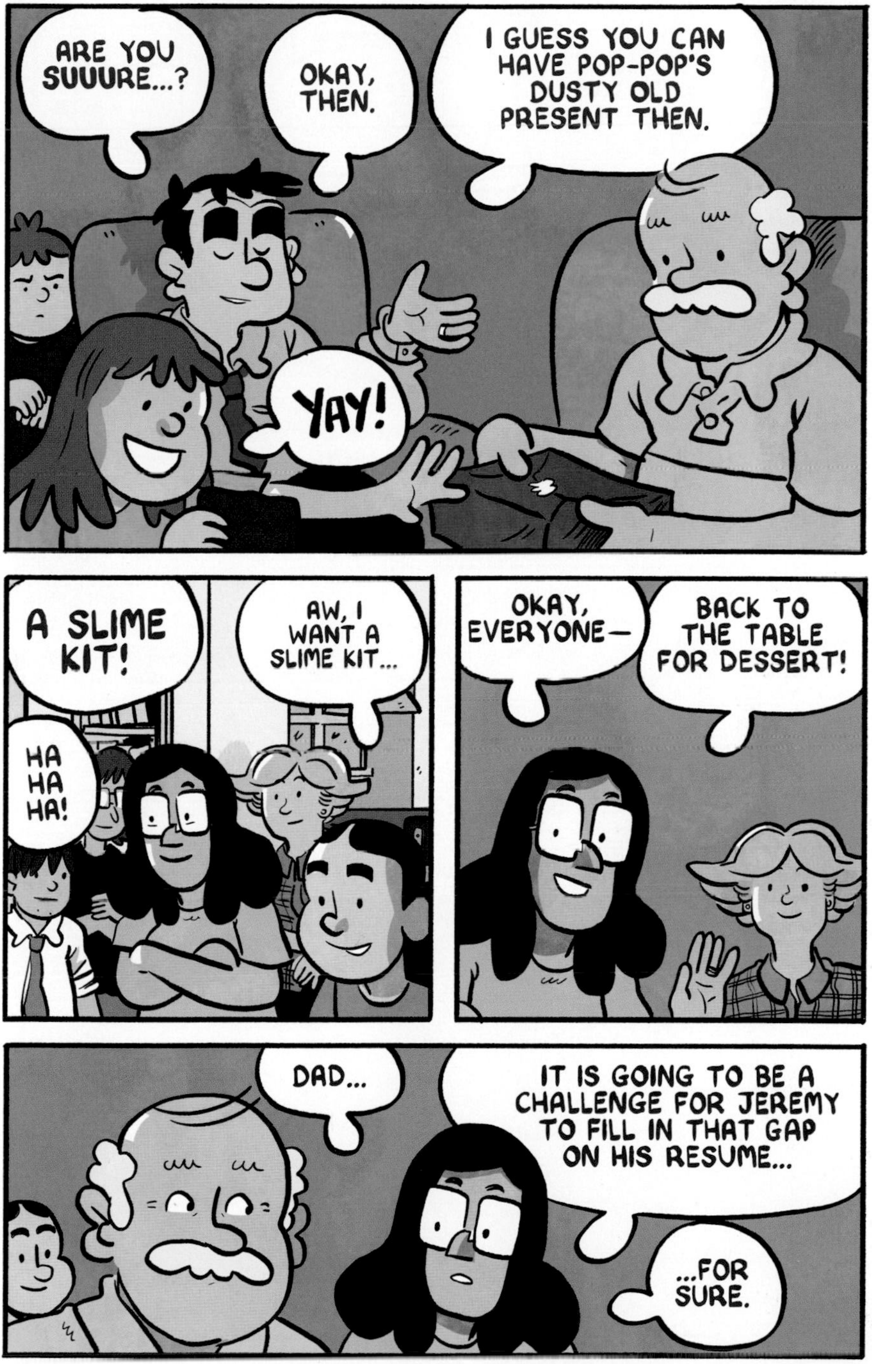
ARE YOU SUUURE...?
OKAY, THEN.
I GUESS YOU CAN HAVE POP-POP'S DUSTY OLD PRESENT THEN.
YAY!
A SLIME KIT!
AW, I WANT A SLIME KIT...
HA HA HA!
OKAY, EVERYONE—
BACK TO THE TABLE FOR DESSERT!
DAD...
IT IS GOING TO BE A CHALLENGE FOR JEREMY TO FILL IN THAT GAP ON HIS RESUME...
...FOR SURE.

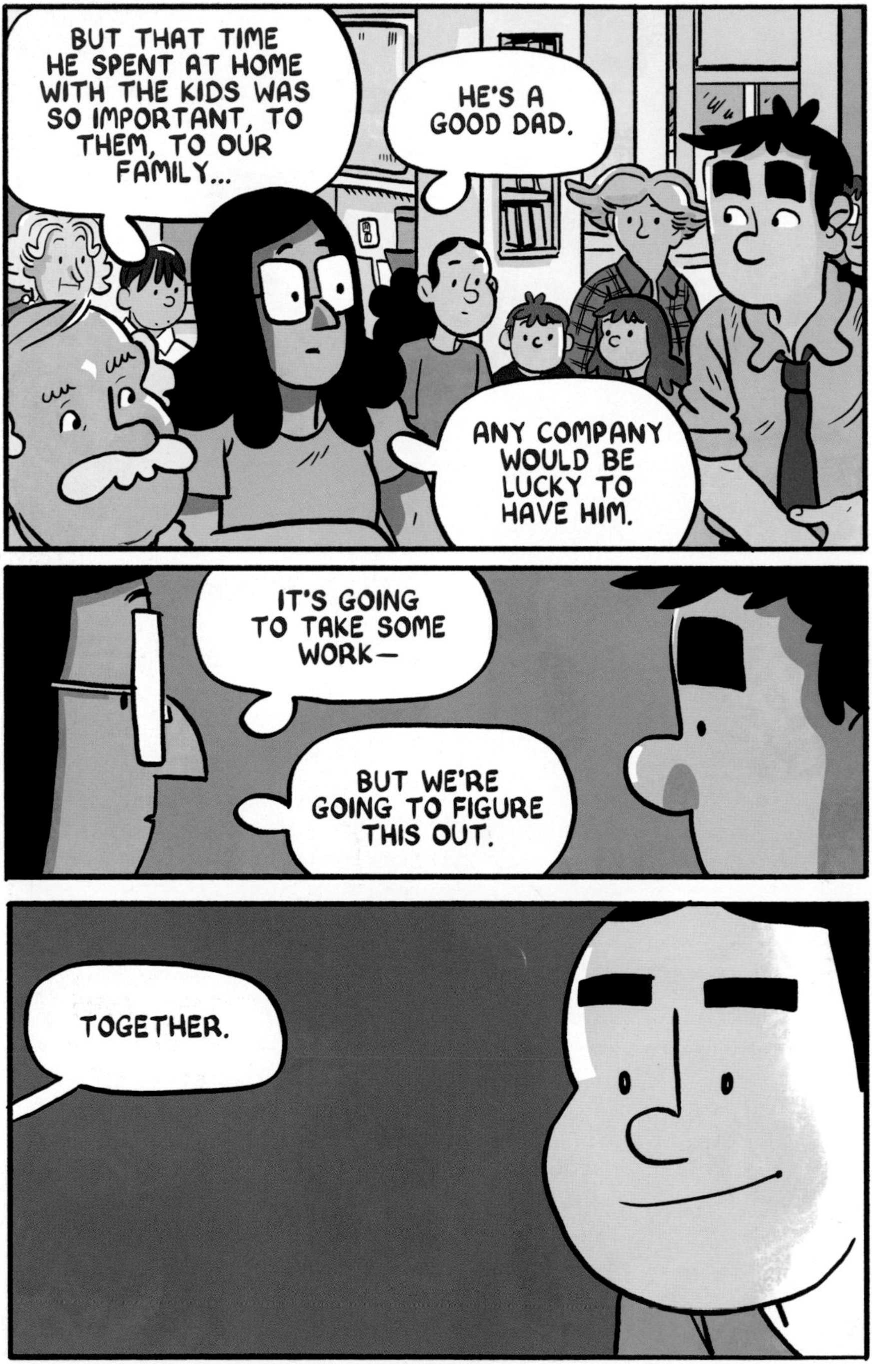
BUT THAT TIME HE SPENT AT HOME WITH THE KIDS WAS SO IMPORTANT, TO THEM, TO OUR FAMILY...
HE'S A GOOD DAD.
ANY COMPANY WOULD BE LUCKY TO HAVE HIM.
IT'S GOING TO TAKE SOME WORK—
BUT WE'RE GOING TO FIGURE THIS OUT.
TOGETHER.

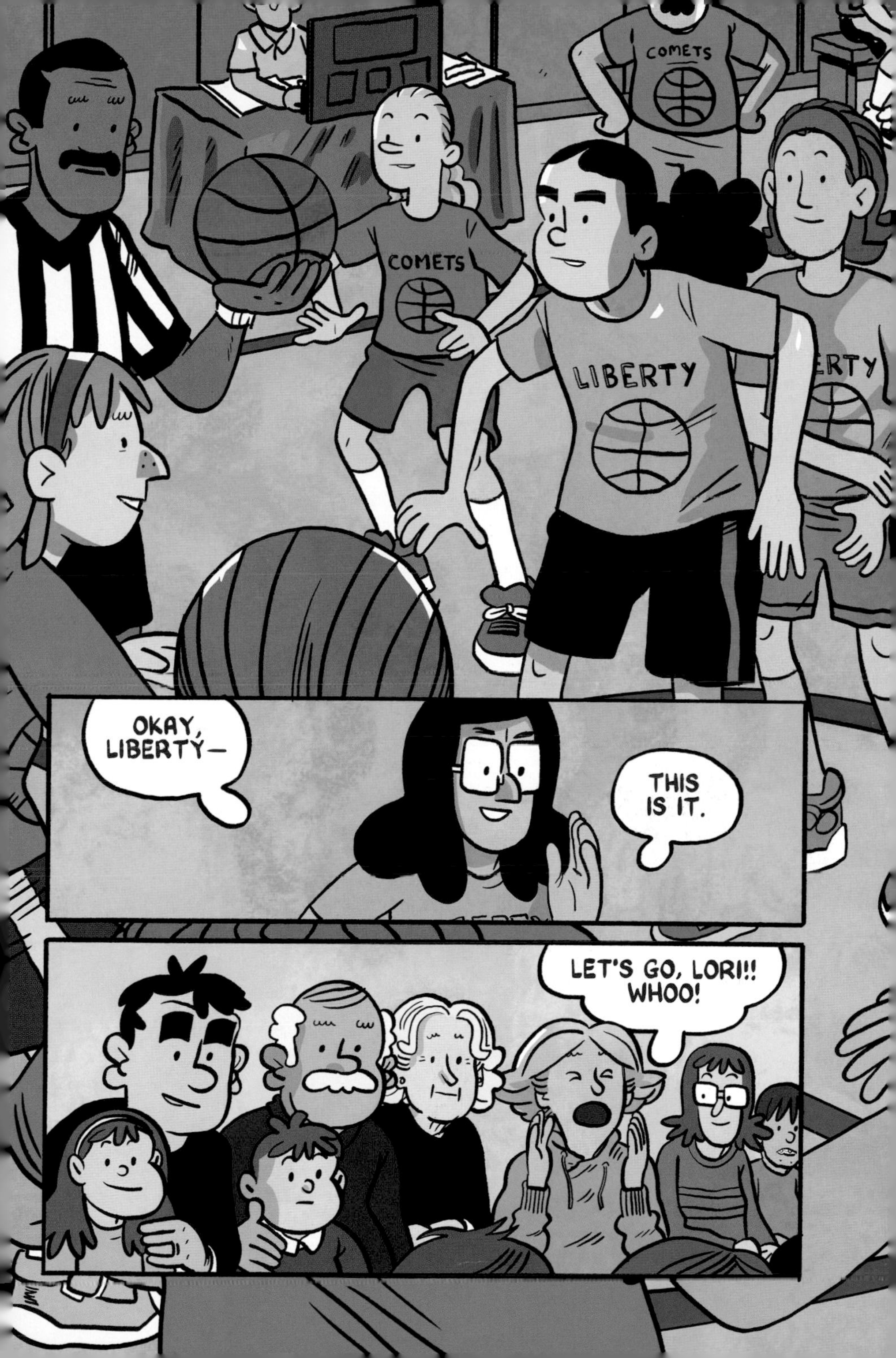
COMETS
COMETS
LIBERTY
LIBERTY
OKAY, LIBERTY—
THIS IS IT.
LET'S GO, LORI!! WHOO!

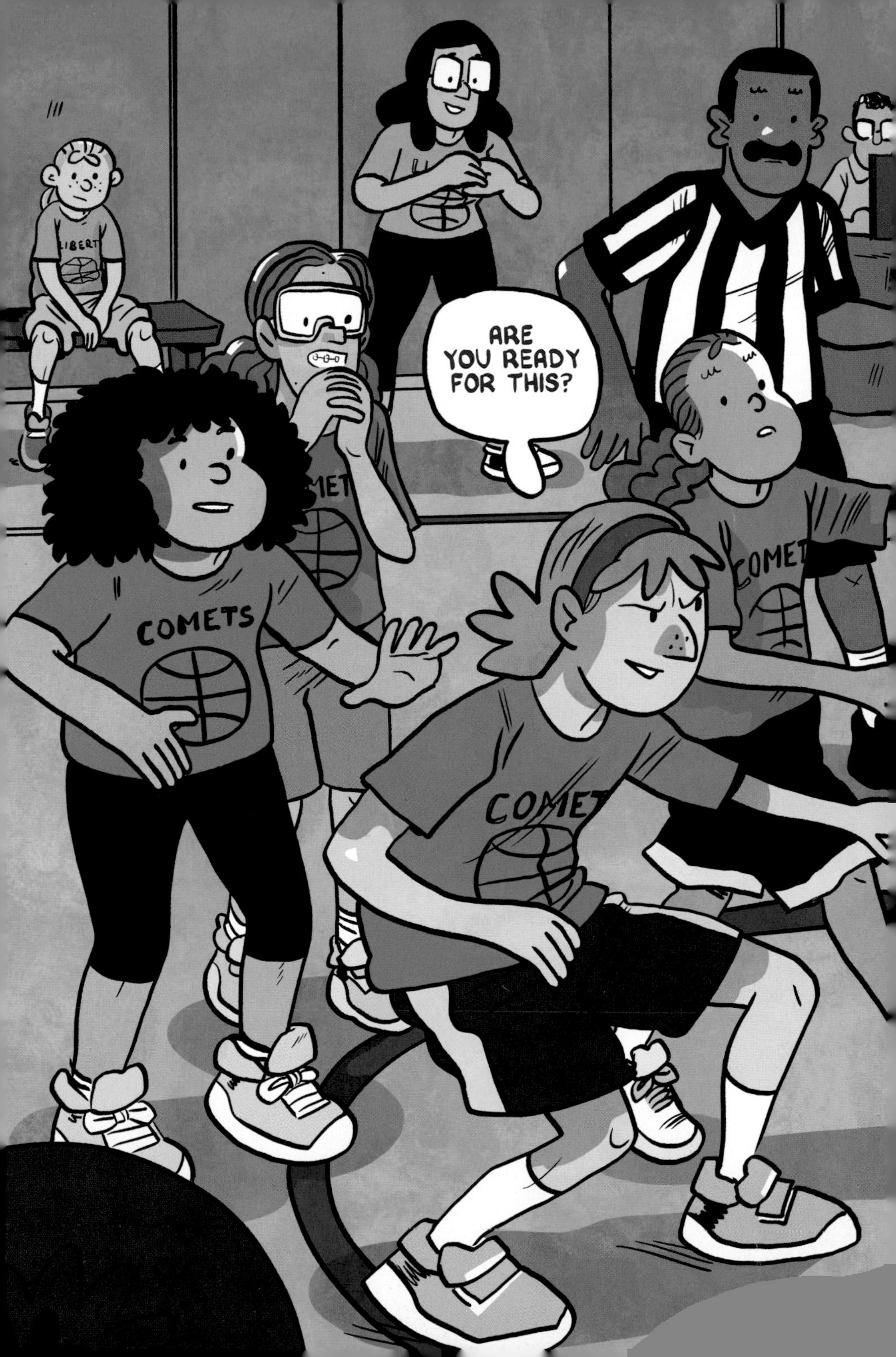
ARE YOU READY FOR THIS?

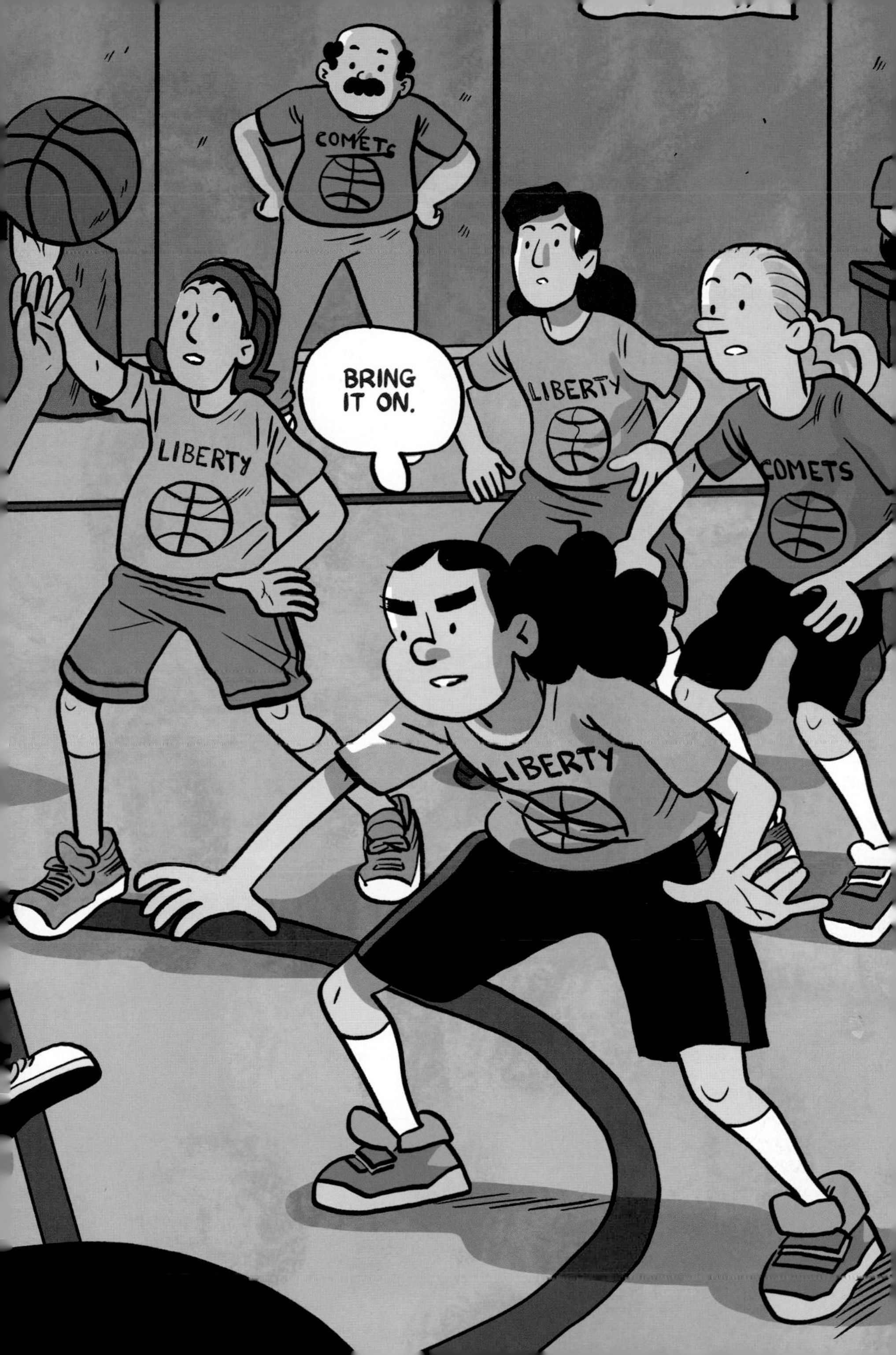
BRING IT ON.
COMETS
LIBERTY
LIBERTY
COMETS
LIBERTY

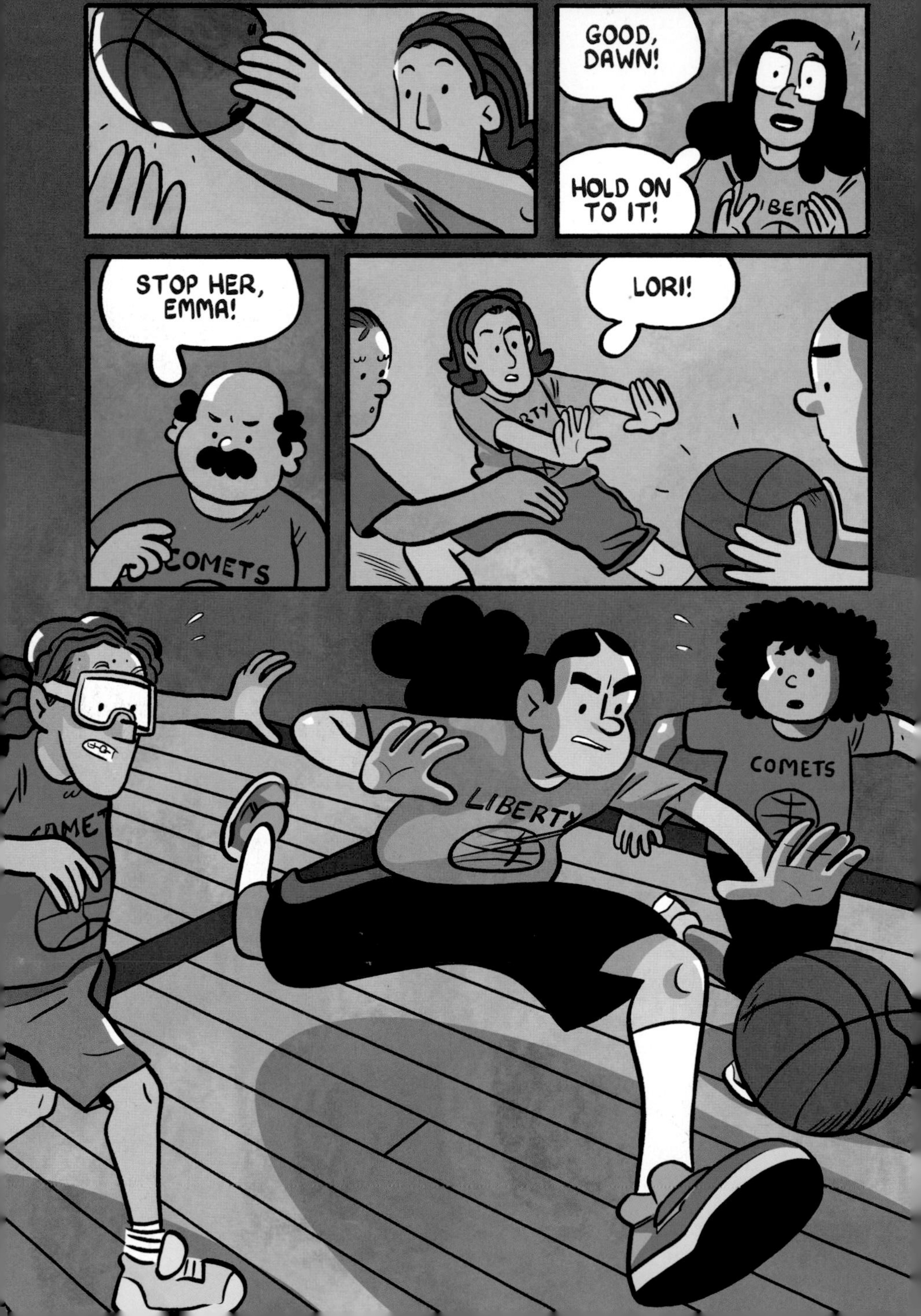
GOOD, DAWN!
HOLD ON TO IT!
IBER
STOP HER, EMMA!
COMETS
LORI!
RTY
COMETS
LIBERTY
COMETS

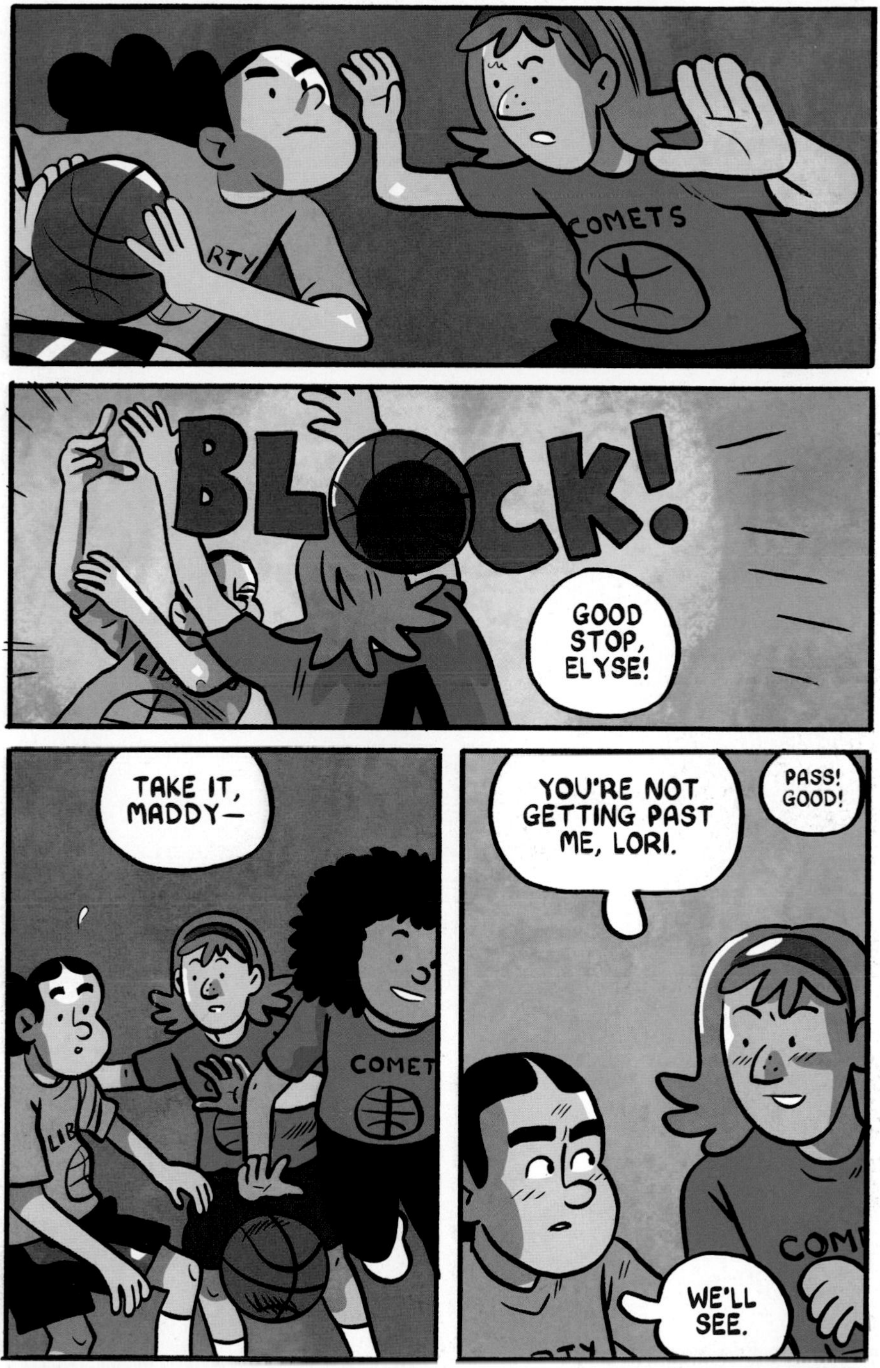

COMETS
RTY
BLOCK!
GOOD STOP, ELYSE!
LIB
TAKE IT, MADDY—
COMET
LIB
YOU'RE NOT GETTING PAST ME, LORI.
PASS! GOOD!
COM
WE'LL SEE.

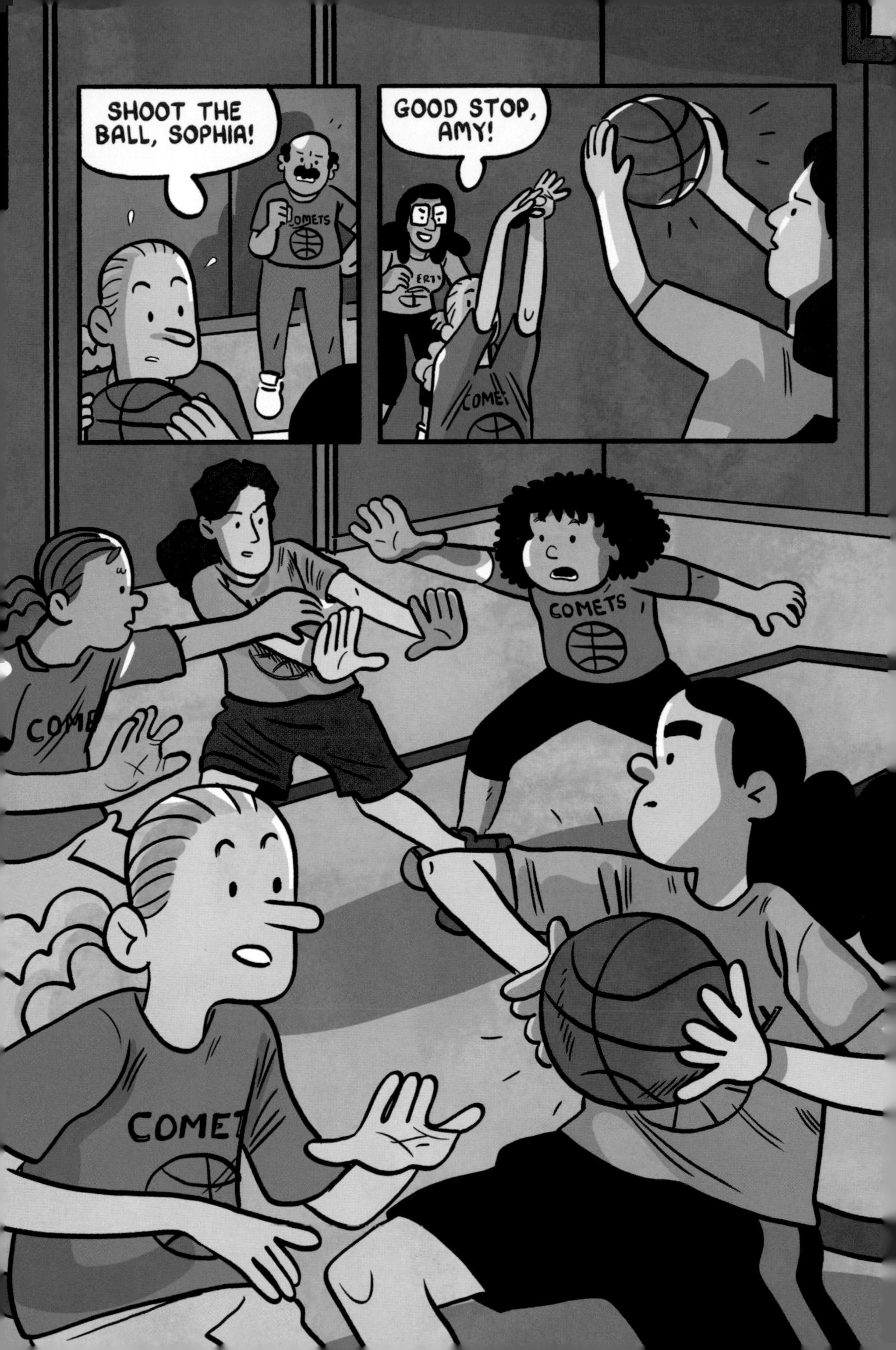
SHOOT THE BALL, SOPHIA!
COMETS
GOOD STOP, AMY!
COMETS
COMETS
COMETS

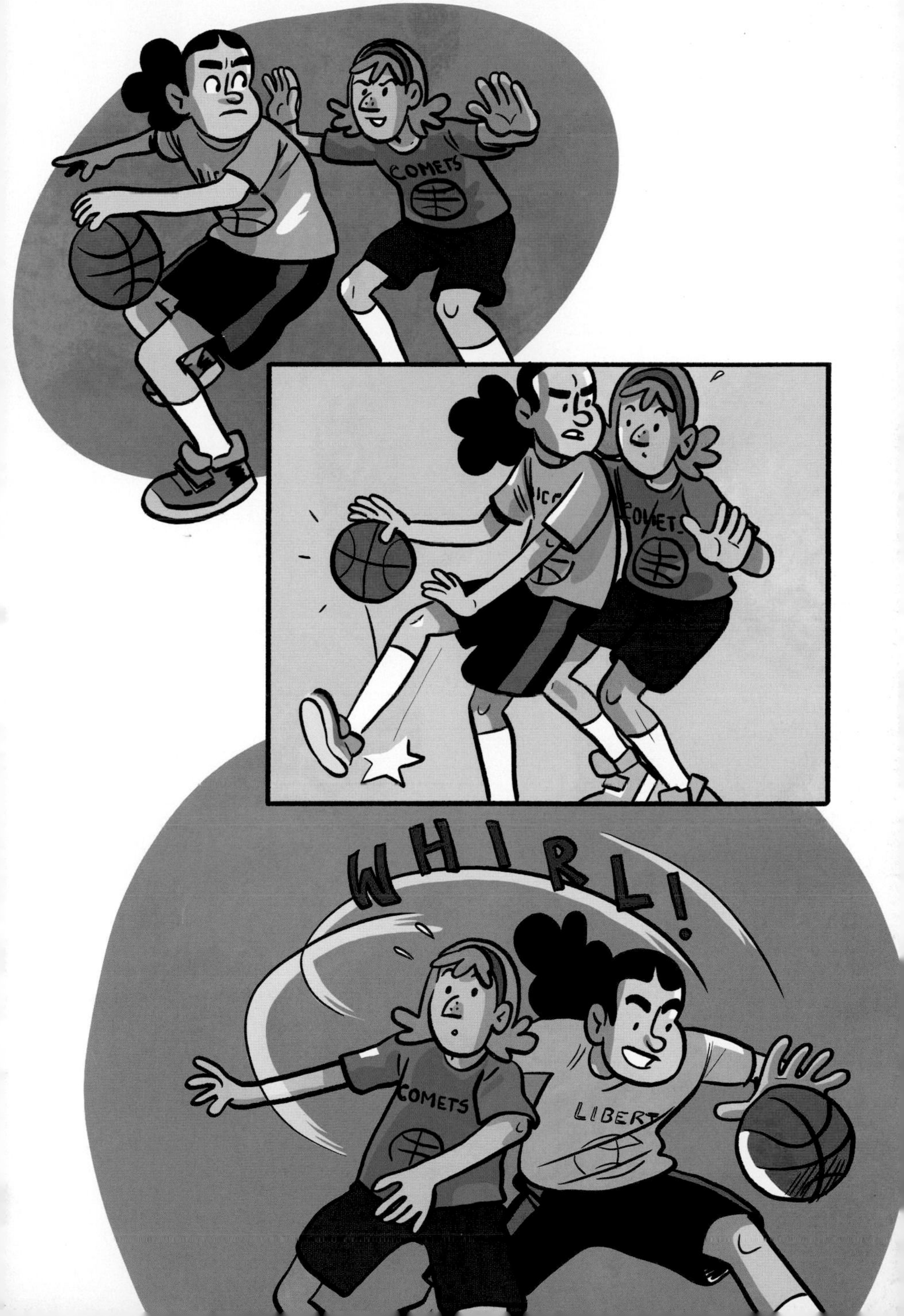
COMETS
COMETS
WHIRL!
COMETS
LIBERT

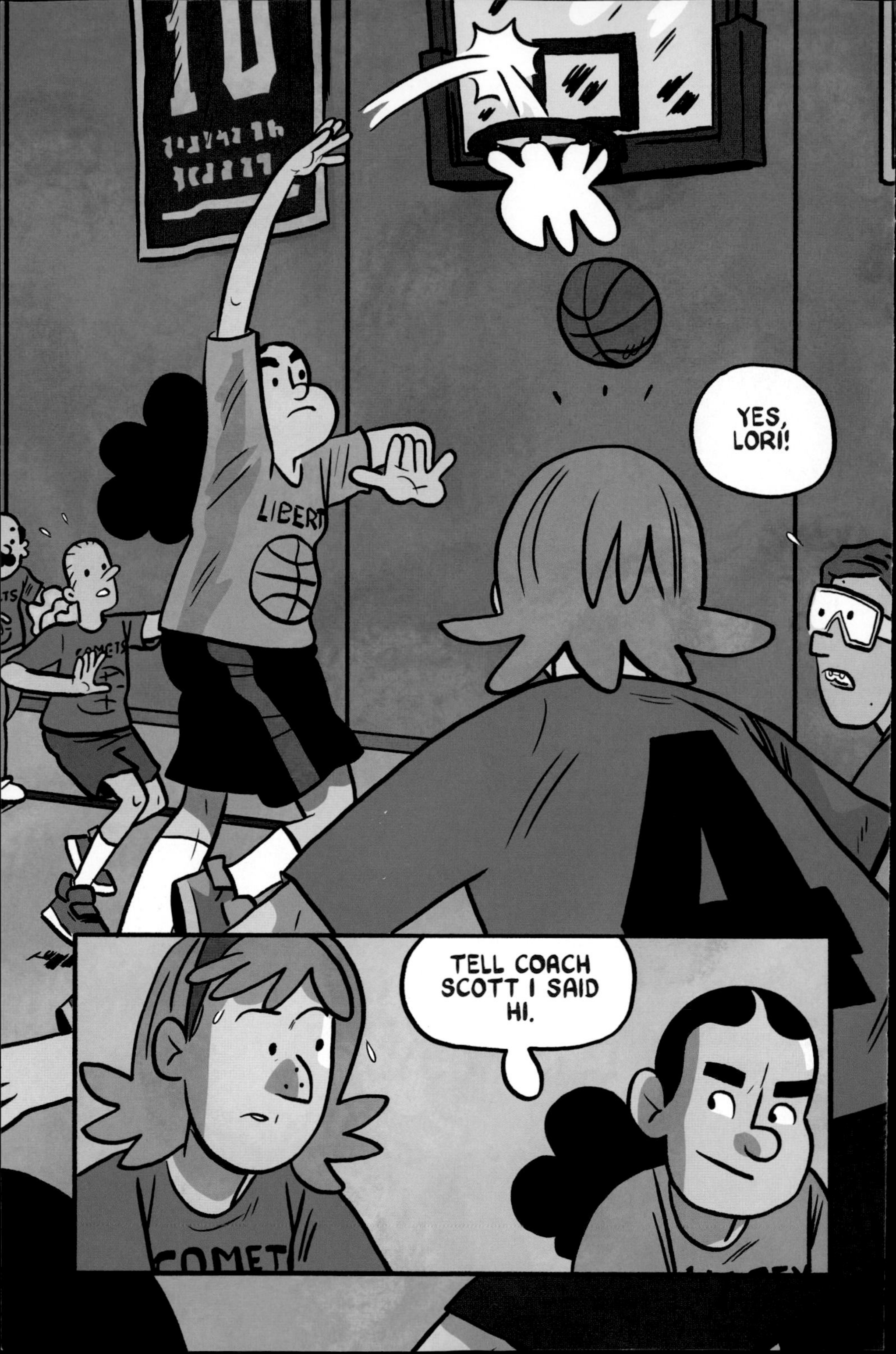
YES, LORI!
TELL COACH SCOTT I SAID HI.

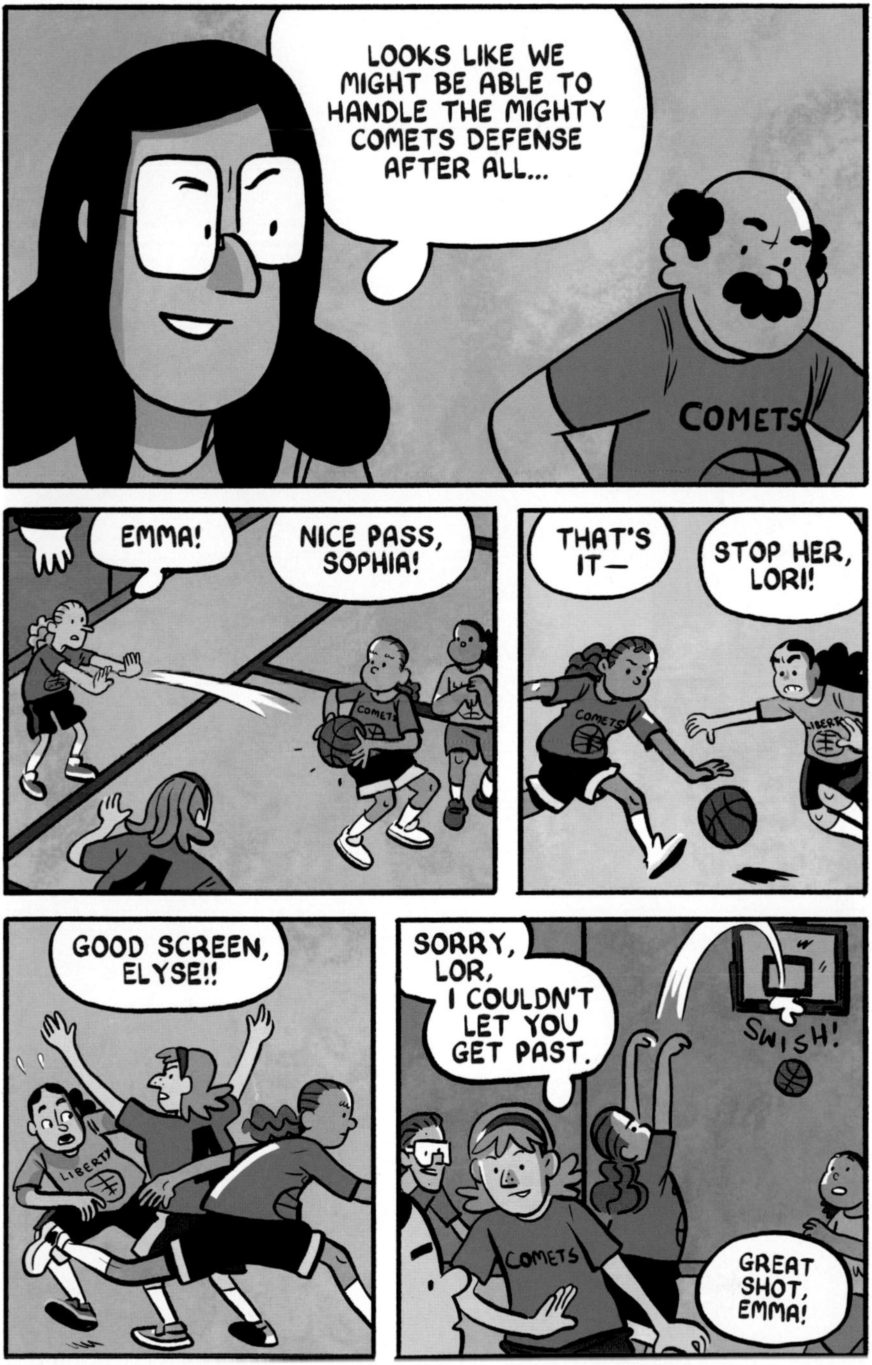
LOOKS LIKE WE MIGHT BE ABLE TO HANDLE THE MIGHTY COMETS DEFENSE AFTER ALL...
COMETS
EMMA!
NICE PASS, SOPHIA!
COMETS
THAT'S IT—
STOP HER, LORI!
COMETS
GOOD SCREEN, ELYSE!!
LIBERTY
SORRY, LOR, I COULDN'T LET YOU GET PAST.
SWISH!
COMETS
GREAT SHOT, EMMA!

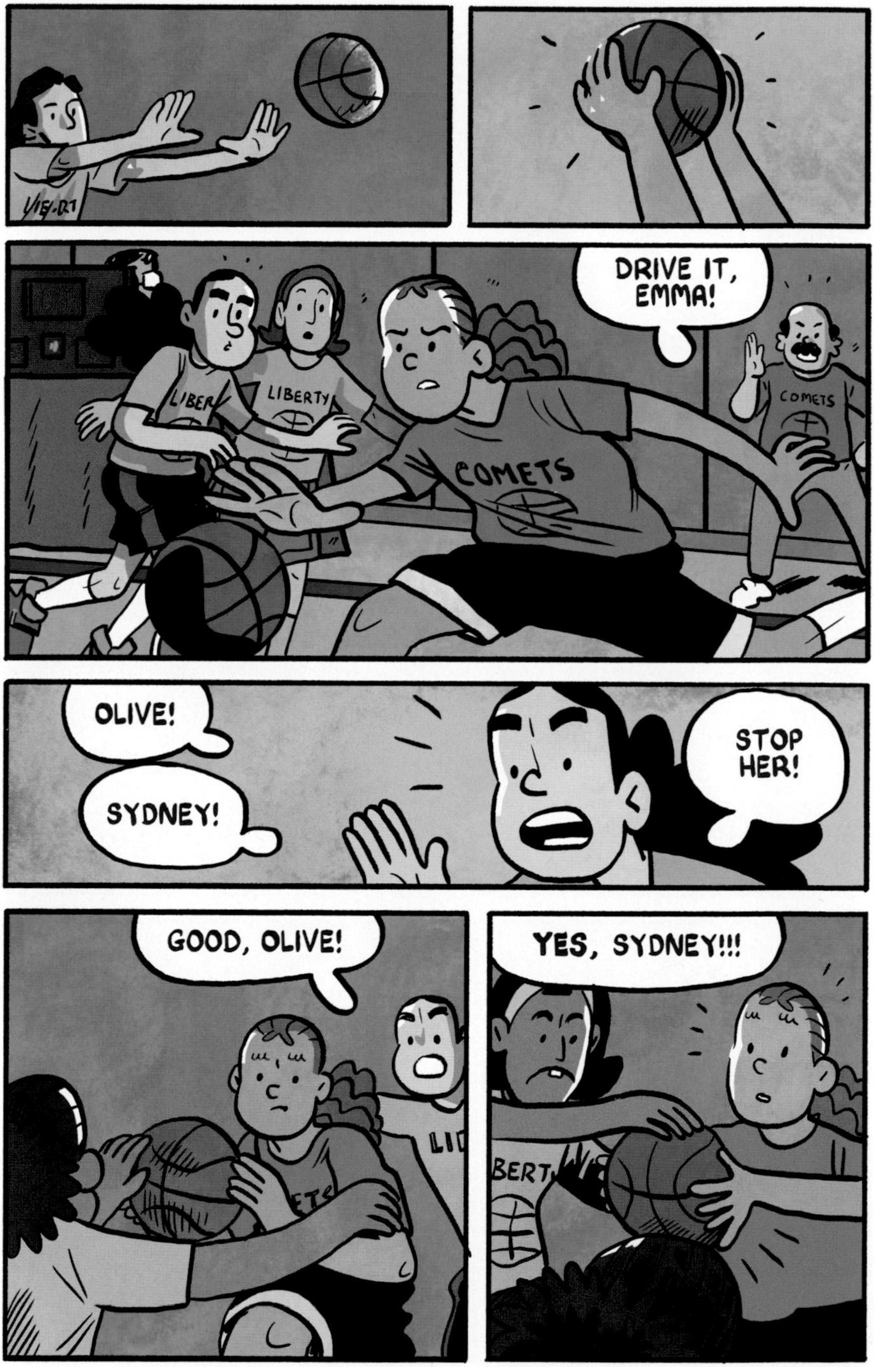

DRIVE IT, EMMA!
LIBERTY
COMETS
OLIVE!
SYDNEY!
STOP HER!
GOOD, OLIVE!
YES, SYDNEY!!!

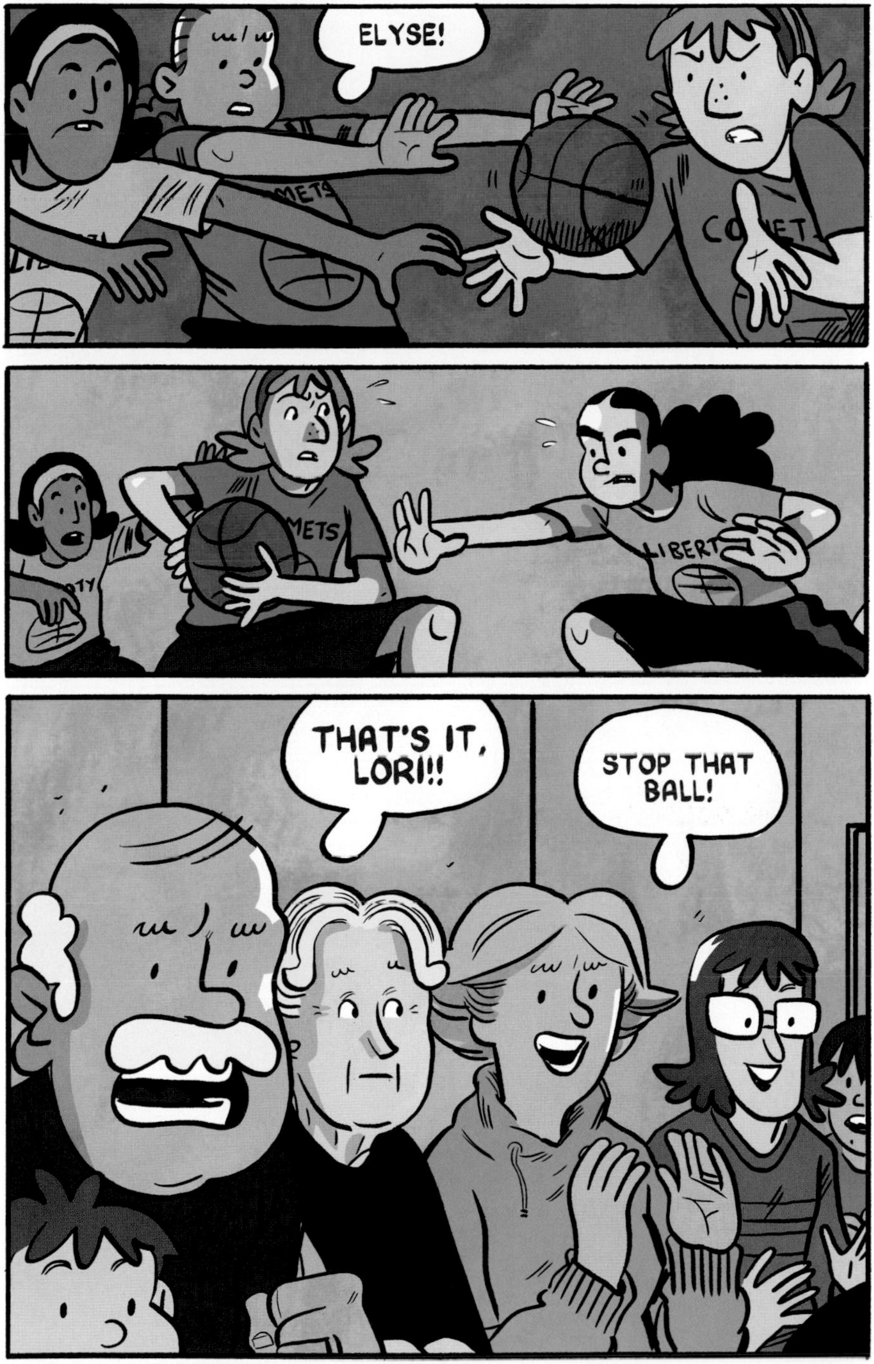
ELYSE!
COMETS
COMET
LIBERTY
METS
LIBERT
THAT'S IT, LORI!!
STOP THAT BALL!

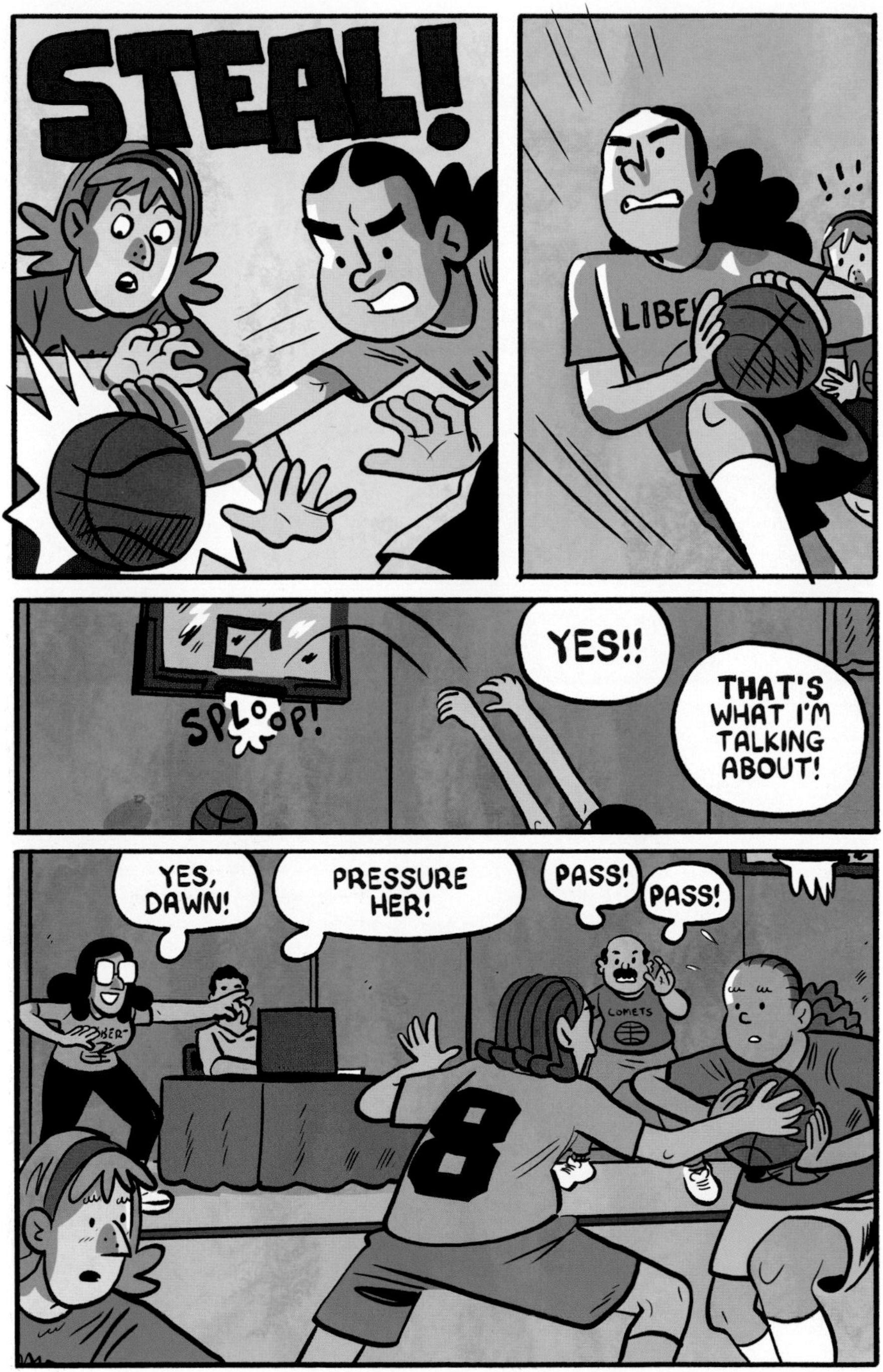
STEAL!
LIBE
LI
!!!
SPLOOP!
YES!!
THAT'S WHAT I'M TALKING ABOUT!
YES, DAWN!
PRESSURE HER!
PASS!
PASS!
COMETS
8

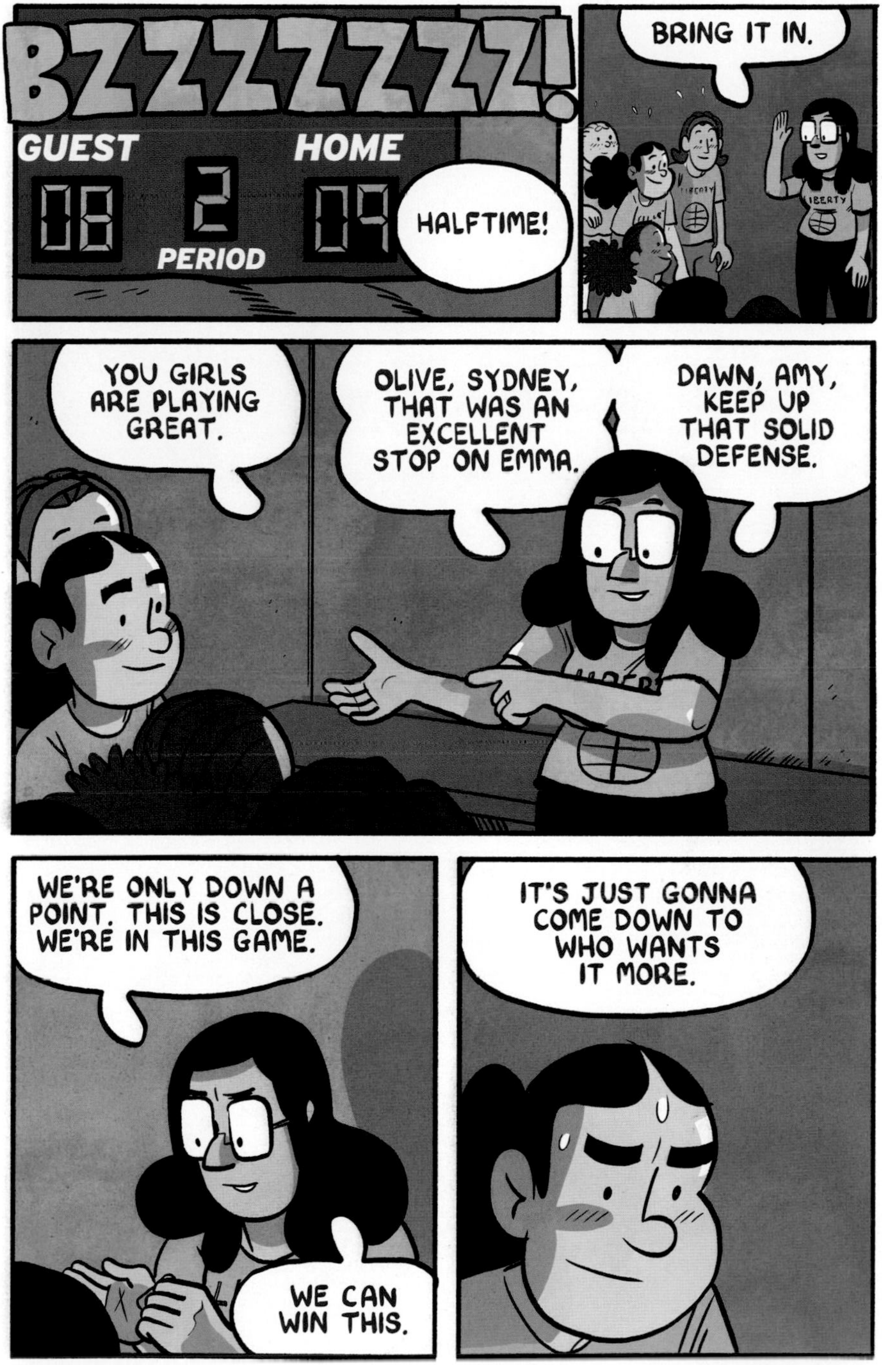
BZZZZZZZZ!
GUEST
HOME
PERIOD
HALFTIME!
BRING IT IN.
LIBERTY
YOU GIRLS ARE PLAYING GREAT.
OLIVE, SYDNEY, THAT WAS AN EXCELLENT STOP ON EMMA.
DAWN, AMY, KEEP UP THAT SOLID DEFENSE.
WE'RE ONLY DOWN A POINT. THIS IS CLOSE. WE'RE IN THIS GAME.
WE CAN WIN THIS.
IT'S JUST GONNA COME DOWN TO WHO WANTS IT MORE.

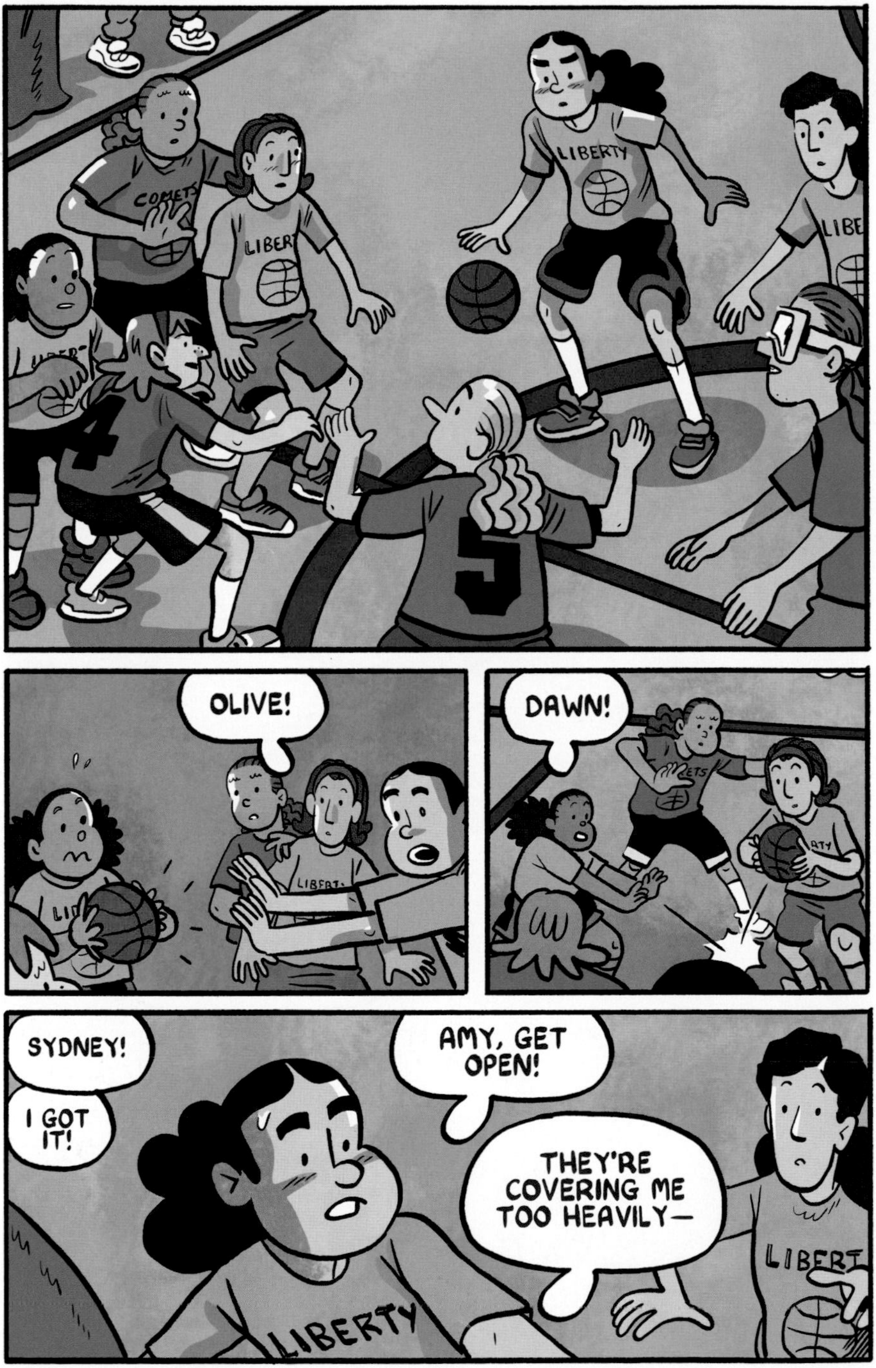
OLIVE!
DAWN!
SYDNEY!
I GOT IT!
AMY, GET OPEN!
THEY'RE COVERING ME TOO HEAVILY—

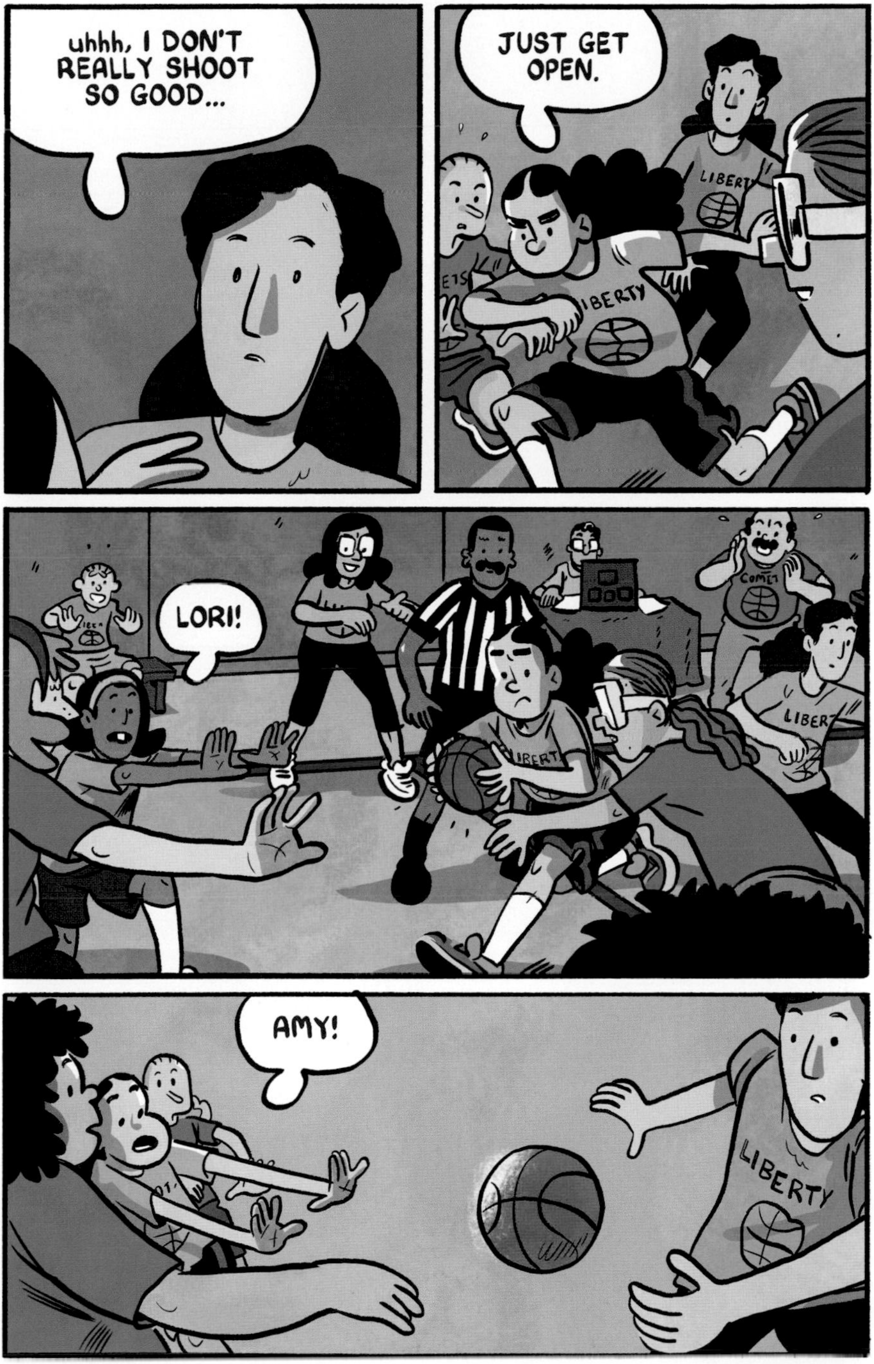
uhhh, I DON'T REALLY SHOOT SO GOOD...
JUST GET OPEN.
LIBERTY
LORI!
COMET
LIBERTY
AMY!
LIBERTY

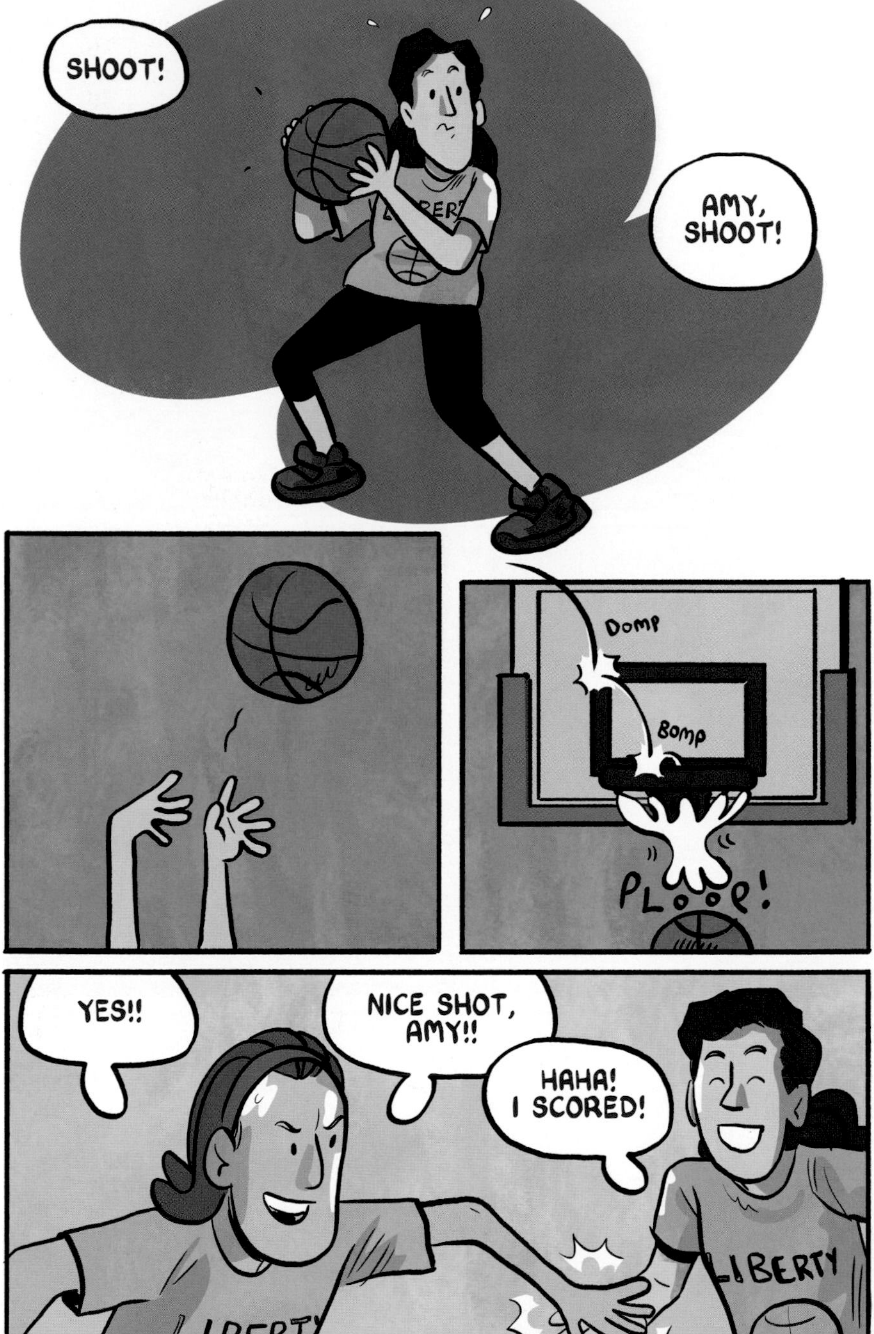
SHOOT!
AMY, SHOOT!
Domp
Bomp
PLOOP!
YES!!
NICE SHOT, AMY!!
HAHA! I SCORED!
LIBERTY
LIBERTY

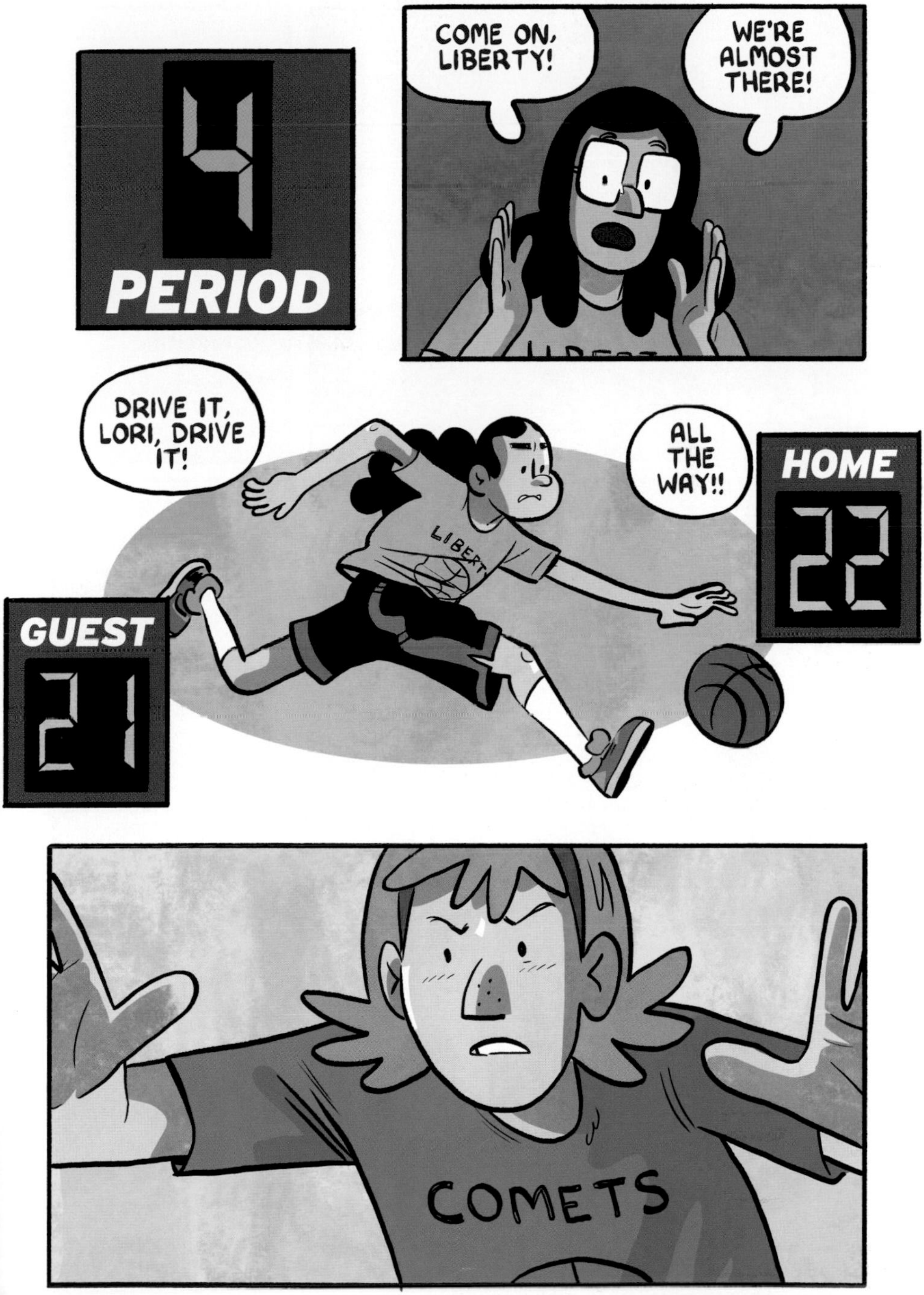
4
PERIOD
COME ON, LIBERTY!
WE'RE ALMOST THERE!
DRIVE IT, LORI, DRIVE IT!
ALL THE WAY!!
HOME
22
GUEST
21
COMETS

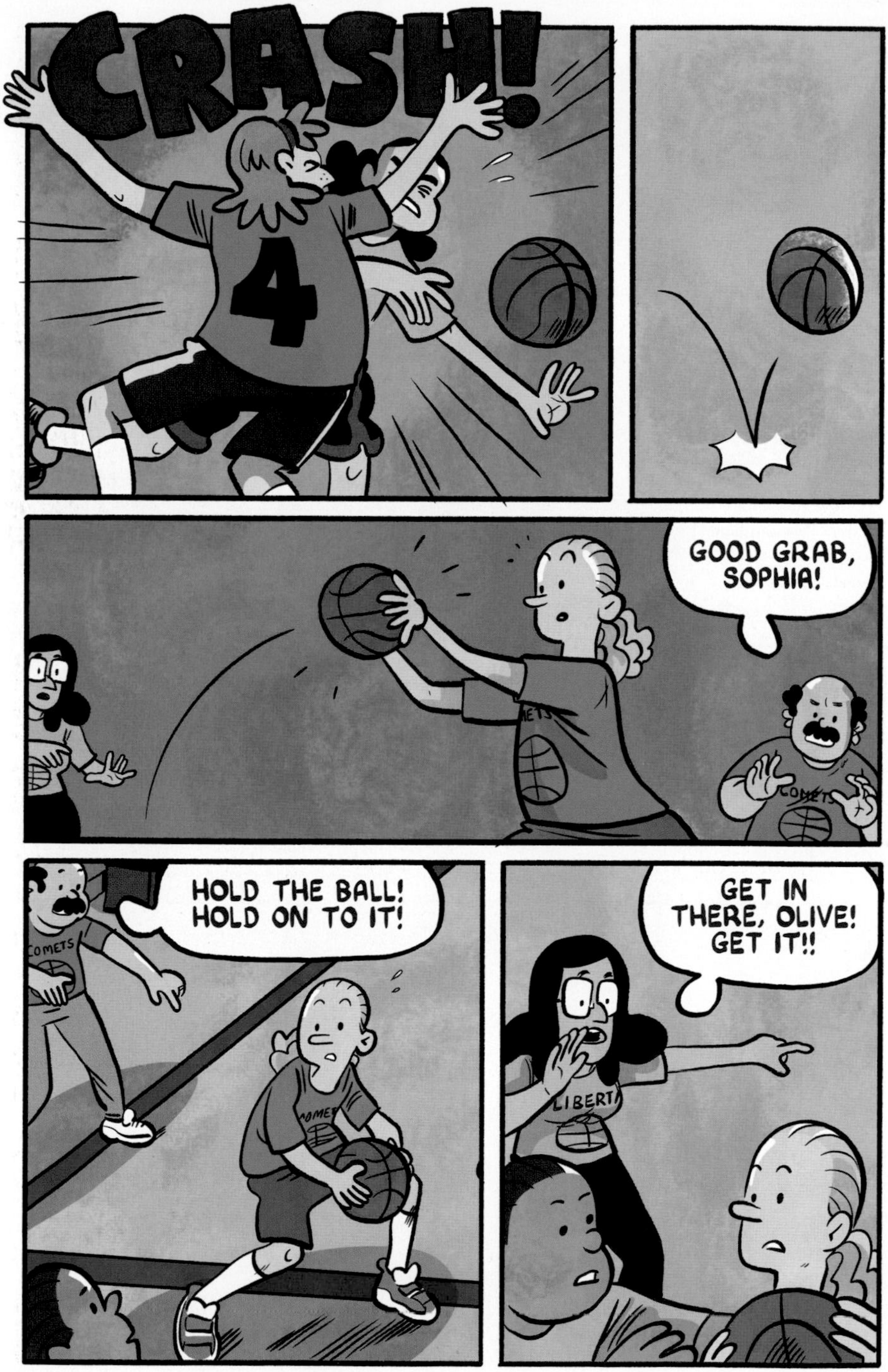
CRASH!
4
GOOD GRAB, SOPHIA!
HOLD THE BALL! HOLD ON TO IT!
COMETS
GET IN THERE, OLIVE! GET IT!!
LIBERTY

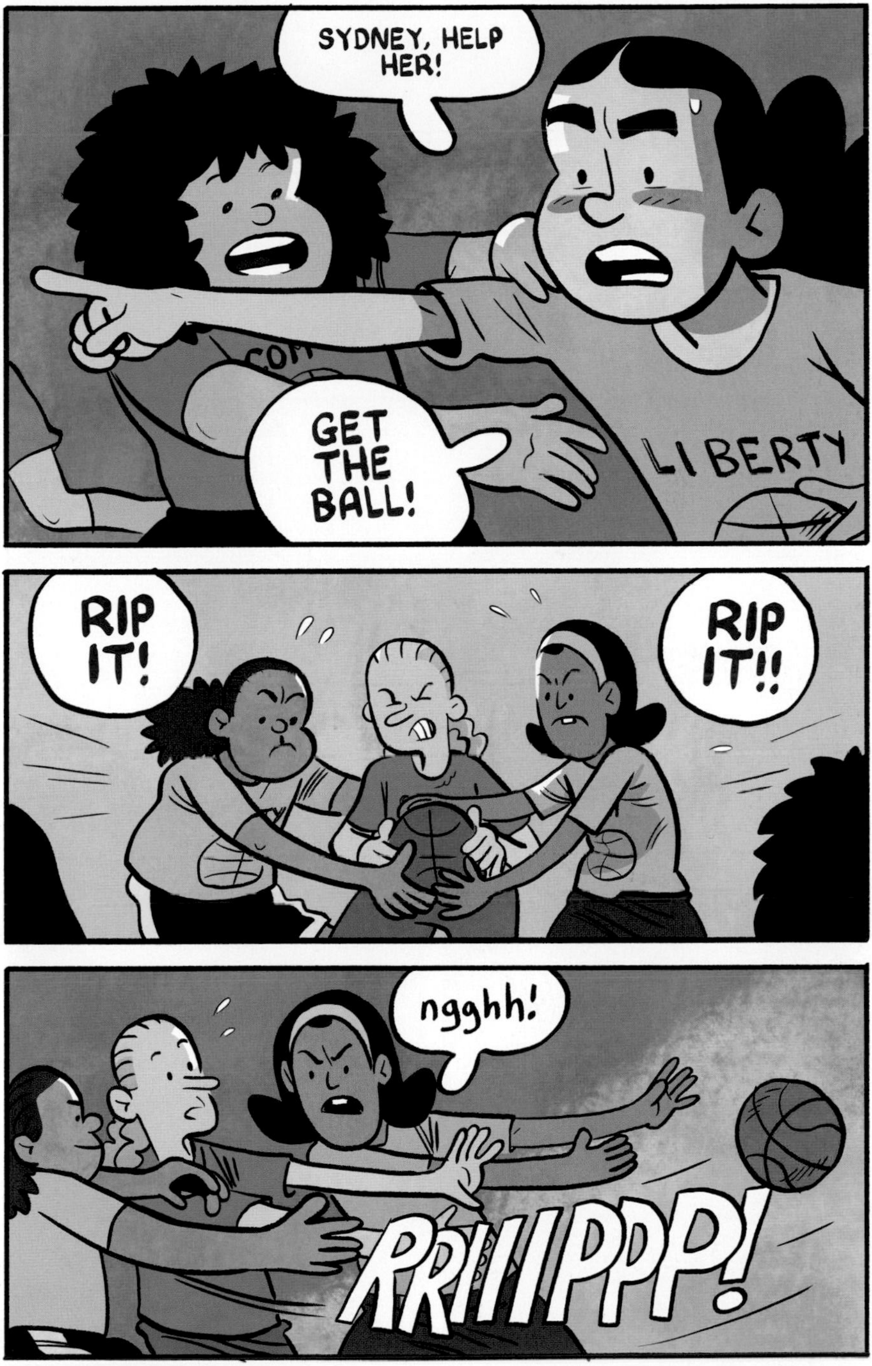
SYDNEY, HELP HER!
GET THE BALL!
LIBERTY
RIP IT!
RIP IT!!
ngghh!
RRIIIPPP!

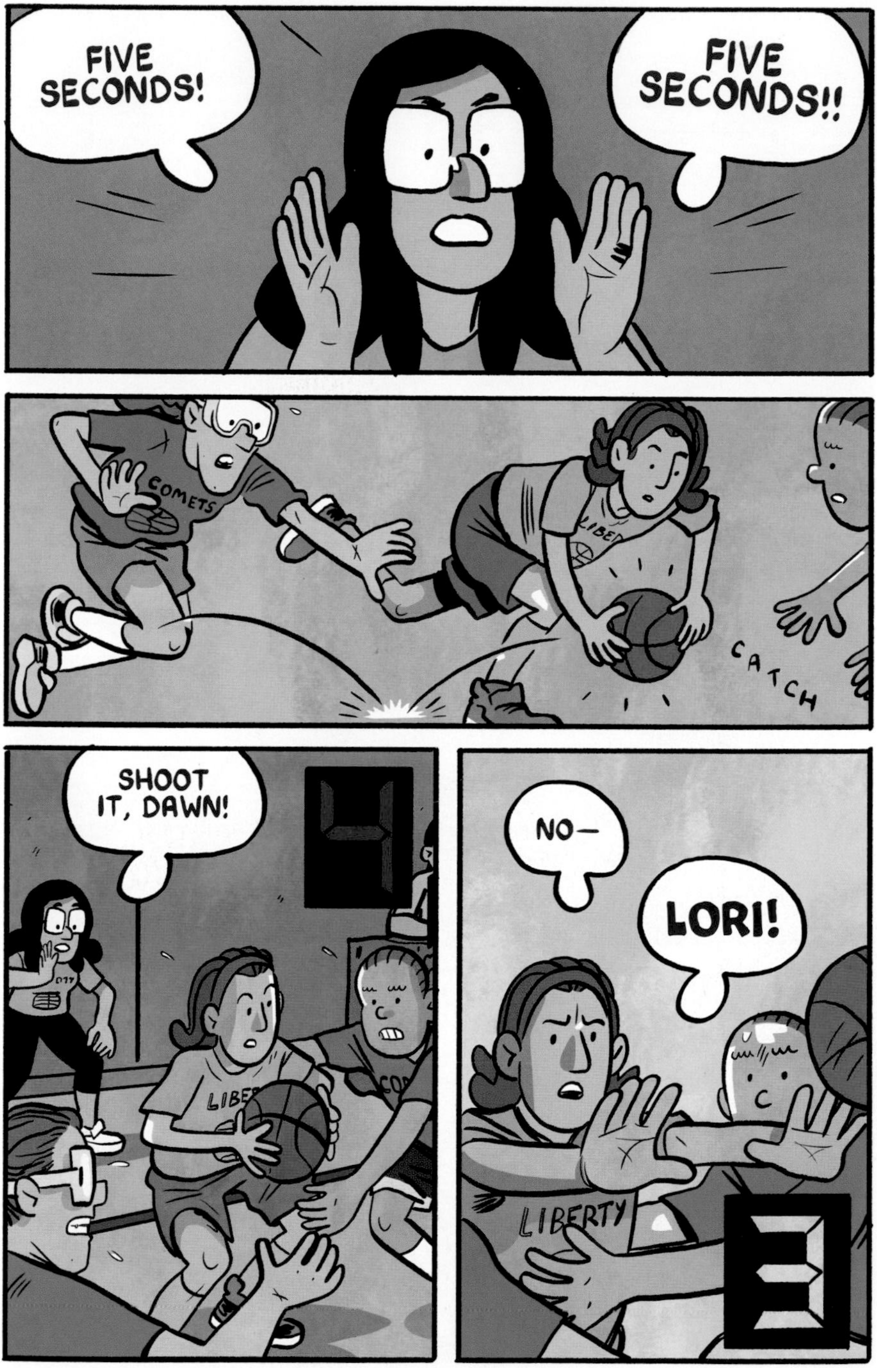
FIVE SECONDS!
FIVE SECONDS!!
COMETS
LIBE
CATCH
SHOOT IT, DAWN!
LIBE
NO—
LORI!
LIBERTY

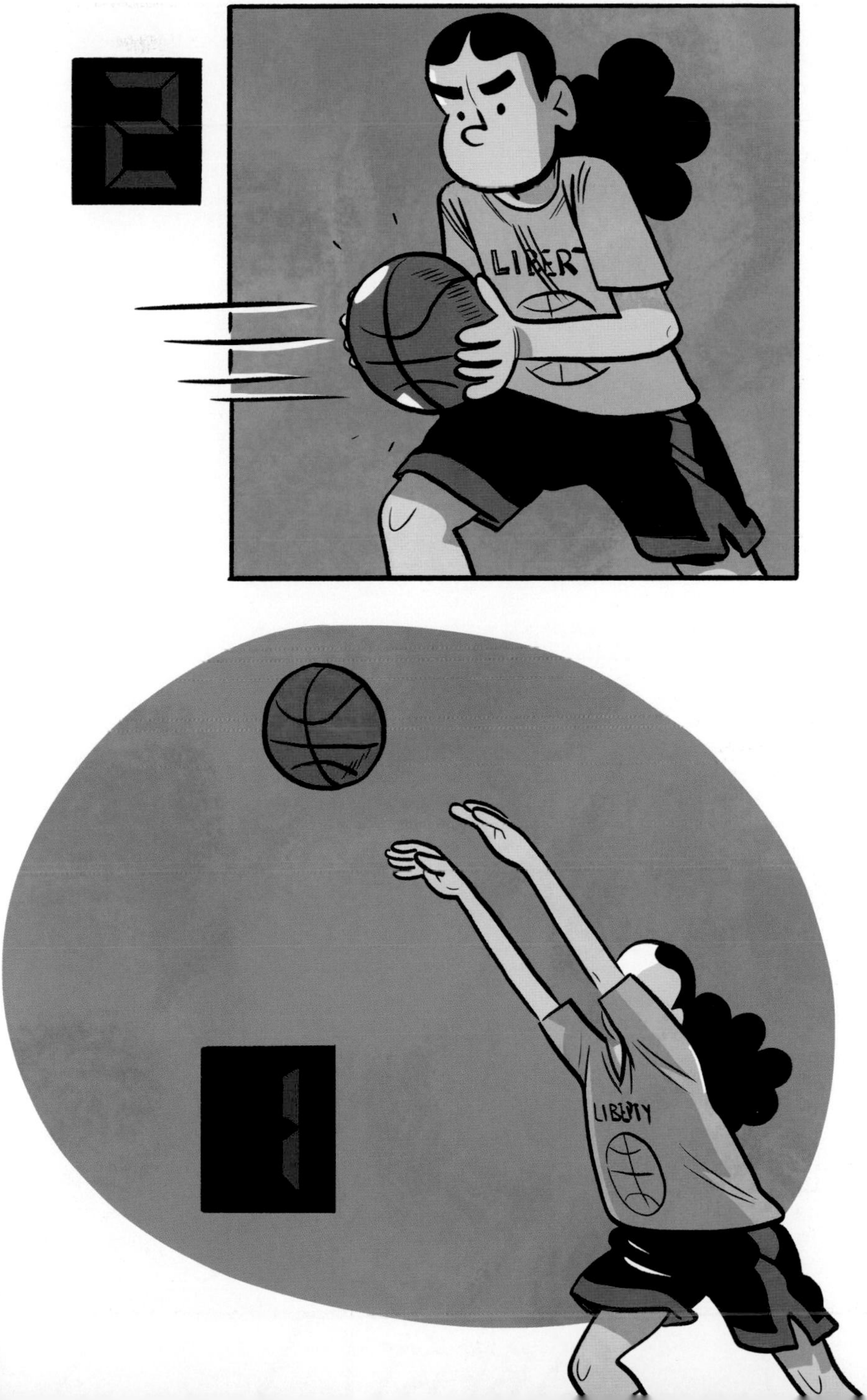
2
1
LIBERTY

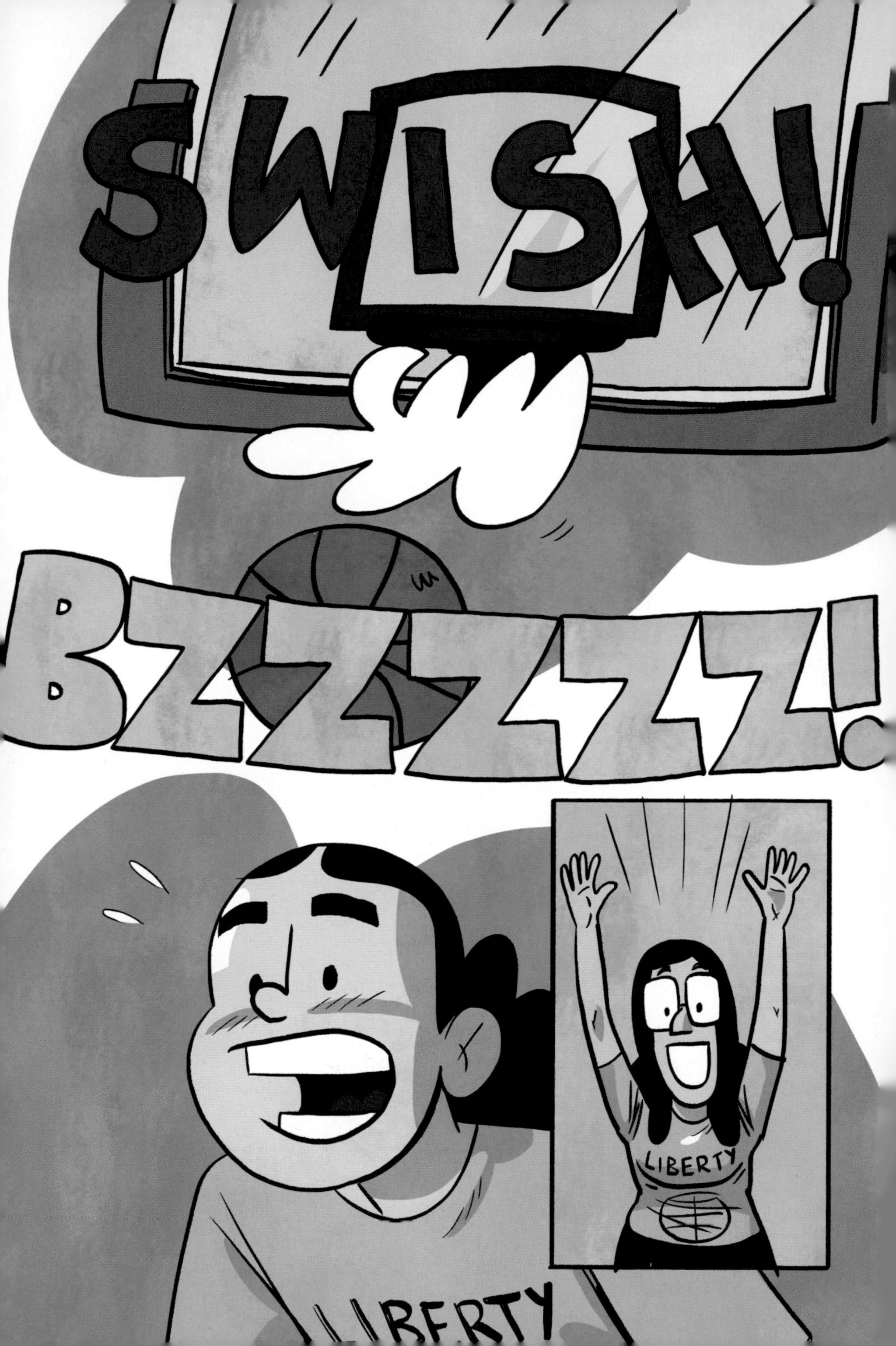
SWISH!
BZZZZZ!
LIBERTY
LIBERTY

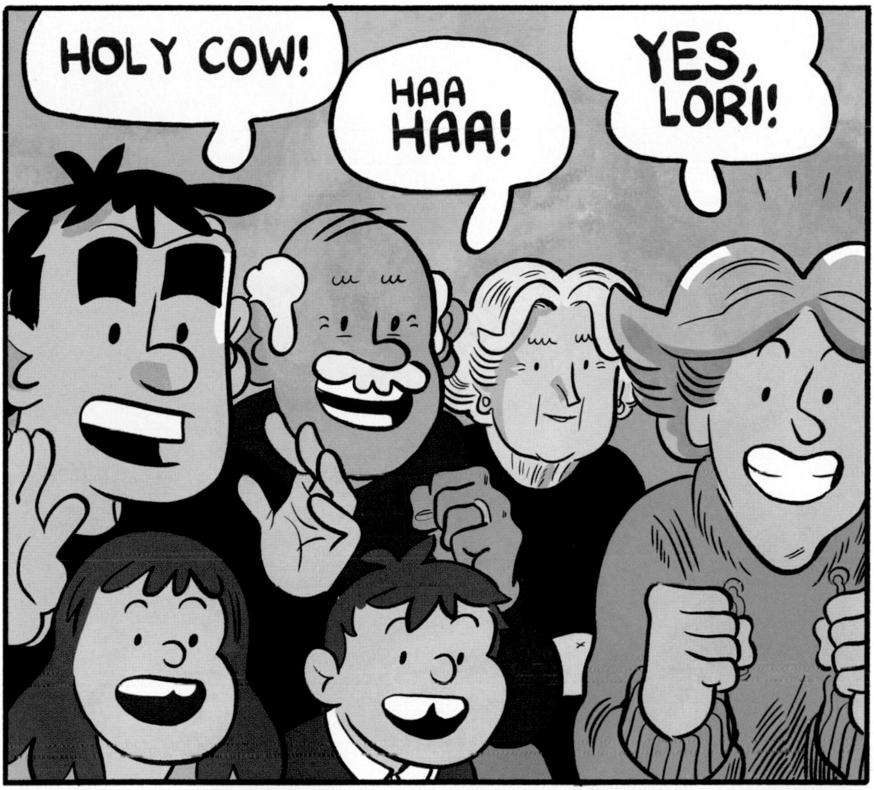
HOLY COW!
HAA HAA!
YES, LORI!

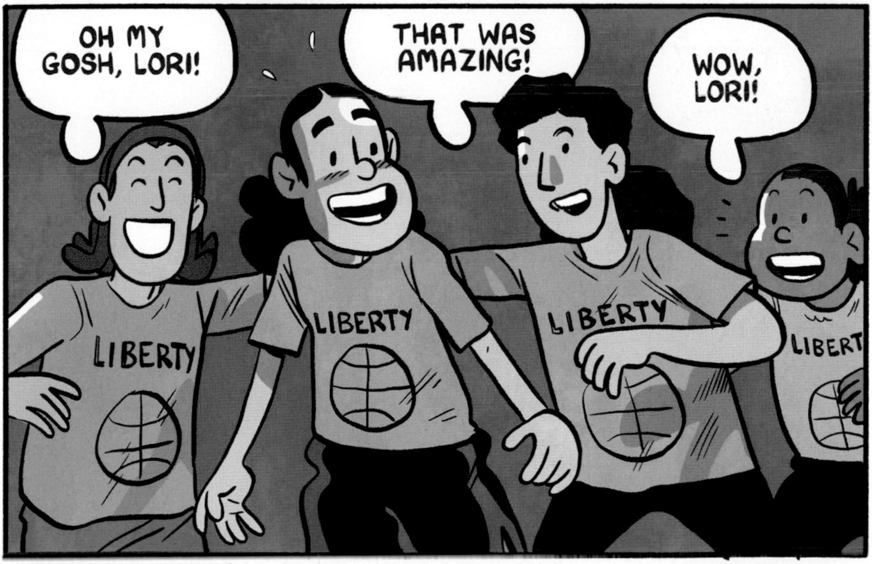
OH MY GOSH, LORI!
THAT WAS AMAZING!
WOW, LORI!
LIBERTY
LIBERTY
LIBERTY
LIBERT

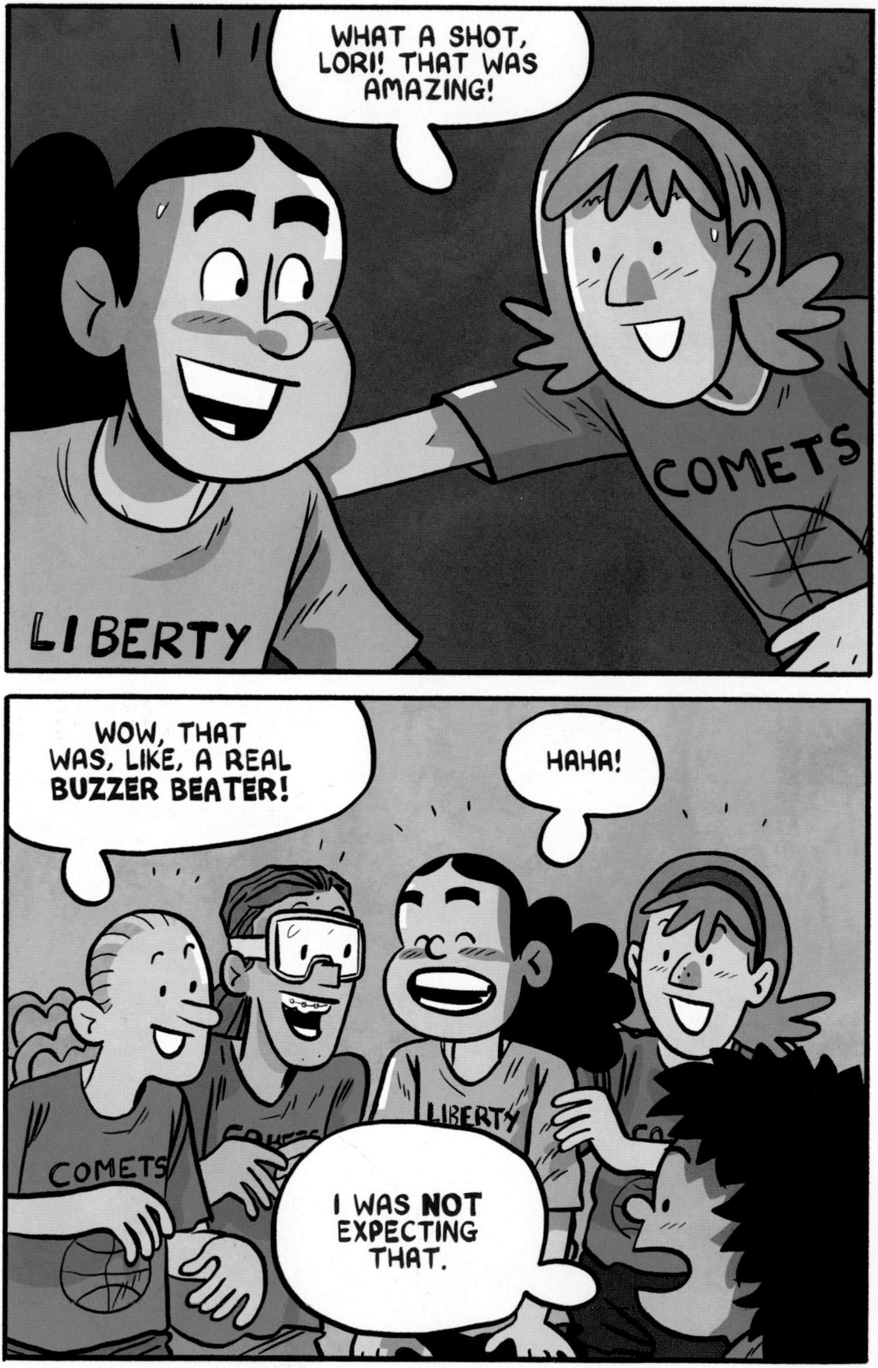
WHAT A SHOT, LORI! THAT WAS AMAZING!
LIBERTY
COMETS
WOW, THAT WAS, LIKE, A REAL **BUZZER BEATER**!
HAHA!
COMETS
LIBERTY
I WAS **NOT** EXPECTING THAT.

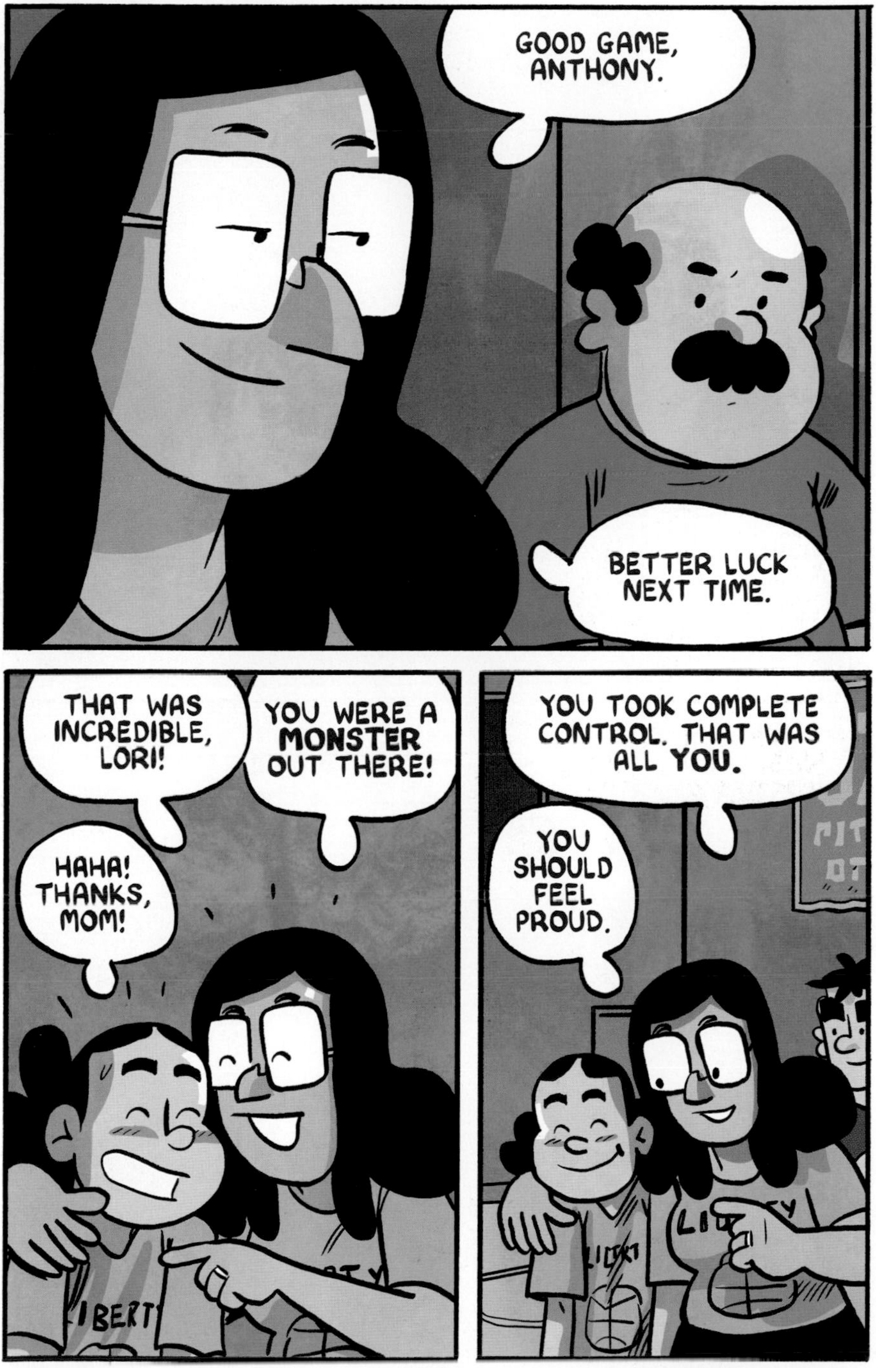
GOOD GAME, ANTHONY.
BETTER LUCK NEXT TIME.
THAT WAS INCREDIBLE, LORI!
YOU WERE A MONSTER OUT THERE!
HAHA! THANKS, MOM!
YOU TOOK COMPLETE CONTROL. THAT WAS ALL YOU.
YOU SHOULD FEEL PROUD.

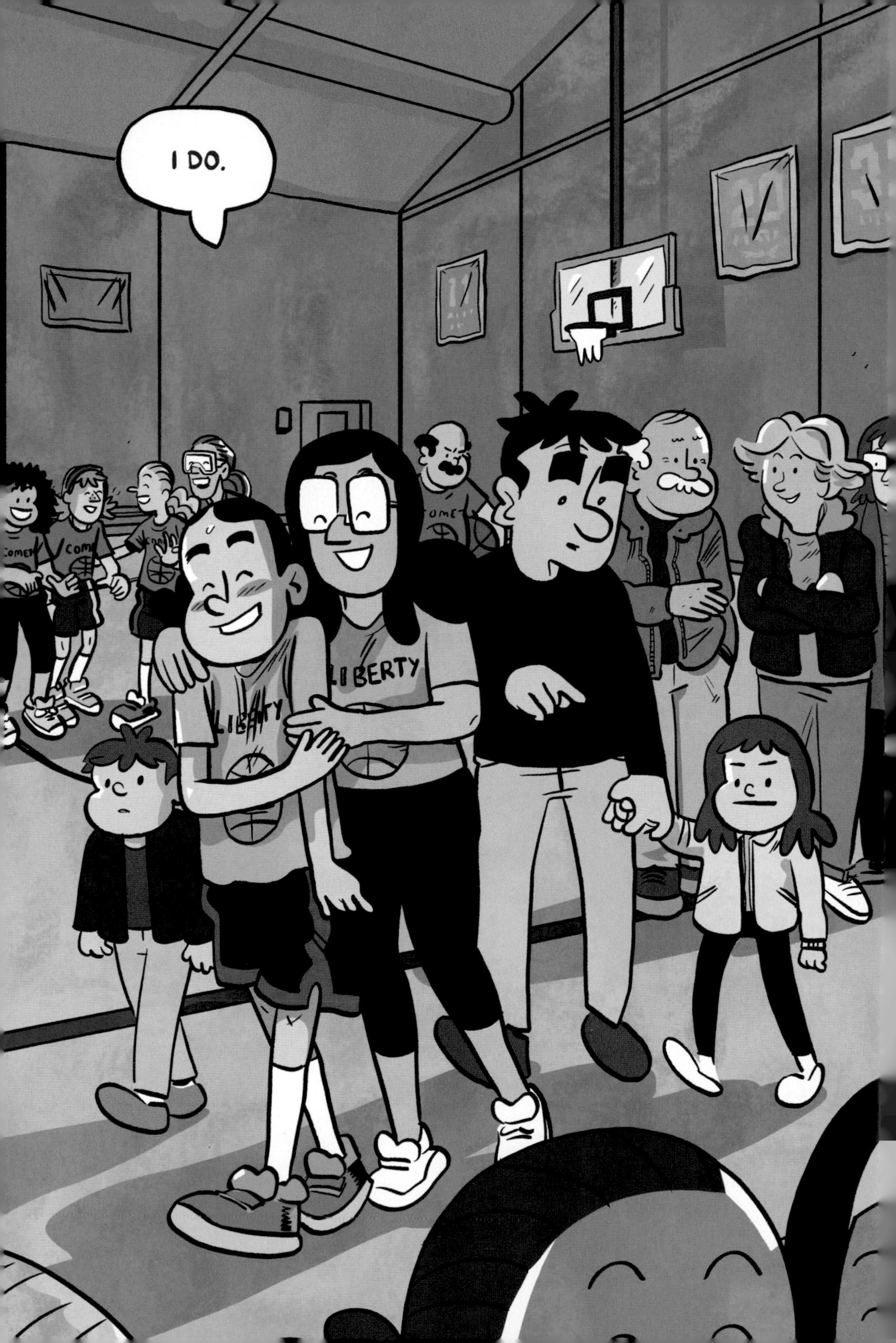
I DO.
LIBERTY
LIBERTY
COMET

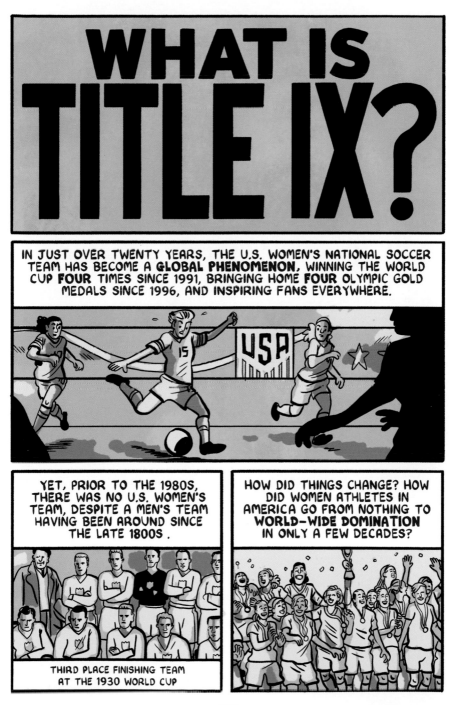

WHAT IS TITLE IX?

IN JUST OVER TWENTY YEARS, THE U.S. WOMEN'S NATIONAL SOCCER TEAM HAS BECOME A **GLOBAL PHENOMENON**, WINNING THE WORLD CUP **FOUR** TIMES SINCE 1991, BRINGING HOME **FOUR** OLYMPIC GOLD MEDALS SINCE 1996, AND INSPIRING FANS EVERYWHERE.

YET, PRIOR TO THE 1980S, THERE WAS NO U.S. WOMEN'S TEAM, DESPITE A MEN'S TEAM HAVING BEEN AROUND SINCE THE LATE 1800S .

THIRD PLACE FINISHING TEAM AT THE 1930 WORLD CUP

HOW DID THINGS CHANGE? HOW DID WOMEN ATHLETES IN AMERICA GO FROM NOTHING TO **WORLD-WIDE DOMINATION** IN ONLY A FEW DECADES?

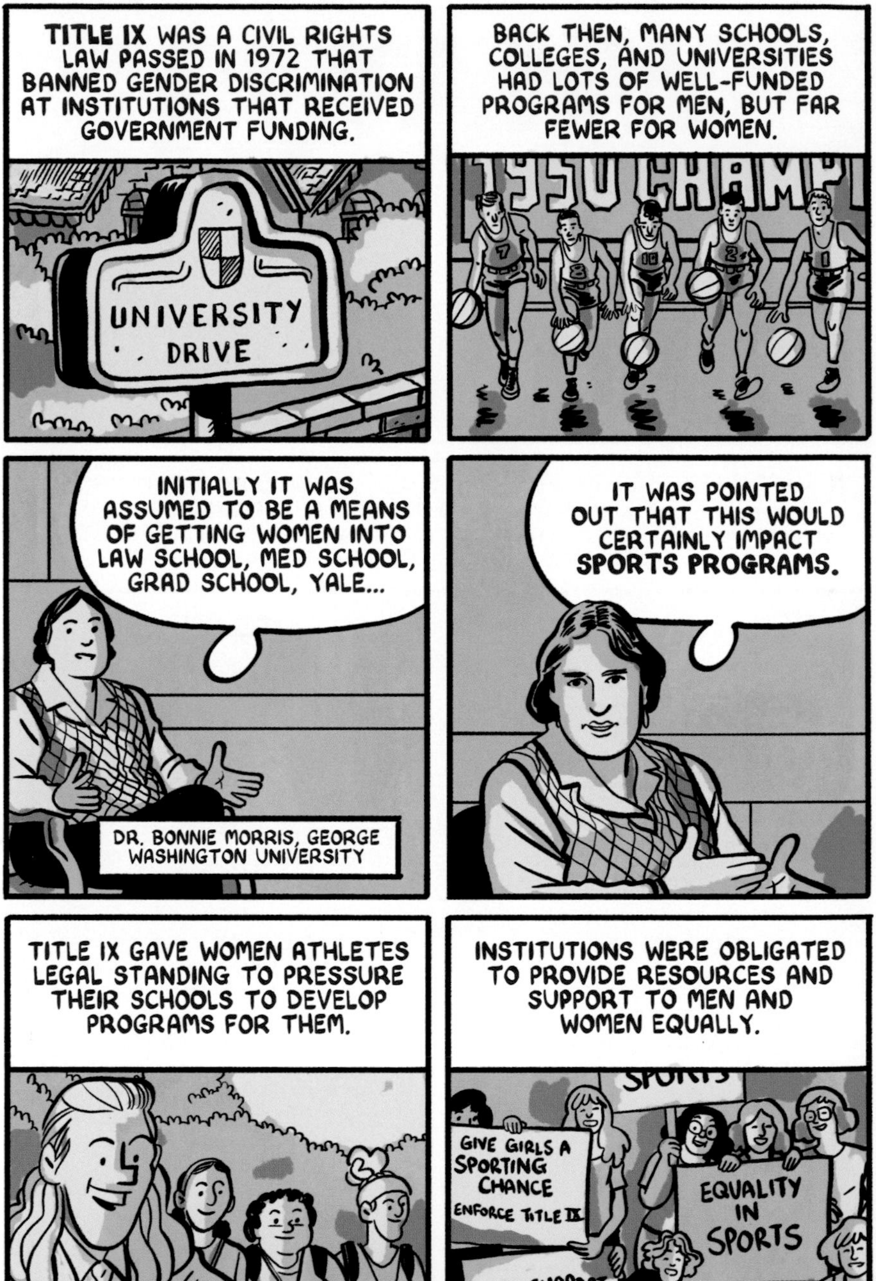
TITLE IX WAS A CIVIL RIGHTS LAW PASSED IN 1972 THAT BANNED GENDER DISCRIMINATION AT INSTITUTIONS THAT RECEIVED GOVERNMENT FUNDING.
UNIVERSITY DRIVE
BACK THEN, MANY SCHOOLS, COLLEGES, AND UNIVERSITIES HAD LOTS OF WELL-FUNDED PROGRAMS FOR MEN, BUT FAR FEWER FOR WOMEN.
1950 CHAMP
INITIALLY IT WAS ASSUMED TO BE A MEANS OF GETTING WOMEN INTO LAW SCHOOL, MED SCHOOL, GRAD SCHOOL, YALE...
DR. BONNIE MORRIS, GEORGE WASHINGTON UNIVERSITY
IT WAS POINTED OUT THAT THIS WOULD CERTAINLY IMPACT SPORTS PROGRAMS.
TITLE IX GAVE WOMEN ATHLETES LEGAL STANDING TO PRESSURE THEIR SCHOOLS TO DEVELOP PROGRAMS FOR THEM.
INSTITUTIONS WERE OBLIGATED TO PROVIDE RESOURCES AND SUPPORT TO MEN AND WOMEN EQUALLY.
SPORTS
GIVE GIRLS A SPORTING CHANCE
ENFORCE TITLE IX
EQUALITY IN SPORTS
WE SUPPORT TITLE

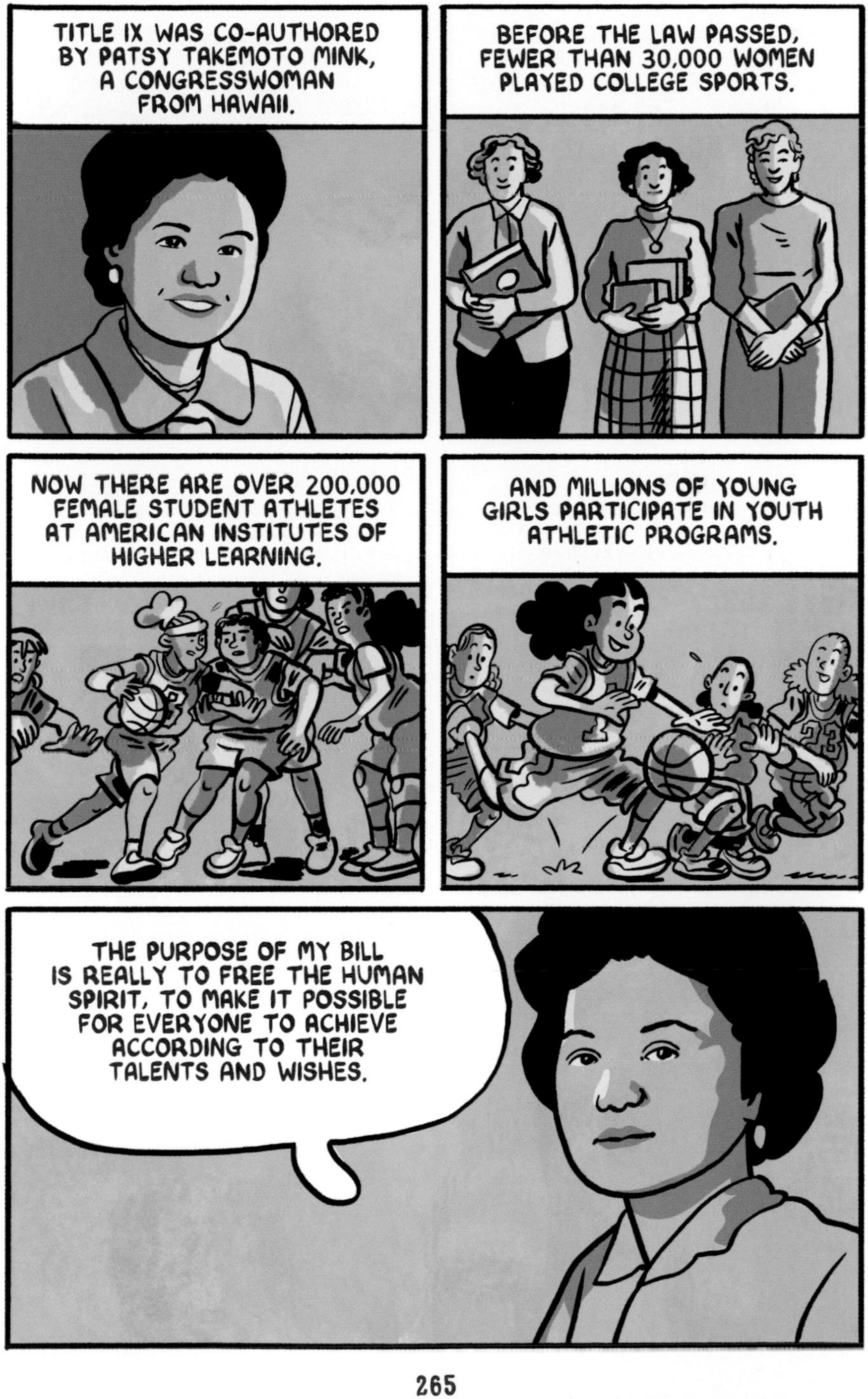
TITLE IX WAS CO-AUTHORED BY PATSY TAKEMOTO MINK, A CONGRESSWOMAN FROM HAWAII.
BEFORE THE LAW PASSED, FEWER THAN 30,000 WOMEN PLAYED COLLEGE SPORTS.
NOW THERE ARE OVER 200,000 FEMALE STUDENT ATHLETES AT AMERICAN INSTITUTES OF HIGHER LEARNING.
AND MILLIONS OF YOUNG GIRLS PARTICIPATE IN YOUTH ATHLETIC PROGRAMS.
THE PURPOSE OF MY BILL IS REALLY TO FREE THE HUMAN SPIRIT, TO MAKE IT POSSIBLE FOR EVERYONE TO ACHIEVE ACCORDING TO THEIR TALENTS AND WISHES.

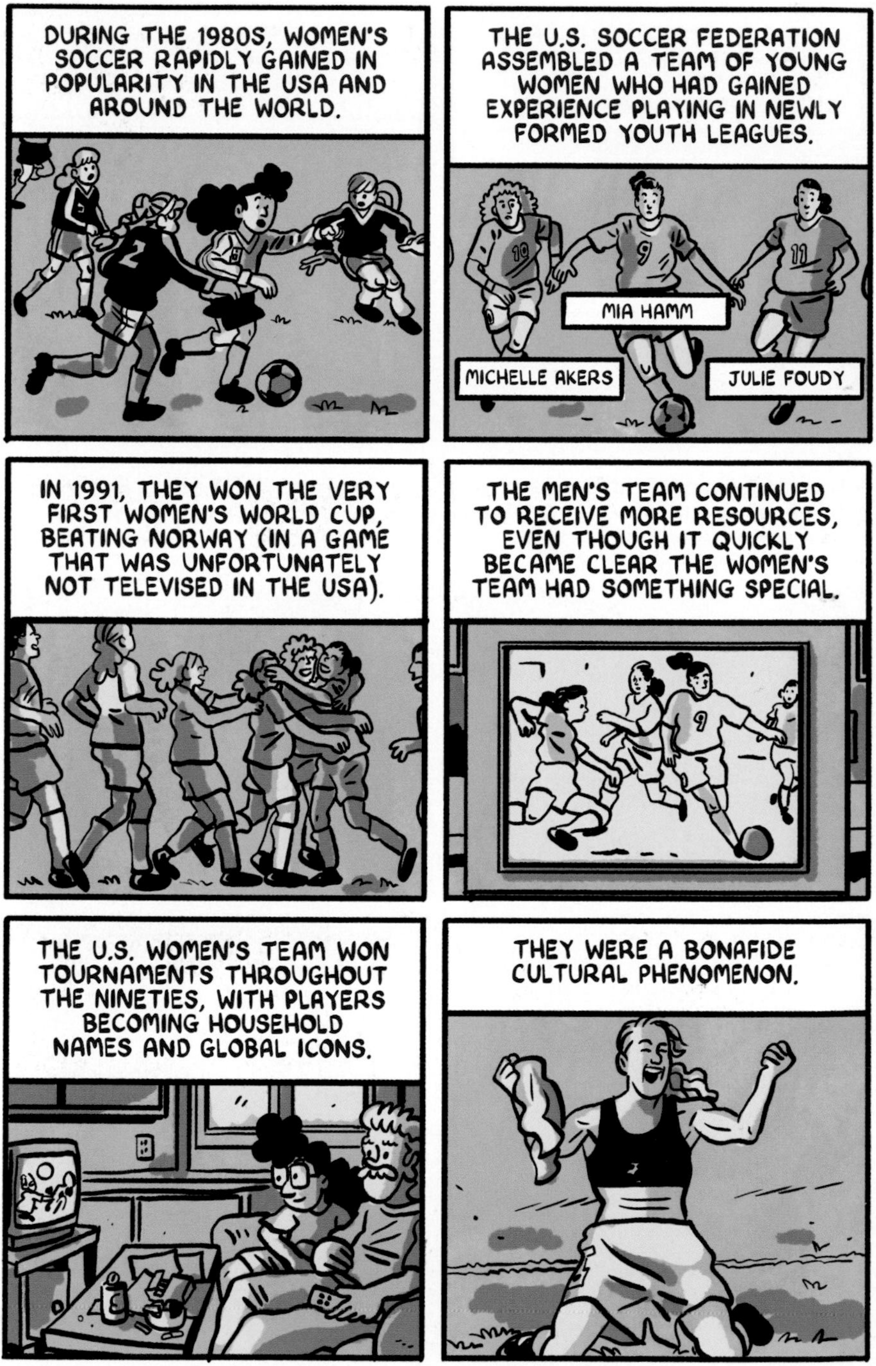
DURING THE 1980S, WOMEN'S SOCCER RAPIDLY GAINED IN POPULARITY IN THE USA AND AROUND THE WORLD.
THE U.S. SOCCER FEDERATION ASSEMBLED A TEAM OF YOUNG WOMEN WHO HAD GAINED EXPERIENCE PLAYING IN NEWLY FORMED YOUTH LEAGUES.
MIA HAMM
MICHELLE AKERS
JULIE FOUDY
IN 1991, THEY WON THE VERY FIRST WOMEN'S WORLD CUP, BEATING NORWAY (IN A GAME THAT WAS UNFORTUNATELY NOT TELEVISED IN THE USA).
THE MEN'S TEAM CONTINUED TO RECEIVE MORE RESOURCES, EVEN THOUGH IT QUICKLY BECAME CLEAR THE WOMEN'S TEAM HAD SOMETHING SPECIAL.
THE U.S. WOMEN'S TEAM WON TOURNAMENTS THROUGHOUT THE NINETIES, WITH PLAYERS BECOMING HOUSEHOLD NAMES AND GLOBAL ICONS.
THEY WERE A BONAFIDE CULTURAL PHENOMENON.

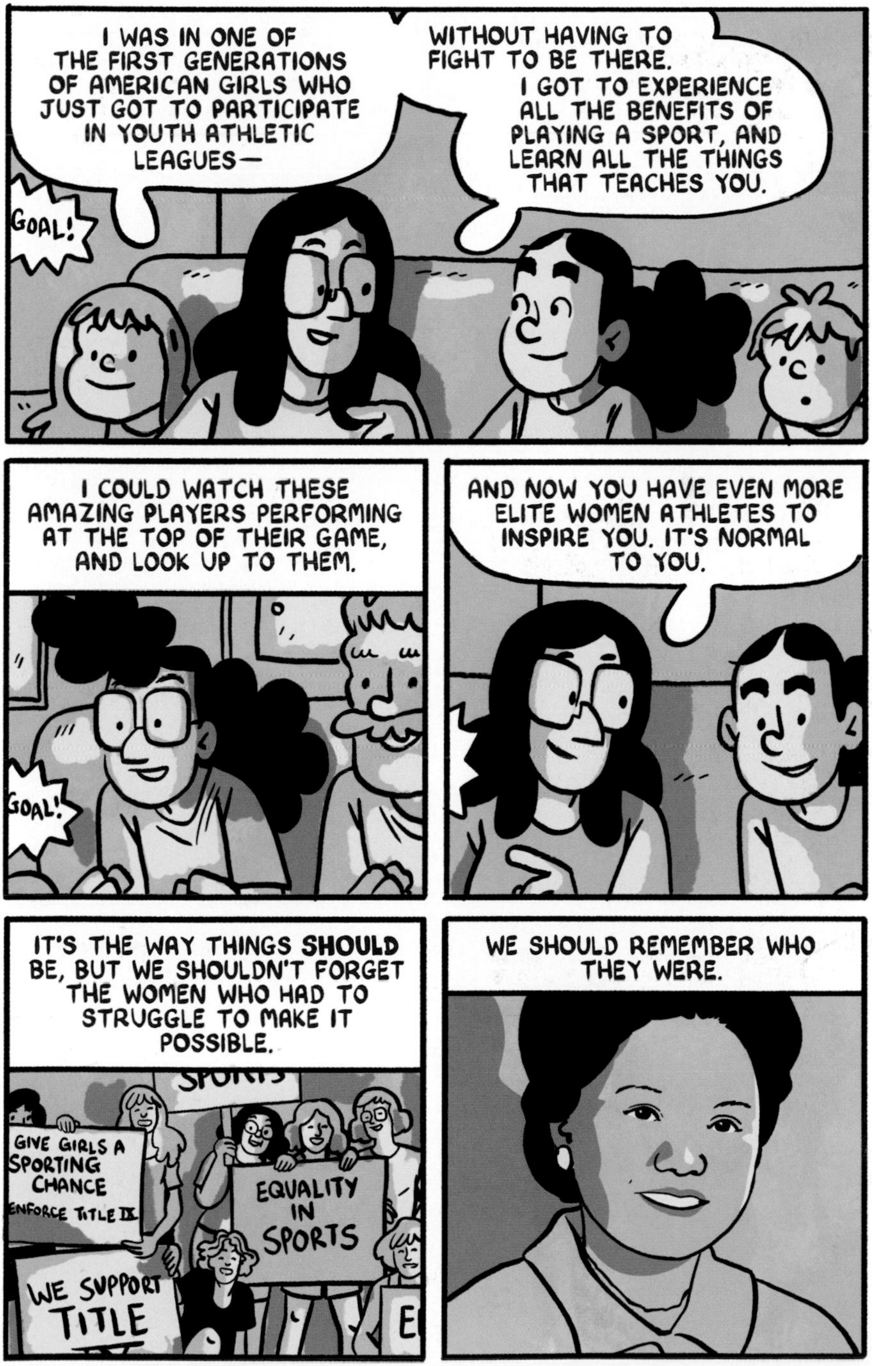
I WAS IN ONE OF THE FIRST GENERATIONS OF AMERICAN GIRLS WHO JUST GOT TO PARTICIPATE IN YOUTH ATHLETIC LEAGUES—
WITHOUT HAVING TO FIGHT TO BE THERE.
I GOT TO EXPERIENCE ALL THE BENEFITS OF PLAYING A SPORT, AND LEARN ALL THE THINGS THAT TEACHES YOU.
GOAL!
I COULD WATCH THESE AMAZING PLAYERS PERFORMING AT THE TOP OF THEIR GAME, AND LOOK UP TO THEM.
GOAL!
AND NOW YOU HAVE EVEN MORE ELITE WOMEN ATHLETES TO INSPIRE YOU. IT'S NORMAL TO YOU.
IT'S THE WAY THINGS **SHOULD** BE, BUT WE SHOULDN'T FORGET THE WOMEN WHO HAD TO STRUGGLE TO MAKE IT POSSIBLE.
GIVE GIRLS A SPORTING CHANCE
ENFORCE TITLE IX
EQUALITY IN SPORTS
WE SUPPORT TITLE
WE SHOULD REMEMBER WHO THEY WERE.

FRIENDS! MUSIC! MYSTERIES!
These great graphic novels have it all!

BE PREPARED
by Vera Brosgol

Come along with Vera as she goes to summer camp for the first time ever!

STARGAZING
by Jen Wang

Meet Christine and Moon, two friends who have a lot in common, but who couldn't be more different!

JUKEBOX
by Nidhi Chanani

Fly through music history with Shaheen and Tannaz in this time-traveling adventure!

CICI'S JOURNAL
by Joris Chamblain and Aurélie Neyret

Join Cici as she explores the secrets and mysteries hidden in her hometown!

Great graphic novels for every reader

© 2016 BY TED TERRANOVA

MIKE DAWSON is the author of several graphic novels and comics collections. His work has appeared in *The Nib, Slate,* and *The New Yorker,* and has been nominated for multiple Eisner and Ignatz Awards, as well as the *Slate* Cartoonist Studio Prize. He lives at the Jersey Shore with his wife and children. mikedawsoncomics.com